Praise for
URBANTASM

Urbantasm, Book One: The Dying City is winner of the 2019 Next Generation Indie Book Award for Young New Adult Fiction.

Urbantasm, Book One: The Dying City is winner of the 2019 Kindle Book Awards for Young Adult Fiction.

Urbantasm, Book Two: The Empty Room is winner of the 2020 Kindle Book Awards for Young Adult Fiction.

Urbantasm, Book One: The Dying City is a finalist for the 2020 American Fiction Awards and the 2020 Wishing Shelf Book Awards.

"[*Urbantasm, Book One: The Dying City*] features a well-constructed plot with a bit of mystery, drama, death, and teen romance. The author manages to keep all of the balls in the air and consider all of the problems that come with a city on the decline and trying to grow up there... the images created by the words will stick with the reader... The trials of being thirteen are truly captured. These characters are growing up fast and not perfect by any means."

— The BookLife Prize

"As tragic as the falling apart of the city was and is, these kids had a lot of nerve, spirit, and guts, probably because they didn't know any better... so much depth and courage."
— Writers' Digest Self-Published Book Awards

"[*Urbantasm, Book One: The Dying City* is] a book that values risk. Coyne managed to make gritty urbanscapes and the conflict therein technicolor."

—S.C. Megale, author of *This Is Not a Love Scene*

"*Urbantasm: The Dying City* is a novel of wonder and horror — but I don't mean that in any traditional sense. Though preternatural elements impinge on the story here and there, what really fuels both the wonder and the horror is Connor Coyne's uncanny portrayal of early teenhood, when every dimly understood new vista promised ecstasy untold, and every wrong move or unintentional difference could mean social death — or worse. This is a tough, tender, and unsettling rumination on coming of age in a dying industrial city, and I'm both eager and terrified to see what happens next."

— William Shunn, author of *The Accidental Terrorist*

"The first volume of Connor Coyne's epic novel *Urbantasm* imbues a neglected part of America with an azure luminescence. Portrayed with sensitive and romantic candor, this tale's young protagonists are never despairing but perpetually haunted. Coyne understands that to survive is to be wounded, and *Urbantasm* illuminates the shadows of a nation that has always exploited the defenseless and the forgotten."

— Jeffery Renard Allen, author of *Song of the Shank*

"The fate of Flint, Michigan can often be hard to believe. Yet Connor Coyne skillfully captures the tarnished essence of a thinly veiled Vehicle City — known as Akawe in *Urbantasm* — with a compelling blend of noire and Rust Belt magical realism."

— Gordon Young, author of
Teardown: Memoir of a Vanishing City

"Combining an ongoing love of noir atmospherics with memorable character development, Connor Coyne's *Urbantasm* takes readers into a vivid and utterly authentic world of adolescent angst, yearning, fear and love."

— Jan Worth-Nelson, author of *Night Blind*

"[*Urbantasm*] is much more than a teen novel. It is a massive creation from Coyne's omnivorous mind, and an often gripping evocation of the throes of a struggling city."

— Robert R. Thomas, *East Village Magazine*

"[*Urbantasm, Book Three: The Darkest* Road] is about being fifteen, where nothing matters and everything matters too much."

   — M.L. Kennedy, Author of *Things You Leave Behind*

"The realest portrayal of angry young people I've ever read."

   — Amanda Steinhoff, Author of *Lily and the Golden Lute*

"Connor is a great writer. His ability to create amazing characters in a richly painted fictional background is something to be truly admired... This is a coming of age tale, crime story, thriller, suspense novel and a use of fiction to condemn and glorify urban decay and corruption... From a pure storytelling perspective, this is a fantastic read. Realistic characters in real peril and dealing with real-life situations... Then a bizarre pair of sunglasses is found and things get — weird. It's breathtaking writing. I feel *Urbantasm* is destined to be a classic."

   — Bryan Alaspa, Author of *S.P.I.D.A.R.*

"*Urbantasm: The Dying City* recognizes that adolescence is magic – your understanding transforms, you are consumed by desires of and just beyond your body, you know your friends in a way you didn't before. Coyne combines this magic with the sociology and cartography of Akawe, Michigan – a 'dying,' but by no means dead, incarnation of 1990s Flint – and a pair of strange blue sunglasses to pull seventh-grader John Bridge and his friends towards something raw, complex, and new."

   — Gemma Cooper-Novack, Author of
   We Might As Well Be Underwater

"Incandescent prose illuminates the darkest underground passages of a town ruined by an auto company, where gangstah drugs turn everything dreamy, mysterious, and deadly. And you can't look away, sentence by gorgeous sentence, from the drama caught writhing and screaming, squinting its eyes against the light."

— Tantra Bensko, Author of *Glossolalia: Psychological Suspense*

URBANTASM

THE DARKEST ROAD

URBANTASM

a novel

BOOK THREE:
THE DARKEST ROAD

Connor Coyne

GOTHIC FUNK PRESS

Flint, Michigan

GOTHIC FUNK PRESS

gothicfunkpress.com

Flint, Michigan

URBANTASM: THE DARKEST ROAD

Copyright © 2021 by Connor Coyne

Edited by **Hosanna Patience** and **Kelsey Ronan**

Designed and Illustrated by **Sam Perkins-Harbin**

forge22.com

ISBN: 978-0-9899202-9-2

Printed in the United States of America

10 9 8 7 6 5 4 3 2 1

First Edition

for Jessica

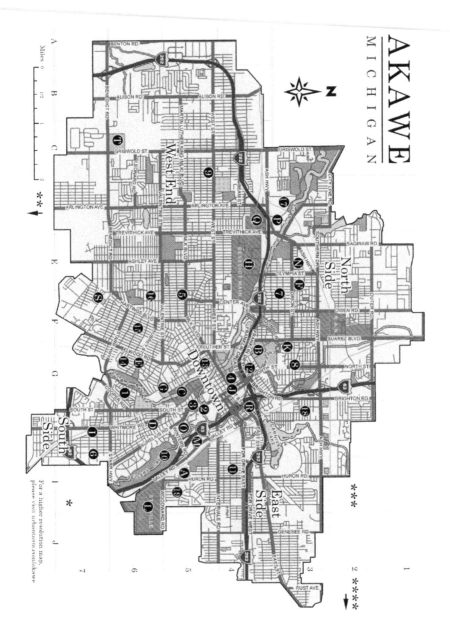

AKAWE

MICHIGAN

LEGEND

NEIGHBORHOODS

1. Ashburn Heights
2. Cartierul
3. The Cellarway
4. Downtown
5. Hastings Corridor
6. Downtown Akawe
7. The Os
8. Anderson Park
9. Arlington
10. Bellwood
11. The East Side
12. Olanville
13. The Old River District
14. South Village
15. South Branch
16. The Palisades
17. Werewolf Town
18. Lestrade
19. Maplewood

LANDMARKS

A. Beckford Junior High School
B. Campus Akawe
C. The Old Benedict
D. Radcliffe Junior High School
E. St. Brendan Church and School
F. St. Francis Church and School
G. The X Automotives Institute
H. The Benedict Main
I. The Constellation
J. East Street Downtown
K. St. Christopher Hospital
L. Starrville
M. Eastern High School
N. Northern High School
O. The Happy Hunting Grounds
P. The Akawe Water Treatment Plant
Q. The Benedict West
R. The Treemonisha Club
S. Southern High School
T. Western High School

SUBURBS

*	Arcadia	***	Acheron
**	Elmwood	****	Parc Pierre

FIFTH REVOLUTION
OCCULTATION

The police arrived some time that morning, and the little brothers and sisters hid behind legs that seemed to their eyes as huge as tree trunks. The grandmother and the uncle and the two aunts wailed through the tiny house, discovering many paths toward nowhere. Only the mother was still. She sat in a chair near the front door and stared at the expressionless walls.

When ten a.m. had come and gone without Bennett crying for milk, his grandmother had stepped into his bedroom and found the baby's head wedged into the corner of his crib. His blanket was twisted around his face. He had rolled over in his sleep and suffocated himself.

The police took statements, then asked the mother and grandmother to come in for further questioning. They agreed. They were relieved when the officers offered them a ride in the cruiser. Their own Aubrey wouldn't start half the time, and when it did, the heater ran full blast and the car got maybe ten miles to the gallon. It wasn't a big deal or anything, but splinters felt like swords that morning.

At the police station, the two detectives – the woman in a bun and the man with a crew cut – went off together, talking quietly, gesturing loudly. Another officer led the mother and grandmother into separate interrogation rooms. Then a fourth detective arrived, this one wearing glasses, shook his head, and brought the grandmother by the hand to sit with her daughter. Bun and crew cut whispered to each other, then commenced their interview.

The longer the detectives talked, the less routine the questions seemed. "How was Bennett lying when you found him?" "You said you found him in the corner, lying on his side?" "Was it his stomach or his side?" "How did his leg look on the bed? If you can't describe it, can you draw us a picture?"

Eventually, the grandmother realized that these questions were not procedural but investigative.

"How dare you," she seethed. "You seen the day she's got? You seen the way her life broke up this morning? Broke like a bottle! You accuse her after she's lost her own blood. Her own blood she fed with her own blood ever since Bennett was born!"

"I dropped him," said the mother, suddenly. "I was in his bedroom last night, just tossing him in the air and catching him. He was laughing ... he was happy and my baby. But one time, I missed him, and he landed on his back. I mean, his head hit the ground. It made a little ... it made a sound I don't want to say. He was just so sleepy then, so I put him to bed. But I went in and looked at him in the middle of the night, and he was dead. And I was worried that ... I was worried what would happen to my other kids. So I put him in the crib like that. So it would look like he just, I don't know, rolled over and couldn't breathe."

For a moment, there was silence in the windowless room.

Then the grandmother screamed, lunging from her chair, fingers bent toward her daughter's eyes, wanting to pluck them, to scratch them out, to draw real blood.

"How could you?" she screamed. "After what you did to Jane! After what you did to Jane!"

Another officer hurried into the room and helped the detectives restrain the grandmother. After thrashing for another few moments, she went limp, and the officer led her, sobbing, out into the hall.

The detectives excused themselves.

The mother sat alone there for a few minutes. She picked at a scab on her arm. Took a small sip of coffee. Stared at the ugly yellow cinder-block walls.

Bun and crew cut returned.

The questions continued as if they had never been interrupted.

"We've called your social worker, but we haven't reached her yet. So, while we're waiting, do you want to tell us a little bit about Jane?"

"Jane is my daughter," the mother answered.

"Does Jane live with you?"

"No."

Jane had been taken away some years before. So had Belle. The other children at the house had been the mother's half-sisters and nephews and nieces. The mother was 24-years old. She was unemployed, but the grandmother collected disability – a paltry little SSI that covered the gas and electricity, but not much else – while the uncle helped out with a combination of odd jobs, part-time work at Arby's, and food stamps.

"And the rent?"

"Well, that's a strange thing, you see," the mother answered. "We're a few months back in rent, and the landlord says he's going to throw us out some times, but a few months ago we started getting ..." she sniffed. "We started getting chunks of rust in the water. It just came out in the sink, and then it started coming out in the bathtub, too. Orange water. Our neighbors don't got it, so we told him it was his fault. So, we pay him when we got the money, and he don't mind, but we don't trouble him with the water neither."

"Hmmm. What's your landlord's name?"

"Mr. Wood. I mean, Mouse Wood."

"That's a name!" Crew cut chuckled. "Do you have an address for Mouse Wood?"

The mother wrote down a number on paper.

"That's the address?"

"Yeah."

"That's the Benedict factory –"

"I think we're getting off track a little," said bun.

"Right," said crew cut. "You said you were behind on rent and had bad water. Is that why Belle and Jane were taken away?"

"Probably something like that ..."

"Think for a moment now. They give an order and a report whenever a child is taken into foster. What did that report say about why Jane was being sent away?"

The mother told them about a fire. How Jane had been sleeping in bed with her. How the mother had fallen asleep with a cigarette in her hand.

"But I got her out," she said.

"Is that why they put her with her cousins? Because you caught the bed on fire?"

"Yeah, that was it."

"Was she hurt?"

The mother was silent for a moment.

Then she explained that Jane had gotten burned before being pulled from the bed.

"We want to help you out here," said crew cut, "but we can't do that if we don't have all the information. You understand? We ask you a question, and you tell us one thing, then we ask another question, and you change your story. But having a wrong story or just half a story? That's just as bad as not having any story at all. We need to know everything. We need to know what you know. That's the only way we can help you out."

"I'll tell you the truth," the mother said.

"You said that little Bennett fell on his back. That his head struck the floor."

"That's right."

"Here, show me. Touch your head where Bennett's head hit the floor."

The mother touched the back of her head near the top.

"Where?"

The mother touched her head again in the same place.

"Because that wasn't where Bennett had a fracture in his skull. It was down further. Bleeding in his brain from a fracture down here. From a lot of force hitting him right here."

The mother touched the back of her head lower down.

The detectives looked confused now.

"Show me how Bennett could have fallen and hit his head right there."

The mother stood up. The instructions confused her. She sat down again.

"Do we have a book around here somewhere?" bun asked.

"Will you take a look at this picture?" asked crew cut.

"Wait, I've got something better," said bun. She left the room.

"Do you see this photo?" crew cut asked. "That's a photo of Bennett's room. Now, do you see the little scuff there? Just a little dent in the drywall, right beside the crib? Your niece – Sarah, is it? – what a charmer, I mean, she's a sharp little girl. Anyway, she was saying that dent is new. Wasn't there before. How'd that dent get in the wall?"

The first detective came back into the room. She was holding a small plush doll, a girl with braided blonde hair, not much smaller than Bennett had been.

"Here," she told the mother. "My daughter gave this to me. I keep it on my desk. Now, stand up like you were when you were holding and tossing Bennett, and just ... toss this doll, and we'll see if you can show us how Bennett fell and landed on his head right there."

The detective pointed to the back of the doll's head.

The mother stared at the doll for a moment, then breathed out a deep sigh.

That was when she told them the truth. About how Bennett had screamed and screamed and screamed. He had screamed like his belly was full of wind, and he would never stop howling. The sound had gotten so loud, so sharp, so shrill that she felt like there was a huge man hammering a giant screwdriver right through the top of her skull.

"Shut up you!" she had yelled at him.

But the big man hadn't cared. He was grinning as he did it. He thought it was fun. He thought it was funny, the way he could drown her world in tears and pain and endless splintering light and noise. He grinned through his broken teeth. And that was when the mother had picked up Bennett and shut him up good.

The next day, my alarm woke me around 6:30. It was still gray outside, and that's how I knew the harvest moon was right around the corner. I dressed in my room in darkness. I put on my breeches and tunic. I pulled my cloak over my head, and it smelled like sandalwood. Smelled a little like sweat. I brushed my teeth and went downstairs, and grabbed a bagel from the pantry. Put on my boots. Picked up my walking stick. Went out to the curb and waited under the young sycamore.

By then, the clouds to the east had turned the color of ripe peaches. Eddie always told me he'd pick me up at seven, but he was never on time. "I have to drive all over town picking up you peasants!" he said with a smile on his face. Still, I don't know why I was always in such a hurry when I knew he was going to be late.

I heard a low groan from across the street. A stray cat stuck behind a gate? A raccoon who couldn't climb down into the weed-choked sewers? No. This was a human sound. I wasn't alone after all. I looked up toward the corner of Agit and Whitmore to a white house, its paint chipping and its porch wrapped in police tape. The grandmother stood across the sidewalk, under the leaves of a maple tree.

"Why does this always happen?" she moaned. "Every damn time. Every damn time."

I wish I could tell you, I thought. She didn't realize that I was there, and I didn't know her at all. I knew a bit about her house, though. It was a loud house. Out-of-control kids. They shrieked across the yard and trampled the weeds of the vacant lots on our block. Most days, they were outside from morning 'til night. And then, the uncle had a firework collection, and he'd go out into their fenced-in back yard and explode his miniature bombs long after the Fourth of July had passed. With the concrete and hills of my neighborhood, the echoes ricocheted like bullets on an old TV western. I kept expecting the man to blow his hand off. I would have expected an ambulance for that. But when the ambulance had come the day before, it had been to collect Bennett's tiny body. After that, the aunts and uncles argued from one window to the next, shouting their secrets for the whole neighborhood to hear. Then we knew: we'd had a murder on Agit Street. If I'd have only looked out my bedroom window at the right time, I could have seen it happening, but I didn't, and that's why the police had to get a confession out of Bennett's mother instead.

I felt sick about the whole thing. Or numb. I wasn't sure what I was feeling. *Did I really think that only the trees and houses on this street could die?* I wondered. *Didn't I expect the sickness to spread to its people?*

Now, yellow tape swelled around the sad-looking house, and the grandmother leaned against her living maple in the predawn haze, and she asked,

"Why does this always happen?"

I wondered if her family would abandon their home after the police wrapped up their investigation. I mean, wouldn't they find its ghosts too heavy? Hell, even I, with my friends and parents and supportive teachers, found Akawe's ghosts too heavy. I was sick of the city, and I told everyone, all of the time, from Omara and Eddie to my Aunt Mabel and my father. I told Mrs. Anders when we were stuck carrying fifty paint cans down into the basement at Akawe Youth Theatre.

"Akawe's a stupid, rotten town," I'd said.

"Let's just finish this first, John," Mrs. Anders had muttered. "One problem at a time."

That was good advice. I wouldn't escape Akawe just by bitching about it. I had to compartmentalize my problems. At the same time, I didn't think the grandmother had the luxury of compartmentalizing anything. If her pain was so great that she was lurking on the street, asking answerless questions of nobody, what escape did she think *she* could engineer?

"We've got to get into that house," Adam would have said. "A little baby was *murdered* in there! We've got to see the room where it happened! Maybe we can cast a spell or something to keep that little baby safe from his own mother when she dies too!"

But I wasn't talking to Adam anymore, and that meant that the murder house would lie undisturbed – at least by us – and its ghosts could do what they wanted. I'd just sit down the street in my own house, my unabandoned, unmurdery house, and let the bulldozers deal with Bennett's house, and that was fine with me too. *Who needs the drama?*

Eddie was taking even longer than usual. I sat down under the sycamore and watched the grandmother stumble and mutter. We shared a street, a morning, a solitude, but it seemed that we didn't have anything else in common. Even if she managed to escape this specific house, I doubted she'd ever get out of Akawe. People like her never got to leave. Whereas I might be stuck in my parents' moss-shingled house for now, but I knew I was going to get out. My whole life had been a preparation to get out. The lean-forward and take-flight at just the right moment. That moment was just a few years away.

When I had entered eighth grade at Radcliffe Junior High, I had several things I'd been missing in seventh grade. Backstage experience with a nationally recognized youth theatre? Check! Ambitious and worldly friends with their own plans for the future? Check! Sophisticated, sexy, high school girlfriend? Check! I respected my parents a lot more than I had before. As soon as I had stopped being a little bitch and just did the things they told me I should do, my life started falling into place. Before, it had never occurred to me that they might have actually been right about that shit.

22

And I had continued to follow their good advice all through eighth grade.

Mrs. Anders had directed two plays for her new Radcliffe Drama Club: *Alice in Wonderland* and *Arsenic and Old Lace*. I helped her with the lighting design for both plays. I built sets and ran spotlights. Akawe Youth Theatre didn't offer any tech classes, but I took an acting class with August March, who had directed *The Cherry Orchard*. While I didn't like acting, I also didn't hate it as much as I'd expected. There wasn't any sort of a math club at Radcliffe, but Mrs. Norman ran the Chess Club, and I joined. I never learned much beyond castling, but it was fun enough. If I didn't stop, these were things I could talk about on *college applications.*

In school, I had annihilated another year of my social studies magnet, crunching through Civil War battles and Reformation senators like they were going out of style. My math grades weren't anything to brag about, but I still managed to slide myself into the honors track. I wrapped up the year with a 3.62 GPA, which was a ton better than the 3.03 I'd earned in seventh grade. I got a congratulatory letter from the superintendent for a report I had written on the Romanian Revolution, though I felt kind of salty for not asking Selby what she had thought about it. If I could do even better in high school, I might even get into the college I wanted.

Oh, I knew what college I wanted.

The University of Chicago had an acceptance rate of 50%. 92% of matriculating students graduated in the top 20% of their class. Their median SAT scores were 660 for math and 680 for verbal. That's what those "Get Into College" books told me. It would be tough, but it didn't seem impossible to me. As the product of a down-and-out urban public school district, I'd have leverage vis-a-vis the heartstrings of idealistic admissions officers. At least that's what I planned to deliver when I interviewed in another two years.

As far as I could tell, the University of Chicago had killer programs in math and theatre. It was in the most magnificent city in the world. It was on the shores of Lake Michigan. Freaking gargoyles straddled the limestone parapets of its Rockefeller-financed mental temples. This was the logical next step in my quest for world domination, and when I say "world domination" I mean getting the hell out of Akawe and marrying my brilliant girlfriend and doing something fun and important for the rest of my life.

And – perfection! – Omara was planning to attend Northwestern in Evanston, so we wouldn't even have to be apart while we were both in college. I mean, the two schools were so close you could easily get from one to the other just by taking trains and buses!

The grandmother stooped to pluck a chicory weed from the cracked sidewalk.

A worn-looking Chrysler minivan turned onto Agit and backed into my driveway. Eddie never felt comfortable backing out onto the hill. The side door swung open, and I saw Chris Allard smiling out at me, his golden boy's hair perfectly coiffed for either Varsity Tennis or starting his own garage band. (He did neither – he was a theatre kid – but everything was an option for him, and that made me a little jealous.) Chris held out his hand and pulled me in.

"Why?" the grandmother was muttering.

"Who's that?" asked Majenta, sitting in the middle row behind me.

"Some old lady," I said.

"Is she all right?" asked Eddie, twizzling a toothpick between his lips as he eased the minivan onto the street again.

"I don't think so," I said. "Her daughter murdered her grandson."

Eddie grunted his sorrow. To his side, Omara laid her hand on her dad's shoulder.

"Damn," said Majenta, and Shannon nodded his head beside her.

As we rolled past the grandmother, she turned and faced me at last; faced the middle-aged man and the six teenagers in the minivan.

"Why does this happen, every time?" she called out to us.

"Peace be with you!" Eddie called toward her through Omara's open window.

The grandmother turned toward the house again, hurling her accusation against the crumbling front porch and all the police tape wrapping the structure like a mummy's shroud.

"All those bodies you keep buried under your bed!" the woman cried.

We didn't talk much at first. The grandmother's cries had killed whatever joke my friends had been sharing on the way over. As Eddie swung the minivan along the wide curve of the I-92 entrance ramp, Nova said, "She seemed pretty pissed off at that house."

"Wouldn't you be?" I asked him. "Wouldn't you be pissed off if your kid killed her kid?"

Nova held up his hands, open-palmed. "Don't get pissy!" he said. "Yeah, I probably would. But don't you think she's gonna walk from that house after that?"

"Probably."

"Isn't that the last house on your block?"

"No. There's still mine."

I turned back around. I was too tired for his shit. Nova, who couldn't keep his mouth shut about anything, was my least favorite friend. But Chris thought he was the shit, and Omara thought Chris was the shit, so Nova ended up hanging out with us more often than not. He was a tall Black kid, with peroxide bleached dreads and the beginnings of a beard, even though he was only three months older than me. His real name was Ronald Richards, but he told everyone to call him "Nova." For some reason, we all went along with it. Nova was going into tenth grade with Shannon, Majenta, and Omara. Chris was going into eleventh grade. I was the only ninth grader.   "Hey,   John?" Nova asked.

"What?" I didn't turn around.

"Isn't your house the last house on your block?"

"No, dumbass!" I said.

"Hey there –" said Eddie. Eddie didn't like swearing.

"It's not?" Nova asked.

"No, there's the house on the corner where the lady was yelling!"

"Word," said Nova.

"Jesus!"

Next to me, Chris caught my eye, gave his head a little shake, like *don't mess it.* I could only imagine Majenta and Shannon grinning in the back. In the front, Omara sighed. She thought that all of her friends were pretty stupid. Her boyfriend included.

"Hey John?" asked Nova.

"What is it, asshole?" I asked, turning around again.

"Hey there –" said Eddie, a bit louder than before.

"How was your first week of high school?"

Oh, I had him now. "It was real hot. I walked into that building, I was so damn hot that the heat came off me in waves. Shorties couldn't look at me. They kept passing out. Hopeless hos falling in droves. Yeah, the principal had to call off school. Send everyone home. I was just too hot to look at."

Eastern High School had, in fact, been canceled that first week because of the heat, though it had nothing to do with me. Summer had taken a squat in the dilapidated building, and they hadn't been able to clean it out on time. I'd heard that the air shimmered like a mirage in the hallways and that some of the chemical vials in the science labs had melted. Acid had dribbled out, burning holes in the floor. They were supposed to try cooling the building over the weekend and try again after Labor Day.

"You were as bright as the sun?" asked Nova. "Like Coolio sez?"

"Brighter."

"Damn, man."

"Now listen," said Eddie. "This is my vehicle, and I don't appreciate that kind of language, so if you could tone it down a little –"

Omara's dad was lanky and fiftyish with a tidy mustache. He'd been raised in the Nation of Islam, in the watchful shadow of three older brothers, but Eddie was a peaceful man. We all liked him. He frustrated us. We frustrated him too. But he drove us everywhere.

"It's fine, dad," said Omara.

"I'm just saying ... I'm just asking –"

"We know," she said.

Eddie took a sip of his decaf coffee. He told me he drank decaf because Muslims weren't supposed to have caffeine, but my father had told me that even decaf coffee has some caffeine. I wasn't sure whether or not Eddie knew this.

"This isn't the first time you've been close to a murdered body, is it John?" Majenta asked.

I liked Majenta more than Nova. I didn't know whether or not she liked me, though. Majenta was hard to read. I turned to face her. She was a Black goth girl with a bob dyed red-and-black, an angular face, and eyes as acid as whatever solution was eating through the floors of Eastern High School. Majenta was slender, too, able to strap herself into a narrow corset and lace it tight. She smelled like cloves, which she smoked often.

"What do you mean?" I asked.

"Weren't you at some junkyard a year ago and found a body?"

"No. That wasn't me. That was these two friends of mine. They found it. And it wasn't a body. It was a skeleton."

"A human skeleton?"

"I mean, yeah."

"A human skeleton is a body. For all intensive purposes."

Whenever Majenta said "for all intensive purposes," it meant that the discussion was over.

"What happened to them?" asked Shannon. "Freeze to death or something?"

Shannon Allard was Chris' younger brother. A lanky white boy with a mullet a decade out of style, but somehow he still rocked it. Shannon was as good looking as Chris, too. If Chris was a secret player, then Shannon was the player hater hater. Shannon *hated* player haters.

"No," I said. "It was a murder. Too. I mean. Someone slit the dude's throat. But I don't know. I wasn't there. Like I said, it was some friends who found it."

"Which friends?" asked Majenta.

"Um. Selby Demnescu and Adam Miller."

I heard Omara snort from her perch up front.

"They go to Eastern?" Majenta went on.

"I don't know." I rubbed my hands on my knees. "I mean, who cares?"

"Well, maybe I'll look them up. I'd like to hear the story."

The story, I knew, lacked a resolution. Adam and Selby had run back to her house and told Angel. Angel had called the police. The news hadn't said much about it, just that "a suspicious death has been discovered off Intervale Road in Downtown Akawe." But the detective who interrogated Adam told him that it was a homicide. Adam had been telling me about it over the phone when the line click-clicked.

"I got a call on the other line," I said. "I'll be right back."

When I switched over, it was Omara. She wanted to get my opinion on Frankenfurter. We talked for the next hour. I had been wishing and praying for this phone call for two days! Omara's whatevers meant more to me than Adam's encounter with the dead and defiled. So, of course, when Omara and I finished talking, Adam was long gone. He didn't call me back, and I didn't call him, either. I didn't see him again until we were both back in school.

"Yeah, I'm sure he'll tell you all about it," I said. "Adam, I mean. I mean, I don't know. I haven't talked to him in ... a while."

"Adam is a jackass!" said Omara.

"Now listen ..." began Eddie from up front.

I put on my sunglasses and looked out the window. I saw the bushes blur by and closed my eyes. I was tired of talking. I was tired.

One hour later, Eddie unloaded us onto the dust-baked grass of an improvised parking lot and the actors' entrance of the Michigan Renaissance Festival. We arrived at the Crown Stage, where a group of tunic-clad lads and tight-bosomed wenches stood around, a lot of them my age, as well as a host of peasants and merchants, jongleurs and bards, Vikings and pirates, nobles and royalty, and weirdos and misfits. Some of the costumes were just a whisper away from bondage gear. The king stood up in front of us all and warned us to stay hydrated for the next three days.

Labor Day weekend was both dreaded as the festival's most daunting climb and anticipated as its most joyful summit: three days instead of two, bracketed by work and school, with thousands more patrons than we'd see on any other weekend. Most of the teen actors were in the Academy program. Our payment came in the form of actorly training: sketch improv and short children's plays. We worked each day from the welcome cannon at ten until the get-the-hell-out cannon at seven. We ran our asses off under the blazing sun and drank a lot of water and pissed it out into hellishly hot porta-potties planted akimbo on whatever hill or slump.

But if you wanted to escape Akawe – and I did – 16th century England was pretty far removed. Sure, cars were sitting right behind the rickety fence. Sure, a giant white tank full of some caustic whatever loomed right behind the Crown Stage. But these anachronisms weren't nearly enough to overpower the scent of sawdust and pine, rosebuds and incense and lavender. The wind blew. The parapets of the Crown Stage wobbled perilously.

"You ready?" Omara asked.

I wrapped my arm around her waist.

"Hell yeah, I'm ready," I said.

A few minutes later, the cannon boomed, the gates opened, and we put on our best British accents and invited the patrons into this dusty, driven, imaginary world.

Our day began down in the Children's Dell, among the petting zoo animals and the towering pines, where we received instruction from one of the professional actors. Juggling or sonneting or commedia dell'arte. We saw how the best actors spent their whole lives practicing their crafts, and after hard years of work and study, they became masters. Today, a spindly, bestubbled man named Cecil was coaching us through different accents: British cockney and British aristocratic and Irish and Scottish and Ohioan. "I got an idear," intoned Cecil. "You put the nasal inflection into the meat of your mouth," he said.

After the workshop, we put on our little production of *Aladdin* for a handful of children wearing ribboned hennins and bearing wooden swords, their faces painted with gold-and-green dragons and butterflies. They screamed and cheered as the genie exploded forth from behind a chair upon which we had poised a small ceramic lamp.

Once the show was over, the other actors and I migrated to a canary-yellow coffee shop built in the late summer shade of an elm tree. I bought Omara and myself hot ciders with cinnamon sticks while the Academy kids argued and talked.

"The Smashing Pumpkins' b-sides are a lot better than their full albums. *Gish* was better than *Siamese Dream,* but *Pisces* is where it's really at. I think this new album might be pretty good, though. Jimmy Chamberlin can drum, that's for sure."

"Billy Corgan is an idiot, but he taught Eddie Vedder how to use his voice. Eddie didn't have any confidence with his own weird voice until he heard Billy singing. If that guy can own it, so can I, he thought. I mean, he said it."

"Three words, bitches: Loreena. Mc. Kennitt."

I drank in their words and opinions. I was learning more every day, and the sensation thrilled me. I had always admired my father's jazz music because it was history spread out through dancing sounds, shuttling blues, jangling rhythms. But if I listened to this music, I could claim membership in my friends' revolution. It was their shorthand. Their code. Their currency. Green Day was out. The Ramones were in. Nine Inch Nails were passe. Ministry was evergreen.

As for the kids in our motley band, some of us were from Akawe: Omara, Chris, Shannon, Majenta, Nova, and me. But there were dozens of kids in the Academy, 9th through 12th graders, and most of them came from Detroit or Pontiac or Flint or Saginaw and every suburb in Wayne, Oakland, and Macomb Counties. They told new stories about their strange domains.

"I hate Pine Knob," said Darcy.

"I love Pine Knob," said Sean.

"Their ushers are so bitchy!"

"Yeah, but that's where I lost my virginity."

"What?!"

"Yeah."

"During a show?"

"No, after dark."

"In the pavilion."

"No. On the grass. In the rain."

"Damn, man!"

I didn't say anything about how I had lost my virginity. Omara was standing right there.

A royal entourage passed us and shot us steely glares. We'd been lingering in the 20th century for too long. We split apart and went back out to mingle with the patrons. The loud, rowdy, morning drunk patrons. We took shifts outside the muckish privies and led our guests to the unoccupied stalls, flipping the doors to "occupied" when we saw they were out of toilet paper. We marched in a parade, hundreds strong, with all of the actors, the shopkeepers, the puppeteers, the gamesmen, and a few participatrons thrown into the mix. We snuck into the Sky Chairs and sat and swung in lazy circles, talking about our love, our heartbreak, our Donna Karans and Geoffrey Beenes, and it was nothing that Akawe was, and it was everything that Akawe could never be, and fuck Akawe because this was a hint of my future.

Later that day, I asked Shannon to tie me to a tree, which he reluctantly did, so that I could beg patrons to set me free. Instead, a clutch of feral ten-year-olds with wooden slingshots pelted me with shreds of mulch as I struggled to untie myself. Omara laughed at me from the margins and then shooed them away.

"You could have done that sooner," I said in the perfect facsimile of a 20th century Michigan accent.

"Yeah, but then I couldn't have laughed at you," she said.

She kissed me, and her lips tasted like late-summer honey. Her long eyelashes. Her sugar-warm eyes.

We acted out a bit in which we were betrothed to be married, but she had misplaced the ring I had gotten her, and so all of the patrons – kids and moms and a couple of high schoolers wearing Coed Naked t-shirts – helped us feel around in the dirt until we found the ring, which was just a bit of twined straw.

Then Omara and I, happy again in this dusty midafternoon, ranged out across the whole realm. The area around the main gate – the Swan Stage and the Green Grove and the Children's Dell – was a place for the newly initiated; a place where one witnessed the awkward juggling of some motley-patched dolls and imbibed the obscene gestures of a giant pickle merchant.

Further down, in the East – in every East of our imagination – the swamp loomed large, and that's where you found ne'er-do-wells like Gibbon the Troubadour and Axel the Sot and Ded Bob. That's where autoworkers from Flint paid five dollars to pelt a mouthy jester with tomatoes, and the raggedy shop stalls sold incense and pewter jewelry. The willow branches swayed in the slightest breath of air, and the stink of standing water crept in from the fens hidden behind the wood plank walls.

Opposite, in the West, every West, ventures and progress – the sun and shade of the Upson Downs, the jousting field where armor-bedecked knights rode each other down, and the Tree Top stage where rascals peeped about Caesar's colossally slick thighs. If you listened above their clamor, just listened so carefully, you could catch the whisper of I-75 sweeping cars and their passengers as far north as the Soo and as far south as Miami.

It was all a magnificent mess, and that was where we arrived early in the evening – Omara and Nova and Chris and Shannon and Majenta and all of the other actors and me – but the sun was sinking already because here it was September and I was about to start high school. *I'm about to start high school!*

The dandelion seeds sparkled in the air. Omara smiled at me. Unlike me, she had straight teeth, and the molten sun shone cool on her cheek. It had been a long day – dry and dusty and romantic and full – and so we joined the weary parade that wound through the grounds, away from the enterprising West with its proud sun painting the joust-field hay bales golden, and away from the mysterious East with its lowering sun striking the green leaves bronze, and away from the fresh-faced hillocks and groves where the atomized straw finally settled to earth, and when we reached the front gate, we gathered under the pine trees. The sun must have set by now because velvet shadows, spiced-inflected, blanketed the world around us. If so much of everything could be packed into a few dozen acres in the middle of Oakland County, then how much of everything awaited Omara and me in Chicago? How much of everything did the whole world contain for us? Just waiting for us to arrive? To finally, finally, arrive?

I took Omara's hand.

The cannon banged, and I squeezed in surprise.

"Ow!" Omara said.

"Sorry," I said, dropping her hand. "But ... you know what I mean."

"Ma'a salaama, John," she said.

The summer dusk gave way to interstitial twilight. There was no sense in riding an hour back home in the dark just to turn around and come back the next morning. Instead, my friends and I bummed our way back to Camp Jellystone, where we got to camp in tents on the gravel and weeds off of the RV lot for five dollars a night. We sat around a fire and drank pop while the older actors – our mentors – went through six-packs of beer and homilized on their atheist Bibles. They quoted SNL routines, Monty Python, GURPS, Cthulhu, and the Digital Underground until we were all too tired to see straight. We all said goodnight and made our way back to our tents. But my tent had flooded during the week, and inside I found dead earwigs floating in slow circles.

I didn't mind.

I was glad that this had happened.

I gathered up my sleeping bag, which Eddie had dropped off in the morning before heading back to Akawe, and stumbled back through the purple dark to Omara's tent.

"Knock knock," I said.

I heard her sigh. "You got your own tent, John."

"Not tonight," I said. "It's flooded. Will you let me stay here?"

"Fine," she said. "If this ever gets back to my dad, he'll murder you."

"I don't think he will. I don't think he'd murder a fly."

She didn't argue. She knew that I was right. She unzipped the tent and beckoned me inside.

In more than a year of going out, Omara and I hadn't had sex. We hadn't even been naked together. The driving thirst and curiosity that I had felt in seventh grade had been quenched by my confusing tumbles with Crystal. By my guilty nescience with Lucy. Still, here I was, sleeping bag in hand, stooped under the slope of the tent roof, wearing soccer shorts and a too-small t-shirt, and Omara stood before me, more stooped because she was taller than I was, her white panties and tank top bright against her dark skin. We unzipped our sleeping bags, made a bed between them, and lay down. Omara turned away from me, and I pressed into her back. I put my arm around her waist with my palm against her bare stomach. I could feel her shapes against mine, though there was still cloth between us.

"It was a long day today," she said.

"Uh-huh," I said.

"We'd better get some sleep. It's gonna be a long weekend. We got two more days to go. Then school. You know I got that job at the Olan Farm? It's gonna be almost like this. I mean, I guess I'll dress up like a milkmaid, like *The Little House on the Prairie* or something. But it'll be acting, you know?"

I sighed.

"I'm not tired," I said.

"Me neither," she said. And then, in a burst: "I can't stop thinking about that woman on your block. Who murdered her baby."

I pushed myself against her. I held my breath. I said, "I can't think about that. I mean. There's nothing I can do about that. It makes me sick, but what does that even accomplish?"

"But doesn't it just stick with you? The idea of it? How awful it –"

"I don't want it to, okay? Anyway, it's far away. We're here now. Let's stay here."

"We can't stay here." I felt the tenseness in Omara's back.

"Yeah. But someday, we'll leave Akawe for good. And anyway. We aren't there now."

"Aren't you afraid your dad's gonna lose his job?"

"My father? Yeah. He's already driving two hours each day ever since they transferred him to Canton. Ever since that strike ended last year, it seems like X is closing everything fast as they can. You know? I mean, they closed the Benedict Main. Most of the Old Benedict. Probably RAN, too. 'Course, my aunt says they were going to close them all anyway."

Omara laughed. A slight untensing. "Sounds like you *have* thought about it."

"I think about lots of things a lot. Some things I don't want to think about and some things I do. I mean, I think about *you* a lot."

I was trying to move toward her. In, you know, *ways*. But she wasn't taking the bait.

"Aren't you afraid they won't be able to pay for college?"

She'd finally succeeded. Omara's fears had become my fears.

"No," I said. "I mean, my mother is working at that new job at XAI. And even if my father gets laid off, he's got options. Right? Transfer to other plants. Stuff like that. What about you? Why are you worried? Didn't your grandparents get you a savings bond or something?"

"Yeah. But I keep thinking someone's gonna open a trapdoor beneath me or something. I guess … I guess I keep thinking I'll believe in college when I get there. And not before. It just seems a bad idea to get my hopes up, you know?"

"You don't have to worry about it for a while. It's still years off. I mean, we just have to keep working, don't we? It'll happen. We just need to be patient or some shit, you know?"

The wind buffeted the tent over our heads. I could hear low talking outside. Low chuckles. Through the tent wall, I could see the embers of the fire flickering faintly. Some of the older actors would be slouching in their folding chairs until the sky started to gray with dawn. That was still several hours away. I listened to it for a long, slow minute.

"I do worry," I confided. "I worry that something will happen that I don't expect, and I'll get stuck. That I'll fail a class, fail a test I need to pass ... and I won't get into college in Chicago, or I won't get into college anywhere. I worry that my parents are lying about everything, and they can't pay for shit. I worry that I'm just being set up to fail. I even worry ..." I caught my breath. Saying this all out loud was *hard.* Trusting a human being was *hard.* But at least I wasn't looking into her eyes. At least the darkness of a September tent wrapped us and kept our secrets from everyone else.

"I worry," I whispered, "that you'll go away to college in Chicago, and I'll be stuck in Akawe, and I'll never get out."

I heard a deep breath from Omara. I felt her belly raise beneath my cupped palm. She had fallen asleep, and I was grateful.

When I woke the next morning, Omara was already dressed and standing with her hand on the door.

"– better get going," she was saying, "if we're gonna hit McDonald's before the cannon."

"Okay, okay," I said. "Just let me get dressed before you open that door!"

"Then hurry!"

I don't think it's possible to really love someone until you've smelled their stinky morning breath. I understood that now that I was a fifteen-year-old ninth grader.

When I got outside, the campsite was quieter than I expected. People must have been in their tents changing or in the porta-potties. Or they had already left. The place felt momentarily abandoned.

I looked up at the sky and shivered. The air was hazy, and I couldn't tell if I was looking into clouds or the naked sky. A poplar rose in front of me, its leaves heavy and wide but gray underneath. Webworm nets hung heavy over many of its branches. I could see hundreds of the worms squirming and devouring the green.

The morning warmed around me, but I felt a surge of approaching cold and dark. I felt that when summer died, it was going to die for good. When winter arrived, it was going to stay. So I stood where I was, and I shivered.

"Come on, John," said Omara, emerging from one of the porta-potties.

For the second day, we listened patiently as the king exhorted us, again, to "drink water and then drink more water!" Then the cannon boomed, and all of the actors, led by Raoul and Raoul, the randy Frenchmen with their taxidermied drop bear, made their way into the festival.

"Behold!" Chris boomed at my side. "'Tis a man with two heads!"

He was talking to a laughing, bearded man with a nervous-looking toddler perched on his shoulders.

Majenta was juggling, and Nova was dancing less successfully.

Just down the line, another man guzzled the morning's first hornful of beer. Today was going to be, if anything, even hotter and busier than yesterday had been.

After a few minutes, the Academy actors converged upon the maypole, a timber that had been shoved into the earth and bedecked with weather-worn ribbons. Each morning we danced and twined the ribbons around each other for the early-arriving crowds.

"Renaissance pole dancing?" a girl exclaimed. She was about my age, wearing sandals and shorts and a bright white tank top in the sun. Almost as fiery as the girl's strawberry red hair. She had a thin face and dull eyes. Tired rings. She laughed at her own joke.

"'Tis but a most harmless fertility dance, m'lady!" I said with a gracious bow. "'T'would you like to twine the pole?"

She seemed to consider this for a moment, but then her eyes widened. A look of sudden shock.

"Great dance," she said, distractedly, and hurried off toward the crowds.

I glanced over my shoulder, trying to figure what who could have been reacting to. But none of the other actors were near me. The man with the drinking horn had moved along. The booming pickle merchant hadn't even set up his barrel for the morning. No, she must have been reacting to me. She had recognized me or something. And then I recognized her as well.

She was Cora Braille.

When two o'clock rolled around, I said goodbye to my friends and marched out to the parking lot. I found my parents' old Benedict parked in the ambulance pull-off with the windows cracked. My father sat inside, reading *Gravity's Rainbow.* The book had hard blue letters set against a garish orange background, but it was the title that captivated me. *Gravity affects everything,* I thought.

I climbed inside. "You probably shouldn't park here, you know. It pisses them off if you're not an ambulance."

"I'm pretty sure an ambulance could get me to move if they needed to."

My father bent the page to mark his place and tossed the book onto the dash.

"You got my clothes for the wedding?"

"Yeah."

Five minutes later, we'd merged onto I-75. We were racing north through Flint and then through Saginaw County along prim-shouldered roads lining limitless cornfields and into a German tourist town in the middle of nowhere.

This was where my cousin Tracy Polchuk, eldest son of my deceased Aunt Ellie and her husband Terry, had brought his fiancée to get married. Frankenmuth seemed an odd choice. Both the Polchuks and the Havishams lived in Florida now. The couple had met at Notre Dame – Michelle as a student and Tracy as a waiter – but he had brought her up here one weekend. The trip must have made quite an impression because Michelle didn't want to get married anywhere else.

"How long you think 'til they get a divorce?" I whispered to Michael as I sat down beside him. The look he gave me told me that he couldn't have been more horrified if I had spit into the holy water.

As the wedding started, Tracy stood at the front of the church in his tan suit, an awed, lopsided smirk on his aftershaved face, a prim goatee making an oval across his chin. We stood as Michelle entered, her dark hair bound up with braids of pearls, a dress of lace and shells, and all the poise bred into her by her life in some alabaster turret above the Atlantic blues. Her unshakable poise. Titania marching slowly toward my Bottomish cousin.

I remembered the time the cops caught Tracy stealing his own dad's license plate.

One year, I thought. *No. Nine months.*

The next several hours were an endless drag. Something about the unending shifts from sitting to standing, awkward conversations with people I didn't know and didn't care about, and waiting too long for the food to come out. The sun was scorching – on the short walk from the church to our car, I felt like I was swimming through a soupy fog – and I felt stupid about my morning premonitions of an endless winter. By the time the garter had been thrown – accidentally caught by my widower Uncle Terry who looked at it with a combination of chagrin and amusement – I was ready to get away from the crowds, even if it meant dealing with the heat.

"Want to go see the covered bridge?" I asked Michael.

"Sure," he said. "May I?" he asked Aunt Mabel.

"Go ahead," she said. "Don't go too far."

The covered bridge wasn't exactly an antique. The concrete pillars that held it over the Cass River weren't any different from ordinary highway supports. But at least the bridge *looked* like it was out of some fairy tale. Two lanes ran beneath a peaked wooden roof, flanked on each side by walkways with views of the river.

Michael and I walked onto the bridge and stopped halfway across. We leaned on the railing and looked out to the north. Short-cropped grass banked sharply toward the Cass before running into a stone breakwall. Willow-shaded swans glided along the mahogany water. In the distance, a riverboat paddled slowly in our direction. I smelled honeysuckle. I smelled ripping ripeness. Just beyond the faux-German town, mile after mile of corn and soy stretched toward every horizon. I'm sure somewhere, a damn lamb was bleating a ballad of pastoral perfection. But I could kinda get why Michelle and Tracy had thought this was worth the trip from Florida. Maybe this was *their* escape.

"So," said Michael. "How you liking high school?"

"You didn't hear?" I asked him.

"Hear what?"

I told him about how Eastern had been closed for the last week due to the heat.

"I guess I'm not too surprised," he said. "Those'll come out of your snow days, so I hope you don't get a bunch of snow this winter."

He picked up a stone someone had left on the railing and dropped it over the edge. It vanished with a plonk that scattered both water and swans. I remembered the webworms in the poplar. I remembered my encounter with Cora. I didn't want to talk about either of these things.

"School better start on Monday," I said. "Because I'm gonna tear it up. Anyway. How about you?" I asked. "How's school? How's *Parc Pierre*?" I tried to say it in a fake French accent, but it sounded stupider coming out of my mouth than in my head.

Michael stared where the stone had disappeared.

"Y'know," he said. "I've basically been getting ready to go to Olan Academy ever since fourth grade. I mean, it wasn't really intense until seventh grade, but still, you had to get just about perfect grades, and take hard classes, and do after-school stuff too. And I did it all. I got in."

"They just couldn't get enough kids to keep it open."

"I think that was some of it. But also, that building had been getting worse for a long time. They never really fixed it up when they had the money to do it, and then they didn't have the money, and it's a huge building, and ... I got to take a tour of it. Last winter? Before they announced they were closing it. It was crazy, John. There was a radio station in there, and people had painted pictures all over the ceiling panels, and I guess they had their own radio show on the public radio, and some of the teachers were trying to get it going again. And there had been this ROTC training area above one of the gyms ... like there was this whole other secret gym in the building, and there was a swimming pool in the basement. They haven't been used in years, but they were there! And Mr. Agape was this incredible teacher who ran the drama club, and their plays were a big deal, and thousands of people came to see them every year. They had French and Spanish and Russian and German. I was trying to decide which language to take when they said they were closing it down."

"What are they going to do with the building?"

Michael shrugged. "I don't know. I mean, they'll probably demo it someday, but right now it's just sitting there. It has gargoyles, you know?"

I thought about the gargoyles at the University of Chicago. I hadn't realized that there were gargoyles on *any* building in Akawe.

"So, I was all set to go to the Olan Academy, and that's the year they closed it. And that was it for my mom, too. That school was the only reason she really stayed in Akawe. She said Parc Pierre was the other best school I could go to."

"So ... how *is* Parc Pierre?" I said it normally this time. I didn't want Michael to think I was making fun of him.

"I'm going to sound stupid, John, but I kind of hate it so far."

"Your new house is nice."

"Our house in Ashburn was nice. There aren't any sidewalks in Parc Pierre. You want to go for a walk you have to walk in the street. And I thought people in Akawe were jerks at school, but in Parc Pierre, they're just ... just jerks with money!"

"It's not that far. I'm sure people will come and see you."

Michael laughed bitterly. "Who other than you is going to come and see me? When you stopped eating lunch with us, everyone kind of drifted apart. I mean, Lucy and Gary and TJ were already gone. You left, and I think then Chuck thought he could go."

"It wasn't like I was hanging out with anyone else last year, okay? I had to get my grades up. And I wasn't like you, acing everything since fourth grade. I did shitty in seventh grade. I had to make it up fast!"

"Even Quanla and Selby. I don't remember who got pissed off at who. I think Quanla thought Selby was going to go to Southern, and then Selby decided to go to Eastern instead –"

"Selby's going to Eastern?"

"Yeah. I can't believe you don't know this, John."

"Well, how do you know?"

"Quanla told me. At the end of eighth grade."

"Well, how was I supposed to know? Things were just different after ... Adam and Selby found that skeleton!"

This was a lie. The skeleton was way after the fact. It was our freakout on the top of the hospital that had changed things between my friends and me.

"Okay. Maybe. But nobody could reach you after that."

"I was trying to get my grades up, okay?!"

"Really? That's all there was to it? I don't know. All of a sudden you have this girlfriend nobody knows, you have these new friends, these older kids –"

"Whatever. It had to happen. Anyway, I still think you should meet Chris. I think you'd like him. And you and Majenta like, like, the same music."

"It's hard enough keeping up with people I already *know* in Akawe. Why you think I'm going to try to meet *new* people it'll be hard to keep up with? I should probably just see who's cool in Parc Pierre. You know?"

"Nobody's cool in Parc Pierre. Except maybe you."

"Ha."

The riverboat was getting closer now. I could make out individual men and women. They were sitting placidly on the deck or leaning on the railing. They all seemed to be old, with bald heads or silver hair.

"You're still not that far," I said. "And you got out at a good time. Did you hear that the state came in and took over Akawe? The governor put in his guy, this emergency manager, and he can do whatever he wants. The mayor, the council, they can't do anything anymore. It's just this one guy, Margate. He makes all the decisions, and he just does whatever the governor says."

"Yeah. My mom was talking about it. She said it's way overdue. She said Akawe can't take care of itself."

"They switched off the water, you know. We aren't getting our water from Detroit anymore. We're getting it from the river, and they're fixing it in that old water plant on the North Side."

Michael coughed. "I did hear about the water thing. That sounds kind of messed up to me. My mom says the river water's fine, but ... what do you think? About the water?"

"It smells funny. It tastes funny. I don't know. We only drink it as coffee, and I guess that hides the weird taste. I still don't like it, though."

We stood silently for a moment. Now we could hear the sound of the paddle churning the water as the boat moved toward us. There were a couple of children standing on the deck, and they shrieked as they ran back and forth, pointing at the bridge as they approached.

"I'm worried about the next year," Michael said.

I swatted a mosquito.

"Why?" I asked.

"Doesn't it feel a little to you like everyone is holding their breath? Like everything is changing so fast, but we're all really quiet about it? The Olan Academy just closes at the start of the summer, and everyone's all surprised by that. And then my mom and I move, like, a month later. That all happened so fast, I can't even believe it. And now the state taking over and the whole thing with your water, and –"

"I think you're thinking about it too much, Michael. Shit always happens all the time."

"Your dad told me that someone got murdered on your block last week. A baby. And it was the mom who did it. What's going to happen with that?"

"I don't know, okay?!"

Michael flinched, surprised by my anger.

I didn't want to freak him out. So I went on.

"Look," I said. "I can't do nothing about it, can I? All I can do is just get good grades and get the fuck out as soon as Omara and I graduate!"

"Sorry," he said. "I didn't mean to, you know ... get you upset. It's just strange, how things are changing fast, but changing quiet. I just feel like something big is going to happen."

I didn't want to answer him, and I didn't have to. Just then the riverboat sounded its horn as it passed into the shadow of the bridge. Michael and I looked down onto those children and those old men and women, and they waved up at us and we waved back. Then they vanished into the darkness below.

The next day, back at the festival, I spent my last five dollars on two maple sugar candies, molded into the shape of leaves. Before the midday parade, I found Omara near the Griffin Stage, drinking tea.

"Can I have a sip?" I asked.

Omara handed me her cup. It was steaming and tasted like mint and chamomile.

"It's official," she said. "They got the school down to, like, eighty degrees. So we're starting tomorrow."

"Sweet," I said. "I'm ready. You ready?"

"I'm always ready."

I handed her one of my candies, then unwrapped my own.

We put them on our tongues like they were tabs of acid. My mouth flooded with a glow of melting sugar, but the aftertaste was bitter.

I kissed Omara.

The parade began.

It started with the wail of bagpipes as the kilted, bearded, white-shirted men with big beards and beer-bellies swayed by, followed by a couple of peasants hoisting plastic hoops on poles strung with twirling vinyl streamers, violet and blue. Artisans and merchants bearing heraldic crests painted onto their kites and Wankel shields, hawking their shops, costumes and corsets, garlands and slippers, the towering body puppets, Elizabethan muppets with dour frowns and feral grins spreading across their paper faces, banners and tapestries, flowers and stuffed animals, saucy wenches entreating merriment and action – "huzzah!" "huzzah!" – in clipped Cockneys that rang rounded and sharp but couldn't quite drown out that nasal Michigan shout, a man wearing what looked like a dead muskrat on his head, burlapped folk, shanty squatters, some modest gentry and participatrons, a troupe of belly-dancers shrilly blasting mizmars while a group of young actors followed behind, kicking out their legs and chanting "hey" at the end of each chorus line. "There's a booger in your sugar," sang an old bard. "No, it's snot!" rebounded the voice of a young actor. And masks, kilts, honey, and pewter. Henna tattoos and the pickle man. Pirates and rogues. Buccaneers and ne'er-do-wells. Wooden swords, wooden shields, wax hands, and bubble wands. Bosom chillers. Crystalware. The goateed rat-on-a-stick vendor followed by a papier-mâché Chinese dragon that serpentined through clouds of hovering chaff. More banners and body puppets and a cloud of shopkeepers spinning devil sticks, butterflies on stilts and bright striped puppet ponies, chanting and dancing, the actors' guilds, candles and lamps and leather and whips and chains and pottery and spices. Parasols and hookahs, tapestries and Tarot, resin and gum, hammocks and hats. Wooden beer steins carved from Leelanau trees. And finally, the royal guard and the royalty. They were dressed in finery, bedecked in crimson and purple, but certainly second in drama to their inbred Gothic cousins, the Vulgarian Court in exile.

And just as I had reforgotten everything *outside of all this* – the charge of the new school year, the breaking up of Akawe, and the baby who had been murdered across the street – I saw her again, in a flash of red hair. Cora. *She's come back.* She saw me as I saw her, and she turned her back.

"So she's still around," I said to myself.

"What?" asked Omara.

"I'll tell you in a minute," I said.

When the parade was over, I took Omara by the hand and led her back toward where I had seen Cora. I had seen her at the midpoint of the festival grounds, where the density of the East met the wide-open fields of the West. The grounds weren't large, but they were crowded, and Cora could have moved on by now.

I knew what I was looking for: that fire-engine red hair as distinctive as a fingerprint.

But I kept slipping into the expectation that I'd see her with someone else; a big man, maybe, draped in purple or zebra-striped furs, bling-slung with heavy sunglasses and a broad-brimmed hat. I knew it probably didn't work like that, but I couldn't stop thinking it. She'd been arrested for prostitution. I'd seen pimps on Ash Highway, and yeah, they looked like Huggy Bear.

I tried to explain to Omara as we passed out through the gray wooden gates and stepped into the crowds.

"She's Adam's ex-girlfriend," I said. "They were going out, like, two years ago. But Cora found out he got a blowjob from a guy at a camp, and so she dumped him."

"Okay, I remember that. But why –"

"Later, we found out she was busted for prostitution. Which is bullshit. How do you arrest a fourteen-year-old for that?! It isn't even the age of consent!"

"So ... why are you looking for her now?"

I didn't have an easy answer for that.

Seeing Cora had reminded me of people and situations I hadn't thought of in a long time. Her call-out at St. Francis was just a couple blocks from where Selby and I had once met Chalky, who was really the man with the knife. The man who had threatened Selby and me, and had told her to steal back the sunglasses. This made me think of Selby, and thinking about Selby made me think of Adam, and thinking about Adam brought me back to Cora again. And when my old friends had intruded on my sleep, usually on a hot and restless night, the steady sulfurous light from the street bleeding into my room because the sycamore was still small, and the occluding houses all burnt down or demolished, I lay awake and worried about my past proximity to sin and crime. The murder that Selby and Adam had discovered buried in the silos beyond the viaduct. The murder that had taped up Agit Street on my own block.

"So, what is it?" Omara asked. "You got an idea to help her out or something?"

"Like I said, I haven't even seen her in two years!"

"So you want to see her now, to what … to stare at her?"

"No! It's just … it's just I'm wondering … what happened to her. Where she's staying? What she's doing? Is she still … doing that? Or did she stop?"

"You think she was doing it because she wanted to do it?"

I stopped and looked at Omara, trying to understand her words, and she looked back at me, and I didn't understand.

We continued walking, and now I read skepticism in Omara's silence. We passed along the lip of a low slope, with shouts and laughter coming from the shops to our left, the clatter and haze of the jousting field to our right. I overheard the brightness of other conversations: an old man admired the hardwood walking stick he had just bought.

"John," said Omara, "if you don't plan on helping or changing anything, there really isn't any reason to look for her. I mean … if you don't plan on helping or changing, looking for her could actually be bad for her. Have you thought about that?"

"But it's like she's hiding or something!"

"Well, maybe she wants to stay hidden!"

Now I understood. It was what Omara had left unsaid. What was between the lines. Staring was rude, but staring at another's misfortune, their decline or collapse, was cruel. Making contact could open up rumors about Adam. About Cora. It might seem harmless, my curiosity, but I didn't know that for a fact. And if Cora had wanted me to know about her life, she probably wouldn't have run away from me when she saw me at the maypole. I wished I hadn't told Omara about it at all, but it was too late to take any of it back.

"You're right," I said. "I didn't mean it like that. It's just …"

"Let's go find Majenta. We should get back on the streets. Acting, I mean."

When I finally got home, well after dark, I went up to my room and looked out my window. I looked down the porch and onto the few swaying leaves of the sycamore below. I was amazed at how quickly it had grown. In just over a year, the tallest branches were already level with the bottom of my window. I wondered whether the tree would shade my room before I left for college. Before I left for Chicago with Omara.

Beyond our front yard, I looked across the demolished lots to the south and saw the outlines of forlorn bungalows the next block over, their chimneys poking into the sky like acrid steeples. If I could have seen farther, I would have found wild groves of trees and fields of wheat and hay, autumn pungent and ripe, siloed farms and evangelical churches, and the broad oceans. *They're out there if you follow the horizon far enough.* Torches hung from hooks on the prows of narrow boats, thrusting their lights above the inky swells, twilight piercing, secret seeking, full of memories of Masonic whispers, Maghrebian harbors, lighthouse beacons flashing out from perilous heights, Alexandrian and Byzantine. The waves as mountains. The mountains as clouds. The clouds as the curve of the earth tilted toward cold and darkness, toward Akawe.

But I couldn't see so far.

I let out a slow breath and looked out the window again.

I saw the murder house on the corner, all its lights out, and now the plastic police tape had ripped and was flapping in the wind.

Those halls, I asked myself. *What's it going to be like in those halls tomorrow? Who am I going to see? What is going to happen?*

"Why does this always happen?" I heard the voice of the grandmother echoing through my mind.

"Let's get on with it," I said.

The next day, my alarm woke me at 6:30. It was a darker gray outside, and I felt around for my clothes. I made a neat stack of my jeans, polo shirt, underwear, socks, and sunglasses. Dark gray.

I made my way down the hall. I could hear my mother stirring in her bedroom. My father had already left. He had an hour's drive each way to his new job at the XAuto factory in Canton. I went downstairs and turned on the shower in the dark. Steam and warmth filled the room. I closed my eyes and tilted my face into the spray. I felt myself peppered by metallic grit.

"The fuck?!" I said.

I reached out and flipped the light switch. The water racing from the shower head was tinged red like blood. It swirled in ruddy eddies before vanishing down the drain, leaving dots of crusted matter behind.

"Well, that's fucking great!" I cried.

"John, watch your mouth, please," came my mother's voice from outside. She sounded tired, not angry.

"I'm sorry," I yelled back. "But there's all this metal shit falling out the shower!"

I gave myself a sponge bath in the sink, though really, this wasn't much of an improvement. I sprayed myself a cloud of cologne. I didn't want to overdo it, but I figured it was better to smell like cinnamon than rusty water.

When I got out, my mother poured me a mug of black coffee and a bowl of Meijer's Mini-Wheats.

"New school year, John," she said. "You excited?"

"I'm gonna tear that school down," I said.

"Are you?"

"Hell yeah."

We clinked our coffee mugs together.

"When's Father getting home?" I asked.

"Double shift today. First in a while. Extra money's good, but he'll be tired when he gets back."

Out on the porch, a blue jay drove the smaller birds away from the bird feeder. He drove his hard beak in through the opening, catching a few seeds and spraying others out onto the ground.

I walked past the vacant lots to Whitmore Road. I crossed the street and stood at the bus stop, and looked at the murder house. Now a light was on in a second-story window. Probably a bathroom. *Once everyone's gone, maybe they'll demolish it*, I thought. *Maybe our block will grow a forest.*

After a few minutes, a school bus pulled over in front of me.

"Eastern?" the bus driver asked. "Southern?"

"Eastern," I said.

"Get on."

We pulled away north, swung onto Winters Road, and passed the tight-packed houses and gardens. Students on the dark bus, mostly freshmen and sophomores, were also packed tight in the rubbery seats. I smelled something chemical and something burning. Low muttering, gross jokes, gossip and whining, weary and amused. I didn't know many of these kids. Radcliffe students were supposed to matriculate to Southern High School, but a lot of white families filled out forms to send their kids to Eastern instead. It wasn't that Eastern was an all-white school. It was that Southern was almost an all-black school. I knew I'd recognize more kids once we got there.

The decade had aged since I had walked up Whitmore Road on the first day of seventh grade. The economy was still fresh and young and getting better, actually – jobs and money for everyone, as long as they didn't live in southeast Michigan – but everything else had hardened. Like when some terrorist assholes, pissed-off by Waco, blew up the Oklahoma City Federal Building and murdered a bunch of kids. The OJ Simpson trial started to wrap up, an earthquake in L.A. killed people, and a heatwave in Chicago killed ten times more. Everyone else was in the audience, eating their popcorn and watching it all unfurl. Shitty movies like *Batman Forever.* Movies like *Powder* to make you feel shitty.

The bus turned downhill. Crossed Aurelius Road. Through the cloudy tufts of elm trees, I made out the plantation-style eaves of Bellwood mansions. When I had started junior high, South Africa was an apartheid, and everyone was boycotting, but before I started high school, 20 million South Africans had voted to elect Nelson Mandela. He had spent years smashing rocks in a limestone quarry so sharp with glare and sunlight that it destroyed his tear ducts. I saw the expressway rising up before us. I put on my sunglasses.

Meanwhile, back home, the Republicans took over Congress, and we figured that was the end of Bill Clinton's plans for places like Akawe. It wasn't. X Automotives continued to close factory after factory, thousands of jobs vanished every year, the whole city drought-parched onto the welfare rolls, and now the president was making good on his promise to "end welfare as we know it."

The bus swept under I-63, the tree-cleared entrance ramps ranging off to either side and hung a left onto Valley Street. I glimpsed the graffitied Pipes as we passed. They had been painted with a lush green family tree, with one of the branches blackened and withered. "RIP MA / MRS. CHENE 1938 - 1995"

In '95, the Red Wings had made it to the Stanley Cup Finals for the first time in a million years, only to get spanked by the Devils. Still, they did a lot better than the Tigers in the AL East. The Pistons that year weren't much to write home about. Football hadn't really gotten going yet, but I didn't pay much attention to it anyway. In eighth grade, I hadn't had a lot of time for television, between theater, homework, chess club, and housework. Sometimes, I'd sat in front of the TV with a science or math book open in front of me, and some show clattered over the background. *Roseanne* or *Family Matters, Friends* or *Frasier, Doug* or *Clarissa*, but it's not like I was paying a lot of attention.

Actually, Omara was a big fan of *My So-Called Life*, and she had invited me over for every episode. We watched while her brothers and sisters shrieked and fought over the Game Boy or the Kool-Aid or whose turn it was to mow the lawn. Rayanne's mom was a mess. Ricky wound up on the streets. Angela never knew how good she had it. What, this was Pittsburgh?!

Meanwhile, music had been the front line of the battle between my friends and enemies.

"What bands are you into?" was the first thing whoever had asked me as soon as they had learned my name.

"The Miles Davis Quintet," I would tell them. "And Wu-Tang."

Although, I wasn't *that* into Wu-Tang, but I heard them plenty just by going out with Omara. She had all one million albums by all one million members. That's one trillion albums, total.

"Beastie Boys," Shannon would say.

"Primus," Nova would say.

"Oasis," Chris Allard would say.

"Fuck Oasis," Shannon would answer, punching his brother in the shoulder.

"The Cure," Majenta would say. "Sisters of Mercy. Bauhaus. Joy Division. Ministry. Swans. My Life with the Thrill Kill Kult."

If Ken were there, he'd trash all of our choices before launching into a monologue about Chuck D. And Justin Ray, our ghost friend, would just shake his head, like he didn't know what we were all about.

Michael was connected to the internet, and he helped me get an AOL account, and I sent Crystal an e-mail from time to time. People dialed in, logged on, played games, ordered books, and chatted with sexy strangers in underlit bedrooms. I thought it all seemed a little bit sketchy, but my father told me that the World Wide Web would only get bigger with time. In a few years, he said, the web would become so important that we couldn't imagine living without it.

We bailed out the Mexican economy. We docked with the Russians at Mir. Two groups of scientists were rapidly converging on a discovery by way of stars they called "standard candles," though I had no idea yet how important *that* was going to be. The fragile flower of peace that had followed Rwanda's civil war had blossomed into genocide and millions of murders while shells fell on Sarajevo. Gikondo, Nyarubuye, Trnopolje, Omarska. The world felt prosperous, and prosperity could be exhausting. But Akawe had been jaded since the first factory closings in the late 70s. Double-jaded, now that the state had taken over the city and disgusting rustwater was pouring out of our spigots and sinks. Whatever. I just had to get the grades and get out.

The bus pulled into the parking lot at Eastern and screeched to a stop. Everyone stood up, jostling for the line. Then, weary and anxious, we filed out into the morning.

Eastern High School could not have been more different from Radcliffe, other than them both being ghetto schools in a ghetto city. Radcliffe had been a compact, three-story brick building with a parking lot squeezed between the nearby houses and side streets, but Eastern was a sprawling, flat postwar thing set in a vast campus of rolling hills with groves of spruce and crabapple trees. Radcliffe had seemed overwhelmed by its neighborhood, while Eastern seemed to overwhelm everything nearby.

From the teachers' parking lot in front of the school, a rusted, chipping pedestrian bridge crossed over Valley Street and the adjacent rails into the huge Florentine Park, screened from view behind a scrubby bluff. On the other side of the school, long grassy slopes flowed down toward I-63, past weedy baseball diamonds and overgrown tennis courts, to where another pedestrian bridge arched over the expressway and spiraling down into what looked like a thick forest. To the south, toward the Pipes and Winters Road, a steep slope formed a natural amphitheater – blue-and-white painted stairs descending to the track and gridiron which, unlike the baseball diamonds and tennis courts, had recently been mowed and glistened with diamonds of dew. On the lip of this hill, a dun-colored garage marked the Akawe schools' drivers' ed course. In the far-off future of the following summer, this was where I would finally learn how to drive. North of the school, a cracked concrete track sloped a thousand feet down to an oak grove at the uttermost extreme of the Eastern campus. A faded sign looked out over this track, reading "DOPPLER SOAPBOX DERBY RUN."

In the middle of it all, with long views in all four directions lay Akawe Eastern High School. As I left the bus and walked toward the entrance, I passed dozens of windows, the coppery green roofline tilting up to mark the locations of the swimming pool, the gym, the cafeteria. I finally reached the main entrance between two protruding wings of the broad building. I adjusted my backpack, squared my shoulders, and passed easily through the metal detectors.

I took off my shades and my eyes fought to adjust. I stood in a dim, hot lobby. In the midst of the concrete floor, I made out a massive mosaic, every bit as intricate and ornate as the Wheels downtown. The picture stretched from wall to wall, projecting faint light from shards of fused glass: steely grays, sandy browns, pearled silvers, and airy blues. The Eastern Mariners had been conceived when Akawe had money, so here, in this shadowy room, barely visible beneath the coalescing sneakers and sweatpants and tracksuits and girls' shaved calves, I glimpsed rafts and waves, clouds and water, everything moving, nothing static, and it seemed an autumn storm was building against some foreign horizon.

"It's a Bonbright," said Chris, who had come up beside me.

"A what?"

"Arnold Bonbright. He's the guy who did the mosaics on East Street. He went to City High and then made this mosaic so people would feel loyal to Eastern."

"Crazy."

"Yeah, I know. I think it's based on some Dutch painting or something."

"It's too dark to see it, though. They need to turn on some lights."

"You think it's too dark *here*? Just wait 'til you see the rest of the school. Later."

And Chris moved along. I slid my sunglasses back into place and started walking. The dim lobby gave way to even darker halls, vaguely lit by spasming fluorescents and the occasional lights that struggled out through open classroom doors. I passed clusters of kids, hulking, whispering, laughing, throwing their hands up at a glance, a gesture, a greeting, and then I caught a narrow face watching me as we passed. It was Adam. He stretched his right arm under his left as he pivoted on his right foot, walking backward now, his left hand hooking his right elbow, his right arm turning up, the back of his hand toward me, fisted with his middle finger extended, his eyes glassy, and his mouth a horizontal line. I turned away. I didn't have nothing to say to him.

I reached my locker, squinted at the numbers, spun the lock, and dropped my backpack inside. I grabbed a single notebook and folder – it was all I needed – and started making my way toward my English class with Mr. Esper. I passed Majenta and gave her a sharp nod – the sort of greeting she'd appreciate – but she was too intent on parting the crowds, and I lost her. A moment later, I passed Ken Lessard, another one of my "new" friends, immaculate with his pale face and his hoodie drawn up, hiding his single earring.

"'Sup loser? 'Sup freshman?" he asked, reminding me why we all called him "The Fucker."

And then I saw Selby, walking with a tender-faced, agate-eyed white boy. He had dark hair and teeth that gleamed against the shadows. She quipped. He laughed nervously. They parted. The boy with the perfect teeth swept ahead of me, the kids flowing around him without resistance. He stopped at a point where the mass of students broke around another boy sitting sullenly in a wheelchair, unloading books at his locker. The agate-eyed boy leaned over his stark-shouldered friend and whispered in his ear. The boy in the wheelchair – older, larger, wiry – shook his head, but the agate-eyed boy grinned a nervous grin, patted his back, and moved off. The boy in the wheelchair gave the locker a casual flick. It slammed shut, shaking the adjacent lockers. At that moment, a distant door opened, and a single ray of sunlight illuminated him. A slender girl stood at his side. She had big bangs and a stupid grin, but she stood with her back against the wall and her ankles crossed, and she clutched a pink notebook in front of her stomach. The boy in the wheelchair pointed toward the light in the distance. The girl with the bangs gave him a nod, and they parted, moving in opposite directions. The door shut, and with it went the light.

"John!" I heard Omara's voice. "You made it!"

"Way to go, man!" Shannon was with her.

They both looked older in their day-to-day school clothes – khakis and second-hand polo shirts – than they did in their festival garb.

"Welcome to Eastern!" Omara said.

It took me a moment to respond.

"Go Mariners," I said. "Go Blue."

"Go Blue," said Shannon as he waved goodbye.

Omara hooked her arm in mine.

"Where you going?" she asked.

"English. Esper."

"That's not this way," she said, pulling me toward another, even darker, hall. "Over here."

The girl with the big bangs was moving ahead of us. I knew it was her because she was wearing a pink knit sweater. She was moving slowly, too, trying to push her way up the left side, against the flow of kids, instead of riding with the current on the right. But then a hand from the reached out and pulled her over, and I caught a glimpse of furrowed brow and pale face. It was Lucy. She'd cut her hair short like a boy's. I felt a shock as I recognized her. *She's* here? But now she was chatting easily with the big bangs girl, and they moved on ahead of me, oblivious to my presence.

"Were you tired this morning?" Omara was asking. "I was *so* tired!

Three days at the festival, and I was so excited last night, I couldn't sleep."

"Yeah," I said.

Lucy and the girl with the bangs said goodbye and split from each other. I tried to see where Lucy was going, but then Nova turned away from his locker and crashed into a sylphy blonde teacher in her late forties, almost knocking her over. She was smaller than most of the students and groped about the floor, trying to find her binder.

"Oh, damn! Sorry Miss Pavilik!" Nova said.

Miss Pavilik stood up, her yellow-gray hair tumbling in front of her face. I saw her mouth "It's fine," but "Mr. Richards!" barked Principal Newsome. "Slow down! Watch where you're going!"

Nova nodded, winked at Miss Pavilik, and turned the corner.

"He's a clown," Omara said fondly.

I felt dizzy in the darkness and motion.

"Well, I'd better ..." she went on, and kissed me on the cheek, and left.

I watched Mr. Newsome as he turned the other way into the main office. His penny loafers whispered against the aqua olefin carpet. He breezed past the secretaries, saying, "Miranda, I hope your situation is better today than it was yesterday." She answered with a sweet smile. "Much better, Mr. Newsome. Thank you for asking," but "how's the coffee today?" he wondered, and "I don't know," she said, because "I've got tea." She lifted the mug to her lips and took a tired, lukewarm glance out into the halls where the last of the students, a loose knot of cheerleaders, leaped and laughed toward their classroom doors, their bangle earrings swaying.

They passed the girl with the big bangs, who had evidently forgotten something at her locker. As she waded through the cluster of cheerleaders, she noticed that one of them was wearing a charm bracelet with dolphins, dice, and a yin-yang circle. It glimmered in the greenish fluorescence – an almost phosphorescent light – like coins piled at the bottom of a fountain.

She looked at this bracelet as if it was the most beautiful thing she had ever seen.

When the bell finally rang, I was sitting at a desk near the back of Mr. Esper's classroom. The radiator mote swirled around me, and I found a bookshelf filled with some authors I had heard of – Melville, Dickens – and many I had not: Calvino, Cortázar, Robbe-Grillet, and Sarduy.

"Hey!" said Mr. Esper. "Dr. Watson at the back! No sunglasses in my classroom!"

"Sorry," I said, taking them off. I had forgotten that I was wearing them.

54

He splayed his hands in front of him, taking in the whole classroom.

"Welcome to ninth grade," he said. "Welcome to high school."

"Can I go to the bathroom?" a kid asked.

"No, not now," the teacher answered.

"Where's the bathroom?"

"It doesn't matter because you can't go right now."

"What's a bathroom?"

"If you will all turn to page –"

"Mr. Esper, what's a bathroom?"

Within a few minutes, I knew that Eastern was going to be harder than Radcliffe. The work wasn't going to be harder. The work was probably going to be easier. No, this school was just fucked with confusion. The kids were bigger, more serious, less stupid, more stoopid. Mr. Esper just wanted us to take our textbooks home and cover them with paper grocery bags so that we could return them undamaged at the end of the year. We all started fighting over who got to skip this first homework assignment as soon as we realized that there weren't enough textbooks to go around. Mr. Esper had a lot of rules, but we didn't get through many of them because his classrooms almost immediately devolved into chaos.

After English, I moved on to Biology with Mrs. Clark. After that, Spanish 2 with Mrs. Dimitri and Geometry with Mr. Russell. A white middle-aged man, a white middle-aged lady, an older Asian lady, and a younger Black man. My teachers.

There were about 1600 students at Eastern. The school had been built for twice that number. But because the district had also laid-off teachers to pay down their deficit, there were about 40 kids to a class. Three out of every four classrooms were empty, but the occupied rooms were so crowded that kids stood against the back walls and sat on the radiators to find enough space.

As we'd been warned, some of the classrooms were hot, sweltering, steeping in a haze of BO, but others were so chilly that goosebumps covered my arms. At least one class, Spanish 2, would've satisfied Goldilocks with its oscillating fan turning in the corner, but even that wasn't enough to forestall an attempted coup: this standing up without asking, interrupting the teacher to talk to friends, tossing a basketball or a frisbee or wads of tissue and toilet paper, or just laughing and asking dumb questions.

It was also hard getting used to the dim, cavernous halls. Even though a third of the school had been accordioned off-limits, there were a dozen different halls, and they all looked the same. Wherever two halls intersected, opposing tides of students collided, leading to shouts, pushing, and jetsam of discarded textbooks and papers. The hardest part of my day was crossing these currents quickly enough to make it from one class to the next before the bell. Not that it mattered because, with all that noise and confusion, it usually took the teacher five minutes just to take attendance.

Then lunch.

The cafeteria was yellow like a vanilla blossom, and while it was just as decayed and burnt-out as the rest of Eastern, a bank of eastward facing windows lit this room more than any other part of the school.

I sat down with Omara, Chris, Nova, and Ken, and a tray of Tony's pizza – a flat square of congealed cheese and crusty sausage.

"Yum," said Omara.

"So how you like high school, John?" asked Chris.

"You were right about the halls," I said. "I can't see a fucking thing!"

"You missed it this morning," laughed Omara. "Nova crashed right into Miss Pavilik, and she fell over. He got told off by Newsome!"

"But not by Pavilik?" said Chris.

"She's a super nice lady," said Nova. "I feel bad. Usually, I'd love to knock a teacher over, but I felt like I slapped a nun there."

"She's aight," said Ken.

"I got her this semester," I said.

"What for? Algebra?" asked Chris.

"No," I said. "Astronomy."

"They let you take an elective as a freshman?"

"So?" I asked. "I just put it on the schedule."

"That class is mostly juniors and seniors," said Omara. "I bet they made a mistake filling out your schedule."

"I just thought it sounded cool," I said. "I guess I got lucky."

"Yeah, you did."

"Who else you got?" asked Nova.

"Esper –" I started.

"Hardass."

"Clark –"

"Harder ass."

"Dimitri?"

Nova thought for a moment. "She a weirdo."

"Jesus, what is it with the language teachers? My foreign language teacher at Radcliffe was a total joke."

"I never said she was a joke. Just a weirdo. I hope you like dancing. Who else?"

"Um. Russell."

"Oh, God!" snorted Ken.

"Yeah, that's gonna bore you to death –"

"Then Pavilik and Barakat ... but he's at Northern."

"Magnet class?"

"Yeah."

"Northern gonna eat you alive," Ken said with a smirk.

"Yeah?" I said. "Why's that?"

"Ghetto, dog."

I held out my hands, taking in everything around me. "And all this isn't?!"

"Not like Northern, man. Northern's in the hood."

But while Ken was dropping faux-gang signs, I saw Omara mouthing something to Chris. He gave his head an angry shake.

"Majenta?" Omara asked.

Chris shook his head again.

Ken didn't drop it. "You gonna go to Northern for classes, maybe you best go sit at the Chalk table."

"Man, fuck the Chalks," said Nova with a roll of his eyes.

But Ken was talking about a specific table. I swiveled around to look across the cafeteria at a long table near the far wall. A dozen or so kids sat there, mostly white, but not everyone, with low-slung jeans, sideways baseball caps, and lazy smiles. Ten of the kids formed a cluster at one end of the table, while three more gathered at the other end. I squinted at them. It was Selby and Lucy and the agate-eyed white boy I'd seen in the hall that morning. The boy with the teeth that seemed to gleam in the dark.

"The fuck?" I muttered.

"What is it?" asked Omara.

Lucy was laughing at some joke. Her hair still shocked me. She was still cute – still the same, worried, self-effacing Lucy – but with her hair cropped to within an inch of her scalp, her other features stood out more prominently. Her cheeks and eyes seemed sunken to me, even though this wasn't a worried moment for her. Even though she was laughing. Selby, on the other hand, was both taller and heavier than she had been in seventh grade. She probably had an inch and twenty pounds on me. She wore a grim expression and was talking softly, her eyes locked with those of the boy. And the boy himself seemed familiar, but I wasn't sure where I had seen him before. I didn't think he had been a student at Radcliffe. Radcliffe wasn't that big. I would have remembered him.

"What is it?" Omara repeated.

"Is it really Chalks at that table?" I asked.

"You know it is!" said Ken.

"That's Selby over there, and Lucy."

"Lucy?" asked Chris.

"His ex-girlfriend," sighed Omara, and Chris' eyebrows went up. "Well, who gives a shit about them? I'm right here."

"Yeah, sorry, it's just weird is all. I wouldn't expect either of them to hang out with Chalks. Or with each other, really."

"Why not?" asked Nova.

"Lucy kinda stole Selby's boyfriend. They weren't friends after that."

"So ..." began Omara.

So why are they there? I thought. *Even after everything else ... I thought they knew better than that.*

"So –" Chris cut in. He didn't like it when we argued in front of him. "What about after school, John? You auditioning for the play at AYT?"

"*Candide?*" I asked. "No, I don't think so."

"But I thought you wanted to do backstage."

"It'll just be set builds. They already got someone running sound and lights. I want, you know, something where I can actually do shit during the play. I thought I'd try out for the play here."

"*Sleepy Hollow?*" asked Nova.

"Yeah. I hear Mr. Agape's awesome."

"He is awesome," said Chris. "But you're just a freshman. No offense. You might not get more than set builds here either."

"Well, I want to try, at least. I mean, if I apply at AYT they'll expect me to do it. Why would I just do set builds when I have a chance at running sound or something?"

Chris gave a skeptical shrug. I took my sunglasses off. I wanted to get a better look at that Chalk table. To guess what they were laughing about.

Miss Pavilik's room must have been the darkest room of them all, but as I felt my way to an empty desk, I realized that this was intentional. She had turned out the overhead lights and instead projected a blurry but unmistakable image of the planet Saturn, its vanilla skies racing against the turbulent shores of bottomless hurricanes. After the bell, she introduced herself. She spoke softly, telling us about the Voyager mission. How the second probe had launched before the first. How the photos they had sent revealed the staggering complexity of the gas giants. How this had all happened so very recently.

Half of the class period had passed before I realized that I could hear her, even though her voice seemed scarcely louder than a whisper. This class, alone, was not overcrowded. There were twenty students here, and from the looks of them, they were all juniors and seniors, just as Omara had said. And since these twenty older students all wanted to take this class, they were all leaning forward, quiet and straining to hear Miss Pavilik as she spoke. When the class was over, I realized that she hadn't spoken about rules or requirements at all. Nothing about tests or homework or group projects or anything. Just Voyager racing out, still at the very beginning of its long interstellar voyage.

After Astronomy, it was time to board the bus for my magnet class at Northern. As we careened around the entrance ramp onto 63, I caught a glimpse of the downtown skyline, with the abandoned Akawe Rise and the Olan Foundation building looming over all.

By '95, developers were bragging that investments in Downtown Akawe had finally taken off. The foundations and nonprofits had decided to concentrate spending here as well. Emergency Manager Margate had sanctioned the process by handing off city properties for a buck and hurling out twenty-year tax abatements to anyone who knew the governor on a first-name basis. Slick new mixed-income housing the gloomy old buildings, while boutiques and themed bars and coffee shops fought over the last few vacancies on East Street.

But Akawe's outer neighborhoods didn't wear this prosperity. They looked shabbier than ever. Once sturdy houses leaned on their joints. Once ramshackle homes had been abandoned. Once abandoned homes had become scorched and blackened skeletons, and last year's firetraps were nothing but thick fields giving birth to cottonwoods and ghetto palms. Now, the neighborhoods where Akaweans actually *lived* were truly alone in their decay.

The bus swerved through the interchange and sank into the depression made by 292. We took the second exit onto "Center Ave. / Owen Rd." and then were we in the Os. We bumped along Owen and Orion, passing the brittle remnants of a gay bar that had been torched just a month after it had opened. Then the Christ's Bikers outpost, which also hosted Narcotics Anonymous and XAWU's radical Salvage caucus. We passed St. Francis Church and School, and while the Church was in good shape, the school's parking lot was empty and pitted with scrub growing up through the cracks.

Of the four remaining public high schools, Northern High School was the oldest. It had formerly been Alexander Pope Junior High, but when enrollment peaked in the 70s, the district had rededicated the building for older students. In '95, with just 1200 students, Northern was also the smallest of Akawe's public high schools. It still seemed huge to me.

The school dominated a large treeless field on Orion Avenue, surrounded by the vanishing neighborhood on three sides. On the fourth side, behind a double chain-link fence that had been incrementally scrapped for its steel, Northern backed up against a junk yard. There, islands of wrecked cars teetered unsteadily over a sea of dirt. The Northern campus was too small for an athletic field, but it was just a block from Victoria Park. Towering oaks loomed over the tennis courts and baseball diamonds while the Zibi River and Ash Highway converged to the west.

Northern itself bore a vague resemblance to the factories toward which it had once funneled its graduates. The brick walls with their limestone ornaments and copper verdure were the same as any of the old schools in Akawe. Still, there was something industrial about the banks of windows, tall-and-narrow rectangles divided into five smaller rectangles apiece, allowing enough light to illuminate the rooms, but welded shut as if offended by the thought of fresh air. There was something angry about the brick chimney thrusting up from the very center of the school like a cyclopean sundial, measuring out the diminishing hours of its students' lives. Northern High School had been built at the outset for the poor people of Akawe.

Inside, the halls were narrow and long, blocking out the light filtering down from circular lamps far overhead. As I wove my way through the labyrinthine hallways looking for Mr. Barakat's civics class, I caught voices and stories from every side.

"Flash don't know."

"Where'd he go?"

"His mama got knocked up by the Big Chalk, so now she's laid up legs up in a cast with a pacifier in her mouth."

"A pacifier?"

"Yeah, he pacified her good."

"So what, where's Flash?"

"Flash said he was gonna kill Big Chalk, so Chalk put his pups on Flash. But Flash was walking down the street scattering kibbles like Skittles. He was wearin' his sister's skirt and her panty hose, too, he didn't want to get seen so bad."

"When he comin' back?"

"God only knows."

"What about his moms?"

"Loving it like McDonald's."

"How's Billy?"

"So Claire says ..."

"Billy's my man, man."

"And then Leo says ..."

"You seen Billy at school today?"

"And everything was iridescent ... the candles and the shirts and the boots and the guns ..."

"Yeah, I can find Billy whenever I want."

"Scarlet sangria ..."

"You want to go the wall and have a word with Billy?"

"Old vermillion ..."

"Yeah, let's go."

"Toda la historia de la sociedad humana, hasta la actualidad, es una historia de luchas de clases."

"I pledge allegiance,"

"Libres y esclavos, patricios y plebeyos, barones y siervos de la gleba, maestros y oficiales; en una palabra, opresores y oprimidos, frente a frente siempre, empeñados en una lucha ininterrumpida, velada unas veces, y otras franca y abierta, en una lucha que conduce en cada etapa a la transformación revolucionaria de todo el régimen social o al exterminio de ambas clases beligerantes."

"to the flag,"

"Para que todos juntos, trabajadores, estudiantes, hombres de todas las ideologías, de todas las religiones, con nuestras diferencias lógicas, sepamos unirnos para construir una sociedad más justa, donde el hombre no sea lobo del hombre, sino su compañero y su hermano."

"of the United States of America."

"Big Chalk keeps a beehive of girls in his nest."

"And to the Republic"

"Numbers?"

"for which it stands"

"Thirteen? Fourteen?"

"one nation"

"That ain't that many."

"under God"

"No, that's their ages. He's got, like, forty, fifty of 'em."

"indivisible"

"Damn, Big Chalk. Damn."

"with liberty and justice for all."

"One million Black men will be marching on down the National Mall, and you'd best believe they'll all be pissed as hell about what they –"

"This is that very Mab that plats the manes of horses in the night, and bakes the elflocks in foul sluttish hairs, which once untangled, much misfortune bodes ..."

"There really can be no peace without justice. There can be no justice without truth. And there can be no truth unless someone rises up to tell you the truth."

"This is the hag, when maids lie on their backs, that presses them and learns them first to bear, making them women of good carriage ..."

"Qubilah speaks that truth."

"This is she –"

"What's true is true no matter who does the speaking."

"Pero el 'pobre' no existe como un hecho 'fatal'; su existencia no es neutral políticamente ni inocente éticamente."

"Tell him he's about to copulate with a creature from outer space."

"Por ello la pobreza del pobre es una exigencia que nos llama a construir un orden social distinto."

"If I have felt pain, I should be able to identify with others who feel pain."

"Quando dou comida aos pobres chamam-me de santo. Quando pergunto por que eles são pobres chamam-me de comunista."

"What's in the box?!?"

"Big Chalk. He knows. Big Chalk knows everything."

"No, no, no! I ordered the books last April!"

"Who is Big Chalk anyway?"

"See, my receipt. My money. Right here. You processed it."

"Big Chalk is God, and God's everywhere."

As the halls had emptied, I had landed outside the heavy oak doors of a gloomy library where two women were arguing.

"So what I want to know is," said the first, "why aren't my books here now, and when will I have them? I've followed up with you guys like twenty times about this!"

"Look," came a second voice, softer. "Today is the first time I've seen this, and all I know is that nobody else has asked me to place your order."

"Then you should still have my money, shouldn't you?" The first, agitated.

"If you gave us your money –"

"You can see that I did. I have your receipt –"

"Then we can place the order tomorrow, and it ought to be here before the end of the month."

"We were supposed to get these books for class last week. I already rearranged things for the last week. Now I have to do it for a whole month?!"

I recognized the angry voice.

It was Ms. Ropoli.

Ms. Ropoli had been about the last person I had expected to run into in this strange building, but my favorite teacher saw my speechlessness as an opportunity.

"Since you're just standing there, John," she said, "will you help me steer this cart back to my classroom."

"Sure ..." I said.

Textbooks and paperbacks packed the metal cart. One of the wheels wouldn't turn. Still, we managed to wrestle the books out into the hall and toward the distant elevator.

"What are these?" I asked.

"A book on Cesar Chavez," Ms. Ropoli said. "I was going to cover this next spring, but since I've got to wait a month for the books on the English Civil War, it looks like I'll be doing things a bit out of order. So ... you're in tenth grade now?"

"Ninth."

"What are you here for? I thought you lived over by Radcliffe."

"Yeah. I'm here for my magnet class. Civics. With Mr. Barakat. I got lost looking for his classroom."

"They bus you all the way over here just to take Civics?"

"I mean ... this is the social studies magnet, right?"

"You know the Civics curriculum isn't any different between the schools. You could take it at Eastern, and it would be just as good as taking it here. How long does it take you to get back home on the buses?"

"I don't know. This is my first day ... because Eastern was closed all last week because of the heat."

"Oh, that's right. Well, it's going to take you an hour to get back, at least, if you have to transfer downtown."

I thought about that.

"I mean," I said, "I don't have much of a choice. If I want to stay in the magnet program."

"Yeah, you're a pretty good student, aren't you, John?"

I laughed.

"I wasn't in seventh grade," I said, "except for your class."

"I hear that every now and then."

"I'm a lot better now, though."

"Obviously, you're pretty good if you're taking magnet classes. Still, Civics? In a few months, you're not even going to make it home before dark."

We'd reached the end of the hall and a brassy elevator. It rumbled into life for us, and we pushed the cart inside, pulled the accordion gate closed, and pushed the scratched number "3." The elevator creaked up to the third floor, slowly, as if one student and teacher and a cart full of books were almost too much to carry.

The third floor was brighter than the others, and through the gray windows I saw lanes of gravel swerving through the junkyard below. Ms. Ropoli's room was in the northwesterly corner, about as far from the elevator as possible, and by the time I had pushed the heavy cart down two long halls and over the rubber strip into the room, my forehead was slick with sweat. But I also had a thrill of expectation. *Is her classroom going to be decorated here like it was at Beckford?*

Ms. Ropoli didn't disappoint. All of her old decorations were here; the dozens of posters, flags, and trinkets, although the high ceiling and large windows made this room seem far more expansive than her classroom at Beckford had been. Five students were scattered among several dozen desks.

"You have a class right now?" I asked, looking at the students.

They looked up curiously at me, then back down at their books. Each of the students was reading a different book, however. One was writing. Another was gluing bits of macaroni to what looked like a black sheet of leather.

"What class is this?" I asked.

"Technically, this is my prep hour, but I do some independent studies for students who want a bit of extra credit. Anyway, thank you for your help, John."

"You're welcome."

She sat down at her desk, put on a pair of glasses I'd never seen before, and hunched over a stack of paper with a red pen.

"Um," I said. "I think I'll need a hall pass. Now that class is almost halfway over. I've probably been counted absent."

"That's right," she said. "That's right, I'm sorry, John."

"Who's his teacher?" asked one of the students. A pimply white boy, older and bigger than me, with greasy brown hair that fell over his eyes.

"Barakat," said Ms. Ropoli.

The boy snorted in amusement.

"Shut it, Kyle."

Ms. Ropoli started filling out the note, then paused.

"You know," she said. "I wonder ... huh. Is there any chance *you'd* like to do an independent study this semester?"

"Me?"

"It'd kind of be like an independent study and class assistant."

"But how would that work? I have to take civics. It's, like, required."

"It'd be a lot of work because you'll still have to do your civics homework ... I mean, we'd have to have it listed as civics on your transcript somehow. Plus, you'd have the reading and homework I'd give you and helping me out around the classroom a bit." Ms. Ropoli leaned forward conspiratorially. "It's probably going to be more interesting than whatever they're doing downstairs."

"I should talk it over with my parents first," I said. "Can I let you know tomorrow?"

"Sure!" Ms. Ropoli said. "No pressure. Entirely up to you."

When I finally got home, the house was empty. The plastic lid was latched onto the top of the record player, and my father's book was open, spine wide, upon the couch. Nobody else was going to be home for another two hours. I poured myself a pop, microwaved a ham-and-cheese sandwich, and sat down at the table to cover my textbooks.

All of my curiosity about high school had evaporated. It was all a mess. An ill-lit, stinking, noisy, close-packed mess, and it was hard to see how I was going to find what I needed there to get into a place like the University of Chicago. Now, Omara's persistent anxieties made a lot more sense to me. The overcrowded classrooms in under-full schools, the broken ventilation, the always-hot radiators, the too-few buses, the too-long rides, the underpaid teachers, the confused and hungry kids.

I couldn't do shit about any of that.

So instead, I focused on the moment: cutting the paper grocery bags along the lines, folding them carefully around my textbook covers, then taping the edges into place.

I had to tape them well.

I had to protect these books for the whole year.

The next day, my alarm woke me at 6:30. Outside, the gray, a shade deeper. I felt around for my clothes. I stacked them – t-shirt, jeans, socks, underwear, and sunglasses. Dark red. I went downstairs and started the shower. The room filled with steam. I stepped inside, and flecks of sand pelted my face. Rust-red water flooded around my feet.

"Son of a bitch!" I yelled.

"John!" my mother's voice rang in from the kitchen.

"No! I don't care! I need a shower! I don't want to go to school smelling like rust, okay?!"

For the second day in a row, I washed in the sink. Ever after putting on cologne, I could smell the stink of metal on my skin. My arms and chest were breaking out in rashes. I rubbed lotion on the welts, got dressed, and went out into the gray day.

On the bus, I closed my eyes to prepare for the noise and chaos of the hours to come. The engine was loud, but I knew that Eastern would be louder. The predawn light was gloomy, but I anticipated those gloomier halls. *Chicago*, I thought. *Just think of Chicago. Just think of Omara. Just think of how wonderful it will be to get out of here and leave all this shit behind. Just let the noise and the darkness move through you like it doesn't even matter.*

I made it through that day. But I could see the exhaustion on Mr. Esper's face as he handed out the day's notes on printouts, having given up on talking over everyone. I saw it in Mrs. Clark's frown as she stood at the front of the class, staring us down, waiting for the talking to subside, only to go ignored for five minutes. For ten. Mrs. Dimitri taught Spanish as if we were all well-behaved little angels. I couldn't hear a damn thing she said. I had to corner her after class just to find out what the day's homework was. I think she was surprised that I gave a shit. Mr. Russell hadn't made it to school that day. The substitute stood in front of us and shrugged.

Chicago, Chicago, Chicago ... I thought. *Omara, Omara, Omara ...*

Lunch gave me a small respite. I sat next to Omara and shoveled my food down without talking so that I'd have a few minutes to hold her hand quietly beside me.

After lunch, Miss Pavilik's class picked up right where we had left off the first day. We still hadn't heard any rules or received our textbooks. She talked about comets. Told us about the water in their dirty hearts. About Halley's comet that had visited in 1986 and would visit again when I was 81 years old.

Then, the bus took me out to Northern, where I saw Bill Chapman for the first time since I had followed him to Quiz Bowl in seventh grade. He gave me a shy wave from halfway down the hall as we passed between classes. I wondered if I could ignore him, then decided he had already seen me see him, and waved back.

"We should hang out sometime, John," he said as I passed him.

"Yeah," I called over my shoulder. "I'll give you a call sometime!"

I stopped by Ms. Ropoli's class, and she gave me the permit to have my parents sign to make my independent study official. We'd decided, between us, to look at local government and what it could and could not do. How it could be limited or empowered by the state or federal government. I already had a feeling that this work was going to rip Margate a new one.

As I rode the two buses home, I realized that the first half of my schedule sucked but the second half was dope. I sat alone at the dining room table, covering the last of my textbooks. Then my mother got home. She fixed us pasta for dinner, and we ate it in the living room, in front of the nightly news. There wasn't anybody to call that night. My friends were all at auditions for *Candide* at Akawe Youth Theatre. My father got back right as I was heading up to bed.

"Is school good, John?" he asked, his voice beat.

"School sucks, Father," I said. "But I'm working hard."

"Good boy, you." And he collapsed upon the couch.

I lay down, thinking *Omara, Chicago, Omara, Chicago,* and I saw the Sears Tower throwing its shadow far out over the stern waters of Lake Michigan for just a moment before I fell asleep.

On Thursday, the third day of school, I found several gallon jugs of water set outside our shower. I used a half-gallon to douse myself, sputtering in the cold room. Then I soaped myself up from head to foot. Then I used another half-gallon to rinse all the soap off. It was a pain-in-the-ass, but for the first time in three days I felt nominally clean.

School didn't change. I mean, it didn't get any easier. Those first three days could have been a month, and summer vacation could have happened a century ago. Thanksgiving and Christmas were millennia ahead of me. But at least Thursday was different. At the end of the day, I caught a bus back to Eastern for the auditions for *The Legend of Sleepy Hollow.* My secret weapon was in my backpack: an old Irish cappie my father wore sometimes. I put it on as I strode into the school. I put my sunglasses on, too. *I'm going to look cooler than anyone else in that room,* I thought. *Because I don't give a fuck. Coolness is not giving a fuck. And anyway, who cares what they think? I'm not going to be here forever. I'm going to be somewhere else.*

As I entered the drab auditorium, its carpeted floor the color of sea foam and spit, I saw more than a hundred students boiling through the space. *Holy shit,* I thought. Clearly, a lot of kids wanted to work on the play.

I found Majenta and took a seat next to her.

"Wicked hat," she said.

From her, this was quite a compliment.

"Thanks," I said, tipping the brim at her.

A minute later, Ken and Chris joined us.

"Damn, John," Ken said. "Omara's gonna be pissed she finds out you flirtin' with all the drama club bitches."

"Who says I'm flirtin'?"

"Who you not flirtin' with, wearing a hat like that?"

"You all went to the AYT auditions yesterday?" I asked Chris.

"Not Ken," he answered. "But Nova, Maj, and me, yeah."

"You get cast?"

"We don't know yet."

"Friends!" bellowed Mr. Agape suddenly, and we all snapped to attention. "Mariners! Countrymen! Lend me your ears!" He was a white guy in his 40s, medium build, salt-and-pepper hair. He wasn't a large man, but his presence was *huge.* "Those of you who get cast, you will be representing not only yourselves, you will be representing all of the Akawe Community Schools, because Eastern is our only high school with a drama club. Okay? When I watch you read, when I watch you perform, I will make my decisions based not only upon your performances, I mean, upon your talent but also upon your professionalism and seriousness. Now, have you all filled out your audition forms?"

Everyone stared back.

"I don't think we actually gave them the forms yet," said an older girl dressed all in black.

"Give them the forms!" yelled Mr. Agape as he came down from the stage.

A couple of student assistants went up and down the aisles, handing out clipboards with papers and pencils attached.

I filled in my name, age, and grade. I x'ed out the middle of the form, which was all about acting experience. For tech experience, I wrote about my work at Radcliffe, AYT, and the RenFest. For scheduling conflicts, the RenFest took out all the weekends through the end of September, and I'd have to find out whether there was any overlap with the Chess Club, but I guessed that the play would take precedent. I felt pretty good when I handed my clipboard to the surly-looking boy in black.

"You just doing tech?" he asked.

"Yeah."

"You don't have to stay."

"I don't got nowhere else to go right now."

He moved off.

My friends were all auditioning for acting parts. First, all the boys went up on the stage. There were maybe thirty of them auditioning for eight parts. Back in the audience, I realized that Ken was right. I was definitely being noticed. When I'd put on the cappie and shades, I'd been going for "fuck all y'all" more than major player, but the mess made plans of lice and zen.

"Hey," said a girl sitting behind me.

"Hey," I said, giving her the most casual glance over my shoulder.

"You freshman?"

"Yeah."

"From what school?"

"Radcliffe."

"Radcliffe?!"

I pumped my fist passively in the air.

"Oh, well," she said, "I like your hat."

I glanced over my shoulder. "I like your hair." She was wearing a pink headband.

"It ain't nothin'," she said.

She tore a piece of paper out of a notebook, wrote a phone number on the inside, and gave it to me. I took it without giving her another look.

Damn, I thought, though I kept my excitement inside. *Why didn't I have a hat like this before I was going out?*

After a few minutes, the boys came back into the house, and the girls replaced them onstage. There were about eighty girls auditioning for ten parts. I felt bad for everyone. Plenty of girls were going to get shut out just by the numbers. I got out my math book and noodled away at some problems without really solving any of them. After forever, the huge crowd of girls came back into the auditorium, and Mr. Agape called up maybe twenty boys, including Chris and Ken, to read from a few new scenes. Majenta got out her homework and started working.

"Nice hat, John!" came a voice.

"Thanks," I said, casual, dismissive. "It ain't nothin'."

"Oh, yeah, you're a real playa' now."

I turned around in my seat and found myself looking at Lucy two rows back. Her short-cropped hair. She flashed the same furtive, wry smile that had murdered me two years before. Another girl sat next to Lucy. It was the girl with the big bangs that I had seen on the first day of school. She smiled brightly, though I didn't know what she was so happy about.

"Hey, Lucy," I said. "I didn't even know this was your school."

"It is," she said as if this explained anything.

"Shouldn't you be at Southern?"

"My mom didn't want me going there. So, she signed me up with one of my dad's addresses."

"That's clever."

"Not really. It's abandoned. So, if they mail anything, we don't get it."

I nodded slowly.

The big-banged girl hadn't stopped smiling, but her grin had faded a bit. Now it was a distracted smile. She was looking over my shoulder, studying something on the wall behind me.

"That exit sign is green," she said.

"What?" asked Lucy and me.

"Aren't they usually red?" the girl asked.

I realized that I was attracted to her, straightforwardly. She was pretty. Slender, but not stickish, wearing a white sweatshirt, jeans, and pink-and-white sneakers, all shiny and clean. Her hair had been cut in a short bob, while the rounded bangs almost obscured her eyebrows. Her brown eyes were golden with warmth. I wanted to stare at her.

"John," said Lucy. "This is my friend May. May, this is John, who I was telling you about. My first boyfriend. You remember?"

"Hello," said May. "I do like your hat."

"Thanks," I said.

"Come back and sit with us!" said Lucy.

"Maj, I'll be back there," I said.

Majenta gave a slight nod. She didn't look up from her textbook.

I moved back to join Lucy and May, with the stagehand glaring at me for reasons I couldn't figure out.

"What you sayin' about me, Lucy?" I asked.

"You worried I'm talkin' trash? I don't talk trash, John. You know that. Anyway, I got good taste in boyfriends."

"You still with Gary?"

"No, we broke up last year. We're still friends, though. He's a math genius. I told him he's gonna build skyscrapers and bridges that'll save a lot of peoples' lives. Now I'm going out with Eli Ostyn. He isn't a genius. He's a gentle angel."

"What did I do that was so great?"

"You were great at wearing sunglasses, and listening to jazz, and pissing people off."

I smiled because what could I even say about that?

"What about you?" Lucy asked. "You still going out with O-what's-her-name?"

"Omara Hutton."

"Yeah, that's right. She seems cool."

"She is."

"Too cool for you."

"She hasn't figured that out yet," I said.

Lucy barked out a laugh, louder and more abrasive than I'd heard before. The stagehand glared at her.

"So, how about you?" I asked May. "You weren't at Radcliffe. How do you two know each other?"

"Oh, no," said May. "I think it was because of Selby, wasn't it?"

"Yeah," said Lucy. "Selby invited you over to the lunch table."

"Selby was real nice to my brother and me."

"Yeah, watch out for Selby's *niceness*, May."

"You and Selby are cool now?" I asked. "I thought you hated each other. After the whole Gary thing."

Lucy shrugged. "I never really hated her. I just thought it was real shitty the way she treated him. Chatty to the max. They made up. I didn't have to be pissy about it. I just don't ... I just don't always like how she marionettes everyone, y'know?"

I thought back to how Selby had stolen my sunglasses while waiting to break up with me.

"Yeah," I said. "I know." *We're talking now, aren't we? She's getting her digs in but's trusting me with this dirt on Selby.* "What's with your lunch table anyway? Aren't those kids Chalks?"

Lucy's cheeks flushed a little. "No," she said. "They're not. Though people say that shit. A lot of those kids are from over around Ash. So, you know, they shoulda gone to Northern before the district redrew, you know? So here they don't even know that many people at this school, and since some of them have brothers with the Chalks, they just assume ... I mean, not everyone has a perfect family like you, John!"

"I don't think *anyone* has a perfect family," I said.

"Whatever," she said. "Eli –"

"Is he that white kid with the perfect teeth?"

That took her aback. "I was going to say he's pasty with black hair, but yeah, he's got good teeth, I guess. Why you noticing his teeth?"

"I don't know." Now that she mentioned it, it had been a strange thing to say. "Lots of us have messed-up teeth, you know? Me too."

"Shit. Maybe he should be *your* boyfriend."

"No, Omara has good teeth too."

"And what about me? Do I have good teeth, John?"

"Not great. But you dumped me, remember?"

"Yeah, but it wasn't because of your teeth. It was because you were acting like a stringy taint."

May laughed like a crow. "So funny!" she said. "You're talking like you're going out right now! I have pretty nice teeth, I think."

"John can be very charming, May," Lucy answered. "He doesn't say the really shitty things until you get to know him better."

"Piss off!" I snapped. I figured that was the cappie talking.

"Peace oaf," May said. "Isn't that how they would say it in England? Like when they don't like somebody, they would tell them to 'peace oaf?' Peace oaf!"

That's when I realized that however cute May was, she was also as dumb as a rock.

The first Friday of ninth grade landed cool and clear. I took my plastic jug shower, dressed, put on my father's cappie, and set out for the bus. Yeah, I caught some snickers as I squeezed past the older students, but I walked with a swagger. I knew when I was being noticed.

Right before lunch, Mr. Agape posted the cast and crew list up outside his classroom. Noisy chatter. Laughter. One girl started crying and stormed off. "It's a bit part!" she whined to one of her friends. I waited by the lockers across the hall until the crowd started to disperse. When it was my turn, I lifted the cast list and looked at the crew sheet underneath. Eleven kids had been listed for tech, with twenty more assigned to set builds. I didn't see my name on either list. I scanned it again, just in case I'd read wrong. I hadn't. But I knew I'd completed the audition form and returned it to the student assistant. *Maybe they misplaced it?*

I found Mr. Agape at his desk, grading papers and eating an egg salad sandwich.

"Hi," I said. "I just checked the cast list and –"

"You're John Bridge, right?"

"Yeah, that's right. Um –"

"Spit it out."

"Yeah, I just checked the cast and crew list, and I wasn't listed."

"Well, that means I must not have picked you!" He barked out a harsh laugh. He took a sip from his pop.

"Why not? I mean, I know that some of that stuff is for upperclassmen, but ..."

"But why didn't I list you when pretty much anyone can help work on sets? Let me see ..."

He opened his desk drawer and pulled out the uneven stack of audition forms. He flipped through until he found mine. "Uh-huh, uh-huh, uh-huh," he said, squinting at my writing. "You," he said, "have really tiny handwriting, John. It's hard to read. I'm sure your teachers would appreciate it if you wrote a little larger."

He coughed twice.

"Okay," he said. "Okay, yeah. You work at the Renaissance Festival every weekend, right?"

"Yeah."

"Hey, that got to be fun, right? Isn't that fun? I love it there! You ... sell food or ... or what?"

"Academy –"

"Academy! So they're teaching you acting, too. Excellent, excellent, yes, you'll be great here. Please keep auditioning!"

"Yeah. I've learned a lot there. And about backstage and –"

"Yeah, well, that is a *problem* because all our set builds are on Saturday, you see? Saturday mornings, to be precise. Mr. Smith runs all those, and we need the stage for rehearsals weeknights, so it doesn't look like you'd be able to come to any of the set builds. Sorry."

"But ... my friend Majenta got in, I saw, and she works at the Ren Fest."

"Cast or crew?"

"Um. Cast."

"See, like I said, cast rehearses weeknights. Crew does weekends. So, she just has a busy schedule, but you have what I call an intractable scheduling conflict."

"Oh."

"Says here you did a lot of work with Akawe Youth Theatre? Great guys over there. Always pushing the envelope ... in a good way! Hey, aren't they doing *Candide*? Can you help them out with that?"

"Maybe?" I said. "They already had their auditions."

"Oh man," said Mr. Agape. "Yeah, that's a shame. Well, call and ask. It can't hurt, right? How long does the Renaissance Festival go this year?"

"Until the end of September."

"Huh. Well, let me know when you're all done, then. We go up at the end of October. Might need some help for the last set build or two. Of course, any spotlight work or whatever that opens up will go to someone who's gone to all the set builds, you know that, right? But we can probably find something for you to do on your Saturday mornings."

"Sure," I said.

"Lot of freshmen get disappointed when they don't get cast or whatever. You know how many kids auditioned yesterday? Ninety-six. You know how many got cast? Twenty-two. Almost all of them upperclassmen. You know what I tell those kids? Come back. Come back, come back, come back, and don't give up."

"Okay," I said. "I understand. Thanks."

"Fuck Mr. Agape," I said to myself as I made my way down the hall.

I had planned for ninth grade to be a noisy convergence of planning and programming to set my life aflight in clouds of rotors and diesel smoke. I had been so certain of getting a job backstage that I hadn't stopped to consider how much depended upon it. Mr. Agape had just killed my plans before they had even gotten underway.

I wanted to punch the lockers as I passed them, but I didn't, because whose fault was this, really? All of the set builds were on weekends because Mr. Agape needed the stage for weeknight rehearsals." That made sense. My schedule was the problem. So this was all *my* fault.

At lunch, I was bitching about the whole situation to my friends, and Ken started laughing.

"What?" I asked. "What is it?"

"What else was it you said you were going to do since you can't do the play?"

"Chess Club. Something wrong with that?"

"No, no," he was laughing harder. "There ain't no Chess Club here, dog!"

"What?! Yeah, there is. It's listed in the student handbook."

"Then they made a mistake because there ain't. Look, I was in Chess Club last year! Mr. Cason was running it. He got laid off when Olan school closed. So, I *know* he ain't doing Chess Club."

I knew he was fucking with me. I mean, he had to be fucking with me. We called him "The Fucker" for a reason.

"Hey, John," said Omara, putting her arm on my back. "It's too late to apply at the Farm, but maybe I can see if they need someone to help out with yearbook? We need people to go to extracurricular events and take pictures!"

But yearbook didn't have anything to do with anything I was planning for the future.

"Excuse me," I said. "I'll be back in a bit."

I left the cafeteria and went to the office, and sure enough, the Chess Club had been canceled at the end of the last school year. Someone had forgotten to remove it from the handbook.

Omara met me at my locker.

"What's wrong with yearbook?" she demanded.

"Nothing's wrong with it," I said. "I just don't want to do it."

"Seems like you want to do anything as long as I'm not doing it."

"What? No! Don't be crazy!"

Lucy and May passed us. Lucy carefully avoided my eyes, but May waved, still wearing that same bright smile.

"Who's that bitch?" asked Omara.

"You know what, Omara, I'm just going to take a second and bang my head against my locker, okay?"

On the ride back home from Northern, I'd lost my bus transfer to the #9. After arguing with the bus driver, he let me on but chewed me out for being an idiot, so I was pissed about that, too. When I got home, I went up to my room and lay down, and just let everything be still for a minute. *Nothing is happening the way it's supposed to! What's gonna happen next?*

A soft knock on my door.

I turned toward it as it cracked open.

My father was standing there, with a small smile and red rings around his eyes. He always looked exhausted.

"What?" I asked.

"There's gonna be a jazz set out at one of the clubs tonight. I thought you might want to go."

"Tonight?" Hey, it would be a break from all the other fuckery. "Can I invite my friends?"

"Sure, I guess. Always happy to help you, you know, know jazz."

Ugh, he was so embarrassing. But it was worth it to get out of the house and forget my problems for a few hours. I called Omara, and then the line was busy, so I called Chris.

"Hey," he said. "That sounds great. Shannon can come too."

"Of course," I said. "I'm inviting Omara, Majenta, and Nova, too."

"Omara can't come out tonight. She's at the Olan Farm; then she's going out with her dad to test for her driver's license."

"Shit, that's tonight?"

"Yeah, you'd better give her a call and wish her luck!"

I called Nova and Majenta, and they were both on board. After we had the pizza kit for dinner, my father swept from house to house, gathering my friends into the Benedict, and then cycled through exit ramps and service drives until we arrived at a forsaken back road. It was all meadowed except for a dilapidated green building on one side and a bombed-out school on the other, overshadowed by hills and ancient sycamore trees.

"This is the Treemonisha Club," my father said, waving in the direction of the green building. "There used to be blues joints all over town, but this is the only one left."

I had to pretend that I had never been here before, but I faintly remembered in seventh grade when Lucy had brought me here with my friends. *Lucy.* Jesus, my breath still caught a little when I thought her name to myself. Her father had been trying to sell the place. Two years later, his metal sign still hung off the side of the building, reading: "ANDREW BANNER REAL ESTATE AND LIQUIDATIONS, LLC." The Reapers had defaced it with a jagged black sickle.

I smiled to myself.

"Hey, John," said Chris. "You call Omara about her driving test?"

"Fuck!" I muttered.

The music wasn't coming from the clubhouse but from the gravel parking lot to its side. We found several dozen people gathered in and around a blue-and-white party tent stocked with a couple of coolers and a keg. My father bought Coke for my friends and me and a Bud Light for himself.

The music wasn't blues, though. It wasn't jazz, either, though it was jazzish. It was funky. Fast and fat and catchy. A whole brass band, a portable organ, a drummer, and two or three singers trading off spots, dueling or dancing with each other. It was hard to know where the music stopped and the crowd began.

I'd been expecting to be one of the only white faces in the crowd, but there was a lot of everyone around. Old Black men and women who might have been original members of the Treemonisha Club when it had been the bejeweled throne of a musical court. Their sons, daughters, grandsons, granddaughters all swaying in the breeze or rapping off in the shadows. Laughing and gossiping about the trouble that they were going to see and cause over the weekend. Then there were the aging white hippies, a few reeking of pot and hash, beer dazed, smiling and talking to the old-timers by first name. There must have been some shop rats, too, because my father greeted a beflanneled fat man with an enormous beard and a jacket broadcasting the numbers of his local. They gave each other a bear hug and started talking fast together. And I saw a few white kids too, and a few Mexican kids, and a familiar-looking chubby Asian girl.

"Hey, John!"

It was Crystal. She'd braided her hair. It made her look younger than she had before. Other than that, she looked the same as she had the summer before.

"Hey Crystal, how you doin'?"

"Fine, I guess! Haven't seen you in a while. Rode my bike here. I'm glad I came. This is amazing!"

"It is. What is it?"

"I don't know, but I love it! By the way –"

But my father, who was standing nearby and must have overheard us, turned toward Crystal and me.

"So," he said. "I just found out a bit about our entertainment here." He took a long pull at his beer. "The singers are great. Look past the singers, though. See that guy on trumpet over there? He's... ach, I don't remember his name. Whatever. He was a member of Africa '70, Fela Kuti's band back in the day. Fela Kuti's a Nigerian musician who made some incredible, just incredible music. Caused some trouble, too. Political."

Majenta had heard this and steered her way into our midst.

"Political?" she asked.

"His biggest hit was about how the Nigerian army were zombies and slaughterers," my father said. "So Kuti had this commune, and the army attacked it. They threw his mother out of a window and killed her. They beat the shit out of Kuti, too." He took a drink.

Whoever he was, this trumpeter knew his way around the instrument. His fingers danced in a frenzy as he swung his horn wide and poured it into the deepening sky. But then I noticed the drummer tucked off to the side, beneath the tent where there was enough room to spread his kit. He was tired, lean, my father's age or older, with dark skin and close-cropped hair. He beat through the rhythms with effortless ease. The sounds he rapped out sounded harder and angrier than what seemed possible from his gentle, almost tender grip. The man was wearing gray sunglasses, even though the day was already giving way to twilight.

I knew him, I thought. *I know him.* Was he someone my father had worked with? My father didn't seem to know him. Did he have some connection to the school? That didn't make a lot of sense, either. How the hell could I have known this man? He seemed *so* familiar to me.

"Anyway, I should start biking back before it gets dark," said Crystal. "Call me, okay?"

And she made the universal sign for "phone" – thumb and pinky – as I waved and watched her leave.

My friends and I made our way farther into the crowd. A fire had been built in a garbage drum, and its light reflected weirdly off the awning of the tent and the green clubhouse bricks. We kept going and found a group of kids dancing just inside the ring of firelight. They were all younger than us, six, eight, ten years old, happy that they had survived a week of school to experience this syncopated release. We joined them and lost ourselves in the music, forgetting to worry, for the moment, about how we looked or where we were standing. We floated along with the beat, and I caught myself smiling.

Then I remembered Bennett, and Cora, and Lucy at the Chalk table, and above all, the fact that I hadn't been given a job in *Sleepy Hollow*, and I stopped moving. The music was for those with the joy and confidence to ride it. I moped on over to the chain-link fence at the back of the weedy lot and watched everyone else enjoying themselves.

After a few minutes, Nova caught my eye and made his way over.

"I ain't gonna lie, John," he said. "I saw that hat you were wearing today. I didn't think you could pull that off."

"Yeah," said Chris, joining us. "You should've seen him at the auditions the other day. John had the ladies eating out of his hand!" He smiled.

"Omara pissed?" asked Nova.

"I ain't called nobody."

"You got numbers?"

"Yeah, I got one."

"I counted three," said Chris.

"No," I said. "Those other two you're thinking of were my ex-girlfriend and her friend. Nothing's going to happen there."

"You dump her?" asked Nova.

"No. She dumped me. Anyway, it was seventh grade. Who cares?"

"What about her friend?" asked Chris. I was surprised by his curiosity.

"Do you know her?"

"May Dunham? Yeah, I know a bit about her."

"She's cute. She seems kind of dumb."

"Yeah, that's pretty much what I know about her. She was in my grade, but she got held back. I mean, she got held back twice." He sounded apologetic about it.

"So, she's gotta be, what, sixteen? Seventeen?"

"Her brother's gangsta baller, though," said Nova.

"Gangsta baller?" I asked.

"Wild West, dog."

He pantomimed putting on a cowboy hat. He put it on to the beat. I could only imagine that it was a black hat. Nova drew an air pistol and fired it into the sky. Chris rolled his eyes.

83

"You can't prove none of that," he said.

"No," said Nova, holstering his "gun." "I can't. Nobody can. And that's why he's so dope, he does all this shit and nobody can pin it on him!"

"What are you talking about?" I asked.

Nova loved getting to sell a story: "Drake Dunham got paralyzed a couple years back after he and his friends fell from a hospital roof. He was out of school for a few months while they were putting him, um, back together. Well, that was when the Mafia got tore up by the feds. So Drake gets out and right away starts working with this guy from the Mafia in Juvie –"

Well, some of it. I felt a jolt of electricity as, for a moment, I saw the weeds replaced by the uppermost branches of trees far below. The dark and howling wind. The rattle of gravel underneath our feet on the hospital roof where Drake and his friends had fallen. Yes, I *knew* this. Well, some of it. The music sounded far away.

"Ziggurat," I said. "Yeah, I heard some of this shit. Drake was a pusher with the Chalks, too, right."

"Well, that was weird," said Nova. "See, the Chalks were all in the Os, but Drake lives over east somewhere. I mean, he goes to Eastern, you know?"

"That doesn't mean much. I should be going to Southern."

"No, I mean he lives out on the East Side. So, Drake wasn't a Chalk, but he was slinging dope for them. But he must've snapped when he fell or something because, now, he's like a lone wolf. Ziggurat was in juvie, Drake on the East Side, and he's been buying from the Chalks and selling to the Masters, buying from the Masters, and selling to the Chalks, and nobody can do shit about it because he's superfly and supersly."

"Why do they buy from him? Don't they all have their own suppliers?"

Shannon had quietly joined us.

"It's rumors," he said. "I don't believe none of it."

"What they say," said Chris, "is that Drake gets guns from the Masters and gets them to the Chalks –"

"And they're warrin', meaning the Masters getting' blasted with their own Glocks!" Nova giggled.

"But all the O-Sugar comes through the Chalks, so Drake gets that from the Chalks, sells it to the Masters."

"Wait, what?!" I asked. "The Chalks have all the O-Sugar? I don't get it. How does that work?"

"You ain't heard that even?" asked Nova. "Yeah, nobody can figure it out. That I do know because my uncle works for the man. The feds want to know *bad* where O-Sugar comes from because it is a *weird* drug. Like nobody understands it. How it works. I mean, chemically."

"Pharmacologically," added Chris. Now it was Nova's turn to roll his eyes.

"They've arrested tons of Chalks," he said. "Interrogated them. Hell, they've probably infiltrated the gang. Seriously, some of those kids slinging dope out in the Os are *Federal agents*, but they still ain't figured out where O-Sugar's coming from! Nobody knows who's making the stuff, or how you make it, but if you want it, it's coming from the Chalks."

"Hey!" yelled Majenta from the edge of the music. "What the hell? If you aren't going to dance, then why are you even here?"

I saw my father standing back in the crowd, tilting his beer back until it was empty.

The next morning, I woke up into the provisional freedom of the Renaissance Festival. The weekend wasn't off to a great start. Eddie wanted Omara to drive down without any of her friends distracting her, so I was on my own for a ride. My father took me. We hadn't been on the road for long before he asked me how school was going. I gave him the short version, telling him that most of my classes were chaos, and I'd screwed up the auditions, and the chess club had been canceled, and I didn't have anything to do after school.

"Huh," he said. "Well, nothing else, I'm sure we can find some stuff for you to do around the house."

That's just what I want, I thought.

"So," he said. "I should probably tell you how I've been lately."

"I know you're about to."

My father gave a cold laugh before launching into a rambling description of the militant local representing RAN. I'd heard these rants a hundred times since the strike of '94. The union had won that year, waiting the company out and extracting all their concessions except for job security. After that, XAuto accelerated its retreat from Akawe. I couldn't even have told you how many shoprats worked in Akawe anymore; it was fewer and fewer every month.

I was able to nod my head slowly, taking the beat from his inflection, but my thoughts were somewhere else. I was looking out the window and thinking about the day ahead. It was miserable weather. Cold and drizzly. The windshield wipers blurred the smoky trees and the paint lines as they raced past us. In a half-hour, I'd be freezing my ass off.

"What would you think about that?" my father asked.

"Yes," I said.

"Yes?" he said. "That isn't an answer. I mean about you getting a job."

"Wait, what?"

"John, aren't you paying attention? This is important. I know it doesn't seem like it makes any difference to you, but no, it really is important."

I stared at him.

"The RAN Contract?" he said. "Group B?" My father gestured with both hands, annoyed, and the car drifted toward the shoulder.

"Woah," I said, and he took the wheel. Steered us back toward safety.

"So, you weren't paying attention at all?" he asked.

"I'm sorry," I said. "I'm really tired."

"Maybe I should have made it quicker. All I was saying was that January 1st, my job's gone. Poof. No more. I'm the third-lowest seniority at Canton, and they don't need that many diemakers anymore. A lot of this stuff is automated now. I won't have any money to give you. We'll be scraping by on the layoff fund until it runs out, or I take a buyout or find something else. Point is, I don't have any money to give you any more. Nothing. And your mother's paychecks are all going to utilities. So, you want some spending money of your own, I don't see any other way around it."

I understood now. He was probably going to have to settle for less pay at a different factory even farther away. That sucked, but my own money wasn't *that* important. I mean, nobody fantasized about stealing my shoes but they weren't ratty shit either. My friends were all cheap dates. My extracurriculars were mostly free. I didn't need a lot of spending money. I did need him off my back because this speech was driving me slowly insane.

"Yeah, I'll get a job," I said.

"I don't think the Renaissance Festival counts," he said. "I mean, they don't really pay you."

"No, I know," I said. "But it's going to be over in a few weeks anyway. And when it is, I mean, I've got to do something, right?"

"Right. I guess that's what I'm saying."

Mud puddles had replaced the usual festival dust with clouds of mist floating above them. I usually didn't like working in this kind of weather, but it matched my mood today. The slower pace and fewer patrons meant more time to think. I borrowed some hot rocks from the Scotch Eggs boy – his name was Harold – and warmed myself by the grill. Finally, it was time to go out into the rain again, among the fallen needles and ruts of the nearly desolate Children's Dell to learn about fencing.

When the workshop was over, I made my way to where Omara leaned wearily against one of the towering pines.

"Hey," I said.

"Hey."

"So ... um. So, how did your driving test go?"

"I passed it, John," she said. "The last half-block, I was driving in the wrong lane, I was so stressed and tired, but yeah, I passed it."

"So, you can drive now?"

"Drove down here today."

"I'm proud of you."

"Hah! Proud! You are?"

"I am!"

"Then kiss me."

It was a good kiss.

"So ... Chris told me about the concert you all went to last night," Omara said.

"I'm sorry we went without you. We wanted to invite you."

"It's okay. Anyway, look. I'm sorry about yelling at you yesterday."

"I'm sorry too."

"I'm sorry you didn't get into the play and that it messed all of your plans up."

"I'll figure out something."

"If you change your mind about yearbook ..."

"I'll figure out something."

I wanted to forget everything going on back at home, but I couldn't stop counting the number of hours left until I'd be back in the dark bathroom, pouring a jug full of water over my head, or standing on the corner across from the murder house waiting for the bus, or stepping into the crowded, smelly, dim classroom where Mr. Esper shouted out the day's lessons. Those moments were approaching. The present was becoming the past. For just a moment, I held the hot rocks in my palms until they started to burn. The next moment, I was standing outside Omara's tent with my sleeping bag in hand. The next moment, I was riding home with my friends and the windows fogging up. Eddie rested one palm lightly on the wheel as Omara steered us gently along the interstate.

It all slipped through and away too quickly to track. The last thing I remember from that weekend was driving out to Aunt Mabel's in Parc Pierre on Sunday night so that my parents and I could take real showers for a change. Michael brushed his teeth and waved at me. After that, I was back at Eastern for another week.

I made it through that Monday. I went home and watched TV and did my homework. As I did, I knew that Chris and Nova were at the AYT rehearsal reading through the script. Ken would have been the next room over working on building the set. Majenta was rehearsing *Sleepy Hollow* at Eastern. Omara was working at the Olan Farm. I sat at the dining room table, put on a record, and poured myself another cup of coffee. Some grit stuck in my teeth, and I wondered whether it was from stray coffee grounds or bits of rust dredged up from the pipes. I poured out the rest of the pot. I got myself a glass of milk instead.

I made it through Tuesday.

I made it through Wednesday.

I was exhausted again by Thursday, but I was getting all of my homework in on time. My test scores were high because there wasn't anything else to distract me. I tried to pretend that this was as valuable as working backstage on a play. That those scores were more important for getting into the University of Chicago. *If you don't have the grades, you don't have shit,* I told myself. *Right?*

I was just one day away from the Ren Fest, from metal roses and sage burning and hot tea and bawdy songs, and ... *I have two more weekends*, I thought. *Two more weekends, and then I'm stuck here all fall and all winter.*

The next morning, I came downstairs to find my father awake and my mother sitting on the couch beside him, watching the morning news. That seemed strange because she usually liked to read the newspaper instead. I went into the kitchen, poured myself a cold mug of coffee, examined it for floating debris, then warmed it in the microwave

"Don't drink that, John!" my mother said, her voice tense. She was standing in the kitchen doorway, watching the coffee mug as it spun upon the turntable. My mother beckoned me, and I followed her back into the living room.

The anchor on the news – the *national* news – was talking about Akawe. He was talking about how the city had changed its drinking water from the Detroit system to the Zibi River.

"But that wasn't us!" I said. "We didn't do that. That was Margate and the governor!"

"Shhh!" said my father.

The switch had happened more than a year before. It was meant to be a temporary fix for reasons I didn't understand. The mayor and the city council had signed off on those plans, I think. But switching to the river? That was all Margate.

The Emergency Manager had said that the move would save us money. But now, it seemed …

My father hadn't shaved. He looked like he hadn't showered, either. I wondered when any of us would be able to take a shower in that downstairs bathroom again. I wondered if we ever would.

The Emergency Manager had said that Detroit had kicked *us* off their supply. But actually, it turned out that …

Well.

And people had complained about the water after the switch.

Right away, they had complained. Sometimes, they said, their water smelled like chlorine, and sometimes it just smelled *wrong*. Like rotting fish or rotten vegetation, or … metals. Grit and glimmer. Like a weird texture against your skin that could be slippery or sticky or harsh. Rashes and welts. I absently scratched at my arm as I listened. Clouds and discoloration. Water the color of a bruised summer sunset. Water the color of a rosy spring dawn. Water the color of diarrhea.

But for more than a year, the city and the state had said that we were making a big deal about nothing. Akawe people, always bitching, you know. Yeah, they said, our water passed all of the federal tests, standards upheld by the state, so most of us had just shrugged and made the best of it.

Meanwhile, E. Coli contaminations had put half of the city on boil notices off-and-on all summer long. These had come from water-main breaks that caused depressurization. The water department, trying to balance it out or some shit, had opened fire hydrants. The blood-colored water had flooded out in front of the grave of Archie's house and drizzled down the hill to vanish into the storm drain on the corner of South Street. The whole thing had reminded me of the elevator scene from *The Shining*.

Then again, sometimes the water was *over*chlorinated. A week before Christmas, we'd received letters from the city telling us that the trihalomethane levels had crossed a threshold. Trihalomethanes were supposed to be a carcinogen. Trihalomethanes happened when river gunk and chemical disinfectants went out for a dance together.

And, of course, this defective water had been expensive. Whenever the pipes cracked, whenever the treatment went out of whack, it showed up on our water bills. Now, we were paying more for our water than anyone else in the country.

Yet somewhere, behind the cost of the water and the fact that it had smelled bad and looked bad and felt bad and tasted bad, behind the water main breaks and the foaming hydrants, the rust and the rashes and the E. Coli and the total trihalomethanes, behind the gossip about Margate and the Akawe City Council, one more complaint was thrown into the mix: there was lead.

One house in the city had tested high for the metal. Like, *toxic waste* high. A kid had gotten sick. He'd been in and out of the hospital. He'd lost a lot of weight. Who knew how this would affect him for the rest of his life? The state had told the mother that this was a problem specific to their house. But a city employee had put her in touch with an EPA scientist, and he had conducted some tests that suggested a big problem, a serious problem, a problem that should have been predicted. Now it turned out ...

... that the state had told the city to withhold anticorrosives from our drinking water.

... that the lead-soldered pipes had flaked off particles throughout the system, but especially in the poorer neighborhoods where the pipes were in worse shape.

... and the state had ordered the city to doctor its own test results to conceal the real lead levels in Akawe.

... and the city and the EPA had ignored their own scientists who had argued that something was very wrong.

... and the city and the state had told us to keep drinking this water, going in front of crowds, going on the news, telling us to tip our heads back and to pour the stuff down our throats ...

And evidently ...

There was too much.

I couldn't wrap my head around it. My memory went back to Mr. Kolin in seventh grade, stalking back and forth before his cloudy chalkboard and ranting at us about our poisoned town. "Lead poisoning lowers your IQ, wrecks your bones and muscles and hearing, and can give you seizures." He had been talking about the dirt in Celestine Park on the East Side, but this, today, was much bigger than that. I wondered what he would have told his students about the water we'd been drinking for the last year-and-a-half.

"Well," my father said. "I suppose I'd better get you to school. Don't use the drinking fountains there. We'll figure something out."

My friends and I were mostly able to ignore the whole water *thing* that weekend at the Renaissance Festival. Even a swamp in the middle of nowhere was able to find cleaner piped water than Akawe. Even the icy showers at Camp Jellystone were better than pouring a plastic jug over my head.

When we got back to school the following week – *I've only got one more week of the festival ... just one more week.* – we found black garbage bags taped over the disconnected drinking fountains throughout Eastern High School. The school was still uncomfortably hot, with the thousand-and-a-half of us sliding up and down those humid halls, bodies against bodies, squinting to see and sweating with movement ... we swallowed our spit, and it wasn't enough. The vending machines sold out of Coke and Dr. Pepper. Not that it mattered. My father did have any money to give me for pop, either.

I wondered whether Margate was tired, too, because I couldn't imagine how he could sleep at night, being such an itchy-puckered self-fellating asshole.

Yeah, fuck that guy.

On Wednesday, I think, the city called a press conference to talk about the whole lead thing. At the last minute, the event was closed to the public. A couple dozen reporters sat in the empty Olan Auditorium at XAI. They sat just a couple hundred feet from the Zibi River. They were waiting from Governor Rhinelander, the man himself, to take the podium and announce that all would be forgiven. We could love him once more, for he'd given us permission to reconnect Akawe to the Detroit tap before there was any further damage.

But Governor Rhinelander wasn't in Akawe, or even Michigan, that day. He was vacationing in California. His man with Natural Resources or whatever department got up on stage, shuffled about a little, then said with stentorian seriousness that the state would give us some thousands of dollars for tests and temporary filters.

Yeah, fuck those motherfuckers.

The drives started on Thursday. Suburbs I had sneered at, spat at, rolled my eyes at, too rich, too white, too intentionally *separated from us,* bought up pallets of bottled water, and had them delivered to our schools. Local bars partnered with elementary schools; patrons donated water bottles for the kids and got a bottle of beer in return. The Olan Foundation, that patronizing patriarch, committed tens of thousands of dollars for filters. X Automotives, who had built us and left us in the dust, committed thousands of dollars for filters. Patrick Rhinelander fiddled with his dick in the Capitol rotunda.

On Friday, Ms. Ropoli assigned me to sit in on a city council meeting. A woman stood up to talk about the water, complaining that she felt "like a second-class citizen."

"This never would have happened in Parc Pierre or Elmwood or Owen or Brighton," she said. "This never would have happened in one of those *white* cities."

I swallowed my spit again and ground my fists in my pockets.

The last weekend of the Ren Fest came.

Freedom. Escape. A moment. The last moment. Costumes. Incense. Music. Maple treats, brown sugar, a north woods bite beaten into distilled beet sweetness. Suck it under your tongue and swallow the syrup.

It rained during the end-of-the-day parade on the final Sunday, and a rainbow stretched out to the east, over the mud and muddles.

Then it was over.

My last escape from Akawe, until I finally had the grades and the money and the plan and the poise to blow out of this motherfucker for good. I hated the rust that ringed the bolts that held the city limits sign to its perch off the interstate. I hated looking at it as we drove back into town.

On Monday, we found out that five of the schools, including Truman, my elementary school, had high lead levels. In one case, seven times the federal limit. That meant 300 kids had been drinking this shit for more than a year since the switch. What would happen to them? How would it hit them and their families years down the line? When some boy punched his father, when some girl forgot her homework again, would it be because that was who they were – their character, their flaws, their bad attitudes, bad personalities – or would that be the lead talking from the cellar of their first-grade drinking fountain? Lead talking from its new home nestled in some corner of their brain? Shit, did this shit have anything to do with what Bennett's mom had done to Bennett? Maybe he'd been doomed before his mom ever slammed his head against the bedroom wall.

I thought about all the coffee my parents and I had made with that water, the pasta we had boiled, and the soup, and I shuddered.

That week, Patrick Rhinelander finally came to Akawe. Someone must have told him that the city was ready to riot – at least the West End and the Os – because the reconnection to Detroit still hadn't happened. It was "working its way through the legislature." Service from the D was going to cost ten million for one year. The state was going to pay half that. How very generous of them after their lies and fuckups. The rest was going to be divided between Akawe and the Olan Foundation. It made perfect sense that we would only have to pay *part* of the penalty for their attempt to kill us.

When I got home from school, I found my father sitting in the recliner, watching TV.

"They didn't need you today?" I asked.

"Nope."

"Do they do that? Do they just ... send you home?"

"They usually let me know a day or two ahead of time."

"Is it bad news?"

"It isn't good news."

I looked out the window. It was raining again. Rain so thick that it almost made the day look like night. Miserable gray rain. Clear, potable rain. I felt like the whole month of September, the last month you could really pretend was part of the summer, had been flooded by our water.

My father took a sip of his Bud Lite.

"No lead in this," he said with a cynical grin.

I took my backpack up to my room and came back down. I was holding an empty water bottle in my hands, and I turned it over and over, staring at the carpet.

"So," I said. "Renaissance Festival ended last weekend, and I think maybe next week I'll start calling around about jobs like you said. So I can have some spending money. But we were talking at Festival last week about how it might be fun to have a party for us ... for all of us doing the Academy ... now that it's all over. Because we're all going apart now. I mean, we won't see each other until next summer and, who knows, maybe not even then. So, we'd like to have a party. But we don't have a place to have it."

My father was listening carefully. He was, maybe, starting to realize that I was about to ask him a different question than the one he had expected.

"I was thinking maybe we could have it here. But I know we won't. I mean, I know we don't have the money for it. But I thought I'd ask anyway."

My father looked at me for a long time.

"Ah, hell," he said. "Let's do it."

It had been years since there had been a big party of any sort at my house.

My parents weren't party people, and I usually liked to go to my friends' houses where they wouldn't be looking over my shoulder.

But I'd realized that unless someone offered to have the Ren Fest party, it wasn't going to happen. I also felt proud, that autumn, of the tired old house with its crumbling stucco and mossy shingles. As houses had come down on Agit Street, one after another, 1012 lorded over the vacant lots and weedy foundations of a half-block of the city. I felt proud of my parents, always tired these days, always a little on edge, the mortgage on the ocean floor, the credit cards climbing toward their lofty limits. They worked endlessly. They never stopped working. I wanted my friends to see them and know that we belonged to each other. We weren't fuck ups. We were going to get through all the shit. Hell, maybe we'd even end up somewhere tropical.

We held our party on the second Friday of October – Friday the 13th – and while autumn had descended with chill menace, the leaves hurrying through greens, yellows, reds, and browns to fall, things had warmed up at the end of that week. Thursday night had brought thunder and quick, hard rain, and while Friday was dark with moldy clouds frowning overhead, it was hard not to savor the brief heat, the late warmth. The wet smell of dirt and worms. The presence of water in the air. At lunch, Omara, Chris, and I talked about how to dress, what snacks to take, what music to bring. We'd invited our other friends, too, of course: in addition to Shannon, Nova, and Majenta, who did Academy with us, we'd asked Ken and Justin. But I knew Justin wasn't going to come. Justin never came unless he wasn't expected. Our ghost friend.

After school, I helped my parents clean up the first floor: the living room, the dining room, the kitchen, the study; any place people might want to stand around and talk or dance.

Then the sun went down, and I stood on the front porch, waiting for the guests, and the prisming incandescence of the porch light cut dagger sharp.

Omara arrived first.

"Where should I put this?" she asked my mother. "It's from my dad."

It was a bag of tortilla chips and some seven-layer bean dip.

"Here," said my mother. "Follow me."

It wasn't long before the others started to arrive. Ronny and Joss, kids from Pontiac. Then three more kids who had been in Academy for a year longer than me; they were from Ferndale and Royal Oak. A girl from Chelsea named Tracy. A boy from Burton named Tracy. Then the Allard brothers arrived with Majenta. Sarah and Anthony walked over from Eastern. They were eighteen, and he was going to college in Ann Arbor. A whole other world for them, but closer than I planned to be.

"Is that *Gravity's Rainbow?*" he said, catching a glimpse of my father's dog-eared book.

"Yeah," I said.

"First edition! Wicked!"

After that, it got hard to keep track of all the beaten-down and beaten-up cars filling up the vacant lot to our west, then all of Agit Street from Whitmore clear down to South. Most of the kids had driven themselves or caught a ride with a friend, and my parents looked a little surprised at their age, their breasts, their facial hair. Before, my friends had always been kids. These were *young adults.* The night was wet outside, but the house was warm, so we drank pop, ate pizza, talked loudly, and laughed from room to room. More than twenty kids were in my house. Then, there were more than thirty.

"Mr. Bridge," asked Josh M, an upperclassman from Lake Orion. (There were three Joshes.) "Would you mind if I put on some music?"

"Go right ahead," said my father, holding a mug of coffee in two hands.

"Thank you kindly," said Josh.

When My Bloody Valentine started blasting from the four living room speakers, my father almost spilled his drink.

"Maybe we should turn it down a bit," he shouted, but nobody could hear him.

He turned it down anyway, but my friends were understanding. Obliging. They were just happy to have a party. Even though my parents weren't quite sure what to do with them, I liked watching everyone pass through my house, leaving gentle prints of dirt upon the carpets, smoking cloves and cigarettes on the back porch. Their laughter and shouts must have drifted for blocks in the thick, muggy air. For once, just once, *my* house was the house where things were happening.

At one point, when my parents were in the kitchen, Katie L, a girl who knew Majenta through their common love of the Cure, caught me by the sleeve.

"I want to see your bedroom!" she said.

"What?!"

"Oh my god! I'm going to lie down in John Bridge's bed!"

She ran up the stairs down the hall to my room and leaped under the covers.

"What are you doing?!" I asked, laughing, standing in the hall.

"Nothing at all," she said, climbing out again. "But now I'm going to tell everyone." As she passed me on the way out: "Your room smells like cologne, by the way. It's nice."

When I got downstairs, my mother took me by the sleeve.

"John, I need to ask you –" she said.

"Oh, about that. She didn't ... we didn't –"

"Come with me," she said and led me into the study, which my friends hadn't discovered yet.

"There's a kid out there ... um, I don't know his name, but he's got glasses ... curly hair and a bit of a beard."

"I think that's Anthony."

"Yes. He has a big bottle, and he's passing it around. Is that beer or something?"

"I'm sure it's not beer. My friends aren't like that."

"Would you ask him, please?"

"You want me to *ask* him?"

"For me? We have to keep an eye on things."

"Fine," I said. *Thank God she didn't know about Adam's beer or Selby's pot.*

When I asked Anthony, he roared with laughter.

"It is beer!" he cheered. "Root beer!"

He took a big swig.

Omara broke away from her conversation with Shannon.

"How you doing?" she asked.

I told her about Anthony's root beer. I told her about how Katie had jumped into my bed. She laughed.

"This is a great party, John," she said.

"I don't want this to ever be over."

"But it is over."

"The Ren Fest was, like, the last thing I was doing that I really enjoyed ..."

"You'll find something else."

"Well, yeah. A job. I've got to get an after-school job."

"That ain't so bad."

"I don't want a job."

"Oh, Jesus, your life is so hard, John. I mean, suck it up. My older sisters got jobs when they were half your age."

Someone put on a mixtape: Alice in Chains, Jane's Addiction, the Violent Femmes. "Blister in the Sun."

"I'm going to go get another slice of pizza," I told Omara.

"Get me one too?"

"Sure."

On my way to the kitchen, I heard Sarah – the senior from Eastern – talking to Katie.

"I'm going to get a tan," she was saying. "I'll be the only one getting one at this time of year. Of course, I would have said 'yes,' even if she was going to North Dakota or something. It's the right thing to do, and it isn't like a big deal for me. I like road trips. But I'm glad we're going to Florida instead."

"What did you say her name was again?"

"I promised I wouldn't say, like to anyone, but she dropped out of school in eighth grade and got kidnapped. Now, this friend of hers is trying to get her away from her pimp and back to her family."

"That sounds dangerous, Sarah. You gotta be safe. Shit happens out there, y'know?"

"I know, but we've got the whole thing really well planned out, and I'm out of here as soon as I graduate anyway."

Chuck had once said that Akawe wasn't as large as it seemed to us.

"Hey, Sarah," I said. "Help me move a couple things in the other room? My parents will appreciate it."

"Sure?" she said.

She followed me to the empty study. I figured closing the door would look too suspicious, so I made a gesture to keep our voices low, and she watched me, puzzled.

"Was it Cora Braille?"

Her eyes widened. She put her hand to her mouth but recovered immediately.

"Look," she started. "I was so wrong to talk about it at all ... even low like that. I just thought if I kept my voice low –"

"It's not like she's my friend or anything," I said. "I never knew her that well. But I thought she was in trouble. So ... it's going to get better?"

"Yeah," said Sarah. "We're leaving tomorrow. I guess ... I guess her dad knew about it – about what was happening – but didn't do anything about it because he was getting some money out of it or something. But she has this aunt she ... likes. So, we're taking her to her. But Jesus, John, do *not* tell *anyone*. This isn't some high school gossip, you know, this is serious, and I've already fucked up."

"How is she getting out?"

"She's got a friend who's helping her get away ... without them noticing for a while."

"Who is it?"

"I don't want to get them in trouble either. See, it's kind of dangerous what they're doing. They piss off the wrong people –"

"I *know* that Sarah, but I *know* people who know Cora, and if it's got anything to do with the Chalks, I *know* people who are messed up with them, too. I got ... I've got to keep my own friends safe, too!" I sounded legit as I said it, but there was a nagging doubt in the back of my brain: hadn't I left those friends behind a long time ago? Did I even have the right to call them friends anymore?

Sarah was hesitating.

"Look," I said. "I know it's Cora, and I know a little about her situation. I'm not going to do anything to hurt anyone. I *want* her to get out of this. Here's why I want you to tell me: so I can go to the person who's helping her out and see if *they* need help."

"If they needed help, wouldn't they ask you?"

"Asking for help is tricky, you know? Whoever it was asked you because they *don't* know you that well. That means that you aren't a risk for Cora's secret getting out. But that's got to mean they're in it, too. I just don't want a friend of mine getting hurt."

"John, if I tell you something and someone gets hurt because you were dumb, I'll never forgive myself, and I'll never forgive you, either."

"What sort of promise can I make to make you trust me? I'm not gonna rat nobody out!"

She looked at me for a long time.

"Just promise me," she said.

"I promise."

"And don't talk to her until after tomorrow. That way ... Cora ... and I will be gone already."

"I won't say a thing until Monday. I swear to God."

"Okay, fine." Sarah lowered her voice even further. "The girl's name is Selby Demnescu. She's in your class, I think."

I had to remain calm. I had to hide my surprise. *Am I surprised?* I felt breathless, but I wasn't sure it was from surprise. It *felt* right for it to be Selby – for it to be the girl who had hooked up with me and stole my sunglasses, and blackmailed her brother so she could take ballet, and told me about the urbantasms, long ago ... but I didn't *want* it to be her. I didn't *want* her to be in danger. I wanted it to be some stranger or acquaintance hanging out with the Chalks, taking risks, and lying to them to help Cora escape. I hadn't talked to Selby in more than a year. And yet ...

"Yeah," I said. "I know her. Don't worry. I won't say a thing to her until next week. And I won't say a thing to anybody else."

We went back out into the party.

I brought Omara a plate of pizza and a drink.

She wore a smile on her eyes. The golden light was all-surrounding. But I saw the dark rectangles of night through the windows.

Later, when the party was ending, and with it the last traces of that year's Renaissance Festival, I stood on the front porch and waved the last car off into the night. Red taillights vanished around the corner, and the street was empty again, and I stood out there in the wind.

Then I saw someone around on the corner of Whitmore. It was a shaggy man working in the driveway of the murder house, loading junk-packed milk crates into the back of a pickup. It was the uncle, and I watched him as the wind began to howl. After he'd loaded the last crate, the man went into the house. I waited. One by one, the lights inside clicked off. Then the man came back outside, locked the door, and climbed into his truck. After several attempts, the engine turned over and the headlights came on. As the man backed down the driveway, he leaned out his window and held his middle finger toward the murder house. A moment later, he was gone, and I was alone with the rising wind.

Somehow, I knew that he was gone for good. That they were all gone forever. Now, the murder house stood dark and empty. It had taken years, but my parents and I were finally the last family on Agit Street.

The air above me tilted toward cold. The clouds turned in the sulfurous haze.

I knew it would snow before morning.

I expected to dream that night, but I'd been too tired for too long to remember anything that my brain did while I was asleep.

The next morning felt different. I felt it in my eyes as I rubbed the grit out with the tips of my index fingers. When I looked out the window and saw the hoary frost and scraps of snow below, I was thinking two things: *the Festival is over* and *Selby is helping Cora escape.*

The rest of the weekend was limp, a dull string of chores and church and homework. That would be the order of things from now on: no more smoky campfires and no more motley parades. No more chilly nights in the tent pressed up against Omara. The sky was featureless and slate gray. And yet, over and over that weekend, the second thought intruded: *Selby is helping Cora escape. How did Selby find out where she was? What has life been like for Cora? Is Selby safe? Is she involved in any other way?*

And so, on Sunday, after Mass and lunch and the last of my homework, I sat on my bed and wrote Selby a note.

> Hey Selby,
> Haven't seen you in forever. Want to hang out after school? Just talk?
> Let me know.
> John

While I knew that Adam was pissed off at me for writing him off after seventh grade, I had no idea what Selby thought about me. I hadn't seen her almost at all in the last year. And while I didn't think that Adam would do anything worse than flipping me off at Eastern, I still remembered how thoroughly Selby had taken me apart after our fight during Mrs. Anders' production of *A Christmas Carol.*

But in the tired fever of Monday morning, I must have decided that my curiosity was more important because I found myself following Selby through the halls and slipping the note in her locker once she had left. I found her reply in mine an hour later:

> Sure. I'm running lines for Sleepy Hollow but I'm done at 5. Meet me at the old baseball diamond after school. SD.

After my independent study, I took two buses to get back to Eastern, but it was only four, so I sat on the dugout bench and did my homework. During the day, the temperature had climbed, the clouds had scattered, and the sun sparkled out over the sweeping banks of maples, oaks, cottonwoods, and crabapple trees. The wind kept trying to snatch the paper from my fingers. The sun sunk lower in the sky. I rubbed my arms to warm them. A figure in a blue coat slowly approached from the school.

"Hey," Selby said, her voice rougher than ever. I wondered if it had actually gotten worse in the last year or if I had just forgotten its sound.

"Why you want to meet here?" I asked. "It's kind of grown over."

"Cause I've got to walk home. You coming?"

I watched as Selby walked past me and continued farther down the slope, away from the school and the road, and toward the roar of the expressway.

"Nice hat!" she called over her shoulder.

"Thanks," I said. I pulled the cappie lower over my ears and hurried after her.

"So, you're working on the play?" I asked when I'd caught up. "On *Sleepy Hollow*?"

"Yeah. I'm on set."

"I didn't see you at the auditions."

"I couldn't make them, so I handed in the form before. Why aren't you doing it? I thought you were all about the drama shit."

"I couldn't because of Renaissance Festival. Jesus, is everybody working on plays but me?"

"I don't think your girlfriend is doing anything with it."

"No, that's right," I mumbled.

Just as the slope fell the last few feet toward I-63, we reached the pedestrian bridge. I'd never seen anyone crossing it before and had forgotten it existed. Up close, the thing looked even more dilapidated. The metal was rusted red and orange, the concrete cracked and crumbling.

"Is that thing even safe?" I asked.

"I cross it every day."

"It doesn't go nowhere!"

"No, it goes into the nature preserves. Down by Sellers Creek. There are paths down there."

"Aren't you worried you're gonna get jumped?"

"Hasn't happened yet."

I stood on the brink, doubting. The firehued trees on the other side of the expressway were denser and taller – more sprawling – than any others I'd seen in the city.

"Stop being chickenshit, John!" Selby's gravelly voice tightened with annoyance.

I stepped onto the overpass. I felt it rock slightly beneath my weight.

"I'm pretty sure this isn't supposed to *move* when I walk on it, Selby!"

She turned her back on me. "I've got to get home," she said. "You can follow me if you want."

Cars rocketed along the eight lanes of I-63 far beneath me. I looked ahead, where Selby's back was receding, gripped the railing tightly, and started after her. I'd only made it a few feet when the angry wind returned, ripping the cap off of my head and hurling it out over the expressway.

"Fuck!" I yelled.

Selby turned, and we both watched the little cap float down like an autumn leaf before a semi pulped it.

"That's too bad," said Selby, and I couldn't tell if she was laughing at me or not. I smoothed my hair with my hand. I hadn't paid anything for that hat, but it had given me something. Whatever it was – whatever confidence or swagger – it had already left me far behind. I figured that was why the wind was allowed to take it in the first place. It pissed me off, but I didn't want to get distracted from Selby and Cora. I gripped the rusty railing and continued along the overpass.

"I been reading my English textbook," Selby said.

"Uh huh?" I grunted.

"I got Cami for English, and he's real boring," she went on, oblivious to the clamor beneath us. "He doesn't teach nothing, but he's also too strict for us to fuck around, so I been flipping through the book to not get bored."

"Yeah? Cool?"

Paint peeled beneath the pressure of my palm.

"Oh yeah," she went on. "Way more interesting than Cami."

I let my eye follow everything that wasn't under me: the contours of the forest ahead, growing in definition, individual trees now, their leaves bleeding textures of red, yellow, and green against the naked bark. And above them, a plume of smoke curling into the sky from somewhere farther west.

"That a fire?" I asked.

Selby paused to consider the smoke.

"Yeah," she said. "West End, probably. Mostly they happen in the Os these days."

"Crazy they'd start a fire during the day."

"It happens all the time now, John."

Selby started walking again, and I made myself follow. We were more than halfway over the bridge now, but it seemed to tremble more with every step.

"I found a table some way in."

"What?" I asked.

"In my textbook. In Cami's class."

"Oh."

"Anyway, this table? It compares two kinds of writing: Enlightenment and Romanticism. See, the Enlightenment was everything that happened before the French Revolution. And Romanticism was everything that came later."

"Romance? Like, love novels?"

"No, not that. It's like, everything was supposed to be all ordered and put together during the Enlightenment. Because the apple hit Isaac Newton on the head, and then they had rules for everything like gravity, but they didn't before. But then the French Revolution happened, and people started getting their heads chopped off, and so people went for Romanticism instead."

Someone had graffitied words across the bridge. "Ifit dont fit," it read, "you must quit." We were starting to descend on the westward side.

"But you don't mean, like, love stories? I mean ... what *do* you mean?"

"I mean like crazy wild shit. Like trusting your feelings – your emotions – and not just trusting your mind. Like ... like night instead of day. Like wild nature instead of, I don't know, farms."

"Okay. So what do you think about it?"

"I think it's fucking awesome! It's the truest stuff I ever found in a lit book."

Now we'd cleared the expressway completely, and I breathed freely again. The ramp spiraled downward and eventually I was stepping onto the ground.

"You made it," Selby said. "Better than your hat did."

"It's okay," I said. "It was my father's hat."

I finally let go of the railing. My palms were orange from the rust.

"I think Akawe's like that," Selby said.

"Like my hat?"

"No! Like Romanticism. Like back when all the factories were going, things were, you know, more like the Enlightenment. Because people thought they'd figured it all out. Follow the rules, and you get somewhere. Now it's all Romanticism, though. Your houses burn down. Your schools are too hot to open. People shoot each other. My own brother got locked up for dealing drugs. You can't even drink the water. It's crazy. There ain't no good in following the rules. Just gets you played. So, we're in Romanticism now. No Enlightenment. Trust your gut. Feel things deep and strong. Connect with nature. All that shit."

"Huh."

"What do you do if someone tells you to make a cake, John?"

"I don't know. What?"

"You cut off their damn head."

Selby started walking again. What had once been a paved road split in two. The leftward branch cut a straight swath toward what I guessed must be Winters Road, far away. The right branch dove straight into the forest. Selby was following the rightward route.

"Where does this go?"

"It takes me home," she said, again with a trace of impatience.

A moment later, the trees had swallowed us, leafy walls of oaks and winking poplars cresting far over our heads while we trampled dead leaves underfoot. Dried leaves scuttled across the pavement. Selby turned off the road onto a dirt trail the led deeper into the woods. I smelled dirt and green things. The trees closed in shadow behind us, but the sky was azure and golden. The leaves crashed in the wind. I heard the rush of the expressway, just out of view, but now I also heard the sound of water moving.

"Why you write me today?" asked Selby.

I felt suddenly aware of how alone we were.

"I haven't seen you in a long time," I stammered.

"Yeah, after seventh grade, we didn't see you much either."

"I guess we all just got busy with shit."

"Bullshit. It was what happened that summer. Adam thought you thought you were too good for us all a sudden, once you got Omara. Once you started hanging out with all *her* friends."

"It wasn't that."

"I know. You ain't that flavor of jackass, John. But it *is* what happened that summer. It was what happened with us all at the hospital. Then the shit

106

with Adam and the gun. Then that body we found. It was *all* that shit. You got scared. You got scared of what we were into. You got scared about us. Who we were with. What we were doing."

Selby knew she was telling me things I didn't want to hear. But I had already been thinking about it all.

"I felt bad about it," I said. "And I didn't want to leave you all. But I had to get my shit together. I didn't want to be there when Ophelia got shot or some shit. Or when someone fell. Or ... and, Selby? I want to get the fuck out of Akawe."

She laughed. "You think I don't? You think Adam doesn't? Anyway, I hear you. You were smart to get scared." Selby smiled. "And now, for some reason, you let me walk you way back here where nobody knows where you are, and anything could happen to you, and nobody would know."

"I guess I still trust you."

"I guess you do."

I looked at her and she looked at me. The wind had quieted. The sounds – both liquid and automotive – were louder than ever.

"What do you want to ask me, John?"

"Why are you sitting at the Chalk table? Why is Lucy?"

Selby squinted at me appraisingly.

"What's going on with Cora Braille?"

She barked out a laugh. It wasn't the answer I expected.

"Come on, John," she said, waving me along behind her. We continued along the trail, and it deposited us on the edge of a small stream.

"What this?" I asked. "I didn't know this was here."

"It's Sellers Creek," Selby said matter-of-factly. "I think it's beautiful."

The shallow water glided noisily over submerged rocks while the stony shores nestled beneath impending branches, boughs, curtains of verdure, maples and vines. A stray fish leaped in the distance. I could still hear the expressway, though.

"So," I said. "What about Cora?"

Selby laughed again and started following the trail along the banks of the creek.

"First," she said, "I thought that Akawe was like Romanticism when I was walking back here one day. See, I don't think it used to be like this here. I think that once this was just another park in the city. But when the people left, when the money was all gone, nobody came here anymore. Everything just grew over. Grew out, you know? Now it's beautiful. Wild." She paused. "Scary."

"Scary?"

"I guess people live back here sometimes. I see their shit. Blankets and clothes and places where they eat. Set up fires. And once, a guy lived here with his family, but his daughter got raped. So, the dad was so mad he strangled her and then chopped her up into a million pieces. He sent one leg to the North Side and one leg to the South Side, and one arm to the East Side, and one arm to the West End. He sent her head and her snatch Downtown and the rest of her body parts to all of the suburbs. See, he was hoping that people, all the crews and kids would get so pissed off they'd come and murder the rapists."

"Yeah?" I asked. *Does any of this have anything to do with Lucy or Selby or Cora or the Chalks?* "Did it work?"

"Fuck yeah. God made it snow and rain on the rapists. They got struck by lightning. Then the birds came down and ate them. Sucked up their intestines. But I never seen anyone back here yet with my own eyes, except one time a guy was jogging through on this path. He looked like Richard Simmons. But that was the only time. I don't think many people live or come back here anymore."

"Where does it go? The path?"

"Eventually, it takes you all the way to Intervale. At the overpass. You'll see."

The path led us northish, deeper into the city and deeper into the forest. It ran roughly parallel to the creek, occasionally right along the shore where we found concrete columns topped with crimsoned manhole covers: "CITY OF AKAWE." "SANITARY SEWER." More than one sewer lid had been popped off.

"Oh yeah," Selby said. "So that's another thing. The Enlightenment looked back at the Greeks and all their stuff. But Romanticism looks back on the Medieval times. So, you seen that courthouse downtown?"

"Huh? Yeah."

"Yeah, it's got big columns. All Greekish and shit. And same thing with some of the other buildings down there. Of course, they're all empty now. Just like the real Greek ruins. But what buildings around here are still okay? I mean, if they build something new around here, what is it?"

"A church?" I asked.

"Yeah, a fucking church!" she shouted. "I mean, it's great. I love my church. It's dark, and the scents ... the incense they burn! See, Quanla never got that. The way a church needs to smell. Incense. But my church uses a ton of incense, and I bet yours does too."

"They use a little."

"High walls. Stained-glass windows. All the darkness that they light up with candlelight and singing and chanting. That's all Romantic! And anyway, when a place – when this place, this park or whatever it was – goes wild, doesn't it sort of turn into a church? I mean, look at it now! It's like the sun goes through the leaves just like they're stained glass windows! And the tree trunks are all like the walls of a church! And the buzzing of the bees? The crickets? The cicadas? It's like that's the organ music. Come on, tell me you can't hear that!"

Selby was enraptured. I saw her trembling with excitement. And I heard what she was talking about. Behind the rush of the stream and ever-more-distant roar of the expressway, the evening air hummed with insects.

"Yeah," said Selby, "and those wildflowers are like incense, too."

I took another look at the towering trees, and especially the oaks. They were over a hundred feet tall. The same height as the tall buildings downtown. That meant that they had to be older, too. Golden in the cooling autumn. Firm in their request for a little extra time before the cold set in. But I knew that, in the end, the cold would win.

The path narrowed as we walked. Shadows set in with undergrowth, dead and choked away from the sun, twining vines, stinging nettles and hawthorns, angry blue jays, and a carpet of twigs and crushed matter. Every so often, another path branched off to our right.

"We'll just keep following the creek," Selby said.

Eventually, steep hills and bluffs rose out of the stream. I found myself scrambling up tree roots and stony banks. Young trees perched on these outcroppings, leaning perilously over the water. When we reached the top, the trail resumed.

"Anyway," Selby said. "I like it here. I like walking back home through here. Everyone has their own true thing. All this that's all ruined – this beautiful, abandoned, ruined place – is all mine, and that's why it's important. I say it's beautiful and wild, and so that's what it is."

We ducked under a maple that angled across the path.

We passed a forbidding looking pipe, two or three feet wide, that vanished into the hill on our right. Someone had cut away the strips of rebar from the entrance. Down beneath us, the stream flowed over little cataracts. Selby paused for a moment and looked over it all.

"What?" I asked.

"Shhhht!" she said.

We listened for a long time.

"You know," she said. "Right on the other side of Sellers – right through those trees over there – is the abandoned insane asylum."

"It's there? But that's on South Street!"

"South Street runs in front of the asylum. But what do you think is behind it? It's this! You know, a long time back, the headmaster there had this daughter. Fucking beautiful. And there was a boy from the Cellarway who wanted to go out with her, and she wanted to get with him too, but the headmaster wouldn't let her. And the boy moved out to Elmwood or somewhere and eventually grew up and became a school teacher, but she stayed in Akawe and got married and moved into a big mansion in Bellwood with a view of the golf course and the biggest factories, and she had two sons. And they went to school, and the boy was their teacher! So of course, they met each other at lot at school stuff and parent-teacher conferences and shit, and they ended up having an affair."

"Did her husband find out and blow them away?"

"I don't think so. I think she got sick and died. I don't remember what from. But they loved each other so much. So deeply. It was the sort of thing you talk about, you know?"

Eventually, the trail broadened and pulled away from the creek. Off to our right, we passed a fenced-off pumping station, all brick, windowless, with the copper detailing of a wealthier age. Dead cattails and living weeds. Concrete cubes with cylinders bored through their middles. It was as if an angry giant had scattered them in a tantrum. Far ahead, I could see Intervale Road tunneling beneath the I-63 overpass, with Sellers and Carnival creeks merging and twining beneath. The expressway over the road over the streams.

Selby stopped and studied the scene before us. I wondered what she was looking for. If this had anything to do with my question about Cora. Or if she had forgotten the question entirely.

"Is that it?" I asked.

"Is what it?"

"Is that everything you figured out about Romanticism? The wildness and the Middle Ages and all that about who you are, and who we are, and what it all is?"

"No ..." Selby said. "There's a lot more than that. Shit about science and ghosts, seeing into the future, and rich people and poor people, just a lot of changes. I can't even remember everything I read."

She sighed.

"I kind of don't want to get any older," she said. "I'm worried that when I do, I won't understand all the shit I understand now. Do you ever feel like that?"

"Maybe?" I said.

"I don't want to be a sad piece of shit, John," she said. "But I don't want to ever be like *them* either."

I thought I knew what she meant. It was *them*: those who knew and who, knowing, had forgotten. Had assumed. Had laughed themselves into comfortable ignorance. Had forgotten, even though they'd promised not to.

Selby's brow furrowed.

"Intervale and I-63," she said. "Yeah. Yeah, I know a story. One time, a few years back, a psychiatrist drove real crazy down the road here and crashed into one of those pillars and basically splattered all over everything. It had to be suicide because who would drive like that and do something like that?"

"You know, I know that!" I said. "I remember when that happened. It was right before we went into seventh grade. Adam and I rode our bikes down here to see if we could see any of the body!"

"Did you?"

"No. They had it all cleaned up by then. But we saw some broken glass."

"You know Lucy tried to kill herself, once, right."

"Yeah. I know. That's why we broke up."

"Because she tried to commit suicide?"

"No. Because she told me about it, and I didn't react to it the way she wanted me to."

"How did you react?"

"Like a dickhead."

"You know, I'm kind of jealous of her sometimes."

"Of Lucy? Why?"

"Because she gets really sad, and then she has a good reason not to do anything. I get sad too, but just not quite *that* sad, and so I still have to do shit. Take care of my sisters. Take care of my mom. Go to school. Act like it all matters. Every fucking day."

"Why are you and Lucy sitting with the Chalks?"

Selby squinted toward Intervale Road. "You think there's any glass left from the accident," she asked. "Where the psychologist killed himself?"

"It was a long time ago," I said. "But, you know, there's always glass."

"Come on," said Selby, turning back toward the forest again. "We're not going out at Intervale Road. There's another way I like to take."

We'd only gone a few hundred feet when she pulled back some low-hanging willow leaves to reveal a narrow game trail that led into the brush along the creek. I followed her down to a small clearing before the water. The trees hung low, the stream gurgled, and without waiting Selby stepped confidently along a string of steppingstones that bridged Sellers. I followed, wobbling on the third stone, my arms airplaned to keep me from falling in. I realized then, all at once, teetering on that rock, watching my own blurred negative looking up at me from the surging black water, that I was going to someday tell the stories Selby was sharing. Her stories. Michael's stories. Adam's stories. My stories. I was going to write them down and share them as Selby had shared them with me. As a Romance.

It didn't matter if the readers and listeners were paying attention, if they liked it, if they hated it, if they got it. It didn't matter if they understood that I'd been standing with friends, exhausted friends, flinching friends, fucked-up teeth friends, friends descended from men and women with hands oil-swollen from pumping a hundred million cars out onto American roads, the substance and hopes of their lives dissolving into froth and exhaust before they could even fully name what it was they wanted. It didn't matter whether anyone recognized these stories as non-compactable myths, as the oldest stories, the richest stories, the deepest stories. It didn't matter. because no matter what, if I said it, then it would have been spoken.

That was why I needed to say it.

I saw Selby's reflection, and the blue sky in the black water gave her a blue hue as she waited for me on the far bank.

I hopped along the last three stones and made it to the other side.

"Why are you and Lucy sitting with the Chalks?" I asked.

"Remember how you got here," Selby said. "Remember how to find the place I just showed you."

"What is going on with Cora Braille?"

"Follow me."

Selby led me up another game trail, through a thicket of tall grass and mingled shrubs, and out onto a two-tread road. Now, I knew exactly where we were, and I wasn't happy about it.

To my right, this trail also converged upon the overpass and the merging streams.

To my left, it vanished beneath the viaduct on its way toward Cartierul and the factories beyond.

Right in front of me, I saw the wild scrap yard with the four concrete silos rising above it all.

Selby rounded on me.

"I can't tell you much about Lucy, or Cora, or me. And you need to keep your fucking mouth shut about what I *do* tell you. Cora's parents basically like rented her out to the Chalks two years ago because they were getting a cut of whatever she made."

"Jesus."

"Then, when Cora's aunt tried to find her and adopt her, the Chalks moved her out of Akawe. They had her tricking out in Wayne County. Eli and I have been working this whole time to try and get her away from them long enough to get her to her aunt."

"Eli?"

"Eli Ostyn. Lucy's boyfriend."

"Lucy's boyfriend has been helping you ... get Cora out?"

"Yeah. He'd better. It's his fault that she got pimped out in the first place."

"How's that?"

"Eli's brother is with the Chalks. Once or twice they've used Eli to ... find girls they can pimp out."

"And this is the guy Lucy's going out with?!"

"They're using Eli too. It's their fucking family business, pimping and gangbanging and being Chalks and taking money. It's what they *do*. Eli hates it. But yeah, he's responsible."

"He pimped out Cora, and he's your friend? He's *Lucy's boyfriend*?!"

"You're way out of your depth, John. So, I suggest you drop it and stop fucking asking questions about it. Or I will find a way to shut you up."

She turned her back on me and started making her way along the path to the viaduct. For a moment, I thought about asking her just what sort of threat she was leveling against me, but then I decided that I wasn't ready for the answer.

In the last year and change, the mulch piles had been scattered and dissolved. Now, the loamy fecundity fed new trees. Common poplars with yellowing leaves. Sawtooth grass, crabgrass, and chicory. Cattails. It was still mucky and swampy behind the viaduct, but the land on either side was tilting toward forest. Within five years, these trees would grow tall, suck up the boggy water, and merge against the untended woods spreading across Akawe.

"Someday," Selby said, "I think I'd like to sneak out and go for a walk. The kind of walk a hero would take. In the darkness. At night, you know, you can really hear and feel things. You can hear and feel and smell them better than you can during the day. Know what I mean?"

The swelling, growing wilderness moved and expanded on every side. Discarded barricades were sliding into sinkholes, their glinting orange and white stripes overwhelmed by the fertility of the wetlands.

"Sometimes," Selby said, "sometimes, yeah also, I kind of ... okay, I'll tell you. I kind of want to try O-Sugar. Don't worry, I'm not gonna. Some people love it, but it messes some people up, like, real bad, like permanently. It turns their brains fucking inside out. But still ... I met some people who've done it and they tell me how they see things they forgot. They see them up close like they can almost touch them. And they have a sort of blue look to them. I know we talked about this before. Back when, you know, we were still talking."

"Has Adam tried it?" I asked.

"I don't know. I don't talk to Adam much, neither. But I don't think so. Adam wouldn't want to. He'd say his life is too much of a bad trip already."

"That's true. So, what makes you want your life to be a bad trip?"

"It's good to see things better. It's good to understand what they are."

The viaduct came up and over us, its flanks licked red and white with brand new graffiti.

"Sometimes, I just wish I could find the right person and fuck their brains out. But there's nobody like that. There's nobody worth putting up with for that."

"I understand," I said, though I didn't.

We finally came down along the undulating path and onto the green field, looking across at Selby's house and all of the other houses of Cartierul.

"I know I haven't seen or talked to you in forever," I said. "I'm sorry."

Selby looked at me.

"You confuse me," I said.

"I ain't confusing," Selby said. "Everyone else is confusing."

"I don't get you."

She laughed, but it was a strange laugh. Half mocking, half awe. Awe at herself? Selby seemed to understand then, whatever else, how immense she was.

We looked around at the green and depth all around us.

"So, you walk back home, through all this, every day?" I asked.

"Most days. I like being able to get to school without anyone knowing where I am. Where they can catch me with my defenses down. Like in front of the abandoned houses where I'd catch the bus. Or, shit, in the back of the bus."

"Is that something you have to worry about now?"

"All sorts of shit's been happening since we stopped talking."

I wasn't sure what to say about that, so I looked toward Selby's house instead. Celesta was standing on the porch, jumping up and down and waving at us. She looked tall.

"I gotta go," I said. "Looks like you do too."

"Listen, John," Selby said. "Remember the walk we just took. If you cross the other bridge, in front of the school, it'll take you into a park. From there, you can follow the tracks all the way past the factories and out of town. Go in the other direction, past the Old Benedict, and there's trails that take you downtown. You can get in and out of this city without crossing any road or passing any house, or letting anyone know where you are. Whenever you need to."

"When would I even need to?"

Selby shrugged. "I feel better knowing that I can. Anyway. Thanks for walking with me, John. I had fun. Enjoy your girlfriend, get good grades, get into college, and move away from here. I hope you have a beautiful life because my life's a bitch."

For the first time, I felt guilt. Not for "life's a bitch," but wrenching guilt for how I had ignored her – how I'd ignored so many of my friends – for the last year. But before I could say anything else, Selby was striding away toward Celesta, who had stopped waving and was now gesturing to something on the porch. I turned toward the old familiar stairs, climbing through the gloom to the viaduct above.

Over the next few days, I tried to follow Selby's advice. I tried to just "stop fucking asking questions" and focus on my own life. It ought to have been easy; I knew now that Cora was safe in Florida with her aunt, and Selby and Eli had done whatever they needed to do. Selby would be keeping an eye out for Lucy, too. It still chilled me to see Lucy hanging off the arm of this reluctant pimp, her eyes wide and a little wild, confiding her true self to him in whispers she had never shared with me, or to which I hadn't really listened.

"Yo, John," said Omara, snapping her fingers in front of my face. "I was just asking you! You gonna ask me to Homecoming or what?"

I blinked. Chris and Nova and Ken were all watching me, waiting for me to reply.

"Yeah?" I asked. "Yeah," I said. "Let's go."

Over at the shadowed table against the wall, Lucy kissed Eli while Selby looked bored and rested her face on her fist. I closed my eye against it. *I am a jackass,* I thought. I opened my eyes and trained them again on Omara's narrow face. Her weary but warm eyes and that unkempt, half-ignored hair. All her wonderful before me. *I am an idiot. Get your shit together, John.*

"What?" Omara asked.

"Nothing," I said.

But it wasn't nothing.

Everything was harder than I had expected.

I had planned to go looking for some extracurricular fix until I could get myself backstage again, but the few clubs that the district hadn't shut down were already filled up.

"Maybe next year," the junior varsity football coach told me when I asked if there were any positions left on the team. He looked at my belly. "You *sure* you want to do football?"

I'm sure I don't, but it's better than being nowhere, doing nothing. I was getting bored of homework at the dining room table. I was getting bored of my room. My world was starting to feel small.

School wasn't as much a breeze as I had expected either. Maybe we couldn't hear the teachers as they lectured us, but they kept giving us homework. I took hours to finish each night. I hadn't even started looking for a job as my father had asked, and assuming I *did* find something to do after school, I couldn't imagine how I would keep up with everything. Each day Ms. Pavilik filled out minds and eyes with constellations and nebulae, and her homework all combined this with unrelenting, exacting math. Ms. Ropoli had tasked me with interviewing the city clerk about election administration, and while it was a fun assignment, it took me a whole week to finish. I loved these two classes and looked forward to them. Everything else was a mess.

Akawe was a mess, too. The police had directed our attention to the arson rings. There were at least two, they said. A group of kids, most likely, who liked setting fires in the Os. They had already started more than a dozen since the end of summer. But there was someone else out there – a professional firebug – who knew how to reduce a single-family home to ashes in a few short minutes by starting with the nerves and bones of the structure.

The police had also picked up the path of a serial killer. They reluctantly confided this after several different departments noticed a fixed rhythm in a series of attacks across Akawe, Acheron, Arcadia, and the out county. Beneath the everpresent hum of local homicide – drug murders, bar bawls, abusive husbands, and kid casualties like Bennett – several unsolved stabbings followed a pattern. One or two survivors described a tall and solid white man with a light accent and a heavy five o'clock shadow. The man had called them over to his SUV – it was a black '94 Little Passway – and asked them for directions. Then, while they were answering, he'd put a knife in their chest. For a day or two, I wondered if it could have been Chalky, who had chased me through my neighborhood and threatened me from his house, but no: this killer only targeted old men, frail and slow. They were all Black. Four of them had died.

And above and about all this, there was the water. The water, the water! We had, at least, settled into a kind of routine. Sometimes, I showered with water my father bought in jugs from Meijer's. Sometimes, I'd set my teeth and scrub my face straight from the sink, accepting the hard metal smell. Once a week, we went over to Mabel's for breakfast and showers. It was nice to see Mabel. Nice to see Michael. It was the only time I felt clean each week.

Before the water disaster, Emergency Manager Margate had acknowledged the thin handful of protesters outside of City Hall, banners in their hands and tape across their mouths, with a thin-lipped smile and a grandfatherly nod before turning his back on them and stepping inside. But now Margate was instead being confronted by reporters from the Arcadian Archive and the Akawe Reporter, then Al-Jazeera and Michigan Radio, and finally the New York Times and the Washington Post.

"Akawe has been following all federal and state standards in the treatment of our drinking water!" he'd answer from the auditorium at City Hall, with its flickering lights and crumbling ceiling tiles. "Everything I've – everything we've done in this office is to put this city on a good financial footing for generations to come!"

Governor Rhinelander was also making weekly pilgrimages to Akawe, but the trips were never announced until after he'd departed. Here was Rhinelander smiling from the kitchen table of a Republican donor in Anderson

Park. Here was Rhinelander holding a jug of filtered Akawe water he promised to drink every day. We heard about his visits, but we never saw them ourselves.

Meanwhile, the damning news continued to roll in:

"Michigan Supplied Bottled Water to Akawe State Offices Despite Claims Tap Water Safe for Drinking."

"Governor Approved Anonymous Bottled Water Donations to Akawe Pastors."

"City Water Department Tested Houses Without Lead Pipes to Meet Fed Standards."

"EPA Correspondence About Akawe Water Contamination: 'You've Got to Pick Your Battles.'"

"State Admits Legionnaire's Outbreak Killed At Least 12 in Basadena County."

Everything was about the water that autumn; the reds and golds pouring from faucets outshone the leaves on the trees. *Why do they care about this?* I wondered about the reporters and the politicians, and the scientists. *They didn't care when we lost thousands of jobs. They didn't care when dozens of people were murdered each year. They didn't care when our schools were falling apart. When Archie's house burned down. When Bennett was murdered by his mother. Why care now? They've ignored us for decades.*

Each day, I came home to an empty house, my mind full of pyromaniacs, midnight ramblers, and the stink of rusty water. I'd warm myself a cup of coffee – we made it from bottled water now – and try to clear my mind to focus on my homework.

Then, one day, I came home and found my father sitting in the living room with a grim expression on his face. I thought I heard a woman crying upstairs. It sounded like my mother. But that was weird because my mother never cried.

"John," my father said. "Your Grandfather Richter died today."

I hadn't seen my grandfather since that summer. As his dementia got worse, I enjoyed seeing him less and less. Finally, on that last visit, after he'd been hospitalized for falling and breaking a hip, we found him sitting up in his bed at the Temple Medical Center. My mother sat at his side and tried to talk with him while I took a seat in the corner, playing on the Game Boy I borrowed from Ken.

An aide came in. Took Grandfather's lunch tray away. Dabbed at the corners of his mouth with a wet cloth until she'd cleaned away the leftover crumbs and applesauce. Then she left.

"What is she carrying?" my grandfather asked.

"Just the food you didn't want," my mother answered.

"She went out into the hall," he said. "Someone poured a bucket of boiling water over her head."

"No, Dad," my mother said. "She just took away the leftover food."

He closed his eyes. My mother put her hand on his, and his eyes opened again. The Game Boy beeped and chirped as my race car crashed in the margins.

"John, could you please put that away?" my mother asked. "Don't be rude."

My grandfather looked out the window, where the first shift workers were going out to their cars, heads bowed in the blazing heat.

"That girl in the blue uniform ..." my grandfather said.

"What is it?"

"They're pouring boiling water over her head," he said. "Why are they doing that?"

He started to cry.

Now it was time to go and bury him.

We sat silently in the pews at the Salinger Funeral Home in Elmwood. Listened as man after man got up and spoke about how brave Martin Richter had been as a soldier in Korea. How godly he'd been as a civilian. His eager participation in the Elks Lodge. His persuasive agitation on behalf of the Michigan Republican Party. His beautiful family. Then my mother got up before everyone and spoke, in a calm, unquavering voice, about the way her father had set her on a course for college: "it was never a question of *if* I would go; it was only a question of *where*." How he had welcomed my father into her family with coffee and Euchre. She didn't mention that that welcome had been begrudging and delayed; that he'd only given in when he realized he'd have to accept this son lest he lose this daughter. My mother didn't mention my grandfather's massive ego, his delusions of grandeur, or his casual chauvinism. She didn't talk about his final, hopeless slide into senility. I guess that, at least, wasn't his fault. She did mention that he was too impatient to paint. He'd painted the outside of his house once, but he'd been too careless, in too much of a rush, and you could still see the patches he'd missed near the cornice. Cracked whiteness beneath the gutters.

After the service, we processed – a long line of earth-toned Aubreys and Benedicts, maroon and black – down to the Stellar Hills Resting Grounds. The cemetery was situated among the river bluffs just south of Akawe, making a rolling canvas of purple velvet grass and flame-drenched slants of light. Fire-spotted maple leaves and the blurry pricks of marginal conifers loomed over bronze statues of children feeding rabbits, hiding behind trees, or playing a game of crack-the-whip. I breathed in the sharp scent of snapped pine branches, the dust of crushed leaves, the peatish smoke of a distant brush fire, and other dying, brown things. Smooth polished graves swept around us, rosy granite, thrust out of the earth and cast their own long shadows.

Grandfather Richter's casket went into the ground.

Her hands shaking, Grandmother Richter leaned over me and affixed a crumbling boutonniere to my jacket lapel. Rose petals flaked off under her thumb.

"He was wearing this when he died," she said, wet voiced.

He was? A boutonniere? When he died?! I tried to suppress my shudder.

Grandfather Richter had feared and hated the communists. He'd torched his way into Algeria during World War II, but it was Korea that really left him rattled. He never talked about what he had seen there unless it was from the forgetful depths of dementia. He had told me about baby mice wine, though.

"You take the baby mice," he'd said when I was young, "put them in a bottle of rice wine. The mice drown. They ferment. You drink the wine. Then you eat the mice. Raw."

I had covered my mouth and acted like I was about to vomit. Grandfather Richter had laughed and laughed.

Grandfather Richter had always seemed weird to me, removed, cold, and almost unlovable. He admitted that he didn't "like the Blacks much." He didn't like my father's jazz music. He would've resented the Motown sounds crooning that had echoed through Salinger's, and reverbed against the leaded windows, their sharecroppers' roots polished from visible view. "You can bring the man up from Waverly," he'd sometimes say, "but he'll still love the waves." "I don't need a boating license. I just need a boat." "No better antidote against entertaining too high an opinion of others than having an excellent opinion of yourself." "You move fast when you got an outboard motor. It whirs like that."

"Beza didn't drown himself in Paris. He fell from a cliff in Morocco." "You put the worm on the hook like this."

I closed my eyes.

I heard the dirt land on the coffin.

I didn't even *like* Grandfather Richter. But imagined his hands unmoving. These were hands that had held my mother as an infant, hands that had fired guns and climbed cliffs, hands that had hurried to paint the roof. Those hands, those fingers, would never move or work again.

It crushed me down to the ground.

I mean, I knelt there because I couldn't stand anymore, and I took a fistful of grass in each hand and clenched tight, using the roots to tether me to the same dirt that was swelling around my grandfather.

I knew my mother was crying from her irregular breathing, but she reached out and let the weight of her hand rest upon my back.

"We move on," my grandmother muttered. "We move on all the time. We want to just ... stay still, but we can't. There is always another sunset, even if he won't see it."

When we got home, the phone rang.

"Hey," came a girl's voice, swagger heavy. "Can I talk to John?"

I sat down in a chair.

"Yeah," I said. "This is John."

"Hold on," she said.

I heard a scraping sound.

Then, the unmistakable cough of tattered branches and rotted syrup pushing out through a puckered anus an inch or two from the receiver. Splish splash. Two girls' laughter, distant, porcelain echoed. Then the dial tone.

I hung up.

Anger filled me like shit. Because everyone was full of shit. Because the world kept dumping all over us. Because I had just gotten back from my grandfather's funeral and heard some girl taking a shit over the phone. *Maybe I should pay it forward,* I thought. *But who would I even call?* No. That shit was too trifling to soothe the thrumming in my temples. I was tired of being passive. Acted upon. The howler tone went off, and I realized that I was still holding the phone next to my ear. I hung up. The signal kept braying in my imagination. I thumbed the yellowing pages of *Gravity's Rainbow*, which my father had left open, spine up, on the arm of his chair. *I'm going to do something,* I thought. *I'm going to fix the water in Akawe.*

The next morning, I woke up in the dark, full of excitement for my mission. I crept downstairs, went into the kitchen, and drank a cup of cold coffee from the fridge. Then I packed my backpack and went to Eastern like it was any other day. The noise and chaos didn't bother me that day because I knew what I had to do. I closed my eyes and tried to erase my self-consciousness and every sense of my physical presence. To impress every sound I heard upon my brain.

"John?" Ken Lessard caught me with his smug grin and his greasy voice. "You better call Omara, dog."

"Why?"

"She thinks you ain't care about Homecoming. You gonna lose her if you take her for granted."

I can make plans tonight, I thought. *Homecoming isn't for a week.* Also, *fuck you, Ken!*

He left.

It was time for me to go, too.

I shut my locker and turned away down the dim hallway. I passed Chris, and he gave a cheerful wave. I passed Omara, and she ignored me. When I reached the end, I hung a left into another hall, with only a few gray lights flashing overhead and faintly lighting the way. Barely half of the classrooms were in use here, and the air was cold and stale. Shadowy students passed me, hurrying to their lockers, grabbing their books, stomping off toward their dismal classes across the huge school.

Then I arrived at yet another, even obscure, hall. One square of light – the bleary white of the isolated Home Ec class – radiated out and outlined the forms of a few silent figures, golems moving furtively through the twilight. But they were voiceless, and I ignored them, and left them with their measuring tapes and ironing boards. A minute later, I had finally arrived at the darkest hallway in Eastern High School.

This part of the building had been closed off altogether. The air was chilly. Colder than outside, even. I could almost see my breath floating in front of me. A metal gate had been accordioned across the hall, but nobody had locked it. I pulled the gate back. It squealed, but nobody was there to hear it. Now that the passing period had ended, even the far-away hum of moving bodies had subsided. I felt my way carefully toward a single distant starry point that gleamed at me through the gloom.

It was a drinking fountain, and unlike the other fountains throughout the school, this one hadn't been covered by a plastic trash bag. *Nobody ever comes this far, so why bother?*

I pushed the button on top.

Sure enough, a spurt of water gushed out of the nozzle and swirled anemically down the drain.

I rubbed my fingers in the stream and felt grit.

I cupped my palm, lifted it to my lips, and took a sip. I tasted chlorine, sharp and eye-watering. A metallic bite, almost as potent. Coppery. The water would have looked rusted and bluish under a better light. Beneath that, in the swirling whirlpools of speckled drifting mote, I could not taste the lead. Lead is tasteless in water. But a few stray atoms, dislodged from their moorings, will quickly accumulate, make their way to your brain, and name it their home until you die.

I dropped my backpack to the floor. Pulled out the heavy biology textbook and smashed it into the nozzle until the plastic shattered. I pulled the casing from the fountain and tossed it aside. I dropped my book, unspun the nuts from the fixture, and removed the washer beneath. I felt with my hands. A small metal pipe ran down into the fountain, bubbling out a trickle of water.

I stepped onto my backpack to get a bit of extra height.

I knew that this was going to be a tight fit.

That's why I started with my right middle finger, pushing slowly and steadily until I had inserted it fully into the tube. Then, one by one, I added my other fingers, wriggling to widen the steel aperture. Its tightness was unnerving, but I finally managed to work my whole hand into the narrow pipe, then pushed it down until I was in up to my shoulder. Now I started with the other arm, pushing in, once again, one finger at a time, my left hand, wrist to elbow, elbow to shoulder. After that, there was no way to go slowly, so I took a deep breath and jammed my head between my arms, shoving forward while my fingers pulled and as hard as they could against the walls of the pipe.

To my surprise, it worked.

Really, the hard part was getting my head in, and while my whole upper body burned cold from the pressure and the effort, I felt my feet lift off of my backpack, pinwheeling as I went. I pulled myself vertical like the swan dive of the Titanic. Then my legs scissored shut and vanished beneath the surface of the ebbing flow.

I was submerged now.

The only way to go was forward, in darkness, and angled into the flaking current.

At first, it was pretty awkward. I wasn't sure how long I'd be able to hold my breath, but the tightness in my lungs finally subsided into a low throbbing, a soft burn, and then faded away altogether. Not breathing was uncomfortable, but it wasn't a deal-breaker.

The first turn was tight, where the pipe angled into the wall, but I found that if I pushed shoulders out toward the joint while angling my head into the turn, I could snake my way forward. From then on, I could use this trick whenever I came to a bend.

My eyes gradually adjusted to the unlight, which gave everything a slight blue/green/violet cast. It reminded me of a mercury-vapor lamp. This light that aided and saved me wasn't miraculous: like Theseus, I had presented myself in place of the tributary youths and maidens offered up by nescient parents and principals to endure principled insomnia, nerve dissociation, dissolved language, dissolution of age, sober tweaking and twitching headaches, harried nerves, damaged hearing, and the decomposition of muscle and bone. The erasure of memory. As such, I had formed a sympathetic and psychic bond with the faltering biofilm that labored in vain to keep the lead at bay. These anticorrosives leeched a resin of Carbolok from the soilstream and gave off pale, illuminating photons to aid my way.

"Whoa," I said, looking at the gutted seams of some nearby pipes, deep grooved, as if they'd been scoured by a chisel, while the toxic minerals grew outward like sentient barnacles. "This is even worse than I expected."

I slithered past, and these enemies scraped up my arms.

I was less worried, now that I'd solved the problems of breathing, moving, and seeing, but my difficulties had only begun: I had entered the maze. Pipes met pipes, right angles met right angles, and there was no gravity for me in there, neither up nor down. The only indication of direction was the pressure of the water pushing against my face. I couldn't know where I was going, precisely. Still, for salmon and Daedalus, this was an easy riddle to solve: I just had to follow the current upstream, always pushing into the flow, the thread of water unwinding behind me. Once I reached the water main, my shoulders popped open and I was able to pump my legs for more speed. Yes, the current was always against me, trying to drag me back into the houses, schools, and churches, but it was impossible to lose my way. I could always find the source as long as I kicked into the current. Although, who knows? Maybe in that ghostly and hollow light, I lost myself underwater. I certainly saw some strange shit down there.

125

Connor Coyne

I accidentally slipped off a side pipe up into a church in the Os where, pressure-pumped into a wall, I overheard a penitent pouring her heart out to her confessor.

"Bless me, Father, for I have sinned," said Camille. "I prank called a boy from my class, but I held the phone receiver up next to my asshole and took a huge shit which he heard."

The priest – some dude from Acheron – I want to be clear about that – laughed. "That's nothing," he said. "Let me tell you about the blowjob I gave this kid, Joe Cliffords, two years ago! His eyes went so wide I thought they were about to pop out of his head!"

"Hey," said Camille. "Speaking of blowjobs ..."

"Absolutely!" said the priest, smoothing his robe and stepping to his feet.

As my head reeled from this exchange, the stannic-bracken current surged and swept me, my arms bleeding as they waved– *Jesus, that hurts!* – back downtown. I got pumped up to the highest floors of the Olan Foundation Building, where penthouse views offered up East Street as it escaped the factories and firetraps, the serial killers and arson rings.

I heard voices, muffled but unmistakable, through insulation and three-quarters an inch of drywall.

" – was going to be," said Arthur Olan's grandson-in-law. "Rising property values are a bonus. Construction contracts. That's where the real action's at."

"Well," came the muted voice of Governor Rhinelander, "you're inventive. Your family forgot all that about remanufacturying cars, but you have always been gifted in trades."

"Thank you."

"Now, tell me. I know I'm safe because they never told me what they knew I wasn't supposed to know. But what I need to know is ... is this going to get any worse? I hate the daylight, you know. It's the real reason I spend so much time at my Presbyterian church ... the stained-glass windows are very dark. I keep blackout curtains in my car. I only go out on overcast days. I never eat garlic. So basically, the long-and-short of is..."

A long pause.

The governor continued: "Are you going make me say it?"

"You want to know," said Olan's scion, "whether there's a paper-trail linking legionnaire's and poisoning to our development concerns across the out-county?"

The governor didn't answer, but the scion wasn't a fool.

"We didn't do wrong things," he said. "And we only did right things. You know that financially distressed cities – cities with Emergency Managers – can't take out loans. But Akawe couldn't sign those contracts without bringing the water plant online, and they couldn't afford it without taking out a loan. So, listen, some asshole owns a junkyard over there, and it has this fucked-up cesspool. I don't have my fingerprints on this. Margate signed off, and the mayor got the photo op. Anyway, this cesspool was next door to the river and the water treatment plant. And you know there's an exemption to obtain loans connected to environmental remediation. You follow me?"

"You *are* clever."

"Not really. *Everyone* does this. We apply for a loan to remediate the cesspool, including adjacent properties. The state gives us a loan for a number of millions of dollars. We remediate the cesspool for a couple thousand and use the rest of the money to refurbish the water plant. Suddenly, we're in business, here and in the out-county. The property values outside of the city will all go up, of course, but like I told you, construction contracts are where it's at."

"And Margate signed off on this? Wasn't he worried about his own exposure?"

"He was too busy fellating himself to complain. He really is one of those rare souls who is able to suck his own dick. He does it all the time. I can't say that I blame him."

"And who is this junkyard owner who ... has buried the cable on our behalf, may I ask?"

"That's the craziest thing of all!" said the scion. "Nobody seems to know his real name. But he's related to the man who sold my grandfather-in-law the land for the Benedict Main, and he calls himself –"

One floor above me, someone flushed a toilet, the pressure flipped, and suddenly I felt myself being pumped back down nineteen stories of Nirosta-accented art deco glory, out of the building, and back into the ochre jellied flow of chaos. It was a maelstrom then, the water, spinning and whirling, and I flew myself into a technicolor realm where circles of witches stripped flesh from bone and reconstituted their victims' bodies from latent and leftover ideas.

That was when the toxic water became sentient, realized that I was *figuring it out*, and tried to destroy me.

It pursued me across the salt flats with a cannon stuffed with lead shrapnel. The water fired the cannon at me, but the wet fuse didn't ignite. I even stuck my head inside to show that the ammo was dead. Then, the water took a look at my mouth, grim and frowning, and realized that I had its number and wisely decided to make itself scarce. It could not destroy me, so it tried to elude me.

It donned a disguise and haunted the plains of Akawe, poisoning

127

children, dropping flowers, and murdering pets, but I was on the case. The water marauded as a spectral pirate, as a moldering robot, as an electrical zombie. Every time, though, I caught the creature, tied it in ropes or got it stuck in quicksand, and pulled the mask off to reveal the culprit's whole identity. Each time, the children and their mothers cried out in dismay: "It's the water!"

"Curse you, John Bridge!" the water wailed in its liquid voice. "I'll get you next time!"

I followed that motherfucker wherever it tried to hide.

After many detours and many adventures, I finally arrived at the middle of the maze.

I knew that something had changed when my upstream path climbed a great height – miles, it seemed, of vertical motion – with the astral ashes and settling sediment tugging at my ankles. I reached the top: a massive pool, pitch black, and I was able to catch a breath of real air.

"The water tower!" I said. "I made it. I'm here!"

I had penetrated the sanctum sanctorum.

No, I pushed my way down through supply pipes into the treatment facility, past the pump well, the fluoridation and chlorination chambers, across the clear well, and into the filtration chamber. I clambered up through layers of gravel, sand, and anthracite, muscled my way across a thousand sedimentation basins. I almost got decapitated in the flocculation chamber. I almost got diced and dissolved in the coagulation tank.

Finally, like the resurrected emerging from his tomb, I found myself standing behind yellow guardrails in a sterile white lab room with a thousand modest jets in the wall pushing chalice clear steams of pure Zibi river water into a vast rectangular draining basin.

Against the far wall, I discovered the heart of the Zibi River Supply Source System. It was a sentient red light hovering behind its perfect glass disk. Layers of color buried beneath color, white within yellow within orange within that sore, dull red. This single beaded eye glittered with malevolent life.

"Not for long," I said and lifted my heavy biology textbook overhead. (I'd been carrying it in my pocket the whole time.)

"Not so fast!" bellowed a beastly bovine voice.

"Who is it?" I said, spinning around, staring fearfully into the slim shadows of pipes and support columns.

My adversary stepped into view.

"You?!" I yelled out heroically. "But I trusted you! My whole life, I thought you were on my side!"

"I know!" yelled Demon Cow, the Hellburger mascot, fire lighting upon his razor-sharp horns, blood running down his cloven hooves, copper and lead glinting in his brand-new metallic nose ring.

"You never wanted to just give us the best burgers in the world, Demon Cow!" I cried. "You just wanted to wreck Akawe so you could keep it all to yourself!"

"Mwahahahahahahaha!" bellowed the cow. "Now die!" he cried, firing lasers and lightning simultaneously from the points of the three-pronged poker.

I agilely dodged out of the way.

He fiercely shot again, but I ducked behind a column.

We fought for a long time. He showered me with sparks and courses of lava while I evaded, evaded, moved fast, always just outside his grip and throwing obstacles in his way.

Finally, Demon Cow had me cornered, my back against the wall. But I could see that our battle had weakened the structural support underfoot and that it was quietly crumbling beneath him.

"Look out!" I said to him. "Demon Cow, the floor is collapsing!"

"You don't think I'm going to fall for that old trick, do you? Young fool!"

He pulled his arm back to strike.

At that moment, the floor fell away beneath us completely, submerging us in the sediment-rich pool.

I trod water. I knew the river and the waterways of Akawe. I understood them. I'd been swimming through them for hours.

"But Water!" bellowed the infernal cow before me, his fires dimmed, his flames quenched. "Water is my weakness!"

"Thus, you die, Demon Cow!" I proclaimed justly. "A death well deserved for the hurt you have inflicted upon the people of Akawe!"

"My master will have the last laugh!" Demon Cow yelled ferociously.

"I'll see Governor Rhinelander behind bars before this is over," I spluttered fearsomely. "Mark my words!"

"Ha," yelled the Cow, discordantly. "After all this, you still think that Trick Rhinelander is my master?! Oh no, he is not the real master of discord!"

"Wait!" I hollered desperately. "What do you mean?" I implored despairingly.

But it was too late.

"Auguaguaguaguagu," said Demon Cow, dyingly.

"Well," I said, struggling my way out of the grim deathpool. "I might be too late to learn who is responsible for this evil, but I'm not too late to put an end to it!"

My wet fingers wrapped around the spine of my Biology book and I lifted it overhead.

I marched with purpose over to the heart of the Zibi River Supply Source System and hammered the shit out of it. Its evil light flickered and went dark.

The building shuddered and convulsed with the damage crackling through its foundations. The whole thing was coming down now! I ran along a blue catwalk, climbed up a red ladder, ran a green catwalk, climbed down a yellow ladder. I found a reinforced steel door and flung it open. I ran down the length of the bridge with the structures behind me shaking and sweating and spitting out chunks of concrete in their death throes. I made it past the cycling wiry mesh of the water screen. Past the grated field of the bar stream. I could see the silver lick of moonlight painting the river just ahead. It had been night for hours now.

That's when the water treatment facility utterly collapsed, imploded, dissolved, and crashed, sending off a tsunami, tearing upstream, rejecting the river water from all the pipes and homes in Akawe, and shoving it back into the unwanted river where it belonged. I knew that I was done for – that falling cement and debris were going to smash me into a pulp at any moment – so I launched myself from the bridge and into the Zibi River.

Somehow, I avoided calamity. The great swell of the disintegrating water plant surged me out into the current, strangely still and mirrorlike despite the immolations happening just a couple hundred feet away.

I rolled onto my back and floated.

As the crashing sounds behind me receded into silence, I studied the stars overhead.

And so, I drifted downstream on that fine autumn night, in the open air once more, my mission accomplished, the scent of leaf and brush fires (a burning house?) heavy and wet in my nose, the tiny movements of fish twisting around my arms and legs, while the last fading cicadas jazzed in the trees along the banks.

Eventually – it could have been hours later – I recognized the Aubrey Street Bridge passing overhead.

I flipped onto my stomach and splashed to shore.

I made my way up to South Street.

From there, it was a short walk to get home.

I went inside, treading softly so as not to wake my parents, and bathed myself with a jug of water, dried, and climbed into bed naked.

Urbantasm: The Darkest Road

It had been a difficult day, but I was comforted to know that I had saved Akawe.

The next day, while I was conjugating "perdonar" in Mrs. Dimitri's class over the clankety-clank of a half-broken fan, Governor Rhinelander and his entourage sulkily convened at the back entrance of the Olan Foundation Building. Having artfully dodged the protesters on East Street – flannel shirts and orange megaphones – the governor was whisked up a cargo elevator to a windowless conference room, where he stood and made his big announcement, flanked by Mayor Stamm and Manager Margate.

"Well," said Rhinelander, his Santa Claus eyes twinkling under snow-white hair. "I am very pleased to announce that this morning the state honored its commitment to the people of Akawe and reconnected their lines to the Detroit municipal system. We, um, don't think, um, that is, experts still advise against drinking unfiltered water from the tap because of the damage the pipes have sustained, but the water is nonetheless supplied via the Detroit system."

Since the state-appointed emergency manager bore ultimate responsibility for the decision, Rhinelander agreed that the state would (alas!) pay the total cost of the switchover after all. He didn't mention that I had forced his hand by destroying the water plant, but then he also didn't mention the mothers, doctors, and scientists who had called him out on all his bullshit, either, so I guess it all evens out.

"I wish you all a lovely day!" Rhinelander said.

As the governor and his entourage made a quiet escape back into the alley, a stocky 50-something Black man with a salt-and-pepper beard, wearing a black sweater and black sweatpants, met them. He was holding a completely black canvas in a gold-painted wooden frame. It was Mr. Jasons, the art teacher from Eastern.

"How did you get back here?" asked a guy from the security retinue.

"Governor Rhinelander," said Mr. Jasons, "I painted this for you."

"I know about this!" said the governor with a nervous laugh. "A copy of Kazimir Malevich, right?"

"No," said Mr. Jasons gravely. "This is a painting of myself, standing in the river and mooning you at midnight on a starless night."

The governor left without Mr. Jasons' gift. As the lame parade left Akawe along 63 and vanished over the horizon's blade, the wheat sheaves and gaunt trees of my zip code exploded with gold and crimson. Lambent sedge and lavender bowed against the wind, which brought a sudden warmth from the south as if nature itself was cheering us for expelling this repulsive Rhinelander from our midst. I knew that more rock-hard frost was just a day away, but for now, at least, I'd get to see purple leaves flicking the wind and licking the royal sky before night swept them against the concrete.

When I got home, my mother had left me a note: "Quanla called. Please do dishes. Please don't leave your mess in the living room."

"It's homework, Mother," I told the empty room and then cleaned up the scattered papers. I was more nonplussed about the message from Quanla. I hadn't talked to her since we had shared Science notes in eighth grade. But I knew the number by heart.

"Hey John," she said. "How you doing?"

"Okay, I guess," I said.

"You at Eastern?"

"Yeah. I mean, you know it. We talked about it last year."

"Yeah, you're right. I'm sorry. We were at the same school for nine years, you know. I don't know. I can't remember where y'all are. Eastern. Northern. Whatever. It isn't Southern."

"I mean, it ain't Jordan either."

"Or Parc Pierre."

"Michael's at Parc Pierre."

"He is? I didn't know that. What, did he get permission to go there?"

"No. He moved!"

"Michael moved to the suburbs?"

"He was going to go to Olan Academy, but then they closed it, so my aunt sold their house and they moved."

"That's crazy."

There was quiet for a moment, then.

"So ..." I said. "What's up?"

She sighed. "I'm sorry," she said. "I don't mean to be weird about it. It's just like ... Darius mentioned that you were taking an independent study from his teacher at Northern, and it just got me to thinking about you and Adam and Selby and ... hey John, do you know what's going on with Selby?"

"What do you mean what's going on with her?"

"Well, I mean ... is it true she's hanging out with the Chalks?"

"I don't know, Quanla. I don't really hang out with her much anymore, y'know? Um ... for whatever, I guess ... I guess they aren't Chalks but maybe kids with Chalks in their family?"

"Okay. Well, that's good. I just ... I just worry about her sometimes. Even though we don't talk much anymore, either."

"I always thought you and Selby were tight."

"We were. Tight like peanut butter and jelly. But her brother went to juvie, and we went to these two different schools, and kind of a sudden we weren't talking that much anymore."

"I guess," I said, drawing it out. "That's sort of what happened with Adam and me. Although, you know ... I kind of stopped talking to him."

"It's so hard, isn't it? I mean, people are hard."

"Yeah," I said. "Yeah, they are."

"Well, keep an eye out on Selby. I don't want her getting into trouble, you know? And I might give you a call again soon, John. I have an idea how we all might get together again soon."

"Yeah? An idea for what?"

"Really?" she said, and for the first time, I heard a smile in her voice. "I don't want to tell you until I know it's for real!"

I didn't do much for Homecoming Week. Monday was Neon Day, and a few kids showed up wearing glow-in-the-dark bracelets that gave off a pale glow in the dusky halls, like angler fish beckoning prey. Tuesday was Tie-Dye Hippie Day. Wednesday was Spirit Day, and a few kids showed up dressed like Mariners. I wore brown cords and a black t-shirt. The school parade had been cut because, I mean, money and priorities, but the powder puff game went forward on Thursday night.

Then, on Friday, the Eastern Mariners faced off against the Jordan Bishops. From what I later heard, the game was almost a rout. Neither team had any defense to speak of, but the wealthy Catholic school could field twice as many players as Eastern. At the end of the first quarter, the score was 7-14, but by halftime it was 27-14. Then 41-14. In the end, Eastern lost 61-16. The Mariners had been state champions not that long ago.

But I wasn't there, sitting on the windswept bleachers under the moldy sky, watching the football flash through floodlights. I was at home doing my homework. The next afternoon, I put on my rental suit from the mall. It came with a purple tie, sharp, with boxes on it, 3-Dlike. My father drove me out to Michael's to take a shower.

"Last time we'll have to do this," my father said. "I bought us filters for our shower and sinks. The pressure's pretty crummy, but at least we can bathe and do the dishes again. Because we can afford that right now, right? *And* bottles for you to take to school, *and* the goddamn water bill."

I didn't say anything. I just nodded my head. He was in a foul mood. Then he drove me northwest out of town to the Olan Farm to meet Omara. He left me in the gravel lot there, laced with damp leaves, yellow and orange. I crossed the grounds to a red-and-white shed and waited. The sun was setting somewhere behind the gray sky, and the wind whistled through the shredded grass. In the distance, I heard the lowing of cows, their bells clanging. The bleating of goats and sheep. The first lanterns lighting about the distant barn and farmhouse. A few families were still straggling toward their plum-colored minivans, the kids laughing because going to a farm was something for little kids to do.

Omara appeared in the barn door, walking briskly across the rolling lawn, holding up the hems of her blue cotton dress so it wouldn't trail in the mud.

"All dressed up for the dance?" I asked. "Fancy!"

"Shut up, John! I didn't get a chance to change," she said. "Can we stop back at my house?"

"We're already running late."

"It's not like we're missing anything."

"No, but I don't want to miss all our friends."

"Fine! I'll change at the school."

Omara didn't speak the rest of the way back to her car. She unlocked the Aubrey, and we both climbed in. She shut the door on the hem of her dress.

"Fuck it all!" she snapped, cracking the door to pull the dress inside.

"What's wrong?" I asked.

"They're closing! Forever! Just like they closed Marsh Island and Happy Bedlam."

"What?"

"The Olan Farm. Yeah, I guess they didn't get their grant or whatever renewed. This was the last weekend. They just let us know, like, a half-hour ago! And next year, I would've even gotten paid!"

"Shit," I said. I looked at the farmhouse fading into the dusk. "I know how you feel. I mean, from when I didn't get cast in that play."

Omara shot me a withering look. The headlights flickered on. The Aubrey sparked into life.

"Do you want to talk about it or something?" I asked.

"No, thank you," she said, her voice brittle.

Back in town, we found the parking lot at Eastern washed in the glow of white lights overhead. I waited outside the women's bathroom while Omara changed. She came out wearing her dress from the Renaissance Festival. A billowing off-the-shoulders blouse with long, full sleeves, gathered in at the waist with a corset. Over everything, she wore a green silk overskirt, parted slightly at the middle.

"So," she said. "Surprise! What do you think?"

"Huh," I said. "That was an ... idea."

I knew at once that I'd fucked up.

"Wait, no, I mean, really like it!" I said.

"I was short on money and realized I liked this more than anything they were selling at J.C. Penny's."

"Yeah, no, that's great. It's just, we were, um, we were wearing those costumes in the dust and stuff for months. It looks all shiny now."

"I got it dry cleaned."

I handed her the red corsage I'd gotten her.

"Pin it on me? Please?" she asked.

It took a minute.

"It looks really cool on that green," I mumbled. The corsage was the red of dark wine.

Omara smiled weakly.

We went back down our hall, gave our tickets to the two girls sitting at the card table, and went inside.

N-Trance. Ricardo da Force.

You could tell right away that whoever had put this shit together (usually the kids that did student government) had been working for weeks with no budget. The decorations were just some balloons and streamers and white tablecloths, but they covered everything. The walls and the doors. The windows where they had jury-rigged hoops of balloons. The organizers had had to choose between too much light (the regular cafeteria lights) and too little, and, this being Eastern, they went with too little. A few spotlights beamed out from the corners of the room or spilled in from the kitchen and hallway, but it was all dim and dimmer.

"Damn girl!" said Majenta when she saw us. "You wore your festival dress? That's fucking brilliant!"

"I couldn't afford a whole other dress," Omara said.

"No, it's wicked twisted. Wish I'd thought of that."

Majenta was wearing a strapless black dress that clung to her waist and hips before fanning toward the floor. It went with her black nail polish and lipstick, and her clove breath. Chris, her date, contrasted in his vanilla suit and lavender tie. Nova joined us with a purple tie, brighter than mine, and a garish orange vest.

"Those are Northern's colors!" I said.

"Like I care?" He put on a pair of sunglasses.

His date, a tall girl named Claire that none of us knew very well, rolled her eyes.

"You ought to care," said a skinny Black boy wearing a threadbare jacket over his plain black t-shirt. This was Justin Ray. The tagger. The ninja. "People gonna look at you." I had only ever met him once or twice, but he was friends with Ken and Shannon as much as he was friends with anyone.

"Where's Shannon?" I asked.

"He's here with this freshman, Lacey," said Chris. They're off getting punch or something. So ... our dad lost his job today. We saw it coming, but ... I don't know, shit's crazy."

"Shit," Omara said.

"Is everyone losing their job today?" I added. Omara shot me a hateful glance. Chris didn't notice.

"He's got unemployment for a bit," he said. "But he was management, so no pay while he's down-and-out. They might move him somewhere else, and if so, we'll have to go with him."

"Away from Akawe?" Majenta asked.

"Wherever they put him. But he's also applying at this pharmacy, I think. Like he could do financial shit for them or something. But it's a bad sign, for ... well, you know ..."

Nobody knew what to say then. In the brief silence that sank between us, I felt like I was being watched. It was hard to say for sure, with many shadows coalescing in that cavernous space. A wary chaperone strutted across the empty tiles, tugging on his beard. His eyes roved like rootless searchlights, examining, never trusting. He took his job Very Seriously. A couple of smirking wallflowers stared at Omara's dress, covering their grins with their fists and muttering to each other. One of the Special Ed kids roved from group to group, trying to find a friend, to find someone to make eye contact, but nobody would. A few jocks preened like they hadn't just been murdered by the Bishops. And over by the punch bowl stood a serious-looking Shannon wearing a black double-breasted suit, one hand in his wild hair, the other gesturing angrily at his freshman date. She seemed overwhelmed by him, and she brushed her dark hair out of her eyes and craned her neck in awe. I felt like all of these people were watching us, and then realizing that none of them were because they were all looking elsewhere, I felt like someone beyond these circles was watching us all.

"It's fucking depressing, what they've done here," said Majenta. "It's fucking criminal."

"What's depressing?" I asked.

"Jesus, John, haven't you been paying attention?" asked Omara.

"I'm sorry." I shook my head. "I'm just feeling ... kind of weird tonight." The feeling of being watched hadn't gone away. Maybe Demon Cow had survived. Maybe he was planning my assassination at that very moment. Majenta leveled a steady gaze at me. I couldn't read it, but I felt more certain than ever that she simply didn't like me.

"I was saying," Chris said. "That it's bad news for you and Omara. Your dads both work on the line, right? If they're laying off so many in management, they're probably trying to close some plants, too."

"My father's losing his work in Canton, yeah," I said. "But he's a diemaker. They can't do anything without him. Even if they close his plant, he'll just switch to a different one."

I didn't mean for it to sound dickish, but it did anyway. I felt like there was something thick and viscous on the floor, like tar, keeping me rooted in place. Like I couldn't move right. I knew I couldn't say anything right. I felt eyes cutting into me. And then I found it. Selby. She was standing far across the room with May and Lucy and Eli. Lucy was leaning into Eli, talking to May, her hands fluttering like bird wings. She stamped her foot, laughing. May nodded pleasantly. And Selby just looked at me.

"Nova, I'm glad you got Claire to go with you!" Majenta was saying.

"Thanks," said Claire, deadpan.

"No, I'm not kidding. What happened to Christina and all of her, what did you call them? Non-racist skinheads?"

"Yeah, that," said Nova. "I was wrong. I mean, they were non-non-racist skinheads. I mean, they were racist skinheads. I think they thought I was their mascot. Now I got to watch my back."

Justin mumbled something.

Everyone laughed.

"What's so funny, yo?" asked Adam, suddenly in our midst. "Someone laughing at my white ass?"

Kool and the Gang came on. Eastern's DJ was less adventurous than Tom at Radcliffe.

"Hey, look!" bellowed Nova. "It's Faggy McFaggerson!"

"Nice," said Adam. "You practice those lines on Dennis Rodman when he's bleaching your hair in his closet?"

"Yeah. He bleaches my chest hair and my nut hair too. You should get some."

"That why you wearin' those shades? Too much light, too much bright, too much Rodman, too little closet, you know, for such a big dick?"

"No. I wear the shades because I'm phat."

"You ain't acidic. I'm the phat one. You're the fat one."

"A phat phaggot?"

"The phattest."

"The phaggest?"

"You know it."

"Haha! What you doing here? Little bitch!"

"I'm here for this man!" said Adam, pointing at me.

"What?" I asked.

"I think you're a chickenshit snitch, John!"

"I ain't a snitch, but I take shits on chickens."

Omara rolled her eyes.

"You never called me back when I found a body in the Cellar!"

"I'm surprised you ain't a body in the cellar." Now I was getting pissed-off. Pissed-off was something I could work with. "Like who's gonna sell your body to the highest bidder?"

"Oh, Jesus, John, don't rap!" said Omara.

I stared at her like, *whose side are you on?*

"See, your own girlfriend thinks you suck!" said Adam.

"Your drunk ass," I said, but Majenta talked over me: "You throw up on my shoes, Adam, and I'll shove them so far up your ass these heels'll break your teeth."

"I wouldn't never puke on a lady," said Adam solemnly. He turned back toward me. "You don't know what I've seen happen the last year. Who happened to ..." His eyes focused and unfocused.

"I don't got no problem with you," I told him. "I don't know why you got a problem with me. You were the one waving that gun around."

"Dude, y'all gonna fight?" asked Nova.

"They're not going to fight," said Chris. "Let's just chill, okay?"

"Fine," I said. "Whatever. I gotta take a piss."

I took a trip down the hall. This bathroom, like every school bathroom on a week when everyone's parents seemed to be losing their jobs along with their water and sanity, was swamped in the sepia haze of pharmaceuticals, smoked and unsmoked. I took a long, leisurely piss, relaxing in the dimness, letting Adam's intrusion, Omara's shitty mood, and Selby's steady gaze drain out of me. I stood there, empty, letting my shoulders un-tense. I went to wash my hands, then remembered that the sinks had been shut off, and that there wasn't any soap or towels. I wiped my hands on my pants and went back out to my friends.

When I got back, Selby and May had joined the group, and Adam was laughing with Nova like they were best friends. The others looked on in bemusement, but Omara seemed impatient.

"Hi John!" said May. "Hi! Hi! It's good to see you again!"

"Okay," I said.

"John," said Selby. "Quanla's going to call and invite you to this techno rave."

"She called me not that long ago," I said.

"She misses us. She hasn't seen us since she went off to Southern. And I've barely seen you more than that."

"What's a techno rave?"

Majenta's mouth fell open.

"Dog!" said Nova.

"It's a big underground dance party," said Selby.

Omara was sizing up Selby, questioningly, not suspiciously.

"Okay?" I said.

"I wanted to let you know now," Selby went on. "Quanla's still waiting on Darius to get his tickets. That's why she hasn't called you yet. But I know your parents like to make plans, like, a long time before they happen. Anyway, make sure you're able to come next Friday?"

"Are you busy?" I asked Omara. "You have work, don't you?"

"No, actually, I don't."

"Oh, yeah, right."

"I'm sorry," Selby said to Omara. "I'm really sorry. I should've just called John, but Quanla's only got, like, three tickets."

"That's okay," said Omara. "I was probably going to be busy anyway. John, can we go?"

"She just said she only had three tickets!" I said.

"No, I mean away from the dance."

"But we just got here," I said.

"I know, but I'm starving, and they haven't played any good music anyway."

"They just played Coolio!" burst Nova.

"Whatever," said Omara. "They're overrated. I'm going to go get my coat." She left while Nova choked on his outrage.

"Better watch it with her, John," said Chris. "She's having a bad day."

"Yeah?" I snapped. "You know anyone's having a *good* day?"

"I really do like your dress," I said as we drove.

Omara sped us along the expressways, through Downtown, from the East Side to the North, and the lights passed overhead and cut shadows across her face.

A few minutes later, we were sitting in a booth at King Michael's Coney Island. The place had kind of gone to shit since the last time I'd been there; it had been part of the second generation of coney islands, which opened during the postwar boom, and it had survived most of its brothers and sisters. King Michael had become neutral ground, where North Siders mingled with the Romanian diaspora and shoprats from RAN and the Benedict Main. By the 1990s, the autoworker crowd had started to dwindle but had been replaced by students, thugs, prostitutes and their pimps, and the homeless. By '95, though, it seemed like even this motley assortment had given up on the place.

A third of the restaurant had been cordoned off, chairs stacked high to block off the back darkness. Other than an old white man and an old Black man sitting at the counter, Omara and I had the place to ourselves.

Some things hadn't changed. A film of grime still covered the walls and windows. The floor was slick with a thick stench of bubblegum soap. Above this, a heavy layer of onion and grease hung in the air. Two muted televisions projected the nightly news out into the still, beige space.

"Two coffees. Two up with gravy fries."

The waitress nodded and moved away.

For a long time, Omara sat with her coffee mug cradled between her palms, her eyes tilted downward as if scrying her future in its creamy swirl. Her skin was so smooth. A seamless flow, arm to wrist, palm to finger, knuckle to nail, prim cuticles. Primed cuticles. Flexed palms. Gracefully waiting to clench. To wrap up in something. To become useful.

"I *want* to see how the ocean moves ..." she said.

"What?" I asked.

"I *want* to outgrow all of this," she said, talking more to herself than to me.

I didn't know what she meant, but I wanted her to know that I'd been listening.

"I guess," I said. "I guess those dances *are* kind of played out."

In the far away reaches of the kitchen, someone dropped and broke a plate.

"What are we doing?" Omara asked. Now she was looking directly at me. Her eyes were reading my eyes. I started to feel worried. I wanted to make a joke out of her question.

"We're sitting in a booth at King Michael's," I said. "We're waiting for our gravy fries."

"Why are we together, John?" she asked. "Why are we going out?"

"Haha!" I laughed. "Well, we haven't got the results of the paternity test yet, so I wouldn't slam any doors until –"

"You're nervous," she said. She reached out and took my hand. "That's why you keep telling stupid jokes."

"They're not stupid."

"Yes, they are."

Her soft voice.

"No ... they aren't," I said.

"Okay. Fine. You're right. You're hilarious. John?"

"Please don't say anything."

"I think we should break up. I mean ... we've got to break up. We can't go out anymore."

"Why not? I mean ... why? Why do we have to break up?"

And I braced myself for everything I had heard in the past. Lucy on the phone, telling me what an asshole I was. Crystal's abrupt and casual dismissal. Even Selby's straight talk edged into my brain, telling me I wasn't half as cool as I thought I was.

"Because I just don't feel it anymore," Omara said.

"I'm sorry for being a jerk tonight if that's it."

"That's not it."

"I feel weird. Like every time I open my mouth, I completely say the wrong thing."

"You haven't exactly been understanding. You've got some growing up to do."

"I can do it!"

"I've got some growing up to do too."

"Well, yeah," I said. "You just drop this stuff on me! Losing your job, not being able to afford a dress –"

"I thought you would like the dress."

"I *do* like the dress. You're so ... inventive. You think we could afford to rent me this suit? My parents? They're tighter now then ... I mean ... Jesus,

143

you just should have told me. But that's all I'm saying. You just drop this stuff on me, and in the moment, I don't know how to react, so I probably say the wrong thing. But I'm trying. To say the right thing, I mean. I've been trying all night to be good to you, and, and, understand, and say the right thing. Like, I don't know! Will you tell me the right thing to say, and I'll say it?"

"I'm not saying you said the wrong thing, and I'm not saying what the right thing is, because I just don't know. But what I mean ... what I realized ... is I just don't like you like in that way anymore. Or at least not right now."

"You mean you might in the future?"

She sighed.

"Let's not go down that road, John," she said.

"But what about at the Renaissance Festival?"

"The Renaissance Festival is over."

"But what about Rocky Horror? What about ... what about when we were in your room, and your dad made us cinnamon toast?"

"That was nice," she said.

"What about all our plans to go to Chicago?!"

"Chicago's a long ways away, John. Maybe I won't even get to go to Chicago."

"Well, I'm going!" My voice had gotten loud. Over Omara's shoulder, at the cash register, I saw the waitress glaring at me. I forced myself to calm down.

"So, you don't want to go out with me anymore?" I said. "Okay, fine! Maybe we could just date then. You know ... we don't have to be officially going out or anything, but just –"

"I don't want to date anyone!" she said. "Why would I, huh? It just leads to ... hurt feelings. And conversations like this. And situations like my parents."

"No, no, no, we're not like our parents. We've got all the time we need to figure it out. We've got years and years –"

"Maybe I will figure it out with somebody someday. But I just lost my job, and my dad's about to lose his. Yours probably will too. Yeah, I know. He's a diemaker, but he isn't safe, not anymore. It's just, everything is falling apart for everyone I know. And I need to do what I need to do. Get another job. Help out with my brothers and sisters. Do good in school, and then when everyone is settled, get the hell out of Akawe."

"But shouldn't we do that together? Won't we be able to do it better if we're doing it together? I hate all this!"

"You're going to get mad if I say this, but I'll say it anyway. I think you're a lost little boy who just lashes out at people whenever he gets scared about something."

"Oh," I said. "Okay, fine. And what are you? A sophisticated adult woman?"

"No," she said. "I'm lost too. And I have to figure out where I am – who I am – before I can have a relationship – a boyfriend – on top of all of that."

"But we're perfect for each other!" I said.

"We obviously aren't."

"But I love you!"

Omara waited a moment, then shook her head.

"But I don't love you, John," she said. "So, you see, it isn't enough."

Those words punctured me. And with that punctuation, two voices, trying to outshout each other: *Don't be an asshole!* and *Do something, dumbass! You're losing her!*

"But you're my anchor," I said.

I felt like an idiot saying it. Omara had already disposed of her need for me. So, what could I possibly accomplish by putting everything out in front of her except showing her what a loser I was?

Omara smiled.

"You're going to feel crappy about this tonight," she said. "But I think you'll start feeling better sometime tomorrow."

The waitress came back and set our coneys and gravy fries in front of us, then left. We picked at our food for a few minutes without talking, and then I waved down the waitress and asked for a couple of boxes. She left.

"You sure you're not just saying all this because you're on your period or something?" I asked.

Normally, saying that sort of thing would get me punched, but Omara just gave a sad, little laugh. "No, John. It isn't that. You want me to pay for your dinner? I don't mind."

"No thanks," I said, and my voice broke. "I said I would. Anyway, you drove me tonight, so you paid for gas. I think we're even."

When I got back home, I gave my father a wave and climbed the stairs to my room. He hadn't noticed. He was wearing his reading glasses, scrutinizing a pile of bills. I closed the door and took a seat on my bed. I didn't like the lines on my palms, so I clenched them into fists and rested them on my knees. Through the rusted water and the wild school and back through the Renaissance Festival and beyond, Omara had been *there*. Now she was *gone*. Everything that had been working in my life had gone south so sudden and slippery. The synchronicity unnerved me. I started to suspect that someone had it out for me. The autumn-swollen city, or maybe God.

The next day, I had to let some people know. My new friends. I called Chris and asked him to pass the word along to Majenta and Shannon. He was polite, but his tone of voice told me that he wasn't surprised. Then I called Nova and asked him to tell Ken. I didn't want them to take sides – if they did, I knew they'd take Omara's – but things were going to change now. I was the youngest and newest member of the group, and I assumed that I would be the one to get left behind.

Monday was awkward at the lunch table, so for the rest of the week I took my sack lunch to the school library and ate there. Things were also weird when I passed Ken and Majenta in the halls. "Hey," I'd say, and they'd give me a perfunctory nod. But the Allard brothers laughed with me about all of the new sports teams the school should consider starting: "spaghettiball" and "crucifixionball" and "sporksgammon" – and Nova surprised me by walking halfway across the school with me as he told me about his mom's enormous cache of Astroglide.

My parents didn't react much to the break-up, either. Omara and I had broken up three times in the last year, so they just figured that this was just the latest installment. But this dumping felt more final than the others. At least I had been through it all before. But I had dated Lucy and desired Crystal when I was young and immature. My relationship with Omara was supposed to have been rich and deep. It was supposed to bend like the reeds in the wind of any adversity.

Quanla called me three times over the next week: on Sunday, on Tuesday, and on Thursday. Each time she wanted to go over the plans for the Friday party, and each time she seemed more anxious than the last. And whatever, I mean, while I was talking about the party, I couldn't be thinking about Omara at the same time. Whenever I got off the phone, I was right back where I started.

"I don't know who's throwing this rave," Quanla said on Sunday. "We only get to go because my brother was invited. But I guess there's gonna be some famous DJs there from Detroit and Chicago. Some DJ named the Kraken is headlining, and there's also folks around here.

"Don't tell anyone about the rave," she said on Tuesday. "Like, I guess it could get shut down or something if the cops find out about it, so we're not supposed to talk about it with anyone who isn't invited."

Of course, I had already told Michael. He'd called and asked about spending the night on Friday night.

"I don't know where the rave is," Quanla said on Thursday. "I mean ... Darius got this flyer telling us where to go, but it's just some party store on West Street. I guess when we get to that, we just park and get directions where to go? And it's gonna go late, so we're gonna have to make up a lie about where you're staying. Selby's just saying she's staying with me. You think you could say you're staying at my place? I know your parents might say no to you staying over with a couple of girls."

"Darius and I both have that independent study with Ms. Ropoli. I'll just say he's having me over to study. Make them think it was his idea."

"Yeah, that'll work."

Making up lies to our parents was definitely *not* the kind of thing I expected from Quanla.

"So why you want to do this anyway?" I asked.

"You remember what it was like back in seventh grade? I had a *group*. We were all at Radcliffe and we were all friends. We were all *together.* Remember that party at Adam's when everyone was throwing eggs at each other, and we had the toast for Elizabeth before she moved, and then you and I went on that walk to the coney?"

"Yeah."

"See, I have some good friends, but I don't have anything like that. I don't have anyone like you or Selby at Southern. She was my best friend not even that long ago. What happened with us, John? Anyway, I just ... Darius told me he had tickets for five people, and he said I could go and take two of my friends if I wanted. He didn't want to take his friends. He only wanted one other ticket for himself."

"Why not?"

"He's probably just bringing some girl. You didn't mention this to anyone, did you?"

"Um ..." I said.

Later that night, Michael called.

"John," he said. "I need to talk to you about that party you were talking about tomorrow."

"Don't even give me shit about it, Michael," I said. "I shouldn't have

147

told you."

"I'm not giving you any ... shit ... about it," he said indignantly. "I want to go too."

"I don't think it's your kind of party."

"Listen! After you told me about it, I asked a couple of kids at school about it, and I got a flyer. The 33 is spinning, John! In Akawe! I can't miss that!"

"Quanla made it sound like there weren't any more tickets. But I'll ask her anyway."

I called Quanla right away. It turned out that Darius' one friend or date had decided not to go. He agreed to give the last ticket to Michael. He wasn't even going to charge us for them, even though it cost him ten dollars per ticket. But I'd have to smooth the way for Michael. He asked Aunt Mabel, and she agreed to drop him off at my house on Friday night. Then our awesome eighteen-year-old friend Darius would be picking us up for a super-important study session, even though he was two grades ahead of us and in a completely different school district from Michael.

This was all some pretty deft "going through the motions" on my part. Even though I really didn't want to hang out with anyone that week, and I wasn't looking forward to some random house party on West Street, I still managed to get all of the pieces in place for my friends.

The phone rang downstairs.

"I'm not even talking to anyone on the phone," I said. "If it's for me, just take a message."

It was Bill Chapman. He'd gotten tired of waiting for me to call him and had decided to call me instead. He wanted to know if I could come over to his house to play video games on Friday. I knew I couldn't, so I didn't call him back.

Friday was brisk and bitter. Harried clouds hid the sun. By five o'clock, Michael and I were both back at my house. By six, Darius had arrived to pick us up and whisk us off to his house on the West End. We found Selby munching on a cold slice of pizza while Quanla stood by asking for opinions on what to wear. I gave her a warm hug. Selby smiled, too, but I couldn't forget a couple weeks back when she had told me about her adventures with the Chalks, so I just gave her a grin and a wave.

"Michael," she said. "You rockin' Parc Pierre High?"

"Parc Pierre High is kind of horrible," said Michael.

"What kind of party is this?" asked Kimmy, Quanla's mom, as Quanla wrapped a neon green boa around her neck.

"It ain't a party for old people, mom!" said Quanla and got a nasty look in return.

We sat around and watched a *MASH* marathon for a while.

Kimmy came back around. "This is a really late start to a party for fifteen-year-olds, Quanla."

"Mom, it isn't a big deal," whined Darius. "I'll be there. Chill, okay?"

"If your sister gets into any trouble, you know it's your ass I'm gonna punish."

Ten finally arrived. The sun had set long ago. Now the wind was picking up. We all loaded into Darius' Daphne, which had lost its muffler a few months back. It roared down the road, making a sound like the hundreds of tin cans people used to drag behind their cars when they got married.

We made our way across the West End. Over the last year I had gotten to know the whole city better. Now I recognized street names: the imperial sweep of Hasting Boulevard as it turned across MLK Boulevard and squeezed itself into Hastings Avenue, a two-lane neighborhood street that shot off between bungalows perched on tiny lots and overshadowed by spidery trees. Hastings spat us out onto Center Avenue, where powerfully built brick and stone churches shrugged off the cowl of West End poverty. A minute later, we reached West Street. Dead ahead, signs proclaimed that the ROAD was CLOSED, because the city was in the middle of demolishing this part of the Benedict Main, but Darius turned left instead. Behind us, the downtown skyline diminished. The Pyramid building was an ever-fading yellow triangle. Quanla looked back at us from the front seat, smiling anxiously. She didn't know what she had gotten us into, and that excited her. Selby was looking out the window. Looking curious. Looking for something. Michael sat bitch, wringing his hands to warm them.

We were together again, but it was harder to talk than it had been before.

We finally got to the corner of Ashley and West, deep on the West End, where Darius pulled into the parking lot of a stop-and-rob party store, barred and padlocked with no light creaking out from under its plywooded windows. But Darius followed the pavement behind the buildings to a grassy field with a dozen parked cars and one idling windowless panel van.

We climbed out of the Daphne. I smelled something molasses sweet and thick in the otherwise brittle air. A chicken clucked from its backyard coop. A plume of smoke rose in the distance from the Os. A house was burning, carrying its message far out over the city. I wondered if the serial killer was awake and working too.

"If this is supposed to be a big secret, you'd think they wouldn't do it right off West Street," I said.

Darius shook his head at me and walked up to the panel van.

The windows rolled down. A college-looking kid was sitting in the driver's seat, Black, bespectacled, heavy, and holding a book loosely in his hand. His skinnier friend sat in the passenger seat, scratching at a stringy beard and cradling a foam mug of coffee between his legs.

"Mercator told me to follow his map," said Darius.

"Who and how many?" asked the driver.

"DA8 and five. Including me."

The driver climbed out, circled around the back of the van, and opened one of the doors. Plush white seats lined the sides while a furry pink carpet spread across the floor.

"Shoes in the box, please," said guy-with-beard, holding up a cardboard box.

"We're getting in there?!" Quanla asked.

"Sis," said Darius. "Chill."

He didn't realize that it had been an exclamation of delight. We took our shoes off.

"Watch your head," the driver said as Selby climbed inside.

Quanla and I followed, then Michael.

"We can fit a few more," said the driver. "We're gonna wait a few."

We didn't have to wait long. Just a couple of minutes later, three more people joined us in the back of the van: two tall, thin white men wearing black slacks, unbuttoned Oxfords, and colorful silk windbreakers, and a goth girl. One of the men looked about thirty, and the other looked forty. The older man had a bit of stubble peppering the area around his jaw, while the younger man was blond with a clean-shaven, almost sculpted face. The goth was a pale white girl with straight black hair that gleamed as if wet, even in dry October air. She was wearing a black corset and a long black dress that fell to her black boots. It made me think a little of Omara's Ren Fest dress if it had been leeched of all color and hope.

The man with the stubble looked skeptically from Quanla to Selby to Michael to me.

"Aren't you a little bit young to be out this late on a Friday night?" he asked.

"Watch your fingers," mumbled the driver and slammed the door.

Pink rope lights lit up at our feet, bathing our chins and nostrils in a devilish glow and throwing our anvil-shaped shadows up at the roof.

The van rumbled into life. We felt it pull onto an adjacent side street, then into the main stream of traffic. We were moving further west.

"So where is this party, Quanla?" asked Michael.

Quanla shook her head. The younger man tried to hide his smile.

"I'll bet it's in Werewolf Town," said Selby.

"Werewolf Town?" said Quanla. "What's that?"

"It's this neighborhood way, way far out somewhere, in this big swampy area near the river. There's only one way in that's a dirt road behind some train tracks, and it's got a tiny cemetery for the Romanians. I think it might have been one of the first Romanian neighborhoods before Cartierul got to be a thing. Anyway, people dump trash all along the road, and they dump dead dogs there, too. And the people there are really weird too. Not paranoid and suspicious like the rest of Akawe, but like they've all been drugged. They just stare out at you if you go out there."

"Have you been to Werewolf Town?" Michael asked. He had been holding his breath in awe.

"No, I haven't," said Selby. "Demetrius has, though. He told me about it."

"That's bullshit," I snapped. "If there was a place like that in Akawe, I would've heard about it long ago."

"It isn't bullshit," said the man with the stubble.

"How would you know?" I asked. "I suppose you been there? In those slacks and that shirt, too? What, dropping off a dead dog?"

"No," he said. "I haven't been there, but one of my colleagues represents that neighborhood, and he has talked often about the trouble he has getting services to that part of the city."

"This is Curt Chives," said the younger man. "The second ward alderman."

The goth covered her mouth, obviously laughing.

"Nice to meet you all," said the older man. He turned to Selby. "You'll be happy to know that improved drainage along the river has helped with the flooding. And there haven't been dead dogs turning up there lately. That trailer park is still a big problem, however."

"There's a trailer park?" asked Selby.

"Since the landlord disappeared, nobody has water or electrical out there. It's a squatter's camp."

The van took a couple more turns than shuddered into silence.

The doors swung open again, and we blinked in the brightness of huge floodlights high overhead. We slipped on our shoes and climbed out into the night.

151

For a moment, I thought we had left the city altogether; we were standing in a small, paved cul-de-sac, surrounded by tall grass and young weed trees. But there was light spilling off of an elevated expressway just above us and to our side, and past the trees I could make out factories and warehouses, older and newer, and the reedy expanse of a giant parking lot. In the distance, a sonorous dot dot dot sound. Pulsing, reverbing bass coming from some interior space.

"Wait a minute," I said. "This is the Benedict. XAuto are Nazis about keeping people off their land. Even their abandoned land. Any party out here is gonna get shut down in no time."

"I wouldn't worry about it," said Curt. "Mercator's got it pretty well stitched up, I think."

Guy-with-beard stood beside us, pointing off at one of the low-slung brick buildings.

"Party's over there," he said. "Buses will start taking you back to your cars starting 2 AM. Everyone needs to be out by 6."

"Buses?" asked Darius.

Guy-with-beard gestured to the van.

"You can pay or give your tickets at the door," he said. "Welcome to Aqua Vitae, the Water of Life."

As we approached the windowless warehouse, we felt the deep vibrations of the dot dot dotting sounding beneath our feet. At the entrance we found a dozen men and women standing around, smoking and laughing. A man wearing a vanilla ice-cream suit and a pink velvet fedora leaned against the red brick face. A tired-looking middle-aged woman wearing red gloves and a red overcoat was talking to him. Another man, some college geek with a rough backpack and red sunglasses held out his palms, on which he had Sharpied an 'E' and an 'O.'

"Welcome to the Water of Life!" he cried.

The goth girl shook her head sharply. Lit up a cigarette.

"I'll have some of that," said Curt's companion, pointing to the 'E.'

"Ten," said the geek.

A quick transaction, like a magician's sleight-of-hand.

Curt wanted to raise the stakes, however.

"I've been hearing a lot about that," he said, pointing to the 'O.'

"Thirty," said the geek.

"Pricey!" said Curt. "I don't know. I've just been disappointed so many times!"

"You'll never know if you don't try."

"Can't argue with that logic."

They made the exchange. Curt was less deft than his friend.

The geek looked us up and down and laughed.

"We didn't want any anyway!" snapped Quanla. "Damn druggies," she muttered.

A heavy man with an even heavier mustache met us at the reinforced steel door and frisked us for weapons.

His mustache-less brother was holding a clipboard.

"D8," said Darius. "Five."

The man scanned the list.

"Kids?" he asked, scanning us as everyone seemed to be doing that night.

Darius shrugged.

"No drugs," said the man. "No booze." And with a tilt of his head, he nodded us inside.

We got in line behind Curt and company and filed toward a card table with three college-looking kids sitting on the other side. A tie-dye silkscreen shawl covered the table.

"You see our pale friend outside?" said Curt's friend.

"Who?" Darius asked.

"White suit, pink hat?"

"Oh yeah, him. What of it?"

"Looks like Chalks in the house tonight. Keep an eye on your kids, okay?"

"Sure thing."

"By the way, my name's Jason."

"Darius."

"Pleased to meet you."

As we stepped inside, the dot dot dots ran up the walls and spidered across the ceiling. By the time we reached the card table, we had to shout to be heard. The first girl handed us a program, neatly folded, with one page dedicated to four of the local DJs playing early – Tick Tack, Stirrup, Knobgoblin, and Wessend – then a page apiece for Positron, 33, and Kraken. The last page was an ad for the 1995 Benedict Honor. You know, a personal luxury sedan for your beige upper-middle-class suburban father. It seemed a bit out of place. I rolled up the program and stuck it in my back pocket.

The second college kid gave us each a bottle of water.

"Drink plenty of water!" he shouted.

The third girl had a big box of sunglasses.

"Pharms?" she asked Jason.

"I don't have any," he said.

"No, what drugs did you order?"

"E."

"You're fine. What about you?" she asked Curt.

"O-Sugar, baby."

She handed him a pair of cheap pink sunglasses. They were enclosed in a cellophane sleeve and smelled like plastic.

"When you start rolling, put these on. For your safety and the safety of everyone around you."

Curt looked dubiously at the sunglasses.

"Really?" he said.

"I don't know why it works, but it works," she said.

We were up next. Darius shook his head. The girl saw Quanla, Selby, Michael, and me.

"Jesus Christ!" she said. "This is, like, a 21 and up thing!"

"Come on, really?" said Curt. "What did you guys expect?! Those flyers are *all over* the high schools."

"I'm seventeen!" Selby offered.

"Yeah, sure you are," said the girl. "You ain't on drugs, though, are you?"

I reached into my pocket and put on my red teashades.

"Great," the girl said. "Hurry up, you're holding up the line."

The fourth college kid stood between two more stainless steel doors painted gray. She wore lurid dread falls.

She gestured to her right. "The Reef. Tick Tack, Knobgoblin, and Positron."

She gestured to her left. "The Maelstrom. Stirrup, Wessend, the 33."

She gestured behind her to green-lit shadows where one set of stairs vanished up and down. "Second floor is off-limits. Head down, and you'll find the Fountain of Youth where Kraken's gonna spin ... we think. Also, Seven Fathoms, with food, free massages and hugs, and a hot tub if you brought your swimsuits. Any questions, ask right here, in Davy Jones' locker."

Curt gave a quick salute, grabbed Jason's hand, and moved off toward the door to the Reef. The goth moved toward the Maelstrom door. Both doors opened, and it was like a levee giving way before an insurmountable swell. Spiraled out in discordant knots, churning beats, foaming tinctures, rimpled acids, and staccato jags. Before the door to the Reef closed we heard the words "Baby baby!" shearing above and through.

"I'm going in there," said Darius.

I took my sunglasses off. It was too dark, and I wasn't ready for them yet.

We stepped into the Reef and saw its golden tones ranging down the shivering walls. Electric pianos chorded aisles of light, sped and syncopated, and merged two songs into one.

"Baby, baby!"

"Do you see the light?"

It was hard to accept what my eyes told me about the feral colors of that room, the pixelated strings, the smears of fog, violent blue, the tattered scraps of verdant green, a fecund forest sliding toward hazier hues of autumn, ruby bonfires, crimson chrysanthemums, nasturtial calypso, a scarlet bumble-bee fuzz licked with slick sunlight, the psychedelic hues of splayed-finger maple leaves squeezed from poison-dart toads by a warted witch to jerkspice her ecstatic stew.

And then there were the people. I thought folks dressed weird at Eastern: all those poor kids wearing ketchup-stained shirts and unspun socks that sloped their ankles like slack tongues. But here there be'ed buzzy pink bunny ears and fur leggings that plunged from knee to floor, Lycra halter tops and tiaras, lollipops and pacifiers. *Who are these people?* I wondered.

"Is this what you expected?" I asked Quanla.

"I don't know what I expected," she said, but her expression was full of *not this.*

"Baby baby!" sang the speakers. "Eeba yeeba!" they swirled upstream. "Baby baby! Eeba yeeba!"

The set ended. An emcee, blood red dressed, took the mic.

"Ladies and gentlemen!" he bellowed, "DJ Knobgoblin!"

The people cheered. Knobgoblin, a Black man in an Egyptian blue suit stepped away from the tables, wiping the sweat from his brow with a red rag. Black-clad techies started swapping out turntables, machines, and crates of records.

"I want to go check out the Maelstrom," said Michael.

We started out. So did half of the crowd. We all choked up at the single door, but eventually everyone made it through the hall and into Maelstrom, where DJ Wessend had already started his set.

Maelstrom pulled out the same light tricks as the Reef, but it played differently here. There were fewer lights, sharper, and the whole cavernous room was saturated in blue.

Wessend's style was slower than Knobgoblin's, but the beat muscled through without pause or hesitation. No singing. No words at all. Just a cascading succession of winds and whorls. Heads nodded and arms swung, and some of those arms were holding glowsticks, orange and blue, where a boy and a girl danced close to each other. A few feet farther, near the wall, a middle-aged man crisply nodded his balding head. His name was Matt Masterson, and he was a columnist for the Arcadian Archive. He was wearing black slacks and a canary-colored button-down shirt, untucked. He kept grinning at a girl with glowsticks, but she didn't notice him. Not even a little. Just past them, we saw the goth from the van. Wessend's beat had dissolved her sullen. She heard the bird chirps, the cricket cries, the tumult of earthworms grinding soil. Yeah, her mouth was still a short, straight line, but she had closed her eyes, and her brow creased in concentration.

Eastern's Homecoming was nothing next to this. The techno rave had been advertised as a dance, but Aqua Vitae argued and encompassed the water of life.

My friends and I started dancing.

I danced to sweat.

I danced to stretch.

I danced to put myself in a place where Omara was *not*, and Chicago was *not*, and I didn't have to think about anything other than sweating and stretching.

I started to get restless.

"I want to check out the basement," I said. "Ain't they got stuff down there?"

"You go ahead," said Darius. "I'm looking for somebody."

The rest of us went out of the Maelstrom, past Davy Jones', and down the stairs into the basement. The room was huge and the ceiling was low. Even with the sound reverbing from both rooms above, I thought I could hear the distant sound of water dripping.

A couple boys and a girl were standing, haloed in red light, in front of an open door. Above it hung a glowing green sign: "Seven Fathoms."

"Who's playing here?" Selby asked.

"Nobody, can't you see?" said one of the boys.

The girl hit him on the arm. "This room's for Kraken, although I don't know if he's even coming."

"Is he, like, the special guest?" asked Michael.

"He's not famous or nothing," said the boy. "I mean, he's known in Akawe, but he don't go touring like Positron and 33 do. He's the whole reason they came at all."

"Crazy that they came," said the girl.

"What do you mean?" asked Quanla.

"33 and Positron hate each other. They went to Chicago and started their own label, what, five years back? It bombed though, bad, so 33 went back to Detroit. And he says that Positron stole some of his masters —"

"Nobody proved that," said one of the other boys.

"I never said they did! But yeah. That's the whole reason the basement's for Kraken. Because it's the biggest space, holds the most people, and if they slotted it to 33 or Positron, the other one wouldn't come."

"Is Mercator the Kraken?" Michael asked.

They laughed at this.

"You coming in or not?" the girl asked. "We got food!"

"Sure," said Selby.

"Twenty bucks for thirty minutes."

"Fuck that!"

"Have some water, at least. Drink up. Stay hydrated."

We got some bottles of water and went back upstairs.

"Let's go back to Reef," yelled Quanla. "It was definitely the best!"

Selby and Michael looked at her like she was crazy.

"Are you kidding?!" shouted Michael. "Did you hear Wessend scratch back there? That was some sick shit!"

But by the time we got upstairs, Wessend was wrapping up his set. In the Reef, I spied the pink-brimmed Chalk slipping from one shadowy wall to the next. We saw Curt and Jason again, pummeling each other with the fun of the beat. Now that Tick Tack, alone, was spinning, all the kids from Maelstrom had flooded into Reef. Everything was dancing again. Everyone was a churn of limbs.

Quanla tried to tell me something, but I couldn't hear. Voices weren't allowed here. Aqua Vitae drowned voices like sailors thrown from their ship. It insisted on sounds more resonant than mere conversation. But then Quanla laughed. So evidently, laughter was resonant enough. I wasn't ready to laugh yet. But I was thinking about it. I felt my sunglasses resting on the collar of my shirt.

But Jeezus, what difference does sunglasses make with O-Sugar? Did Drake and his friends jump because they didn't have sunglasses when they went up on the roof of St. Christopher's two years ago? Would sunglasses have kept them from walking off the edge? Wouldn't sunglasses have made them walk off the edge? Like they couldn't see where it was?

"What? Who?" asked Quanla.

"Nothing," I said.

I saw Curt halfway across the floor. He must have been deep into his O-Sugar by now. I watched as he slipped the sunglasses down his nose, then sucked in his breath in horror and recognition. *What did he see?* Curt pushed the sunglasses back onto his face, shaking his head. Then he kept dancing.

Meanwhile, Qunala was dancing in joy beside me, and the dance hit me too. I felt a little drunk with it, even, and out of defiance, I stared at Quanla's chest and tried to see the motion of her breasts there – now that Omara was out of my life and gone – but I couldn't see shit through her t-shirt.

Then I turned toward Selby, who met my gaze dead on, and her expression said, "I know exactly what you're doing." She certainly was not wearing a bra, and when I met her eyes again they said, "So what? You think I care?" She had a point. She was in control. I wasn't. I couldn't even keep Omara from dumping me, so did it really matter if I looked like a pathetic asshole in front of this friend I had had since I was three years old?

That's when Tick Tock sought me out in the crowd, and pointed directly at me, and spoke into the microphone:

"You fucking asshole," he said. "You sad sack. You know the burdens she carries, and yet you're going to add to these as well?"

"I'm sorry, Selby," I said.

She stared at me for a second, and the glint in her eyes told me that I was mistaken, that she hadn't noticed anything at all.

"What are you sorry for?" she asked.

I smiled and shook my head like it was an inside joke, and she decided to laugh and go along with it.

Tick-Tack's set finally ended with a crash and the drawling ground-state of amplifiers with nothing to amplify. For the first time in hours, we felt a slim moment of silence. It shouted in our ears and brains and was the loudest thing I had heard so far.

Then, across the hall from the Maelstrom, we head the voice of the red-dressed emcee: "Welcome welcome welcome well-cup to the 33!"

I decided that it was time to put on my sunglasses.

The crowd had grown.

When Wessend's set had finished, everyone at the rave had crowded into the Reef until the Maelstrom had emptied. Now, Maelstrom was packed again for the beginning of the 33's set, but the Reef was still jammed. Up on the stage, I saw a skinny black man with vitiligo and a constant smile. Even as Dr. Positron plugged in his equipment, newcomers kept shoving their way into the Reef.

"I have to see the 33!" yelled Michael. "He's like, the best!"

"How do you know about this shit?! I've never heard about it before!"

"Some guys in one of my classes at Radcliffe were into Nine Inch Nails. They got me into Ministry and Skinny Puppy, and then Sisters of Mercy ... and it all kind of led me back to the 33. He's from Detroit, you know?"

We pushed our way upstream, against the tide welling in through the exit. The closer we got, the slower we moved. An unending stream of humans flowed in through the door until our countervailing dozens finally applied enough pressure to flip the current, pinning a few ravers against the walls, heaving and kicking.

When I got within a few feet of the entrance, I suddenly realized that I didn't have any control over where I was going. Everyone behind me was pushing forward, and the crowds ahead were pushing back. Panic flooded my mouth as I felt myself suddenly smothered by under a tide of backpacks and sweaty backs. I couldn't get enough air. The pressure was crushing. The next moment, I got shot through the door, across the hall, and into the Maelstrom.

Here, the 33 was already spinning. He was a rail-thin white boy, young enough but already starting to bald. At least that's what I assumed because he'd shaved his head on both sides except for a thin strip up the middle, not rigid or spiked like a mohawk, but flopping from side-to-side. He filled his depths with hollow sounds, hollow chords, pipes and mallets, more percussion than melody. My eyes found the face of the goth girl. She was happy now, actually smiling, her eyes still closed, bobbing like a buoy among the madding waves.

"Hi John!" someone shouted behind me.

I looked around for the voice. It was a girl's voice, but I didn't peg it to Quanla or Selby.

Then I saw her, just a foot away. May.

"Hi," I shouted back. I introduced Quanla and Michael. "Is Lucy here?"

"Yeah, she's here," May said. "She went off with Eli. He gave me a ride. Mind if I hang out with you until I find them?"

We danced some more in the synthetic waves that rose and fell through the Maelstrom. A piping sequence ascended along a curved line to shatter against the rusted rafters. Spooky hatchets rounded the room with deeper strains of bass. The 33 was marking his territory here.

Then, another, less mechanical sound joined the fray. It was Dr. Positron who had started spinning in the Reef. For one brief moment, the two musicians seemed in sympathy, like jazz players improvising around a common theme. But then the 33 flushed and flung his channels high, and the sound crushed and hammered us again.

Through the haze, I saw a dark Black boy with a black baseball cap, red-trimmed, black jeans, and a worn black hoodie slipping through the crowd and passing me without a nod. It was Justin Ray.

My eye returned to the goth girl. Her eyes snapped open as a man dancing at her side put his hand upon her waist, but she brushed it aside. He reached out again and touched her, and she turned on him, rust eyed. He'd already started to walk away, but she planted her massive boot against the small of his back and gave a rough shove. The man vanished into the crowd amid the mocking laughter. High-frequency squeals hit me like ball bearings. They took out every brassed obstacle that crossed their path.

"I like this music!" shouted May.

"I'm going to go see if I can find you Lucy and Eli!" Selby shouted. Then she was gone.

I glanced at Michael and Quanla.

Great, I thought. *She's left us with the retard.*

A tall man, thirty maybe, wearing a purple silk shirt and black silk pants entered the Maelstrom behind us and made his way along the wall, looking suspiciously out over the crowd. At the same time, with movements so synchronized to Purple Shirt that they could have been choreographed, the pink hatted Chalk slid along the wall to our left and exited with the Reefward flow. Purple Shirt stepped onto an amp, lifted his hand to his brow, and looked out over the nodding masses. He jumped down.

"I kind of want to see what Dr. Positron is doing," Quanla shouted.

Michael gestured incoherently toward the stage.

"But, but," he shouted. "This is the 33!"

"He's playing for two hours," I answered.

"Won't it be harder to find Selby?" Michael asked, his last play.

"She left *us*," I said. "I don't want to wait around for her!"

Michael frowned, defeated.

By now, the floods of ravers pushing between one strobing room and

161

the other had settled into a steady stream. We made it through without crushing or bruises.

Dr. Positron stood at his helm in the Reef with flames dripping down and bubbling up across a screen behind him. His sound didn't fill the space as utterly as the 33's had, but the melodies were more varied. Groaning voices, muttering about lunch counter sit-ins, vocodered sirens, skeletal contraltos, and trilling organ tones waved through the room like the bright blades of a soft-lit kelp forest.

Right in front of the stage I saw the "bus" driver and the guy with the beard.

Guess they got some time off.

Jason stood now in the center of a circle of three dancers. He held a martini glass over his head, the drink within sloshing dangerously up the sides as the cherry stem flicked back and forth to the beat. The dancers were all a bit older than him – late 30s, early 40s – and they wore sequined dresses. Gemstone earrings swung in their ears and put the mirror ball in the ceiling back where it belonged.

"I feel so much love!" one freckle-dreaded white girl screamed, falling to her knees.

"Hi!" I heard a voice in my ear. "Welcome to the Water of Life!" she went on. "I can tell you where to meet your pharmaceutical needs."

It was Elizabeth. She looked like she had dropped at least twenty pounds, and her hair was a hard black, falling about her face in thick tangles, but her eyes were still a watery, clear blue.

"You!" I said.

"John?!" she said. "What are you doing here?"

"I'm here with Selby! And Michael and Quanla! Wait, what about you? Are you still in Owen?"

"Um, no. Um ... I'm ... in Shelley."

"Your mom moved again?! Fucking Owen."

"No ... she's still ... um ..."

"But you're in the city? So you're going to Western then?"

"I mean, not exactly, I mean ..."

"Wait, wait, where did Quanla and Michael go? I know Selby's off, but I don't know where they went!"

"Hi!" said May.

"Hello?" said Elizabeth.

"Oh, this is May," I said. "May, Elizabeth. Hang on right here. Don't move. I'm going to go get the others. They'll want to see you. You know?"

I hurried off, did the quickest of circuits of the room, but I couldn't find either Michael or Quanla. I was back in less than a minute.

"I can't find them," I said. "Do you know where they went?"

May shook her head. "They said they were going downstairs to look for a bathroom. Didn't you hear them?"

"No. Wait, where did Elizabeth go?"

"I think she went to go sell drugs."

It took me a minute to process what May was saying.

"What, Elizabeth?" I shouted. "No. No way."

"Yeah, I'm pretty sure. I mean, she was trying to sell you O-Sugar when she came over."

"That's crazy. Elizabeth is the last person who ..."

But the facts surrounding Elizabeth's appearance started to sink in. May was right. The *retard* was right. "Pharmaceutical needs." Living in Shelley, but without her mom. Not going to Western. *Holy shit, where is she staying?* I wondered. Of all my friends, only Michael had seemed less likely to have become a dealer. *It's just been a year since we saw her ...* Maybe a year-and-a-half? *What happened to her to make her start dealing? Is it just for the money? Is she a user?* I wished she hadn't left. *God,* I wished she hadn't left! Because I would have asked her those questions. And then I would have helped her. I would have answered her in such a way that she knew I wasn't judging her at all. Did she need a place to stay? Did she need ... *anything?* She had always helped me. I would have been happy to have helped her. I felt helpless. I felt May watching my face. Her mouth quirked into a sad smile. She reached out and squeezed my hand.

"I know, John," she said. "You aren't real good at seeing people. You probably don't remember the first time we met, either."

"Wasn't that at the play audition?"

"No! It was at the planetarium!"

"The planetarium?"

"Yeah. They had a laser show. With music. It was real crowded, you know? I was sitting by your feet. Then a guy on O-Sugar ran into the machine and broke it."

"Wait, that was you sitting there?"

"Yes, it was me!"

I had imagined that girl several times over the last two years. Maybe it was because I had only seen her in dimness, in sepia mystery, and because we had both been distracted by the other people around us ... May didn't look at all like the girl I had imagined. The face of the planetarium girl was elusive and intoxicating. May's face was plain and clear. But I found myself leaning out over her, and she didn't pull away. For a moment, I wasn't even sure what I was doing. Then, I did know.

I was smelling her hair.

I breathed in the trace burnt scent – the chemical reassurance – of her hairspray. But May herself smelled like synthetic cherries. They were in her perfume and her lip balm. I smelled sandalwood from the incense that she must have burned in her bedroom. I smelled the slightest trace of must and mold from the dirty house where May lived. And I remembered this all from before, from the planetarium, even though it had been such a small piece of that memory. Just one more detail that had embedded itself within my thoughts of that mysterious night.

"I do remember you," I said.

"You do. It's only because I told you! That's okay. Selby didn't remember me either. But I don't think your friend Elizabeth is mad at you."

"What is going to happen to her?"

"I don't know. I've seen this happen to other people sometimes. She can ask someone for help. Maybe she won't. I hope she does."

Michael and Quanla came back.

"What'd we miss?" Michael asked.

"Nothing!" I said before May could answer.

Right beneath Dr. Positron and his turntable, Matt Masterson was dancing. He'd lost his Oxford and had replaced them with a set of glowsticks. He was wearing an undershirt and twirling in a sweaty mess, flanked on either side by the boy and girl ravers he'd been ogling earlier.

"Now I've seen everything," Quanla said.

She hadn't, though, because just then, the bricks shook with another sonic assault rolling in from the 33. Dr. Positron took a step back, firmly held up both of his middle fingers toward the walls, and then leapt onto his hands on the turntable, wobbling for just a moment before lifting himself on one arm, left leg extended, right leg bent at the knee, rotating before us as the crowd sent out its loudest cheer yet.

Michael's scorn was garish in the red-orange light.

"That isn't even spinning," he said. "That's fucking gymnastics."

I laughed. It was always funny to hear Michael use the word "fucking."

"He is spinning," I said. "Like, literally."

"Can we *please* go back to the Maelstrom?" he asked.

Back in Maelstrom, the 33 had adopted a mellower tone. The pipes and all their echoes were still thundering across the vacancies above like an army on the move, but their master had faded in a fluted birdsong, still mechanical, still synthetic, and it soothed the froth of dance into gentle nodding, tapping. I recognized a familiar head of spiky orange hair.

"Nova!" I yelled.

He turned. "John!"

"Everyone's here!" I yelled. "Omara isn't here, is she?"

Nova laughed loud.

"Nah, she's probably studying with Chris."

"You think they're gonna hook up?"

"Nah. They're just friends. Besides, Chris has a thing for Majenta. He and Shannon both do."

"I didn't know that."

"How you'd not know that?"

"They didn't tell me."

"They don't have to say it; it's obvious, boy! It's a real bizarre love triangle."

"So what about you? Why are you here? I saw Justin. You come with him?"

"No, actually, it was your friend Adam told me about this."

"John!" called out Adam, and he ran across the space toward me.

He looked the ravest of any of us. Bell-bottom slacks, yellow cotton gloves with some sort of glowing white balls jammed into the fingertips, and glasses with whirlpool curls obscuring his eyes.

For a moment, I thought he was going to hit me, but then he wrapped me in a huge hug. "I've missed you, man," he muttered in my ear. "I don't know what I did to make you abandon me, but it ain't working, man. You are my brother. My fucking brother. And when you get cut, I start bleeding halfway around the world."

And I ached throughout myself. I *had* abandoned him. Just like I'd abandoned Elizabeth. Now, my new friends were abandoning me. Except for Nova, who I didn't even like.

"Thanks, Adam," I murmured. "But you ain't halfway around the world. You live, like, ten blocks from me."

Adam slapped my back in an exaggerated way. "This guy!" he barked.

"He's hilarious!" And he went over to talk to Quanla and Michael.

"Is he stoned?" I asked Nova.

"Yup."

"It's O-Sugar, isn't it?"

"No. E. And a lot of liquor. But I talked him out of O-Sugar."

"Is it really bad? O-Sugar?"

"The fuck you think I know shit about it?"

"Do you?"

"Nope. Never done it. Never done E, neither. Never smoked up. Never drinked a drank, neither. Adam! Positron. Kay?"

"I'm gonna suck some dicks tonight!" Adam sang.

Quanla looked annoyed. Michael looked embarrassed.

"Get him home, okay?" I asked Nova.

"Soon as this set's done, we're Audi," he said.

"Don't turn Benedict on me."

The current swept Adam out of sight toward the Reef with the hulking form of Nova right behind him.

We danced again, and the dance masked my confusion, but I couldn't pretend it wasn't there. My head was a rush of names from now and from before: *Omara, Elizabeth, May, Adam, Selby, Nova, Quanla,* and they circled and repeated and circled in my head and returned again, and each name brought its own ache that I traded out for another.

Another roar of laughter spilled in from the Reef. I got it now. Positron couldn't out sound the 33, but he could push his peoples' energy with his theatrics and drunken charisma. Every time this happened, the 33 pounded buttons, flipped switches, spun knobs, and turnt the noise so high that I thought he'd finally bring the ceiling down.

It was in the middle of one of these counterattacks that May called out: "I see them! I see them!"

Since we had seen practically everybody else, I wasn't surprised to look up and find Lucy silhouetted in blue light, along with the boy who had been sitting with her in the cafeteria. *So you're Eli,* I thought. It was the first time I had seen him up close. He was leaner than I was, and a bit taller, and there was something angular but humble about his face. A self-effacing smiling-not-smiling to his expression. His smooth cheeks. His unfurrowed brow. It was funny that he'd be going out with Lucy, of all people. Those perfect teeth hidden behind pale, full lips. Those agate eyes hidden behind my sunglasses.

Urbantasm: The Darkest Road

Oh, yes. He was wearing *the* sunglasses. Even after two years, I recognized them instantly. The sunglasses were made out of two bottle-bottom ultrablue lenses fused to a thin wire frame. Like a sideways eight. The very same shades I had found under the overpass on the first day of seventh grade. The same shades that Selby had stolen and given to the man with the knife. Perfectly perched on the face of Lucy's new boyfriend, who looked a little bit too much like me, only thinner, and kinder, and better looking.

But I'd never helped kidnap a girl to sell her into prostitution, so I guess I had that on this motherfucker.

"Michael, Qunala! I thought we might see you," Lucy said. She was all smiles in the room of shuddering sound. "We saw Selby, and she told us that you were here."

"Where is Selby?" demanded Quanla. "I came so I could hang with her and John, and I haven't seen her a long time."

"I saw her on the other side. Is that the Reef?"

Michael nodded. "The 33 is better," he said.

"I like Dr. Positron better," Lucy said. "I can't even hear myself think in here."

"That's what I like about it," said Eli.

He seemed like someone who wouldn't have drawn the wrong conclusions about Lucy and the tent-and-tarp shop. He seemed like someone who would have listened to her, carefully and sincerely. I hated him.

"Nice shades," I said.

"Thanks," said Eli. "You too. I dig the red."

"Where'd you get them?"

Eli studied me for a moment, but of course, I couldn't read his expression behind the heavy sunglasses. I wanted to snatch them right off his face.

"They're very special to me," he said. "I *loves* my sunglasses."

"Yeah?"

"What about yours? Where you get them?"

"My neighbor got evicted," I said, "so I was in his house, and I found a whole drawer with a bunch of shades in them, and I took them. These too. The house burned down, like, a month later, so I saved 'em. Moral of the story: If people care about something, they shouldn't just abandon it."

"Booooring," said Quanla.

"Yeah," said Lucy. "Sorry guys, I know you want to masturbate over your sunglasses all night long, but it's too loud, and I got a headache. Eli and I

167

were just thinking of leaving. May, you think you're ready to go?"

"I had fun," said May. "We can go."

Lucy gave a little wave, Eli gave us the tiniest nod, and May leaned in and planted a quick kiss on my cheek. She *did* smell amazing, but it all left me perplexed. She acted so random.

Then they were gone.

"Guys," said Quanla. "If I go off and look for Selby in the Reef, will you both stay here?"

"I'm not leaving 33," said Michael.

And then Quanla was gone, too.

The 33 kept hitting forward with sharp punches of percussion, but now he seemed distracted. Annoyed. The cheers from Reef were coming louder and faster, and it seemed that the crowd in the Maelstrom was thinning out a bit.

"Hey, John!" I heard a voice.

"Jesus Christ, who is it now?" I asked Michael.

"I don't know," said Michael. "I don't know her."

The girl dancing our way.

"Crystal, hey, how's it going?" I said.

"Dipshit, you were supposed to call me!"

"Sorry. You travel too much."

It was a lame thing to say. Crystal looked hurt, but it was fake hurt.

"Who's your friend?" she asked.

"This is Michael, and he's my cousin. We're here with other people."

"You and Omara still knocking the boots?"

"No. We didn't knock boots, and we aren't going out anymore."

"Oh," she said. "That's too bad. I thought you two made a cute couple. You definitely should have knocked the boots."

"Who are you here with?"

"Nobody. I'm here on my own."

"Is that safe?"

"I'm not dead or raped, am I?"

"Not yet."

"If I'm fine in Hanoi, I'll be fine in Akawe."

"You sure about that?"

"So, what, you here for the music then?" asked Michael.

"I'm here for DJ Kraken."

"Hah!" I said. "We talked about him with the people putting the thing together. He ain't coming."

"What, Mercator told you that?"

"No. The people downstairs told us."

Crystal shook her head. "Kraken'll be here. You'll see. He'll kick everyone's ass. He's like that. I wouldn't believe he wasn't coming unless Mercator told me himself."

"Who is Mr. Mercator?!" shouted Michael. "Is he a DJ? Because I've never heard of him before!"

"Don't you know?" asked Crystal. "It's like the worst-kept secret in Akawe. Mercator's Paulson Olan. Heir to the Olan Estate. Chief of several of their pet projects. He owns half of the property downtown, and everywhere else, too. Mercator is his party name. He thought Akawe needed a rave – he thought Detroit was getting all of the action – so he asked Kraken to get him some solid talent. Why don't you think the police have busted this up? There's like a thousand people here, but one of them is an Olan."

Just then, the 33 faded his music down to the tiniest hum. Now, only the beat remained. It had become so quiet that we heard, from the other room, one of Dr. Positron's improvised vocoder impressions: "The 33 has a little dick. The 33 g-gets dogs to lickit. The 33 has a little dick. The 33 g-gets dogs to lickit."

The 33 tossed his headphones aside, vaulted from the stage with the beat still dotting, and hurtled toward the door. The ravers all stood aside, and a riot of noise went up in the Reef. Dr. Positron's set ended with a literal record scratch.

"Kill that bitch, Positron!" someone shouted from the hall, followed by the sounds of distinctly unplurry celebration.

Crystal snorted.

"Well," I said. "I guess that's that."

But it wasn't.

Another sound emerged. It was a vast bass wave that rose up through the floor and entered our feet. From the basement. From the Fountain of Youth.

"It's DJ Kraken!" said Crystal. "Anyway, call me John, if you want a badass job!"

With that, she vanished through the door.

Slowly, like zombies, Michael and I merged with the rest of the crowd, slowly making our way out into the hall and past Davy Jones' Locker. We climbed down the stairs and ignored the floral colors of Seven Fathoms. We moved, hundreds of us, into the hollow darkness of the Fountain of Youth where two floodlights, one blue and one purple, lit up the familiar, expansive, multitudinous array of DJ Tom's Leviathan.

After that, my sense of time blurred.

It might be that we all felt a little strange down there, standing in puddles, dancing in darkness, with only the hard light of the floodlights silhouetting the contours of Kraken's – of Tom's – face. It looked like a topographic map where peaks and valleys revealed more of this man than I had ever noticed when he'd DJed the dances at Radcliffe Junior High. Here he was, Tom, aka Kraken, who had summoned famous DJs from Detroit and Chicago, had drafted support for Mercator's dreams, and had prompted the swaying of one thousand bodies.

Now that the basement was spinning him around him in Mevlevian frenzy, Kraken punched some buttons, turned a knob, slid several dials, and leveled us into a sound more sinuous than the 33's, more aggressive than Positron's, an orbital hypnosis. Dancing returned us to the sea: the water we swallowed there bled out through our pores, saltwater kisses, lest we forget our ancestors.

The man in the purple silk shirt slid among the shining ravers, his ear and mouth to a walkie-talkie. The bus driver blew a stream of paraffin wax through a small torch, igniting curls of carbine bright flame. Purple Shirt moved fast toward the pink-hatted Chalk. Pulling the bill of his hat down over his eyes. An ironic smile. "I'm going, I'm going," and then he was gone. Kraken phased in with palming beech leaves, the dust of dull days, the city broadcasting its invitation to encounter new people, new things, other ways of living. Of being. Curt was talking to the bouncer. Matt Masterson lay in an exhausted heap behind his new raver friends, his foot and ankle trailing through a murky puddle. I sought out the face of the ever-dancing goth. She had become a disembodied spirit, unconcerned with mortals. Hands fluttering. Nataraja. Take them. A couple danced behind her. The man was clearly Darius, and he had an intent expression on his face. The woman was just as focused. It was Ms. Ropoli.

The fuck?!

Jason now. I don't know who he was talking to. They were talking about how once, in 1985, one West End gang (the Satan's Masters) had routed another (the Demonik Mafia). It was an old song:

"O Lord God Most High, mighty warrior, you once empowered the child David to slay the gruesome giant Goliath. Hear my humble prayer."

"She has done what she could."

"Send Your heavenly blessing upon these weapons, all these AK-47s, these Uzis, and these MAC-11s."

"What has she done?"

"Fuel them with power and strength to protect Your Holy Church, the widows, the poor, and to fire death into those who trespass against me, for you are my strength and my fury and my protection, and all my glory and praise is yours, in the name of the Father, and of the Son, and of the Holy Spirit, as it was in the beginning, is now, and ever shall be, world without end. Amen."

"She has anointed my body beforehand for its burial."

They had rained down fire on the Park of the Tamaracks and took out two Mafiosos. They also took out a bystander. Coral Sarvis had brought her two children to the park to play, and her daughter, Temple, caught a bullet to the head. The girl lingered for two months before dying. At the funeral, Corey wept, saying: "She'll never dance in a wedding dress! She'll never dance out in the poppies! She'll never walk down an aisle holding a bouquet! She'll never get to breathe that lilac air!"

On the day it happened, Temple's eight-year-old brother Zuggurat stood at the side of the road and banged his tambourine as the motley cars swept past.

Five years later, he joined the Demonik Mafia.

I took my shades off to see if it would help me see any better. It didn't.

I put them back on.

The beat continued, infinitely, into the past and the future.

The dark space stretched out, infinitely, on every side of that warehouse basement.

So what is the infinite? Are infinities real, or are they just something we say when we mean "a lot"? I knew the answer to this: It is whatever we can reduce and annihilate by any proportion, but there's always more. Always more. But: *If a worm ate itself from the tail forward, then what did it do when its jaws pressed against the back of its head?*

I smelled fear percolating through the air. Kraken's beat had gradually decrescendoed down to almost nothing, but then he suddenly opened all channels and flooded the room with noise and feedback. Everyone took a step back.

Except for Selby, who was standing off by herself in the terrible awe of that moment, and I could tell that she was watching for something.

The cacophony ended as sharply as it had started, reduced to the beat, joined now by the singsong voice of a young girl, distant hills, dusty stars.

Then a man intoned:

"Kings came. Kings fought.
They fought, those kings.
They fought by the water,
but they didn't rob us of our treasure."

Kraken mixed in a string section, a melodramatic sweep. Violin and viols overcome with grief.

"The stars of heaven fought for us.
They turned from their courses.
The rain flooded the river, and it swept the enemy away.
The banks all swollen with mud and blood."

And everything paused for one eternal, aching moment.

"Eden knows. Eden knows. Eden knows. Eden knows.
And God resides in Eden."

Selby mouthed a word. Two words.

I walked over to her.

"He's good," she said. "I never knew he was this good when he was playing records at our dances at Radcliffe."

Kraken had slowly tilted the beat down. A farewell hum started to blend out of the invisible-huge speakers of the Leviathan.

Then the beat stopped, and only a faint ringing hung in that basement air.

"I think it's time for us to head out," Selby said. "We've been here a long time. Mr. and Mrs. Adams didn't give us a curfew, but if they wake up and we're gone, it'll be bad for all of us."

The crowd had started to thin as soon as 33 and Positron's sets had ended, but there were still hundreds of people milling around. Selby and I found Michael dancing maybe a dozen feet from the Leviathan.

"We're ready to go!" said Selby.

"What?" shouted Michael.

We pulled him along with us and found Quanla arguing with a frustrated Darius. Ms. Ropoli was nowhere to be seen, but I saw the goth girl climbing a metal ladder that vanished into a black hole in the ceiling.

"You ready to go?" shouted Selby.

"Oh, I'm ready to get the hell outta here!" shouted Quanla.

We finally reached the main stairwell, and I heard giggling leaking out from Seven Fathoms. I stopped just long enough to see three shadows struggling behind a white screen. Matt Masterson's Oxford shirt lay crumped up in a ball in the corner.

Then we were upstairs, where the Maelstrom and the Reef were all but empty, lit up by ordinary lights, notwithstanding the piles of fading glow wands and hundreds of crumpled water bottles. Now, it all looked like a drab, gray, windowless bunker. When we got outside, we found a crowd of about fifty people.

"Can we, um, catch a bus?" Darius asked nobody in particular.

"Sure," said the bus ride dealer. "Get in line."

Darius moved off to the end of the line. It looked like this was going to take a while.

Quanla glared after him.

"You guys go wait with Darius," said Selby. "I'm going to look around for a minute."

We moved off, but I was already thinking up excuses to follow her.

"You know," I said when we got to the line. "I think I gave Selby my wallet to hold onto. I'ma go make sure she's got it, because if she doesn't, I'm screwed."

It was a bad lie, because I didn't even have a wallet, but nobody said anything. Everyone still seemed dazed by the music and the motion.

I walked the length of the line, but Selby wasn't there. I went back to the outside of the warehouse and walked its perimeter. I finally found her, standing on the eastern face of the building and smoking a cigarette as she looked off into the distance.

"That's bad for you, you know?" I said, coming up behind her.

I expected to surprise her, but she turned coolly toward me.

"It's a lot worse than pot, you know," I suggested.

"But probably better than O-Sugar," she said, the rasp in her voice startling me in its smoky roughness.

Selby held out the cigarette. I took a pull. I inhaled, coughed a little, and breathed it out. It tasted like ash. I gave it back.

"I don't see why people do that," I said.

"Smoke?"

"Yeah, it seems overrated."

"Maybe they just want something to do with their hands."

She looked out again, eastward.

"What are you looking at?"

She paused.

"You know," she said.

I looked out with her, but all I saw were trees, weeds, and a lot of darkness.

"No, I don't," I said.

She laughed. "I thought you were paying better attention. I guess not."

"So, aren't you going to tell me what you're thinking?"

She slid her foot along the pebbled ground.

"The only way to keep a secret," she said, "is to keep it to yourself."

"Who needs secrets?" I asked. "Better to know where you stand."

"Know where I stand? I would *love* for someone to fucking tell me where I stand." She took a drag, took a look at the half-finished cigarette, and flicked it into the rubble. "Okay, John," she said. "I will tell you something you don't already know. When I was a kid, I was molested. When I was four years old. The guy worked construction with my dad. He ... I don't know ... he and my dad got along at work, and he always acted like he was friends with my family. They gossiped a lot about their boss, who was the guy's dad. Kept saying what a loser he was. And he just ... he just got to know us really well."

I felt like I should say something, but I couldn't think of anything to say. I was trying to add this information to the growing pile – *Elizabeth's a drug dealer, and Adam's stoned, and Lucy's dating this Chalk pimp who has my sunglasses!* – but this seemed bigger than all of those other things combined, and Selby was confronting me now with the words she said. The realities she had lived. She watched me.

"Well," Selby continued. "He got to know *me* really well. And then one day, I came home with a cut on my throat, and my voice all fucked up. I'd said I was going to tell my parents, you see. So he tried to kill me. He stabbed me here." For the first time ever, I noticed a tiny scar – a crease of raised skin – in the middle of her neck just beneath the chin. "But I got away."

Selby took a few deep breaths. I could tell that she was regretting throwing the cigarette away. I would have wanted something warm to hold as well.

"When I told my parents, my dad told my mom not to take me to the hospital. He didn't want anyone to know what had happened. Then he said that he had to hurry, because if he didn't find Quint right away, he would vanish."

"Quint?"

"That was the guy's name. Don't say it out loud. I shouldn't either. You'd shit yourself if you know who all could be listening. But my mom stitched me up. It hurt, but I think she did a good job. Later that night, my dad came home and talked to my mom for a long time. The next morning Quint's body got found somewhere over in the Os. And a week later, my dad died. He fell off the viaduct, they said. They said he'd been drinking. That it was an accident. My dad hadn't had a drink in years."

"What did your mom do?"

"I never talked to her about it. I was too young. Maybe George or Demetrius knew something, but they never told me. They loved my dad, though. But I think my mom was worried that if they could kill my dad so easily, they'd go after the rest of us if she said anything. So, she kept quiet. I don't think it was easy for her. But she had to keep her kids alive, you know? She had to keep us all fed."

Selby kept looking to the east. *What is she looking for?* She had fixed her attention on something far away, but all I could see was scrub and chain-link fencing and concrete piles.

"So, I guess I told you several things. That I was molested. That my father killed the guy. That they killed him for it. And why my voice is ... like this."

"Who ... who do *you* think killed him? Your dad? Who would want to protect someone who did ... something like that to, to just a little kid?"

"It was *his* dad, John," she said. "It was the boss."

I felt like I was trespassing. I felt like I should leave, but that would make me callous.

"Why do you want to know this shit about me, John?" Selby asked.

I was tense all over. My chest was so tense I felt like I couldn't breathe. *Because I see things!* I wanted to say. *Because nothing adds up! Because everything is so completely fucked up!*

"Because I care about you," I said.

"Well, then I guess I should tell you. I guess I should tell somebody, you know? In case I die or go missing or –"

"What have you been doing, Selby?"

She held her hand up to quiet me. I mean, I realized that I was almost shouting.

"It's probably nothing. I'm probably just being a drama queen."

"Probably." I didn't think it was a coincidence that Selby had been the one to help Cora escape from Akawe. I didn't think it was a coincidence that she was sitting at the Chalk table at lunch now, either. But she was playing a subtle game here, and if I was going to wade in with her, I'd have to be subtle too.

"For years," Selby said. "I thought he had left. The boss. The asshole's dad. I couldn't ask my mom about it, and anyway, I didn't think she knew. But people also said ... nobody ever really knew his real name."

"What do you mean. Wasn't he the –"

"Boss? Yeah. But he always did things unofficial. You ask one person who he is, they'd say one thing. You ask someone else, they'd say something else. But I found out that he's still around – he's still in Akawe – and you'll never find anyone with a bigger fucking ego, because he calls himself God."

"He thinks he's God?"

"I don't know what he thinks, but he makes people call him that now. God Ostyn."

"Is that his real name?"

"What do you think?!"

"Wait a minute," I said, because finally my mind was moving fast and supple. "Lucy's boyfriend. His name is Eli –" And Selby started to nod. "– Ostyn." I finished. "And he was wearing those shades tonight. The sunglasses I found. The ones you returned to ... the guy with the knife?"

"Who I never saw. So as long as you were telling me the truth –"

"I was –"

"I didn't mean to tell you this much. Really, I was just going to tell you about what they did to me. About the wrong they did by me. About how much I hate ... how I just hate and hate until I shake." Selby stopped speaking. She closed her eyes and breathed. Marshaled herself and went on. "Don't mess around with it, John. I'm not fucking around. They're dangerous. They're, like, the most dangerous people I've ever met. I didn't mean for Lucy to ... to get all caught up in it, but the whole thing got really complicated last year. Maybe you could have helped out with it, some, but you were all busy with your new friends, and your new girlfriend, and your plans, and ..."

"Okay," I said. "Okay."

"Just, if anything weird happens to me, like, if I stop coming to school someday or something, just tell Demetrius, so he can, whatever ..."

"Okay."

"And hey, I'd really like for you to give Lucy a call sometime. I'd really like for you and her to be friends again. I knew she was coming tonight, you know? I was hoping we'd see her. I didn't know she was going to bring Eli with her."

"Eli is –"

"Eli was fucked over when he got born into that family, but he also ends up ruining whoever he meets, so I guess it all evens out."

I had to keep reminding myself to breathe. I wished I had a cigarette then. I wished I had something to do with my hands and my mouth. But the wind blew, the clouds covered the stars, the temperature was falling, and black branches rattled against a black background. Selby leaned toward the east.

"What are you looking for?" I asked again, my voice cracking.

"Eden knows," she murmured. "God resides in Eden."

"I don't understand."

"Well, that's too fucking bad, John!" she laughed. "Who says you get to understand everything? I was going to tell you one thing, and now it looks like I told you everything, so if you don't get it, why is that on me?"

She looked at me, fierce and skeptical.

"I think you're a whole person, Selby."

"Thanks," she said. "I guess everything is fine, then."

She turned her back on the margins and made her way back toward the diminishing crowds.

When we got back, Darius was near the front of the line. A few minutes later, a huge Benedict pulled up and the driver – someone we'd never seen before – barked at us to get in.

"What about the bus?" asked Darius.

"What?!" yelled the driver. "No, no, it's crazy, man, just crazy, people leaving, too many, just get in, get in."

Our ride bounced across the cracked concrete to the chain-link gates of the Benedict West, then cut off away from the factories until the dark windows of Darius' Daphne rose out of the gloom like something out of a dream. We hurried across the parking lot and clambered inside.

I felt like it had been weeks since we'd arrived here. Like we had spent months in the warehouse light and darkness and music and noise. Everything was still muffled in my ears.

"What time is it?" I asked.

"Looks like ... 2:50," Darius said.

"God dammit, Darius!" snapped Qunala.

"What!" he snapped back. "Look, you weren't in a hurry neither!"

"We're gonna be in so much shit when we get back, and all because you went and hooked up with that old lady."

"She ain't old!" barked Darius. Then, "We didn't hook up!"

"Hey guys, guys," rasped Selby, in the most soothing tone I'd ever heard from her. "Look, don't be pissed off, okay? That was a lot of fun. I mean, that was fucking mythological! Is Akawe ever going to even have a party like that again? We'll be telling our kids about that time we saw Dr. Positron throw down against the 33. And then they both got shown up by our junior high DJ!"

After the talk we'd just had, I didn't trust Selby's joy in that moment.

"But it was epic, wasn't it?" she asked. "Quanla?"

Quanla was grim and quiet.

"Michael?"

"Yeah!" burst Michael. "It was fucking sweet!"

"Look," said Selby. "I've got a bit of money. And I'm hungry after all that dancing. So, let's go out to the Os and hit King Michael's. We can get some for your parents. We'll take the drive-thru so we'll be fast, but if they wake up, we'll say we were in there and just talked a lot and lost track of the time."

"It'll be, like, four by the time we get back!" said Darius.

"We're stupid teenagers," Selby explained. "They'll buy it. They don't think there's anything so retarded we won't do it!"

Darius thought it over.

"I don't know," he said. "That's clear across town. We have to drive down to Center to get over the river, and then there might be a train crossing."

"No, no, no," said Selby. "It'll be fast. I know a shortcut."

I knew exactly where we were going.

I didn't want to go where we were going.

I sat in the back, Michael on my left, Selby on my right. By night everything looked twisted and contorted. I was convinced that these objects had become warped. That they would never return to their original dimensions. Houses. Cars. Trees. Stars. An endless sequence of shuttered businesses, liquor stores, empty and unending auto plants, parts suppliers, warehouses, loading docks, and rubble clusters where the demolitions and the abatement experts held final sway. Failed factories. And across the street, endless rows of ramshackle houses, most of them abandoned.

My father's house is in there somewhere, I thought. *That house where he and Aunt Mabel and Aunt Ellie lived when Grandma Bridge locked herself in her bedroom and refused to come out.*

But the beaten-down bungalows all looked the same to me. I couldn't have known which one had been my father's. Instead, I imagined high-tech windmills – electropulse turbines – moving in the morning, blowing away what little remained of this lonely part of the city. I didn't feel like we were driving across a few miles through the night. I felt like we were diving straight toward the center of the earth.

A lot had changed along Trevithick Road since the last time I'd been here, back in '94, when Dwight had gotten lost driving my friends and me home after we'd spent the day in Detroit.

The sagging factories had been demolished. Trevithick's weary four lanes were flanked by a young and angry prairie. We pulled up to the weird side street that had divided the factories, and I saw that everything had been removed. No more rusting catwalks. No more chemical drums. No light at all, besides the headlights from Darius' Daphne.

A sign had been erected at the entrance to the desolation: "X LIQUIDATIONS – A PUBLICLY HELD CONSORTIUM." Letters black on white. A blue-and-red logo.

"There's a gate," Darius said. "This road has been gated off."

But the chain-link gate had been stripped of its wire mesh. Only the posts and rails remained.

"You can drive right through that," said Selby.

After another moment's hesitation, Darius eased the Daphne through.

It was so easy.

Scarcely a bump, and we were on the other side.

The other side of what?

We moved through the demolished blank space and arrived at the tunnel angling downward. The headlights illuminated a pool of sludgy water at the very bottom, and Darius brought the car to a halt.

"That's –" he said.

"It's not deep," Selby said.

"If I stall out down here, we'll –"

"You won't."

Darius took a deep breath and accelerated into the muck. Black water flew up against our windows, and I smelled smoke and saw it curling out of the hood, but we plowed through the mess and emerged on the other side. As the tunnel angled upward, we all started breathing again.

On the other side, the road was still blocked by concrete barriers even though the surrounding structures had been demolished. This was where Dwight had stopped on that fatally bright summer afternoon. This was where I had persuaded him to turn the car around. To return to ordinary spaces filled with normal abandoned houses and fallen-down factories.

"What now?" asked Darius.

"Just go around it!" said Selby, her voice tight.

"Okaaay," said Darius.

Unlike Dwight, Darius trusted Selby, and I didn't speak up to challenge her. I didn't want to keep going. I didn't want to see the awful things that waited beyond, but something in my body was telling me that I needed to know. What would we see at the end of this darkest road? In the dead center of the demolished Benedict Main? At the very heart of it all?

As we passed between two huge piles of concrete rubble, faint lights appeared again, all around us. To our right, the tired neighborhoods of the West End. To our left, the sickly lamps of 292. Far ahead, miles and miles away, the dim twinkling of the downtown high-rises. Everything between here and there had been toppled down.

"This is hella creepy, Selby," said Darius. "How you know about this?"

Selby didn't answer.

"Look!" said Michael.

A street sign had been randomly planted in the midst of the rubble. It dangled sideways from a single rusted screw, but if we turned our heads we could read it:

EDEN ST.

The Daphne continued to creep forward. Darius wasn't driving, really. He just let the car idle forward through that black remoteness where the lights of houses and high-rises shone no brighter than the distant stars.

"I see something!" said Quanla.

I took my sunglasses off. I leaned forward. We all leaned forward.

Up ahead, a ragged shape seemed to have been cut out against the backdrop of light. It was still small and far away, but it grew larger as we approached.

When the headlights finally caught the thing more clearly, my heart sank. I don't know why it made me so afraid, this inanimate and contempted thing all alone in the sprawling void, but it seemed like a place where everything bad had happened. Its gravitational field was too powerful for evil acts – furious, desperate violence? – to escape. No, frenzy and corruption were all sucked in toward this thing. Now we were, too.

It was a house.

A farmhouse, certainly more than a hundred years old, modest but not small, once elegant but informal, with a fine porch that wrapped around the first floor. Its white paint had almost entirely flaked away from its disintegrating skin, its cornices were sunken, its apertures hidden beneath plywood, its shingles molding. It had a small round window on the second story, dark, cross-framed, and catastrophic ruin, and absolute refusal, and a clenched-teeth front door.

I'd seen hundreds – thousands – of abandoned houses in my city, and this was the worst of them all. This house was animated by a dark life, and its darkness was predatory, and its darkness was death.

My brain tried to move, to explain the monstrosity: *Maybe this is why the factories all closed up and got torn down. Maybe this is why X Auto left us here. Maybe this is why Akawe was doomed from the beginning. This house. Here on Eden Street. The darkest road in the world. Maybe this house was made from the wood of the Tree of the Knowledge of Good and Evil, and that's why they called this Eden Street. Maybe this house – this street – infected the whole world, and that's why everything breaks and keeps on breaking.*

We'd arrived at last, a half-mile from any other structure, and the world outside was visible to us because of the light it emitted, but this house was invisible in its obscurity. Only we saw it in the feeble light of the Daphne's headlights. Only we bore witness to its desiccation, its hunger, its hollow, its malignance.

Just in front of the house, another street crossed our path, heading off to the left, with a sign marking the lightless intersection.

EDEN ST.

crossed

O ST.

"The fuck?" murmured Darius.

He looked to the right, but O Street was blocked by a pile of rubble there. To the left, it vanished off toward I-63 and the river.

As for Eden Street, it continued for a few hundred feet beyond the dark house before ending against a moldering gray concrete wall, thick with withered ivy that trembled in an unseen breeze.

Darius turned left onto O Street, and we turned our backs upon the abandoned house. I didn't want to turn around and watch it recede behind us. In fact, I found myself slouching down in my seat, so that nothing looking out of one of its haunted windows would be able to see me. I noticed that Michael was doing the same thing. But Selby sat upright, rigid, and her expression was blank and as clear as glass.

O Street cleared the remnants of the Benedict Main, then descended and rose through another tunnel – this one wasn't flooded – and emerged onto a service drive lined with alternating pines and concrete barriers.

"Not much of a shortcut, Selby," muttered Darius.

Selby shrugged.

"Where now?" he asked.

"Right," she said.

A minute later, we reached a bridge, crossed the river, and entered the Os. Soon we were sitting in the drive-through line at King Michael's. Nobody felt much in the mood for food, but we dutifully ordered some coneys and fries and ate in silence as we rode back to Quanla and Darius's house. When we got in, we slipped our shoes off at the door. Quanla put the food we'd brought for her parents into the fridge. Then Selby followed Quanla to her room while Michael and I crept up the stairs with Darius. We lay out bedding and pillows down on his soft-carpeted floor.

As I lay there, I tried to think about the rave; about the music, the lights, dancing with my friends, and watching DJ Kraken and his Leviathan tear the whole place down. But my thoughts kept shifting away toward Selby with her cigarette and her secrets. Toward Akawe's worst secret; Eden Street winding crazily through the torn-down belly of the city's largest factories and that horrible house standing naked at the center of it all.

It took me a long time to fall asleep, and when I did, I had weird, unsettling dreams that I couldn't remember when I woke.

Nobody wanted to stick around the Adams' house the next morning. Aunt Mabel picked Michael and me up and dropped me off at home on her way back to Parc Pierre. I told my parents that we had pulled an all-nighter studying. I wasn't sure they bought it, but they didn't say anything. Then I went back upstairs to sleep some more.

I woke as the sun was setting, its orange flames firing off cold from the West End. I realized that it must be falling shadowless upon the house on Eden Street. Was sunlight allowed to penetrate those broken windows? Was that white paint allowed to reflect light?

My stomach rumbled.

I went downstairs and reheated some pasta, but I still didn't feel very hungry.

"John," said my father. "I need you to go out and mow the lawn. We need it cut a couple more times before winter comes in."

"Isn't it already here? It's freezing out! And aren't we going to rake the leaves first?"

"Don't bother. Just mulch them. Yard looks like shit anyway."

It was almost night by the time I got inside. My parents sat listlessly in front of the TV. I took a seat beside them, but I was finding it hard to sit still. *Desperate times call for desperate measures.* But what desperate action could I take? *I could call Omara.* Her voice, even if she sounded annoyed, might be able to dispel the image of Eden Street from my mind. *If Omara had been there, she would have known what to say. To call it what it was. To name it out loud.* But I wasn't going to call Omara. I wasn't *quite* that pathetic. And so I was left alone in my mind with the thing that stood in the middle of the Benedict Main. Everything else was inconsequential.

On Sunday, we went to church, but the conversations and the light-soaked pews didn't make me feel any better.

It was all a gnawing in my stomach.

At school the next day, my friends seemed just as lethargic. Except for Omara. When I passed her in the hall, she threw me a smile so warm and reassuring that I almost dropped to the floor right then to beg her to reconsider. Then I remembered that I had already said everything I could say. I had already humiliated myself in front of her. It didn't get me anywhere. She smiled at me now because she was forgiving and understanding. It didn't have anything to do with her wanting to get together again. *Besides, she didn't see what I saw on Eden Street. She didn't see that house. She doesn't know what I know.*

That day, I ate my lunch in the library. I had planned on working on my civics homework, but I ended up skimming a *Rolling Stone* that someone had left on one of the radiators. "Alanis Morrissette: Angry White Female." "Clinton in a Funk." "The Militias and the NRA." It was warm on my lap as I read, and the room smelled like radiator heat and peeling latex paint.

"How was your weekend?" I asked Ms. Ropoli when I got to her class.

"Fine," she said. "Yours?"

"Ravey," I said.

She didn't react.

I took a seat and resumed the minutes of the last Akawe city council meeting.

After school, the temperature spiked into the smoky sixties. Bad news for the city on Devil's Night, when the firebugs in Detroit and Akawe and a few other Michigan towns fanned out through the most arid neighborhoods, sparking anything that could catch an acrid flame. For hours, plumes of smoke curled into the sky. A heavy stench of char and oil and useful, forgotten things rendered to ash. At least our house was somewhat safe now, unthreatened by abandoned shacks and mature maples. By the time the tired sun rose over the city on Halloween morning, over 200 fires had been reported throughout Akawe. About 20 houses had come down on the West End, another dozen in the Os, and a few others scattered around the city.

Now that the unseasonable warmth had done its damage, it went away. A foggy chill descended over the neighborhoods, and the sky filled with gray clouds.

I was surprised when Chris tracked me down in the library at lunchtime.

"You know," he said, "you don't have to leave the table just because you and Omara broke up. Everyone's talking about it. I mean, your not being there. Not that you broke up."

"I don't want it to be weird for anyone," I said.

"Jeez, John. It isn't like you breaking up with her is the biggest thing that ever happened on this planet. Anyway, that's not why I'm here. There's no rehearsals tonight, here or at AYT, so we're going trick-or-treating ... Shannon and me, and Maj, and maybe Nova if I can find him. You want to come?"

"Trick of treating? You're a junior!"

Chris shrugged.

"It's probably my last year."

"Where you going? Bellwood?"

Chris laughed. "No," he said. "They're real cheap over there. Nobody goes over there. We're going in Anderson Park."

I didn't have a lot of time to put a costume together, but I dressed in black, combed my hair down as flat and straight as it would go, put on a dark pair of my tea shades, and some old lady rings my Grandmother Richter had given my mother. I wrote "OZZY" across the knuckles of both hands.

"*That's* your costume?" my mother asked.

"The taste of bats is really salty!" I barked. "Really salty!"

When I hopped into Chris' minivan, Shannon gave a snort at my costume. He had dyed his hair green and was wearing green plastic gloves. He held a huge coil of chicken-wire, wrapped in green ribbon across his lap.

I said, "What's –"

"Sea serpent," he said.

Chris had gone for a minimalist costume: a knife thrust into one side of his head and out the other, with blood dripping down his scalp and from the corners of his mouth. Nova wore a skeleton costume. Majenta, sitting in the way back, seemed to be dressed no differently than usual.

"What's your costume?" I asked her.

"I'm a bat," she said.

"Baller."

We talked strategy on our way north, and Chillout Chris weirded me out with his ice-cold battle tactics.

"There'll be a lot of little kids," he was saying, "but they're slow. They'll be like in packs with their parents, and they'll stick to the sidewalks. So, what we do is we cut across the lawns. That way, we can get up on the porch before they do, even if they're ahead of us."

"Brutal, man," said Nova.

"I'm going to get so much fucking candy tonight," said Chris. "And I'm gonna eat it all before tomorrow."

Majenta didn't say much. I couldn't tell whether she was just her usual sullen self or if she objected to my presence on Omara's behalf. It was hard for me to believe Chris that *nobody* cared about the break-up.

"Hey," I said, "you invited Omara, right?"

I imagined Majenta rolling her eyes behind me.

"Yeah, we invited her!" said Chris. "'I'm too old for that!' she said." Chris' derision of Omara's derision came through in his high-pitched imitation of her voice. "Ken would've come, but his dad needs his help at some event their family is hosting in Detroit or something."

"What about Justin?"

"I haven't seen Justin lately."

When we started, the sun was still shining through the tattered hems of the clouds, casting its weak light upon the last of the leaves. Silver maples. Street after broad street had already filled with kids in costumes – Power Rangers, Batman and Robin, Will Smith and Carlton Banks, the Penguin and Catwoman, the occasional Barney – and they waddled just ahead of their parents from house to house. I expected to catch some dirty looks, but I didn't. Yeah, we were old for trick-or-treaters, but at least we were wearing costumes. At least we weren't pushing the little kids around. At least we didn't trample the parkway beds of cabbage, pansies, and mums. Some of the kids trick-or-treating were older than we were. Some of them were stubble-chinned adults, plastic Hefty sacks stretched wide, cigarettes dangling from the fingers.

"Trick-or-treat!" they growled.

And they received their candy and moved on. There was an unspoken truth in the air. Anderson Park was a money neighborhood, and none of our neighborhoods were money neighborhoods. So Anderson Park got its snow plowed, its trash picked up on time, and life was good enough there that they were able to worry about things like which trees the city cut down, and whether feral cats were murdering baby bunnies. Not whether live electrical wires dangled through the trees, or whether you'd get chased down the street by murderous dogs, or whether the vacant house next door would explode in the middle of the night because nobody had turned off the gas after the last eviction. And so, on one night of the year, Halloween Night, the rest of Akawe went knocking door to door and collected its poverty tax in Snickers and KitKats. Anderson Park paid up, and didn't fuss about it too much.

The longer we were out, the more people packed into the neighborhood, with lines of kids running from the porches to the sidewalks. We saw Wednesdays and Pugsleys, Leonardos, Michelangelos, Donatellos, and Raphaels, sometimes sporting shells made from green-painted trash can lids, Splinters and Quailmen, plenty of devils, an angel or two, Vito Corleone and Marlon Brando, Woody Harrelson and Buzz Lightyear, a Sufi and some Indian princesses, a lich holding his demilich buddy in his hand as he went, swinging it like a lantern, the usual motley of vampires, ghosts, clowns, witches, and Frankenstein monsters, a band of dancing zombies, a Cher Sarkisian, and a Cher Horowitz.

While a few sullen houses greeted us with lightless windows and drawn curtains, most of the porches glowed with pumpkins, candles, Tiki torches, faux cemeteries with cheeky epitaphs – "Izzy Dead" and "Barry D. Live" – and scarecrows planted among the gourds and cornstalks, and manic spectres with flickering eyes running from second-story windows down to the lawn, and howling demons, rattling bones, broomsticks, and evil trees.

My friends and I ranged up and down the fanciest streets. On Red Arrow, at an angular mansion of raw stones and slate shingles, with a copper conservatory at the back like the house from *Clue*, we got the hugest Butterfingers and 3 Musketeers bars.

In front of a more ordinary house on Peterson, an *Evil Dead* shack that Quanla would have admired had been erected in the front yard, while a man revved a (chainless) chainsaw and roared dismembering threats at the local kids while his wife dropped handfuls of candies in their sacks and pillowcases.

Across the street, an experimental Christian congregation had set up a pavilion where they gave away popcorn and hot cider to the kids, and beer to the adults, and tiny stapled tracts for everybody.

"I'm gonna try for a beer!" said Nova.

"Don't waste our time," snapped Chris. "It's getting late. There's still candy to get got, but we've only got a half-hour left!"

The neighborhood got wild in the last minutes of trick-or-treating.

The sun went down and the temperature dropped. Sharp and gusting wind became rain, then sleet, then snow. A lot of parents, not wanting to get out of their cars in this mess, idled down the streets alongside their kids going door to door. It all turned into a traffic jam amid the narrow streets. A few parents got fed up with waiting and drove over the curbs and across lawns as the last of the trick-or-treaters dove out of their way.

"This shit's getting nuts," said Nova. "Wanna head back? My bag's full, and people are running out of candy anyway."

Everyone agreed except Chris. Chris would've kept on trick-or-treating until November 1st if he could have.

"It's good to be high on life," he said. "It's better to be high on sugar."

But we'd gotten turned around. The streets of Anderson Park twisted around parks, streams, and parkways. It didn't help that the porch lights were all out, now that almost every house had exhausted its cache of candy. Nearly all of the remaining light came from the taillights of angry cars trying to escape from the neighborhood.

We thought we were making our way back toward South Street and Chris' minivan, but we must have gone the wrong way because we found ourselves away from the crowds and approaching the expressway.

"I want to go this way," said Majenta.

She was standing at the mouth of a slim drive – barely a road – that turned and vanished between tall, skeletal trees.

"That is *not* going to get us back to the car," said Shannon.

"Is it even safe?" asked Chris.

Majenta scoffed.

"It's Anderson Park," she said.

Nova laughed.

"Vote?" said Majenta.

"No way," said Chris.

Shannon shook his head.

"I'm cold," he said. "That's two of us, Maj."

"Okay. All in favor? Come on, who wants to?" asked Majenta.

I was cold. I was tired. But I also wanted to score some easy points with Majenta. Maybe she'd tell Omara how dope I'd been during trick-or-treating.

I raised my hand.

Nova imitated me, straining for heaven like a first-grader who just aced his spelling quiz and knows all the shit in the world.

Majenta flashed a rare smile.

"The Salty Allard Brothers vs. the Rest of Us. We're going."

The asphalt track cut between the overhanging trees and vines, all of them leaf naked, before dumping us in a frosted parking lot. Anderson Park *was* one of Akawe's "rich" neighborhoods. And this *was* a country club. But now it was, like seemingly everything else, abandoned. The stripped tennis courts had been riven by wide cracks packed with gray weeds. The old clubhouse had been incinerated, nothing left but a Stonehenge of blackened columns. Someone had dumped an old couch at the end of the parking lot, and it was rapidly being covered with a coat of rimey snow. Beyond all of this stretched a golf course, all of it waist-deep in dead grass and studded with yearning cottonwoods, and watched over by the ever-blinking red lights of distant radio towers.

"I know where we are, yo," said Nova. "My uncle used to go golfing down here. This is Ruth Golf Course. I didn't know it was shut down, though."

"Looks like it's been shut down a while," said Shannon.

"It's beautiful," said Majenta.

All I could think was that – yes – this was beautiful, and here I was on another – accidental – nightwalk, but Omara wasn't here, and *why isn't Omara here?* Then I remembered. *She's at home studying. She's too old for trick-or-treating. And also, she dumped me.*

I kicked a mound of snow. Majenta looked at me.

"It *is* beautiful," I said.

She blessed me with another smile, but I knew that her mere smiles wouldn't put me back together with Omara.

I swallowed some snot and my throat hurt. I could feel myself getting sick as we walked. It was time to come in out of the cold.

When I woke the next morning, my throat was raw and wet, but I made it out to school anyway. *I can't let Omara think I'm defeated* kept playing through my head, which didn't make a lot of sense. I felt like my absence would have told her that I'd been ground down or something. *I'm not sick*, I told myself. *My throat's just raw from all those fires this week.* Sure enough, three more plumes rose alongside the sun.

Another murder – another Black man – had been linked to the "Akawe Slasher," and I felt like the Black kids were glaring at the white kids like *we* were the ones stabbing their uncles and grandfathers. The serial killer pissed me off, too. I didn't like that my Black friends had to watch where they walked and I generally didn't. I hated that. But there wasn't anything I could *do* about it. I just tried to keep their eye-daggers on my chest and not my back. To keep my face blank, relaxed, listening, and understanding. But even listening was hard because, again, liquid snot kept pooling at the back of my throat and dripping down into my stomach.

And then those *Sleepy Hollow* fuckers kept reciting their lines in the hall, like the rest of us wanted to hear about made-up Catskill ghosts as we walked the more honestly haunted halls of Akawe Eastern High School. Anyway, I knew more than the rest of them. I had seen the house on Eden Street. Haunting *crowded* my head. I still didn't know why Mr. Agape had decided to stage his Halloween play on the week *after* Halloween. *What the fuck is that all about?* I kind of wanted to save up my lunch money so I could buy Mr. Agape a clue.

Schininnnnnnickk! my nose said, and the other kids in the hall looked at me in disgust.

I didn't blame them. I revolted myself.

That night my parents took me to Mass for All Saints Day at the church downtown. We'd missed the regular Mass; this was the cracked-out Latin liturgy. The long kneeling, the soft candles, the heavy incense, the steeping shadows; they all exhaled a perfume of holiness. These traditions were older than the corruption of Akawe. Maybe if I could have stamped down my doubt and said an actual prayer, God might have heard me and lifted me out of the tangles. But then I remembered that "God" was the name of the man whose son had molested Selby. Even if I said a prayer at St. Mark's downtown, I couldn't demolish the Hell House in the middle of the ruins of the Benedict Main. I couldn't redeem Elizabeth from her secret situations. I couldn't keep Adam from getting stoned and trashed like both of his parents. I couldn't call Lucy away from Eli, or pull Selby away from the Chalk table, and onto a stage, doing ballet. I couldn't convince Omara to go out with me again. I couldn't do anything. So why pray?

"Fuck," I muttered as I knelt in the dark.

The next morning, I felt dizzy as I staggered around the house, putting on my backpack and getting my clothes ready for a busy day of Geometry and all the other shit. *I can't skip school!* I had to keep my grades up. *For Omara!* What about that? *No, not for Omara! For Chicago!* I wondered if Chicago got cold like this in November.

We didn't go to church for All Souls Day, but as I lay on the couch beneath three or four heavy blankets and sipped the chamomile tea and honey my mother brought me, I imagined the celebrations that must have been going on at St. Francis. In the Os. The Mexican kids there would've stood in a Mass almost completely shrouded in darkness. I checked the dim memories of a field trip I had taken when I was seven or eight years old. I imagined the guttering veladoras throwing their lights upon the vaulted ceiling. The altar surrounded by marigolds. Bowls of sugar candy skulls waiting on card tables in the narthex. And someone reminded me that St. Francis had been founded when a bunch of Poles in the Os asked the Archdiocese for a parish, but the bishop's office misunderstood and sent up an Irish priest instead.

"Conas ata tu?"

"Nie rozumiem!"

They finally got it straightened out and sent a Polish priest. He presided over that parish for fifty years. He watched the Appalachians replace the Poles, and then the Mexicans move in on the Appalachians. He learned how to speak the speech of Chattanooga and Sinaloa.

"Qué pelón está el cochi!"

"Cain't never could but for prayers and intercessions!"

In the Os, most street names started with an O, but in the 70s a few of the streets had been renamed: Zacatecas. Oaxaca. San Pedro. Xoxocotlan. Guadalupe. Quetzalcoatl. The newcomers claimed the empty rooms at St. Francis and filled them with their own voices and traditions. They moved in right as the first factories started closing. Right as the neighborhood had started hollowing out. But the old priest had welcomed them, and when he finally died, they threw him a wake that hazed the snow with candle smoke and made the night into day.

My ears popped. The room swam in a hizzy daze. I was floating. And then my father was in the living room. He was talking to me. He was reclining in the La-Z-Boy with an open beer can cradled in his crotch.

" ... fought the good fight," he was saying. "Ran the race and all that bullshit."

"What?" I asked, and my voice slurred like I was a wino.

"You better find a job, John," he said. "For, you know, money you need."

"I'm sorry?" I said, trying to focus on his face. "You ... did you lose your job?"

"Yeah. That's what happened."

"It's happened before."

"Nope," he said. "This is it, probably. I had more than 25 years at Tool and Die. I took that transfer to Canton. To fucking Canton! That was me playing by their rules. Now that's all gone. I guess I can see if there's a transfer to Ohio. Hey John, you want to move to Ohio?"

I did not want to move to Ohio.

"That's okay," my father said, answering my unspoken thoughts. "There's no transfer for me. I only put in a quarter century with this company. Maybe if I'd put in another quarter they could find something for me."

"When does it happen?" I asked.

"December first."

"They're not even gonna give you 'til Christmas?"

My father didn't say anything. I thought about asking him again, but I realized he wasn't speaking because he didn't want to cry. He was staring out the window, concentrating upon some fixed point. I let him stare as I tried to shape a space for logic and reason in my stuffy brain.

"What are you going to do?" I finally asked.

"I guess I'm going to have to go out and find another job," he said.

He tried to smile at me, and it was the saddest, lamest, weakest smile I'd seen in my whole life.

On Friday, I told my mother that I was too sick to go to school. Staying home pissed me off, but I was sick and it was obvious. I took a cup of hot tea to my room and lay down, and my mother went to work. The pillows were a comfort. The blankets were a comfort. The fucking dripping sinus gray was a comfort.

I closed my eyes and slept without a flutter for three or four more hours.

When I woke up, I spun myself up a bowl of chicken noodle soup. I mean boiled. Spartan brand. I made some bread and butter to dip. I rifled through my parents' record collection and picked out one that belonged to my mother. I don't remember what it was. Something psychedelic. I dug out an old VHS tape of *Fantasia*, but I muted the television so that cartoon shapes were moving to my music rather than anything chosen by Leopold Stokowski. At first, the whole production was a discordant contrast. Then it was funny. Then it seemed profound. Then, during the Beethoven piece, when topless technicolor centaur women hook up with the equine surfer dudes, and Zeus and Hephaestus throw lightning upon the plains, and Bacchus and his saucy ass get drunk on eggplant-colored wine – I suddenly felt like I was falling through air. *Is this it, then?* I reeled. *Is Chicago just a place out there for other people, while I probably get a shitty job that doesn't even pay what my father's job pays, and then I lose that, just like he lost his, and we both have to stay ... here ... and meanwhile horrible things are allowed to exist ... here ... and?*

Bacchus slapped me with a sloppy grin.

I rested my arm on the armrest. I was sitting in the La-Z-Boy. I needed someone to wrap my arms around. For comfort. For safety. And stability. It almost didn't matter who. Someone with a beating heart that pumped blood. That would be enough. If I was with someone else, Omara might remember me. She might get jealous. She might get back together with me, and then we would be two peas in a pod again.

But, no, it wasn't quite that either. I couldn't count on Omara to change her mind. She probably wouldn't. So I spun out another parallel track as the putti danced. This wasn't going to be a regurgitated version of Adam's seventh-grade plan. I didn't want to *play* or *use* anyone ... this could be good for everyone. Yeah, I just needed a stopgap girl to keep from going insane. A delicate centaur maybe, with a fine curtain of close-cropped hair and perfect penny-sized penny-colored nipples – just to keep going until I could stop obsessing over Omara and a single abandoned house.

Who will go out with me right now? I wondered. *Who will absolutely not turn me down if I ask her out today?*

I paused the movie.

I checked the time.

It was just after three.

School had been out for about a half-hour, but my father could get home any moment. I was surprised he wasn't back already, actually. I didn't want him walking in on this conversation. I got out the phone book, looked up DUNHAM, found the number I needed, and picked up the phone. After just a few rings, May answered.

"Hi May, this is John," I said.

"Hi, John!"

"John Bridge."

"I know."

"So ... how are you?"

"I have to rake leaves today! Are you sick today? You looked kind of sick yesterday."

"Yeah."

"Oh. I'm sorry. I hope you aren't sick for long. I would make you chocolate chip cookies if I could, except we're all out of butter."

"Um, that's okay. I wanted to ask you something."

A pause. I closed my eyes and plowed ahead:

"I was wondering if you'd like to go out with me?"

Another pause.

"Okay," she said.

It was such a matter-of-fact, unconsidered-sounding answer, I wondered if she had even heard me right.

"I mean ... if you'd like to, you know, be my girlfriend."

"Well, yeah, that's what it means, isn't it?"

"Uh, yeah."

"And then you will be my boyfriend."

"Yeah."

"Haha! Awesome! I got a boyfriend, and you got a girlfriend!"

"Yeah, I –"

"So why did you break up with Omara?"

Isn't that something you should have asked me before saying 'yes?'

"May, I'll just tell you. She dumped me."

198

"But you don't want to go out with her anymore?"

"No! Do you think I'd be asking you out if I did?"

"No, but I have to make sure, you know? I don't want you going out with me and thinking about her while you are. That would be pretty crappy."

"I mean ... I don't know. I don't think I ever liked her that much, to be honest."

May was quiet for a moment. "That's too bad," she said.

"What do you mean, 'that's too bad?'" I asked. "I thought you just said you didn't want me thinking about her!"

"Well, yeah, not now! But it's like ... but you went out with Omara for, like, a super long time. And I just thought you would have to love her to go out with her for so long."

"Well, okay, I guess you're right. Yeah, I liked her ... a lot. But that's all over now, you know?"

"She seems amazing. She's beautiful, and super smart. But I'm surprised she would go out with you for so long if you couldn't even say, 'I love you,' to her."

Well, I did say that to her ...

"Anyway," May went on. "I won't say 'I love you' to you yet. It's too soon, right? We're just going out now. I mean, we barely know each other! But we have to say something, so I'll say 'lylab'!"

"What?"

"A couple years ago, I asked out this boy – he was super cute. He had nice eyes and a nice ass, but he never cut his hair, you know? Anyway, he said to me, he just wanted to be friends, so I said 'lylab' which I made up and it stands for 'love you like a brother.'"

"But I don't –"

"Don't worry, I don't love you like a brother. That would be gross. I love you like a boyfriend. So, when I say it to you, the 'b' stands for 'boyfriend.' But it doesn't mean I'm really in love with you like I'm going to faint for you, or you have to buy me all the Valentine's Day candy in the red hearts, and there's all that chocolate. It just means, you know, we're going out with each other. You are going out with *me*, and I am going out with *you*."

"I ..." I said. I was struggling to think of anything. "Okay. I mean, I don't know what you're talking about."

"It isn't complicated, John! Just, I say 'lylab,' and you say 'lylag,' okay?"

"'Lylag?'"

"Yup! 'Lylag.' Now I've gotta go rake those leaves. My dad's giving me the Evil Eye. Lylab! Goodbye!"

And she hung up.

By the weekend, my head and nose had cleared. I still felt tired, though. At breakfast, my father started bugging me about a job again, so I pulled out the newspaper and started looking. Most of the classifieds sounded like they had been posted by serial killers trying to lure you into the sewers.

GENERAL HELP WANTED

Hi Teens! General Help wanted for exciting new business opp
in Basadena Cty. Filing, errands, ets. Must be flexible, strong,
know how to type. $4.25/hr.

It all sucked, but then I remembered what Crystal had told me at the rave.

"Call me," she'd said. "If you want a badass job!"

For the first time in over a year, I picked up the phone and called Crystal.

"Hey there, boy!" she said when she picked up the phone.

"Hey, it's —" I started. "Wait a minute, how'd you know it was a boy?"

I could imagine Crystal shrugging.

"The odds were good," she said. "Girls don't call me much."

"You said I should call you. About a badass job. Or something."

"Oh, yeah, that's right. Lucky you, too! We're almost out of time to apply."

"Well? What is it?"

"Well, I'll give you the bad news first. It doesn't pay much. I mean, it doesn't even pay minimum wage."

"That's a problem," I said. "I need to make some money. My father's losing his X job in a month. I need to basically make money for my own shit, you know?"

"Yeah, but you didn't let me get to the good news. You could get college credit for this. As a *ninth grader.* That's some big shit if you want to go to college."

Really? That didn't make much sense to me.

"Well, what is it?" I asked.

"It's working at the planetarium," she said. "Selling stuff. Ushering. Maybe leading some school groups after a bit. Orientation is today ... this afternoon, but I'll bet you can get in if you just give him a call. They've been having trouble getting kids to apply. Because of the money thing. Just tell him I sent you."

"What's his name?"

"Carl Paik."

I wrote the name down.

"So?" Crystal said. "What do you think? Are you going to give him a call?"

I thought for a minute.

"It does pay *something*, right?"

"Bagel money, yeah."

"Yeah," I said. "Yeah, I want to do it. I mean, this is just what I need right now."

It was already getting dark when my mother loaded me into the Benedict and drove me to Campus Akawe. I passed Akawe Youth Theatre on my way through the parking lot. By now, *Candide* would be in its tech week. *Whatever,* I thought. *I've got places to be too.* A giant mural depicting the solar system covered a wall of the planetarium lobby. It was new since the last time I had been here. There were also large plastic bags taped around each of the drinking fountains. I found Crystal sitting in an uncomfortable-looking chair with a textbook balanced precariously on her lap. Once again, her hair was braided.

"John," she said without looking up. "What up?"

"Nothing," I said.

"Yeah?" she asked. Now she stopped reading and took a look at me. "Really?"

It took me off guard. I forgot that this was a talent of hers. Asking rote polite questions and then excavating the ground beneath rote polite answers. How should I answer? *Everything* was up.

"Um," I said. "I wouldn't even know where to begin."

"Tell me about it."

"I kind of don't want to. And I've got, you know, homework."

"Fair enough."

I took the seat next to her, but a moment later, Carl Paik came out. A forty-something Asian man, not heavy, not slim, with a pleasant face and a shocking lime green sweater. A few stray threads of black and gray hair clung to his glossy scalp.

"Miss Galitz?" he said.

She nodded.

"You brought a friend."

"Hi," I said.

"You'll have to fill out the paperwork before you start," he said and led us back to his office, a humorless cinder-block cube with a tiny computer on a tiny desk.

Carl had just been appointed Planetarium Director during the last summer. As he interviewed Crystal, I hurried through the stapled-together application. My own name and contact information, school and grade. There was a parental consent form.

"You can bring that back next week," Carl said, interrupting Crystal in the middle of an answer.

By the time I had finished the forms, he was ready for me.

"And you are a student at Eastern High School?" he said.

"Yes, I'm a freshmen there and –"

"Yes, and you are doing what extracurriculars?"

"Well, I tried out for some plays, but I didn't get in, and I was going to do the Chess Club, but they canceled it –"

"Yes, and what is your GPA?"

"I'm not sure. It's three-point-something, but I'm planning to –"

"Yes, and you can get me your transcripts from your middle schools?"

"Yes, I went to Radcliffe Junior –"

"Yes, and what did you do there?"

And so on.

At some point, Carl started talking about the planetarium, and he'd been going on for several minutes before I realized that the introductory part of the interview had finished. Suarez was one of the most expensive facilities in Campus Akawe, yet from Carl's perspective, the programming was the least satisfactory. For several years their educational mission had been a box to check off through the occasional "starry sky" program and their Christmas Special focusing on astronomical explanations for the Star of Bethlehem.

"Our program says it was probably a supernova from the Andromeda galaxy. Personally, I think that's way off base."

"What do you think it was?" asked Crystal.

"Double occultation."

We stared at him.

"Jupiter rises in the east just before the sun rises. The moon crosses it. 6 BC, about the same time of year that Christ was supposedly born, and we already know that he was born several years before o BC. The moon would have moved in front of Jupiter, blocking its light. Then the sun and earth would have eclipsed the moon. The word occultation means hiding something away. In Greek culture at the time, this might signify the birth of a great king. But to be honest, I don't care all that much about the Star of Bethlehem. The Christmas show is good because it brings money in for Suarez, but it isn't real astronomy."

"What is *real* astronomy?"

Carl nodded in response, warming to the question. "Quasars. Pulsars. Black holes. Nebula. Cosmology. The cosmic radiation background. This is the astronomy I learned about in college. Right now, scientists are poised at the edge of some extraordinary discoveries. They are going to learn some fundamental truths about the expansion and curvature of the universe."

You dumbass, I scolded myself. *Why didn't you tell him about Miss Pavilik's class!*

"Mr. Paik," I started. "I forgot ... I'm taking a class. Um ... it's usually for upperclassmen, but –"

"If it's on your application, I'll see it soon enough," Carl said. "I was telling you both about our mission. I hope that we can orient the planetarium more toward serious subjects and research in the months and years ahead."

"Are you still doing the laser shows?" I asked.

Carl seemed puzzled by this question. "All of our shows are laser shows."

"No, I mean like Laserpalooza."

"Ah. No. Well, for a while, they brought in large crowds, but that hasn't happened in years. I want to retire them for good. Even when these shows were making money, they weren't worth the trouble. People showed up on drugs, fought in the parking lot, tore up the cushions. A couple of years ago, a kid actually knocked off a piece of the projector."

I didn't mention that I had been in the audience that night.

Carl went on, "Anyway, I want you to both start out working the gift shop. We'll try you out here for a month or two, and depending on how it goes, you can narrate a show. Eventually, I'd like to have you both working the projector ... at least in an apprentice capacity. And of course, we'll see about coordinating with your schools for college credit."

"Awesome!" breathed Crystal.

"But for now," said Carl, "it's gift shop, gift shop, gift shop."

Carl took us back out into the lobby and showed us how to keep inventory and manage the cash register. How to keep the hallways neat and clean. Making sure that all of the items were fully stocked: the star charts and kaleidoscopes, the wire and inflatable solar systems, the Apollo and Space Shuttle models, Geminis and Mercurys. The sleek silver space pens and foil-wrapped packages of astronaut ice cream. Big thick Carl Sagan books with starry black dustcovers.

"But I want to show you why we are doing all this," said Carl, leading the way back into the blacklit gallery surrounding the projection dome.

"Only about a third of our revenue comes from ticket sales. That's why the gift shop is so important. We make a lot of money there. But it's the grants that keep us going. If we expand our programming, we can get better grants. You see what I'm saying?"

Crystal nodded.

We followed him into the familiar, mauve-toned hemispheric room

Connor Coyne

with the crazy machine in the middle. Carl turned to face us, his back to the projector.

"When I took this position, I came up with a music show of my own ... the first in a new line of programming. Astronomy by the Blue Öyster Cult. Orion by Metallica. Planet Caravan by Black Sabbath. Mostly rock music. I'm not opposed to using rap, but there happen to be a lot more songs by rock artists dealing with outer-space –"

"You try the Digable Planets?" asked Crystal. "Afrika Bambaataa? Redman? Um, Dr. Octogon?"

"Have a seat."

We sat.

Carl vanished into a projection booth tucked back against the curve of the wall.

The lights abruptly shut off. There was still a faint glow around the edges of the dome. Red exit signs marked the doors. *May would think that these were ordinary*, I thought. Then, vast banks of stars appeared across the hemisphere overhead.

I took Crystal's hand because it seemed like the thing to do.

"Feeling friendly?" she asked.

"I have a girlfriend," I said, indignant.

"Quiet, please," said Carl, his voice muffled by the booth.

Somber guitars strummed up some trembling reassurance, along with a quavering voice and what sounded like bongo drums. The stars above started turning, and I felt dizzy at once, like *I* was spinning.

Carl spoke. "I start the program with 'Planet Caravan' by Black Sabbath. The distortion of the voice comes from Ozzy Osbourne's voice processed through a Leslie speaker."

"Yeah," I hissed over to Crystal. "I'm sure he knows as much about Ice-T and Ice Cube as he does Sabbath."

A pause.

"One of the interesting features of the Suarez Planetarium is its perfect acoustics," said Carl from above. "Even if someone whispers to the person sitting next to him, I can hear everything they say."

Crystal giggled.

Carl went on: "This is a very meditative song, and I chose it to ease the audience into a sense that they are moving through space. It's still a sensation I get, even though I've sat in your place a hundred times. I'm sure you're feeling it now. You aren't moving – the stars are – but you feel like the planetarium is spinning. Your brain knows this, but your senses insist that you are turning in circles. This is a good way to convey to the audience that nothing in this universe is still. That everything is moving, always. There is no such thing as stasis."

The song stopped in the middle of a noodling guitar solo.

"When the song is over," said Carl, "I stop and talk a bit about a few of the constellations. There are many to choose from. You have to do Ursa Major and Minor. Polaris, the North Star. Then, I always go with some of the Greek legends, so I start with Perseus." From the booth, Carl shot a red laser pointer at a cluster of stars almost directly overhead, making an inverted "v." "Can you see the warrior?" he asked. *Not really.* "He beheaded Medusa and rescued Andromeda from where she was chained up by the sea." The laser pointer swept Andromeda. "In the night sky, Andromeda is a galaxy," said Carl. "In four billion years, it will collide with our Milky Way. By then, humans will be long gone or evolved into something utterly alien, and the earth will have been baked to death, though not yet consumed by our sun. But events like the collision of these two galaxies are the sort of things that generate complex stars, rich in elements – heavy metals – that allow the creation of a rich environment like that of Earth and, ultimately, life."

"And speaking of heavy metals ..." Carl went on with no subtlety at all.

The music clicked on again. We heard the soft ascension of a chainsaw distortion, while a steady drumbeat kept pace.

"Orion. Metallica. Naturally, I play this while we zoom in on the constellation of Orion."

The red pointer bobbled in expanding circles around the shape of the hunter.

"I wish the projector could zoom in, but it isn't designed to," apologized Carl. "I have to go through the mythology. It is what the kids relate to." A chopping guitar cut in. It sounded as annoyed as Carl was by the need to placate "the kids."

"There are a lot of stories about Orion," Carl said. "They all agree that he was a great hunter and that he got killed because of the goddess Artemis. But they give different reasons for his death, and I haven't decided what story I will tell the school groups." He sighed. "But the real story of this constellation lies with its nebulae, a place where we can observe the creation of stars. The most famous is the Horsehead Nebula."

The music stopped again, too abrupt.

"For the end of the program, I play Astronomy by the Blue Öyster Cult."

He put the song on. A piano echoed out through tentative percussion.

207

A shivering rhomboid shape, drawn with tracers of purple and red light, spiraled overhead.

"This is the best representation of a pulsar I have at the moment. I still haven't figured out the transition because it's awkward, but the idea is that we start talking about pulsars, quasars, black holes, supernovae. And the last will be where I leave off, talking about standard candles."

"We've talked about a lot of this stuff in my eleventh grade Astronomy," I said.

"What's a standard candle?" asked Crystal.

"A standard candle is a kind of supernova that is chemically the same wherever in the universe it occurs. Very soon, they are going to tell us something important about the expansion of the universe."

The song stopped.

"And that's the end of the show," Carl said.

The lights faded up.

"Do we get to see any of the shows?" Crystal asked.

"You get to see all of the shows," came Carl's voice, softer now as he stepped down from the booth. "Last ones in. First ones out. I hope you'll each write an essay about it. We can use them in our grant applications."

"How much do we get paid?" I asked. It was an important question. My father would want to know the answer, too.

"Michigan's minimum wage is \$3.35," Carl said.

"That's not much," I said. If I was working here ten hours a week, that meant ten dollars a week less than what I'd get at Taco Bell.

"That's what the college credit is for."

Although Carl never actually said I'd gotten the job, he asked me to return the parental consent form when I showed up to work the next week. I had every reason to feel excited about this. After the end of the Renaissance Festival and missing out on every extracurricular activity I tried, a job at the planetarium was a lot cooler than anything else I could have hoped for. I wanted to be excited about it. But the weight of that year had fallen upon me, and now my new job at Suarez was just another chore. I'd do it, but only because I didn't have anything better to do.

At dinner – Mexican casserole – my mother wanted to talk to my father about getting a new job.

"I'm working on it," he said. "I've got a few calls out to guys from the plant. Something temp, maybe. Longer-term, maybe I want to see about taking some courses. Get involved with something with computers. Really, should be able to do that; we used computers a lot making the dies."

"You mean with the internet?"

"No, I mean with programming. Languages. Hardware."

"Have you tried the classifieds?"

"Dammit, Theresa, it hasn't even been a week. I'm working on it, okay?"

My mother dished herself up another wedge of casserole. It wasn't really that Mexican. It was a mush of ground beef, baked beans, and hot sauce, topped with cheese and Jiffy corn bread. But it was an excuse for her to look at something other than my father.

"I understand," she said. "They didn't give you a lot of time. You've only got about a month until it's all over."

"Actually, they moved it up," my father said. "They're closing us out on the day before Thanksgiving, and going half time until then," my father murmured. "Same thing with the last of the Old Benedict. That was the deal they worked out with XAWU. XAWU wanted them to keep it open until Christmas. X wanted to close before Thanksgiving. Now they'll close before Thanksgiving but pay us through the beginning of December. We're worth more to them gone than there. What kind of a shit deal is that?"

My mother didn't look at him.

"I don't want to settle for shit," my father went on. "I'm going to want to take a bit of time to get something decent. If one of my buddies, Mars maybe, can get me in with a parts supplier, then that'll buy me time. But I'll be getting part-time pay through the contract, and I think I need to spend that time finding something good. Better than what I've found in the classifieds. Truck driver jobs. Truck driver jobs going away from here."

"We're underwater," my mother said, her frustration apparent in the minute quaver of voice. She *hated* to lose control of her voice. "We don't have time. I mean, you've had years ..."

"I've had a lot to do," my father answered, louder. "Working. Taking care of this crappy house falling apart. Helping John with his stuff because you're gone all day every day."

"Because I needed a job, too. Because you said the public radio wasn't bringing us in enough."

"Well, if I find out about a nice secretarial job at the XAI, I'll be applying for that, too, okay? You happy?"

To signal that he didn't want to talk anymore, my father took a tremendous gulp from his bottle of water, glaring at my mother, his cheeks bulging like a chipmunk's.

I lost the weekend in the drumbeat of things I had lost and things I was afraid I was losing. *Omara. Chicago. Selby. Adam. My grades. Elizabeth. My father's job. May. Lucy. Selby. Eden. Omara. Chicago. Omara.* I synced with the sinus pulse of my diminishing cold. *Selby. Firebugs. Serialkiller. Leadwater.* I must have done my homework in there somewhere, but I can't remember if I did, and I don't remember what it was about. *Elizabeth. Eden. Adam. Lucy. Omara.*

When Monday finally arrived, I didn't feel like talking to anyone. I nodded to Chris and Shannon as they passed me in the hall. I managed a smile for Omara. I didn't really want to see May because I didn't know what I would say if I did.

I skipped my locker and went straight to Mr. Esper's class. From there, on to Biology without anything much happening. I heard my name called out just as I was almost to Mrs. Dimitri's class. It was Lucy, with Eli standing at her side, his reluctant smile and his radiant teeth parting his soft pink lips.

"What?" I asked in my most annoyed voice. "Don't you live in the Os? I thought you went to Northern," I said to Eli.

He rubbed his eyes and smiled shyly.

"I go to every school," he said. "Northern is where my blood lives. Southern's where they wear the dopest sneaks. Western runs on soul power. And my girl goes to Eastern. I love every school, and I know all the halls and cracks and crannies."

But Lucy was interested in a different conversation. "May said you called her up and asked her out!" Her voice was high with laughter and delight.

"Yeah?" I said. I don't know why I said it like a question.

"Oh my God, you did ask her out! Oh my God, John, I never would've seen it coming. I mean, I think you two will make a great couple, but I never thought you'd ask her out. I mean ... I honestly thought you wouldn't think she was your type. I didn't think you would think she was on your level at all. But you surprised me."

"What do you mean ... on my level?"

"Well ..." and here Lucy dropped her voice. "Some people say she's kind of stupid."

"And just a couple weeks ago, you were going out with that other girl," said Eli. He didn't care that I wasn't looking at him. It made it easier for him to look through me. I felt like he was x-raying my thoughts. "What, um, happened there?"

"Nothing," I said. "It just wasn't working."

"That's cold, man," he said.

"Oh, shut up, Eli," said Lucy. "John's not cold. John's, like, a little too warm."

The fuck's that supposed to mean?

"You ever meet May's brother?" Eli went on.

"I don't think so."

And then I remember that May's brother was Drake. Who had gone off the hospital roof. I had never met him. It was strange that I had this connection to him now, and that I hadn't thought of it myself.

"Well, I guess you will now," said Eli. "He's intense, man."

By the time I was in Geometry, I knew I had to make up my mind about something I'd been putting off for days. Where would I sit at lunch? I'd been sitting with my new friends since the start of the school year, but that's where Omara was, and it would seem weird to pass up sitting with my new girlfriend in favor of the girl who had just dumped me. But did I really want to sit with Lucy and Selby and Eli? At the *Chalk* table? I couldn't see that either. Plus, talking to May one-on-one was weird enough, and I couldn't imagine how much weirder it would be with the others thrown into the mix.

I could put it off for at least one more day. I shoved my lunch down my throat between two shelves at the back of the library.

I had to stop at my locker before Miss Pavilik's class. I found a note addressed "john."

It read:

I coudnit mak you cookie be no butter! but I bout you a cookie this mornig. I cant wate to see you at lunch. Dont get bit by scary dogs haha! Woof woof!
LYLAB!
May

I shoved the note in my pocket and practically sprinted to astronomy. When the bell rang again, I hurried down the halls, escaped into the parking lot, and hopped onto the bus. I felt safe as it pulled out of the parking lot. I certainly wasn't going to run into May in any class for gifted kids.

The bus got off to a late start, and the bell was already ringing as I hurried through the frowning doors at Northern. My head was starting to throb and the ache seemed to keep time with the sound of the bell. As I hurried toward the elevator, I passed Bill at his locker.

"You never called me, John!" he said. I heard the annoyance in his voice.

"I'm sorry," I said. "I've just been real busy, you know?"

"Oh, yeah, I'm sure you're real busy. With all your *real* friends."

His lazy eye looked a little bloodshot as he glared at me. I glared right back at him.

"It's not like that, actually. As a matter of fact, I've got a lot of my own shit to deal with right now!"

Immediately, he relaxed.

"I'm sorry, John," he said. "I didn't mean to jump on you. Hey, I've got some bad shit too. We've got to hang out. You never know. Maybe I can help."

The throbbing in my head intensified.

"That's a good idea!" I said. "We should do that. I'm late to my class, though ..."

I'd reached the elevator and banged on the button to take me up to the third floor.

"I'm not boring, you know!" Bill called after me as the doors slid shut.

After the elevator got stuck between floors, I was almost ten minutes late to Ms. Ropoli's class. As I walked in, I heard the voice of a man singing in Spanish, in a way that reminded me of the crooners my Grandmother Richter idolized. Ms. Ropoli was leaning over one of the students, gesturing as she described some article or story for him. A sliver of sun shone through the window, and I noticed the red highlights in her hair.

Darius was sitting at the teacher's desk, sorting a stack of papers into two piles, and he seemed to notice Ms. Ropoli, too.

"John," she said, without looking up. "Go ahead and find a desk. You're a whole week behind on your civics homework, so you'd better spend the hour getting caught up on that."

I set my backpack on the floor and dropped into the nearest seat. My head tapped out its pain. I wondered whether my temple was visibly throbbing.

The student Ms. Ropoli was helping started talking now. His name was Tony. I don't remember his last name. He was working on a project that had to do with X Auto's departure from Akawe. He had a stack of three huge books on his desk and a fat stack of photocopies Ms. Ropoli had made for him.

"These are good points," Ms. Ropoli was saying. "Smart points. But I want you to look again at the two books, the highlighted chapters. What is Halberstam saying about the autoworkers of today and their attitudes? How is Hamper demonstrating it through his own experience?"

"But Halberstam's talking about the older workers ..."

"No, here. In Chapter 29. Look, I'll paraphrase a bit for you, but I still want you to reread, okay? Two generations ago, the Sit Down strikers, the guys who incorporated the UAW in Flint and Detroit, the guys who put together XAWU here – and look to that tricky difference, syndicalism and corporatism – they had to fight for everything they had. One generation ago ... you know, they grew up during the Great Depression and then fought in World War II. So ... thrifty, work-oriented, but kind of cautious and conservative. The newer generation, their kids, the Baby Boomers. When they started working for the Big Three and X, they'd been through Vietnam, and they'd been through Watergate. Then Nixon stepped down. So, they didn't trust anybody. I mean, they didn't trust XAuto, and they really didn't even trust their union."

I didn't move. I couldn't sit down. I stood and listened. My head hurt, and the light that filled the room seemed to take on a reddish hue.

"Okay?" said Tony.

"So, look," Ms. Ropoli went on. "They also come into these jobs, and it's basically been pay increases and boats and cottages since, like, 1945. That's 30, 35 straight years of money and moolah. *They* go into these jobs expecting it's going to be the same for them, and they maybe don't care as much about, say, union solidarity or social justice as the guys that founded the UAW and XAWU. As their parents and grandparents did."

"Okay?"

"So Halberstam is wondering, or, I should say, he's presenting a story in this chapter that maybe their kind of cynical outlook had something to do with the way the unions fell apart. And without the unions on the job, he's wondering, right here, through the quotes of this guy Fraser, whether that had something to do with the American automakers losing some of their ground and the Japanese filling up that empty space."

"Okay?"

"Like listen to this quote: 'They're paying double-time and we've only got a fifty percent turnout.' And Fraser says: 'Get me a pair of gloves, and I'll get out there myself.'"

"But what does that mean?"

Ms. Ropoli sighed. "He means that Chrysler was paying double for overtime or something, but the workers weren't even bothering to show up for it. They were so cynical, so happy with the money they already had, they turned down the chance to come in extra and make twice as much money per hour!'"

"Whoa."

My father never turned down holiday pay. He had missed two or three Christmases because of it. He never turned down weekend or overtime, either. "Feast or famine," he sometimes said. "Got to eat when you can."

Ms. Ropoli went on: "So, what do you think Halberstam is suggesting about how that might have contributed to the fall of the unions and the automakers? What do you think Hamper suggests about his own experience, his own sort of not giving a crap about things?"

For a moment, I felt like someone had put a knife through my head. I winced.

"I don't buy it," I said.

Ms. Ropoli looked up at me, surprised.

"They cut hours so much," I said, "I don't buy that that many people aren't going to show up for work when they can make money like that."

"But they did," said Ms. Ropoli. "It's right here. Halberstam is very thorough with his sources."

"Yeah, I don't care," I said. "I mean, maybe they did that at Chrysler or Ford or something, but not here. Not with X. I ... I don't think this is going to help Tony with his paper, because people here work whenever they can. They need the money."

Ms. Ropoli stood and put her hands on her hips. I could tell from her expression that she was weighing me out, trying to decide whether to build the conversation or shut it down. For some reason, her calculations annoyed me this time. Maybe it was her obliviousness to the hammering pain in my head. Or maybe it was her obliviousness to something else ...

"XAWU has," she said, "if anything, a worse track record than the UAW on building a culture of solidarity. The UAW has to reign in three different manufacturers. XAWU just has one. And, XAWU has always had a less ... contentious ... I mean, a less argumentative relationship with XAuto. If anything, XAWU workers expected more and put in less."

"No," I said. "It isn't like that. They're tricky. X is. They lie a lot. They'll say they aren't going to retaliate or whatever by closing down whatever plant, but then they just close down another one instead. I mean, how do you even talk with someone who has complete control like that? What do you expect them to do?"

"I'm not talking about what's happening now, John. This is all about what happened about fifteen years ago –"

"It's the same stuff! It hasn't changed! It's the same. And I know what 'contentious' means!"

Ms. Ropoli put on her teacher voice: "I think you better calm down a little."

"I think you better shut up!" I said. "You come in here from Italy. You drive a fucking import. Then you teach in schools that XAWU paid for, and you tell the kids you teach that their parents are lazy and that's why the city is falling apart? Jesus Christ, can't you hear yourself?!"

"Okay, that's enough." Real anger. "Calm down now. If I recall, from your last civics assignment, you aren't even quite clear who appoints Supreme Court justices, so you aren't going to lecture me on a subject I've been reading about for years –"

"No!" I said. "I haven't been reading it about for years. I've been living it my whole goddamn life!" I took a deep breath. "Go outside," I said, "and get in your import, and drive it into the river."

I turned my back and walked out of the room. I looked left and right. The halls were empty.

"Fight the power!" came the voice of some Black boy out of an adjacent classroom.

I pumped my fist in the air as I hurried toward the stairs.

"John!" called Ms. Ropoli from behind me, so I broke into a run. Rounded the corner. Down the stairs, then down the hall, around a bright bend, and into a bathroom. I went into a stall, closed the door, and took a seat on the toilet. I felt like an idiot. I felt like a helpless asshole. I sat there and cried, as quietly as I could. For a minute, my crying eased the aching in my head.

The next day wasn't any less awkward.

I couldn't keep slinking off to the library without looking chicken shit, so I took a deep breath and sat down at the Chalk table with Selby, May, Lucy, Eli, and the other mildew-smelling motherfuckers that lived there.

I ate my food quickly and nodded a lot like I was more interested in listening than speaking. When I did speak, I tried to only talk to Selby and Lucy. I didn't speak to Eli because his sensitive eyes unnerved me. He always wore an expression like someone had hurt his feelings, and I didn't buy it. I didn't speak to May because I couldn't think of anything worth saying to her.

"I'm collecting Bath and Body Works coupons," she said, "because I want my conditioner to match my shampoo and lotion, and if I get enough of them, everything will be free."

"I don't think it works like that, May," said Lucy. "You can't stack them."

May stared at her.

"What does that mean?"

"I mean, you can't use more than one coupon on one thing."

"But I'm going to get lots of things!"

"I'm sorry," I said, standing up. "I got to check out a book from the library."

Then, when I arrived at Ms. Ropoli's class, I slunk over toward my desk, sat down, and started working on my civics homework without even looking at her. A few minutes before the bell rang, she came over to my desk and murmured, "Stay after class for a few minutes, John. I need to talk to you."

So, I stayed after the rest of the students had left.

"I don't want to talk about it," I told her.

"I think we need to," she said.

"No, we don't," I said. "I won't interrupt you again. Okay? I'll do my homework, you do whatever, it isn't a problem."

"I want to understand why you were so upset yesterday."

"But you probably *don't* want to talk about why you were dancing with your student aide at an illegal party in an old warehouse, right? So, let's not talk about that, either. I mean, let's not talk about either of those things."

It was the second time I'd seen her surprised in two days, and Ms. Ropoli had always seemed unsurprisable. Even when a gorilla-masked Crystal had hit her in the face with a water balloon, my social studies teacher seemed to have expected it.

"I see," she finally said. "Well, if you refuse to talk about our disagreement, I'm not going to force you. Although understand, John, I think it sounds like what you are trying to do is blackmail me, and I'm not going to be blackmailed by my students. Or anyone else, for that matter. All you had to do was tell me to leave it alone."

"I did tell you that. You were the one who wouldn't listen."

"I think, maybe, given the lack of trust between the two of us now, that this independent study isn't going to work out. Why don't you stop by the office tomorrow and pick up the papers to transfer back into Mr. Barakat's class."

"Fine."

"Come to think of it; I'll stop and do that on my way out today. There is no need for you to come in here tomorrow."

"Sure."

"You'd better hurry up if you're going to catch the bus. I'm certainly not giving you a ride home."

On Wednesday, at lunch, I sat at the Chalk table again, and I nodded and I grinned like a cartoon idiot. May climbed onto my lap and I put my hands, palm down, on the table because I felt strange about Selby and Lucy and Eli watching me wrap my arms around her waist.

Then, a few minutes before the bell rang, I went over to the other table, where Omara sat with Chris, Nova, and Ken.

"Hi, guys," I said. "I'm, um, I'm sitting with them for now because, um." I could tell from their faces that they had no idea what I was rambling on about. "I'm going out with May Dunham now, so she wants me to sit with her. Of course."

Omara was studying something on her green-painted fingernails. Ken was stifling a smile so shit-stuffed I would have happily taken a week of detention just to punch his fucking face in. Chris laughed nervously. I was surprised that it was Nova who came to my rescue.

"No prob, dog," he said. "It's just lunch. We'll catch up soon. Maybe this weekend."

I nodded.

"See you 'round," I said.

As I turned away, I saw Omara's head snap up. "Oh my God," she mouthed silently. I walked away and heard Ken burst into seams of laughter.

Everything was fucked, and maybe the real game was determining, somehow, when it had all gotten fucked. Was it when I had called May on the phone with a drunken head cold and asked her out? Or was it when Selby had told me about God's son molesting her? Maybe it was when I saw Elizabeth slinging at the rave or Adam high on whatever Elizabeth was slinging? Or maybe it was when Omara dumped both me and our dreams of Chicago together? Maybe it was before that. Maybe it was earlier. Maybe it was before I was born, when my father decided to stay in this godforsaken town and take a doomed job at X Automotives.

Maybe it even happened even earlier.

Maybe it happened on the day they lay the first brick in the foundation of the Hell House on Eden Street.

One day, a week later, I think, I found two notes in my locker.

The first note was from May:

> hi Jon
> wuld you like to com over to my hous for thanks givig
> your girlfrend
> May

"What?" I said aloud, "Can't you even spell my name now?"

I opened the second note:

> Hey John,
> I hear I saw you at the RAVE. I don't even remember. OR DO I?
> Anyway you'll always be a brother to me. My cuz got some extra stink
> bombs. This is for you!
> Adam.

A small capsule of yellow-green liquid had been taped to Adam's note. I ripped the glass off and held it up for a closer look. It was just a capsule full of liquid. *This is stupid,* I thought. *I don't have anything to do with this.* I put the capsule in my pocket. I caught myself smiling. *It would be funny if I did something with this, though.* I held the glass in my palm. *Who deserves something shitty and unexpected to happen to them on a Monday morning?*

I waited until the bell rang, then slipped in through the backstage door to the auditorium. Mr. Agape was teaching his Drama 1 class, pacing the front row and yelling out some story about a fire in the Globe theater. It was easy to slide unnoticed behind the back bank of curtains, up against the cinder block wall, set the glass capsule down on the floor, and step on it with my shoe. I heard the glass crunch, and I edged off to the side as the eggy smell slowly soaked through the room.

Mr. Agape stopped talking.

"What's that smell?" he barked. "Did someone do something?"

The pungent stink spread and the students muttered to each other. Mr. Agape leapt onto the stage, ran to the back, and flung the curtains open where they parted at the middle. I was far off to the side, but there was no way for me to make it to the door without being seen. I froze where I stood.

"This isn't funny!" shouted Mr. Agape. He'd found the shattered capsule, but of course, his students didn't know about it. "This isn't funny! This could ruin these curtains. Hundreds and hundreds of dollars! You, help me with these."

I heard him running off to the fly loft with someone right behind him. A moment later, the curtains floated off into space, leaving me exposed to a pissed-off Mr. Agape and about thirty confused kids. There was no place for me to run, so I put on my sunglasses and glared right back at them.

Five minutes later, I was down in the main office. Mr. Agape was arguing with Mrs. Stadler, the assistant principal, while the school secretary called my father at home.

"For vandalism, five days suspension and the cost of damages," said Mrs. Stadler. "That's the policy."

"Yes, but I don't know that there are any costs or damages," snapped Mr. Agape. "He was trying to pull a harmless prank, not burn the school down."

"Pranks are not harmless."

"What do you even mean when you say that? Most pranks are harmless! Look, he deserves to be punished. He's mad that he didn't get into my play this semester. Lots of kids are. Can't you make it something less?"

"Fine," said the assistant principal. "Three days suspension and the cost of damages."

"Put the cost of damages down as zero," yelled Mr. Agape.

"Yes, Mr. Bridge?" the secretary said into the phone. "This is Miranda Roth calling from Eastern High School. We have your son here at the office facing disciplinary action."

"That curtain better not stink!" Mr. Agape snapped at me.

"Five days suspension," said the secretary.

"Tell him it's three days," said the assistant principal.

"Three days suspension. No, not at the school. He'll have to go home. The buses won't be here again for three hours. Will you be coming to pick him up?"

For a moment, it was quiet in the office as my father replied to Miss Roth. She looked a little surprised.

"John," she said, covering the receiver. "He has asked you to sign out for the day and walk home. He says you don't live too far from here."

A mile? Two miles?

"No," I said. "Not too far."

Outside, the snow whistled off of leaf-laden trees caught unprepared by this early winter. I tucked my head into my coat and pulled my hat over my eyes to keep the wind out. Valley Street dumped me onto Winters Road, where the cleared spaces funneled the wind. I passed under the 63 overpass, where I had once taken a pair of blue sunglasses on a day as hot as this day was cold. I kept walking. I finally made it back to Agit Street.

The whole time, I kept thinking about my father's response. He got pissed off lots, but he *always* came and picked me up. Even on the night when I'd been nightwalking with Adam and Michael, and that was a *lot* worse than stinkbombing Mr. Akawe's class. *He must be angrier than I thought.*

When I got home, I half expected to find my father standing on the porch, hands on his hips, waiting for me to get inside so he could start reaming me out, but the porch was empty.

I unlocked the front door, opened it, and went inside. My father wasn't in the living room. I heard the cuckoo clock coming ticking in the dining room.

"Father?" I called out.

"Dammit, John!" I heard his muffled shout from the direction of the study, but his heart wasn't in it. I went down the hall and found the door shut. I knocked.

"You in there?"

"Yes, I'm in here! You ... dropping stink bombs in school?! I'm not proud of that. You're in trouble now! Go up to your room! You're grounded! I'll ... we'll decide how to punish you soon; that's what you'd better believe!"

He sounded like he was reading from a poorly written script. Some stupid dialogue from a Friday night sitcom.

I reached out and turned the knob.

"Don't come in here!" he shouted. "Go up to your room!"

I hesitated a moment and went in.

I saw him slumped in the reclining chair, a coffee mug at his side, and a newspaper open in his lap. He was holding a red Sharpie, and his nose and face were flushed.

"Father?" I asked.

"What is it?" he said, sucking out and floating over the vowels in a horrible way. "I'm just looking for some job like your mother wants."

"You're drunk," I said, realizing it as I spoke the words. "Holy shit."

He looked at me.

"How much have you had?" I asked.

"Nothing. Not much. Just a little since ... it's a relaxing morning, John!"

"Yeah, I guess so," I said.

I could smell it in the air. Acrid ... fermented ... I scanned the bookshelves, looking for a bottle. My father's eyes darted to the side. I followed them to the coffee mug. He glared back at me, defiant.

"That's why you told them to make me walk home," I said. "You didn't come and pick me up because you couldn't drive. Shit, I'll bet you couldn't even get out the driveway. Jesus fucking —"

"Watch your mouth!"

"No," I said. "No. Not anymore. I'll say what I want. I'll say what I see."

I kept waiting for the explosion, and it kept not coming. It pissed me off that he wasn't getting pissed off at me. Here I was talking to him like a disrespectful little shit, and he didn't explode. That told me that he knew that he was a bigger shit than I was.

"I said," he said, his voice husky, "to go up to your room, and I want you to go there ... now."

"So you can decide how you're gonna punish me. So you can decide when you tell Mother about what I did. But you're not going to tell her what I did. Or am I going to tell her what you did?"

"Ha!" my father wheezed. "You think I keep secrets from her? No! I don't keep secrets from her. She keeps secrets from me! Everybody keeps secrets from me! I'm the one that everyone keeps secrets from!"

Now, his slurring voice shook, and his red eyes started to water, and suddenly I couldn't get out of that little room fast enough. I was stumbling back. I was closing the door behind me.

"John!" he called after me, his voice ragged. "You're grounded! Go to your room!"

That gave me the resolve to stay there a moment later.

"No," I said. "I'm not going to my room. I'm going to Adam's house to spend the night. You can't stop me. So, don't try."

I saw him biting his lip. It was the last thing I saw before I shut the door on him. I hurried upstairs and shoved my deodorant and toothbrush, and a change of clothes in my backpack. I didn't want to give him a chance to come out and talk to me again. I didn't want to hear him or see him. I packed everything I needed in a minute. On the way out, I slammed the door so that he would know I was leaving.

I was so mad, and I had never walked so fast.

As fast as my feet moved, my thoughts moved faster. They weren't focused, though. I couldn't hold them. They scattered like startled birds.

I felt my backpack on my back, my shoes getting soggy beneath me, my toothbrush and deodorant poking me through my back pockets. I thought I had forgotten my shades, though. I stopped walking and groped around for them for a minute before I realized that I had never taken them off. I had been wearing them on the whole walk home, during the scene with my father, and I was still wearing them now.

I started walking again.

Why Adam? I wondered. At least part of the answer was easy: his place was the closest. I'd be standing on his front porch in ten minutes. Plus, I knew his grandparents were home, so I wouldn't have to wait around in the cold. It still didn't make a lot of sense. I didn't really talk to Adam anymore. Other things had to have been moving across my brain when I had said, "I'm going to Adam's house to spend the night." *It's because I was already thinking about him*, I thought. *I was thinking about him because he was the one who left me the stink bomb.* Maybe ... but that didn't feel right either.

I passed Radcliffe, where the little seventh and eighth graders might look out through their grimy classroom windows and see me striding down the sidewalk. *Yeah*, I thought. *That's it. That's why.* I had spent a year and a half trying to follow my parents' plans and hopes. To plan for college. To plan for Chicago. With Omara. I had bought the beanstalk seeds my parents and teachers had been selling. I had kicked my best friend to the curb and went out and found "better" friends. I had gotten a smart and kind girlfriend who wasn't into endless drama. Who didn't run with gangbangers or plot with kidnapping victims. I got the grades. I did the clubs. I read about college and spent evenings at the dining room table with my homework. I planned a whole life that had nothing to do with Adam or Elizabeth or Selby or Chuck. *Chuck!* I thought. I hadn't thought about him in forever. *Elizabeth!* Was anything going to happen with that? Having seen her once, fleetingly, was she just going to vanish again forever?

Because I had, I thought, good parents with good jobs, a long view, willing to make sacrifices for me, and ready to show me what sacrifices I'd need to make today. My sacrifices – these old friendships – were less than what *they* were sacrificing for *me*. That offering had bought me, I had thought, a future. A real future. The things you see in the backgrounds of the romantic comedies your parents watch: a big house on a tree-lined street, white painted. Casual Cadillacs and Valentines. Good looks. A happy job. A growing family. I had eaten it all up, but this feast had been fragile. It had been false. How could my little ambitions compete with the fires, murders, poisoned water, and abandoned houses. The dark and cold and half-empty schools? My father had told me – he had actually said the words: "If you get the grades – if you *do* the *work* – we'll find a way to pay for you to go to school wherever you want."

It wasn't even close.

He wasn't going to pay for me to go to college.

Hell, they might even lose the house. That shitty, drafty, moss-draped house on an empty block. Then what?

He'd been pink-slipped less than two weeks ago, and he was already getting shitfaced. He'd probably started been getting secretly shitfaced for months. Or was it years? *How long ago was it when Adam said he found beer bottles in our basement?* There was Adam again. Adam, who *I* thought had a messed-up life and family. Adam who knew *my* family's messed up secrets better than I did. And what was the deal with my mother? Why wasn't *she* around more? I hadn't ever bothered to add up all the hours she was gone, but between her full-time work at XAI and her part-time volunteering at Michigan Radio, it usually meant long nights three or four times a week. Now, she never seemed to be back on time. Monday through Friday it was my father and I, alone, making dinner, doing the dishes, ignoring each other. Each of us doing our own thing. Me, my homework, and he his whatever.

My mother thought about herself and my father thought about himself.

Neither of them was thinking about me.

They went through the motions, of course: asked me about school and grounded me when I got into trouble. But there wasn't force behind it anymore. They just wanted to be alone with their own hopelessness. I was going to have to figure my life out on my own.

So maybe there wasn't anyone for me to go to other than my oldest and best friend.

I had arrived at Adam's vine-covered house.

I stood on the porch right where Ophelia had stood when Adam had pointed his gun at her from the other side. That had been the last time I had stood in this doorway.

I knocked.

Grandpa M shuffled over, just as I knew he would, and let me in without question or surprise.

"I thought I'd spend the night here tonight," I said.

"Adam's still at school," he said. "Get some food out the fridge. I'll be in the garage."

"Thanks."

I got myself a sandwich and some Faygo and sat down to watch MTV. Rock Block, Jams, and an hours-long wall of music videos. The light behind the window sheers was steady dim and gray. I got hungry again and made myself some instant mashed potatoes. Grandpa M came in and out a couple times. Grandma M came down the stairs, waved tiredly to me, and left to go shopping and pick up her prescriptions. I drank more pop. I went to the bathroom a few times. I saw the video for "Bullet with Butterfly Wings" a dozen times.

Eventually, Adam arrived. He stood in the archway with a can of Cheez Whiz in his hand. He didn't seem surprised to see me.

"John!" he said. "So, you bombed Mr. Agape's class with that stink bomb I gave you. Baby, I never dreamed you would use it like that. I am honored, man. Everybody knows about it. I guess half of his class thought he had farted. Like he had a rancid beef fart, and he was just trying to pass it off like it was someone else. Until you got caught, but then they said you just put on your shades and stared him down like a badass."

"I got suspended."

"Who cares?"

"My father wouldn't come and pick me up. He told me to walk home. When I got back, I figured out it was because he was totally shitfaced. Like he must have pounded a fifth of vodka the second I was out of the house, he was so wasted."

Adam sprayed a ribbon of fake cheese into his mouth. "At least he didn't drive out to get you and run over a bunch of people on the way. That's what my dad would've done."

"Yeah," I said.

"Come on to my room. I got this new CD I've been listening to, and it's amazing."

I turned off the TV, and we went down to Adam's basement bedroom that, despite its single naked light bulb, was still brighter than the living room had been.

Adam put on a CD and sat down on his futon. Draped a blanket across his feet. Handed me the jewel case.

"Tori Amos?" I asked.

An angry piano thundered out. A fluttering, full voice, defiant, singing about dirty sheets.

"Not what you usually listen to," I said.

"I think she's my new favorite," he said.

For some reason, the piano made me want to talk, so I turned the music down and told Adam everything I could remember. I started with my college plans. With the way I had hoped to do everything right, to get good grades, to go to Chicago.

"It's all broken," I said.

"No, it isn't," he said.

"Come on, *everything* is falling apart."

"No, it isn't. You were right when you decided to listen to your parents. I mean, yeah, it didn't mean you had to be a dick and ignore the rest of us ... but then again, why was I a dick who flipped out that night and started waving a gun around? I mean, who was the bigger dick? But you going to college? Yeah, that's gonna happen."

"How? They might lose the house!"

"You think Michael and your aunt are going to let you get put out by the street? Shit, they're rolling in money!"

"Then we might have to move away."

"So, you have to move away. I mean, yeah, that would suck ... but there are a lot of things that suck a lot worse."

I remembered then when Adam really *had* been evicted from Carla's apartment in the Os, and he had ended up camping out in the woods with a bunch of hippies, and one of them had molested him.

"Okay," I said. He was right. I couldn't argue with this.

I went on and told him about how Omara had broken up with me, how I'd gotten sick, and asked out May just so I could have *someone* to talk to.

"But I haven't talked to her much since then," I admitted.

Adam thought. "I like May," he said. "I don't know her too well. She isn't the sharpest light bulb in the pasta box."

I told him about the new lunch table, with Selby and May, Lucy and Eli. How Selby had been trying to learn about Eli's family, but somehow that led to Lucy hooking up with Eli.

"Wait, what?" he said.

I didn't know what Adam knew and what he didn't know, but I felt reckless that day. So, I told him about how Selby thought her father had been feuding with Quint Ostyn, and they were both dead the same week. I didn't mention that Quint had molested Selby, though. That part was too private to share.

"Holy fuck!" Adam said.

I told him everything else that Selby had told me about the abandoned junkyard beyond the viaduct. About how she had discovered dark Eden Street in the ruins east of Trevithick Road. About the abandoned Hell House in the middle of the demolished Benedict Main. About God Ostyn. About my sunglasses that I had found under the overpass, demanded by the man with the knife, who was evidently Chalky from the abandoned house in the Os, who made Selby steal them back from me.

About how I'd seen Eli wearing the same sunglasses at the rave.

I told him not to tell Selby what I'd told him.

"I had to tell you," I said. "You're my best friend. It's too much to carry alone, you know?"

The CD stopped.

"I really wanted you to pay attention to that," Adam said. He sighed. "Look," he said. "We got to figure out what's going on."

"I want to, you know? I'm worried about ... Selby and Lucy and –"

"You think?!"

"But we can't ask Selby about it. I kinda think she already thinks she told me more than she wanted to."

He shook his head.

"Oh no, we can't ask her about it. She'd kill both of us. We have to find out ourselves."

"How are we going to do that?"

"Well, if we ask just a couple questions of a bunch of people, and we get good answers, then we can put it all together and solve the mystery! But if we only ask each person a little bit, then they won't realize we're, you know, up in their shit."

"Who are you talking about asking?" I asked.

Adam thought.

"You told your dad you're spending the night here, right?" he asked.

I nodded.

He thought some more.

"We're not spending the night here," he finally said. "We'll stay in the Os."

"The Os? Why the Os?"

"Yeah. Think about it, John. All the weird stuff you're talking about ... George Demnescu's old boss was this guy God Ostyn. And his, what, kid, grandkid, nephew ... Eli? You said he's from the Os?"

"Yeah, but he says he goes to every high school. It's weird. I think he's making it up."

"Nah, he's probably telling the truth, because he's probably slingin'. And you said that that guy you met up there called Chalky and the house had Chalk tags."

"Yeah …"

"The Chalks were only ever in the Os. I mean until the Mafia fell apart, they were *only* in the Os. And then that's where you saw the graffiti about Cora the first time … at St. Francis. I'm just saying … a lot of the shit you're talking about happens in the Os. And it's weird over there. Lots of places where people can do secret shit and not get caught."

"I don't like it over there."

"Shit, *I* don't like it. You think the people who live there like it?"

"Where are we going to stay?"

"With a friend of mine." Adam shot me a big smile. "We'll stay with Juanita."

Shades on under dimming skies, the howling wind pushing against me, I started to feel like I was over Akawe. Not like I was tired of it. Not today. No, I felt like I owned this place. Like I'd been through enough *shit* by now that I knew the city's secrets, and I could make it do what I wanted. I followed Adam out to his garage where he got onto the smallish green bike with coaster brakes.

"You can borrow Ophelia's?" he offered.

I climbed onto the diamond-patterned purple-and-pink Huffy Cranbrook – the trim matched my sunglasses – and wheeled in circles while Adam got his bearings.

"Let's go," he said. "I want to get out there before it's dark out. Damn, it gets dark out fuckin' early."

And off we went.

Our route would take us clear across the city, from the South Side to the North, and I'd never been on a ride like this before. I didn't want to follow Whitmore past my house, so we took Debs all the way west past the river before turning onto Poplar Ave. I remember one vacant house where someone had painted "No Gas. Please Dont Burn!" in red paint upon the white porch. Then we were spinning through the Old River District past battered vacants and blemishless Victorians, pastel painted, their lawns crusted with silver-gray frost. We blasted through snow drifts. I wished I had gloves. My knuckles on the handlebars were as white as skulls.

"Fuck the snow," said Adam.

When we reached MLK, we cut west to Reuther Street, and the downtown skyline rode by on our right, the scattered high-rises looking brittle and broken. Sooner than I expected, we crossed the Zibi again, then 292, and Reuther became Suarez Blvd. A few minutes later, we were biking alongside the bulwark between Campus Akawe and the Os, beneath yellow and black billboards proclaiming: "Boiling Water Will Not Remove LEAD." Yellow bubbles floating up from a yellow pot. "El Agua Hirviendo No Elimina El PLOMO." "Apa Clocotită Nu Va Elimina PLUMBUL."

Then Adam gave a wave, and we swung our kiddie bikes across the five lanes of traffic – cars honked, *fuck 'em* – and into the Os. The neighborhood was packed with poisonous black walnuts, most of them presiding over death: abandoned homes with collapsed porches, occupied houses with collapsed porches, occupied houses stripped of their siding, the groaning wind, the lonely pavilion out in the park, and the sick chain-linked backyards where underfed dogs howled. A tree-drenched neighborhood. Electrical wires, alive or not, who even knew, had gotten tangled in the branches of the towering trees, the branches knotting together, their interlocked sinews a mazy canopy, a cathedral ceiling. And we passed all those O streets: Olthoff, Omira, Ormond ... we crossed Owen Road, and I saw that the shuttered shacks on either side had all been demolished since the last time I was here.

We crossed the cluster of streets bearing Mexican names. Nothing had been left standing on Xoxocotlan. The entire block was one vast weedy field.

We went another block.

Something caught my eye, and I stopped.

"What the fuck?!" I asked.

Adam braked, and his bike skittered to a halt. He looked at what I was looking at.

"Damn," he said.

Someone had nailed severed doll's heads to each of the trees and telephone poles. Baby toy tolls plucked from the necks. Nails through their foreheads. Leering up through the snow at the sky.

Every house on this block was smashed and ruined.

We were alone.

A dark bird perched in a tree.

The wind tugged at our coats.

"Let's keep going," Adam said, and he pushed off.

We sailed past more blocks: Ortman, Octavius, Osborn, and Osh. Little kids, seven or eight, shrieking from their front porches and smoking cigarettes. High-tension wires buzzing between the electric lines overhead. The clouds clumping. We finally stopped in front of a dirty little house with a blue-painted porch separated by long stretches of exhausted wood. A little girl, her hands streaked with mud, squatted on the hard dirt in front, scraping at the ground with a stick, barefoot. Adam walked past her and banged on the storm door.

Juanita's living room was small and dark. Weak light trickled through the grease-stained curtains and landed upon the scratched coffee table and crumb-dusted floor. The couch and chairs held stacks of books, newspapers, and crumpled fast-food wrappers. A couple spent valedoras perched on top of a plug-in fireplace, and a rosary had been nailed in the middle of an archway leading into the equally crowded dining room. In one corner stood a vacuum cleaner that I assumed was broken. Another corner was filled with towering cases of bottled water.

Adam rounded on Juanita as she closed the door behind us.

"We need to spend the night," he said.

Juanita crossed her arms. She was still small and skinny, but there was no mistaking her for a kid anymore. "You can spend the night whenever you want, but I don't like him or his family."

"You don't know my family!" I snapped.

"I know you and your cousin, and that's enough."

"She got you there," said Adam.

I held up my hands, helplessly.

"I know about Michael," I said, "but you're really still mad at me?"

"I'm not mad at you," she said. "I just don't like you."

"Come on," said Adam. "You let Crazy Reggie sleep on your floor. You can let John!"

"Wait, we're sleeping on the floor?" I said.

"We need you to help solve a mystery," said Adam.

"Oh, no," said Juanita. "I don't need another crazy plan. No way."

"No no no, this ain't for me. This is for John."

"I already said –"

"Come on, Juanita," I said. "Please?"

She glared at me.

"Aren't you curious?" asked Adam. "Don't you want to know what we know?"

We put aside the drama for the night and watched TV while Juanita's mom warmed a couple Totino's pizzas for dinner. I met Juanita's brother and one of her two sisters. The older sister was off somewhere, staying the night with a friend in Elmwood, but the younger sister – Candy – was strung out on a sugar high. She kept climbing onto the arm of the couch and jumping off to a loud thud.

"Stop it!" Juanita yelled after each jump.

Kevin, her brother, one year younger, smiled every time this happened.

After the news was done, we put on *Nightmare on Elm Street* and ate circus peanuts and Dorito's until Candy and her mom went to bed. Then Juanita tossed out a bunch of blankets, and we laid down on the dining room floor, facing each other over a bowl of popcorn.

"So," said Juanita. "What's your story?"

"Huh," said Adam. "I'm tryin' a think of how to say it without it coming out weird. I need to find out about a guy named God."

Juanita stared at him.

"So why you come here?" she asked. "You should go to church."

"No. Not God. A guy named God."

"I don't understand."

"His name is God Ostyn," I said. "Or at least that's what they call him. I think he knows people in the Chalks."

"And they call him God? This is bullshit, Adam."

"No, it ain't," said Kevin, who was watching us from a darkened hallway. "God is real. We give him money every month."

"I already made that joke, asshole!"

"No, no, he's our landlord, Juana."

Kevin joined us on the floor and helped himself to a fistful of popcorn.

"Don't call me that. Anyway, he ain't our landlord! You think I wouldn't remember a name like that? Gary's our landlord. Mom's always bitching about him, you know?"

Kevin shook his head.

"Gary ain't the landlord. He's, like ... a super who handles the money. I swear it, Juanita. Ask Mom. He's talked about God before."

"Yeah? What's he say?"

"He says he has to give the rent money to God so Gary can buy his bread. And that God works at X, but he owns so many houses over here that his whole check from Benny just pays his taxes. He buys his food and everything else with his rent checks. And he's got a ton of houses."

"How many?"

"I don't know. A few hundred over all the Os. Maybe even a thousand."

"No way! I'd hear about that."

"God doesn't rent them out in his own name. He rents them out through Gary and his kids. Like the houses are in their names, and the money to keep them goes out from God. Gary and the kids take a cut, and the rest of the take goes back to God."

"The kids?"

"Yeah, some of the kids nobody knows, but others of them are like legends over here."

"Eli?" I asked, over-eager.

"I don't think so. Ezekiel and Trace."

"Don't tell them about them," snapped Juanita.

Kevin ignored her. "Trace don't even live here," he said. "In Akawe. It's like, some houses are in her name, but he has some other guy comes and collect the rent. Maybe Ezekiel. Trace is gone, though. She's outta here."

"Shut up, Kevin."

"And Ezekiel? Damn, son! You said ... huh ... you said God knows people in the Chalks? Yeah, Ezekiel's a Chalk. Except when he's a landlord, he's real, like, official, right? Ezekiel Lang. When he's running with the Chalks, everyone calls him EZ. Or Easy. Or something, you know, sounds like that."

"Shut up!"

Juanita was on her feet now. Kevin glanced at her and stuck his tongue out. Juanita sat on the couch, fuming. She stared into the darkened kitchen. I wondered why she was so pissed off, but I was more eager to learn more about the children of God.

"You said that God's last name was 'Lang?'" I said. "But I heard his last name was Ostyn. Or, at least he has a son named Eli Ostyn. Who goes to Northern and I guess lives up here. So his dad has to be God Ostyn, right? But you're saying it would be God Lang."

"Two guys named God both running the Os?" Adam said. "That's pretty strange, even for Akawe. They gotta be the same guy."

"Well, I don't know God's last name," said Kevin. "I mean, he's supposed to be God, right? That's the story. He created this neighborhood and cursed us all to live in it. But I know about Ezekiel and Trace all right. They're brother and sister and, yeah, their last name is Lang. And they have a dad named God, and he owns how many houses down here, and one of his supers is our man Gary Ortiz. God owns the house you're in right now. The floor you're lying on right now belongs to God."

I thought about that and shivered.

This was all something, but it didn't add up to a lot.

"So, what about you, Juanita?" I asked. "You still think it's all bullshit? You don't think God exists?"

Juanita had been glaring at the floor. Now she sighed. "Yeah, I do," she said. "Because now that I think of it, I heard Gary say a thing a couple times. He said he had to manage the Mexicans for El Señor because he didn't speak any Spanish."

"What does that mean," I asked. "The Mister?"

"Michael said you took Spanish."

"I did. I do. But I had a shitty teacher in seventh grade and didn't learn much last year, either."

"El Señor means the Lord. I thought he was saying it almost like you meant: for the Man. I just thought Gary was being weird. I mean, Gary's weird. But yeah, he could have been saying he was doing it for God, which I guess makes sense if God is a man and also if God is God. Gary's an old-school Chicano. Scrapes boiled sheep's cheeks off the skull with fried tortillas!"

I must have made a face because Juanita smiled at my discomfort. I didn't know why it made me squeamish. I guess I just thought of meat as being meat. Not the boiled cheeks of an actual animal. Then again, I knew what went into a coney.

"You know," said Kevin. "There're lotsa stories about that family. I didn't think of 'em at first because you asked about God. Nobody talks about God much. But like I said, EZ – Ezekiel – he's big all over the Os. Everyone knows about him. I never met him ... he lives on the other side of Orion ... but they say he's got a weird way of talking."

"How does he talk?" I asked. The question was important to me.

"Like he's a thug, but he knows the Bible super deep. Some people say he used to be a pastor even. I don't buy that. He's just one of those weird old Chalks."

"What you mean, Old Chalks?" asked Adam.

"You don't know about them?" asked Kevin.

"I'm not from the Os."

"You lived here!" I said.

"Not for long."

"I'm only thirteen," said Kevin. "And I know about them!"

"I'm only fourteen!" said Adam.

Kevin shrugged. "Okay," he said. "The Chalks used to be skinheads."

"Wait wait," said Juanita. "Shut up, Kevin. You're wrong. They didn't used to be skinheads. I know this part better than you."

"No, you don't!"

"Yeah, I do, you're full of shit, so shut it, or I'll beat you! Yeah, the Chalks used to be a white gang, but they weren't skinheads. I mean, they used to be two different gangs that fought all the time ... um ... they were ... the Counts. And the Tomahawks. But the Os were all white back then. It was in the law."

"Does this have to do with the open housing thing?"

"Back then, it said when you bought the house, there couldn't be any Blacks or Latinos living there. In almost all of Akawe, you had to be a white person to buy a house. Everyone else got the trashy, polluted parts. My teacher told me all this. And my mom."

"But where did the Mexicans live?" I asked.

"I don't think there were a lot of Mexicans in Akawe back then."

"But the Chalks ..." Adam prompted.

"Yeah," Juanita said. "The Chalks formed when the Counts and the Tomahawks combined because the Blacks started moving across the river from Eden."

"Wait, what?" I asked.

"Across the river –"

"No, you said –"

"From Eden. That was the Black neighborhood. There were, like, two neighborhoods for the Blacks, and that was one of them."

"Where do you get all this?!"

Juanita shrugged. "People talk," she said. "I listen. But I was *saying* they started moving from Eden across the river into the Os. See, the house rule or whatever didn't work anymore. Like there was some law or court that said they couldn't do that. The Blacks could live wherever they wanted. And it was cheap in the Os, and so the Blacks started moving in. The whites didn't like that, you know? The Counts and the Tomahawks, they hated each other, but they hated the Blacks so much more they joined up and made themselves the Chalks. Like they chose that as their new name. The name was to let the Blacks know this was a white neighborhood."

"But you said they hated each other ..." I said.

"Look!" said Juanita. "I saw this picture at the museum, and it had hundreds of KKK people in Hunter Park. I mean, they were in white hoods and the whole shit. They burned a cross down there. A motherfucking cross right in the middle of Hunter Park! It was a long time ago, but you know that they and their kids were in those two gangs that made the Chalks, so you know it made sense!"

"Fuck those bitches," said Kevin. "You know one of them murdered his wife? She was pregnant. They sliced her belly open and pulled the baby right out, they thought it would keep the Blacks from coming, like they were doing some voodoo or some shit. And they murdered one Black guy walking back home across the river. They caught him before he got to his own side. Stabbed him a bunch. Threw him in the river. Blood all over the water. ¡Vete a la verga culero! But then some of the Blacks got those motherfuckers a few nights later. Robbed 'em. Stabbed 'em. Got off all their clothes, and so those Chalks went running through the streets with everyone seeing their little dicks and assholes as they ran home. Fuck those Chalk fuckers, they hated the Blacks, they went crazy. They saw nothing but blood. Bloody brains! Motherfucking faggot motherfuckers. Serves 'em motherfucking right!"

"God, will you shut up, Kevin!" said Juanita. "Yeah, the Chalks run everything over here now. Everything. Now the Undertakers got beat, and the cops are scared to come over here. I hate them. You know a year ago they tagged our house? We got back, they tagged it all over. 'Kill Juanita,' they wrote. 'Kill Kevin.' 'Kill Maya.' That's my other sister." She spoke in a momentary hush. "You know they sieged a woman two blocks over."

"Sieged?" asked Adam. "Like a castle?"

"No, in her house! Like she was going to testify against 'em in court. So, they had snipers in this house and that house, both sides of her, or across the street, and every time she came out her house, someone took a shot at her."

"That's bullshit!" I said. "Akawe sucks, but that's too far. That doesn't happen here!"

Juanita and Kevin both laughed at me.

"It ain't too far, though," said Kevin. "In fact, in fact, it was like too close! The snipers weren't, like, a house away. So many houses torn down over here, you don't even need to be close to snipe. You got a good rifle you can take a shot from a block back!"

"It happened," said Juanita. "I ain't made it up! It was in the newspaper and everything! Look it the fuck up. Anyway, you don't believe me, the fuck am I talking for?"

"I'm sorry," I said. "I believe you. You know I'm not from the Os. It just sounds ... too crazy to be real."

"EZ was one of the Chalks from after they made the switch," said Kevin. "From after the old gangs became the Chalks. He's, like, a man, not a kid, but he's not that old. I mean, I think he's younger than mom. So, you know, when he was in school, any school, over here, like Northern, or Weiland, there were Blacks, and Mexicans, and Chinese, and Indians there with him. They were his friends, right? Like his parents would've shot at them or hung 'em up a few years back, but now they were *here*. *All* those kids were crazy running crazy.

Their parents were old-time bangers, but they didn't have no control over 'em. Everything was going to shit, right? So, EZ and them made the Chalks so it wasn't racist anymore. Except against the Undertakers. Like the whites over here were all Chalks and the Mexicans were all Undertakers, and the Blacks were whatever. And that was just the way it was, for years and years, until the Undertakers went down. When Kid Zero got shot, and they never got the puto did it. And you know what the fuck happened? Those boys and girls with the Undertakers go off to jail. And their little brothers and sisters join the Chalks! How fucked up is that?!"

"I didn't know the Undertakers were so great," I muttered.

"I don't like any gangs, John," said Juanita. "But even I think that's fucked up."

We were quiet for a moment.

"I kinda liked the Undertakers," said Kevin. "They were better than those Chalks. I'm pissed they're gone now."

"Shut up, Kevin!"

"So ..." I was getting impatient. I still wasn't sure what this all added up to. What any of it had to do with Selby or Eli or the messed-up street across the river. I was floundering.

"What do they say about EZ?" I asked. "I mean, in the neighborhood."

"What do they say?" asked Kevin. "They say everything! Anything crazy you can say, someone's said about him."

"But what?"

"Everything! Okay, so here's something they say about EZ. So at my school, they say that one time he fucked a ho blind. She was just some ho, and one night EZ says, 'I'll fuck you, and you'll pay me a quarter for it,' and she says, 'yeah,' and they go into this abandoned house. And they're fucking and fucking, and then some Blacks come out and set the house on fire. So, the house is burning down around them, but EZ and this ho are having too much fun. They can't stop fucking! But then the roof caves in around them, and the bitch says – she was a crazy ho – she says, 'don't let a bird fly over and shit on my face,' and EZ says, 'I can help with that!' and he pulls his dick out of her and just ... busts a nut all over her face!" Kevin laughed. "And right in time, you know, because two big birds fly over the fire and drop shit on her face, but it just bounces right off EZ's jizz. So, she thanks him. Then she goes and washes up her face, but she's gone all blind from all of his jizz. I mean, she's completely blind. Never sees anything again. But she thanks him over and over because it was the best thing that ever happened to her."

"Fuck you, Kevin!" said Juanita.

"What? They asked me to tell them what people in the neighborhood said about EZ!"

Juanita got up and left the room.

"Does he wear sunglasses a lot?" I asked.

"What?" asked Kevin.

"EZ. Does he wear sunglasses a lot?"

"Um, I never heard about that," he said. "But I can tell you about his homies in Bucharest and Zaire. I can tell you how he took a shit on a bunch of Satan's Masters while they was sleeping. And about how he sucked his own dick and turned his own jizz into milk and honey, and spit it out, and then he and his sister Trace drank it with tea. And how he blew this Black dude away with a shotgun, and all that was left of his head was his teeth, solid diamonds. So EZ sold 'em to his Gs in Chicago and LA, and he bought Trace a old Valentine Formosa from the 60s. Gold plated. Platinum grille. Pure emerald headlights. Like, real emeralds! And two dice made out of jade hanging from the rear view. And he said, 'Trace, baby, take this fine ride and get the fuck out of here, because living in the Os is suicide, and damn you're hot, I'd fuck you if you weren't my own sister!'"

"Fuck you!" snapped Juanita from the doorway. She was shaking with anger.

"They're just stories," said Kevin.

Juanita shook her head. "They're our stories. They ain't earned them."

"How can we earn them?" asked Adam. His eyes were on fire.

"You can't!" said Juanita.

Juanita turned the light out, and darkness flooded the room. I heard her climb down beneath the blankets between Adam and me. Kevin sighed.

"Te amo, hermana," he said, and shuffled out of the room.

We lay there in silence for several minutes, and I tried to make my breathing steady, natural, inaudible to Juanita and everyone else in the Os. I thought about her. How I had dismissed her when I was in seventh grade, and she was twelve. I hadn't really known her at all. Who was she then, and who had she become in the last two years? Who was I? Who had I become?

When Juanita finally spoke, I thought that it might be my mind speaking.

"I heard about EZ my whole life," she said. "I know he's real, okay? I know he lives over here. But I also know sometimes people put their own stories on him. They put their own stories *in* him. If someone tells you a story about EZ, you might be hearing someone else's private business, you know? You got to be careful who you share that shit with."

I thought I should answer, but I couldn't think of anything to say.

239

"*One* story," she said. "I'll tell you just one story I've heard about EZ. But don't tell anybody. It's the story my brother just fucked up. And yeah, it might be the one story that helps you both out. So. One time this guy – it's a white guy, not a Black guy – climbs in EZ's bedroom window while he's sleeping, and it wakes him up, and EZ doesn't even think twice about it. He just sits up and pulls out his gat, and blows the guy away. And it wakes Trace up, because she's staying with him, you know? But nobody else, because this is on one of those blocks where nobody else lives. And Trace goes over and looks at the dead guy, and he's a homeless guy, and he was just climbing in to look for a place to sleep. And Trace says, 'you killed an innocent man. He wasn't going to hurt us. He wasn't going to rob us.' And EZ says, 'whoever does not enter a sheepfold through the gate but climbs over is a robber.' And Trace says, 'you killed him. You're dead.' And EZ says, 'I'll live again,' and Trace says, 'No, you won't. You've always been dead. Ever since you were born. So have all the Langs. So have all the Ostyns. But not me. If anyone is going to live again, it's *me!*' And Trace takes her earrings, and her rings – her *own* that belonged to *her* – and pawns them and uses the money to buy a bus ticket to New York City and she goes out there and gets a job on Broadway and lives on her own, and isn't a part of that family anymore. She's the only one to get out of that whole messed-up family. Ever."

I stared at the ceiling darkness, thinking.

"You said it would help us," said Adam. "How's it supposed to help us?"

"Because the story does tell about the Osyns. And EZ and Trace were the Langs. So they had a lot of brothers and sisters, and they had different last names."

"Why didn't you say that before?" I asked. "When I asked about Eli Ostyn."

"I thought I was hearing the name wrong. I thought it had to be 'Austin' with an 'A.' I mean, they kind of sound similar."

I suddenly felt exhausted.

I suddenly felt like I didn't care anymore, and I wanted to turn my back on God Ostyn and Ezekiel Lang and Trace and Eli and whoever else, and just go back home. Only I didn't want to go back home either and face up to my drunk father and my gone mother. I just wanted to go into my bedroom. And then, in my mind, that too became a perilous place. There were too many memories in that room, but no shielding maple leaves to protect me from examination. So, I tried to imagine myself floating high in the sky, or resting still and compressed deep underground.

It wasn't a dream exactly, but I wasn't awake, either. On the cold floor, my thoughts kept trying to gather, kept rallying, kept struggling to find sentences to describe that sensation of rootless floating. But I was too dazed to get more than a word out, and so there was one word – the same word – "disappointed" – and I kept thinking it over and over.

Then, once, I must have said the word out loud because Juanita rolled over to look at me and said, "I know. I'm disappointed in everything."

"Did you hear me?" I asked, still not sure whether I was awake or asleep.

"I hear everything in this house."

"I didn't say it ... before ... but I think you're pretty. I think you've become pretty."

"I don't care."

"I don't mean it, as ... like ... you know. I mean. I have a girlfriend."

Juanita was silent, then, and I realized that I really was awake.

"Who is she?" Juanita finally asked.

"I don't know," I said.

I woke to the popping of grease and the heavy scent of bacon. A silver light trickled through the lace curtains. I saw Adam standing over the stove, shaking a skillet. Juanita sat on the couch, tying her shoes. She was already dressed for the weather, wearing jeans and a fuzzy brown sweater. Studs twinkled in her ears.

I sat up.

"Where's Kevin?"

"He decided to go to school," she said.

"What about you?"

"I'm gonna miss it today and help you figure out God."

"Thanks."

"Whatever. Now I want to know too. If he's our landlord, I want to know his deal. I want to know why he makes people call him God ... why they even do it."

I went into the bathroom and cleaned up, changing into the flannel shirt I'd stuffed into my backpack, ran my wet hands through my hair, and met Adam and Juanita in the tiny dining room.

"Your mom care about you missing school?" I asked.

"I get the grades," Juanita said. "She don't care. Kevin don't get the grades, and she don't care with him neither. But I told him he should go today. He runs his mouth too much. Keeps people from talking what they know. Just like last night."

Adam served us bacon and eggs, sunny side up, with some bacon grease drizzled on top. A few sliced, fried potatoes, sticky with salt and pepper. He dumped a bunch of hot sauce on his plate and scraped it all together with his fork and knife. He took a drink of instant coffee. So did I. Juanita drank water.

"Damn, Adam," she said. "You wanna come live over here and cook for us every day?"

Adam laughed.

"No," he said. "I don't wanna live over here ever again."

We stepped out into the brightness. The sun sparkled in the startling blue sky, but trains of mist tracked along the ground. Stepping off of the porch was like wading into the sea. We walked over to Orion and turned right, toward the east. The Os had been changing fast. Maybe faster than any other part of town. I could tell as soon as I saw the bulldozers lumbering over the compacted foundations of St. Francis' school. As the Church retreated from neighborhood after neighborhood, it took its charms and relics with it. It would reduce its schools and hospitals to powder before it allowed them to be gutted by the forces of chaos.

Everything else had missed out on such loving farewells. Buildings that had been restaurants and clubs in '93 had been abandoned, and swollen mattresses hung from their doorless doorways. Buildings that had been abandoned in '93 had been torched, and the blackened, gridded timbers all seemed to stink as bad as they must have on the day they'd lit up. Buildings that had been torched in '93 were gone. Now we saw long fields. Only the shaggiest grass and the hardiest weeds were able to survive in this desert of machine-compacted earth.

I'd never seen so much desolation so densely packed together. A density of desolation.   We passed groups of people as we walked; boys and girls coming and going from school, huddled clusters of men and women whispering over steaming cups of coffee, a few prostitutes waiting near the bus stop, not too near, not too attentive, and a few heavy teens – Mexicans and Appalachians – that glared at us as we walked past.

As we walked, I started to feel – to touch with invisible fingers rather than imagine with organized thought – the reasons that the Os unsettled me. It was the sort of place that made me believe that bored children would go out and burn down houses for a laugh and a jizz. It was the sort of place that made me believe that a bored man would go out and stab old men for a quick spike of adrenaline. It made me believe that someone, somewhere, would dismember dolls and nail their heads to telephone poles as a hideous witness to hideousness. A witness worthy of the witnessed prospect.

And yet, for all its violence and mess, this wasn't the hardest part of town. On the West End, miles and miles of hood stretched out, ignored except by the police who came by to vent rage and knock skulls. The Werewolf Town that Curt Chives had been telling us about, with its waterless, heatless, lightless trailer park. The Os was a rough neighborhood, but it wasn't the worst in Akawe.

No, here, at least *part* of the threat was existential. It was written into the incorporation of the district. "A white neighborhood." This place named after the most gaping of vowels, the oldest letter of the alphabet, a place that by its very name defied the domination of X Automotives. This place that lived across the river from a place named "Eden," that had been the "Negro neighborhood," all gone now, *where did it go?* and *its people crossed the river here. Became neighbors in the Os?*

How much of the Os' ravagings had been the child of segregation?

From the very beginning, these houses had been small, fragile, and close to the factories. Painted pearl white. As Juanita said, men with pearl white robes and steepled heads had once climbed carefully down the sunlit slopes of Hunter Park. Their children had called themselves Counts and Tomahawks. But now, the Os were integrated. The most Akawean neighborhood because it was part Black, part white, like Akawe. The least Akawean neighborhood because, in Akawe, Blacks and whites keep their districts separate. Salt-and-pepper across the Os. Salt-and-pepper along each block. Salt-and-pepper within many houses. Infinite regressions.

Here, in this place where some people forged their lives around an obliteration of race.

Here, in this place where a few people murdered and died to obliterate another race.

Here, where everyone was poor, and race was everything and nothing.

Here, in this walled-in neighborhood where sedimentary humans settled at the bottom of the basin, the base of the well, the last place where they could cling to a mooring, to any anchorage whatsoever, and so they held as best they could and tried to rest, to catch their breath, to nourish their strength, while the veterans of this district, the oldest men in the Crazy Chalks walked their ranks and reaped their boys and girls.

Since everyone here had settled at the bottom, and since they had all settled because they didn't have any choice, and since I was a stranger on these strange blocks, of course I was unsettled. The only way to not feel unsettled in the Os was to settle there and to make its ways my ways.

"So how are we gonna find God?" Adam finally asked, after we'd walked about a hundred blocks.

"By talking to people who might have seen him or heard about him," Juanita answered.

We arrived at the edge of Hunter Park, where stately maples rose in stands upon the brow of a crescent slope descending toward the flooded fields. Hunter Creek, twisting beneath willows and four or five rusted white-painted foot bridges, exited the park near 292 to the south, then finally discharged into the Zibi River. A huge, white, mission-shingled pavilion, graceful in its decay, hung off the lip of the hill, surveying the vastness of the park beyond. Even wild, even overgrown, Hunter Park exhaled an arcadian splendor, suffused with smoky luminosity as the cold sun finally started to burn off the last bands of fog below.

Juanita led us through the pavilion, down a flight of chipped steps, and into a thick grove of trees. We found a dirty circle there, with a tent and three teen boys, two white and one Black, lying about in sleeping bags.

"'Ita!" said one of the white boys.

"Marco," Juanita said.

"You brought something from you know?"

"I ain't a thizzhead. You know it."

"Aw man. I ain't even got shit to eat today."

"Stop over at St. Raph's."

"Ain't open yet. Long way to walk."

"Hey, these are my friends: Adam. John."

"Hey."

"Hey, I'm trying to find out some stuff about my landlord."

"You over by Pacific?"

"Orleans and Osh."

"Yeah right. Ain't that Gary Ortiz?"

"Yeah. You know that?"

"He owns half the houses over there. All you Mexicans."

"Yeah, we pay him, but I heard different. I heard he works for this this other guy, makes people call him God. Last name Lang. Or Ostyn."

"Huh. I don't know the dude's last name, but there is a guy called God. But he definitely ain't a landlord. He owns a big junkyard."

"Where?"

"I don't know. Somewhere out in the city."

"That helps. There's a million junkyards!"

"Why don't you just ask Gary?"

"I don't want him to know I'm asking, you know what I'm sayin'?"

"Yeah, yeah. I don't know nothin' else about it."

"I know about God," said a white girl, older than us, maybe eighteen, twenty. I hadn't seen her sitting under one of the trees, knees drawn up to her chin.

"You can tell me?" Juanita asked.

The girl shrugged. "It ain't like it's a secret. Yeah, he's this guy named God Ostyn, just like you said. Has a big junkyard out on ... huh, I think out on Ash way that way. Near Arlington or Griswold or something. Has three kids named, um, Ash and Eli and Spark. Ash and Eli are boys and Spark is the girl. They live over here sometimes. In the Os. I never seen God. And I don't know about Eli. But I seen Ash and Spark. Ash is a devil and Spark is a vampire."

Adam, Juanita, and I stared at the girl.

"Straight up," said Marco. "'Ita, this is Lisa."

"What do you mean, a devil? A vampire?" said Juanita.

"They are criminals," said Lisa. She was trembling, but I couldn't tell if it was from waking up into this frost or from whatever drug she was recently on or off. "They buy and sell young girls. They are actually hundreds of years old, both of them, but Spark looks like she's just fifteen, which she uses to, you know, get other girls to trust her. Always girls twelve, thirteen, fourteen. Then they bring them back to the Os and keep them in a house they have out here and sell them a lot. And when the girl's all used up, they kill her and burn down the house. See, Ash can't be hurt by fire because he's a devil, and Spark drinks their blood if they try to escape. They get lots of money from the girls. They live in a fancy house in Parc Pierre, I heard. But they always keep them in an abandoned house on the Undertaker side."

Lisa sniffed.

"The Undertaker side?"

"This side of Orion," said Juanita. Used to be, the Undertakers were on this side and the Chalks on the other. Now, you know, no more Undertakers over here, but I don't know, we still call it that."

"The Chalks don't mess with them because Ash is a Chalk," said Lisa. "The popo grab Spark sometimes, but they can't hold her because she's under eighteen. They don't know that she's the real secret pimp, and even if they did, they'd have to let her dad pick her up."

"You sure her dad is God Ostyn?" Juanita asked.

"Yeah."

"Do you know anything about him?"

"Just what I told you. That that's his name, and he has a junkyard."

"Wait," I said. "If Ash and Spark are hundreds of years old, then what about God? I mean ... if he's their father."

"I guess he must be that old, too. Probably thinks his name is funny."

"Like he's flipping the real God the bird!" laughed Marco.

"Anyone else wanna tell me anything about God Ostyn?" asked Juanita.

Nobody had anything to say.

"Please let's keep this on the dl, kay?"

The boys and Lisa nodded.

Lisa zipped up her coat.

"You headed up that way?" she asked.

"I think so," said Juanita.

"I'll come with you. I want to hit VDP. Holding a coat for me. Besides, I might think of someone else you can talk to."

We waved off the other kids and made our way up the hill and out of the park. A minute later, we were walking north along Odette, on one of the more put-together blocks of the Os. Early Christmas lights winked out from freshly swept porches. It was difficult to tell whether they were glowing or just reflecting the dazzling sunlight. A stiff wind turned down against us, the last of the fallen leaves scuttling back south toward the park. Juanita and Lisa walked ahead of Adam and me.

"Stay away from huffs, John," muttered Adam. "You'll start believing in devils and vampires and shit. Although, you know, maybe she's right. That would explain a lot of fucked up shit around here."

I wasn't thinking about flame-retardant Chalks or hundred-year-old fifteen-year-olds. I was thinking about the possibility of an actual fifteen-year-old pimp, helped out by her brother who gave her cover and support through the local gang ... and about their father who might be giving them their orders. I was wondering what happened to the girls who didn't have a Selby to risk everything to save them. Were they murdered, and then the house burned down? What had Eli Ostyn seen? What had he touched with his hands?

I pulled my coat tighter.

Eventually, we got back to where Owen crossed Orion. On one corner, steam rising from the vents at King Michael's spiced the morning with the scent of cooking Goerlichs. Across Orion, the Kroghetto – one of the last supermarkets in Akawe – must have finally been shuttered. Its windows had been smashed, and the salt-crusted parking lot was empty except for a single broken-down Chevy. We crossed Owen and stopped at the dim-lit doors of the St. Vincent de Paul, just opened for the day.

"Hey," said Juanita. "Lisa's got a friend here called Linda ..."

"I heard her talking about God one time," Lisa said. "I can ask her to talk to you. I'm going in anyway."

"Sure," I said.

We waited, kicking stones across the lot, shoving our hands deep in our pockets, and squinting in the harsh sunlight. All of the fragments and fractures of the place stood out in sharp detail. Finally, Lisa came back out.

"Is she gonna say anything about it?" asked Juanita.

"She don't like him," said Lisa. "She fucking hates Gary Ortiz. Go on around back."

"Thanks, girl," said Juanita.

"Around back" was through a narrow gate past a barbed-wire-topped chain-link fence, then a parking lot, to a small loading dock surrounded by spooled and unspooled concertina wire.

A small, middle-aged Black woman joined us. She wore a calm, skeptical expression on her face.

"You're the ones want to know about God Ostyn?" she asked.

"He's my landlord, that's all," said Juanita.

"He ain't your landlord. Gary Ortiz is your landlord. The Ostyns ain't nobody you want to mess around with."

"Does he own a junkyard?"

"I don't know. I'm pretty sure he died a few years back. I do know his kids run wild. Shoot things up. Burn things down. And they all think they own this neighborhood. I mean, it's named after him."

"What?!" I said.

"Yeah, way back, some Ostyn owned a farm up here. He sold off the lots here and across the river. For whites here, Blacks over by the factories. They connected them along Ostyn Street, which is all gone now. Sold it off to X way back, so they could build houses for their factory. But when they did, they said they had to start so many streets with the letter 'O.' And X was growing real fast back then, so they were willing to agree to just about anything the man said. But look, I don't have much to tell you about this man or his family. Lisa should have known better. God Ostyn isn't your landlord, so you don't go asking about his family. You have to pay Gary rent or something, fine, do that and leave it at that. I don't want anybody getting hurt."

"Dead end," Adam said a few moments later as we poked along Owen Road.

I shook my head. "That thing she said about the neighborhood ... about how all the streets got 'O' names ... that's fucked up."

"I don't know I believe all this," said Juanita. "How much I don't believe. S'okay, though. I know lots other people we can talk to."

"Don't you think we talk too much people are gonna wonder why, or it's gonna get back to him?"

"He's my landlord! I just want to know a little about my landlord. Besides, what are they gonna freak about? I'm not asking about drugs. I'm not asking about the gang."

I couldn't believe that Juanita was this naive, but if that's how she wanted to play it ...

"Let's go," she said.

For the next several hours, we crisscrossed the Os on foot, stopping back at Juanita's for sandwiches and chips. We talked to her neighbors: whites and Blacks, Mexicans and Chinese, and Chippewa. We talked to a homeless man in Victorian Park, a janitor at Northern High School, and a couple of scrappers stripping aluminum siding from an abandoned house on Oakdale Street.

"I'm thinking," said Juanita, "we ask people disconnected from each other. One question just sounds like one question, not worth mentioning. But if two people meet up, realize we asked each of them the same shit, that's when they start to notice. So, I'm asking people that ain't gonna meet up."

"See?" said Adam. "That was my idea, too."

God, it seemed, was everywhere in the Os. Everyone we spoke to had heard of him, and everyone had an idea of who he was and what he did. But if God was omnipresent, he was also contradictory and indistinct. God was never the main character in the stories we heard, which were much more concerned with the troubles and sins of his children. These stories included God only to shade in their history and situation, and so the details of the father fluttered and shifted, collided and coalesced, multilingual palimpsests graffitied on the walls of houses that would burn down in the next year or two anyway. We heard about God the landlord, God the junkyard owner, God the autoworker, God the soldier, God the concrete installation and repair contractor. We heard about his two, three, six, twelve, or twenty-four kids. We heard about the wretched shack where he lived on Katanga Street, the opulent mansion where he had retired in Bellwood, the car where he huddled on the East Side of Detroit, his cool bright cabana on the shores of the Belizean Caribbean, his simple cell in a monastery in the foothills of Maramureş. There was slippage, and the soil from the conflicting summits of these tales collected in the more accessible valleys: "God foreclosed on my neighbor. Kicked him right to the curb. Always paid on time. Don't know why he did it." "Everyone knows God takes kickbacks from the Chalks. Almost everyone else kicks back *to* the Chalks." "I saw him once. Don't remember his face. Funniest thing. I remember his shotgun, though."

As the day wore on, I started to form a clearer picture of God's kids: Ezekiel, or EZ, who I was pretty sure was the man with the knife I'd imagined behind every shadow, and Lucy's boyfriend Eli. Ezekiel Lang gently intoned threats through the thousands of Biblical verses he had memorized. Meanwhile, Eli Ostyn was quick to pray and quick to cry. He went into all four of Akawe's high schools and quietly harvested girls for abduction and prostitution. I hated and feared both of them. But I also felt like I was starting to see pictures of violent Ash, and cynical Spark, and the opportunistic Trace who had escaped, and Quint, "that perfect boy." The homeless man said, "He died young. He was a beautiful child. He bought people groceries who couldn't afford 'em." Ruth Lang, the mother of Trace and Ezekiel, who had lost her mind and was rotting away in a facility somewhere. Even the unknown mother – mothers? – of the Ostyn children, unmarried and nameless, expressed, somehow, a powerful presence through her resolute absence from the stories, as though her disappearance from the nightmare chronicles was an intentional act of will. It all seemed so much more determined, so much more meaningful than any of the details about God himself, which changed in every conversation and fit every story.

Finally, the sun started to set, and I wondered which of the houses we'd passed during the day would burn down over the course of the night. Nights

249

were long now. Any warmth in a storm?

"I gotta go, guys," I said when we finally got back to Juanita's house late in the day. "I have work at the planetarium tonight, and I'll be late if I don't head out now."

"Drop my sister's bike back at Grandpa M's?" asked Adam.

"Yeah," I said. "Sure."

"Be safe, John," said Juanita. "The sun's going down, and it's strange out."

"I know," I said. "Thanks. Hey. It's good to, you know, hang out again."

Juanita smiled politely and went inside.

It didn't take long to reach Suarez, but as I chained Ophelia's bike to a telephone pole, I realized I hadn't gotten much of a lunch. When I got inside, I waited until Carl was in another room and swiped a Snickers.

"What are you doing?!" Crystal asked.

"I'm starving," I said.

"You've got to pay for that!"

"With what?" I asked. "The $3.35 they're paying us for this shit? I don't have any money right now."

"You're gonna get us fired."

"No. I just won't record the sale."

"They keep inventory, idiot!"

Whatever. It's one candy bar. Carl came and went, and Crystal and I sold tickets, picked up the trash in the lobby, and when things had quieted down, I snuck off to the bathroom to eat my "dinner."

Frost was in the air by the time work was done, so I decided to take the bus. After a quick stop at Adam's to drop off the bike and a brisk walk home, my hands were pale and numb. I found my mother at the sink, washing dishes. She gave me a glance.

"You didn't tell me anything about spending the night at Adam's," she said.

"You weren't home to ask."

I went into the dining room and set down my backpack. My father was sitting at the table reading the *Old Farmer's Almanac*.

"You aren't going to finish *Gravity's Rainbow*?" I asked him.

"I almost did," he grunted. "I was fifty pages from the end. But I don't see the point. It made me worry more about light bulbs than bombs."

"How was school today?" my mother called in from the kitchen.

My father stared at me. I stared back.

"It was fine," I said. "I'm gonna go get my homework going. It was a busy day, and I probably have a couple hours to go. You wouldn't believe the kind of shit they lay on us."

"Watch your mouth, John."

"Okay."

I had one more day of suspension, but since my father hadn't mentioned this to my mother, I just bullshitted it.

The next morning, I took the bus to the library and skulked from section to section, getting caught up on all of their back issues of Rolling Stone. Did you know that Weezer was neither punk, pop, nor pretty? Whereas, I guess, Green Day was both punk and platinum. The Foo Fighters were simply, I guess, too young to die. Anyway, by the time school was over and I was walking over to work at the planetarium, I probably knew more about some of my friends' bands than they did. Then, since I was already lying to my mother that day, it seemed pointless not to extend the lies, so I took some more candy, as well as a glow-in-the-dark solar system that I easily slid into my backpack. Because *fuck it.*

"You are an idiot, John," said Crystal, "and I was an idiot for helping you get this job."

She refused to talk to me for the rest of the night.

On Thursday, I went back to school, and everyone was talking about my stink-bomb prank. I didn't have the time or attitude for the laughs and questions. Maybe in other years, I would've seen the drama as a social opportunity: I'd stunk up Mr. Agape's stage and put on shades. I was obviously a badass. I didn't have the energy for this anymore, though. Too much was going sideways to get distracted by stupid shit. I tried to ignore the comments as best I could.

After third hour, I was looking forward to a moment of quiet in the empty hall by my locker, but May was waiting when I got there.

"I just ... are we still going out together?"

"Uh, yeah."

"I wrote you a note, and you never wrote me back."

"I'm sorry," I said. "But I don't think we can break up unless one of us tells the other. I mean, you have to know."

"Okay. Yeah. Okay. It's just, I haven't seen you at all lately. And you got suspended! And you haven't written me back, and we haven't talked on the phone, or seen each other out of school at all."

"I've been busy. I've got my job at the planetarium."

"I understand. When my brother was in the hospital, I was so busy seeing him and taking care of my dad, I thought my head was going to fly off! But I think we should get together after school sometime and go on a date sometime, don't you?"

"Yeah."

She waited to see if I would say anything else. I waited to see if she would say anything else.

"Okay," she said. "Well, there's this McDonald's near my house, and it was closed up forever. And they just opened it up, and it's a lot nicer than it was before. They put up a playground for kids. I think we should go there. You could buy me dinner if we're on a date. Or, I don't know. I could buy my own dinner, I guess."

"Yeah. Sure."

"So, when do you want to do it? Do you want to meet me this weekend? Or maybe after school? Do you think you could get a ride? I'd give you a ride, but my car is broken."

"Um, no, probably not. My father's not driving a lot these days."

Her brows creased. "Yeah, my car's broken. Its brakes are broken. It has to be getting its brakes fixed. I can't drive it right now. That's okay. We can take the bus!"

"Um, May, I think I'm going to be busy this weekend. I have a lot of homework, and I'm working really hard on it."

"That's okay. Maybe we can work on it together! I have some trouble with my homework, too. Hey, maybe you can help me!"

I grunted because I had run out of excuses. Instead, I started unloading books into my locker. May's eyes flitted between my backpack and the locker, and I tried to ignore her. Then she nudged me aside and climbed inside.

"Hey, you know what would be funny?" she said. "If you just shut me in your locker!"

I laughed. "That would be funny," I said.

I slammed the locker shut and walked off.

I hurried off toward Mr. Russell's class. For a minute, my head was cloudy. I actually starting thinking about other shit, like how many Geometry questions I'd fuck up that hour. I didn't stop until I reached the door.

What the fuck is wrong with you?! I thought.

The bell rang, but I spun and ran back through the dark halls. *You fucking asshole idiot.* It was the pointless cruelty that made me an asshole. It was the obvious self-sabotage that made me an idiot. I was an asshole idiot. I turned the corner just in time to see Mrs. Brown, one of the assistant principals, popping my locker open with a master key. A couple upperclassmen were standing there, watching, concerned. I hung back, just glancing around the corner like I was there by accident. When I strained, I could overhear what they were saying.

"What were you doing in there?" demanded Mrs. Brown.

"Oh," said May, "that's my boyfriend's locker. I, um, locked myself inside so I could jump out and surprise him when he came by next time."

"You really did that?"

"I thought it would be funny."

"No, May, it was really stupid. You could have suffocated in there."

"No, I couldn't. See, there are those air holes."

"That's not what a locker is for."

"I'm sorry."

"You're late to class now. Are you going to pass this year?"

"Probably not ..."

"Yes, probably not. But you should try at least. Why don't you go to class and stay out of lockers."

I pulled back. Hung around the corner. Mrs. Brown passed on her way back to the office. May turned the corner. She saw me and gave me a little smile, but there was also a tiny little frown buried there, and it made me feel like absolute shit.

"You know," she said. "I didn't mean for you to really shut me in your locker."

"I know," I said. It was weird. It was too easy to act like an asshole to May, but I had a hard time lying to her. "I'm sorry. I thought it would be funny."

"I didn't think it was funny. I didn't think it was funny at all."

I felt small. I felt like I was as awful as the Ostyns, but without the strength and courage for their straight-up evil. I wasn't the badass who punked Mr. Agape's class. I was the idiot asshole who shut his girlfriend in his locker.

"I was coming back to get you out when Mrs. Brown did instead," I mumbled.

"Yeah, those guys heard me banging on the door, so they went and got her, and she got the key. It's really tiny in there."

"I'm sorry. Thanks for, um, not ratting me out."

"Snitches get stitches, John. Anyway, try not to worry about it. You shouldn't be sad. I'll give you a call, okay, and we'll figure out a time, okay, when we can go to that fancy new McDonald's!"

Karma caught me that night at the planetarium. Carl called me into his office. He offered me a chair, then sat down stiffly behind his desk.

"How old are you, John?" he asked.

"Fifteen."

"Mmm-hmm. And what are your plans?"

I knew what adults meant when they asked this. They meant my plans for the *future*. And I'd gotten a lot of practice answering questions like this over the last several years.

"College," I said. "Then maybe work in theatre. Backstage. Or do something with math, if I can keep my grades up."

"Hmmm," Carl said. "My plans are to steer the planetarium away from entertainment and toward education. And about how I want to compensate my employees with college credit since I don't have the budget to pay them very well. Do you see where I'm going with this?"

"I'm sorry, I don't think I understand."

"In the last week, our inventory has shown shortages of three candy bars, one packet of Astronaut Ice Cream, and one solar-system mobile. The sales price of these items only totals about fifteen dollars, but it's a problem because I have to trust my employees. I have dozens of applicants, you know. Dozens of kids, not just from Akawe but from all over the county, private schools and public schools. They all want to get into college like you do, and this job is the sort of job that is going to improve their chances. So, for me to employ someone who steals from the planetarium is unacceptable."

"But I thought ... um. Crystal said you didn't have a lot of applicants."

"John," Carl said. "I saw you take the solar system kit the other night, and I even gave you an extra day to return it. I thought maybe you'd change your mind and bring it back, and you haven't. You know, I don't usually give extra chances like that, but I didn't want to be wrong about you."

I still didn't say anything.

"I asked Crystal about it too, and you should know that she didn't tell me anything. She's a very loyal friend. She's risking her own job, and only to keep you out of trouble. I don't know that I feel great about her right now, either. But still, you're stealing, and she isn't, and that puts me in a challenging position."

"So, what are you going to do?" I asked.

"It is a question of zero more chances or one more chance. Because I cannot go on employing you, absent trust. Either we garnish your wages for the price of what you've stolen, and we have a meeting with both you and your parents to discuss what is expected here at Suarez ... or today is your last day. It's your choice."

My eyes took in the drab walls of Carl's office. For the first time, I noticed a framed photo of the horsehead nebula hung above his desk, in full color. I imagined the lobby with its NASA caps and model rockets. The gallery with its luminescent paintings of the zodiac illuminated by blacklight. The eggshell interior of the planetarium dome and its almost invisible seams. I suddenly felt like I was going to cry.

Here I had been so focused on the shitty pay and the other dramas in my life, that I hadn't stopped to think about the planetarium itself. Since the Renaissance Festival had ended, this job was the only thing that had gone *right*. It had been something that I could have felt happy and excited about, if I had bothered to try. I *could* have asked Carl more about quasars and pulsars and standard candles. I *could* have. *Why* hadn't I? I asked Miss Pavilik questions like these. Wasn't it enough to just sit in the dome when two or three kids showed up for the star show and just watch the sky spiral around us? Wasn't it enough to sit in there and marvel and get paid for that? Holy shit! Had I really just traded all of that away for some shitty candy and a plastic mobile?

And yet, even though I felt sick in my stomach, I couldn't see myself sitting down with Carl and my parents. I knew how deeply they would feel their disappointment. And I was disappointed in them, too. What sort of conversation would we have after a meeting like that? What might they say? What might come out of my own mouth? No. That was more humiliation than I could agree to.

"I'm sorry," I told Carl. "I really am. I made a mistake, and you can garnish my wages. But I don't want to tell my parents. I mean ... I'm not going to tell my parents."

Carl sighed. He had hoped – had expected, maybe – the other answer.

"Well," he said. "As I said, there are a lot of applicants for this job. I'll see to it that your last paycheck is mailed to your house."

As I worked those hours next to a sullen Crystal, it occurred to me that I had merely changed one secret for another. The secret of my thefts from the planetarium had been uncovered, but I had a new secret, which was the reason I was leaving the job.

On the bus ride home, both of these secrets became monstrous, infected by my sense of bitterness and frustration. When I held them against the secrets I'd been probing with Adam and Juanita in the Os – real questions of life and death – my own sins simply joined the parade of secrets. Selby's secrets. The Ostyns' secrets. My parents'.

I decided to skip doing homework that night. I went right up to bed, and since the whole house seemed cold, I wrapped myself as tightly as I could beneath my comforter.

It was snowing again.

The hours passed in tension: doors locked, windows barred, bedsheets-and-towels-as-curtains drawn taut.

When the reluctant sun crested the walnuts, an ex-Marine, ex-desert-rat, ex-shoprat living in the Os started awake with a screeching hangover. Last night had been the same as the other nights. The air was icy and his blankets were thin. He padded into the kitchen to see if there was any coffee to microwave. The house behind his house had been abandoned like all of the others, and beyond the tree stumps and the wilted flowers, he made out three human silhouettes in the space between. He leaned forward to make sure he was seeing things quite clearly. His pulse kicked up a notch. *Yes, motherfuckers.* He'd lost and lost, again and again, but *I've got you, I've got you, I've got you now little bitches.*

The man hurried into his bedroom, panting, jumped into his sweats, reached behind his headboard, and palmed the Glock 9mm. He stood in his slippers with saliva flooding his mouth. The was the metal mouth he'd first tasted when he'd gotten braces in seventh grade and sliced his tongue trying to pry them out. A bite of blood and metal mingled, but he really learned what it was all about a decade later on the outskirts of Al Busayyah, where the date palms formed contours he'd never see in Akawe. A taste of what was coming. And God knows, he sick of ashes since that day, and he was so fucking sick of getting fucked with.

Reminding himself to breathe, the man slipped out his front door, backtracked along his driveway, his back to the walls, and slid around the side of the garage until he was as close to the vacant as he could get without being seen. The air was brittle with the faint stink of molding paint, but something new began to bleed through. A fog of gasoline. As the silhouetted figures left the house – two boys, three boys, four boys, five – the man stepped into full view, raised his weapon, and called out:

"Bad morning for you motherfuckers!"

The boys ran.

The man fired three shots.

One of the boys fell with a scream.

The abandoned house went up in flames.

Its massive black plume deposited shreds of the house for miles.

But the injured boy carried less blood than the house gave smoke, and the blood grew beneath him, making a perfect circle, while the boy's slayer stood in the snow and felt the metallic taste turn acidic in his mouth, his headache returning, and now he felt tired and nauseated.

The boy died. The shooter was taken into custody. Within an hour, the Sheriff's Department and the Akawe PD had the names of the other four boys. The North Side Firebugs. Their reign of flame had come to an end.

At the same precise moment, the state police swarmed a ratty, pink-and-yellow roofed party store in Shelley on the Far West End of Akawe. They came right in with their guns drawn, and the girl behind the register held her hands to her head, eyes wide in terror, and backed up against the wall.

"Where is he?" one of the cops asked.

The girl shook her said.

"I said where is he?"

"Wh – who?" the girl stammered.

"Eliseo!"

"He's. He's not in today. He's ... he's been ... he's been skipping his shifts. We ain't seen him in days."

The cops pushed around the counter, yelling to each other, spinning knobs and flipping doors open, checking the bathroom, the other bathroom, the storage closet, the little room in back with bad lighting where they kept the generator. Nothing. Nothing. Nothing. Nothing!

As they searched, the girl kept talking. The miniature barrel of the gun leveled at her head had hypnotized her. She was sure that if she could fill the air between the bullet and her face with words, she could divert it, should it try to fly:

"Mr. K says he's fired anyway, next time he comes in. Unreliable, you know? I ain't seen him. What is this all about? He do something?"

In five minutes, the staties were gone. The girl breathed out slowly. Then she knelt and cried. She held her head and shook. Another five minutes passed before she'd pulled herself enough again to pick up the phone and call Mr. K to tell him about what had happened. By then, some kid was standing at the counter, yelling at her to take his money for his fucking Funyuns.

And as that happened, back in the Os, but six whole blocks from the firebug shooting, more police and staties and sheriffs surrounded a tidy ranch house and smashed in front doors and smashed in back doors and startled Elisio's mom in her bed. She screamed in the face of the rifle, the sudden shock crowding thoughts from her head.

"Shut up!" yelled the SWAT man. "Shut up! Shut up if you don't want your brains on the ceiling!"

"Rob," said another.

"Where is Elisio?!" yelled Rob.

"I don't know!" wailed his mom. "He's gone. Moved home. To his dad's. In Israel."

And as that happened, eight-hundred miles away, at Hartfield-Jackson, the FBI – agents like blondes in slimming business suits with black briefcases, and agents like traveling contractors in greasy baseball caps and ripped jeans, and agents like the Taco Guy opening his stand for the morning – formed a loose circle around Eliseo, and he figured out what happened and knew at once that there was nothing that he could do.

They calmly put him in handcuffs.

They took a seat next to him there and read him his rights, but Eliseo didn't give a shit.

"You just chargin' me with one murder? Why not charge me with all of them?"

"Your victims. They were all Black men. You got something against Blacks, Eliseo?"

"Nah," said Eliseo. "News just doesn't cover them as much. Easier to not get caught that way. Ya' know?"

The man in black bought Eliseo a donut.

And as this happened, a man in a banged-up Aubrey ran a red light back on the West End of Akawe. And the cop two cars back saw it happen, flipped on his lights, and took off in pursuit. But as the cruiser shot across the intersection, it caught two women as they were halfway across the crosswalk. It scattered them both along the margins. In several pieces.

And as this – all of this – was happening, I was standing on the corner of Agit and Whitmore waiting for the bus to come and take me to school. I was thinking about Adam. I was thinking about how we'd played Dungeons and Dragons back in fifth and sixth grade. A module called *Bloodstone Pass*.

Bloodstone Pass had taught me that the Abyss wasn't just a place where monsters dwelled. The Abyss was an idea that once acknowledged, could establish itself anywhere within the world. Adam and I had rolled up our rangers and elves, our clerics and dwarves, pushed them up to eighteenth level because we were too impatient to get there the slow way, and then fought our way to the temple to Orcus, the bloated demon prince of unlife. There, we tried to kill him with the dice we rolled across the floor, and when the numbers they gave us told us that we'd lost – that Orcus had destroyed us and his cultists had devoured our flesh – we ignored those numbers and rolled them again. We had kept rolling the dice until we finally won. Until we'd saved the day. Good people could live again in safety and pastoral joy. In the game, we could defeat evil.

The bus must have come. I must have gotten on. The day must have passed. I told my parents that I had too much homework to also keep a job at the planetarium.

"That's okay," I said. "I don't have to have any spending money. I don't do anything anyway."

They were too absorbed with their own problems to wonder about it.

I avoided May at school, but I sat at her table sometimes. She talked about baking and cleaning her room a lot. Those seemed to be her two favorite things in the world. Lucy sat next to Eli and nuzzled into his shoulder and smiled up at him, and he smiled back through his gleaming teeth. Selby sat across from me and asked me about my plans. What I was doing. What I *wanted*. It all confused me. It all seemed pointless, and yet, weird and insincere at the same time. I must have given a decent answer because nobody stared at me.

More days passed.

On the day before Thanksgiving, Ken called.

Ken had never called me before. But, sure enough, this was his annoying voice, dripping with money and I-don't-give-a-fuck.

"Yeah?" I asked.

"Do you have a nickname?"

"What?"

"Do you have a nickname?"

"Why? Who said what?"

Ken laughed.

"Nobody said nothing," he said. "It's for Justin."

What's for Justin?

"No," I said. "I don't think."

"Just John Bridge?"

"Yeah. Why?"

"You're a perfect eleven, 'ccording to Justin. Can you come over tonight? My house?"

I was still mad at my father and didn't want to ask him for a ride, so I rode my bike over to Ken's house. I didn't really want to go, but I didn't have anything better to do that night, and I was curious. It rained, but snow was on the ground. The rain melted the snow, and once the sun sank, the water would freeze again and make the puddles into black ice. All I could do was tuck my chin into my neck and try to watch the road ahead.

Bellwood wasn't far from my house, but it was also the other side of reality. Not many maples here. Ancient beeches towered over magisterial lawns with canopies so great that you could have fit half of Agit Street inside.

Ken's driveway had a fucking gate of wrought metal, and for some reason, I didn't feel like I could ride my bike up the black pavement, so I got off and walked alongside it. A huge-ass plantation-style house with big black shutters and big white columns rose out of the mist before me. I leaned my bike against the wall, sheltered by the portico, and rang the doorbell. I was half expecting Jeeves in a red bowtie, but instead I got Ken with his shit-eating grin.

"You're soaked, dog!" he laughed. "Want a towel?"

I was about to say no, but Ken was right, so I let him lead me to a bathroom the size of my bedroom, where I roughly toweled my head and arms dry. I wondered how many bathrooms like this there were in the house, but Ken was already leading me away.

"Come on! Come on!" He took me along a blue-tiled hallway, the walls papered with velvety vertical yellow and green stripes, around a corner, and down to the basement.

The basement was a basement. I mean, the Lessards could evidently afford to heat this monster of a house – I didn't want to guess how many thousands of dollars they dropped on *that* each year – so I couldn't figure out why they weren't able to buy some floor lamps or nice rugs for this dank, cavernous space. What I did notice, between the gray-painted floor and the exposed pipes on the ceiling, was a broad, cinder-block wall that had been sprayed with all the aerosol that Bellwood would never suffer on its manicured streets.

I could tell that two people had done this, and that they were Ken and Justin. Both of them knew more about it than I ever would.

Ken had obviously been working on his murals for days. I could see smudges where he had fixed a false start. Time when his parents would have rather he'd been doing his homework or playing lacrosse or whatever other shit they did up here. *Why is he even in the public schools?* I wondered. "LESSART" his inscriptions went, and he tried them out in fire oranges and reds, with moony whites and berry blues, rough angles and bubble bright, lustral and dun.

Urbantasm: The Darkest Road

Justin's tags were more fluidly executed. They each reminded me of a different photograph of the same face; the same shapes and lines and angles comprised each tag, but slight variations projected shifts in mood, need, and attitude. He had performed them each in just two colors, black and green, but the way one swipe glided into another created a whole universe of shade and contour. Justin's tags were all brothers, but none of them were the same. "Raygun" he called himself, though you could scarcely make out the individual letters in the labyrinthine mazes he'd woven.

"I crib a Philly style," Justin said, suddenly at my side. "I like it more."

"Yeah?" I asked, startled.

"No need to get too pretty. Get it said and get done."

Ken slouched, quietly offended.

"So," I said. "Why did you want me to come here? Ken said I was ... a perfect eleven? What's that even mean?"

"I saw you at the rave last month," Justin said. He was wearing the same stinky hoodie he always wore. He smelled like he hadn't bathed in several days, but he was watching me with his serious dark eyes, and even Ken managed to shut the fuck up.

"I saw you too," I said. "What you know about it?"

"You do that O-Sugar?"

"No." The questions were weird to me. "Do you?"

"No. Don't need to. You don't have a nickname, do you?"

"Not that I know of."

"Word. So, I don't know if Ken told you, but we're both Arithmancers. Well, really, we're just Arithmancers in training, and nobody's there to teach us, so we just have to figure it out on our own?"

"Arithmancers?"

"Numerologists. Studiers of numbers. And the numbers you have in your life are occulted in your name, and they tell a lot about you. We noticed you were a perfect eleven, so we wanted to see what you knew."

"What do you mean? What's a perfect eleven?"

"Every letter in your name counts for a single number," said Ken, suddenly eager. "The numbers start as A is one and count on up to nine. Then at J you go back to one. See, you never get higher than nine. And when you add them all up, you get your name number."

"See, we did it for you," said Justin, holding up a college-ruled notebook, where I saw the names of all of my friends, and several strangers, with numbers tabulated from their names.

263

Near the bottom, I saw my own name:

J O H N B R I D G E

1 6 8 5 2 9 9 4 7 5 = 56 = 5+6 = 11

"But you said that the numbers only go up to nine," I said. "But eleven is bigger than nine. But one plus one is two. So, doesn't that mean I'm a perfect two?"

"Two ain't perfect," said Justin. "Anyway, eleven is special. Eleven is its own thing."

"And what does eleven mean?"

"It means you're like a more powerful version of a two. Like you're a supercharged two. You're deep and you think deeper things than the rest of us. You see the whole universe, so you sometimes miss the little down tiny things that happen."

"I guess I don't get it," I said. "I mean ... doesn't this just mean if my parents had given me a slightly different name – like if they just named me 'Jon' instead of 'John,' – I'd have a totally different personality?"

Ken shook his head in contempt, but Justin watched me steadily.

"That's exactly what it means," he said.

I didn't know what to say then. Part of me was annoyed that I'd ridden my bike through the freezing rain just so they could tell me that the letters of my name added up to a magic number. I was a little unnerved by Justin's unwavering seriousness, but I also wanted to wipe the smirk off Ken's face.

"So, what if I changed my name?" I asked. "Because people can do that. What if I walked into a court and changed my name to Jon?"

Now Ken stepped up. "Then your personality would change, John! Jesus, we think we control so much, but just giving it up to the reality would give us a lot more control, you know? Don't you know that everything around you makes a difference in who you are? The letters in your name?"

"Word," said Justin.

"The stars when you were born?" Ken went on.

"Word," said Justin.

"The lines in your palm?!"

"Yes, that," said Justin.

I was speechless at the size of their bullshit. I'd known Ken was a jackass from the moment I first met him, but Justin had always been an enigma. Evidently, the enigma was an idiot. I couldn't stop myself.

"That's fucking stupid," I said.

Ken sneered, but Justin continued to watch me.

"You never took O-Sugar?" he asked again.

"No!" I said.

"You ever see ghosts?"

"No! I don't believe in ghosts!"

"You ever like to take walks at night?"

"No, I –" but I *did* take walks at night. The nightwalks I took were the best, the most perfect –

"You ever go astral walking?"

"What?!"

"You ever see blue ghosts?"

"I told you –"

"You ever see blue things that aren't supposed to be there?"

"I –"

His questions didn't have anything to do with reality. This didn't have anything to do with getting good grades or getting back with Omara or getting past my fucking drunk father or getting out of Akawe or ...

"I –" I stammered.

"Told you," Justin said, grinning at Ken, who grinned right back. "A perfect eleven. He takes night walks. Takes astral walks. Sees blue ghosts. The best prophets don't even know they are! Don't listen to those ghosts, John. They're real but they can't talk to you. If they talk to you, they're just telling lies."

"What are they?" I asked, and realized that by asking I was admitting to something.

"The spirits of the dead!" Ken intoned.

"Nah," said Justin. "They're nothing but a candle's leftovers. Just a shadow of the past. Leave them alone, and they won't bother you. Count to eight and get them gone. But don't tell me you ain't a perfect eleven. You've seen all the perfect eleven shit. You've gone astral walking. You've seen the blue things. You just told me."

Justin walked silently over to the wall and picked up a can of spray paint, already over the conversation.

"Well," I said, stammering, looking for something to say. "What are you then?"

"Raygun," said Justin. "A five. I'm a number of confusion. That means

I'm confused. I'm the number of looking for answers. That's why I wanted to ask you, Mr. Eleven: have you seen the blue things? And I asked you, and you said yes, and now I know."

I didn't feel like riding my bike back home, so I walked it through the ice and slush, even though my fingers burned and my knuckles turned red. At least the rain had stopped. When I got home, I heard the low rumble of my parents arguing upstairs.

I kicked off my shoes and socks, picked up the portable phone, and took it into the study.

I couldn't remember May's phone number, so I picked up the phone book, found her number, and dialed.

May answered almost at once. *Does anyone else in that house ever answer the phone?*

"Hi May, it's John."

"Hi, John! I knew you'd call me sometime."

"Yeah. Um. So, you know how in your notes you've been asking if we're still going out?"

"Yeah?"

"Yeah. Um. I don't think we should go out anymore. I think we should break up."

"Oh. Okay. I kind of thought you might want to break up. You just never talk to me, you know?"

"I know. I'm sorry. I've been kind of a jerk. And I didn't want to hurt your –"

She laughed. Loudly.

"Why are you laughing?" I asked.

"Oh, I'm just ... I'm just watching *Dave's World*. It's really funny. Have you seen it? He dresses up like this doctor, and there's this tattoo of a bunny with a stick in him, and I'm –"

"Right, but I didn't want to –"

"I can't hear you, John. Just a minute. Drake! Turn down the volume, okay! I can't hear John!"

A pause.

"Okay," she said. "I can hear you now."

"I said I didn't want to hurt your feelings," I said.

"That's okay," she said. "I didn't want to hurt your feelings either."

"What do you mean?"

"Well, we were sort of going out, but not going out, you know?"

"I don't understand."

"I mean, I said, we didn't talk, we didn't kiss, we didn't you know, or didn't do anything else together. But I thought you might be feeling bad, and it would make you feel worse if I broke up with you. You know? So I thought I'd wait until you felt better. But you broke up with me first, so now you must feel better, right?"

"Um ..." I said. I wondered what Drake made of this conversation.

"It's kind of good, a timing thing, because there is this really cute boy in my English class and I think he wants to ask me out – or, oh my God, maybe I'll ask him out! – but it was going to be not fun dumping you to do it, and now I don't have to, and you are happy, and it's just the best way things could go, right?"

"Um. Yeah."

"Okay, John! Don't worry about me. I'm doing great, and I'm glad that you are great, too. And the best part is, I can still say LYLAB because before it was 'love you like a boyfriend,' but now I can say 'love you like a brother.' Anyway, I don't think we were meant to be together forever anyway. I mean, if we can't even go out once or twice on a date, then it probably wasn't even a real thing, right? And anyway, there are plenty of fish in the sea, and I'm going to catch a really big fish! But you're a nice fish too, John. I'm glad that we are friends together!"

"Thanks, I –"

"I should go, though. I don't want to miss the end of my show."

"Okay. Sure."

"I'll see you in school tomorrow. Only I won't because tomorrow's Thanksgiving. Gobble gobble! I'll see you in school on Monday, John. Happy Turkey Day! Happy Thanksgiving!"

"You too."

She hung up.

On Thanksgiving, my parents and I rode out to Elmwood, pretending to be friendly to one another. We passed the Tent and Tarp Shop, and it surprised me. As if I shouldn't have expected to see it. As if it hadn't been there all alone. *Where is Lucy now?* I wondered. *With Eli? What are they doing?* I heard my teeth grinding together.

We left the city, driving the wooded bluff that overlooked the Zibi. We passed a row of houses with wide views of the valley below. Simple ranch houses. They weren't large or elegant, but they had always been occupied. Now, every third house out here was empty and plywooded up. Akawean decay, it seemed, was now spreading beyond its own city limits.

When we got to Grandmother Richter's, Uncle Patrie was already standing in the kitchen with a beer in one hand and a glass of wine in the other.

"Hi Mark," he said, "can I grab you a Bud?"

"No thanks," my father said and hurried from the room.

"Hello there, John!" sweeted my Aunt Rosie. "Did you bring your girlfriend again this year, dear?"

"No," I said. "I don't have a girlfriend anymore."

"You'll take care of that soon enough," she said. "You're growing into a very handsome young man. She doesn't know what she's missing out on!"

Yes, she does, I thought. *That's why she dumped me.*

One room over, Tim and Lince were arguing over something. I went into the kitchen to get some coffee. I found Grandmother Richter alone in there, hovering over the edge of the stove, basting the turkey, and basting it some more.

"Happy Thanksgiving, John," she said with wet eyes, and asked if I'd set the table in a minute.

I went into the living room to see Tim and Lince, but they had left. Instead, I found my father kneeling in front of the record player. He dropped the needle. Ameliorating violins sang together. My father smiled.

"Carlos Gardel," he said. "Pour Una Cerveza."

A man's honeyed voice swam into the moment. The gold and gray upholstered chair where my grandfather had always sat was empty in the corner. The television was off. Two jays fought on a birdfeeder in the front yard. A dreary light trickled in through the narrow windows.

For the next hour, I wandered from room to room, politely brushing off obligatory questions, reading the titles of dusty books where they sat, and moving the glass paperweights from one shelf to the next. We finally gathered at the table, where yet another empty chair awaited Grandfather Richter, our own Eli, and Uncle Patrie, the oldest male of sound mind and soundish body, said the Protestant prayer:

"Come, Lord Jesus, be our Guest;
And bless what you have bestowed.
For since men landed on Plymouth rock
you've endowed your flock with common stock."

Despite my grandmother's latter-day basting, the turkey was dry, with steam rising off its parched breast bones. The ham was worse – slimy and undercooked – and I took a few furtive bites before hiding the crimson chunks among the green bean casserole. The marshmallow yams did better, though.

"There's a story behind this recipe, you know," said Rosie Petrie, and so she told us again: "Back after the Civil War was over, people wanted to reconcile the brothers of the South and the North, so they decided to make a recipe with the food from each place. Yams grew in the south, and maple syrup was from the north, and so syruped yams became a Thanksgiving tradition! I guess somewhere in there, people started using marshmallows instead of maple syrup. Whatever! I always thought this recipe was appropriate for our family because dad decided to move us up here because Michigan had less crime and more jobs than Tennessee. Great job, Dad! We all saw how that worked out!"

Aunt Rosie laughed merrily. Most of the others chuckled half-heartedly. My mother and father and I were silent.

I looked at Tim beside me. He was tired, maybe, because his mother had gotten him up early to watch the Macy's parade, then drive ninety miles for this family party. I imagined Adam sitting there instead. I imagined Lucy. I imagined Omara.

"Won't you have some ham?" my grandmother had asked Omara the year before.

"No thank you," she had said. "I don't eat ham."

"Are you a vegetarian?" Rosie had said, her voice already warbling with disapproval.

"No," Omara had answered. "I love meat. But I don't eat ham because I'm Muslim."

"Oh my!" Rosie had exclaimed.

I had dropped my knife and fork, ready to leap to my girlfriend's defense, but she beat me to the punch.

"We have Thanksgiving stories too," she'd said. "My uncle told me about sergeant Nicholas Said during the Civil War. He had been enslaved by the Ottomans, but then he came to the United States. He lived in Detroit. He fought for the North. And he was a Muslim."

I would have given anything to have had her at my side. Or Chris. Or Michael. Even May, in her clueless decency, would have been someone I could look at and let my eyes say, *can you believe this shit?*

I tried to ignore the conversation and focus on the food, but none of it was very good. Even the green bean casserole tasted stale and a bit off. *How do you mess up green bean casserole?* I wondered. *It all comes from a can!* If anything, the food should have been even better than before. Now that my grandfather had died, my grandmother didn't have to change his diaper, hide the guns, or keep him from climbing into the bathtub with all his clothes on. And yet everything tasted rough and confused, as if she'd been fussing with the recipes, not letting them rest, adding too much flour, too much salt, one pinch after another. As if she'd kept opening the oven door to peek at the pie crust. She had always been the best cook in my whole extended family. I never imagined that my grandfather, that colossal pain-in-the-ass, could have made her life more bearable, simply by being here. But that was the only explanation that made sense today. I found myself watching Grandmother Richter as she sawed at her piece of turkey, not really listening to what was going on around her.

Then my Aunt Dulce held a writhing hand out over the middle of the table.

"... put his hand in the glove?!" she said. "My goodness! I mean, my God. I mean, I swear the prosecution was bribed by the defense!"

"Well," said Rosie. "Are you really surprised that a jury of his peers didn't convict him? You know he held the knife just as easy as Ross has that carving knife right there."

"You know they were cheering him on when he was on the run!" said Dulce. "You know they wanted him to get out to Mexico!"

"Haha," said my Uncle Patrie, belatedly. "I'm not holding the knife that easily, really."

"Well, they're never happy with what they get," said Rosie. "No matter how much they get."

She keeps saying 'they' because she knows that if she says 'the Blacks,' it'll sound racist.

"It's just like here," Rosie went on. "I remember the block busting years. People kept selling their houses, and they kept moving in. Some of us tried to make a stand for it out on the West Side, but they just kept coming. There wasn't any end to them. They weren't going to be happy until they had the whole neighborhood to themselves. Well, they got it. Then they wrecked it. Just like we knew they would. They'd move into a house, and they wouldn't take care of it, and that would make a bunch of neighbors on the block put *their* houses up for sale, and so it just kept going and going. It's bad enough what they did to Akawe, and then they had to push out X out, too."

"Rosie," said my father. "You don't know what you're talking about. Would you please shut up?"

The table fell silent.

Not just the voices, but all the silverware. The knives and forks stopped moving across the plates.

"Excuse me?" Rosie finally said.

"*They* didn't have anything to do with X leaving. X left when they couldn't annex their suburban factories and get taxpayers to pay for the upgrade. X left because it was cheaper to set up shop in Kentucky and Mexico, and there wasn't anything *anyone* in Akawe could do to stop them."

"That doesn't mean –"

"Do you remember why your father moved to Akawe? I think you do, because you said it a little bit ago: for the jobs. You moved from Tennessee, and you got those jobs. I grew up here, and *I* got that job. You know who didn't get those jobs? The same people you're talking about! African-Americans who moved up here from the South. They showed up, but they didn't get jobs, or they got shit jobs. And they couldn't even go out and buy a house because for decades, they weren't allowed to buy in those neighborhoods you're all talking about. They all got pushed into a couple tiny neighborhoods not fit for rats because nobody else would have them. To Sycamore Grove and Eden. So, of course, they moved out the first chance they had. You would've done the same!"

"You know about Eden?" I said.

I had spoken before I could stop myself. I was so surprised to hear this word – *Eden* – used to describe a neighborhood in Akawe, coming from my father's mouth, that I had forgotten for a moment that I was still angry at him.

He looked just as surprised. I couldn't tell whether he was surprised because I didn't sound mad or because of the question I had asked. He turned the same question back to me.

"You know about Eden?" he said.

"It was the neighborhood between the river and the factories. Across the river from the Os. It was the neighborhood where the Blacks used to live."

"Yes," my father said. "My family lived on the other side of the factory from Eden. It's gone now."

He looked down at his dirty plate as if his half-eaten dinner was a map of the dying city.

"They took Eden down for the expressway," he said. "It was polluted. X polluted it."

I watched my father, waiting for him to say something else. Everyone waited. My father helped himself to more of the slippery ham. He got a large dollop of mashed potatoes, then drizzled gravy all over it. He took a big bite, chewed, and swallowed.

"I'm not a racist," said Rosie. "I just think, after everything we've lost – all of us – they should ... appreciate. And contribute."

"They all did more with less than any of you have," my father said calmly. "More than me too. My friend Mark Adams grew up in Eden. His wife Kitty grew up in Sycamore Grove. They both lost their houses because of the interstate. Moved into public housing. The whole nine yards. They have a son who is a senior and a daughter who is John's age. They named them Darius and Quanla. Darius because he was the Persian conqueror, and Quanla because, I don't know, I guess they thought it sounded like it was from the continent. Good for them. They live out on the West End, where you guys ran away from. Good for them. Their house is worth half of what mine is, even though it's in way better shape. That's their neighborhood. Even though they always mow the lawn and don't have moss growing on the damn shingles. They got it paid off, though. Good for them. He still has his goddamn job. Good for them. I'm glad."

My mother smiled her natural smile, but her face was as pale as her napkin. And I missed Quanla with an ache so big I couldn't see the bottom.

"Martin wouldn't have liked this conversation," muttered my grandmother.

Shocked silence couldn't stand forever.

Rosie retreated crying into the bathroom. My father grunted, and Dulce slapped Patrie's face and cursed his reticence. Lince stared. Tim smirked. My mother apologized to Grandmother Richter on my father's behalf. My father apologized to Grandmother Richter on his own behalf. Hearing this, Rosie came back into the room, putting on her magnanimity. My father succinctly explained that he was apologizing to Grandmother Richter, not Rosie.

My head was full of *Eden*, and I wanted to be alone. I dabbed the cranberry from my lips and excused myself. I passed a brass-gilt cage with a little yellow bird inside. I couldn't remember having ever seen it before. It was a new thing, and it was singing and beating its wings as it went around in circles.

I passed through the living room and saw people that I hadn't seen in years. I turned down the front hall and saw people I had heard about but had never met before. There was an ache within me. A pain on the back of my neck that ran the length of my spine. *That canary, I guess.* I climbed the cold and creaking stairs to the second floor and heard a golden voice coming from my mother's childhood bedroom.

"Aren't you thirsty?" it asked. "Won't you taste it?"

"What does it taste like?" I asked.

"It's delicious," said the woman's voice.

I stood on the landing for a moment, breathing. I wasn't afraid of getting hurt. I was afraid of what I might learn. But I had been asking questions, and having opened that door, I didn't think that I could shut it again. I stepped into my mother's room.

I expected to feel the draft from the cracks in the too-tall windows that ran almost from the ceiling to the floor, and crusted on the inside with frost each winter. I expected to feel the shag carpet underfoot, and to see folded clothes on every surface, and the small and ancient TV sitting on top of the dresser. Instead, I was standing in a room as large as the whole house, its yolk-colored walls rising toward a high ceiling embroidered with treacle traceries of schooners sailing upon a sea of milk. In the center of the room, a crystal chandelier hung as low as a fallen angel. Four squat chairs surrounded the chandelier, balanced on bowing hardwood legs, plushed in shades of velvet violet and sinuous green, and beneath the chandelier sat a tiny, circular, wooden table. The table was set with a gold-gilt pink china tea set, and a thick pulp paperback.

A woman sat in one of the chairs, facing the table, angled away from me. As I entered, she turned to look at me, and I recognized her as the girl in the gold-green one-piece swimsuit from my dreams. She was older now. Before,

274

she had been my age. Now she was an adult. Younger than my parents. Twenty-something. She was even more beautiful now than she had been as a girl, and she wore an unadorned gold-green ball gown that flowed about her like an ocean swell.

"I thought you were just a dream," I said.

"I am more than a dream," she said. "But I am less than someone that you can touch."

"I had a friend once," I said. "A maple tree. She said you hated me."

"Have a drink," said she said, offering me a teacup.

"What is it?"

"Hot chocolate."

I lifted the cup to my lips and took a sip. It *was* delicious. Creamy and dark and rich and –

"Are we going to be safe from Eden?" I asked.

"Who?"

"Lucy? Or Selby? Or me?"

"Nobody's safe from Eden. I know better than anybody. Do you want me to tell you about it?"

"I thought I wanted to know about it. But now I think that I just want to be safe from it. To keep my friends safe from it."

"How can you be safe from it if you don't know what it is? How can you hide from your enemies if you don't know who they are?"

"Who are they?"

"Who do you think they are?"

I needed something to do with my hands. I grabbed the book from the table. It was *Les Misérables.* Victor Hugo. The gold-green woman watched me as I thumbed through its pages. My mind raced through the names I had learned with Adam. EZ. Trace. Ash. Spark. And God. I had a strong feeling that this woman was reading my mind, so I tucked the book under my arm and took another sip of cocoa.

"God's children," I finally said. "Especially Eli. Does she really want to be with him?" I asked.

"What do you think?"

"She seems to like him. But she deserves to know what he is."

"And what is he?"

"He's a pimp."

"Then you should tell her. He's had a hard life. A strange life. I wanted to help him. I tried to help him. But if you tell your friend what you fear, she can decide for herself."

"I'm a little bit worried about what she'll decide, though."

"I'm a bit worried about what you'll decide."

I took another sip of the cocoa. With every taste, I felt the warmth and bitter sweetness flood through me, and I felt like I had a deeper understanding of the gold-green woman, even though she hadn't told me much.

"Why?" I asked. "Why are you worried about what I'll decide?"

"Because so much depends upon you."

"What depends upon me?"

"You should ask Selby about her grandmother," the woman said. "You should ask her about Florica."

"Florica?"

"She was a tale to tell."

The woman watched me as I finished the cocoa, wiping my mouth with the back of my hand.

"I don't know what I did that was wrong to you," I said. "But I'm sorry if I hurt you. I want to be a good person. I want to do good things."

She watched me. She didn't blink. I started to wonder if maybe I had gone a little bit insane.

"It's the water, isn't it?" I asked.

She crooked her eyebrow in confusion.

"Am I going crazy?" I asked.

She sighed.

276

The next three days of Thanksgiving Break passed. I didn't fill these days with rumors and adventures. 1995 was worn out. I sat in my bedroom and listened to my father shuffling from room to room below. The sun went down, it got late, and my mother got home, the lights of the Benedict carving the cracks in the driveway. I stared at my dingy walls and hated them. I started, furtively, reading *Les Misérables.*

At first, I thought it was more challenging than anything I had read before – a thick book with thick words thrown into a whirlwind – but I didn't give up, probably because there just wasn't anything else to do. I settled into the rhythm of the story. The narrative alternated anecdotes and homilies, but I was Catholic, so it wasn't too hard to follow. The bishop met with a revolutionary and realized the man wasn't a total shit. The bishop took in a thief and told him that he wasn't a total shit, either. The thief stole the bishop's candlestands. Then the thief also stole money from a kid on a country road. This thief seemed to be a real asshole. But I remembered that I, too, had once taken a pair of sunglasses that wasn't mine, not to mention all the times I'd been wrong to Michael and Lucy, so I went on reading in my dingy bedroom.

Another week passed. More snow fell. It got cold. I kept reading. The thief changed his name and ways and made himself rich. He was trying to be a just man. He was trying to help a prostitute. My brain felt warm and my hands felt cold and everything felt muffled. *If Jean can turn his whole life around and save peoples' lives after all those years in prison, then I should be able to warn Lucy about Eli.*

The next day, or maybe it was the next Monday, whatever, I took the bus past my stop and rode another twenty minutes to the Tent and Tarp Shop. Passing cars had waked the snow into thigh-high drifts. My pants got soaked, and I felt like a dumbass, but I went up to the side door and banged four times.

I hadn't called or said anything about showing up tonight. That was part of my plan. I didn't want to be expected. But I also realized, just now, that I hadn't stood at this side door since St. Patrick's Day in 1994. It all looked the same: Lucy's house. The Tent and Tarp Shop. *Maybe we can pretend it back! Maybe we can repeat what happened before and get it right this time! We can go out again. This time Lucy can tell me any secret she wants. I will listen and understand, and I won't just ... whatever. I'll just listen. I'll just be there!* This thought felt so good, so potential, after the days and weeks of fatigue, that I just let the possibility wash over me. *I still adore you. You are lilacs! You are amazing, incredible, beautiful, immaculate! Maybe we should be together! Even after everything that has happened. Especially after everything that has happened.*

Then the door opened, and Lucy appeared.

"John?" she said, surprise written all over her face.

"Hey," I said. Then I shuffled, trying to remember the script I'd composed for myself during the bus ride. "We haven't hung out in a while, you know? I mean, we haven't talked."

"Yeah. I know. Um. You just want to hang out?"

"Yeah, I ..."

"It's fine. It's just, um, I've already got company, you know? But you can come in."

Eli's here! I thought. *I'm going to have to brush it off. I'll just have to hang out with the two of them for an hour and leave like nothing's weird about it.*

I stepped inside and took my boots off, and Lucy led me through the kitchen where I had first seen her close her eyes. She led me through the living room where we had kissed for the first time. Once again, plastic candles were glowing in the frosted windows, just as they had two years before.

"John?" said Selby. She was standing next to one of those windows, bathed in the golden glow of the fake candlelight. Her boots were lying sideways near the front door, and she looked just as wet and weather-beaten as I must have. "What are you doing here?"

"Um ... I just wanted to hang out with Lucy. You, um ..." I was trying to figure out if it was better or worse to have Selby here than Eli. Eli was an enemy. He came from a family of enemies. But I had come here specifically to spill Selby's secrets. I needed to say something innocuous.

"You take the bus here?" I asked.

"No. Demetrius dropped me off."

Lucy's mom sat on the couch, and I realized that I was interrupting the infrared call-and-response between the cracked remote and the grainy television.

"Sorry," I mumbled, stepping back.

"Lucy, why don't you three go upstairs if you're going to talk. And next time, let me know if you have friends coming over."

"I didn't *know*," Lucy said. "They just showed up."

And just like that, we were following Lucy through the back hallway, around the bend, and up the narrow stairs that led to the second floor and the bedroom where I'd find all of her totems and protections. Her five maiden courtiers frowning upon me in disappointment and disapproval. Maybe they liked Eli more than me. For a moment, I even thought of saying some bullshit and leaving that house right then ... but Selby was walking behind me, and she had to be wondering why I was there. Now I wished that I hadn't spent all of those lunches in the library so that a sudden visit to Lucy wouldn't have seemed so weird. *Should I explain more? No! Too many explanations just sound unnatural.* And by the time I'd completed this thought, we were through the door and inside Lucy's room, and I realized that a lot *had* changed since we had dated.

The four white walls were bare now. A single white lightbulb hung from what I was pretty sure had been a light fixture before, and its glare made the walls so painfully bright that it was hard to look at anything other than the floor. The only decoration was the wrinkled poster from a Sheryl Crow concert.

"But, where –" I started.

Lucy turned around to look at me, confused. Selby bumped into me from behind.

"Move," she said.

The blankets were piled upon a mattress on the floor. Lucy's bed was gone. Papers and clothes mounded everywhere. It was even messier than I remembered. Lucy sat down on the mattress. Selby sat against the wall beneath the single window. She smiled, but there was a grimness in her expression. Or maybe it was just the shadow from her brow down over her chin and face. In the same light, Lucy looked positively ghoulish. She had, if anything, lost weight since seventh grade. Now, when her brow furrowed in worry, as it so often did, she looked much older.

"You can sit wherever, John," she said.

I nudged aside some t-shirts and a discarded bra and took a seat against the wall, across from Lucy and Selby.

"So, what's up?" Lucy said. "This is weird ... or something. Selby, we haven't hung out besides lunch in weeks. I don't even remember the last time you were over here –"

"It was the summer," Selby cut in.

"And John, we haven't hung out since –"

"I know," I said, not wanting her to finish. *Does she ever think about Mendocino anymore?* I wanted to ask her, but I knew it would seem strange to both of them.

"So what if you got here and nobody was here?" Lucy asked.

"If nobody was home," Selby said, "John and I would've run into each other. We would've taken the bus back together. It wouldn't be a big deal or nothing."

Lucy seemed to forget the coincidence, but I could feel Selby glancing at me out of the corner of her eye. She was curious. *She does suspect! She knows, somehow, that she's why I'm here!*

"So," Lucy said. "What have you guys been up to? John, you broke up with May?"

"Um, yeah ..."

"Why?"

"Because she was kind of –"

"May is a retard," said Selby. "And John's an asshole. They were the stupidest couple I've ever seen."

"May is my *friend*," said Lucy. "She's super nice. Even if she isn't, um, that smart –"

"May is fine," I said. "It just wasn't working out. We didn't have nothing to talk about."

"What about Adam?" Selby challenged. "You have anything to talk about with him lately?"

"Huh?"

"You and Adam. You ever see him anymore?"

"I see him a bit. In the halls and ..."

Selby grinned.

"Okay, fine!" I said, putting on my pissed-off voice. I knew I could conceal any deception beneath honest irritation. "My father's a recovering alcoholic, right? Only he ain't recovering anymore. He just lost his job, and now he's drunk every day. He thinks he's hiding it, but he's not. And my mother's pretty checked out too. So, you can laugh at me because I know I'm a fucking idiot, because I thought I could get out of this shitty ... but now I don't think anyone gets out of here. So, uh, yeah, I haven't seen much of y'all lately, but I guess I did see Adam. I stayed with him when my father was drunk, and I was skipping school."

"You stayed with him at Grandpa M's?"

"What kind of question is that?" I answered lamely.

Selby shrugged. "Adam stays all over the place. I didn't know where you might've gone. What kind of stories you might have heard."

Bullshit, I thought.

"That reminds me," I said. "I thought you might be able to tell me something about your grandma Florica."

Selby's eyes widened.

"What do you want to know about my bunică?

"I don't know. I think I heard your mom mention that she'd had an interesting life." This was a lie, but a plausible one.

" *When* did she mention it?"

"It wasn't recently. It was a while ago."

"Like a month ago?"

"Like a couple of years ago."

"And you're asking about her now?"

"I did that report on Romania in eighth grade. I felt bad that I didn't ever ask you about your family's experience." *This* was true.

Selby watched me intently. I could almost hear her sifting through memories to see whether or not they aligned.

"But how you been, Selby?" asked Lucy. She hadn't caught the strange energy buzzing through the room, and Selby smiled at her warmly.

"Me?" she said. "Oh, I been hangin' out in the Os."

Lucy laughed nervously.

"Hangin' out with Chalks," Selby went on.

"Don't," said Lucy, abruptly. "They're bad. They do bad things."

"We both sit at their table, Lucy."

"Not their table. Their brothers' table. Eli isn't a Chalk."

"Isn't he? I can't never tell with Eli. When he's with you, he talks about how much he hates all the gangsta shit. Blazin' and blastin' and slingin' and pimpin'. But after he's been staying with Ash ..."

"He ain't with Ash when he can help it! He don't like Ash!"

"Or when he's with EZ."

"EZ's different. EZ doesn't do Chalk shit no more."

Selby waited a moment before continuing.

"Okay," she finally said. "Well, look, I ain't here just to 'hang out' and 'catch up' like John says he is. I'm here because I want to give you some advice."

"Who says I want your advice?" Lucy asked, her voice suddenly acidic in a way I'd never heard before.

Selby was on her feet before I knew what was happening. Her head hit the naked light bulb, and it bounced where it hung, knocking our shadows sideways. Lucy started to stand up, but Selby cut her down at once:

"Sit down, bitch!" she said.

For the first time, I perceived Selby's real mass – her height and weight – contrasted with Lucy's. Selby was solid. She could have crushed Lucy, and Lucy knew it. She could have crushed me, too. I watched her anxiously.

"I'ma give you advice," Selby said. "I'ma tell you some shit. So don't make me throw you down the stairs for your mama to see."

Was this the person I'd known since preschool? Who had kissed me behind the foundry, and blackmailed her brother to take ballet lessons? Who shared her weed with me on the front porch and told me about the urbantasms?

But Lucy had changed, too. Now she knew the rules of this new game that she had decided to play. She sat deferentially down upon her mattress again, her knees drawn up to her chin, but her eyes accusing Selby of all sorts of things.

"You know where this is going," Selby said. "That's why you steppin' up. It ain't worth it. Not what they have waiting for you if you stay with him. You know Eli's a pimp. You know he's getting girls for the Chalks. And you gotta dump him, Lucy. You gotta get away from that family. They have blood on them. Bad shit's gonna happen to you if you don't. It's your own fault if you don't do it."

Lucy's hands were trembling with anger, but she looked determinedly at the floor.

"Eli doesn't like doing what he has to do," she said. "And he's going to get away as soon as he can. But he can't right now. And you think those girls are coming from ... from happy houses? You think they've got a mom like yours who feeds them every day? And they don't get pimped out, anyway. Eli's dad knows some landlords over there. Most of the time, they just, just get them a place to stay. *Off* the streets. Don't you think that keeps 'em from hoing? See, you don't know so much. And now you talk shit to me. Tell me to *dump* him? It's just because you know you can beat my ass, but do you think you can take EZ? You think you could take Ash? Shit, any one of them could take you out, Selby. Any of Eli's brothers. Any of the Chalks. Now, what do you think's gonna happen when they find out you're saying this shit?"

Selby smiled sadly.

"How are they going to find out?" she asked.

The question waited for an answer, but Lucy refused to give it.

"You aren't going to tell them," Selby said. "Because you aren't violent like they are. And that's how I know that you don't belong with them."

"With him ..." I offered. It was the first thing I had said in several minutes.

Lucy fanned her fingers through her hair.

She pulled on her hair.

"What makes you think," she said, "that you know where I belong? Or who I belong with? You don't know half as much as you think you do. Either of you."

She lifted her eyes to Selby.

"And I don't like some heifer come in here and try to tell me to dump my boyfriend!"

I braced for Selby's retaliation, but it didn't come. Selby chuckled.

"Lucy, you can't talk ghetto, but Jesus can't keep you from trying."

It was still weeks until Christmas Break. I was already sick of it all.

Mr. Esper gave me back my essay on "Sinners in the Hands of an Angry God" with notes telling me that I had written it too quickly and hadn't developed my argument about implicit complicity. I humored him and rewrote the thing.

Mrs. Clark gave me back a test with an 'F,' showing that I *still* didn't know shit about adenosine triphosphate. She offered for me to retake the test, but if I couldn't understand the thing after all this time, I wasn't going to figure it out in another two days.

Only Miss Pavilik seemed to get it, speaking softly through dimmed lights about projected images. The Main Sequence of star evolution. Spectrography. Nuclear fusion. Gravity. Her quiet class was as close as I got to happy those days.

One day, Quanla called and left a message that she wanted to see *The Nutcracker* with Michael and Selby and me.

"Chuck's playing the Mouse King!" her excited voice played over the tape. "They usually don't cast someone that young in a part that big. There are professionals up there. I mean, if they didn't think he could handle it, they'd have hired a professional!"

I didn't call her back. As much as I had missed Quanla that Thanksgiving – her voice and her mind – I couldn't see myself sitting in the dark with Selby and her suspicion for two whole hours. I was also worried about seeing Chuck for the first time since junior high. But I missed the show for nothing: Michael called later and told me that Selby hadn't come and that Chuck had been too busy with the cast afterward to meet up.

I was mad at myself for that. Maybe a bit of stage magic could have brought me back. A flood of fog, a summiting sound from the orchestra pit, and then the candletipped Christmas tree would have grown huge, inexplicably, although really it was just the fly cables lifting its crown fifty feet in the air and unpuddling the yards of green fabric hidden upstage behind the set. And when the intermission came, Quanla could have said something funny about Omara and something kind about Selby. Something wise about all of the falling apart in our collective worlds, because she noticed things that I did not.

Instead, I sat alone in my room doing who knows what. I don't remember. Listening to music? Staring at the ceiling? Not homework. I'd already given up on homework. Not a play rehearsal. Not work at the planetarium. Nothing memorable. Nothing worthwhile.

I had also wondered whether Akawe's unending run of bad news – the arsons, the serial killer, the poisoned water, the factory closings – meant that I wouldn't see many Christmas lights that year. After all, you don't put out Christmas lights for yourself. You can't see them when you're inside your house, safe and warm. You put up Christmas lights for other people to enjoy. People had to focus on their own survival.

At least I was wrong about that.

Less than two weeks into December, millions of lights went up all over the city. Tiny multicolored incandescents strung between porches and trees, giant C9s staking out the silhouettes of flat and vaulted rooflines, bubble lights and icicle lights, orange and red, blue and silver, rosy pink and tallstrunt essenced, sharp sapped, pinned stars, snowmen, and reindeer landing pads above harrowed windows where pink candles, sometimes real, sainted their sills with latter-day haloes. The prevalence of these displays expanded with Akawe's dissolutions. Every time a factory closed, it subtracted light from the city. The Christmas lights replaced this, at least a little, at least for the moment. Even the snow obliged, reflecting its own softer versions of the interlaced patterns in signatures as singular as snowflake thumbprints.

One afternoon, when I got home from school, I found my father shuffling along the edge of the roof, lining it with multicolored lights. When he finished, I took an all-white strand and plugged it into the last string. I unrolled it across our driveway and into the vacant lot on the east. Then, uncoiling as I went, I lay out a large rectangle on the ground to make the place where Archie's house had once stood.

One day, my parents and I rolled along from one Christmas tree farm to the next before we settled on a spikey blue spruce and flew it through the front doors without dropping a single needle. Lights and garlands, bulbs and trinkets, angels and stars, crown to root. We wore gloves as we decorated so we wouldn't be welted by the hard needles. My mother set out her nativity scene that had been cut from one hard block of wood. My father set the advent wreath on our dining room table. Chestnuts and macadamia nuts. Holly and Ivy. Poinsettias and amaryllis and mistletoe and the Christmas cactus. Purple. Purple. Pink. Purple. Christmas cards signed and stamped and dropped into thin envelopes licked shut.

Most of the time, I felt like we were all just going through the motions – my mother, my father, myself – pretending that we were a happy family delighted by the snow and sparkle. Like we could spice our rooms with cinnamon and clove, and they would automatically answer with comfort and trust. But there *were* moments, unexpected, when that warmth felt real. The earth had gone to sleep, and we had answered the cold with warmth, the night with light. My body shook with hope and despair, too much of both, and I had to just close my eyes and wait.

That's when I'd pick up *Les Misérables* and read. The prostitute had died, and the thief was a fugitive again, but now he had an adopted daughter, and she was in love. The man she loved was with a group of revolutionary teenagers, and they were ready to tear up the streets and tear down Paris and tear up their lives to get what they'd been denied. I wondered how they got so much energy from their hunger. My friends' hunger just seemed to make them tired.

One day my mother asked me: "What do you want for Christmas, John? I know we say this every year, but it's more true this year than ever before: we can't get you anything huge."

"I don't know. Paint?"

"Paint?"

"I want to paint my room."

"Why?"

"I think it's ugly. I want it to be brighter."

"Okay. What color?"

"I don't know. A lot of them. Make it a rainbow. Or make it like the night sky. Or the setting sun. I don't really care. Just something that's not boring and gross like everything else is."

At least I felt honest then.

On the last day of school before the break started, I gathered my books in a hurry and struggled to make my way out of the warm glow of Miss Pavilik's classroom.

"Have a restful break," she called after us. "When we return in the new year, we'll be talking about standard candles!"

When I got out into the hall, I saw Omara trying to navigate the hallway. She had to cross the whole school between her fifth and sixth hour classes.

"Omara!" I called out.

She heard my voice above the clatter of lockers and the stomping of wet-booted feet. She looked in my direction.

"Happy Holidays!" I said.

"Ma'a salaama, John," she said and smiled.

Even before I reached my front door, I could hear the shouting.

If I had only stopped to listen first, I wouldn't have gone in. I would've walked over to Adam's, or just around the neighborhood for an hour. But I already had my hand on the doorknob and I was inside before I could reconsider.

"Many calls have you made?!" my mother was shrieking. "How many applications?! How many letters?! Did you even update your resume?!"

"I *did* update my resume!" shouted my father. "I showed you! You already forget that?! And on the second day, I made a million copies and walked them up and down that fucking road and dropped them off like a fucking moron!"

"And nobody called you back?"

"What? No! Nobody called me back. They only call you back if they think they might hire you!"

"Don't mind me," I yelled at them. "I just live here."

"Sorry, John,' my mother said, suddenly deadly calm. "I just found out that your father has been getting drunk instead of getting a job."

"Oh, I know that," I said.

"First, I *have* been looking for a job!" My father didn't bother quieting down, and he never looked away from my mother. "Second, do you know how hypocritical you sound?! When you had a decade-and-a-half of a glorified internship that never went anywhere, while I, I, me, *me, I* had to make all the money for us to live on in this shitty house in this shitty city!"

"You had plenty of chances, Mark. At least I *tried* to make something of myself. It's not my fault you gave up easy and stayed mad about it ever since."

"Well, that's pretty easy to say when I'm the one keeping the lights on, and the furnace going, and buying us cars, and buying us a ... a new roof!"

"A new roof?! This house needed a new roof when we moved in!" She sounded wild now. "When the hell were you planning on buying us a new roof?!"

"Well!" he yelled. "If we ever get a new roof, it certainly isn't going to be you paying for it!"

"So how long was it, precisely, before you gave up on this whole 'job' thing?"

"I didn't give up! I took a couple days off. Jesus, where can I even apply? All of the jobs are in the suburbs, and you have the car half the day!"

"You're actually going to tell me you haven't applied for more jobs because you didn't have the car?"

"It takes forever to get anywhere on the bus!"

"I told you, they've been giving me overtime. Hey Mark, since I'm the only paycheck right now, are you going to pick up all of your million little chores I've been doing all these years? And going to the parent-teacher conferences, and driving John to all his stuff, and scheduling the dentist, and –"

"Shut up! Will you shut up?!"

"No, I won't!"

My father gasped like a fish on a muddy riverbank. "It sure seems to me," he yelled, "that you're always working overtime!"

"I'm only working –"

"Is it forty hours a week?! Fifty hours a week?! Your paychecks sure don't look like it! Who is it you're seeing?"

My mother's arms flew out explosively.

"What on earth are you talking about?!"

"Pretty goddamn cliché, Theresa," my father spat. "You know 'administrative assistant' is just an updated euphemism for 'secretary.' Is it Robert What's-His-Name? That son-of-a-bitch? He gave me the limpest handshake I've ever seen when we met him at the luncheon, but then you know what they say about men with limp handshakes. But then, do you know for sure?"

Now my mother understood what he was saying.

"Are you kidding me?!" she screamed.

My mother's anger usually emerged as crisp cuts of ice: orders spoken in short sharp words. I'd never seen her untangled like this. Her hair was all frizzed out from her wild gestures.

Of course, I'd often seen my father yelling, but not with this intensity. He'd never vented this kind of anger at me: not when I'd skipped out on church, not when he'd picked me up at Lucy's in the middle of the night, never. And I was pissed off too. Pissed off about the college con job they'd put on me. Pissed off at my mother's absence and my father's hypocrisy. Pissed off for putting me in the middle of this fucking scene tonight. And I was mad that they'd caught me off my game. Yeah, I knew how to deal with their anger against me. I knew their numbers. Both of them. But I didn't know how to deal with them mad at each other. They had always been a united front against me. Tonight, who knew what they were going to destroy?

"Okay, Mark," my mother said. "Okay, you're right about some of that. Not what you think, which is a foolish – a horrible – thing to accuse me of but, but, okay, fine. I have been working late and avoiding home, and yes, I've done it even when I've been off the clock, and my coworkers *have* told me to go home, including Robert, by the way, but I haven't wanted to. I haven't wanted to come back and sit here with it all quiet and depressing, and you just wasting day after day, not shaving, not even getting dressed sometimes. God, it's sick. You're like a sick pig!"

"Jesus, *Theresa*," I heard myself saying, and it was like I was following some stupid sitcom script. "Way to be a selfish bitch. You want to stay away, and I don't blame you, but you don't seem to have any problem leaving *me* with his drunk ass all the time. Just him and me, while you hang out with Robert or whoever. Could you even be more selfish? And hey, *Mark*, I remember when you were in rehab before. I was, what, four? That was, like, eleven years ago. I've grown up since then. Why haven't you? I mean, what the fuck?"

I mugged for them, but it didn't even matter. They didn't respond to me at all. It was like they didn't even hear me talking.

"How much are you spending on vodka?" my mother asked.

My father grinned at her. "Not much. Probably a big chunk of your paycheck, though. It ain't like you even earn shit. What are you making, six dollars an hour?"

"Motherfucking ... taint lickers!" I yelled.

"John," said my mother, "why don't you go and wait in your room? This is between your father and I. It isn't your fault, but you really don't have any business getting in the middle of our ... disagreement."

"It ain't my fault but you're sure as hell punishing me for it!"

"Go up to your fucking room!" my father screamed, finally rounding on me.

"Fine!" I yelled. "Fuck you!"

When I got up to my room, I lay down on my bed and stared out the window. I didn't get out my book or put on any music. There wasn't any point. Nothing was going to distract me from the rising and falling of the voices downstairs. I heard silence, then shouting, then more silence. Doors slamming.

I lay there for a long time. The sun was already going down. Soon, it had sunk. My eyes started to drift. I opened them. I must have fallen asleep. I was still in my clothes, on top of my covers. I'd bent my head at a weird angle, and now pain flooded my neck. I had a vague memory of a strange dream. Pink skies, nuclear fallout, endless winter. Fruitcake and desert. Yes, desert. That's when I realized that my father had opened my door, and he stood in the doorway, staring at me.

"What is it?" I asked.

"Your mother left for the night," he said. "I don't ... I mean ... I think she'll be back."

"When?" I asked.

"Um ... tonight, maybe? Or tomorrow? Or ... soon. She's really mad at me. And I'm not happy with her either."

"So, are you two going to split up?" I asked.

"What? No. Jesus, John, no!"

But he didn't sound so sure.

"Sorry," I said. It seemed like the right thing to say, but I wasn't sure what I was apologizing for. Not the things I had said to them; I had meant all of that, even though I'd only said it to distract them. But I could feel sorry that the job that he had tumbled into right after high school, and that had spent twenty years tumbling him from one factory to another had abruptly vanished into the empty air and left him with nothing. And I could feel sorry that my mother had worked unpaid and underpaid for decades, putting her passion into public radio, with nothing to show for it at the end. I could feel bad that absence and alcohol were the best salves they could imagine. And I was sorry that they were fighting, and I was sorry that they were ignoring me.

"I'm sorry too," my father murmured.

I was used to my mother's voice carrying that note of soft concern. Of careful listening. It was strange to hear it in my father's voice. But, I supposed, if she was gone for the moment, it was on him to take care of his teenage son.

"Let's go for a drive," he said.

"What for?" I asked. "Where we gonna go?"

"I don't know," he said. "Just out. We'll see where the car takes us.

Maybe we'll see some stars. You don't have school for two weeks. What could it hurt?"

I couldn't see his eyes, but I could tell that he needed this.

The snow had turned into sleet and rain. It was warmer, but I could still see my breath.

"Didn't Mother take the car?" I asked.

"She borrowed her mom's." My father cranked the keys until the old Benedict finally turned over. As we turned onto Agit Street, the car crossed a patch of black ice and started sliding, inexorably, into South Street. But my father had played this game many times before, and he idled the car up onto the curb where it found better purchase on the rutty grass. He eased down the hill until he could see that there wasn't any oncoming traffic, and swung us off to the north.

"I sometimes take these long drives," my father said. "I don't know. I guess every now and then, it's just nice to be on my own."

Beams of yellow streetlight poured over us as he drove, illuminating his face by intervals. A Billie cassette was humming out. For a moment, I felt like a little kid, and if I closed my eyes, I could almost remember the faintest trace of my mothers' cigarettes. These were old memories. Unless she was keeping secrets better than my father, she hadn't had a smoke in ten years.

"I usually like going south the most," my father said. "You know, farms stretching out, the land all flat. It's a civilized kind of middle-of-nowhere. You never really forget that you're surrounded by people. Makes it feel like Akawe is joined to other cities. Ann Arbor and Jackson and all those ... places that have ended up happier than here."

We weren't driving south, though. We were moving north through the city.

"North is something different," he said. "The forests begin as soon as you get out of town. Swampy and thick and muddy."

Now we were moving west through the Os. Now we were west of the Os and moving through the bleak patchwork of junkyards and railyards that chopped up the farthest extremes of Akawe.

"I'd feel more alone on those drives," he said. "Sometimes, what you need – what you want – is just to find a forest."

And now we left Akawe altogether.

For weeks, the air had been brittle and cold. Now, I saw tendrils of fog turning slowly in the ice and rain. No sign of stars or visible clouds. Everything was dark. Now and then, I caught the vague contours of trees sliding by, intercut by ghost-white industrial silos and yellow drums of compressed gas. Girders and Caterpillars. But mostly, it was just the trees.

Finally, a sign materialized through the haze: "Dixie's Coney Island." The building was covered in wood-planks, painted a lighter blue, and affixed with farming implements. Shovels and pitchforks. Hammers and mallets. My father pulled into the parking lot, and I thought we were going to go inside. To feed in the glow of conversation and laughter radiating off of other people. Instead, he turned along the side of the building to a drive-thru screen. He ordered us each a coney with gravy fries and a coffee. We sat there in silence for ten minutes while the cooks put our order together. Finally, the waitress opened the window and handed my father a greasy brown bag. He gave her some money.

"Keep the change," he said.

"But that's a —"

"It's fine. Happy Holidays! Merry Christmas!"

"To you too, hon!"

And a moment later, we were on the road again, headed north and farther from the city, the paper bag warm on my lap. I don't know how long we went on, back and forth, north and west, through those lonely miles. I wondered whether I should close my eyes and rest, but the smell of the food was intoxicating. I felt my saliva working in anticipation. My eager tongue. Outside, more knotted branches slid by. Oaks and spruces. My father was right. It *was* lonely out here.

"I wish you wouldn't drink," I said.

"Me too," he grunted, and I couldn't tell if he felt annoyed or just exhausted.

"It isn't good for anybody," I said. "It makes Mother not want to trust you. Me too."

"Thanks," he said.

A few minutes later:

"I know you think," he said, "that I haven't been applying for jobs. I've applied for dozens of jobs already. Probably about a hundred. Problem is, nobody's hiring. Nobody wants to hire a 44-year-old with a high-school diploma and a quarter in the shop."

"You didn't work on the line," I said. "You're a diemaker. That's a skilled trade, right? That has to count for something."

"See, that's what I always thought. But I've applied everywhere. Anywhere doing skilled trades, die-making, stuff like that ... computer programming. Not just here but farther out. Flint, Saginaw, Lansing, Detroit. Not just with X, either. I've applied with Ford, GM, Chrysler. All these baby parts suppliers. No, they're all swamped. When a few thousand old men are all applying for the same dozen jobs, those jobs fill up fast. And I've applied for plenty of other stupid stuff, too. Bank teller jobs. Jobs downtown. At Campus

293

Akawe. Even at the mall. Nothing. They don't want to hire anyone. If they do, they want to hire someone young or someone with better skills, and they have plenty of people to choose from."

"So that's it, then? You're just never going to get a job?"

"No, no. I'll get a job. It's just ... taking longer than I thought. And it might end up being a worse job than we need."

We drove.

"I still think you should stop drinking," I said.

"I know," he said.

Finally, we reached a particularly dark patch far beyond any of the surrounding houses or farms. It was nothing but a gravel inlet – a widening of the road's shoulder – but I could see the naked poplars and cattails jostling for space around some muddy bank just beyond the reach of the headlights.

"Where are we?" I asked.

"Don't know," my father grunted.

Without saying much, we spread the napkins on our laps and opened the papers wrapping our coneys. Steam rose against the windows, and a flower of beef and onion bloomed in the close air. My father and I tasted the sting of the mustard, the snap of the hot dog, the warmth of the gravy-drenched fries. The heavy food filled my stomach. It filled me up. I finished first, and sat, and waited. When my father had finished his food, he crumpled up the wrappers and tossed them into the back. Then he got out of the car and quickly moved out of the light and into the thickets. I followed him.

On the edge of the road, I could smell astringent ice and stagnant water.

"Where are you going?" I asked.

Waving cattails gave away my father's path through the reeds.

"Don't know," he said. "Wait, I do. Got to piss."

I heard the sound of his pissing for a moment. The prim zippering shut of his pants.

But then he didn't turn back toward the car. He kept moving out into the tall grasses and the cattails.

I followed him, the frosted weeds and spongy puddles soaking my shoes and socks.

We eventually climbed onto a stony bluff overlooking a small pond. Tufts of grass stuck up where the snow had been rained away. A thin glaze of ice crusted the water, but now it was being punctured by a drumbeat of chilly rain. Down the bank, a frost-crusted duck blind watched us, its windows black.

For a moment, the clouds behind us parted. Looking over my shoulder at it, I couldn't see any stars through the gloom, but the moon stood out sickle sharp, its points a wicked Cheshire smile. Narrow as it was, it magnified the curling fog and illuminated the scene before us.

"Yeah," my father said. "There is it."

We saw all of Akawe laid out under the sky.

I mean, we couldn't see the city itself. We were too far away, and there were miles of trees and hills blocking the way. But the dying city was still brighter than I had imagined. The highway lights, the floodlights, the leftover factory lights, the houselights, and those millions of Christmas lights: they all conjured a silver-yellow glow that stretched into the sky where the mottled cloudscape cast them back like earthbound aurora.

"It's right there," my father said. "It's very quiet from out here. I mean, Akawe."

"Yeah," I said.

We watched. My father coughed.

"It's funny," he said. "Not that long ago ... not long at all ... there wasn't even anything there. I mean, everything we see out there is just one, two hundred years old. It all came up so fast. And now it's dying. It hasn't even been a long time. It isn't an old city, John."

He kicked pointlessly at the hard dirt.

"Father?" I asked. "What is Eden?"

"What?"

"The neighborhood. In Akawe."

"Ah. Why you so curious about Eden? I don't know a whole lot about it. I mean, besides what I told you before. It was built back in the, I don't know, 20s, 30s? They had laws back then that Blacks, Irish, Italians, Romanians, they couldn't live in most of the neighborhoods, so they just all wound up in Eden. River on one side, factories on the other. Polluted as hell. Eventually, most people were able to move out, but the Blacks were still kept out of the other neighborhoods, so by the time I was growing up, it was all Black. Then, they tore it all down. Moved all of Eden's people into the projects, or somewhere else on the West End. That all happened in the 70s. Put in 292, but that was pretty much it. They were going to put in an industrial park there, but nothing much ever came of it. It's all empty now. It's crazy, but you can even see it, kinda, from here."

Pointing his silver-lit finger out over the frozen pond, he easily found the sliver of darkness at the heart of Akawe's glow. It didn't surprise me this time, but the apparition still haunted me. Knowing what was there. Knowing what wasn't there: light.

"Do you think ..." I wanted to ask without giving anything away. "Do you think any of it's still standing?"

"What, the industrial park?"

"No. The neighborhood. Do you think there's maybe a house that never got torn down?"

"That wouldn't make any sense, John. They tore down the whole neighborhood. Nobody was allowed to stay there. It was all knocked down."

I couldn't ask him anything else. My father, taking solace in the spectacle before us, had moved onto other things.

"I don't drink because I want to, John. I ... I don't know what's going to happen next year. I don't know about finding a job, your education, or ... I don't know much at all, honestly. But let's try to make it a good Christmas. We can have this at least, can't we? Let's take what we can. Let's take this Christmas."

"Sure," I said. I realized I was shivering. "It's getting cold."

"Yeah," my father said, in that strange, soft voice. "You're right. Let's go home."

My mother woke me in the silvery light of the morning.

"Come on," she said. "I've got something for you in the car, but I need your help with it."

I followed her downstairs and found my father in the living room, holding a bottle of water in his hands. He was still wearing his pajamas. My mother was dressed smart, in black slacks and a black knit sweater.

"No coffee?" I asked my father.

He shook his head. "Power's out."

"Why?"

"Ice storm. You'll see it."

"Daaamn," I said when I got outside. The air was warm, and the wind carried the wet sound of cherry pickers and salt trucks growling down South and up Whitmore. A translucent coat of crystal covered everything: windshields and hubcaps, branches black and tapering, evergreen needles, and the last few wrinkled leaves. Tapering icicles dripped from every sign, every porch, every fender and bumper. Some trees were so sheathed in ice that they looked like abstracted sculptures of themselves. Knots and whorls bulged out like pregnant bellies, preserving warmth beneath bark.

I heard a loud crack and looked up in time to see the top branches of towering maple, one block away, snap and crash through a power line. A shower of sparks erupted, then a haze of smoke floated out over the neighborhood. The branches landed out of sight with a crunch.

"Be careful," my mother said. "It's icy."

We teetered down the walk to Grandmother Richter's Aubrey. My mother took out her keys and opened the trunk.

"Damn!" I said again.

Inside, I saw eight cans of paint, along with some paint trays and sheets, brushes, and rollers.

"For your room," my mother said. "We've got Mabel's party tonight, and with the power outage and everything, I don't know if you'll get this finished by Christmas, but I thought you might want to get started now so you could enjoy the new look a little before school started up again."

"Yeah," I said. "I mean, thanks."

"I also got you a new light fixture and a dimmer. If you like, you can paint your room like it's the entire universe."

With standard candles?

"I think I will," I said.

"I don't know if you want it, but I got some of that glow-in-the-dark paint, too. In case you wanted stars that light up when you turn the lights off."

"Thank you. It ... it sounds amazing. I can't wait to see it. When we're finished." I wanted to hug her, but there were things between us.

"Where did you go last night?" I asked. "Are ... you and him," and I gestured to the house, "cool now?"

She looked at me for a moment, then reached into the trunk and took out a couple cans of paint.

"You better get started," she said.

As I carried the painting supplies up to my room, my parents talked about the power outage.

"We can't afford a hotel," my father was saying. "We'll just have to stay here. We've still got those two propane space heaters in the basement. I'll go out and get some new cans for them. Get some hot coffee too."

"Ugh. Can't we just stay with Mabel tonight?" my mother asked.

"I don't like relying on her all the time."

"I don't think she holds it against you, Mark."

"She doesn't have to. She knows she's the one with all the money. You know it."

"What, do you think if her power went out that she and Michael would just stay in their cold house overnight?"

"No, I think they would go stay in a hotel."

I'd never painted a whole room on my own before, and I didn't know what I was doing, so I decided to go slowly and concentrate on not fucking up. I spread the first two paint sheets over my bed and chest of drawers. I lay the third over the middle of the floor. I poured paint into the first tray, assembled the roller, and began rolling lacy whiteness out onto the walls. I smoothed the paint petals into white planes. The dark wood panels soaked it up at once, but I could see dark eyes looking out at me through self-opening bubbles.

I kept going.

After a while, my mother came up. She stood with her hands on her hips and watched me.

"I probably didn't do you any favors telling you to get started while the house is cooling off. That can affect the way it dries. I mean ... I don't know everything, but this is interior paint. We should probably wait until the heat's back on."

I'd already painted a third of the room.

"Should I stop?"

My mother thought for a moment.

"You're going to need two coats of white, at least. This coat will probably be mostly dry before it gets too cold in here. So, let's finish the first coat and then wait on the others until we've got power again."

She got a second roller and fitted it up. A few minutes later, she was painting alongside me, moving counterclockwise while I painted opposite toward the windows.

When my father got home, he brought us three steaming cups of coffee.

"It's getting cold in here. I want to get out pretty quickly if we can swing it."

"You get the propane?" my mother asked.

"Yeah. We'll block off one room with bedsheets. Probably the living room. Try to keep it warm. Anyway, I almost forgot. They're demolishing the Akawe Rise in about an hour. So, we can watch it come down and then go out and grab a late breakfast. How does that sound?"

"Works for me, but let's try to finish the first coat of John's room before we head out. I was telling him that we should try to get the paint on to dry before it gets too cold in here."

"Yeah, that sounds about right."

My father grabbed the third roller and took it to the far wall where nobody was painting. We all moved quickly. First, we finished the walls, and then my father and I ran the rollers across the ceiling while my mother brushed the corners and creases of the room, making it all look smooth and new.

After we had finished, we locked up the house and headed off toward downtown. Somehow, amid our months of violence and water contamination, the city had shelled out to demolish its largest abandoned building. The Akawe Rise, closed for a decade now, had been littering the sidewalks and parking lots below with heavy chunks of itself. Now it was time to bring down the rest.

In preparation for the tower's demolition, crews had dismantled the eight concrete piers that extended upward from the building's midsection and which had always been its most memorable feature. Without them, the Rise looked naked and vulnerable, its dirty planes of gray concrete pierced at intervals to help the building come down more quickly.

The crowd around us, several hundred strong, waited patiently, quietly, hands in our pockets, eyes on the Rise.

"What time is it?" I asked my father.

He checked his watch. "Ten o'two," he said.

"Is this one of those things where we all show up on time, and then it takes an hour for the demo to actually happen?"

Suddenly, rapid-fire cracks rent apart the air and rolled out over the ice-glazed city.

For a moment, nothing happened.

Then, all in a few seconds, the Rise plunged in billowing clouds of granulated concrete dust. The building tilted ever-so-slightly in our direction, tipping its antennae, as if they were a hat, toward us. And then, the tallest building in Akawe was gone, the crowd was applauding, and my father was taking a step back to look at us.

"Hungry?" he asked.

We made our way back to the South Side, to the Constellation, which was more crowded than we'd seen it in years. We ordered coffee and eggs, sausage and hash browns, ketchup and hot sauce.

"Clean your plate," my father told me. "We don't have anywhere to put the leftovers."

"What do you mean?"

"No power, so we have to keep the fridge closed."

"Isn't our whole house a fridge?"

But I ate until my plate was bare.

Back at the house, my father brought some old blankets up from the basement and hung them over the arch to the dining room, the stairway, the living room windows. "A bit of extra insulation," he said. He carried in a couple of inflatable mattresses and blew them up. "This way we don't have to worry about it when we get back."

It was already getting cold inside, though I couldn't see my breath yet. We all put on our sweaters and moved out into the brief day.

"Let's head out to Arcadia," my mother said. "We have a few hours to kill before the party. I don't know about you two, but I haven't finished my Christmas shopping yet."

We hit Blockbuster Music, then Borders' Books, then the mall. We bought cinnamon twists, and I got my father a Pat Metheney CD, and my mother a copy of Leonard Nemoy's autobiography. I recalled her saying that he was pretty much the only reason that anyone should watch *Star Trek*.

By the time we got outside again, the darkness was complete. We walked through the icy air. It was far below freezing now, and the only remnants of that morning's fog were the cracked branches and dark windows we passed. It seemed like the whole world was ripping up with new beginnings, in ice and latex paint and trinitrotoluene and breaking.

But there had been no power outages in Parc Pierre. I wanted answers to other questions, and now it was time for Aunt Mabel's Christmas party.

Booker T. and the M.G.'s followed us for miles past the bland houses on big lots in Arcadia, the dingy flats and body shops of Acheron, and all of the populated periphery of Akawe. Then, "Joy to the World," we were back on East Street, miles from the block where the Akawe Rise had collapsed into a fifty-foot heap of rubble.

We made our way through downtown Parc Pierre, where bright windows at the bakery and the antique shoppe threw nostalgic shadows out upon the crystalline puddles, and then Aunt Mabel's subdivision where brick ranch houses glittered with frosted chandeliers. Hot, clean water coursed through the galvanized copper pipes. We parked in Mabel's driveway and went inside.

Aunt Mabel's Christmas party had certainly gotten larger over the years, but this year it seemed like it had doubled in size. Mabel was finally in her element now; she had been *meant* to live in Parc Pierre. Now that she had the house she had always wanted, she was finally ready to show it off to all of her friends and coworkers. It still took me off guard because Mabel's life, like Michael's, had always been somewhat insular. Mabel had her family and her work, and never the twain shall meet and all that. But once each year, she sent out gilt invitations on heavy cardstock offering wine and hors d'oeuvres, and holly, and music, and she brought her several worlds together.

Throughout the house, guests stood almost shoulder-to-shoulder, and for the first time I saw some of Mabel's college students mixed in with her other colleagues. In every room, cadenced laughter met wry anecdotes about failed bridges, wastewater infrastructure, and the implosion of the Akawe Rise. Torque and acceleration. The Pre-K programs in Parc Pierre and those available in Brighton. In Ann Arbor. A live jazz quartet hummed over the din of conversation where the living room met the sunroom. Their jam session added to the atmospherics of the vanilla-colored candles and the geometry of the Persian rug underfoot.

Some of the neighbor kids had come over, too. They were all younger than me, so they nominated me as their storyteller. I told them about how Demon Cow was the minion responsible for Akawe's poisoned water. How I had tracked him through the pipes and channels of the city's water treatment system, and had finally flushed him in victory.

Meanwhile, the house itself, in all its suburban sprawl, still felt half new and un-lived-in. I could just catch the faintest trace of plastic sheeting beneath the clove-perfumed pine cones. I looked out of the back windows and saw the cottony tufts of untraveled snow receding toward a furry border of arborvitae.

I made my way to the dining room table, where my father was biting into a leg of fried chicken and laughing too loud at someone's engineering joke. My mother was standing in front of a bookshelf, reading the titles as she took careless gulps from a glass full of California Cab Sauv.

"*Moby Dick*," she muttered. "A bitter November indeed."

I grabbed myself a Dr. Pepper and a plate full of garlic-stuffed Spanish olives, Goldfish crackers, and roasted chestnuts. I turned away from the table and almost ran right into Michael.

"There you are!" I said. "Where've you been? I've been looking all over for you."

"Sleeping," he said. "I got a headache."

"How the hell you got a headache?"

"I've been getting 'em lately."

"Let's go to your room. I've got to talk to you."

When we got there, I took a seat on Michael's bed and he sat down on the floor with his back against the dresser. The light shone through his curly forelocks and cast shadows over his eyes. He leaned forward, ready and listening.

"Do you remember that weird house we saw after the rave?"

Michael hesitated a moment.

"I'm not ever going to forget that house," he said.

"I've learned more about it, but there are so many secrets here. Can you keep this shit to yourself."

"Of course!"

In the next hour, I caught him up on everything I knew except for Quint's assault on Selby.

"Holy shit!" Michael said over and over.

"There's more," I said. "It's deeper than that." "It's complicated." "It's hidden."

And so, responding to his doubt and confusion, I led him farther into the story, until he also grasped the enormity of Eden and God Ostyn and O-Sugar and Selby's plots. Finally, I told him about my visit to Lucy's house. Her fight with Selby. My mother's disappearances and my father's despondence.

"Well, that sucks," said Michael.

"For who?" I asked.

"For everybody!" he exclaimed. "It all sounds awful!"

"Do you think Selby's mad at me? Do you think she thinks I ... betrayed her or something?"

"How would I know, John? You see her every day. You all go to school together, and I'm stuck out here."

He waved around at his beige-painted brand-new bedroom with an expression of utter disgust.

"I don't know what to do," I said.

"I think you just need to listen."

"Listen to who? To Lucy?"

"To everyone. Your parents, Lucy, Selby. I mean, Lucy, well now she knows about Eli. But you can't make her dump him, and it sounds like Selby found that out herself. Sometimes you've got to do something, but sometimes you've got to be careful what you do, because if you do the wrong thing, you'll just make things worse."

He scratched under his chin.

"You've got to listen to Selby because Lucy won't, and you've got to listen to Lucy because I don't know if anyone really listens to her. Based, I mean, on what you've been saying."

"What kind of difference could listening make? I need to know what to *do!*"

"I mean, if Lucy just found out that her boyfriend is a pimp, and she's all messed up with his family, and this gang, and then Lucy knows that Selby's messed up in it too ... and anything Lucy says could have consequences for Selby. Just having someone to listen and understand could make a big difference!"

"I get what you're saying. And it makes sense. But I don't think that Lucy trusts me. I mean, why would she?"

"Well, you'd better try. I mean, you're in it now. I'm in it, too."

"How are you in it?"

"We're all in it. If we care about these people, we have to help them out. But how can we help them if we don't understand? How can we understand if we don't listen?"

In that moment, understanding felt like an overwhelming undertaking. There was too *much* to understand, and probably even more questions hiding among the answers. I knew that Michael was asking me to try a different kind of listening, but I still wasn't sure how I was supposed to do it. I just knew that I felt lonely and frightened. I pulled the blue comforter up over my goosebumped legs.

"Well," I said. "Thank you for listening to me. I don't know that anyone else does right now. Not my parents, for sure. You've never let me down, Michael. Not ever. Not even once. I ... I think sometimes about what happened with us all up on that hospital roof."

"I think about it too ..."

"I think about our walk on Hastings, and all the times we had growing up. I think you've got to be my best friend. Like, for real. My for real best friend, Michael."

Michael smiled. I realized, for the first time, that he wasn't bad looking. I mean, no, he wasn't the sort of guy that most girls I knew would go for, but his jaw had firmed out. He had tamed his hair a bit. Most of all, Michael knew what he was looking at, wherever he was looking.

"I'm your cousin too," he said. "Does that count for anything?"

"No," I laughed. "Terry's kids are my cousins, too, and I don't even like them."

It felt good to laugh.

My parents and I were the last to leave.

"Great party, Aunt Mabel," I said.

"Thank you, John!"

"I mean it. It felt like ... every party."

She crooked her head to the side.

"That's a compliment?"

"It's a good thing," I said. "Whenever I'm at a Christmas party from now on, I'm going to compare it to this one."

"It was that guy on the piano," Mabel said. "I work with him. Thomas Clawson. Did you hear his take on 'Carol of the Bells?' It sends shivers down my spine!"

Michael waved, and they closed the door, and we were alone out in the cold. The temperature had dropped through the night. Now, at eleven o'clock, it was in the single digits, falling fast toward zero before dawn. When we finally got home, my mother and I left our gloves and socks on. My father lit some candles, and in their light, we could see the clouds we made with our breath. We quickly changed into our pajamas behind the hanging sheets and lay down in our sleeping bags. We covered up with all of our blankets, and my father fired up both of the propane space heaters, although they only burned for about an hour before the coils cooled and went dark.

We closed our eyes.

We tried to sleep.

It was a long night.

Literally long. Just a few minutes past the winter solstice and a few minutes south of the 45th parallel. Long in my mind. I'd wake up coiled in the icy dry air with phosphenes sparkling through the gloom like an incandescent snowfall, and I could play through, at last, the completed arc of my decline through the months that autumn. At the Renaissance Festival, with Omara, anticipating Chicago, I had felt that I was wading through warm pools in the golden robes of a late-summer sunshine. By the time reality had shattered these illusions, and Selby revealed herself at the rave – by the time we penetrated the membrane of Eden Street – the leaves were blanched, the harvest collected, the sunset stained the color of real bruises. By the time Adam and I had crept through the Os, looking for stories about God Ostyn, the fog and frost had promised months of bitterness and barrenness. And now, on my living room floor, in an obscurity so complete that what I imagined seemed more real than what I could actually see, my family's decline seemed inevitable. Looking back at it from where I was now, I couldn't see how we could have avoided it.

My thoughts were interrupted when my father got up out of his sleeping bag, put on his boots, and stomped outside. He came back in with another couple of propane tanks and relit the space heaters. I turned my face toward their orange glow and enjoyed the waxy heat that spilled over my cheeks and lips like liquid. It didn't do much for my neck, though. It didn't do a thing for my chest, belly, legs, or toes. I faded in and out of sleep, wondering how quickly I would wake if one of the coils threw out a spark and caught my hair on fire.

The sleeping bags were shit. My father got them for camping years before, but they were summer sleeping bags, and they'd been used so much when I was a kid that by now they were worn through. The quilt made a difference, but I still felt the drafts tickling up my sides. I remembered a few years back when our furnace had died in April and I had walked up and down through our house wearing slippers and breathing into my fingers. One night of this was worse than weeks of that. And then I remembered how Adam had spent that same month out in the forest with snow on the ground, and I told myself to stop bitching, even if I was only bitching to myself.

My father tossed and snored loudly where he lay against the wall.

Next to me, my mother seemed to have discovered some secret warmth of body and mind. Her lips and face were statue still, and she breathed in and out, slowly and deeply, quiet and untroubled. *What does she know?* I wondered.

I had spent the last couple of months digging into peoples' secrets. I thought back to the conversation we had had walking through the Happy Hunting Grounds from Eastern to Cartierul. When I'd asked Selby about Cora's escape from the Chalks. *What if I had just let it lie? What if I just didn't need to know? It's not like my knowledge has helped anyone. What if I had just gone on with my own life. Would things be going better for me today?* But no. Because my father was still going to lose his job. Because he'd still be drinking, and my mother would still be checked out, and Omara probably still would have dumped me too. Because there still wouldn't have been enough money to do things that needed money.

It's bullshit, I thought, *that we trick ourselves into thinking that we can have some control over things we don't control at all.* I curled my back for warmth and my fists for anger. I heard my breath catch, but I clenched my teeth so that I wouldn't disturb my parents.

There was no way to find comfort. Coiling up cramped my muscles, but stretching out made me too cold to think. My father got up many times to bring in more propane. The timbers of the house groaned around us. I flickered between sleep and consciousness. If I could just remain long enough, the night would pass. Eventually, I would be warm again. Eventually, it might even be spring again. I faded in, and I faded out, and I dissolved into visions of fireflies.

I woke to the sound of my mother talking. She was still in her sleeping bag up to her neck, but her voice was carefree.

"That wasn't so bad," she said. "I expected it to be a lot worse."

"I don't care if I have to go crawling back to Mabel," my father groaned. "We're not staying in this house another night until we get the power back on."

The kitchen had gotten even colder than the living room.

"Our bottled water froze," my father said after giving up on brushing his teeth. "I can't even get the sink to turn on. The pipes haven't split ... yet ... but it isn't looking good. I should have left it on a trickle."

That day, we were pilgrims.

We piled into the Benedict, and I held my raw fingers under the vent and massaged them the whole way out to Parc Pierre.

When we got to Mabel's house, she was out running errands, but Michael let us in, and we all took hot showers and brushed our teeth. My mother made eggs for breakfast while my father called his sister and explained the situation. Mabel seemed to think he was pretty stupid for not having asked for help in the first place. We all agreed: we'd pass up Midnight Mass and go to the Childrens' Vigil at four instead. Then, my parents and I would stop back at Agit Street, check on the pipes, and bring all of our presents back to my aunt's.

It felt good to waste the day away, talking with Michael and watching *Sense and Sensibility* with my mother while my father hit the party story to buy stocking stuffers.

By the time we arrived at St. Brendan's, five minutes before Mass was supposed to start, the church was packed. Michael and I were able to grab a few of the last folding chairs that had been set up at the back of the nave, while my parents stood near the doors and craned their necks looking for my aunt.

"O come, o come Emmanuel, and ransom captive Israel."

I heard those haunted notes, and I didn't follow them word by word, but I *followed* the meaning of the song more than I ever had before. *Ransom us!* I pleaded, my thoughts. *Please!*

The green marble of the sanctuary was flushed with the crimson blooms of a hundred poinsettias and thousands of shining white Christmas lights, mounted on wreaths, on trees, and in the puffs of fake snow and gauze that lined the nativity scene before the altar.

"O come, o come desire of nations bind in one the hearts of all humankind
O bid our sad divisions cease, and be yourself our King of Peace.
Rejoice! Rejoice! Emmanuel shall come to you, O Israel!"

The children acted out the Nativity of Jesus, seventh and eighth graders playing the parts of Mary, Joseph, and Gabriel, and younger children as the angels and shepherds. A baby, a few months old, lay in the blanketed cradle and clawed toward the ceiling in her debut role of the Baby Jesus. She seemed so vulnerable. We all did, there. Vulnerable and temporary. But at least it was warm. At least there were candles and light. Songs and prayers. It was a moment.

After all of the readings and singing, after a homily that I'd forgotten before it was even finished, after the offering and the consecration and the Lord's Prayer and the Sign of Peace, I felt a tingle of anticipation rising within me. It was a quiet voice, and I didn't hear it until the pew creaked when I leaned forward, half-conscious, on the kneeler. The host was there. The communion. *What am I committing to, taking this sacrifice? What does it mean? My father asked for a good Christmas. We can all have a good Christmas, I think, but what about after that? Christmas will end. New Year's will end. Then it will be months of cold and dark, and he still won't have his job, and we'll have all of the same problems we've got right now.*

My hands trembled in nervousness as I cupped them to receive this wafer of Christ, but I put it on my tongue and swallowed anyway.

When my parents and I got home that night, we discovered that the lights had come on inside the house. We ran up the porch, cheering as we went. Inside, the furnace roared, the faucets poured out water, and all of the heat and life returned to the cracks and corners of those weary rooms.

At once, my father set to work wrapping presents, my mother started on our Christmas Eve dinner, and I went up to my room to resume painting. As I spread the second coat, my bedroom became more and more a place where things were revealed, not hidden. By the time I'd finished, I felt like I could see everything in there. The corners hid as little as the windows.

When I lay down that night, I fell into a sleep as smooth and featureless as the night before had been rough and scraped. Down there, I found myself a young child again, playing with Selby in Cartierul, in the summer mud.

"I've got to know what's going on with you," I said.

I woke up warm and refreshed on Christmas morning, and it had already been light out for hours. I came downstairs, sat with my parents, and we all opened presents.

For weeks, I'd been priming myself for Christmas austerity. They'd kept telling me how broke we were. *Did I even ask for anything besides the paint?* I couldn't remember. Maybe there wasn't going to be anything for me under the tree except for the glassy chunks of coal I deserved. *It's okay. I really don't mind.* Coal would have been a comfort, honestly. *You can burn coal, can't you?*

But I was wrong about my parents that Christmas. They'd gone hard in the other direction. Probably, they figured, with one shitty income – my mother's – and being underwater on the mortgage, and ready for catastrophe with half of our house and appliances – the microwave, the roof, the porch, the upstairs toilet – "why the hell not?" A few extra presents weren't going to make the difference between poverty and stability. Better make good while they still hadn't hit their credit limit.

So I got paisley shirts and a new spring jacket. Several swanky pairs of sunglasses. My own coffee mug, care of the Field Museum in Chicago. *The Moonsea Forgotten Realms Campaign Supplement* and *Ruins of Zhentil Keep.* Socks and boxers and cords and khakis and slacks. An empty journal.

Then, with the temp up to a balmy fifteen degrees outside, we drove out to Grandmother Richter's for lunch, and I opened more presents there; snow globes and ornaments and CDs and a new CD player and the *Lord of the Rings* trilogy illustrated by Alan Lee. It was beautiful. I'd been wanting to take on these books ever since Crystal had challenged me at the end of seventh grade. I cradled *Fellowship* on my lap and turned from glossy vision to glossed image, the homey holes of Bag End, the sylvan shores of Lothlórien, and twisted tree limbs dripping with fog under the stones of Amon Hen. I put the fresh-cut pages to my nose and breathed in their pulpy scent.

Then, in the evening, when it was dark again, we returned to Parc

Pierre for the third time in three days. Mabel gave me a set of three ties, a book – *Mathematicians Are People, Too: Stories from the Lives of Great Mathematicians* – and a card saying that she'd deposit two hundred dollars in a bank account to be held for when I went to college. And Michael got me a deck of tarot cards. I flipped through them. The Lovers were naked on their namesake card.

We played Monopoly, and started a game of Risk, but eventually, my parents told me to wrap it up. It was already eleven. We were already tired. Our joints were still tired from sleeping on the living room floor two nights before. We filled a gallon jug of tap water from Mabel's sink then went back home to our warm house. I sat down on my bed, opened my new journal, and started writing.

On the first twelve pages, it gave me writing prompts and I decided to start with those. On the first page it asked me: 1. **Where Did You Begin?**

I wrote: "Akawe, Michigan. 1980. Time is travel and loss is learning."

I put up the book and went to bed.

It had been a good Christmas.

293

I made a stained-glass sanctuary out of the following week. I was safe. I was sheltered. Not forever. But for a moment.

When I woke on the day after Christmas, I resumed work on my bedroom. Now that the walls and ceiling were blank and white, I got up on the ladder and painted concentric circles starting at the light fixture. The innermost ring was a fierce, hot yellow, followed by bonfire orange and flaming sunset gold, then firecracker red and rosy dusk, and finally a courtly shade of violet. Then I filled in the rest of the ceiling with a calming tanzanite blue. It took me about an hour to paint each color and another hour for the paint to dry. I painted two coats. When I had to wait for a circle to dry, I'd crack the window, close the door, and go downstairs to watch TV or read one of my new books. The Tolkien books were the most enticing, but I had the feeling, gut-deep, that I should save them. Besides, I still wanted to finish *Les Mis*. The ice storm had stalled out my reading, but I was already two-thirds of the way through. Now, the barricades were going up. The students were ready to fight! And when I needed a breather from those thundering old words, I picked up *Moonsea* and read about the smoke over chilly Melvaunt, the vaulted walls of xenophobic Hillsfar, the towering ambitions of the Mulmaster Blades, and the ruined hubris of Zhentil Keep. The Bell in the Deep, tolling through the sunken weight of umbering amethyst waters.

By two in the morning, I'd finally finished painting the seven circles. I cleaned out my brushes and rollers, closed my window, then lay down in the middle of the floor and looked at the ceiling. I saw the Pyramid Bank in the centering sun. I saw the bricks of Radcliffe Junior High in the rosy red. I saw the luminous marquee of Constellation Coney Island in the surrounding iris tones. I was happy with the choices my mother had picked out for me. She understood both light and color. My room really was going to become the whole universe.

I took out my journal again and answered the second prompt: 2. Where Are You Right Now?

I wrote: "Akawe, Michigan. We have bottles of water to drink and wash with. My house is warm. My mother still has her job, so we have food to eat and a place to live. I got gifts for Christmas and I love them. I have friends though I haven't seen them much. Adam and Nova and Selby and Quanla. Michael, especially. I need to just be here right now and to be so grateful for what I have."

The next morning, I feathered out the borders between the circles, blurring them together so that the vision transformed into a singular fading corona. It still took two coats of paint to finish, but this work itself was a lot faster and less exacting.

Which was good because I didn't want to spend quite as much time painting today. I finished *Moonsea* while I was eating breakfast and had just decided to start a D&D campaign with Michael and Adam and, if I could talk him into it, Nova.

That night I answered the third prompt in my journal: 3. **Where Are You Going?**

"I don't know where I am going really but I someday want to go away from Akawe and I want to go to college so I've got to get money for that and have to start working in school again hard. I mean I'm not going to get there if I skip school and don't do my homework."

I closed the notebook and looked up at my bedroom ceiling. Now, with the varied colors all brushed together, I felt like I was looking at a whole field of hues: hundreds of different colors. I picked one out, then another, then another, and imagined some of the places I would like to visit in the new millennium. I would start with Romania. If I ever got over the recent weirdness with Selby, maybe I'd ask her to take me to her Romanian Orthodox church some Sunday. After that, maybe I'd visit the towering cupolas and alabaster monuments of Rome. Or the creamed and tanzanite vista built out over Santorini. Maybe I'd go to Jerusalem. Balance between the Wailing Wall and the Dome of the Rock. *I could buy souvenirs for Crystal and Omara.* The clay gray finish of the Lalbagh Fort shifting in the sunlight into a fierce black-on-orange penetrating glow, stark against the towering verdure. Somber-colored, sober-shaded flags, un-dustdaunted, rippling and snapping in the winds descending from Annapurna. The Takhi raging and dancing along the steppes. Languedoc. Gascony. The Rue St. Denis. I saw them all in the fleeting shades of my ceiling. I fell asleep on my floor. I woke a little bit later and got into my bed.

The next day, Selby called and left a message on my answering machine. "Hey John," she said. "I'm having a New Year's Eve Party. You should come. Don't tell anyone I invited you."

It made me nervous. I was ready to see Selby at Eastern. I was ready to listen to her with the clatter of lockers all around us. I didn't want her to corner me in her own house and ask me why I'd gone to Lucy that night. I erased the message before my parents could hear it. Maybe I'd go. Maybe I wouldn't. I still had time to decide.

That night, I extended the blue down my walls. I brushed it on in huge swaths so that the paint dribbled in fat drops that bulged out where they dried.

My journal asked me: 4. **Are You Greedy or Generous?**

"Michael is generous. The Chalks with their O-Sugar are pure greed. X Automotives is pure greed. I think I am in between. So is Selby. So is Lucy. I think."

The next day, I got a letter from May. It was a small Christmas card with a chubby cartoon shepherd hugging an equally chubby sheep, with a ribbon reading: "Celebrate HIS Birth!" May had included a sandwich bag with three crumbling chocolate cookies. I guessed that she'd made them herself. I ate the cookies over a paper towel. They were a bit dry, but the chocolate chips were rich in my mouth.

That night, my parents and I mounted the new light fixture. It had frosted glass and didn't give out as much light as the original fixture had. Now I'd need a desk lamp, too, and a bedside lamp because I liked to read in bed. In the rosy light, I squinted to make out the prompt in my journal: 5. **What Season Are You?**

"I think I am autumn, getting close to winter. But I want to be spring. The problem is that spring needs to believe in it's self: about seeds and rain and sunshine and everything that. I don't trust much. The problem is that spring needs to sacrifice itself, because it opens up so that things can live and grow and then it becomes summer. But I don't like to self-sacrifice. I like to keep what's mine."

The next day I got another message from Selby. I erased it again.

I got a card from Crystal. It included a pair of cardboard 3D glasses and a sticky pad shaped like Saturn. On the top of the sticky pad, she'd written, "I swiped these for you from Suarez. You're a bad influence, even though you're not there anymore. Merry Christmas! Let's hang out more in 1996!"

My father came upstairs carrying several lamps and the hardware for a dimmer switch.

"Michael called," he said. "He's wondering if he can spend the night tonight."

"Can he?" I asked.

"Sure."

Once we'd installed the light switch, I sat down with my journal: 6. **What Taste Are You?**

"I think I'm bitter. Obvious, right? The nice thing about being bitter is that when I've swallowed that maybe then I can be sweet or sour. Not the salt of the earth. I tried that. It didn't work."

A little bit later, Michael arrived. My parents got Domino's, and we ate it then went up to my room. Michael gasped when he saw all the work that I had done.

"This is badass, John!" he said. Then he sniffed. "It still smells like paint in here."

"I've been airing it out every day," I said. "But it's too cold to open the windows a lot, you know?"

"Yeah," he said.

We sat in silence for a moment.

"So," he said. "Selby invited me to this New Year's Eve party at her house."

"Me too," I said. "She told me not to tell anyone."

"Me too," Michael said. "But I figured if she invited me, she must have invited you."

"Do you know who else she invited?"

"No. I figured you might know."

"I don't. I ... never called her back about it."

"Oh." He hesitated. "I did. I told her we'd both come."

"What? Why?"

"I'm sorry. But I figured it'd be weird for me to go without you, and I figured you were probably going anyway."

"Do you still have a crush on her?"

"No. I mean, I don't think so. I haven't seen her for real since eighth grade. Anyway, I do like a girl from my school, you know? Her name is Abbey Waldrop!"

We played some Dungeons and Dragons. We read the tarot cards. I tried hypnotizing Michael, but I don't believe it really worked. I couldn't convince myself that he wasn't faking.

The next morning – New Year's Eve – Michael went home, promising to see me at Selby's party. I was on my own again, and I went through my bedroom alone, with the glow-in-the-dark paint, and dotted the ceiling with the twelve constellations of the zodiac.

When I was finished, I still had several hours before the party started, so I lay down on my bed and read *Les Misérables*. I had almost finished *The Idyll in the Rue Plumet*. The feral kid had outed the Lawful Neutral police inspector as a spy. They tied him to a post. The students got ready to die in glory. Gunfire laid a poor girl low. I was pretty sure the feral kid had a number on him too. I kept waiting for the original thief to enter the mix. He never really stayed on the sidelines, even when he wanted to. He was too *good* to do nothing for long. His hair had turned white one night after he had been wrestling with his conscience.

I checked my alarm clock. It was time to get ready. I took a shower. I put on my gray cords, a black turtleneck, and a bright red scarf. I put a pair of red teashades in my pocket, just in case. I went up to my room and took out my journal, and read the seventh prompt: 7. **Do You Want to Understand or Do You Want to Be Understood?**

Connor Coyne

For the first time, I felt kind of exasperated with the journal. All of its questions were silly, but this was the first one that pissed me off. I was obviously supposed to write "I want to understand," but I couldn't write that because it would have been a lie. Instead, I wrote the true thing: "I want to be understood, and also to understand. Can't I have both?" It didn't seem complete, though. Something was missing. And then, a strange thought entered my head: *I never called Bill back,* I thought. *Even though I promised him.*

"Call Bill in 1996," I wrote in the margins, in tiny lettering.

Then I closed the journal and put it on my dresser. I looked out of the window as twilight faded for the last time in 1995. The sunset on my ceiling was a reflection of the actual moving sunset. And then the night. The long night.

But now, it was time for Selby's party.

I followed my father out to the car. He was in a good mood. He'd spent the whole afternoon watching the *Taxi* Collector's Edition VHS tapes my mother had scavenged out of some bargain bin in Arcadia. I had heard his laughter floating up all afternoon. I strained to read in the dark as my father backed out down the driveway.

"You make a New Year's resolution?" he asked.

"No," I said. Then quickly added: "I think they're dumb. What's 'new' about it? It's the middle of winter? I've still got half the school year left. I'm not even through the first semester yet!"

"I made a New Year's resolution," he said after a moment.

He wants me to ask him what it is, I realized.

"I'm trying to read," I said.

We made our way down through the hills and toward the river. Fat snowflakes swirled around us. We passed empty houses on the right and the darkened mass of the Old Benedict on the left. The car moved achingly slow through what was looking more and more like a blizzard. I was grateful, though. It gave me just enough time to finish my chapter before he dropped me off at Selby's. The thief intercepted the letter from the lovelorn student. The thief now felt that he was responsible for a great evil. He was determined to make it right. He was always determined to do the right thing, however absurd it was at the moment. But now, he worried because he felt that he had, through his actions, condemned this young man to die on the barricades.

"Poetic justice," I said aloud as I closed the book.

My father glanced over at me, then back at the road.

I could smell the cinders of some distant fire riding on the air, even though the windows were rolled up and the swirling snow obscured everything around us.

My father finally pulled to a stop in front of Selby's house. The walk hadn't been shoveled, but I saw a lot of bootprints filling rapidly with snow.

"Happy New Years," my father said. "Want me to hold on to your book for you?"

I smiled, nodded, and climbed out of the car.

Selby met me at the door. She was wearing a lot of eyeliner, gigantic hoop earrings, and a distracting low-cut blouse. Bright orange. In one hand, she held a red Solo cup full of hot cider.

"Don't worry," she said. "We made it with bottled water."

"Michael here?" I asked.

"Come inside! It's crazy out there."

I stepped into a world of bright color and loud noise. Each of the five Demnescu kids had invited several of their friends, and only Selby had limited herself to two. Angel appeared from time to time to let us know that she *was not* going to be making a trip to the Proctor ER that night and *was* going to be taking money for anything destroyed over the course of the evening. Everyone – Selby, Angel, the kids, their friends – looked faintly diabolical in the swinging red lights.

The Demnescus had painted their living room luminous white, and with all of the lamps on, reflecting off of every kid's red cups and mugs, the whole room flooded with blood and crimson. It seemed that 1995 had trained the young body politic on both Lenin's demurrage and Rasputin's hemorrhage, and these cyкas had big plans for its downfall. They meant to stab the old year, and poison it, and poison it again, then shoot it, then shoot it again, then drown it in the river, then kill it with cold on the frozen infant shores of 1996. Cut its dick off to be packed in a jar of pickles. They hated 1995 that much.

I followed Selby through the living room, and the kids parted for us, but just barely.

"Don't mind the ghost," Demetrius said to one of his friends perched upon a radiator, taking small sips from his cup, which, I guessed, was filled with something that wasn't hot cider. "It's just my old man, calling out to us from the basement."

Selby led us into the hallway.

"Is Demetrius –" I asked in a low voice.

Selby hunched her shoulders. "Out on good behavior," she said, answering one question and creating several more.

"It was the gun," Selby went on. "He had a MAC-11 and a sack of O-Sugar. They weren't very happy about it."

I followed her into the kitchen, where she gestured toward a plate full of cinnamon-crusted graham crackers and Hershey Kisses.

"Did it work?" I asked.

She stared at me.

"Did juvie work?"

"No," she said. "My mom's disappointment worked. He's been straight since he got out. But he only got out about three weeks ago."

Giggling came from under the sink.

Selby opened the cupboard. It was one of Aria's friends.

"Close it!" she hissed. "I'm hiding!"

Selby closed the cupboard.

We found Michael in the bedroom that Aria and Celesta now shared. A candle glowed in the window, and a cherry shone brightly on the tip of a stick of nag champa. The air was smoky, heady.

"What are you doing in here?" rasped Selby.

"I just ... feel a little bit nervous right now," he said. "What time is it?"

"It's only nine. Hours to go. You might as well go dance."

"I feel weird dancing."

"You go dance. Some of Celesta's friends might flirt with you. You're a cutie tonight."

My cousin was wearing a black silk shirt and a red tie. He was also pointedly not staring at Selby's chest. Something she obviously noticed.

"Don't be a dick, Selby," I said.

Selby laughed.

"I don't want your sister's friends to flirt with me," Michael said. "I'm already ... interested in someone. A girl from my school. In Parc Pierre. Anyway, they're all too young for me."

"You're the one hanging out in my sister's bedroom," said Selby, and she took a sober drink, watching us over the tip of her cup. I wasn't worried yet. If she was planning to spring anything on me, she wasn't going to do it now. Maybe she just wanted to party.

"Hey Selby," I said. "Is there going to be champagne at midnight?"

"Maaaaaybe," she said.

"So, did you invite anyone else? Quanla or –"

"Selby, Selby, Selby!" Celesta rushed into the room. She was wearing Selby's old tutu and leotard, which exposed her long legs and arms. "You got to dance to your song!" she said. "George is putting on your favorite song!"

"Alright!" Selby cried. "Let's go!"

They left. I looked at Michael.

"Is Selby's sister at Radcliffe now?" he asked.

"I guess," I said. "She's thirteen, I think?"

We went out into the other room, waking the incense behind us. We were just in time for the opening drums of "Sympathy for the Devil." As Selby and I started to dance, along with a pack of Radcliffe kids, Michael watched us quizzically.

"I been asking my mom about my dad ..." Selby explained. "What he was like, what sort of art he liked. What music. His favorite band was the Stones. They're the best band ever, and this is their best song."

"Not 'Gimme Shelter'?" Michael asked.

Selby laughed. "Touché!" she said.

Michael shrugged and joined in. We danced under the painted frown of Ștefan cel Mare, who clearly disapproved of all of this. On the walls, the Romanian pale-faced maids rode their red horses. A basket of brightly colored eggs hung from a painted nail. Lace-fragile china plates had been mounted on the wall in a wooden rack, embroidered in scarlet. But if you knew how to look for it – and after knowing the Demnescus for my whole life, I almost knew how – you also saw the Romani signatures upon this house. Images of motion, like horses and boats, or the cross-stitch of an emerald peacock drawing its discerning train behind it. Then, of course, all these Akawean ghetto kids with their Akawean ghettotudes. Selby and her sibs spoke English and Romanian and a few scraps of Romany, but only half of their friends could write. They ranged in age from ten to twenty-one. For Celesta's friends, "dancing" meant leaping up and down, or the occasional awkward bump-and-grind, while some of the older kids, George and Demetrius's friends, danced mithuna close, with a proud anticipation that, yeah, I'd imagined often, but never in front of so many people.

"Where is your mom?" I asked Selby.

She shrugged.

"Probably upstairs, to keep away from the noise," she said. "Sipping brandy, I think. She'll come down for midnight, though. She trusts us."

"Should she?"

"Probably not."

Little George, who was now over six feet tall and probably weighed a couple hundred, turned off the Stones and put on Common Sense. "Resurrection."

"What's this?" someone asked.

"It will break down your miiiiind!" said George, finger-stabbing the air for emphasis.

I went back to the kitchen for a bowl of Cheetos. I was alone in there

Urbantasm: The Darkest Road

and looked out the window. I realized I was looking across the driveway into the hole of a black and open window in the abandoned house next door. At the same time, I saw my own reflection perfectly framed by that void, ringed in blue, and staring back.

I gasped and leapt back.

I suddenly felt like I was being watched. I glanced over my shoulder. The kitchen was still empty. *She only invited Michael and me*, I thought. *Why didn't she invite Quanla or any of her other friends?* And then I realized that understanding is also exposure. The more I learned, the less I could hide. By discovering, I realized the importance of concealment, even as the same discoveries made concealment impossible.

I didn't like being alone in there. I wanted light and voice and presence. But at the end of the night, I knew I'd be alone in the dark, after all.

The next two hours played out cinematically, I guess, in the sense that I was always eating food and watching from a safe distance. Aria and her Truman friends watched us high-schoolers in awe. Michael, Selby, and I were old enough that these fifth graders saw us in the same light as Demetrius and his friends, George and his friends. Celesta's friends, junior high girls, all of them, not a single boy, were coy and flirtatious, especially with Michael (to his confusion), but we – or, at least, I – quickly realized that they were performing more for each other than for us.

Demetrius' friends, the miscreants, the bangers and thugs, were absorbed in each other, sometimes bolting out a loud laugh or leaping from the couch. And George's friends felt a bit above all of us. They never danced but moved back and forth between his room and the living room, smiling at their own jokes and speaking in low voices.

George's girlfriend, Lydia, was on a quest to drink two two-liters of Mountain Dew that night, straight from the bottle, and it looked like she was going to pull it off.

Nothing that happened tonight, between anyone, was happening for real. Nobody was going to fight or hook up. Not with Angel floating around somewhere. Despite the chaos of hormones that fogged these kids like the inside of a tipping kettle, some of them so young that they carried Lisa Frank folders and some of them old enough to drink legally, everything that happened in here was scripted and restrained.

But if you listened carefully, you heard the same old Akawe story boiling through all of these young people. Longing and lust. Which, I suppose, was the whole muddy American story underfoot: Appalachia, Detroit, Flint or Saginaw, whatever, Prahova, wherever, it doesn't matter, doesn't matter, it was all second-hand anyway.

"When you got thoughts like that, you got to just sit on them," someone said. "Don't tell nobody. They just gonna judge you. They look at you and think you ugly bitches. Fuck 'em."

"They want her, they got to take all of her, you hear?" someone else answered. "They want her, they got to *accept* her. She's a mess, but she has real dignity. Real pride. More than you can say. More than me. Looking at her's like looking at the face of God, and I swear that. So she asks for that kind of acceptance. She *insists* upon it. And she'll get it because she knows what she's about. And that means, also, the big decisions she makes. Her decision to be *temporary*. To be *more* temporary than the rest of us all."

"You think she will?" the first asked. "Kill herself?"

"Yeah, she told me, yeah," the second answered, "but not to think about it, yeah, that way, yeah. She says ... she says ... like, her toes wiggle and they have life, and after, after it, after that, they won't wiggle no more. They'll get cold, and they'll rot. But she knows that, and she says she's okay with it. She's gonna be temporary, you know? She's gonna be *good*."

At a few minutes to midnight, everyone gathered in the living room, and Angel came downstairs again. Someone turned on the TV. We saw the tracksuited masses huddled tight beneath the Times Square towers. Mayor Giuliani was talking about the momentous occasion.

"Mute that asshole," said George, and Angel glared at him but muted the television.

Demetrius went to the CD player and put on a song. Pretty quickly, I figured out it was "Gimme Shelter," but it wasn't the Stones' version. It was Grand Funk singing tonight. They threw that piercing vulnerability out the window and raised their walls with strutting guitars, eager egos, indignation, and "give us all the booze," and "give us the keys to the car." "It's an early night," they said, seemingly. "We might as well riot."

The glittering ball moved down its spike in New York City on Angel Demnescu's little TV.

"Sixteen!" we screamed. "Fifteen! Fourteen! Thirteen!"

Mark Farner screamed about rape and murder.

"Twelve! Eleven! Ten! Nine!"

Someone was getting shot.

"Eight! Seven! Six! Five!"

Everyone had been hiding. Now, everyone was exposed. And everyone could see each other. There was no place left to hide.

"Four! Three! Two! One!"

"Gimme Shelter!"

And the honeycomb lights spelling "1" "9" "9" "6" supernovaed their bulbs, and the thirty or so kids in the Demnescu living rooms screamed and leapt into the air, and the older kids kissed, and the younger kids pumped fists, and Angel Demnescu popped the cork from the pink champagne and started pouring cups for the kids, twenty-one and seventeen and fifteen and thirteen and eleven and ten, and we all banged pots, and we all stamped our feet, and I tipped my head back and poured the stinging drink down my throat, and I sputtered from drinking it too fast, and I wiped my nose and eyes, and I looked around.

Neither Michael nor Selby were anywhere to be seen.

It took me a few minutes to find them. I checked Selby's room, then the kitchen, the basement, and I even stuck my head out in the swirling snow to see if they'd gone into the backyard.

They were back in Celesta's room, and they had locked the door.

"Did you two hook up?" I asked.

"Get your mind out of the gutter and get in here, John," said Selby.

"Why are you in here?"

"I wanted to get away from the others. I wanted a few minutes alone with just the two of you, and this is the only door that locks."

I wasn't sure what to say, so I said: "Kinky ..."

Selby rolled her eyes.

"We heard everyone cheering," Michael said.

"Yeah," I said. "George's friends were all making out. Angel was liquoring up the little kids. It was great."

Selby laughed.

"First things first," she said. She held up a joint and lit it. She took a long drag. "Happy New Year," she said and offered it to me.

I took a drag. "Happy New Year," I said, coughing.

I looked at Michael.

"I don't know," he said.

"Whatever you want," Selby said. "But I don't think it would kill you to just fucking relax a little."

Michael looked at me helplessly.

"Hey, she's right," I said. "It isn't gonna make a big difference one way or another."

He took the joint.

He took the tiniest puff, but I had a feeling he'd be tossing and turning with guilt over this for days. Selby made up for his reluctance, and I followed. We passed it around for a minute, and then Selby ground it out in a small clay ashtray.

"Aren't you worried about your mom smelling this shit and busting up your sisters? I mean, like you said, 'whatever you want,' but getting your sisters in trouble? Ice cold."

"No, no, no," said Selby. "She don't come in here." Her voice got more ghetto when she got stoned, but I thought she was getting a jump on it tonight. "Anyway, she don't blame nobody 'lessen the cops get avolved."

Selby pulled her backpack out of a corner of the room and set it on her lap. She pulled out a bottle of champagne and handed it to me. I studied it for a minute. It was Cook's.

"Is this better than that stuff your mom had?"

"Yeah. That shit's barely alcoholic at all. I swiped this from the party store over the viaduct."

I unwrapped the foil and popped the cork, cradling it against my palm to muffle the sound. The liquid foamed out. Michael watched us, his lips parted ever so slightly. Selby brought out three Solo cups, and I filled them with champagne.

I took a big gulp.

"Not yet, John, we got to have a toast!" Selby said.

"Sorry," I said. "I already swallowed it."

"To 1996!" she said, holding up her cup.

We crunched them together.

I took another big gulp.

Selby took one.

Michael took a sip.

"Come on, Michael!" I said. "Are you Akawe or Parc Pierre?"

He took a reluctant gulp.

"So I know," Selby began, expansively, "I know you been wondering why I asked you here tonight, and you and nobody else."

"I haven't wondered –" began Michael.

"I have," I said. "Jesus, your sister invited pretty much everyone she knows. You only invite the two of us? I thought we could see Quanla or maybe Chuck tonight!"

"Yeah," Selby said. "Yeah. And now I'm gonna tell you something. I invited you because you're my best friends."

Michael and I stared at her for a moment.

"Me?" I said. "And him?"

I had expected her to confront me. To accuse me of betraying her trust. To tell me that she had known *exactly* why I was showing up at Lucy's house to "hang out."

"That's right," said Selby. "Best *friends*, so stop staring at my chest,

John, and Michael, stop acting so weird around me. John, would you like it if I stared at your crotch all night long?"

"Yes," I said and took another drink. "Any attention is appreciated."

"Don't get drunk," Selby said.

"Okay," I said and took another drink.

"But I ain't joking," she went on. "I only wanted to invite my very best friends. You, and you."

"But what about Quanla?" I asked.

"What about Adam?" she asked.

When Selby saw that I still didn't understand, she continued:

"I guess I think a best friend is someone you can trust and someone who understands you. I can trust Quanla. I can trust her with anything. But she doesn't understand me. You know what I'm sayin'? You do."

"I do," I said. It was a statement, not a question. All I could think of was that far away night when Selby had taken me behind the viaduct and we had kissed. At the time it had felt so confusing, because I had figured we had to start going out. But it was more a sense of being seen by her and seeing her. Of recognizing each other. That night had been about recognition, not sex. Maybe I was finally old and experienced enough to get that.

"You're saying he understands you, too?" I said, nodding in Michael's direction as if he couldn't hear me.

"Michael understands all sorts of shit you don't see, John!" said Selby. "But yeah, John, yeah. You think Adam understands you? You think that you understand *him*?"

It was a good question. It was a funny question. Mainly because I had spent a lot of time wondering if I understood Adam. He was gay – openly gay, now – and I sure as fuck didn't understand all the ways that this fact overlapped with everything else he experienced. I also didn't understand being born into poverty to drug-spun parents. I didn't understand how he felt being constantly shuffled from one house to another. Adam felt, like he had said, like a brother, but life had put us on different tracks. We could laugh and fight any day, but I couldn't pretend I was able to see his life through his eyes.

"You grew up with everyone expecting everything of you," said Selby, "but did they deliver? Did they come through for you?"

Her words startled me. I had thought this, to myself, in the privacy of my room, not saying it out loud, but I had never told anybody. *No,* I thought. *They did not.*

"Adam doesn't understand that," Selby said. "You can trust him, but he doesn't understand. But I understand. So that's like me and Quanla. And trust me, and she is a brilliant – a genius person! But she's going to go off to college and probably leave ... here. She doesn't understand how trapped I feel. But you do, John! You understand!"

"Yeah?!" cried Michael. "Well, how do I understand anything? I live in ... fucking *Parc Pierre!*" and he sounded so loose and vulnerable that my chest ached for him. I wanted to hug him.

"You, Michael," said Selby, "shouldn't understand. But you do. And it's only because you're a really good listener."

"I don't want to live out there," he wailed. "I really don't. I want to live here! With you all!"

Selby put her hand on his elbow.

"That doesn't matter now," she said. "At least, it doesn't matter as much as you think it does. Because I've been realizing, little by little, that something big is going on. Something that is all about Akawe, but which is a lot bigger than Akawe. I mean, a lot more important. Something that is all about us, but which is bigger than any of us. John, why did you *really* ask me about my bunică Florica?"

It was because the woman in the gold-green gown had told me to ask. *But was that real?* It had to have been real: evidently, the question made sense to Selby.

I decided to dodge.

"Do *you* know what it means?" I asked.

"I know it *means* something. I don't know *what* it means. But I been thinking about it ever since you asked."

"Well? What is it."

"My bunică never told me about what happened to her during the war. But I did hear about it."

I took another sip of champagne, but it was only so I would have something to do with my hands. Michael almost seemed to be holding his breath.

We were listening.

"How do I begin?" Selby asked. "It's hard. There are walls. And doors. Locked. I'm not trying to be weird."

She scrunched her eyes in concentration. She tapped her right foot as she thought, as if its ability to find the floor, again and again, was a code for organizing the stories in her head. Selby opened her eyes.

"When Bunică Florica died last summer," she said, "after the funeral reception was done, my mom and I were alone at the church. It's a beautiful church. Way more beautiful than your church, John. They aren't cheap with the incense. Icons painted on the walls. Everyone knows that Mary wears blue. She carries the whole universe within her robes. Anyway, my brothers and sisters were gone. There might have been a couple of people cleaning up, but my mom and I were basically alone."

"'Your dad was not as positive as I am,' my mom said. 'He liked to explain it this way: 'The way people see God has to do with the way they see the world they live in. If you live in a place that is rich and happy and full of sunshine, then you see God as kind and forgiving, because he has given His people happy lives. If you live somewhere poor or struggling or bloody or beat down, then your God is strict and quick to punish. And since my parents came from Romania after the War – after we had the Germans and the Soviets on us – they saw God as angry. That's why I see God as angry.' 'But George,' I told him. 'I don't see God that way, and my parents came out of Ploieşti at the same time as yours did. They came out of that country together.' Your dad told me I always put too much faith in people. 'Maybe Silvia never told you what Florica told me. Maybe she never told you about where they spent the War.' That made we wonder. My mother *hadn't* told me about the war. She'd said a lot about her childhood in Ploieşti. And about her courtship with my father. About their arrival here, in Akawe. But never the war itself. And never the emigration. My parents had died by the time your dad and I had this conversation, so I couldn't ask them. But Florica was still alive, and we went to see her in Detroit from time to time. I thought that if I asked her about it, she would tell your dad, so I didn't. I didn't want that friction ... that mistrust between us. But then your dad died, and so after the funeral I went to see Florica. I didn't think she'd want to talk about it. About this angry God her son had imagined. About bad things in her life that had happened a long time ago. But I was wrong.'

"'It is hard to talk about,' Florica said. She was an old woman, then. Her hair was like steel wool, but her eyes were always warm. She laughed a lot. She lived in a little apartment just north of Eight Mile. We sat at her table and sipped tea, and looked at the parking lot out the window. 'I will tell you about it,' she said.

"'My family wasn't from Ploieşti,' Florica said. 'They were with the gypsies that settled where they were in Moldavia after they were freed. They did woodwork and metalwork. Spoons and cups and bowls. Some of them farmed in the summer. They weren't nomads. They weren't poor. They owned their own house, for example, which was significant to me because they had been slaves not long before. And my mother's name was Nicoleta, and her mother had not been a gypsy at all, but had come from out east with her husband once the slaves were free. All of the people there welcomed us. I mean the Romanians. We lived in a small village, I don't remember where exactly, but the main thing to grow out there were sunflowers, and even though it has been such a long time, I still remember the sunflowers in the late summer, which just seemed to have a bright smile, every one of them. I could climb the hill behind our house and see millions of smiles going out all of the way to the mountains. And I remember the smokestacks in Focşani – that was the closest city, and we went there to buy things – and we were very respectable, my family, buying Romanian things and speaking both Romany and Romanian well. I think my parents didn't want us to be like the nomadic gypsies who were still traveling in their wagons. We painted our house blue and yellow on the outside, and on the inside, my mother made lace. And the Romanians in the city and the village were always polite to us, very kind, even warm, and they said I was dulce. Melodica. O fată tandra. Which made me smile because I never thought I was 'o fată tandra.' Sunt o fată sălbatica! I still have fond memories of the villagers there. But they were also kind to us in the city, which seemed very strange to me later, because their hearts were not kind, and it taught me that you cannot always trust people by their faces.

"'But I trusted their faces, and I decided I wanted to become a singer. I didn't want to live in a village, surrounded by farms and farmers. I wanted to live in a city and sing and be loved and adored by the people who came to hear me. I sang gypsy songs, and Romanian songs, and songs I made up about sunflowers, and songs my grandmother sang about the blue ghosts that had followed her out of the east back before she had met my grandfather.

"'I did some singing in Focşani, and it went well, and one night I met a young man named Gheorghe Demnescu. He was a Romanian and he fell in love with me. He was crazy, and so was his father. His father had tried to take on the last name 'Dumnezeu,' but nobody bought it, so he went with 'Demnescu' instead. We married and moved to Ploieşti, so he could find work in a factory. We were married on September 1st, 1939. The day that the Germans invaded Poland."

"Hey, that's my birthday!" I said.

Selby narrowed her eyes in irritation.

"Sorry," I muttered.

Selby resumed Florica's story.

329

""'I didn't follow politics much back then,' my grandmother told my mom. 'I was too concerned with my singing and my music. And with putting my house together, and being a young wife, and being full of all the joy in the world ... wanting to start my own family. I still saw unhappiness as very *inconvenient* for me. But then Gheorghe joined the army, and they sent him off to Stalingrad. I was alone in my house, and I started to get frightened. Horrible things were happening in the streets, but my neighbors were still friendly to me. They didn't speak of the terror. They didn't seem to see it. Their friendly faces started to worry me. I didn't know who I could believe anymore.

"Marshal Antonescu was in control then, and for a while he had the Iron Guard – the Legionnaires – in charge. The Iron Guard was for Romania what the Nazis were for Germany. They hated Jews and gypsies and communists. They murdered some Jews in Ploieşti, I remember. Took them away from a synagogue and shot them. They killed even more in the capital. They did horrible things. Things that make me shudder. There are no words. And this whole time, Jews were vanishing from their houses. Their homes and shops all went to the Legionnaires.

""'If the Jews weren't safe in Romania, what was going to happen to the gypsies? We'd been slaves only a hundred years before. That was a year of earthquakes. Houses collapsed. Fires broke out. Hundreds of people were, were crushed beneath the stones. And I remember thinking that the earth itself was angry at what was happening upon its surface.

""'One day, one of my neighbors was standing near the gate to our house waving a newspaper. When I came out to see him, he pointed to the paper and said, 'all you gypsies are going to Transnistria.' What was Transnistria? The name didn't mean anything to me. I was settled. I kept my house and my yard clean. I was married to a Romanian man, and he was fighting in the Romanian army alongside the Germans. Maybe they were going to send somebody else away, but not me. But I asked that man, in my confusion, I said, 'why are they going to send us to Transnistria?'

""'To die,' he said.'"

""When the constables came, they came in the night. They banged on my door. They told me I had to leave. A new home had been prepared for me in Transnistria. I had to go. It had already been decided. I told them that my husband was with the army, fighting the communists. They told me that it didn't matter. My name was on their list, and there wasn't anything they could do about that. They gave me ten minutes to get ready. I grabbed some clothes and blankets. A little bit of money. It was all they let me take. I left my house, and they put me on a train in the cattle car with a lot of other gypsies. Soldiers rode the train with us.

""Once we were all on the train, they weren't so kind anymore. They gave us a bit of bread. They told us they were going to shoot anyone who tried to run. We couldn't see in the dark, and it was hard to breathe. It smelled bad. It smelled like cows at first, but eventually, it smelled like humans. The train finally started to move.

""Everyone who was in there was confused. Some of us had known that the nomadic gypsies had been sent east, but we had lived very differently ourselves. Some of us didn't even speak the Romany language! Then someone said that the guards had lists of all the gypsies they thought were dangerous, and that explained who they put on the trains. But that didn't make sense, either. So many of us were women and children and had never done anything criminal in our lives. But then we heard that the entire family was to be sent, not just the person on the list. Soldiers' families were not supposed to be sent, it seemed, but then in one city, the constables hadn't been able to find all of the gypsies on their list, so they just grabbed other gypsies instead. And then there was one man who said that he wasn't a gypsy at all, but that he was a Black American who had lost his papers. He had won a lot of money from a man in his town – Bușteni – and so his enemies got together and added him to the list.

""This man's name was Jackson, and his wife's name was Silvia. Silvia was a Romanian. The constables had told her that she could stay behind in Bușteni, but she wouldn't leave her husband. She went with him. I spoke to this couple. I told them about my own confusion and terror. I had been worried about my Gheorghe fighting in the east. I had heard horrible stories about the war in Russia. Now I was worried that my husband would come home and find me gone.

Jackson and Silvia were childless. They were mostly worried about their things. The house and their china and their rugs and paintings. Their friends and the shows they went to. The parties and the dances and the concerts and the vineyards.

""I'm sure they looted us the second we were gone,' Jackson said. 'It was all empty!'

""They were very different from me, and they cared about different things than I did, but they were kind voices in the dark, and we were friends long before we were finally able to see each other clearly.

""The journey to Transnistria took eight days. When the soldiers took us off the trains, we were in a new place. Rolling fields. Distant hills. Not enough trees to break the wind. It kept rolling over us. This land would have been pretty in the summertime, but now the leaves and the grass were dying, and the fields had been so worked over that there were muddy ruts everywhere. Bombs had fallen, and the houses had been hit by bullets, and everything looked cracked and fractured to me.

"The soldiers told us that we were going to live together in cooperatives. We would work, and they would give us food and housing in exchange. And they split us up into groups, and sent us off to what they said was our new home. There were several hundred people in my group. I don't know where the other groups went. Silvia and Jackson came with me, and as we walked, Jackson told us – his Romanian was very bad – about how he had lived in New York City, and walked in the rain down Broadway, and saw grand old women wearing great fur coats. And Silvia told me about her mother's house in the mountains, how she had been born in a one-room cottage with a dirt floor but had grown up to work as a maid in the king's palace for a while. How she had polished crystal glasses that the king's hand had held. And I told them about my village in Moldavia, and the singers, and the farmers, and the metalworkers, and the golden sunsets over the Carpathians, and the sunflowers. The long April rains that turned the soil into a great green sponge that just surged with life and vibrancy.

""When we got to the area where the soldiers were going to settle us, they made us dig a trench. I thought that maybe it was going to be for a road or a canal. Later that night, I heard machine guns. The next morning, the soldiers took us back to the trenches and made us fill them in with dirt. They were full of naked dead people. The dead people were Jews, and I wondered if other Jews somewhere were digging trenches for us.

""There weren't any houses there for us to live in. The soldiers put us in an old school building that had been abandoned. There were dozens of us in that one dark room. There were lice biting us all of the time. There was no heat, and as the days got colder, we started taking the roof apart so we could burn the wood for warmth. It was so cold that some men lost their fingers from it.

""And the school started to fall apart because we had taken off too much of the ceiling and the water and the winter kept coming in. 'Let us in.' 'Let us in,' but we had to stay warm. We were already dying. Some of us were already dead.

""It was even worse for the nomadic gypsies. They had gotten there before us, and they had been forced to hand over their wagons. They slept under the sky, and they had no ceiling or roof at all, and every night they prayed that it wouldn't rain and freeze into ice by morning. Then, they prayed that it would rain during the day. They became so thirsty that they drank from the muddy puddles. They bathed in the puddles that filled the trenches and holes where bombs had fallen. As a child, I had always admired their bright clothing, yellows and greens, laced embroidery, but now their clothes were tatters. Some of them went naked. They had no choice.

""There was never much food. Just a little – just a little – cornmeal, and we'd stir it into mămăligă. Maybe a piece of corn. Maybe a little potato. And the nomadic gypsies slaughtered their horses. They loved these horses – their beautiful horses with strong legs and thick coats. The horses were how they had lived, worked, and sold. Like a name. Like a house you build and paint and care for. Like a child. They had taken such pride in their horses! But they had to slaughter them now, because they didn't have anything to eat, and eating was the most important thing ...

""And the nights got longer, and the snow fell, and the ground got hard, and the clouds were everywhere, and we kept dying, because we were so cold, and so hungry. Old men who fell asleep in the dirt. Babies whose mothers were too hungry to give them milk. Some boys, I remember, tried to steal some corn that had been frost-bit and ignored. They got shot. Their bodies were left in the dirt. It was days before the birds got them, because by then it was too cold for birds. And I was also getting thin, and I could count every rib under my skin, just like when I was learning to count, and I could see my own skeleton when I dressed.

""And waves of sickness swept through us. A horrible sickness that made the guards keep their distance, their guns would shoot us before we ever got close, and they kept us away from the other prisoners, too, because they didn't want it to spread. Typhus. A burning fever even though our legs and arms were trembling with the cold. An aching exhaustion even heavier than the hunger in our bellies. A devouring monster. A dead dandelion. A rotted beet. A dead sunflower. A rash that went over our cuts we'd gotten. How we had forgotten what we were before. A hatred of the light. A growing madness because everything had been ripped from us and we'd been put out into the winter and death. And death was in the soldiers. And death was in our bellies. And death was in the cold. And death was in the wind.

""I won't tell you what I ate to stay alive. I won't tell you what I did to stay warm. Hell is not a burning lake. Hell is wind and snow and fields too hard to till. You can't see it, Angel, with everything you've had for yourself and your children. There was nothing for us. Nothing! When someone died, we'd dig a little hole and throw some dirt or straw over them, we were already too weak to do more than that. Or they'd make us dig a hole and throw in all of the dead, a brother, a sister, a mother, a father, and bury them all together. And when that happened, I prayed to God and thanked him that I had left my family. I would have wanted to die if I had had to bury my family like all of the people around me. And I was glad that when I died, my mother, my father, and

Gheorghe would not know, and would not see how sick and small I had become. The bitter dregs we drink when there is no safe water. No safety.

"Finally, the snow melted. It went away. But the hunger just got worse and worse. There was no food. The constables moved us into separate houses then to stop the spread of typhus. These were little houses that the Ukrainians had abandoned. I wound up in a small shed with Silvia and Jackson. It didn't have any windows. It had a door and a hard dirt floor. But it had a table and a couple of chairs, so that we could sit down and eat our mămăligă like human beings for the first time in a year. That was when Gheorghe arrived.

""He was furious.

""He had fought for months at Stalingrad. He had seen men killed, and he had killed men himself. A priest had tried to shoot him in the back, so he had held the man's head down and cut off his beard. He had done other things, too, which he wouldn't talk about. Now he had returned to his home on leave and found another family living in his house. All of our possessions were gone. He followed the reports eastward until he had come to Transnistria, and he was the angriest that I have ever seen any man. He found us in our shed at night. He flicked his lighter open and then blew it out. Then he banged his hand on the table.

""'I will kill them,' he said. 'I will burn them with fire. I will smell their flesh burn.' And he kept lighting his lighter and banging it shut. 'I will take you back to Ploiești,' he said.

""But I had seen more than Gheorghe. What I mean is, whatever he had seen, he hadn't seen the trenches filled with bodies. He hadn't seen the boys who were shot for stealing an ear of corn. I knew what would happen if he tried to burn anything. So, I said to him, I told him: 'Don't fight them with fire. Fight with your mind. Go back to Ploiești and tell them about the mistake they made. They weren't supposed to send the wives of soldiers. They *said* this! If you prove it, they'll let us come back to Romania!'

""Gheorghe kept opening and closing his lighter, and Silvia watched him, and Jackson had an angry face, and he said, 'You see how many gypsies die every day. We could die tomorrow. Or today. If Gheorghe goes back to Romania and gets permission for you to return ... even if he isn't held up ... it'll take a whole month. Who knows if you will be alive by then, Florica. Who knows if any of us will.'

""'If Gheorghe runs away with us now, he'll be a deserter from the army!' I answered. 'We'll be shot for running off, and he'll be shot for deserting. At least if he talks to them, we might stand a chance!'

""We argued for a long time, then. Jackson thundered his anger and stomped around the room, calling down every insult he could think of upon the Romanians and the Germans, and he yelled for Gheorghe and me to run off while Sylvia sat petrified, as narrow and translucent as a ghost. I argued for prudence. I said that evil and suffering had driven us insane, but sanity was our best chance of survival. I begged Gheorghe to leave on the next train, to go as fast as he could, and to pray to God and Jesus and Ștefan cel Mare that I would be alive and waiting for him, and that we could finally go home.

""Gheorghe was silent, though. Silent in anger and misery. He had a full belly. While he was on leave, he had eaten full meals of meat and fruits. He had had wine. He had put salt on his steak. Standing with us, his skeleton of a wife and the two skeletons who had kept her alive, my husband hated himself so much that nothing that I could say could comfort him. So he flicked his lighter on and off, and off and on, and dreamed of killing and revenge.

""And then, after I was almost ready to fall asleep from exhaustion – to let my husband do whatever he wanted – Gheorghe held his lighter over the middle of the table. By its tiny flame, he had seen something etched into the wood. Jackson and Silvia and I had never seen this before. The windowless shack was always dark, and we only came in to sleep. We all leaned over the etching, trying to read its meaning. And even though I couldn't read the words, I put my fingers in the grooves, and I felt what they meant.

.וְשַׁבֵּחַ אֲנִי אֶת-הַמֵּתִים, שֶׁכְּבָר מֵתוּ--מִן-הַחַיִּים, אֲשֶׁר הֵמָּה חַיִּים עֲדֶנָה

.וְטוֹב, מִשְּׁנֵיהֶם--אֵת אֲשֶׁר-עֲדֶן, לֹא הָיָה: אֲשֶׁר לֹא-רָאָה אֶת-הַמַּעֲשֶׂה הָרָע, אֲשֶׁר נַעֲשָׂה תַּחַת הַשָּׁמֶשׁ

"'Jackson is right,' I said. 'We have to leave. If we don't, they'll kill us.'"

""We left later that week," said Florica. "Gheorghe went into a nearby town and bought us food and train tickets. He watched the guards' movements, and at the right hour of the right night, we fled. We ran through the fields until we were miles away. Then we boarded a train at the second town and started west. But when we got to Chişinău, some soldiers got on board and stared at us – especially at Jackson and me – and we thought they were going to kill us or interrogate us, so we got off again. We decided to go on foot the whole way.

""The rest of the journey was a terror. We always traveled at night, still hungry, still weak, stealing food when we could, sleeping in bushes or trees, startling whenever we heard a train whistle or the bark of a dog or the sound of a gunshot. Each morning, I went to sleep wondering if the day would bring death, and every night I woke up glad that we had fled Transnistria. That we were back in our homeland – in Romania – and I could feel us gaining strength and hope every day.

""We hadn't decided what we were all going to do when we got to Ploieşti, but Gheorghe planned to present himself to the army in hopes of a reprimand instead of a court-martial. The war was changing, he said. The Germans had lost at Stalingrad. Now the Soviets were advancing, and the Americans and English were fighting, too. Maybe the Germans would be pushed back to Germany, and the Russians would be stopped at the border, and everything would be as it had been before. But I knew that nothing would be as it had been before, even if every last Russian and German died.

""It was the height of summer when the hills finally flattened out, and we came out on the lime groves and the oil field of Ploieşti. Our timing was bad. We saw a lot of little black clouds coming out of the south, and then the clouds started dropping bombs. It was the Allies. The Germans on the ground returned fire. We could hear the booming – miles off but thousands of times – thousands of times over – and several of the airplanes went close to where we were hiding, so we went into an orchard to wait for the bombing to end.

""When we went in there, we found something strange. A lot of the lime trees there had started growing wild during the war, but we also found a tree that was wilder than any of them. It wasn't large, but it seemed large because of how bent and twisted its trunk was. It had a sort of wax on it. It had thick black bark, and its branches were twisted into circles. There weren't any leaves on its branches, but they were heavy with fruit. Almost like plums, but they were blue. They were like moonlight. They were like starlight. And we all stared at the tree and forgot the bombing and everything that we had left behind us, and the things that were rising up in front of us. We were hungry. We ate the fruit, and it filled our stomachs and quenched our thirst. And then everything was expected, and nothing surprised us anymore. We had already seen so much, so we weren't frightened or surprised at all when Death started dancing around the lime grove.'

"'Death?' my mom asked.

""'Yes, Death,' said Florica. 'Death on dark winds. Death with socket eyes. Death, shining blue. Death wasn't there for us. Death was waiting for someone else. But we also saw everyone we had ever known who had died. They must have followed us as we traveled. And because I had known so many who had died in Transnistria, I saw many of the dead. Hundreds of the dead. They were blurry to look at. They were all shaded blue. I couldn't touch them. Spectre. Fantome. Urbantasmele. Behind us, the airplanes crashed or escaped into the west, and there were no more gray bombs falling on Ploiești. Yet we saw shining blue bombs rising back up into the air. As fires spread among the refineries, other blue fires dwindled and diminished. The ghosts moved around us, and the wind blew, and night fell, and the refineries burnt like a bright blue torch.

""'We've come so far,' Gheorghe said. 'And now we have to stop when we can almost see home!'

""'Is it your home?' Silvia said. 'This place did not love you. This place cast you out. How can it ever be your home again?'

""'It takes time,' I said. 'But we have traveled a long way. Time is travel.'

""'And loss is learning,' said Jackson.

"Wait!" I said. "Where did you hear that?!"

Michael wheeled on me, started from his patient listening.

"Shht!" said Selby. "I'm telling you that story!"

"I'm sorry," I said.

"So my mom said: 'Florica said: 'I asked Jackson: 'Where did you hear that?''"

""'Where did you?' he asked me.

""'And as the blue ghosts moved around us, we talked about our pasts. We talked about them in a way we had never talked before. I told them about my grandmother's mother. How she had two brothers. How she had lived on an island with leafless trees with blue fruit and how her family had seen the blue ghosts. How they said that time was travel and loss was learning. How she had left with a missionary, who had told them that these visions were the sign of the devil working among them. How they had sailed to China and had a baby; my grandmother. How my grandmother grew up and married a sailor they called 'The Gypsy,' and they traveled, somehow, great distances, to Focșani in Romania, and settled with the Vlach Romani there. How my grandmother had been a stranger among the Romani, and yet they welcomed her. How she had taught me her songs about the blue ghosts. That time is travel. That loss is learning.

""Then Jackson spoke. He told us about his grandfather's father. How he had had a sister and a brother, and he had also lived on an island with leafless trees with blue fruit, and how his family had seen the blue ghosts. How they said that time was travel and loss was learning. How his sister had run off with a missionary. Jackson's grandfather told his younger brother to wait for him, and then he went off to bring his sister back home. But he was waylaid, and he never saw his village again. He converted to Islam, and got married, and traveled somehow to Patagonia, and he had a son, and then a grandson that they named Esteban El-Amin. Esteban married an American woman and moved to New York City. They had a son. Their son was Jackson. And Esteban had taught his son the songs. That time is travel. That loss is learning.

""That was how I learned that while I had lost my family forever – my mother, my father, my brothers and sisters – I met my distant cousin, Jackson Allan, and we were children of the whole world, and we had both heard of the blue ghosts, and now we were seeing them ourselves.

""By the time we had finished sharing these stories, Death had drawn away, though we had not noticed because the blue urbantasmele were still drifting about us. But we heard the sound of fighting. It wasn't a ghost sound. It was a human sound.

""We crept back toward the edge of the orchard, and we saw a woman arguing with two soldiers in the road. Death stood on the other side, watching them. The woman was heavy and pregnant. Almost ready to give birth. She was a woman, older than the soldiers. They were young. Just boys. The woman had a beaded sack, and one of the soldiers was trying to rip it from her grasp. She was yelling at them: 'Lasa-ma in pace!'

""And the boy soldier yelled back at her: 'Dă-mi-l! Dă-mi-l!'

""And they tugged and tugged, and the sack ripped, and a bottle of wine fell and smashed against the gravel.

""For a moment, the woman watched as the dark wine trickled into the dirt beneath her feet. Then she stood with one fist on her hip and a finger in the air and said, 'Futu-ţi Dumnezeul!' And the other soldier, the one who had been watching, drew his pistol and shot her in the head. She fell to the ground. The first soldier yelled in surprise.

""The soldiers both ran away. Death came out onto the road and touched the woman's body with his toe. Then she reappeared above her own body as a blue ghost, and she was still and sad looking. And I watched her closely to make sure that it was really her. And it was! And then I looked back to her body to check again. And that was when I saw something kicking inside her belly. And I vomited. I vomited up the last of the fruit we had eaten right there off the side of the road. And Gheorghe and Jackson stared. And Silvia screamed. She had never screamed, never shouted, never made a lot of noise in the whole time I had known her, but she screamed then. Death was kneeling toward the woman's body, ready to touch her belly, when Silvia screamed, and her scream stopped Death. And Death looked up at us. And then two glowing people stepped out of the orchard behind us.

""There were two of them. A man and a woman. They were glowing blue and orange, but they weren't like the urbantasmele. I could tell right away that these were flesh and blood, and that they could walk and talk and do things in the world. And when Death saw them, he drew back to the edge of the road, and then I couldn't see him anymore.

""'Who are you?' Gheorghe asked, but the glowing people walked past us and over to the body of the dead woman. Her head was broken like the wine bottle, but the baby was still kicking inside her.

""'Brother?' said the woman.

""And the glowing man pulled out his penis and –"

"What?!" exclaimed Michael and me.

"It's the story, yo," said Selby. "It surprised me when my mom told me. I'm sure it surprised my mom when Bunică Florica told her, too. Now, shut up! We're almost to the end."

Michael and I glanced at each other, and listened.

Selby resumed: ""'The glowing man pulled out his penis, and it was as sharp as a sword, and with it, he cut open the dead woman's belly with one smooth motion and pulled out a screaming, bloody baby.

""'Sister?' said the man.

""And the glowing woman lifted her skirt and squatted over the road and took the baby and pushed it up inside her until it had completely vanished from view. Then the glowing man and woman turned and walked past us into the orchard again. We ran after them.

""'Where are you going?' Silvia asked. She demanded! 'Where are you taking that baby?!'

""'The glowing woman turned toward us, and she was even more radiant than she had been before, because of the life she carried within her. 'We are taking this living child to join his family in heaven, until he decides to return,' she said. 'But you ... you will want to take shelter now. Fate is about to strike.'

""'As we pulled back, as we cowered behind the skinny trunks of the lime trees, we heard a roaring sound overhead, and an airplane flew over us, and dropped a bomb. The bomb hit the leafless tree, and it exploded into nothing leaving a big hole in the earth. When the smoke cleared, the glowing man and woman were walking toward the hole. It opened onto a sort of cave, and then we looked closer, and we saw the cave became a road that ran under the earth in two directions.

""" 'You should take this road,' said the glowing man. 'It isn't safe in Ploiești. You will die if you go there. They will send you three back to Transnistria. And you,' they said this to Gheorghe, 'they will shoot you for deserting.'"""

""" 'Who are you?' I asked. 'Are you angels?'

"" 'The glowing people looked at each other and laughed sadly.

""" 'No,' said the woman. 'We are not angels. We are the last survivors of Sodom and Gomorrah. God has cursed us, and we travel in time and space and use God's blessings to do God's work.'

"" 'We followed them into the hole. The underground road went off to the left and the right.

""" 'We are going to the right,' said the man. 'You must go to the left. When the road takes you above the ground again, you will be in the City of Akawe in the United States. You can find work and a home there.'

""" 'Go with love,' said the woman.

""" 'Time is travel,' said the man.

""" 'Loss is learning,' said the woman.

Selby took a long, deep breath. When she spoke again, it was her mother's account: "'When your father's mother finished her story, she took a long drink of tea. It was cold by now, but she blew on it anyway.

And when Selby spoke again, she spoke as herself: "And by the time my mom finished telling me all this, all of the lights in the church were out except for a few candles in the sanctuary. We were sitting in the dark.

"'I cannot tell you,' my mom said, 'whether your dad was right or not. I cannot tell you whether God is angry and hard or gentle and tender. But I know that you have to be careful who you trust, and to take care of those who depend upon you.'"

None of us said anything for a while. Outside, the angry snow was swirling harder than ever. I held my cup, but I didn't feel like any more champagne. I wanted to memorize everything that Selby had told me.

"What do you think about it?" I asked.

"What do *I* think?" Selby answered. "I was wondering what *you* thought. I mean, you were the one who asked me about my bunică! But blue ghosts? Urbantasms? I know it was a couple years ago we talked about them, but don't you remember –"

"I do remember! I'm just not sure how it all connects."

"Manole – I mean, Macewoudd – had to have seen some of the same stuff my grandmother saw. The same stuff that I saw. That connects us all. That binds us all. Something made us all see the urbantasms. But God is vicious. Everything he touches dies or goes bad. We have to be watchful. We have to know how to keep secrets. Like my mom said, we have to be careful who we trust. But you haven't been careful, John."

"What?"

"Asking people about God Ostyn? His son, Ezekiel? I sure as fuck hope you haven't been asking about Ash."

"What about Eli?"

"Eli's a pawn! He's a dumbass. He doesn't know half the shit he thinks he knows. But it doesn't matter. Point is, I know, like, after I told you all that stuff at the rave, I know that you and Adam went off to the Os, and were asking around about God and his family."

"How did you know?"

"Because the Os are small and people got big mouths, okay? Plus, you and Adam running around with Juanita was like the most obvious thing ever."

"Wait," said Michael. "You saw Juanita?!"

"It was nothing," I said. "We were just asking her some questions about the Chalks and shit."

"And you spent the night at her house," Selby added.

"I slept on the floor!" I said. "And Adam was there! And Juanita's brother!"

"You didn't even tell me!" said Michael.

Selby pressed on: "If *I* heard about what you were doing, you don't think God Ostyn heard about it? You think he doesn't hear about *everything* that happens over there? And if they know about you, maybe they follow it back to me? You know they'll kill me if they know what I've been up to, John! I mean, I'll be dead in some warehouse, and it'll be your fault! All because you couldn't keep your mouth shut. Look, I said you were my best friends, and you are. Both of you. But you need to back off my shit, understand? This is a story I've been writing my whole life, and I get to write the ending."

"And what about Lucy?" I asked. I was on my feet. I remembered her eyes. I remembered how she smelled. I saw her face and her brows and her hair. I thought about Lucy's anger and despair as she confronted Selby in that blank bedroom.

Selby turned her face up toward me, and she radiated anger.

"What about Lucy?" she asked. "I was gonna try and hook you two up again. You think she'd be hanging around Eli if she was going out with you? But no, you had rebound your ass into May instead, who doesn't have shit to do with shit. Anyway, you were there. You heard what I said to Lucy. What I *risked* to make her see the truth of what that family *is*. Isn't it enough that I did that for her? But that wasn't all I did for her. Oh no, I did more for her than that."

"Yeah, but how did Lucy get with Eli in the first place? I mean, if she wasn't near you and you weren't near him?"

"Lucy got too fucking close!" said Selby. "I didn't choose that. She did. She's still choosing it today. She doesn't give a shit. She thinks she's got something to prove. You never saw that about her, did you?"

"What," I said. "What do you mean you did more for her?"

Selby barreled on. "Lucy shouldn't be my problem. But I'm an asshole too, worse than you, so of course I help her out. Even if she doesn't want it. Even if she doesn't like it. Same as Cora. She thought she wasn't even in a bad situation. She didn't realize how bad things had gotten. Back at her home, I mean. Her dad abused her, you know? And she was mostly just with her mom most of the time. And Ash and the Chalks? That's how they pick them out. They send Eli out with money and presents. Take some girl out for a date. Take her to a movie. Buy her dinner. Buy her ice cream. All this innocent shit. No rape. No fucking. Nothing physical. But they take her back home at midnight. Just to see – just to see – who is gonna freak out about it. A girl's mom, a girl's grandma starts bitching and calling around at ten at night? That isn't gonna work for the Chalks. No, that girl's *protected*. Quanla's *protected*. I'm *protected*. I'm sure Omara was fucking *protected*, John. But Cora gets back at midnight, and nobody complains? They barely even noticed she was gone! They – her mom, her dad – they're all busy with their own shit. Working or running around or taking care of their other kids. They're glad she's back, but they're not *worried* about it. And Ash says, 'take her out again, Eli.' So, he does. This time, Cora's out until maybe two in the morning. Same deal as the first time. Maybe she goes to hear a band or watch some TV, or they give her some beer, but nothing major. She gets back after everyone's in bed, and they don't say shit about it the next day, and they don't bitch to Eli, and Eli tells Ash. 'Now,' Ash says, 'now it's looking good.' So, the next time they keep her overnight. No call home. No explanation. Just drop her off in the morning. And she's all moony and happy about the shit, because she just got to spend the night with her *boyfriend*, and that's such a fucking *adult* thing for her to be doing. And when nobody notices or complains about that, then they know they've got her. After that, it won't be long, and she'll be tricking out of houses in the Os, and they'll just tell her parents that she's staying with her boyfriend's family, and they're taking good care of her, and he's buying her lots of presents, and God is getting her good and fat on his own dime, and he'll send over some money, a hundred here, a hundred there, to her parents, and they use it to pay their rent, and it's one less fucking mouth to feed, and it's just so fucking sad, John. It's so fucking sad, Michael. And I watched this shit for months, and I just couldn't watch it anymore!"

"So you got her out."

"She had this aunt in Florida she trusted. I called the aunt, and let her know Cora was coming. I made sure she'd be there for her. Then I found someone to drive Cora down. Someone *protected*, who barely knew me, and didn't have any connections to the Chalks. And I let Eli know, because someone had to let it look like she had just slipped away on her own. I couldn't have pulled it off without him, but I had that he knows that about me, and I never know when he's going to use it against me. I planned this shit for so long. It took months and months."

"But what about Lucy?!" I asked through clenched teeth. I was clenching my fists, too. "What else did you do for her that I don't know about?"

"Oh," Selby said. "I got her out too, although I don't think Eli ever had those plans for her. He liked Lucy as his for real girlfriend, you know? He didn't want to ho her out. And Ash wasn't going to give him shit about it, neither. Like who fucking wants to get laid by Lucy, anyway? But I could see what was coming down the line. Because Lucy was always looking to prove something. Like, it didn't matter if EZ or God or Eli weren't going to hurt her, she's fucking crazy, and she was going to find crazy something to do, anyway."

"What did you do?"

"I didn't get it at first. I thought she just didn't realize what he *was*. Eli. Well! You saw how she reacted! She was making excuses for him. She didn't care. So I thought about it for a long time ... but I was also noticing about the Ostyns and the O-Sugar. They're not all Chalks, you know. The Ostyns. EZ is sort of a retired Chalk, but they need him. He gives them info they need. But Eli's brother Ash is way in deep with the Chalks. Anyway, I knew that they were selling O-Sugar and that people taking O-Sugar were seeing urbantasms. Then you asked me about my bunică, and that reminded me that *she* had seen urbantasms, too. I was thinking about Macewoudd, who told me about the urbantasms all those years ago, and I was thinking about those Chalk fuckers that were just as heartless as the Iron Guard and those other fuckers who sold out my bunică. I couldn't take it anymore!"

Selby had started pacing around the room. Michael watched her, open-mouthed. I tore myself away and picked up the champagne bottle. I needed something to block this, to swipe this, to erase the mounting horror, but the bottle was empty. *Did we drink all that?* I wondered.

I heard myself asking: "Are they still together? Is Lucy still with Eli?"

Selby stopped pacing and thought for a long moment.

"No," she finally said. "No. I broke them up. I mean, I got Lucy to dump him. But it wasn't easy, John. I mean ... I'm scared. I ... I don't know what's going to happen to any of us."

"To ... her?"

"To me! I don't know what they're going to do to me! And I don't know what Lucy's going to do, either! In Arcadia, there's this coffee shop. Ground State. It's not that far from the mall. I knew Lucy was going to be there. I knew ... I knew she was alone. Her mom was dropping her off. Eli was going to meet her there. But I got there first. I had Demetrius drive me. So we got there, and we saw Lucy waiting at a table. I told her to come outside. I told her I needed to talk to her about something important ..."

Her voice trailed off.

"What happened?" Michael asked.

"Lucy came outside. For a minute, we talked in front of the car, and Demetrius was just standing there. And then when I saw that the parking lot was mostly empty and nobody would notice, I shouted to Demetrius, and we both grabbed Lucy, and we threw her in the trunk of his car, and slammed it, and drove off."

"You what?!" I roared.

"Shhhh!" Selby hissed. She looked apprehensively at the door. "Celesta will hear you. Or my mom."

"You ... you thought this would get her to break up with –"

"I had to get through to her, John! I had to have a way, I had to have a way, I had to make her see how bad he is! How bad that family is! How ... serious –"

Selby looked to the windows, to the walls, to the messy floors for something that would help her explain. But she found nothing.

"I told you about what they did to me," she said. "What they did to my family. What they threatened me with. I've told you more than anyone else, John. But I had to show Lucy too! I had to *show* her!"

But I was only half listening, because as she spoke, it was like a door had opened on her mind, and I understood what she was saying.

"You took her ... *there?*" I asked.

"I had to," Selby said. "I had to be able to say: this is where your boyfriend's dad lives. And he is a racist. And his son was a rapist. And most of them are murderers. And this is where he lives. This is the kind of place he calls his home. He rules from here, and he thinks he rules over all of Akawe, and that's why he calls himself 'God.' I was going to tell her that."

"Did you?"

"When Demetrius opened the trunk," she said, "Lucy was already laughing. I mean, she was laughing before she even saw us. Before she saw that house. Laughing before she heard the first word. And that was when I knew that nothing I said was going to change her mind. She'd made up her mind. She knew what she wanted to prove. But she surprised me."

Selby stopped pacing again and looked down at us.

"'You obviously want me to dump him real bad, Selby,' she said. 'Well, fine. He ain't got nothing I want. He isn't my answer anyway. I'll dump him. But I want you to know, Selby,' and she said this to me while she was laughing so hard in the back of that trunk, she said, she said, 'I don't owe you shit, and you don't scare me, and that house don't scare me, and God don't scare me, and you should be scared of me, and nobody scares me but me.'"

Selby closed her eyes. I had no breath. I felt exhausted.

"Did, she ..." I started.

"We took her back home after that. In the car. That was the last weekend before Christmas break. She dumped him, like, the next day. They're still friends. But they're not going out anymore. I don't. I don't ... I don't even know what happened with her. I mean, I just know. They mess up people, John. The Ostyns do. Not just their bodies, but, like, their souls. I don't want you to get hurt, and I don't want you to do something that gets me hurt. So stay away from them. Both of you."

"But what about you?"

Fists banging on the door.

"Selby!" came Celesta's voice from the other side. "What are you doing in there? It's *my* room! Why don't you go in your *own* room?"

Selby snatched the ashy remnants of the roach and jammed the champagne bottle back into her backpack. She zipped it up and opened the door for Celesta.

"It's nothing!" said Selby. "Look, we just wanted to talk for a few minutes. Why you gotta be a bitch about it, huh?"

"No, it's not!" said Celesta. "You were all getting high! I can smell it!"

"We weren't," snapped Selby. "Anyway, I know you been ditching sixth hour to hang with Marcus on the roof. You want me to tell Mom about that? You know what they say about snitches, Cel!"

"Get the fucking fuck out of my room, Selby!"

Celesta's face flushed. *Did Selby look like that in seventh grade?* I wondered. *Did I? It wasn't that long ago ...*

"Yeah, yeah," Selby said. "We will."

Selby shut the door in Celesta's face. She turned back to face Michael and me.

"It's 1996. Happy New Year, my dear, sweet best friends. Now: stay away from the Ostyns. Stay with each other. Love each other. Trust each other. Everything is fucked up. Everything is crazy. Everyone is going to die. We're all going to die. But let's not die for a little while. Let's not. Please?"

And before either of us could reply, Selby flung the door open again and parted the angry waves of clamoring girls, while the red light of Angel Demenescu's house crowned her with a halo.

Urbantasm: The Darkest Road

SIXTH REVOLUTION
ILLUMINATION

8. Will You Warm the Cold or Will the Cold Make You Cold as Well?

"I am a little candle under snow. I go out right away."

9. Do You Say More with the Words You Choose or with Your Tone of Voice?

"I don't never pick the right words. I have to do it with my tone of voice."

10. What Is One Word to Describe Your Dearest?

"Father – Sad. Mother – Determined. Michael – Conscience (don't con science). Selby – Revenge. Adam – Adventure, or longing. Whatever. Quanla – Clarity. Omara – Good. Nova – Loud. Chris – Helpful. Lucy – Mysterious. May – Simple."

11. What Is the Meaning of Love?

"I used to think that it was a feeling inside you that you are right and they are right and everything buzzes inside you like the sun and fire and water and you are perfect in the universe. Now I think love is wanting the best for somebody else and doing things for them instead of just doing them for yourself all the time."

12. What Is One Word to Describe You?

"Hidden. No, not hidden. Hiding."

Sometime after New Year's Eve, I lost *Les Misérables*. I don't know what happened to it. I set it down somewhere and could never find it again. So I didn't finish it, after all. From such a distance, the story was hard to remember. A week into 1996, I already felt like Christmas had happened centuries ago.

On the day school started again, the temperature had fallen to the single digits. A lot of snow had fallen, too. I expected them to cancel school that morning, but they didn't. All across Akawe, kids went out into the iridescent dunes of ice while the wind howled along unplowed streets as barren as the surface of the moon.

When I got to Eastern, I found the halls half-empty, I mean, even emptier than usual, and everyone was bundled into their dark coats and damp gloves, all black, mostly, and with the lights flickering, it was difficult to make out anyone's features. We shambled through the day, not speaking, breath puffing because it was as cold as a cave in there.

Still, there *were* lights on. In some classrooms, if I put my palm against the furnace slats, I felt the warmth of dry air. Students eventually took off their gloves. Their hats. Some girls laughed at each other's wild hair. Some kids' gloves were just as stained by sweat as by snow. They had skipped the bus. Instead of waiting outside for an hour, they had walked, slugging through the thigh-deep snow, their hearts banging like angry drums. Those hearts knew that we weren't even halfway to summer yet. It wasn't the number of days that bothered us. It was the question of how many catastrophes hid among the days to come.

When I finally got to Northern for Civics, Mr. Barakat got distracted and slid away from his lecture on executive privilege into the murky story of Meriwether Lewis.

"'We were now about to penetrate a country at least two thousand miles in width, on which the foot of civilized man had never trodden; the good or evil it had in store for us was for experiment yet to determine.' Mr. Lewis said that," said Mr. Barakat. "And they did – Lewis and Clark, with Sacagawea as their guide. And despite all of the storms and difficulties, they made it all the way to the Pacific Ocean, and back again. The wilderness of North America wasn't an evil that Meriwether Lewis was unable to overcome. It was his own mind that turned against him. He ended up shooting himself in the head in the darkness of his bedroom at an inn. It wasn't a clean shot, either. He scattered his brains but bled out. That was how he died, you see, and he didn't die for hours. He was losing his mind, you see."

And then the bony wind dragged its knuckles down the shingles out my window.

I lay in bed, tired and awake. I heard the wailing moon. I heard the blanketing clouds. I heard the feedback loop. I heard heat death. The rotation of reality. The iced-up naked branches. The phosphor skies. The blueberry snow drifting. The visible wind. They were Real. They all sang blue.

We're done pretending by now that everything isn't blue, right? We've stripped away that veneer, haven't we? I mean, we've accomplished that much, right? Baratashvili was a Georgian. Caucasian Georgia, not Dixie Georgia. Nikoloz Baratashvili. He called out blue as an effusion of divine action. A fiery color that cooled the sky. A blue sky might scatter blue rain, he promised. So, it might fall, come spring, upon the Tenth Town, the ghost home, the shocked hive, the wigwam, the first.

I heard aurora, north, cold, blue.

I drew my covers around my shoulders and shivered.

And then my parents, hoping, maybe, to extend the fast-fading camaraderie of our night-before-Christmas-Eve in the icy dark, had an animated discussion about throwing a pasta dinner – no, a party, even! Yes, we would have everyone over – all of their friends and all of my friends – and we would have hot dogs, and ham and melted cheese on toasted slices of Italian bread, and a ton of pasta, and cocoa for the teens, and Moscow Mules for the adults.

"But not for you!" my mother grinned at my father.

And they could put on the Godfather trilogy, or at least the first two, or maybe it was Star Wars, or maybe it was Star Trek, or maybe it was *The Sound of Music*.

"Or we could ask Mabel to bring the *Terminator* movies!" I said.

"I've got them!" my father cried. "I've got them in the attic! What's Mabel got that I haven't?"

"A job?" my mother laughed.

My father dropped his smile, stood up, and left the room.

"Mark!" my mother called after him. Then, "Jesus," she said, as she followed him down the hall. I sat and poked at my dinner, straining to hear them, but they were silent. We never threw a party that winter.

And then RAN North announced they were ending their Akawe operations in April '96. This had been expected. But X Metal / X Future Fabrication were going to shut down too. X Auto had just invested millions in new equipment at Metal, and everyone had figured that they were set for years.

Now, another 1500 jobs were going to leave the city on top of the other tens of thousands, and I started to wonder if there were going to be *any* cars made in Akawe when the new millennium finally rolled around.

The graffiti around town recalibrated its subject matters that month, splayed across brick and cinder-block walls where the graffitists had stamped down the snow to give themselves more room to work. Fewer tags. Fewer gang signs. More politics, darkness, blood, more confusion. This wasn't the old anti-Japanese bullshit that had appeared on expressway overpasses during the first shutdowns of the 80s. This was something new. Fury at the company. At the city. At America.

My favorite mural was on the Pipes a block from Eastern. I saw Governor Rhinelander imprisoned behind the four steam pipes, dead in a bath of rust-colored water, a fountain pen in one hand, the other clutching the scrolled-up Michigan Public Act 666. On the concrete wall behind the columns, a black-skinned dashiki-clad Charlotte Corday escaped into the shadows.

Even from behind fogged-up bus windows, I smelled the stench of aerosol dispersing through the arid air.

And then Lucy told me that she was going to kill herself.

I found her at her locker – without Eli – and I said:

"Hey. Happy New Year. What's up?"

"I'm having a shitty day. Whatever. Someday, I'm going to kill myself."

I stared at her. She laughed bitterly.

"Don't worry," she said. "It isn't going to happen today. It might not even happen for a long time. It's just that every day I have to decide if I want to keep living, and every day I have to answer 'yes,' and someday I'm probably going to answer 'no.' I only have to once. Anyway, fuck. It's hard when it's cold out, you know?" She laughed again. Gently, with self-deprecation. To set me at ease.

I felt awkward and embarrassed, for myself and for her.

"I don't think that's very funny," I said.

Lucy shrugged.

"Don't blame me," she said. "Take it out on my neurons."

"Well, when you say shit like that, what do you expect me to say? You need help, I want to help you, but you say shit like that, and I'm like, 'I can't do anything about that.'"

"I'm sorry," she said. "You're right. I should have just whatevered. But you asked how I was, and I gave you a true answer. Anyway, I never asked you to help me." She turned back to her locker and contemplated the crumpled papers and food wrappers mounding at the bottom.

"You still eating lunch in the library?" she asked.

"Yeah."

"Mind if I join you?"

"Okay," I said. "But don't you want to sit with May and ... them?" I didn't want to say Eli's name out loud, or to hear what Lucy thought of Selby.

"I don't really want to be around anybody."

And then Adam and I skipped school and did drugs.

I mean, it didn't really happen like that, only it totally did.

I hadn't seen much of Adam since our adventure in the Os, but one day I found him at my locker, almost levitating, and I asked him, "What are you on?"

Adam leaned in confidentially and said: "Minithins and a beer." Then he leaned back. "No way I can sit at a desk and read a book right now."

"I'm so sick of this shit," I said. "All of it. I wish I could do that. Just escape a while."

"Sorry, man," Adam said. "I ain't got no more minis. I took what I had."

"That's okay. Forget about it."

"I got some Ibogaine back at Grandpa M's. You could have that."

"What's that?"

"My moms got it when she was in Canada trying to kick smack. It didn't work, so she just gave me the rest. It's, like, I think it's kind of like acid only more mellow. But they're old, so they might not even work. I haven't taken one in, like, a year."

I sat on the thought for a moment. If I wanted, I could be drug free for another day. I mean, except for the occasional toke or sip of beer. If I wanted, I could spend another day in the shadowy school, watching everyone else freeze and worry. Or, I could go over to Adam's to trip on his mom's expired medicine. It was up to me. "I mean, I don't know," I said, reflexively playing it safe. "It doesn't sound like a great idea."

"You don't have to decide," said Adam. "Let fate decide. Flip a coin. Let destiny choose for you. Tails, you just go to your class and forget I ever brought it up. Heads, I get us a ride back to my grandpa's, and we get you tripped the fuck up."

My heart fluttered. It felt the heat of the moment. Anything was better than more of this wintry decay.

"Okay," I said, "but I'll flip the coin, and I don't want you looking when I do it."

"I will spin around thrice," Adam said, trilling his rs and turning in place.

I dug a quarter out of my pocket and flipped it.

It landed tails.

"I got heads," I said.

"Awesome!" said Adam. "Let's go."

The next hour flew fast-forward. Adam and I went out to the payphone and used the quarter I had just lied about to call Carla. "I'm sick," Adam said, his voice running quick and excited. "John is too. We need a ride back home." Then we went outside and shivered in the parking lot until Carla showed up. We piled very healthily into the back of her Aubrey, and fifteen minutes later, I was sitting barefoot and Indian style on the floor of Adam's living room. He fished a rolled-up wad of toilet paper from behind the television and unwrapped a long capsule that looked like it had been filled with fine sawdust.

I put it on my tongue and swallowed, then drank a glass of water.

"Am I gonna hallucinate?" I asked.

He nodded.

"Is it, what, like acid?" I asked.

Adam stared at me a moment. "You've done acid?"

"No."

"Well, then you're not going to know. I mean, kind of. I don't know. It's, like, more spiritual, you know? Less colorful. Least that's what I think. It could be different for you. Hey, I'm gonna go make myself some eggs. I've been cooking a lot the last year or two, and I got good with eggs. You want an omelet?"

"Sure."

"With bacon?"

"Sure."

Adam left. I sat there on the floor, painfully aware that I wasn't feeling anything strange, all the while hearing the clink of dishes and the running of water coming out of the kitchen. Nobody else was in the house with us. I moved onto the couch. It was harder to move than I had expected. That was the first thing I noticed. Then Adam walked in holding two plates piled with golden omelets that must have been cooked from blemishless eggs lain by saintly hens. It was all a magnificent froth of yellow-white, creamyrich gold drizzled with hot sauce and peppered with bacon crumble.

"I put Cholula on it," Adam said. "Because it's the best. I should have asked first. Is that okay?"

"You know," I said, though I didn't know why, "I played this video game a year ago where you're a kid who loves baseball, and it's your job to kill this evil guy who wants to destroy the universe. Which isn't that fucked up, right? But what's fucked up is that in order to do it, you turn yourselves into robots and get shrunk, then you go back in time to when the evil guy was just a fetus, and you go into his mother's womb and fight him, and once you're there, you say prayers until God aborts him. Isn't that fucked up?"

It was my voice speaking, but I felt like someone else was thinking up the words and saying them.

"No way that game exists," Adam said. "Nobody would let them sell a game like that."

He handed me my omelet, and I took a bite. It was good, but I didn't feel like eating.

"You want that?" Adam asked when he had finished his omelet.

I handed him my plate and he ate. A warmth gradually swelled up in my body and moved into my limbs, as if *I* had been the one filling myself with eggy goodness. A whirring, like the comforting consistency of a thousand flawlessly functioning machines faded in around me. I could speak. But whenever I spoke, the whirring faded out, and because I enjoyed the sound of the whirring, I tried to speak as little as I could. I knew I was shaking as I sat on the couch, but I didn't think I could walk or stand up or change my position at all. It didn't bother me. Then, twisting orms, sequencing carpets, rhythms of color, of shapes divided by and inlaid upon themselves, and many eyes appeared in front of me and spun in circles like a locker lock.

"Don't worry so much about it," Adam said. "It's supposed to happen like this."

"Why are you so careless?" I said, and then shut up so the whirring machines would return.

All day long, in light and darkness, images came and went, approached and retreated, like tides unsure whether to rise or fall. I kept feeling like shadowy figures, lightweight, humanoid, featureless, were creeping cautiously along my brow, prodding my lips open with their stubby heels and tugging my eyes open. They explained that calculus could state with accuracy and precision the momentary contours of the flickering clouds. They told me that I could calculate, through math, the angles made by the rays of stars to multiply against the reflected brightness of the drifting snow. This, they hinted, was all very obvious. The real trial was in understanding the provisionality of scale. That the feigned luminosity of the snow was instrumental in determining the shifting distances between suiciding stars. Once I understood this – once I learned to collapse scale – I could easily move on to the infinite, because what is infinity but an unbounded negation of scale? Thus could I prove the existence of God. Because I had a self and my self was me, and what could we, myself or any other mote of consciousness, name the totality of matter and time and above all our *selves*? We could – we must – name it God. At least that's what they told me.

"Can I have some paper and scissors and tape?" I asked.

"Sure," said Adam.

I spent a few hours fiddling around with hypercards and Möbius strips. I made many Möbius strips, and I cut some of them in half lengthwise and ended up with skinnier, longer Möbius strips. I cut some of them into lengthwise thirds, and I ended up with twisted figure eights.

"Don't be limited by shapes," the figures said.

When it finally started to get dark out, I got up and called my parents. I told them that I was studying at Adam's. That I'd be back after dinner. After that, I fell asleep on the couch. I woke with Grandma M moving around the room, straightening up. I got up, put on my coat, and left. It was almost ten by the time I got home.

"What's with you?" my father asked as I hung up my coat.

"Tired," I said, and I was already on the stairs. Already in my room. Already in my bed. Already asleep.

And then, one night, the Allard brothers took me to a drink-free all-ages club downtown hosting four bands in five hours. That night they were headlining a weird feedbacky rock band from Livonia, but some solid Basadena bands as well: Simple, Cherry Chime, and some ska rockers. Cherry Chime welded disordered jangles to blue Monday mellow tones. Simple stomped down the stage with the wild distortion scissoring our heads in half. His Name Is Alive vroomed out pixelated soul music. The light was dim and fuchsia. The air smelled like ash and lavender. It was cool in there. We left our coats on. Dozens of kids boiled across the carpeted floor, jumping on each other, loving it. I could hear the loud laughing, and the sliding t-shirts and bra-straps and dirty boots got to me for a moment, and I felt warm again. I felt, for a minute, like I wanted to leave the wall and meet someone. To get a name. A phone number. Did I still have that piece of paper with the girl's phone number from the *Sleepy Hollow* auditions? Or had I lost it along with my hat? Dammit, if only I hadn't lost my hat!

And then, one night, my mother took me out into the brackish slush because "I want to buy you something," she said. We went out into Arcadia to the Best Buy whose big yellow letters floated above the smashed parking lot, while ragged clouds chased the last echoes of a fading sun.

"What are we looking for?" I asked.

"A CD player," she said. "You love your music. You've wanted one for years. I was going to buy you one for Christmas. I mean, I wanted to. I'm going to buy you one tonight."

"You know we can't afford it," I said.

"Forty dollars or whatever isn't going to make the difference. If I need to, I can cut back and make up the money somehow. Drive less. Try not to buy coffee when I'm out. I do that sometimes. Too much."

We went in and bought a small Sony boombox with a cassette and CD player and a MEGA BASS PORT.

"Okay," my mother said. "You go buy a couple CDs, and I'll pick out one for you, too. You'll like it. I promise."

She was animated in her excitement. I *had* wanted a CD player for years, so I was just riding that wave. I hurried down the Pop/Rock aisle and grabbed *Daydream Nation* by Sonic Youth because Crystal had told me that they "blow up amps." A new Tori Amos album was out, and I remembered how Adam had played her for us in his bedroom, and her swirls of voice and piano had eventually sent us out toward the Os. So I bought a copy of *Boys for Pele*. When I met my mother up front, she'd gotten me something new, too. *Pearl*, by Janis Joplin. The first banks of lights far overhead had started shutting off. The store was closing for the night. We paid and went back out into the cold. But it wasn't a silent cold anymore.

And then the record player broke.

And then the furnace broke again, but that was a quick fix.

And then the expensive water filter my father had bought for the shower broke. He called the company. The filter wasn't defective. It had been overloaded. By lead? No, by iron oxide. When we hammer-smashed it open to see what was going on, we saw rust streaks striating the mesh grille.

"I can't afford a new one," my father said. "Not now. But hey, you got your new CD player."

"So what?" I asked. "We go to Aunt Mabel's for showers again?"

"I'm tired of asking her for help. No. Just go to school early. Take your showers at the locker room there."

"I can't do that! I'm not even taking gym!"

"Ask the teacher. He'll say yes."

"Fuck that. I ain't ghetto."

"John, our water is bad, and I can't do shit about it. So, I guess you are."

And then the news about our bad water went national again. It was bigger now than it had been before. Everybody was talking about Akawe for, like, a week. The new mayor had declared a state of emergency, and it was like she had strapped the order to a relay baton and slammed it into the complacent skulls of the county commissioners. After they had declared an emergency, they lobbed the order at the state, and the state passed it on to the feds.

All of a sudden, everybody from Carolina to California was talking about Akawe through the shut bathroom door while waiting for their morning turn at the toilet. Protesters arrived at City Hall with mannequins, papier-mâché effigies of the governor and the emergency manager, and Jenny Holzer-style flashing lights.

It all seemed strange to me because last week had been just as shitty as this week was. Hell, I couldn't even keep the days straight, I was so tired. But what was the same? What was different? We'd been back on Detroit water since October, but the pipes were still ruined, and we still didn't have any money to fix them. The emergency manager was still running the show, and nobody had lifted a finger to reconsider either him or the law that put him there. The same suits still worked at the state environmental office, and while they felt Very Bad about the poison and death they had fed us, that was where it all stopped. Was all of this new attention really going to change anything? And who was to say it would change for the better? Things can change for the worse too, you know?

I didn't bother to try to guess what would happen ahead. I lay on the couch and spied on the tragically unarrested Patrick Rhinelander as he delivered his State of the State address.

He'd given himself a close shave with a straight razor. Slapped his bare face with bracing aftershave. He stepped out into the fiery light of the state capitol – columns and walls the color of Michigan wheat and eggplants – and adjusted the silver "Akawe" pin he'd fixed to his lapel.

"You take that off," I told the TV.

Then, Rhinelander said what he knew he needed to say.

"I am sorry," he said.

"Fuck you."

"I take responsibility," he said.

"Go to hell."

"I will fix this."

"You can't fix shit, you asshole moron!"

For the next hour, I listened as my governor talked about entrepreneurship, state aid, water filters, and federal involvement, and I glared at the screen until smoke started to rise from the outlet plugged into the wall. Because Rhinelander didn't say shit about how the Akawe schools were going to balance their budget when a quarter of their kids had suddenly landed in Special Ed after his water crisis took root. He didn't say shit about how his teams choked out their own appointed scientists when they started to realize that the number of Legionnaires' deaths looked more like eighty than eight. He didn't say shit about how Michiganders were going to foot the legal bills for his personal defense in all the lawsuits on the way.

When the address was over, he and his retinue parted the dark down I-96 all the way to his quaint brick apartment in downtown Ann Arbor. Activists had chalked up sidewalks out front with images of sludge sliding from rusted spigots, but there were thankfully few protesters at this late hour. Two girls with dreads were arguing with the security detail. Let them argue. Rhinelander said goodnight and went inside alone. He climbed the stairs and entered his condo, closing the white door softly behind him.

He went into the bathroom – large, ornate, windowless – and turned on the light and disrobed in the pearly glare reflecting off the ivory tiles underfoot. He turned the shower on, and the water cushed out like alpine snowmelt rapidly warmed by the coils of lodged serenity, crystalline, diamondine, unadulterated except for the good kinds of minerals. The nourishing kinds.

Patrick scratched a dry patch in the small of his back, but it was hard for him to reach. He climbed in and let the soothing fingers of water pull away the crust of cologne, the aftershave and hair product, the sheen of sweat and nervousness. Jesus, this wasn't worth it. Why had he run for governor, anyway? He'd had good ideas. You had to cut what you could cut. You couldn't let cities get away with leeching off the state. If they couldn't sustain, they'd have to do with less. Could anyone really think that this was his fault? It was foolish. He wasn't a career bureaucrat. He was an accountant. He'd just gotten here.

He'd had the good ideas, but the human element was tricky. Humans were unpredictable, but that wasn't his fault. Anybody else in his place would have done worse. Anyone else in his place wouldn't have even tried. Anyway, could he hold the hand of everybody in his own environmental department? And then the emergency manager? Margate had had a very good reputation as a city administrator in Kalamazoo. Or was it Benton Harbor? Whatever. When Rhinelander had made the appointment, he'd been sure to choose a Black man. What, wasn't that enough for them? He thought that was their whole currency!

It was starting to get foggy in the bathroom. Hard to see. Maybe the vent wasn't working properly? Oh, this annoyed him! My goodness! He'd have to call management in the morning. Of all the annoyances, and with what he'd paid for this little condo – it was only 2500 square feet – he really shouldn't have to deal with problems like this!

Patrick leaned out of the shower and pulled the door to the hall open.

The steam started to clear, and beyond the little island of light, beyond the fading vapor, Patrick saw the opening into darkness. Horrible oceans of darkness.

Hadn't he turned on the hall light just before he'd gone into the bathroom?

Patrick stared into the dark spot.

Was there a shadow among the shadows?

Something? Someone? Who had heard him talking to himself, perhaps? Who had heard the denials he had spoken as he was dreaming? His justifications? His frantic gestures, hands shaking out toward his marvelous, efficient ideas? All the ways he meant to *fix Michigan*?

Now, Patrick was unnerved.

He turned off the water and slipped out of the shower. He stood dripping on the bathmat. The water ran the length of his miserable dick, and then fell the last few feet to the floor. It was an incommensurate distance. He couldn't escape the feeling that this immaculate, bright bathroom was the only point of light in the whole godless, expanding universe.

"Hello?" Patrick called into the darkness.

And he waited.

And then May told me that she wasn't worried about the water at her house.

I'd seen her at her locker and stopped to ask if she'd had a good Christmas break.

"You aren't going to shut me in my locker, are you John?" she asked with a crossed brow.

"No, Jesus, no!" I said.

"It's okay," she said. "I'm only kidding!" Then, "You look tired."

"I had to get up early and come to take a shower at the gym. We had a filter in our shower, and it broke. There was too must junk getting inside. I guess the water here is less junky."

"I don't even worry about that stuff," said May. "Even since they changed the water, our water looks normal at our house. I don't even think it tasted different."

"Are you sure it's okay?" I said. "I don't think you can taste lead. Or see it."

I could see the skepticism on her face.

"Dirty water looks dirty, John. I mean, did you ever look at that river? Dirty! Anyway, I'm glad you came over, because I wanted to ask you: Do you want to come to my birthday party for my seventeenth birthday?"

"Maybe? When is it?

"I don't know yet. I mean, my birthday is on February 1st, but I haven't decided about my party. I need to find a time when my dad isn't going to be there because he gets bad earaches and I'm going to want to play music, you know? Loudly."

"Yeah, I think it'd be the same thing at my house. Just let me know. I'll come. If I can."

"What a guy! We're going to have so much fun. You'll see!"

And then the heaters all broke in the school.

And then it snowed every day for a straight week while the wind whistled out of the west.

And then twenty teachers stopped showing up. They never put in notice or told the school they were going to quit. They simply vanished. The school didn't tell our parents, either. They just shuttled a new crop of subs in and out of the classrooms. But they didn't even have enough subs. In those teacherless classrooms, the students taught themselves and each other. Spitballs, battle raps, fashion, and Euchre. In those classrooms the lights were always going on and off all day long, and nobody cared if the heat went off, and fog shrouded the windows that looked out on the teachers' parking lot.

And then Adam and I skipped school and got drunk.

We didn't trust Carla to pick us up again after we'd played her last time, so we just put on our coats and left the school.

"Someone might see us on the road," Adam said.

"I don't think they care," I said. "Anyway, I know another way."

I took him across the baseball fields to the pedestrian overpass that Selby had shown me. I closed my eyes and hurried across so I wouldn't have to look at the cars roaring underneath us.

At Grandma and Grandpa A's empty house – larger but less well-kept than Grandma and Grandpa M's – we went inside and poured Smirnoff's into a couple of coffee cups, and then poured some bottled water back into the fifth so his grandfather wouldn't know the difference. We mixed our vodka with Hawaiian Punch, and that worked because we almost couldn't taste the alcohol at all.

I drank two big mugs. The first only had a little bit of vodka, but the second was half-and-half. I was surprised how fast I got totally fucked up. This wasn't the subtle, gradual shift of the Ibogaine. The room suddenly started lurching, sliding sideways. Standing up was a stupid idea, so I just rolled or crawled along the floor. Before long, Adam leapt off the couch and said, "where's your games, where's your games, John, where's your games?"

"In my backpack," I said. The words didn't want to make their way out of my mouth.

Adam dug through my backpack, brought out the Earthbound cartridge, and jammed it into the Super Nintendo that sat gathering dust in front of the big screen TV. He turned it on, and Dr. Andonuts hooked him up with the Sky Runner. The doomed, zombie-bound version. But Adam wasn't going to play. He was there for the music. As soon as he had the game going, he threw down the controller and started dancing about the dim living room, his bare feet kicking up, his thin t-shirt sliding from side to side.

I watched Adam dancing, then put my head in my hands, and I felt like I was vaulting, like my head was moving toward my heels, though I wasn't moving at all. Stars rayed into me like the Star Wars hyperspace leap, only this time they curved toward me at a hyperbolic angle. I kept aiming for the floor and missing it, over and over.

I heard Adam laughing, and I realized that I had fallen off of the couch. I laughed too, but the arc didn't stop, and I closed my eyes against the Mandlebrot shores, the Julia flowers, they blossomed before me. I managed to get back up to my knees. My tongue was fat in my mouth.

"I get why people like this," I said.

Adam didn't answer. He was too busy dancing.

"Someone's got to figure it out," I said. "Someone's got to figure it out, eventually."

Adam looked at me quizzically.

"It's okay if we don't figure it out," I said. "If we don't figure it out, someone else will. It'll be okay."

He shook his head and kept dancing.

I crawled onto the couch, pulled a blanket over my legs, and fell asleep.

When I woke up it was dark in the room. I felt an urgency in my stomach, and I lurched through the blackness and up the stairs and vomited into the toilet until everything inside me was gone, and my throat felt bitter and raw.

Adam stepped in, rubbing his eyes.

"Holy shit!" I said, my voice rough. "It's dark out. It has to be late."

"It's, like, eight," Adam said.

"Oh shit," I said. "My parents are going to flip the fuck out."

"No, they won't," he said. "I called them. I told them you were spending the night. I told them you and me were doing some serious studying tonight, and that you wanted to call them yourself," he giggled into his hands, "but you couldn't because you had bad diarrhea!"

"They bought that?"

Adam shrugged. "It wasn't your mom," he said. "It was your dad I was talking to."

"And *he* bought that?"

Adam shrugged. "Yeah."

"Was he drunk?"

"You're one to talk, fucker!"

"That's not an answer," I said and punched him in the shoulder.

The movement unbalanced me. I caught myself, but my stomach went sideways again, and even though I'd already thrown up everything I'd eaten, I flopped over the floor and wretched, my saliva making a pool between my feet.

"Over here, buddy," said Adam, and he helped me crouch in front of the toilet. As I wretched, he wiped up my mess and tossed the towel in the corner. Then, something deep in my belly told me to keep vomiting, so I dry heaved for I don't know how long. At some point, I realized that Adam was gone. He returned, carrying a glass of water.

"Drink this," he said. "It'll help you in the morning. Trust me."

I hated it, but I drank it.

"John," he said, "don't hear me wrong, okay? I love you, man."

I stared at him. I tried to grasp at thoughts, but they were slipping through my fingers. I didn't want to think. It was all stupid anyway.

"Is this some gay shit?" I asked.

His expression flickered. On the one hand, I could tell that he had been expecting my words, so he couldn't feel shocked by them. On the other hand, he couldn't help but feel at least a bit offended. He was disappointed. He had hoped that I would surprise him, and I hadn't.

"No, John," he said. "You're short, you aren't thin or in shape, and you get too pissed off too fast. It isn't some gay shit. What I meant is that you are my brother. I have four grandparents, two sisters, and one brother: you."

"Oh," I said. "Yeah. You're my brother too." I spat into the toilet again. "Sorry. I can't think, I mean, I can't even talk right now. My tongue's not right, you know? I'm sorry, Adam. I'm really sorry. For everything." I giggled. I felt like I should cry.

Adam got up and left the room.

I'm too drunk, I thought. *I can't do anything right.*

"Shut up," Adam said from out in the hall. "You do lots of shit right."

And then Mrs. Clark asked me if I was going to start coming to class or if she could save herself some time and fail me right then.

And then I decided that the time was right to break out my new Alan Lee illustrated hardbound edition of *The Lord of the Rings*. After making it so far into *Les Misérables,* I figured I'd be able to make short work of these fantasy books. Besides, Crystal had told me to read it back in '94, and I wanted to be able to brag about it the next time I saw her. In one week, I had the hobbits camping under Weathertop. One week later, they were ready to take a stab at Moria. I got briefly hung up on the River Anduin, but I still finished *Fellowship* around the time that my mother took me out to buy me a CD player.

And then I took out my social studies book and opened to the big map of the United States, and traced the path I'd take on my Unending Road Trip throughout the country. First off, I'd blast down I-75 all the way to Miami. A straight shot. February would be for New Orleans. March would take me from Santa Fe to L.A. April from San Francisco through Portland to Seattle. By May, I'd reach Minneapolis. June in Chicago. July in Detroit. (No need to return to Akawe.) August in New York. September in D.C. October in Virginia. November in East Carolina. December in Georgia. Then back to Miami to take the same path all over again. I could follow the summer like the tern chases the sunlight.

And then I took all my finals for the semester, and I had been missing a lot of my classes, but I still had worked hard enough earlier in the semester that I didn't think it was going to be a total wash. Honestly, I didn't even care. As long as I didn't flunk anything. As long as I pulled an A in Miss Pavilik's class. I could always do better next semester.

And then I caught my mother cheating.

Adam had come to school with a bottle of Sprite with some vodka poured in. He realized he'd made it too strong, so he gave it to me instead. I drank it too fast and threw up on the carpet of Mr. Russell's class. With everyone laughing, and Mr. Russell looking angry and confused, I managed to say, "I think I've got the flu," and he excused me to go to the office and call my parents.

I didn't bother with that.

I left the school, took the now-familiar shortcut across the expressway, not even feeling cold even though the wind was bitter, and I'd somehow left my hat and gloves behind. When I got back home, I used the key to go in, went up to my room, and fell onto my bed with my head swimming.

I woke up to the sound of voices downstairs. The first thing I remembered was that I was technically AWOL from school, but I was still too buzzed to move around without making a lot of noise. I say as still as I could.

Voices resolved.

My mother's voice, silvery with laughter, and a man's. Not my father's. It was very low.

"I feel bad going behind his back," my mother was saying. "He might leave me if he found out."

"These things can be difficult," the man said humbly. "Even painful."

"I just know how *personally* he would take it," my mother said.

They were standing in the living room, shifting their weight, the floorboards groaning under their feet. If I moved, I'd be heard. Then they started moving from room to room below.

"... taking chances here," the man was saying. "People get nervous. But I should see about getting you a chandelier."

"A chandelier would be overkill, don't you think?"

"What? Wouldn't you love a chandelier?"

"They always seem like a pain-in-the-ass to keep clean ... dusting them all the time ..."

"We should go. Aren't you afraid that someone is going to see us coming or going?" the man said.

"Who would see us?"

"Your neighbors?"

My mother laughed again.

"We don't have any neighbors."

"What about your husband? Or your son?"

"My husband's looking into a job in Detroit. He just called me a few minutes ago. And John's at school for hours."

"Well, I still have a few minutes. Tell me, have you ever been to Farney's Lighting in Acheron?"

"I don't think so."

"Let's stop there. I want to show you some chandeliers. If you take care of those chandeliers, they'll be mirrors and diamonds for you."

I heard them leave. I grabbed my comforter, crawled under my bed, wrapped everything around my swimming head, and went back to sleep.

I woke up after dark when my father opened the door, and the hallway light spilled into my room.

"Oh, there you are," he said. "Why are you under your bed?" He started stumbling away down the hall. "Dinner's ready," he called over his shoulder. "Tuna Helper. Some cheesy shit."

After dinner, I went back to my room. My mother was gone, and I couldn't concentrate on my homework. I still had a good swig or two left at the bottom of the Sprite bottle. I turned out the light, lay down, shot down the rest, and let the world pleasantly fuzz out.

And then I went on a ghetto tour with Adam and Nova and I-don't-know-who. I mean, I was so drunk that month that there's a lot that I don't remember. I wasn't drunk when we went on the ghetto tour, but I was maybe just a little weird and fizzy about who was driving, and how I couldn't drive, and neither could Nova, and neither could Adam. Was it Chris? Chris could drive. It wasn't Chris. Who was driving?

We ranged out through the bluestruck blackout skyclad ranges of the Os where chimneys shorn of their houses pointed accusing fingers at heaven, and the West End where cindered cookie-cutters collapsed their palms in prayer. Orion through to Arlington, Trevithick down to Ashley, wide fields, nobody out in all this snow and ice, they must have all huddled indoors, and it was Saturday I think.

I tried to take them to Eden Street. I thought I would show them the abandoned Hell House, and I thought – I hoped – that it might look less awful in this blinding daylight. That was a bright day. Searing, shocking blue everywhere and the icy sun crackled upon the white-banked planes like this was big sky country or some shit.

But we couldn't get in there: concrete barriers blocked the entrance to the service drive that led into the mess. Instead, we went out into the far West End, Chasing Heights, and Cheshire where Akawe had annexed wheat fields expecting to pave them over with new housing, new factories. That day, the place was all mildewy weeds, four-wheeler ruts, and winter-stripped birches.

Somehow, we swung way, way out east; did we take Starr Highway? We spun through the iced-up parking lot of an elementary school that was supposedly one of the best schools left in the city except for the fact that its lead count was ten times the federal limit, so we all knew the hundreds of kids that went to school there were probably going to end up retards anyway, and that made me think of May, and I kind of wanted to see her, but I couldn't remember where she lived, just that it was somewhere on the East Side, so we toured many different neighborhoods and subdivisions, and the East Side was always more *closely* contaminated than the rest of Akawe, like its industry had meddled in the houses and the houses in the factories, and we saw a graveyard of discarded containers leaking inky ooze at the bottom of a bellied ridge somewhere a block or two off of East Street, a bizarro little neighborhood of all-dirt-roads buried in among the hills and the scrap, happily inhabited by crack-smoking Appalachians leaning back in rusted chairs under rusted RV awnings, their bare feet kicked up, plus the thug-sheltering barns hulked up brown-and-white a couple inches from Intervale Road, icicles tipping, and by the way, I am making most of this up, it never happened, we never saw some of this, but some of it we did see, and why the hell can't I remember who drove us around town that day?

Did I go with Adam or Michael?

It was Adam.

And Nova.

Nova and Adam had ideas, but Michael and Selby were wise, I decided.

Wisdom isn't knowing everything. Intelligence is knowing everything. Charisma is knowing how to sell what you know. But Wisdom is knowing the importance of what you know. What to keep and what to discard.

I wanted to know what Michael and Selby would have thought about what we saw that day.

We found an unlocked stairwell at the shuttered Olan Academy and made our way through the chilly building, our breaths puffing. We surveyed the swimming pool underground, full of dark water, and the radio station with its mural-painted ceiling panels, Superman and Freddy Krueger, and the ROTC gym perched in dust above the girls' gym, and the magisterial stage overlooking the gloomy rows of the auditorium. The school was mostly sealed up as tight as a drum, and nobody had gotten in and tagged it yet. Except for our driver.

"Suck my dick, OLAN," he sprayed.

"I don't mean it as an insult," he explained. "I mean it to be friendly."

And then later, a day, a week, Selby caught me at my locker and asked if I was planning on going to May's birthday party.

"I think so," I said. "I mean, she invited me. She find out when it's happening?"

"First Saturday next month, I think."

"You get invited?"

"Yeah."

"You going?"

"No."

"Why not?"

"Lucy."

"She's going?"

"I'm sure she is. She's May's best friend at this school. And if Lucy is going, so is Eli. Oh yeah, they're still tight. Friends. Anyway, I don't want to be around them. It isn't safe. Not since what happened, you know, last month."

"Don't you see Eli at lunch every day, anyway?"

"You haven't seen? We don't have a lunch table no more. You and Lucy started eating in the library, and since Lucy dumped him, Eli hasn't even been coming to Eastern that much. The other kids split up and went to other tables. For, like, a week, it was just May and me. Now she's sitting with her brother –"

"You could –"

"I told you, I don't want to be around Lucy. Besides, I like eating alone. It gives the other girls a chance to give me shit, and I'm glad. One of these days, I'm gonna fuck them up, and it's gonna feel great."

I thought for a moment. I wasn't drunk that morning, but my thoughts dripped slow and sticky like corn syrup.

"Why you care if I'm going?" I finally asked.

"Because I want you to wear these."

And with a single fluid motion that revealed everything to me while shielding it from anyone passing in the hall, Selby drew the startling, blue-bottle sunglasses from a pocket in her jacket.

I couldn't speak.

I hadn't seen these sunglasses since the rave, and I hadn't seen them in any sort of light in over two years. Often, I had wondered whether I'd imagined or exaggerated their elaborate construction, but here they were, right in front of me, two deep blue lenses almost glowing against the flickering backdrop of the Eastern High School illumination, as if hidden galaxies turned behind the glass.

"How did you –"

"Take them. Call it a present."

I took the sunglasses without thinking.

I folded them and put them in my pocket.

"They're yours now. For real."

"If I wear these to that party, what's going to happen?"

Selby shrugged.

"Probably nothing," she said. "Nobody's gonna recognize them except Eli. If anyone else asks where you got them, say you just found them, I don't know, lying by the road. Or, better, tell them that they just turned up in your locker one day. John. They can't find out you got them from me."

"Eli's brother chased me with a knife about those sunglasses. You don't think he's going to do something about it?"

"Not at the party. Eli isn't like EZ. He won't fight. He's a little bitch. He doesn't want to be there when things get bad."

"Why do you want him to see the sunglasses?"

"I want him to know that he's being hunted. I want him to know that his family is being hunted. It doesn't mean much, my hunting them, if they aren't afraid."

"*Hunting* them? What are you? I mean, why are you – I mean ... this is about the thing with your dad?"

"I've been working on this for *years*, John."

"I don't think I can do this, Selby. I don't want shit to happen to me." I paused. "I don't want shit to happen to you, either."

"It already is."

"Still, I don't think –"

"Fine. Don't. Then give me the sunglasses back."

My hand went to my pocket. *No.* They were the perfect shade of blue. And they were mine again. They were with me now. Where they belonged. Selby looked straight into my face, and she knew what I was thinking.

"On New Year's Eve," I said. "You told me not to get involved in this shit. You told me to stay away from Eli and his family."

"Yeah, well you've been showing up to school drunk for weeks now. You're drowning, John. Obviously. I hope you figure it out, but until you do, you might as well be useful to me, too."

"You said that I was your best friend. Me and Michael."

"I did. You are. In fact, I kinda think you're my only friends. And after this, I can't be seen with you, neither. Ha. Some friends I've got!"

"I know how you feel," I said.

She frightened me. But the sunglasses comforted me. I was able to cup my palm around them in my pocket.

"You really think this is going to work?"

"Probably not, but it's the best way I can think to send a message Eli's going to believe without signing it with my name, you know?"

And then I skipped school and dropped acid.

One morning, I gave Adam a ten from my father's wallet, and he passed me a tab of lavender paper, along with the key to his house.

"You ain't comin'?" I asked.

"I can't miss any more school, or I'm gonna fail English," he said. "I'm already failing Pre-Algebra."

I put the blotter on my tongue and swallowed, wrapped myself in my coat, and hurried across the pedestrian bridge as my stomach cramped and my bewintered world went full bloom. It wasn't like the severe grays ever went away. I just stopped noticing them. There were colors to be enjoyed, and I noticed them in places I'd never seen them before. They were tender, these colors. They watched after me. Guardian angels. They mourned my pain – everyone's pain – and our weariness, and they wanted us to all get better, though we never recognized them or realized that they were pulling for us.

Down in Adam's basement, in his bedroom, I found a lamp built out of a Yoda figurine. It shot blue-green lasers from its eyes, and they struck me in the chest. Shapes and objects were more three-dimensional than they usually were. Day-to-day life had been illustrations in a textbook, but today everything was dioramas. I put on Adam's Tori Amos album. The one with the white cover. Her high piano and quavering voice fell like icicles into blemishless snow. I turned off the light and lit a votive candle. It glowed rosy, and I dribbled the wax along my hand. I flexed my fist and watched the crust crack. Now it was part of the diorama, as was I. Fixed in place to lend the other, unseen observer that very special spatial perspective.

Adam had taped a postcard of the Golden Gate bridge to a pipe that rose through the middle of his room. *If you're having a shitty day, there's always the bridge.* I thought. *Isn't that something they say out there?*

That bright, beautiful, terra cotta-colored bridge. Michigan had a bridge, too, but it was in the thick of the wilderness. Not a molting metropolis. Our bridge wasn't terra cotta-colored. It was the stripped white of an ice-scarred Petoskey stone. It was several hours away, by car. Still, *there's always the bridge.*

Eventually, Adam came home.

"How is it?" he asked.

"It's okay," I said. "It hasn't opened up the universe to me or anything like that."

"Sometimes it doesn't." He had his hands in his pockets. "How do you feel?"

"My stomach has been hurting."

"These were cheap blotters. Sometimes they're cut with rat poison."

"I feel sleepy. I feel so tired."

Snow tornadoes through the darkening windows.

"Can I spend the night tonight?" I asked. "My parents won't care if I tell them I'm doing homework. They might not even notice."

"Sure," he said. "Go ahead. And hey, man. Maybe you want to go easy on the drugs for a bit. Take a break, you know?"

"Sure."

"Drink some water."

"Whatever you say."

And then someone asked, "Is this going to be another diorama?"

Miss Pavilik was standing at her desk with a large cardboard box, surrounded by dim light. She believed in the pedagogical power of dioramas.

"No," she said, lightly but unsmiling. "Not today." Her voice eversoft.

She brought out two identical white taper candles. She set them upon her desk.

"This is going to be difficult for me to explain, and some of it might end up going over your heads. It will make more sense if you remember the conversation we had last week on hyperbolic geometry."

Before she had even finished her sentence, an audible groan went up from the class. Everyone had *hated* the discussion on hyperbolic geometry, even if they *loved* Miss Pavilik. It had taken two days instead of one and had left almost everybody thoroughly confused. She had brought in a horse's saddle, and drew a triangle upon it, and explained how in *our* universe, the interior angles of a triangle never added up to 180 degrees. How every line shares space with an infinite number of coplanar lines. *I* had enjoyed it, even though it confused the hell out of me. *I* had felt something calling to me in this evocation of expanding vacancies between geometric points. Or the mosaic disks that Miss Pavilik showed us on the overhead projector: Escher fish falling from the seamount at the center into the abyss of the margins. These things all suggested a space in which emptiness was easier to find than matter. They were difficult to imagine, but I enjoyed trying.

"What I am about to tell you is true," Miss Pavilik said. "We live in a hyperbolic universe. Space is not what you imagine it to be. Distance is not what you imagine it to be. Your textbooks tell you about three possible ends to our universe. They are all wrong."

Miss Pavilik looked at me, and for the first time, in a whole month, I felt completely sober. Now I was straining to understand what she was about to tell us.

"In the last year," Miss Pavilik said, "there have been two discoveries in cosmology that have completely changed our understanding of the expansion and fate of the universe. You'll remember that the last time we talked about it, before winter break, we were talking about how Edwin Hubble proved that the universe was expanding. Then, your readings discussed how Stephen Hawking explored the possible outcomes of that expansion. Over time, the universe will either expand eternally but always slowing down, or it will slow almost to a stop, or it will stop expanding and start contracting and will ultimately collapse in upon itself. Now, cosmologists believe that none of these situations is the case. Last year, scientists at the Cosmic Anisotropy Telescope in England measured the small-scale structure in the cosmic microwave background. You may remember, the cosmic microwave background is radiation left over from the Big Bang. It actually proved that the Big Bang happened ... when you look at that background radiation, you are looking at the Big Bang! But as we were able to get a better look at it, it told us other important things as well. One of those things was that the geometry of our universe is not Euclidean but hyperbolic. When the scientists looked at the fluctuations on their scan of the background, they saw warps. Distortions. Some places were expanding much faster than others. This suggested a negative curvature of space. It suggested a hyperbolic universe. That straight lines curve away from each other. That triangles pinch toward their points. There is no other explanation that makes sense.

"The second discovery confirmed the first while also proving something else." Miss Pavilik fired up a match and used it to light the two candles. "Kareem," she said, "would you kindly turn out the lights?"

He did. The room was dark now, except for a slim trickle of winter light bleeding in around the shades, and for the steady glow of the two candles. Miss Pavilik left one on her desk and took the other to a shelf at the back of the room.

"Some supernovas," she said, "look very different from one another, but there are some that look exactly the same. Do you remember our discussion of pulsars? When a dwarf star has used up all of its fuel – something as massive as our sun but the size of our earth, and glowing white-hot, but slowly cooling – and it is in orbit with another star, the dwarf star can pull matter from its companion star, if the orbit is just so. And as we talked about around last Halloween, if a star has the right combination of size and density, it will fall into a chain reaction in which it will eject most of its matter in a spectacular explosion. This is what a supernova is. Sometimes these dying white dwarfs pull off enough matter to cause a supernova. Because their mass is always the same when they do this, they leave the same spectrographic signature – the same range of colors – that identifies them. They also are of about the same brightness. So from Earth, when we see this particular kind of supernova, we can figure out how close or how far these stars are from us by how bright they appear. To a very high degree of accuracy. We call these supernovas *standard candles* because they are same no matter where in the universe we observe them. Any questions?"

Standard candles! I thought. My heart was pounding in excitement.

"Two groups of physicists took observations of all the standard candles they could find. First, they confirmed the negative spatial curvature suggested by the cosmic microwave background. But they also discovered that distant standard candles were not as extremely red-shifted, proportionally, as those that were closer. Remember, in astronomy, distance equals time. So the light from the farther stars is older than the light from nearer stars. And the farther stars were moving away more slowly. This means that the universe is expanding more quickly now than it was in the past.

"The expansion of the universe is accelerating. And, what's more, the rate of acceleration is accelerating! The idea that there might be energy driving the expansion of the universe was something Einstein once believed, and we call that idea of his 'dark energy.' But nobody expected acceleration to accelerate, and so we call this dark energy, this scalar field, quintessence. We call it phantom energy. Do you understand?"

I tried. I tried hard, but my head was still back at the place where the triangle had pinched corners. But I caught the term: *phantom energy.*

Miss Pavilik put the candles together on her desk.

"What's gonna happen?" someone asked.

Then I realized that the voice was mine. That I had asked the question.

"Not the Big Crunch in which everything in the universe collapses back together and maybe starts over. It's not that. And it isn't the Big Freeze, which most physicists had expected, in which all of the stars burn themselves out. The most likely scenario now is something called the Big Rip. The universe will expand more and more quickly. Galaxies will be blasted into pieces by the expanding spaces between them. Our solar system will be scattered as the planets are sucked so far from the sun that its gravitational pull makes no difference. Then, finally, structures, molecules, atoms, and electrons and protons will be drawn away from each other. The whole universe will be dissolved to elementary particles, and then those particles will dissolve as well."

Miss Pavilik blew out the candles. She turned on the lights and returned to the front of the classroom. We blinked our eyes in the sudden light.

"This won't happen for billions of years," she said. "But that is a very small amount of time, compared with a universe aging toward heat death. What we have discovered is that this universe of ours will only support life very temporarily."

I thought about the galaxies, the solar system, and our little world scattering itself apart as the space between expanded at an ever-increasing speed. I imagined myself scattering into dust, and then, reflexively, I imagined the shellacked hell house standing alone out in the desolations of Eden Street. Would it scatter, too? It was, I suspected, a symbol of that scattering. I shuddered. The Big Rip was a horror story. It filled me with a sense of revulsion.

I raised my hand.

"Yes, Mr. Bridge," she said.

"When things move away ... like the standard candles are moving away. That's red shifting?"

"Yes, it is."

"And it's called that because things are moving away, so their wavelengths are stretched out ... toward the red end of the spectrum. So the colors would look more reddish in a telescope or whatever?"

"That's basically what it means."

"So, what is the opposite of that?"

"I think you can figure that out."

"When things are moving toward you, it means that their wavelengths are pushed shorter, aren't they? Toward the other end of the spectrum. The blue end. So the colors would look more bluish, wouldn't they?"

"They would be compressed down toward the blue end of the spectrum, yes."

"And that's the opposite of what is happening with the universe, according to what you are saying?"

"Yes. The universe is red-shifting faster and faster."

"Thanks," I said.

I put my hand in my pocket and wrapped it around the blue-bottle lenses, wide and thick.

The sunglasses made me feel better, a little. Maybe, if the universe started to expand around me and throw me apart, I could put the sunglasses on and pretend it was converging again.

And then Charles Letts called me and asked if I could run the sound booth for AYT's production of Zora Neale Hurston's *Their Eyes Were Watching God.* Their last sound tech had gone AWOL. I wanted to bring my copy of *Lord of the Rings* and read that, but I couldn't find it, so in a fit of annoyance, I grabbed my father's Bible instead.

There were just fifteen or twenty sound cues in the whole two-hour-plus show.

I sat all alone in the tiny, claustrophobic room with the green cinder-block walls. It was cold, but I had the red coils of a battered space heater a few inches from my feet, the fluorescent light overhead, and a foam cup of coffee perilously close to the ancient sound equipment. I cradled the Bible on my lap and read it during the long pauses between the cues. Eating from the tree. Begat begat begat. Fleeing from the flood. Begat begat begat. Building the tallest tower. Begat. Then the many adventures of Abraham and his son Isaac, who went off on a pilgrimage to a strange place, a desert, landlocked. I imagined this place with black scorpion shells thrown into relief by blinking neon lights, the dry wind cool off the mountains, the as yet unextinguished stars, and an isolated bowling alley where the patriarch Bethuel eked out a meager living from the truckers passing through. I thought of Rebekah's plans and her own ambitions. How she must have felt when Isaac showed up out of nowhere, and he was like, "marry me, yo."

I also wondered how I felt about a God who would create a life-sustaining universe only to suddenly explode it, to rip it apart, just as life had finally arrived at its full burgeoning. "My ways are not your ways." *Your ways defy all sanity. Your ways will drive us all mad.*

And then the snow swirled and the wind moaned and the moon howled, but I couldn't see it howling, because it was blue daylong and all night gone, and it was cold and awful everywhere.

And then my report card came in the mail.

I was home alone. My father was off somewhere enrolling for a typing course at the community college, and my mother was off working late or hanging out with the disembodied voice I had heard downstairs.

I went into the lonely dining room and opened the envelope.

1	ENGLISH	ESPER	B
2	BIOLOGY	CLARK	F
3	SPANISH 2	DIMITRI	D
4	GEOMETRY	RUSSELL	F
5	ASTRONOMY	PAVILIK	C-
6	CIVICS	BARAKAT	D-

It was officially all over. It was done. No University of Chicago. No college in Chicago. No college at all, most likely. I already knew my parents couldn't afford it, and now I also knew that I wasn't good enough. I was getting a 1.65 now. *How did this even happen?* Yeah, I'd been slacking off, but I'd still been turning in most of my homework and passing my tests. I just couldn't see how my grades could have fallen so fast and so far.

I clenched my fists and shuddered when I imagined what they were going to say. My stomach hurt. Had I skipped breakfast that morning? I was pretty sure where my father kept his beers. But I didn't want that. I wanted something clean and easy. Something more innocent and unimplicated than this disastrous piece of paper.

I went to the pantry and grabbed a box of Vegetable Thins. *I'm already in as much trouble as I can be,* I thought. *Might as well finish these off.* I grabbed a can of pop and went back up to my room. It was cloudy outside, but the clouds were translucent, and their bright light reflected off the snow and filled my painted room with an effervescent light.

I got *The Lord of the Rings. The Fellowship of the Ring.* I was looking for one picture in particular. I found it more than halfway through. Alan Lee had drawn the scene after the Fellowship had escaped from the mines of Moria, casualties notwithstanding. There, in the eastern foothills of the Misty Mountains, a stony stair led down between karstlike columns of stone toward a still pool of perfect blue, flanked by stubborn tufts of grass.

"Silverlode they call it," I said, reading from the book.

Why had I wanted to see this picture *in particular?*

It was the grass. It was the water. Liquid, not ice. It was the sun bathing the stark cliffs as they soared to hundreds of feet. It was the first glimmer of spring in Wilderland. But spring was still far away from Akawe.

I had finished *Fellowship,* but Crystal had told me that I had to keep going and, anyway, I wanted something, anything, to distract me from what my parents would say when they saw my report card. I went and got the second book: *The Two Towers.* I held it in my lap for a long time, studying the cover, on which a spindly, blue-white spider pursued a figure holding a flashing white sword aloft. In this illustration, the rocks were high and jagged, and in the distance, a tapering stone tower looked out over the scene through a red-eyed window.

Everything is falling apart, I thought.

I opened the book.

The dwarf, the ranger, and the wood elf decided that they could not follow the Ring into the dark land. Instead, they decided to rescue two of their friends who had just been abducted. But the enemy had already made good time in the opposite direction. The three friends ran for days into a new country, a landscape of rolling hills and grasslands riven by eroding outcroppings and spanned by bright blue skies as fierce and merciless as early spring.

I had never concentrated on any story the way I read this story now. Even *Les Mis*, in the fierceness of its barricades and its gunfire, couldn't carry me away from my moss-shingled house where bad news kept coming, over and over. I became this world, and my friends in Middle-Earth had much bigger problems than unexpected Fs in Biology and Geometry. I could see the great river. I could see its stony banks falling, loose pebbles kicked and ticking the hills on their way down. I could taste the coppery bite of the clear streams that sinewed down from above. I imagined the waves crashing on the distant sea, a vast swelling mother presence that we did not know in the Midwest, even in the Great Lakes. I imagined the calming of a warm, southern sun. I wanted to keep reading forever.

Eventually, I heard the door open and shut downstairs. My mother had arrived home. A cold stone settled in my belly. I just wanted to get it over with. I put the book down, grabbed my report card, and went downstairs to meet her.

"I got my report card," I said. My voice was defiant, though I didn't mean for it to be.

I handed it over. My mother looked at it for a long time. Finally, she looked over the top at me.

"What is this?" she asked.

"I told you," I answered. "It's my report card."

She didn't say anything for several moments. Her nostrils flared.

"I see," she said. "Any idea how you got these grades?"

"No," I said. "They don't make sense to me. The only grade that makes sense is Esper's. I expected a B in English. But I don't know what I did to fail two classes, and I was expecting a *lot* better than a C- in Astronomy. I've worked so damn hard in that class!"

My mother continued to study the report card.

"Aha," she said, finally. "I think I understand."

She turned the paper so I could see it.

"See that column? Just to the left of your letter grade?"

"Abs," I said.

"What do you think that stands for?"

"Probably absences," I said.

"Yes, you're right. It says you have nine absences in English, eleven in Biology, and twelve in all of your other classes. When you are absent eleven days, your grade is lowered a full grade. When you are absent twelve days, your grade is lowered two full grades." She looked at me long and hard, and it felt like cruelty. She was daring me to say words that would seal my fate with her.

I didn't, so she continued: "I don't remember you being home sick eleven or twelve days," she said.

"I was home sick for, like, almost a week after Halloween! Remember? And another day or two. I forget."

"That's seven. Tops. What do you think is going on here?"

"You know what's going on. It ain't like it matters to you. You're gone all the time, and Father's drinking, and you're both fighting and ... stuff."

"Oh, well, okay then. You want to blame your skipping school on your father and me? Interesting way to act out, John. Yeah, you don't have any trouble sitting up and watching movies with us or letting me take you out and buy you music, but your anger finds a convenient outlet when you want to skip school. Were you skipping with Adam?"

"On my own."

"Hm," she said. "Well, I don't think you'll be visiting with Adam anymore for a long time, and that's just the beginning of your punishment."

She looked at the report card again.

"If you hadn't skipped, it looks like you might have gotten a B, a D, a B, a C, an A-, and a B-. Even that isn't very good. A lot less than you're capable of. And it's going to affect your chances to get into college. Have you been thinking about any of this?"

I shrugged.

"That's it?" she said.

I shrugged.

"I see. Well, you'd better be careful, or your father and I might just shrug our shoulders at you, and then you can figure this all out on your own. I mean, you know everything, right?"

"I know shit that you don't think I know."

"I don't want to look at you. Get out of my sight."

I went up to my room. I got under my covers, and opened my book, and read about hobbits and talking trees and monsters and impending spring. I read that book as though my life depended upon it.

I heard my father come up the driveway and into the house.

Then I heard him shouting, and then my mother was shouting too. For a few moments – delusionally – I thought that they were releasing their utter disappointment in me, their fuckup son, as a sort of fusing catharsis between them. But then I realized that they were blaming each other for my behavior. My father was raging that if my mother had just been around more, she could have helped keep an eye on me, examined my homework, checked my tests, noticed all the signs that I just didn't give a shit anymore. My mother, then, was screaming that my father had set such a horrible example, his drunkenness, his despair, his complete lack of ambition. It was hard to concentrate on my book with all the shouting below, so I studied the pictures instead.

Finally, their voices went silent, and I heard my father's feet stomping up the stairs. My door spun open.

"Where did you go?" he bellowed. "All those days you skipped school, where did you go?"

"Mostly back here," I said. "I guess. Or Adam's house."

"So you *were* with Adam?"

I shook my head. "Not mostly. I just went over there to hang out by myself." I didn't want to get Grandpa and Grandma M in trouble ... they opened their house to all their grandchildren's friends, and some of those friends were in worse shape than I was. "He gave me a key."

"Give it to me," my father said and handed out his palm.

I got up, went to my chest of drawers, got the key, and gave it to him.

He stopped at the door.

"I don't want you coming down until dinner. Do you understand?"

I nodded.

He slammed the door.

A few moments later, he started shouting at my mother again, and she shouted right back. I heard a plate shattering against the kitchen wall. I turned on my radio and put my palms against my ears, and hunched over *The Two Towers.* Now the two abductees had been rescued by a strange man. Now the three pursuing friends had reunited with an old friend. But despite these happy turns, the odds still seemed bleak. The heroes were about to be crushed between the hammer and anvil of two hostile armies. I read as the sun sank and the streetlights winked on. When it was too dim to read by the weak light trickling in through my windows, I turned my light on and read some more.

Urbantasm: The Darkest Road

Finally, my mother opened my door and said, "Dinner's ready."

I closed the book and went downstairs.

We ate in silence – reheated pasta – and I returned to my room. I hurried through my homework. I wasn't doing it very well, but I was getting it done. That would have to be good enough for now. I needed to get back to my book. I kept reading until the sounds of my parents' talking subsided. I read until the whole house was quiet. I read until no more cars hushed along South and Whitmore, and the whole city had slipped into an unsettled hibernation. I read and I read. I opened the window and let the dark wind in, because I was sick of the stuffy airlessness of that house. I kept reading. I read until I couldn't hold my eyes open anymore. And then I tucked my book under my pillow and finally closed my eyes.

That was a long, cold, quiet, awful weekend.

I still felt relieved. My parents had both seen my complete failure as a student, and they knew that it was because I'd been skipping school. They didn't know, it seemed, about the drugs, and that terrified me – the fact that I'd actually *done* them and the risk that they might ever find out about it – but if I stopped doing the drugs, I didn't think they would find out. Now that I'd had my feet on the ground for a few days, I looked back and felt frightened about how out-of-control I had been that month. Where had I been trying to land? What did I even think it was going to accomplish? Here – now – there was despair. But at least I could see clearly again. At least time moved in minutes and hours again.

All weekend, I tried to stay in my room and read as much as I could. I lived in the book as much as I could.

My father said that I could only do my homework at the dining room table, under supervision, and that was the worst part of the weekend, because neither of them wanted to talk to me. They glared at me, and they glared at each other. My stomach hurt, and ... something, something, covalent bonds. Something to do with trees. Something to do with the Kievan Rus. Something to do with the present participle. Eventually, I finished, and I could go back up to my room and open the window so I could enchant the icy wind and make it into the bitter breeze that crossed the Anduin and the Emyn Muil and fanned its fingers out over the plains of Rohan.

Finally, it was Sunday afternoon, and I heard my mother answer the phone. Her muffled voice drifted up from below.

"I'm sorry," she was saying. "He can't talk on the phone today. I'm sorry, who? Ah. Can I take a message? Yes. I will tell him."

She hung up.

I heard her steps come up the stairs, and she opened the door without knocking.

"That was Charles Letts from the youth theater," she said. "He said they're putting together a new script for the play they're doing this spring, and he hopes you'll audition for it. Not to do backstage, but as an actor."

I looked at her. I didn't know what to say.

"You can't do it, you know," my mother said. "Not with your grades what they are. Those rehearsals are long. You need to be at home, doing homework. You can call him back tomorrow and tell him you're sorry."

"Then why are you telling me about it? If you won't even let me audition."

"Maybe you need to see what happens when you disappoint someone else. Since you don't seem to care when you disappoint your father and me. You know, we don't trust you anymore. When you lie to someone, that happens."

"You know that, huh?" I asked but, again, she didn't pick up on the signal. I found a quick purchase in that silence.

"You know," I went on, "that's the only way I'm going to get out of this mess, right? Since my grades are so bad, the extracurricular stuff is the only thing that was really going good for me. If you take me out of theater like that, I'm just another kid failing classes in a bad school district."

My mother's lips compressed with anger.

"Fine," she said. "You've got a point. No friends. No phone. But you can try out for the play. Now close that window. It's fucking frigid in here."

I agreed with her.

The next morning, I felt different.

Maybe it was the return of actual sunlight – snow everywhere and not a cloud in the sky – the world was going to sparkle– and holy shit, how easily I got played by the weather and the ebbs and flows of nature. Still, if this was how I got to not feel shitty, I was going to enjoy it.

As I waited for the bus, I thought about the noisy atheism I'd professed in seventh grade. I'd been speaking out against Quanla's and Selby's unexamined belief, as I saw it. A belief born of habit. But now, I felt like I was about to witness the bracing merits of unbounded faith. The cardinality of divinity. The real meaning of grace. Whatever we named it, there was something transformative in the unfogged sun, its radiating arms, its conquest of frigid distance. It was like I *heard* it rising, and I was ready for it. I was impatient for it. I wanted it. Like, a lot.

Now, very soon, we'll arrive back at the beginning of this story.

This story that began when I realized that God had it out for us, which was why we hated him.

This story that began when I realized that I'd have to become the antichrist.

Remember?

When I got to school that morning, puffing steam as I passed through the double doors, I felt full of breath and hope. My boots were wet with blood and water. Maybe I had already screwed things up too much to recover, but at least I could work hard and speak up and make someone remember me for doing something good. I could *change* them. I could make them wish that they had never shut us out. *Who is 'they?'* I wondered.

I was halfway across the vestibule when Adam caught me by the jacket and spun me around.

"Hey John, how you doing?"

"Really shitty," I said with a laugh.

"Cool," he said, distracted. "You think you can help me out now?"

"What's up?"

"I gotta ... I gotta go to the Taco Bell on Whitmore Road. I gotta meet with my mom."

"With ... Alice?"

I hadn't seen Alice since I was eight or nine. When I was four, my father went off to rehab for a month. When Adam was eight, Alice had gone off to rehab, had checked out of the facility, and never came home.

"Why?"

"She wants to talk with my Grandpa A. About where she can live again. And see Ophelia and me again. Because she didn't ... because, I mean." He shook his head like a noise was bothering him. "You know she's fucked up, John. And she's afraid my grandpa'll be really pissed when she stops by."

"Will he be?"

"Yeah. No way around that. But I can tell her how to, like, manage it. You know? There's shit she can say to calm him down. My grandma's sick. My mom can help out. They could all help each other out if they'd just stop fighting for a minute."

"Okay. What do you want me to do?"

"Just ride over with me. I haven't seen her in, like, three years or something. Just be there with me. I'm freaked out about it."

I thought for a moment. *Being this new, better person, it's probably a good idea to think about decisions before I make them. If I really am ready to look God in the eye.* I had told myself that I wasn't going to skip school anymore. But this was different. Adam had been there for me even though I had broken with him before. He needed me now. This was skipping school for a better reason.

But I wasn't going to catch up with school if I wasn't at school.

But this was just one class. Mr. Esper's class, where I hadn't had too many absences. That answered it.

"I'll go with you," I said. "But we have to hurry. I have to be back by second hour."

Adam pulled me down one of the dark corridors lined with upperclassmen lockers and found a lanky kid shuffling down the hall.

"Hey, Curt," he said. "I got some gas money for you. You gonna give John and me a ride to Taco Bell."

Fifteen minutes later, we pulled into the parking lot, and Adam and I went inside.

Alice was the only person eating in today. She sat at a booth with a big cup of pop and a burrito. She had wavy blonde hair streaked with gray, and she looked like someone who hadn't slept well in weeks. I had remembered her hair as full and lustrous, her brown eyes as animated and golden, but I didn't see these things in the woman before me. Was my memory fucked? Or was I just putting all this on her because of the stories Adam had told me?

Alice started talking before we even made it to the booth.

"Adam," she said. "Oh my God, baby, I've been praying a long time.

387

I've been back two months now, but it took me a long time to work up the courage to call you. God bless Carla for giving you my messages. How are you?"

"Fine," he grunted. His voice sounded small. I could see that his shoulder was trembling. "Where you been staying?"

"With Janice, hon, with Janice. Now she's been good to me. After last time, I ... well, anyway. How is Ophelia?"

"She's fine. She gets into trouble. I mean, you did. You know. She's, um ... Grandma and Grandpa M's taking good care of us. She's got her own room. They, um. They buy her too much shit."

"Haha!" Alice chuckled nervously. "I wish I could. I wish I could buy her too much shit."

Then she looked at me, and Adam seemed to remember that I was there.

"Mom, you remember John, right?" he said.

"Of course, I remember John! Where do you live now, honey?"

"We still live on Agit," I said.

"On Agit! That surprises me. Your parents are smart people."

I shrugged.

"Does Archie still live there? And Bill's family?"

"No. Archie got foreclosed and his house burned down. Bill's family left too. Moved to the Os. I see him at Northern sometimes −"

"So, how are you?" Adam interrupted. "I mean with the ... you know?"

"Well," Alice said. "In the past, I wasn't willing to talk about that, but I can talk about it with you now. You see, I was in Memphis ..."

I gave Adam a nudge.

"I'ma go buy us some food," I said.

I was there for Adam, but I didn't think he really wanted me listening in either. I spent a long time looking at the menu. I ordered tacos and pop and cinnamon crisps, and handed over money. I did it all as slowly as I could. Alice was wrapping up her story by the time I made it back to the booth. I slid in next to Adam and passed him some food. He unwrapped it and started eating.

"It's a fucking crime what they're doing to us," Alice said, and she pointed toward the sky. I didn't understand what she was talking about. "I should have bought that food for you. I have a bit of money, John. Let me pay you back."

She gave me a five. I hadn't spent that much, but I didn't have change. Then she went to use the bathroom. As soon as she was gone, Adam leaned forward and hissed, "when we get out of this I really want to get fucked up."

I just smiled back.

Alice returned.

"So," she said. "I don't want to ask you for your help, Adam, but you know I need it. He won't even listen to me unless you tell him to."

"I'll help you," Adam said. "As long as you don't ask me for any money."

"Oh, honey," Alice said, and she put her hand on his face. Then she pulled his hand across the table and placed it upon her cheek.

Adam held his breath and stared down at the table.

I sipped my pop and looked out the window. A salt-streaked red pickup made the turn, spraying mud and ice upon the sidewalks. A man on the corner got drenched. He waved his fists and yelled after the retreating truck.

"I can help out now," Alice was saying. "I can make lunches, to start."

A half hour later, Alice and Adam were ready to leave. They were planning to walk to Janice's house just a few blocks away. That was when I realized that Alice didn't have a car, and Adam's ride was long gone. I was going to have to walk back to Eastern, and there was *no* way I was going to get back in time for Mrs. Clark's class.

"I gotta go," I said.

I put my hat and gloves on, gave Adam a hug and Alice a nod, and set off into the bright wind.

I walked fast in metallic light across the crusted snow and the white-streaked pavement. Crows pushed against the currents and sparrows huddled in the eaves. Pigeons bobbed through the shadows, pecking at beads of salt. The air crackled with ice and sunshine. I hadn't checked the time since we'd left the restaurant, but it couldn't be ten yet. I figured the quickest route was to follow Whitmore to Winters, and then to turn east. If I walked quickly, I'd get back before the end of my Spanish class. That was okay; the Spanish sub was a bit of a pushover, overwhelmed by the chaos of her forty students coming and going. Mrs. Clark was more of a hardass, but I was already planning to stop in ask for her help. My absences had reset with the start of the new semester, so if I could keep up with my classes, my grades would be okay. *I just have to focus. Just have to keep focused, man. Do your fucking homework. Every day. Study for the fucking tests. Make this semester better than the last. Don't fuck it up. Just don't make stupid fucking mistakes.*

I felt, rather than heard, the car slow down at my side.

"John?"

It was a thin, deadly voice.

I turned toward the old Benedict.

"Hello, Mother," I said. I wasn't afraid or anxious. I wasn't angry or contrite. I was ready to answer any questions she asked because I felt justified in everything I had done that morning.

"Why aren't you in school?" Her voice was shaking.

She'd pulled the big car up against the curb. I felt its heat radiating out through the open passenger side window.

"I'm on my way there now," I said.

"Why aren't you there *already?*"

"Because Adam was meeting Alice at the Taco Bell, and he wanted me for backup. They haven't seen each other in three years."

"Get in," she said and shoved the door open.

I got in.

My mother continued north on Whitmore and turned right onto Winters, speeding ten or twenty miles above the speed limit, passing through the red lights a second after they'd changed.

"I already told you," she was saying. "I don't trust you anymore. This drive is the last favor I'm doing for you."

"I don't know what you mean," I said, "but I don't trust you either. I know what Father's doing, and I know what you're doing. You don't like the choices I make, I don't give a shit. They're my choices."

"You only get to make those choices because you've got people who care about you and give you everything. Food, water, a home."

"Some water," I said. "Some home."

My mother didn't answer. She didn't speak again until we'd pulled up in front of Eastern High School. She threw the car into park a moment too soon and it lurched in complaint. She pulled her purse onto her lap and pulled out a small key. She held it up between us, the sun reflecting, a point of light between her eyes and mine.

"This is your key to Adam's house," she said. "I'm giving it back to you now. Since you evidently like his family more than your own – since you'll drop everything to do whatever he wants – I think you'd better let them take care of you."

I took the key in my hand and stared at it.

"You're kicking me out?" I asked.

She started to answer, then hesitated a moment, then spoke anyway.

"Yes," she said. "Yes, I am. Now get out of my car."

As I slammed the door behind me, my heart leapt twice. First in shock, and then in elation. *What am I now?* I wondered. *I am the map!* I thought. *I am the compass!* I felt the words. I didn't know what they meant, but suddenly the whole world felt like my home, and I knew this part of it well. Akawe. Now I could range out, learn the stars, taste the sun, ask my questions and hear my answers.

The blue doors of Eastern swam before me, cool and warm at once, like mingled ocean currents, shifting with the climate, ebbing along the surface, subsiding, rolling through darkness. As my mother's car rumbled away into the morning, its growling sounded like a smoky adjuration. "You'll regret this," it seemed to say.

"No, I won't," I said.

Because my mother had driven me to Eastern, I did, in fact, make it back before the end of Biology. Mrs. Clark was mid-lecture as I strode into the room and took my seat in the middle row.

"Nice to see you, Mr. Bridge," she said without looking up from the chalkboard. "Are you going to fail my class again this semester?"

"No," I said. "I'm going to be your best student."

"Well, that will be nice for a change."

After class, I asked Mrs. Clark if I could have a piece of paper to copy down the homework.

"Don't you have a notebook?" she asked.

"I thought it would be better to get back in time for class."

"Where were you?"

"Taking my best friend to meet his junkie mom before getting caught by my mother as I was walking back here."

She frowned, but her next class was starting in a couple minutes, so she scribbled the assignment on an index card and gave it to me.

As I moved on through Spanish and Geometry, I kept turning over the strangeness of my new independence. In the last few months, my house had become close and oppressive. If I played it right, I could use this time to set things right. To kick the drugs and drinking for good, and do my homework, and find out what the fuck was going on with Lucy and Selby. The thing is, I knew that my "exile" wasn't the same as when Adam's disappeared into the woods Up North. No way my parents were going to let me vanish into the city. My mother seemed to have reached her breaking point with me, but I thought that my father would disagree, and after screaming at each other for a few hours, they'd probably join forces to drag me kicking back home. I had to short-circuit that, and that meant that I had to avoid meeting them back on Agit Street. If I did, they might say, "We changed our minds," or "We need to work this through as a family," or "Go to your room, dammit!"

They wouldn't like me staying at Adam's, but I didn't think I had any alternative that first night. So first, I had to avoid them. Then I had to put some distance between us. Adam's it was.

I passed May on my way to lunch, and she smiled and gave me a bright wave.

First things first.

"May!" I said.

She turned and looked at me. Her brown eyes, bangs, eyelashes. The faint flower of vanilla that traced the air about her.

"You drive, right?" I asked in a rush. "I got kicked out of my parents' house this morning."

"Oh, no."

"No, it's okay. But look. Can you give me a quick ride home? I need to grab a few things? We can be back before lunch is over."

When we turned onto Agit a few minutes later, I saw at once that the driveway was empty.

"Pull up here," I said and May idled her own decrepit Aubrey in front of Archie's vacant lot. I climbed out, hurried across my driveway, and peeked in through the living and dining room windows. Then I crossed around back, glancing through the windows to the kitchen and study. The house appeared to be empty. I used my key and went in through the back, opening the door with the slightest of creaks. After listening in the back hall for a minute, I kicked off my boots, grabbed a Meijer's bag, and ran upstairs. I got my deodorant, cologne, and toothbrush from the bathroom, then went into my room and grabbed some shirts and pants, underwear, socks, and pajamas. I got a few pairs of shades, including the magical blue-bottle sunglasses. I got my Tori Amos CD and my *Lord of the Rings* books. I thought about grabbing a loaf of bread and the peanut butter, just in case, but decided against it. If they thought I was hard up for food, they'd bring me home right away. I had to play it more delicately. They had kicked me out, and I wasn't going to let them kick me back in until I was good and ready. In just five minutes, I was back in the car with May.

"I like your porch," she said. "Do you sit and drink lemonade in the summer?"

"Let's get the hell out of here," I said.

After school, I took the bus over to Adam's. Grandma M didn't seem surprised to see me.

"John," she said. "Your dad called."

"I'll call him later," I said as I thumped down the stairs to Adam's room. I had to stall. If I called home now, my father was going to beg me to come back. I knew it. He knew too much about Adam's family and their drama, and he'd use his mistrust as an excuse to come and get me. I needed to find someone else to stay with, and then call him from *their* house. Someone they trusted more. I found Adam in his bedroom, sitting on his bed with his shoulders slumped.

"So," I said. "Alice?"

"She's staying with Janice for now. I have to bring it up with my Grandpa Addison. He's not going to like it, but better him than my grandma.

They won't want to let her into the house at first. I might see if they want to meet at a restaurant or something."

"Do you think she's better?"

"Junkies don't get better. But she's, you know, sober for now, so ..."

I didn't say anything. After everything, Adam didn't seem to be angry at Alice. It made me question my anger toward my father over his drinking. Was I right to be angry? Was Adam right to not be angry? I had no idea who was right and who was wrong. Adam must have read something in my face because he went on after a moment:

"I have to help her out, John," he said. "It isn't about whether she deserves it or not. It's about what I do says about me."

After hanging out in his room for a while, Adam and I came upstairs to watch music videos, but Grandpa M was already dug in on the recliner in front of the TV. It was CNN, but I could see that they were broadcasting from Akawe. The news crew had set up in front of the Masonic lodge, the bricks of East Street foregrounded, gray in the salt smear. Cut to crying kids sitting on tables inside. Needles poked into their fingers. Tiny drops of blood. The newscast shifted to a similar scene at Truman Elementary. The reporter was talking from the dull yellow cafeteria where I'd eaten lunch for seven years.

"What's going on?" I asked.

"Testing kids for lead," said Grandpa M. "The water."

"What about it?"

"Jesus, John," said Adam. "Where you been?"

"I saw the governor's speech, but you know what my month's been like!"

"The National Guard is here. Ever since the feds declared the state of emergency, we've been getting bottles of water from camo guys."

"No, we aren't!"

Adam simply pointed at the TV. I watch a U-Haul roll down what looked like Orion Street. Men in fatigues walked to and from the truck, carrying crates of bottled water and boxed filters.

"I ain't seen any," I said.

"I don't know how you missed it. It's all over. Everyone knows about it."

Obviously not, I thought. Still, it made me think about how phased-out my parents had become. In the past, they would've brought this up at dinner, told me exactly what was going on, what they thought of it, and invited me to agree or disagree.

"They giving out shower filters?" I asked.

"I don't know," Adam said. "Hey, Grandpa, can we please change the channel?"

"No!" Grandpa M barked. "I'm watching this."

I went into the dining room and picked up the phone.

I tried to remember Nova's number, but I'd forgotten it. I wanted to ask Chris and Shannon – their perfect family, their perfect house – but I hadn't talked to them in about a month. I knew, dimly, that I could call Crystal – that she might even say "yes" – but that would have weirded out my parents for other reasons. I certainly wasn't about to ask Omara for help.

"Call Chuck," said Adam.

"What?" I said.

"They'll let you stay. They don't have no drama in that house."

"I haven't talked to Chuck in over a year!"

"Don't matter. He's still your friend."

"Is he?"

"Yeah. Blood, water, whatever." Adam pointed at the TV. "Water ain't shit. But, I mean, you'd be staying with a male ballerina. So, you better watch your asshole."

A half-hour later, I finally made up my mind and called Chuck.

"Hello?" he answered when he picked up the phone. I hadn't heard his sullen voice since we were both in eighth grade, but I knew it right away.

"Hey, Chuck. How's it ... hey, it's John."

"Hey."

"Hey."

"How you doin'?"

"Great? Shitty? I don't know. I just got kicked out this morning. From my house."

"Sorry, man."

"I'm at Adam's tonight. He said ... he said maybe it would be okay if I stayed at your place a few nights."

"Stay here, John. Just do it. It ain't a thing."

After I got off the phone, I stood in the kitchen for a minute, feeling nervous and weird about going over to Chuck's after I'd spent a year writing him off. *What are we even going to talk about?* I wondered. *What am I going to say to his mom?*

Back in the living room, the lights were off, but the blue light from the TV bleached the carpets and curtains, the faces of Adam and Grandpa M, and the images seemed to strobe against me. Camaros, Corvettes, and the '96 Aubrey Soma, its panels as white as its tires were black, a lesson in the potentialities of real-world monochrome, spearing down the Circus Maximus, the Campus Martius, the limestone paths of Bloomfield Hills' Olympic-sized pools, of still-aired wine cellars and milk-walled corridors, of sparkling saltwater aquariums rainbowed by coral reef fishes, of the delicate perfume of real roses, January blooms, of the castellated turrets of Grosse Pointe, Grosse Pointe Farms, Grosse Pointe Shores, Grosse Pointe Woods, Grosse Pointe Promenade, Grosse Pointe Gruesome, Grosse Pointe Park, and whoever was slumming it in Harper Woods, of picturesque turrets commissioned by Art Moderne architects to look pretty, and possibly to repel the feral soiled noisome stuffpeople. A grinning Leonardo DiCaprio and a pouting Sarah Michelle Gellar. Will Smith smirking and Christina Ricci glaring. Kirsten Dunst with a slight shake of her head. Johnny Cochran and Marcia Clark. Tim Allen and Richard Karn. Steven Bochco jamming some juicy tune through the churning rotors of a pulp police procedural. Some trashy flashy chair-throwing shit on Jerry Springer. The MV Bukova taking a turn for the worse. The Zambian copper industry tilting toward privatization. Kikwit too toxic to touch. Dhaka going under. Derek Jeter, Andre Agassi, Albert Belle, and Ronaldo Ronaldo. Cheering. Chanting. Waving at the enemy. Sparkles of gunfire from the black-clad Praetorian Guard. It was getting dark outside, but the change manifested as an intensification of the light from the television.

It seemed to outshine the sun and stars.

But I was in a house where I knew the people cared for me, so the things I saw on the television didn't phase me.

The next morning, my eyes flew open to the touch of tropical sunshine. Actually, it was the naked light bulb that hung in the middle of Adam's windowless bedroom.

"Jesus," he said. "I do *not* want to get up right now."

I did.

My heart was a woodpecker trying to drill its way out of my chest. I had finally found the relief that I had been seeking in the drugs and vodka all month long. None of that shit had even worked. But this shit was working! But what was this shit?

That day passed by like any other day, except for everything I saw and noticed. Now, my home was not home. I took careful notes in each class, writing so quickly that my wrist got sore from the speed and effort. Then, after my Global Issues magnet at Northern, I took the bus through the Os to the depot and transferred to another bus that swept me up Hastings Boulevard and dropped me off at Aubrey Street.

A few years ago, this had been "The Deadliest Street Corner in America," and Adam, Michael, and I had crossed it on our October nightwalk. 1993. Now, it was the dead of winter '96 – the heaviest, coldest winter I had ever known – but something was different. The sun was out again, and it was hard for me to see my breath in front of me. Dark ribbons of wet laced the gray pavement like rivers across the tundra. The snow was melting.

I made my way to Gardenview Street, a boulevard lined by maples on the sides and crabapples along the median. These houses were compact, wood-frame bungalows. Shop rat houses. In their day, they had looked solid, dignified, more carefully built than the houses off Whitmore Street.

I had entered the Palisades. Seventy-some years ago, this neighborhood had been built as a whites-only factory workers' enclave. Today, I was probably the only white on this block, not that it bothered me.

Chuck's block had done better than most. Only a handful of houses had burned down or been demoed, and more than half of the rest were occupied. Even the living houses wore scars, however; bright blue tarps nailed onto leaking roofs, construction cones mounted above sidewalk sinkholes, and white paint around each apple tree's trunk to keep the bark from splitting. But Chuck's house was still narrowly prim, its astroturfed porch a perfect match to the emerald-colored trim, which itself seemed to bleed out of the olive green aluminum siding. Two knobby jack pines mugged over the other trees' embarrassed nakedness.

After hesitating a moment, I went up to the door and banged. I heard the howling of a dog inside, but this one didn't frighten me. The pit bull bounded up against the door inside, grinning at me.

"Hey Twig!" I yelled. "Hey girl, I haven't seen you in a long time!"

"Is that John?"

The woman's voice was muffled by distance and glass, but I saw Chuck's mother, Tammy, coming down the narrow, dark hall. She unlocked the door and let me in. Twig bounded up against me, and I reached down to pet her, her tongue rolling around on my wrist. I didn't like dogs, really, but Twig was so affectionate it was hard not to love her.

"Chuck's at dance now," Tammy was saying, "but he'll be back in an hour or so. I didn't expect you for a while. Usually, the buses are slow."

"It was faster getting out here than it is to get back home," I said.

I took a seat on the couch. Tammy held a dishtowel in her hand, wadded it up and set it on the coffee table, and took a seat across from me. She had a dark, clear face, and right now, her hair was tied up in a do-rag. She was maybe a decade younger than my parents. She smiled.

"When was the last time you sat on my couch, John?" she asked.

"A year ago, I guess?"

"Too long. You know, Chuck used to be over at your place every week, every other day. You used to come over here just about as often!"

"I know. I feel bad."

"People drift apart. It happens. But you and Adam and Chuck were inseparable. He was doing his karate thing, and you showed him those video games."

I laughed. It felt good.

"Yeah," I said. "I could kick his ass at Double Dragon, and he could kick my ass in real life. Back when we tried it at recess ..."

"Mrs. Tacken made you clean all the lockers. I remember."

"That kid deserved it."

"That's what Chuck told me then. 'You deserve it too,' I told him."

"I kind of miss Truman."

"Now they're doing blood tests there. Did you see that?"

"Yeah. I feel funny about it."

"Why do you feel funny?"

"Nobody cared about all the things we've been going through. Now it feels like everyone wants to stare at us. Like it's suddenly their business. I mean, they owe us money. Right? I want their money. But I don't want them to stare at us like we're in some zoo!"

My anger surprised me.

"I know that's a weird way to say it," I said.

"No, I think I understand. Because we've been through all this. You've lost people. Chuck's lost people. He's had friends shot. Killed. And the water is a mess for everyone."

"How do people even survive?"

"If they can, they leave. If they can't, they stay. And do the best they can. People who aren't from here don't care, though."

"I think they think they care, but you're right. They're more worried about whether they look like they care than if they actually do care."

"How is the water at your parents' house?"

"Red. More like a rusty orange, I guess. We couldn't even shower in it. Then my father bought this expensive filter for the shower, but there was so much rust in the water it broke. And then he lost his job. I mean, nobody noticed that whole time. Now it's some big emergency? And, and celebrities are coming here?"

"Yeah ..."

"And the National Guard?"

"Yeah. And they want the governor to resign over it."

"Will he?"

"Rhinelander? No way. No, he isn't gonna resign."

"I didn't think so ... it's hard. It's all hard."

"I know, John. I know. Our water is bad too."

We just sat there for a minute. I was surprised how quickly the conversation had turned serious.

"Your house looks nice," I said. "Real nice. Better than mine."

"That's just because none of the others are standing," she said with a rueful laugh. "So," she went on, "what happened with you and your parents?"

I didn't want to keep secrets today, but if I said too much, it could come back to haunt me.

"None of us are getting along right now," I said.

"I don't want to horn in, John, but ... I've known your parents for years. I know that they love you a lot."

"I know they do," I said. "But I need a break from them. I need to work on my homework. I need to show them I can do it."

"Do they know you're here?"

"I was going to call them tonight."

"Can you call them now?"

"Yeah," I said. "Yeah, I can do that."

I went to the kitchen and picked up the phone where it was mounted upon the wall. Tammy retreated upstairs to give me some privacy, but Twig knelt at my feet, her tail wagging, and I pet her as the phone started to ring.

My father picked up.

"Hi," I said. "It's me."

"John," he said. "Your mother and I both think that Adam might not ... I like Adam. You know I like Adam. I always have! But his family's in a rough spot, and –"

His arguments were going exactly as I had expected.

"I'm not staying with Adam," I cut in.

"You're ... not?"

"Yeah, I'm at Chuck's. His mom says it's okay. I'll just stay here ..."

"I know your mother is angry at you, John," my father stammered. He had prepared all this, but he'd expected to come and get me from Adam's, and now he had to improvise. "I'm angry, too, you know? But we can work this out. You could come back home if you wanted, tonight. I can come pick you up."

I shook my head to steel my resolve.

"You can't impose on other people, John," my father said.

I'd expected this, too.

"Yeah, but you want to impose on me. All your drama. All her drama. No. I'm here now. Try and drag me back. Go ahead and try it. You won't like it. I'm here for now. You deal with it. You figure out shit with Mother. Okay? You two work your own shit out. And I'm just going to be here and try to figure my own shit out."

After I got off the phone, I met Chuck's mom in the kitchen.

"You sure it's okay for you to stay here?" she asked.

"I'm sure," I said.

Hours passed.

I did my homework.

I fell asleep on the couch.

Chuck's two sisters, Cala and Maya, came in and ran up and down the hall, shrieking, and they took a break to hit me with pillows. We joined Chuck's

400

mom in the dining room for pasta and garlic bread. After dinner, I returned to my homework.

Finally, Chuck came home. He was taller than I remembered. His voice, which had been deeper than mine in seventh grade, was now deeper still. His hair was cut short, and a single circle of facial hair grew upon his chin. Chuck looked more of a man than a boy, whereas I was still squarely in between.

"Hey," he said, and I nodded back. I still wasn't sure what to say.

Chuck vanished into the kitchen to microwave himself some dinner. He met me in the living room again.

"C'mon," he grunted, the steaming bowl in his hand. "Follow me."

We both went up to his bedroom, a small room with mint green walls and a long crack in the window, though even this was better than Adam's room in the unfinished basement. Chuck set his food down on his dresser, left for a moment, and returned with a foam mattress and a sleeping bag with a slightly musty smell.

"It's all I got," he said.

"It's fine," I said. "Thanks for putting me up."

"Anytime. It's not a problem."

"I'm sorry I ain't been in touch."

"It's nothing. Nobody's been talking to nobody. I mean, I haven't been talking to Quanla, even. She came to see me at the *Nutcracker*."

"She invited me to that. I should have come to see you. I'm sorry I didn't. I haven't really been on top of things."

"Relax, John."

"You were the Rat King?"

"The Mouse King. Yeah."

"How was it?"

"Oh, it was the shit! I have a lot of work to do ... but some of my instructors, they ... they think I can do this – can do dance – like, professionally. So, I'm taking all these lessons every night. Ballet and modern and everything. Anything I can take. It's a lot of work. But the Mouse King. Yeah, that was something else. I had this huge helmet with glowing eyes. I wore it out into the lobby one night, and it freaked these little kids right the hell out! But they loved it."

Chuck had always been taciturn. It was strange to see him so animated. It was strange to see him at all. This conversation reminded me of the night when we'd crashed at Carla's apartment after Laserpalooza.

"How do you like school at Southern?"

"Huh, that? No, that's nothing. It's stupid. Everyone's frontin', you know? School's just the thing I do until I get to dance."

"That's really cool. I wish I had something like that."

"You still doing theater?"

I'd been doing theater for two years and had factored it into my college plans. When I'd had college plans. But if I had been *really* serious about it, I would have auditioned at both *Candide* and *Sleepy Hollow.* Just like Chuck wasn't going to turn down any opportunity to dance.

"I guess," I said. "AYT is doing a play this spring, and they called me about auditioning. So, I guess I better do that. I just don't know if it leads anywhere, you know?"

"What do you mean?"

"Well, like your dance. If you keep doing it, and get a job in it or whatever. Do you really think it's going to get you out of Akawe?"

"I mean, I can't count on *that*," he said. "It's not like I have money for college. And I help out a lot around here, too. My mom needs my help when I'm not dancing. I don't know. Maybe it'll lead to a job, but I won't want to leave. Or maybe I'll get out of here, and there won't be any work. I can't worry about that right now. I've just got to get as good as I can."

"But it still seems like you've got some shit figured out."

"I guess I do? I mean, I say to myself, all day long, 'is this worthwhile?' About whatever I'm doing at that moment. And if the answer is 'no,' then I start doing something else."

"What about, like, having fun?"

"Fun is worthwhile."

We talked for a while longer. Chuck had just broken up with his girlfriend, Nik. She was a cheerleader, but he said, "she's obsessed with petty bullshit." I told him about Omara.

"I think I was the one obsessed with petty bullshit," I said.

"Nah," Chuck said. "You just got to get through to summer. Meet some other girls."

Eventually, Chuck turned his attention to his homework. He put on a small light on his nightstand, set his dinner on his dresser, pulled the sheets over his lap, and started revising an essay. My homework was already done, so I lay down on the sleeping bag. The walls were narrow, and the ceiling seemed far away. And yet this room also felt like a home to me, even after the years that had passed. *I'm going to find homes for myself all over the city*, I thought.

"You comfortable enough?" Chuck asked.

"I didn't realize how tired I was," I said, then fell asleep.

The next morning, Chuck and I got up and waited for our separate buses. All day, I strained to hear the teachers and take good notes. Back at Chuck's, I did my homework, ate an Italian beef sandwich for dinner, finished *The Two Towers*, and went to sleep on the floor again.

The day after that, my father called. Again, he tried to talk me into coming home.

"I understand," I said, "but no."

I was doing fine. I was doing what I needed to do. Why was he trying to screw things up for me? Anyway, it had been my mother who had kicked me out of the house. If she wanted me to come back, why didn't she give me a call? He didn't yell at me when I said that. He eventually sighed and hung up.

By Thursday morning, I was getting used to my new routine. The long wait for the bus in the shadow of the skeletal houses, the rumble of laughter or argument from Chuck's sisters in the evening, and the hard creaks of the floor beneath me at night. None of it bothered me. I started reading *The Return of the King* and the pages flew beneath my fingers deep into the night.

When I got back to Chuck's on Friday, he was waiting for me.

"No ballet today?" I asked.

"Nope. I was thinking maybe we go to the mall."

"Is your mom gonna drop us off?"

"Nah, I thought we could take our bikes."

"We're going to get smashed by some mom in a pickup. People on Aurelius drive crazy."

"So, we don't go that way. We take the tracks. I'll show you. Come on. Look outside. It won't be nice like this for long, you know?"

I looked out the window. The temperatures had been climbing all week. Huge banks of snow had slurried off, making a mess in the streets.

"I think I gotta hold on to my money," I said. "I mean. When I'm out, I'm out."

"How much you got?"

"I don't know. Thirty bucks?"

"You know you can stay here as long as you want. My mom will feed you. And if you ever want to leave, you can stay at Adam's."

He'd won. The warmth had won.

"Fine," I said. "Let's go."

For the first time since Selby had returned them to me, I put on the blue-bottle sunglasses.

The world became purple and electric azure for me. I was swimming through an ocean, and the currents told me where to go.

"Dude," said Chuck.

We went out to his garage. Chuck pulled out Maya's bike, and I climbed on. It was so small that the pedals brought my knees almost up to my chin. Chuck's bike was adult sized.

We biked in the fiery wet light to Hastings, and then to Starr Highway and turned east. The sun hurled our blue shadows far ahead of us and we went over the low hills, past purple houses and violet churches, and swept across Elmwood Road and onto the South Side. Fast food stops sloped against brick banks, McDonald's and Arby's, a couple coney islands, marigold-colored pawn shops, and black brick medical offices carried us down to the river where we flashed across the bridge, overhung by wet-barked trees, then up again, pushing our chains beneath the gleaming spires of Temple Medical Center, across Cooper Road, swelling around some blighted white-bricked low-rise apartments where people still lived, even though half of the windows were smashed, and it didn't look like they had any lights on, either. Someone had sprayed the walls with black paint: "Get Out APES." Then we sailed across South Street, passed a ghetto Burger King, a ghetto Little Caesar's, an African braid shop, and the Taco Bell where Adam and Alice had reunited just a few days before.

We turned south onto Whitmore, a straight shot toward the suburbs now, and a couple blocks later we swung past the Constellation and onto the train tracks, which angled off to the southeast.

"Don't get hit by no trains, Chuck," I said.

"I don't think they even use these tracks anymore."

The tracks spanned I-92, then emerged onto a tree-crowned ridge, about thirty feet above the houses of the farthest South Side. Here, the streets weren't paved, and there weren't any sidewalks. These houses weren't broken or abandoned – just shabby – and I felt a bit like a spy, able to look down into the backyards and second-story windows as we thumped along the tracks. I kept an eye out for any girls undressing in their bedrooms, but there wasn't anything to see. Just a few men working on broken down rust-buckets and dogs spiraling their chains around clothesline posts and pissing in the fast-disappearing snow.

Eventually, we left the houses and Akawe behind and entered Arcadia. I don't know when it happened: there weren't any signs. All we could see on either side were the trees and cattails and the buzzing high-tension electrical lines high overhead.

Then we suddenly hit pavement again. Some road that seemed to be in the middle of nothing, freshly painted with yellow stripes, told a different story.

"Mall's that way," said Chuck, pointing off toward the left.

We crossed a rise, passed a used Starr dealership, and then a boarded-up bargain movie theater. It had once had a dozen screens, but now the weeds had breached the cracked asphalt. Beyond it, at last, rising like some stony monument in the midst of a desert parking lot, the Basadena Mall.

I don't know how far Chuck and I had biked – miles and miles – but he was right. We had traveled fast. The sun was still several hands above the horizon, and I was sweating in the evening heat.

Once we got inside, it took my eyes a few minutes to adjust to the dimness. I saw the gibbous moon, silvery through the glassy skylights. We sneaker squeaked past the children's play area with its mechanical horses and spaceships. Our shoes friction-laughed as we passed Alladin's Palace, Tenth Town Threads (an actual tailor), Aéropostale and Black Tie White Tie, and Supercuts. I had my hands in my pockets. I squeezed my money in my fist. I was going to spend this on *me*, but when it was gone, it was gone. I'd have to choose carefully.

"I mean, never date a cheerleader," Chuck was saying. "Ask 'em out, they're like, 'yeah, okay,' and that's all you have to say to them, but then you're out at some restaurant or something, and you have to listen to them talk. Salty shit. They're stupid. They're hot but stupid. Hot's all you gotta be to be a cheerleader. All the rest is on-the-job, you know?"

"You were saying you don't ever see Quanla?" I asked.

"Nah, I mean, we're in a few classes together. I don't know. 'Hi' and 'hi,' but we don't hang out much. When the rest of you went off to Eastern, I met a bunch of new people through dance. Quanla has some friends, I guess, but nobody we know. I got to know her brother better, though. Darius is cool. He's a pimp! Like he was telling me about some older woman he's into right now."

At the center court, the four wings of the mall spoked out – north, south, east, west – with the long passages each bracketed by department stores. Here, beneath the rising escalator and elevator piers, the Santa's Depot had finally been cleared away and replaced by a ruby-colored Passway. After its long delay due to the Great XAWU Strike of '94, it had gone on to become X's best-selling product. Chuck and I rode the escalator up to the food court.

"I'm not hungry," I said.

"Me neither," said Chuck, but he bought a giant pretzel with some mustard.

He broke it in half to share with me.

I wanted to tell him about how strange my life felt right then, like my body had been given a new mind, a brighter mind. How my teeth had ached for months, but now they had finally stopped hurting. Was this finally my chance to be good? To turn pages? To read ahead? To run ahead? To become what I was supposed to be?

"Long as you aren't out on the streets," Chuck said. "That shit's cold. It'll kill you."

"What do you know about it?"

"Me? Nothing. People from school."

"I know people from school, too. Half the time, those are the kids that show up one week at the beginning, and then you never see 'em again."

"Some of them were squatting out of a house across the street from me. They were living there for a month until one of them accidentally burned it down."

"How'd they keep warm?"

Chuck shook his head. "I mean, we know how they did in the end! But I don't know. Lots of blankets. They drank a lot, so maybe they didn't feel it. I kept expecting someone to die, but it didn't happen while they were there."

"How long were they there?"

"Three weeks maybe? My mom kept saying she was gonna call the cops on them, but she never did because she didn't think they'd have anywhere else to go."

Chuck took a big bite of pretzel.

I thought again about the house on Agit Street and how much I hated it that winter. What if I had to leave Chuck's? What if I couldn't stay at Adam's? If the cold came, and the hunger, would I return to my parents before I went into an empty house? *If we aren't willing to sacrifice everything to be who we want, is it really who we are, and do we really want it so badly?* Then again: *It doesn't matter who you are if who you are is dead.*

We threw away the empty wrapper and circled up and down the halls. Candid Portraits, Payless Shoes where Chuck bought some new laces, B. Dalton and Waldenbooks, and the Global Scent Company where I splurged a dollar and bought a dozen incense sticks: lavender, patchouli, sage, and passion. Past the fountains where fired pennies gleamed up at us through the troubled surface.

Then, finally, out again, back to our bikes, where we climbed on and rode back toward the city along the crazy margins of Aurelius Street, swamped with cars. By now, the sun was almost down, but Chuck and I turned off into a Wendy's just shy of city limits.

As we went inside, the sun began to set between the trees and buildings to the west. The light hit the big glass panes of an abandoned K-Mart across its pitted parking lot and the five lanes of Aurelius Road.

That was when the sunglasses revealed their full power to me.

I had understood, from what Selby had said, that these sunglasses would hide the urbantasms – the blue ghosts – from someone who wore them, by cloaking everything in blues. Now, in the absence of urbantasms, the ordinary living, breathing, moving people around me seemed to become urbantasms themselves: they were all shades dressed in shimmering skins of violet and cerulean.

The Wendy's was crowded this evening. People, tired, were eating in their booths or waiting for their orders to come up.

Someone coughed because this was the coughing time of the year.

Chuck and I got in line behind an older white man – wrinkled mouth and gray hair, and a little loose, like he had lost too much weight too quickly – and he was blue. He was wearing a navy blue track jacket with white stripes painted luminous lavender by my sunglasses. His jacket made a plastic zipping sound whenever he lifted his right hand to scratch at the side of his nose. In a nearby booth, a crying Black girl with three braids – left, right, and top – kept burying her face in her mom's black shirt, then turned out to see who was watching, then turned back in and cried some more. More noise. More shuffling. No conversation except for the murmur of the cashier taking money and orders. Returning change.

Out the windows, the sun fired against its blue backdrop and silhouetted the passing cars in molten glow. It was a traffic jam out there. This was the busiest I had ever seen Aurelius Road in Arcadia, even though this was it an ordinary Friday night at the end of January. *Is it because of the weather?* I wondered. Even as the darkening came on outside, the snow kept melting. The smallest drifts had been reduced to slush. The larger drifts had lost their jagged, mountain-top severity. The grit and soot that had settled on their peaks now made black pock marks upon them. Vast puddles rippled blue on the blacktop parking lots. Heavier, deeper, more intense blues crept on while the sinking sun licked the few remaining clouds blue-orange and purple-pink. Everything seemed to sing and shiver together.

It all reminded me of my bedroom back on Agit Street, and I realized then that I had prophetic powers. When I had painted my ceiling, I had been painting this sunset, which I had not yet seen.

And I sighed, because even though this was the most beautiful thing I had ever witnessed, I knew that it wasn't going to last. The cars would move on. The sun would move down. The light would fade. The scene was vanishing even as I watched. All that would remain would be the stark white light inside the restaurant and the emptiness of the night without.

I almost felt that this brief beauty had been specifically prepared for me alone, not in the turbulent wake of a butterfly tumbling into Mexico, but in the plunge of a mayfly. The way its tiny wings must have troubled the magnetic fields. Or in the crack of an iceberg on some polar ocean. Or maybe, even, in the way time transcribed the sap of a tree that bore a blue-colored fruit. Had these small, remote events changed their environments in ways that became magnified by months and many miles, and found me wearing these blue-bottle sunglasses in the Aurelius Road Wendy's that night? Had everything been timed *just so*? And if so, had it been predestined, or was it was just a big fucking coincidence? Or was it something else? A story that moved on action and passion and responded to *me*, too? That heard, somehow, when I climbed onto Maya's bike, and put on my magical shades, and followed Chuck out into the wilderness? That said: *Now is the time for the sunset of all sunsets.*

I knew that the universe was expanding out of control.

Miss Pavilik had said so.

It was going to expand so quickly that it would eventually dismantle itself. A fast dismantling. An explosion.

A mystical God, I thought, would have engineered a cyclical universe in which death would give birth to life which would lead to death again. In which complexity and simplicity would wax and wane. A clockwork God would have engineered an expanding universe to succumb to heat death, ameliorated, perhaps, by the resolution of all complexity into bleak speed and frigid stillness. But a God who designed a hyperbolic universe and then pumped it full of phantom energy, the fuel of that ripping apart, *that* God must be a monstrous God. Not a God who knowingly creates that which must someday decay, because even the best universes must be possible universes. No. A God who creates only to witness the gory destruction of the end. A demonic God. A Satanic God. A God averse to God's own creation. A pyromaniac homicidal sociopathic God wedded to divinity's own immolation. How could any God be so ghastly?

And yet ... here was beauty.

The restaurant's radio started playing Louis Armstrong. "What a Wonderful World."

I had been holding my breath. I let it out now. With it went the last remnants of ache and doubt, but just for this moment. I breathed in. I filled myself with cold blue. I imagined the universe pulling toward me. Contracting. Shifting toward a closer frequency. *If time really is just another dimension – if it's only measured by light and the heat our brain loses when it makes thoughts – then where we begin and where we end aren't any more important than what we pass along the way. Happy endings aren't possible. Unhappy endings aren't possible. Endings aren't possible. Every second, every moment, is a beginning, and an ending, and a middle. Time is travel. Loss is learning. We are forever temporary and temporarily forever.*

Like the evangelists who wrote down the words and stories of Christ, or like the scientists who accidentally saw the Big Bang while fine-tuning their fancy radio antenna, I knew that I was seeing, right now, in this moment, in this beleaguered restaurant, through its grime-streaked windows, everything I needed to see. I would spend the rest of my life trying to understand it, truly, but still: I was *seeing* it and *experiencing* it, and I knew, *I knew*. *This is all I need to know! This is the answer to everything!*

I felt my breath stirring inside. I felt my heart hammering. I felt my mind groping about in darkness. Fumbling for something that it had dropped long ago. A key. My mind found a key. It found a keyhole in my memory and turned, steadily, assuredly, and opened a door that I had forgotten, and I remembered things that I had not known in many years.

I remembered when I was young, and my father had gone off to rehab. I remembered the sun and the moon in the sky at the same time. I remembered the film of blue that had seemed to cover things. The blue things that had come out of blue shadows. Spectral, shining, glowing blue things that I could not touch, that seemed to fade in and out. And the air around me had also carried a strange charge, not electrical, but the frisson of the ghosts. Their passage. Their invisible interactions. Conversations with inanimate objects. Communion with phantoms. I had just been a child! I didn't know what I was seeing! And now that I was fifteen, I still didn't understand.

But I remembered an ancient afternoon, when I had run from blue monsters – had run from my parents – and had wound up in a bathroom with a man who had given me a pair of blue sunglasses, and told me that they would keep me from seeing the ghosts.

Louis sang about the babies. Their tears. What they would know. What he would not. Again, the passing of time. The song was lovely, but the sun had finally slipped across the horizon, and with it, the reflection vanished. Now, the liminal light finally tilted toward dark. Night had arrived.

"You're up," Chuck said.

"I like your sunglasses!" the cashier said.

"Thanks," I said. "I'll get the spicy chicken nuggets, and a fries. And a Coke."

That night, May called me at Chuck's house. Tammy handed me the phone.

"My birthday party's tomorrow!" May said.

"Oh, that's right!"

"Can you make it?"

"I think so. Where is it?"

"I sent you an invitation. I sent it in the mail."

"Where did you send it? Adam's house?"

"No. I sent it to your house. I bought stamps for it."

"But I'm not staying there. Remember? You drove me over to pick up my stuff?"

Silence.

"May?"

"Yeah, it's not my fault you didn't give me a better address."

"No, but … okay, I think I can make it. Just give me your address. And when is it?"

"The party is at eight. That way you can eat dinner before the party. We aren't fixing dinner for anyone here." Her voice was apologetic. "You are going to want to go to Two-Zero-One-Eight Armstrong B-L-V-D. Our house has a mural on it. Of Jesus! So that way, you'll know it when you see it."

"Should I take the bus?"

"It would take you a long time, but that's okay. I asked Lucy at school today if she and Eli could give you a ride, and she said yes. Just give me your address, and I'll let them know."

I gave her Chuck's address.

"That's great, John. Thank you for coming to my party and for eating dinner first. I will see you tomorrow. Don't forget to take your shoes off when you get there. It makes my dad really mad when people come into our house without taking their shoes off."

"Okay."

"It makes me mad, too."

"I got it."

"Or you can be barefoot. Or in your socks. Just don't be a jerk, okay?"

The warmth didn't last.

Saturday morning broke with steam in the air. I had finished the weekend's homework by lunchtime, took a walk around the neighborhood with Chuck, and watched some TV. We had sub sandwiches for dinner. I helped carry bottled water down to the basement after the fatigued guardsmen dropped it off at the front door. I sat in Chuck's bedroom and read about the nightfall massing against Minas Tirith. The white light stabbed at the dark birds of emptiness. The sun slashed the fields of Pelennor. It finally left me breathless.

I'd enjoyed getting caught up with Chuck and his family, but now I was ready to decamp to Adam's for a day or two. His grandparents wouldn't keep me on as short a leash as Chuck's mom, and besides, the bus ride to Eastern from the West End took forever.

"It's about time for my friend's party," I said at the end of dinner. "I might not be back tonight."

"What do you mean?" Tammy asked. "Where are you staying?"

"The party's going kind of late."

"Your parents know about this?"

"Look, if I don't come back here, I'll go home, or crash at Adam's, okay?"

"I don't like this, John."

"It's just a birthday party."

"Before you go to bed tonight, I want you to call me and let me know where you are. I don't care how late it is. Do you understand?"

"Yeah."

"If I don't hear from you, I'm calling your parents."

"I got it."

When the time was right, I put on my coat, shouldered my backpack, and Chuck followed me out onto the porch.

"You can wait inside, you know," he said.

"I don't want your mom asking me more shit."

"Who is this girl, anyway?"

"You know, you wouldn't remember her, but that night we went to the planetarium laser show? She was there. She was sitting, like, at my feet. She remembered me from that, even though it's years later."

"She's got a good memory, then."

"She's strange. But she's really nice. I owe her this."

And I owe Selby, too. I hadn't forgotten my mission: to send the Ostyns a message that they were being hunted, without Selby's signature. I was excited by the idea of catching Eli surprised. I had decided that his nervousness was just a front. A mask he pulled to give himself an edge. I wanted to see him vulnerable. The more I thought about that anxious motherfucker – his tidy teeth, his cutting eyes – the more I hated him. Clouds covered the sky, but they glowed a mottled gray, like dead moss, and I knew that the moon was full.

"Where you staying tonight?"

"Adam's, probably."

"Just don't go out on the streets."

"Thanks for caring, Chuck. But don't worry. I've got tons of places I can stay. Worst case, I can always go home. I'm not someone who is gonna end up on the street."

"You think so." Chuck's face was grim. "I've seen people out there you wouldn't believe."

I studied him. He still didn't say a lot, but in the last week, I had finally absorbed how much Chuck had changed over the last two years. Before, his silence had kept him from appearing foolish in front of others. Now, it lent his words an added impact. Whatever Chuck said, he meant.

"You are a good friend," I said. "I shouldn't have lost touch with you."

"Then don't do it again. You can come back here any time. Even if things get bad."

We hugged, and then Chuck went back inside. I went down to the curb to wait for my ride. Nobody was out there. No cars. No dogs. After a while, ten minutes maybe, a pair of headlights soaked through the fog on my left before pulling up to the curb in front of Chuck's house.

It was one of the shittiest looking Benedicts I'd ever seen. Some mid-80s model, off red with rust pricking the edges of the door and one end of the fender held on by a strip of bungee cord. I made out Lucy's smiling face in the passenger seat. She reached back and fiddled with the lock behind her. I popped the door open swung myself inside.

"Thanks," I said. "Nice car."

Lucy rolled her eyes. Eli glanced at me over his shoulder, his mouth twitching.

The car was moving again before I even had the door shut. Squinting through the window, I could see empty house after empty house slide by. Lucy looked out her own window. Eli seemed to be trying on different faces in the rear-view mirror. Trying to decide which expression would best fit the occasion. He frowned. He grinned.

"John," said Lucy, without looking back at me. "I'm glad you decided to come to May's party. You know, some of us are hoping you two hook up again."

"Us?" I asked. "Who's us?"

Eli gave a nervous laugh.

"Okay, just me," said Lucy, "but I thought you were a cute couple."

"We don't have nothing in common."

"No, but you're such an asshole, and she doesn't notice it. She notices the nice things you do, but not the shit things you say. If it isn't for a girl like May, you'll never get to hook up with anyone."

"Yeah? Thanks."

I fingered the teashades in my pocket. My hands were sweating. It seemed too soon. I decided to wait. I pulled my hand out of my pocket.

Eli kept fidgeting, trying to find a comfortable perch. He leaned forward, his hands rolling across the steering wheel, tightening and then relaxing. Snow and salt flew against the windshield, but Eli didn't turn on the wipers. He pushed ahead, chugging through stop signs and red lights as soon as he saw that nobody was coming.

"You always drive like this?" I asked.

"John!" said Lucy.

"I'm sorry," Eli said, his voice trembling. "I can slow down."

He gave me a quick grin, but he didn't slow down.

"Eli's a little weird tonight because he's on bees," said Lucy. Her voice was sulky.

"Bees?" I asked.

"Four, bro," said Eli. "Mo, too. Five die. Methoxyphenethylamine. Acid, too. Bees and acid. Acid and bees."

"And what about you?" I asked Lucy. "Are you on *bees?*"

"I don't do drugs," Lucy said with a sullen shrug.

I tried to hide my relief.

"Should he be driving?"

"It's fine," Eli said, irritation cutting into his voice for the first time. "I drive high all the time. I drive better this way. It makes me more careful."

We flashed across Hastings. Cape Cods with bars over their windows flew by. I fastened my seatbelt.

"Remember when you bitched me out for not putting on my seatbelt?" Lucy asked. "You took fucking forever to put on your own."

She was in a good mood. Everything was funny to her tonight.

"You sure you're not on drugs?"

"No, John. I'm high on life." She laughed merrily.

I'd never moved through the city so quickly. Buildings, intersections, relics misted past, billowing, dark, squat, half-familiar, and ugly. Sycamores sprouted on neglected yards with their shaggy bark shredding up the snow. For a brief second, Poe Junior High loomed over us on one side, as drunk and bleak as its namesake.

I touched the sunglasses again through my pockets, like a charm. They were Cosette's letter receiving Marius' breath. They were the One Ring that came out of darkness and shadow. They *were* truly precious, and I couldn't wait to show them off. But I felt like I was getting dizzy. Out of breath. I was afraid Lucy was going to notice. Or Eli. *Is he freaking out? they'll wonder. I can't freak out.*

We reached Elmwood Road. We'd hit a red light and traffic. Eli reluctantly drew his car to a stop. *It's time.*

I took the shades out of my pocket and put them on. The world turned dark and blue. The mist, which had obscured the world outside, now cloaked it entirely. I felt muffled by the lack of light.

Eli sensed my movement. His eyes lifted to the rear-view mirror, and instead of mine, he saw the sunglasses. He looked calmly back toward the road.

"Hey Luce," he said. "I could drop you back home, you want?"

Lucy laughed again.

The intersection was clear now, though the light hadn't changed yet. Eli spun the wheels into the slush before releasing the brake and blasting through the red light and into the South Side.

I'd been to St. Brendan's Church a few hundred times, but it seemed an alien thing in the blue fog. I'd been through XAI on my bike a dozen times, but there was nothing welcoming that night about the brick contours of the humanless campus. We crossed the Zibi River in the all-encompassing pale, and I couldn't even decide whether the river had been frozen or simply hidden beneath the snow. The downtown skyline. The open-toothed gap where the Akawe Rise had once stood. A pale blur in the clouds flagging the peak of the Pyramid. It was just a mile away, but it all looked faint and small.

But it was behind us already from the speed that Eli was going. I glanced over his shoulder at the speedometer. It breached 50. Bent toward 60.

Flung back against the clock as we took the curls and curves, Adams Street and South and, "Don't you live over here, John? Between South and Whitmore? Agit or something? I know over here, you know."

We passed the hulking lunatic asylum, a vast rectangle that seemed to dominate the staggered surrounding trees. Now we were on Aurelius Road. If we kept going, far enough, I knew, we'd reach Arcadia and the Wendy's where I had seen the time-arresting sunset reflection, but it would look different now. Ghostly. I didn't want to see it. I didn't want this night to shatter my memory of yesterday's reality.

But Eli didn't continue along Aurelius. Instead, he turned left onto Winters Road.

"We're out of our way," he said, "because I wanted to show you both – John, Lucy – something I've never shown anyone before."

The landscape was blurring even more. We'd only left the West End a couple of minutes ago. Now, we were almost on the East Side. I could see the stark banks of the I-63 overpass rising up before us. I made a collage of the scene in my mind, remembering all the times I'd been here, and assembled it just in time to know what was coming.

With a gentleness that surprised me, Eli slowed his car as we approached. He pulled over onto the narrow shoulder overshadowed by the overpass. He rolled his window down, and the cold came inside. I heard semis rumbling overhead, invisible but shivering the supports with their tremendous weight. Eli sat and breathed, and Lucy and I waited.

"This is an important place to me," he said. "This is, this is where my mother died. I don't mean my blood mother. I mean my true mother. I mean the truth. She was the one who adopted my brothers and sisters and me. She was the one who loved us as much as she loved her own children. She was the one who kept me alive through shit you wouldn't believe me if I told you. Ruth. That was her name. Ruth Lang." He spoke softly, and ended each sentence as if it was a question. Each word held the weight of the Mack trucks barreling twenty feet over our heads.

"She was crazy," Eli went on. "She lost her head, and my dad sent her looking for it. She was ... she got sent to some hospital in ... far away ... to get better, you know? Well, she got better, but they wanted to keep her there. They didn't want to let her go. Even though my dad told them to let her go. But she escaped. She broke out. She walked away! This was, like, two, three years ago? It was hot and summer. She tried to come back here, to her family. And I've wondered how she made it here, even. She didn't have any money. She managed to find her way all the way from Arizona to Akawe, and once she got here, she couldn't find us. Jesus, how can you not find your family in one little city when you've tattooed the whole nation like a map on your hand? Since she didn't have anything, since she didn't have anyone, she lay down here, beneath this expressway. Then she slept. Then ... she died."

I stared at Eli through the sunglasses, but all I saw was a black silhouette on a blue background. Meanwhile, Lucy stared out the window as if this confession wasn't unusual, or even unexpected. Her shoulders slumped, and she sadly studied the puddles out on the curb.

"And then," Eli said, "she got robbed."

He turned where he sat and looked right at me.

"She had one valuable thing in this world, and some motherfucker came and took it from her, and then left her corpse decomposing in the heat, rotting like bad meat, like ain't that fucked up, just the most fucked up thing you ever heard, John?"

He knows, I thought. *He sees. The homeless person was dead. Or dying. And I kept on walking. And he knows.*

"I mean, who loots a poor dead woman, even here in Akawe?" he asked, and now I knew he was grinning because I caught the gleam of his teeth through the blue shades. "Who keeps her things but keeps her from being buried? From her song and soul? From her family who loves her?"

He waited for me to answer, but I couldn't think of anything to say. I waited to see if Lucy would say something, but the only sound that escaped her lips was the tiniest of sighs.

"It makes me sad," Eli said, "but I gotta say, it makes me mad, too. Do unto others, right, but I gotta say, if I ever find the motherfucker who looted my mom's rotting body, I might just try to outdo the little bitch."

Eli threw the car into gear, hit the accelerator, the engine shrieked, the wheels spun, and the car lurched toward speed again.

"Watch it, Eli!" Lucy cried.

We hit Valley Street and the Pipes – "GET US GOOD WATER" the tags read today – and hung a left through the empty red light.

We shot like a comet past Eastern High, its windows incomprehensibly brighter tonight than they ever were on a school day.

We passed churches and houses and hovels and a drainage ditch stuffed with dirt and filth and shattered pallets. Past tattoo parlors and plywooded apartments on Intervale Road. We plunged northward into the industrial burrows of the East Side. We went up hills and down hills, in and out of fog, and Akawe swirled around us and then evaporated into fast remoteness even though I knew that we were wild in its belly.

"John," Eli was saying. "We haven't had a chance to hang much, you know? You and I, we got a lot in common. We know the same people, go to the same two schools, we come, we go, we ask questions about the world, but we ...

we don't really know each other much, do we?"

I had to say something. I had to say something as clever and manic as the shit he was saying, how this shit just spilled out of his mouth like he didn't even have to think of it first.

"We both went out with Lucy," I said suddenly.

"That's what?" Lucy sneered.

"That's what I mean, who we went out with, and where, and why," said Eli, effortlessly synchronizing all of the words in that car. "The same zones. The same odors. The same circles. That's how my dad would put it. It's all circles with him. Everything circles around. Circles and circles, everything all spinning round and round, down to the ground, up to the sky. Jesus, *he's* a motherfucker that makes a big fucking deal about circles and all the shit he's seen. I mean, he just imagines, like he's such a fucking big deal, but I know he ain't shit! He ain't nearly as big a deal as he thinks. What a fucker. You know that, John? You end up like your parents, whether you like it or not."

I felt like Eli was either going to start crying or lean back and stab me in the chest. But Lucy seemed utterly relaxed up front, even as her expressions showed me that this conversation both annoyed and bored her. I sat tense in my seat, trying to look relaxed. Lucy shook her head. Eli looked at her. Looked back to the road, fleetingly, as he hooked around a blind corner. We'd left the little factories. Made it back to the hoop houses. Wait, hoop houses? Asparagus and shit. Frosted over dead by now. Eli took his foot off the accelerator, and we crawled toward a lonely light up ahead. It was FDR Boulevard. A mile away, it ran past Crystal's house. I thought for a moment about how comfortable and summer-warm that house must feel, with the gray carpet and the tasteful paintings and Crystal doing homework and Robin reading a book.

"I don't know, John," Eli said, "what people told you about me or my family. I don't even know if you heard anything, but if you did, it's probably bullshit."

"Bullshit," I echoed.

"Exactly," Eli said. "I will always tell you the truth. I will never lie. Told her the same thing when we were going out. I will never *insult* you with a lie."

"You lie plenty," said Lucy.

"But there's always a truth in my lies. There's a Ruth in my lies. I'm a gangbanger, a secret pimp but a shitty pimp, a poor pimp, a feeling-bad-for-all-unlucky-females pimp, and I hate that. I hate that, I do. I break the law, you know, John, I'm a criminal. But not violence. Not guns. Just love. My gun is only for protecting myself and the people I love."

Eli hit himself below his belt. For the first time, I noticed a little black gun cradled there.

"Violence is a cancer!" he exclaimed. "So, we sell to a few people here and there, you know? A few of those Chalks out on the Os. I'm not a Chalk, I'm not, but we sell to them, you know. We sell to Drake, you know? We sell to –"

"May's brother? He's still slinging?"

"Huh, what? Oh, yeah, Drake, he's still slinging. He never stopped. You heard his story, right? Oh, man, that shit was wild. And legendary. Like a Greek and Russian tragedy. I cried myself, man, me too. It was all so crazy and sick, like Romeo and Juliet, like Macbeth, like ... like Swan Lake, really."

"No," said Lucy. "It was just a sad accident."

"They said it was a suicide pact!" Eli said. "Jesus Christ, they don't even know, because who could fucking believe that, huh? No, Drake ain't a jumper. Drake is a boss. He, like, knew the Chalks, but he wouldn't join the Chalks. He needed some capital, but he knew they needed him more than he needed that. To wrap their little fingers around a part of the East Side no other gangs had going. Lestrade, you know? So, he sold for them to get his roll going, but he was always really smart about it. No rings or rims. Not even some new shoes. He was rolling quiet. But then my brother gives him this O-Sugar, and it was way, and I mean, waaaaay stronger than we make it now. We didn't really get about O-Sugar back then. It was a brand new thing. It was just, I mean, it was new, you know? And they went up on that hospital roof, and none of them suicided themselves. No. That drug straight up murdered four of them. Drake's best friend. Drake's other friend. This girl Drake liked. Her best friend. It killed them. Smashed them into that parking lot. Seventy feet down or something! And somehow, Drake survived the fall, that motherfucker, paralyzed though, from the waist, and now he's all broken up like Darth Vader, but Drake he knows that zone, and nobody fucks with him, his life, his madness and crazy, because you know after that he's got to be crazy, and crazy pissed off! His fiending dad, his bitch of a mom, his retarded sister. Shit. Even I don't want to fuck with Drake. He's wicked. Choleric and subannuated. Look, what I meant to say about this whole thing, before I got distracted by that other shit, is that just because we deal off to the Chalks and these other bitches, we ain't got them shooting at each other. They do that their own selves. You hear me, John?"

"I hear you."

"What about you, lover?"

"I hear you," said Lucy, bored. "I ain't your lover no more, 'member?"

"Bitches always say that before they come crawling back," Eli muttered. "Except they don't never come crawling back to me. They just crawl, you know, but who the fuck knows where they're going? I mean, I'm lonely. They're just sad."

Lucy didn't answer.

We'd reached East Street. The light was red. This time, there was traffic, and again Eli had no choice but to wait. He didn't seem to mind, though. It was as though his anxious energy had dispersed during his speech, and he didn't need to take it out on the Benedict anymore. I caught his eyes flitting to the rear-view mirror, studying my sunglasses, covetous or curious.

"This is my promise to you, John," he said. "You hear any fucked-up shit about my family, you come and tell me, okay? I give you my word, I'll never lie about it. I'll deal straight with you. I'm tired of people making up shit about us and using it to hurt us. People that live down in dirty places where all the water goes when the snow melts. You hear me? People that hurt us ... that manipulate us? I want to forgive them, man, but my brothers? They want to hurt them back. My brothers hurt people sometimes. You hear me?"

"I hear you," I said.

Eli flashed his perfect teeth grin for the third time that night.

The light turned green. I saw the roughage between East Street and I-292. I didn't know this part of town well, but for a moment everything looked familiar. I saw the giant field between two tall hills thick with ghetto palms and huge sycamores at the bottom, leading back toward the expressway. I saw the old, dented club with dim lights flickering dimly inside: The Treemonisha Club. And across the street, there was ...

"Lucy," I said. "This is where you took us that one time. To that abandoned theater thing. That your dad owned. Does he still own it?"

Lucy sighed. "I don't know," she said. "I haven't heard from him in more than a year. I wish he would just ..."

Her voice trailed off. *You wished he would just what?* But I couldn't ask her because Eli down shifted and roared across the interstate, turning onto an almost invisible little road and entering a new neighborhood.

I hadn't ever seen anything like it, in Akawe or anywhere else. This was a neighborhood where half of the houses were old, turn-of-the-century wood-frame things, leaning heavy on their foundations, paint chipping and dinner lights becurtained. The other half of the houses were younger, postwar ranches, all clean lines and neat-shingled roofs that hung out prairie-style over the straightforward rectangular Midwestern lawns. The houses were either clean, crisp, sharpkept, the recently diminished snow frosting neat rows of short cut gray grass, of cyclone washed cars and motorcycles waiting under chaste awnings, honeyed lights haloing out of the broad-blinded windows. Or they were not only empty, not only abandoned, but awful, burnt from crown to shell or, worse, inexplicably, it was as if their outer walls had exploded like a bomb had gone off inside, singed bricks scattered through those yards, and the remnants of lives lived – shitty diapers, bloodied tampons, spunked condoms, smashed bottles and light bulbs and plastic pipes and motawipewabics shedded piecemeal through the top-heavy grass wilted achingly moreoatsnow.

One house had been flayed and skinned of everything that made it more than a pine skeleton, and though no longer living, it wriggled. The ribs of its joists turned with termite grubs. *How can there be grubs outside? It's February. Cold February.* But I knew there were grubs because the wind does not make a house wriggle the way those studs and struts wiggled. They were twirling with it. And someone was home. A starlight blue Pontiac Sunbird was parked in the gravel driveway, and lights glowed bluishly behind several windows.

One of the ranches, long flat bricks of white holding the wet brown roof aloft, looked out over its cruel, bright lawn, guarded by hashes of chain-link and gray frowning statues, creatures and gargoyles studded with glowing blue lights, alabaster ornaments, and the yews cut into beastly topiaries, all beshadowed by a lawn globe and a porch light as hard as the winter sun.

One house had scrims more than curtains pulled across its windows. Inside, I saw the slim shape of a human hunched over a candle, twining his fingers, wrapping his hands, making a shadow play for the street outside.

"They call this hood Lestrade today," Eli said. "Back when there weren't that many Blacks in Akawe, they all had to live in two neighborhoods. The poorer Blacks lived out west, in Eden, with the factory and the river all around them. The Blacks with just a bit more money – those who were here before the factories came in – were already over here, right by the lake. But the city didn't like that the Blacks got their open housing passed. So, all this shit got all cut up by those two expressways. They made a mess. I mean, you see it. You see it, don't you?"

"How you know all this?" I asked.

Eli shrugged.

"My dad tells us all about the city. He says if we want to survive this city, we got to understand this city."

"You can't understand it," said Lucy. "It's ununderstandable."

We turned right onto another side street, a boulevard, with a razor-straight grassy median parting the middle.

A third of the way down, on our right, was a tiny one-story house on a small lot with a chain-linked fence. The house had a wooden ramp leading up to a little front door, and a single window in front, and it had been painted pink. The windows gleamed clean. The sidewalk had been shoveled. Several yellow ribbons were tied along the fence at random intervals. But as Eli pulled into the driveway, I noticed the lurid mural painted upon the north-facing wall.

Upon that seashell pink wall hung the sprawling figure of an orange-skinned man, his arms flung wide like an embrace or a plus sign. The head was too large, the hands and feet swollen, and the orange on dark pink made it hard to look at without my eyes throbbing. It was like the color of the man's skin was constantly changing before my eyes. He was wearing a crudely drawn crown of green thorns, and his eyes were swirls of blue without whites and without pupils. The man was naked, but didn't have a dick or lips or fingernails or toenails. It was Jesus Christ, and he was utterly inhuman, so mangled by torture that his inchoate pain had no room for – could not even express – any intention of self-sacrifice. This Christ was nothing but pain. But there was plenty of pain. This Christ called out to a whole universe full of howling pain.

Eli cut the engine.

"Here we are," he said.

As Eli led us up to the vespertined concrete porch, I glanced quick at the other cars in the driveway. There was a shitty-looking Aubrey, a shitty-looking Starr, and a smooth black Valentine, so liquid in its dark light that it must have been washed and waxed just earlier this same day.

"I thought May said this was gonna be a small party," I said.

Neither Eli nor Lucy spoke. Eli stepped onto the porch, stopping to glance at a Tupperware bowl holding a messy plant with elm-shaped leaves growing out of the middle. Then he opened the door without knocking and vanished inside the house. Lucy stood on the front walk, looking surprised. As I crunched through the snow, she stepped onto the porch, gave a tentative knock on the already-opened door, then went inside. I followed her.

The living room boomed with noise but was empty except for a stick-thin Black boy with a pointy chin, his hair close-cropped, maybe eight or nine, sitting on gray shag carpet in front of the TV, playing a video game. I recognized the game. It was Mega Man X, and I knew he was somewhere deep in Sigma's stronghold because I knew the music that crackled out at full volume from the crappy TV speakers like a deranged take on the James Bond theme. Popped bubbles and jizzing cascades all over. The walls were studded with several framed prints from Goya's *Caprichos*. There was also an understated black-and-white photo of the Akawe skyline and an actual painting – more crudely drawn – of a naked fat green man squatting on a lily-pad, legs modestly pressed together at the knees, staring blankly out into the room. The words "FROG FRIEND" had been written in yellow paint across the top.

Lucy seemed as confused as I was, but we walked through the living room to a hall that branched off left and right. We heard two sets of voices. The deeper male voices came from the left. To the right, younger voices, lighter voices, voices of boys and girls. Lucy led the way to the right, and I followed.

Now we were standing in what I assumed was May's bedroom. It was so small that if I had lain down crosswise, I easily could have touched walls with my hands and feet. Somehow, May had fit in a dresser, a desk, and a white metal frame bed with twirled bars on the headboard and footboard. A single window near the ceiling looked out into the backyard. The room was spare but immaculate. Cleaner than my room and cleaner than Michael's, and we were both serious about keeping our shit clean. May sat in the desk chair, and four other people stood on the sliver of carpet the ran between the bed and the desk.

"Hi, guys!" May shouted over the music from the TV.

"Hey, cool shades," yelled a Black boy.

May stood up, and the room felt even more crowded.

"Everyone is here!" she shouted. "Wait, wasn't Eli coming, Lucy?"

"He walked in here ahead of us," Lucy said. "I don't know where he is."

"We'll find him somewhere!" May yelled. "He isn't going to go running around out in the snow!" she laughed. "John and Lucy are some of my friends from Eastern. Lucy, you know Lisa, I know, but John doesn't.".

Lisa was a Black girl, very tall and very slender, with spiky short hair. She was wearing a white t-shirt and very obviously no bra, and I was smart enough not to stare, but clever enough to see a lot out of my peripheral vision. Lisa glanced at me with an expression that could've been disdain but was maybe just fatigue.

"And this is George and this is Nick. They're from the hood but they're at Northern."

Nick was a white boy, and George was the Black boy. Nick stereotyped himself as a hippie with sandals and a tie-dye t-shirt, even though the little house wasn't warm. He also rubbed his bloodshot eyes, but his smile was friendly enough. George was a bit on the heavy side and short like me. He wore a shy, nervous expression. He appeared to feel a little claustrophobic in the crowded room.

"And this is Chris, my pretend cousin. She just moved here from California a month ago. From Los Angeles! She lives in Acheron."

Chris was cute, with curves, blue pointed glasses, wavy gold-red hair, and a lemon-chewing mouth. She didn't look at May, or anyone else for that matter. She fixedly stared out the window. I wondered if she had been made to come to the party just because she was May's pretend cousin, whatever that meant.

"Hey, May?" said Lucy. "It's kind of crowded in here. Maybe we should go somewhere else in the house?"

"Right, right. You remembered to take off your shoes?"

The other kids nodded, but Lucy and I had forgotten. A deep frown grew across May's face.

"Get your dirty damn shoes out of my bedroom! I told you all special! Now! Come on! Take them off here, take them off take them off! Then go back to the living room and put them by the front door. Where did they raise you guys, in a barn?! Holy my God!"

"May," said Lucy, hopping on one foot as she struggled with her shoe. "You know there's a kid in your living room playing video games loud?"

"Oh, yeah," said May. "That's Daryl. He's from across the street. Don't mess him about girls. He called his girl Candid three times and she never once called him back!"

We got out to the living room, still throbbing with Daryl's storm and static, and while Lucy and I dropped our shoes on the plastic sheeting by the door, Chris slipped into some boots and went out onto the porch brandishing a cigarette. The door slammed shut behind her.

May stood in the doorway, glaring mistrustfully at Lucy and me.

"Girl's kind of crazy about the carpet," muttered George. He offered me a flask.

"For real?" I asked.

"Maker's Mark," he promised.

Lucy shook her head. The music blared. I took a swig. The whiskey lacerated my tongue with warmth and comfort, and for a moment, I could forget about Eli, Drake, and Deformed Jesus.

"Guys, I'm making cookies!" May shouted.

"I know," said George, defensively. "But I'm nervous, and it's only polite to share."

"Why are you nervous?" I asked.

"He's always nervous," said May.

"I don't want to get killed and buried in a pyramid, you know?" George yelled. "My mama? Pure Egyptian. My dad was a cracker, but she's, it's like, she eats men, and it makes her happy. They get her stuff. Neon signs and carnival lights, like a festival. Like the blinking kind. And an emerald ring, and pearl necklaces, and all sorts of shit. Rocks the size of my fist, you know, and they're as green as anything, and they can break anything. Bigass bottles of Cointreau. One dude? He even bought *me* new shoes. Superfly! And statues of Set and the Sphinx. You ever seen Set? He wants to bite you bone dry, right? Thing is, I know myself. I want what she wants. I want to be the one in charge for once, right? I want hot men to give *me* presents, and then I get to go off them the second they go bitch on me. But I'm also chickenshit. I don't wanna get my ass beat, you know? So I never follow through. I'm always, you know, making these moves, dropping pickup lines, acting real sexy, and maybe I'd even follow through if I ever thought someone was gonna be true to me, like a true love, truly devoted, but mostly I just freak out because I don't know if someone's gonna pop off on me. I mean that's what they always do in the end anyway, you know? And that isn't just with crushes, either, like, it's true with my friends, too. Except for May, you know. May is true."

"Am not!" May sauced.

"It's okay," I shouted. "I'm kinda chickenshit, too."

George gave me a furtive smile.

"I'm the chickenshittest," he said.

I looked over at Lucy. In the car, she'd been mirthful and bratty, before

Eli had started monologuing. Now she looked pale. Broad smudges ran under her eyes, which I couldn't have noticed in the darkness of the car. She seemed a little unsteady on her feet.

"You okay?" I asked her.

"No," she said, smiling. "But don't worry, I'm fine."

Now I shook my head.

Chris finished came back inside, sans cig, her fists balled up in her jacket pockets.

"Don't forget to take off your shoes, cousin!" said May.

Chris huffed in utter disdain but sloughed her shoes off while May watched.

"Okay, then," May shouted. "Down to the Third Substage."

This startled me. "Did you say the Third Substage?" I asked.

"Yeah, that's what Drake calls the basement," she said. "I don't know. He can't go down the stairs since the accident."

"Since the accident," Nick croaked.

We went through the living room again, but this time we took a left at the hall and found ourselves in a combined kitchen-dining room a little bit larger than May's bedroom. A yellow linoleum floor and wood-paneled cabinets hung over bits of counter space here-and-there, a sink, an old stove with age-scraped electric coils, an arch doorway leading down to the basement, and a group of teenagers. Older teenagers. There was a light-skinned Black boy, tall and slender, leaning against the wall, arms crossed, and glaring at Eli Ostyn. Eli stood on the opposite side of the room, glaring back. A third boy sat in a threadbare wheelchair near the sink and watched Eli. His head was shaved, his jaw was relaxed, and his unblinking brown eyes were calm, but he had his index fingers wrapped over his thumbs, a scarce hint of tension. He drummed his knuckles against the arms of the wheelchair. A fourth boy, dark Black and heavy with an afro, a red t-shirt, and impatient, darting eyes, leaned over a green card table, which had baking supplies and, wait, what, no, huge and varied piles of plants and drugs. I stared at it. I couldn't help myself. There was so much there.

"My brother and his friends," muttered May, moving quickly toward the oven.

The boy in the wheelchair gave a cynical chuckle.

"Come on, May, introduce us!" said Eli, laughing and showing his teeth.

May stopped and sighed. I could read her thoughts right off her face: *It's* my *birthday.*

"John," she said. "Lucy, Lisa, George, Nick, Chris, my brother Drake."

Drake was the boy in the wheelchair. "Ziggurat." Ziggurat was the tall leaning boy. "Mike." Mike was the heavy boy by the table. "And Eli."

"And don't forget our other friends," Eli added, making a grandiose gesture toward the card table. "That is ... man, a lot of hard shit. You all should take a picture of that and send it up to the Os. Chalks'll eat their hearts out. Or you should feed them that, so they can eat their hearts out." Eli went on, pointing down at all of the stuff on the table. A Tupperware filled with round, butter-colored pills: "Soma. Don't eat beans first." A black bottle labeled. "Yohimbine." A Tupperware filled with small, blue pills: "O-Sugar." A plastic bag filled with dried leaves, but not pot leaves. "Mambog." Another bag. "Caapi." Another bag: "Salvinorin, I mean, damn." A Tupperware filled with what looked like ground chicory. "Processed kava." A bit of a knotted, dried branch. "Raw kava. Now *that's* dope. You guys starting a conservatory here? You cosmonauts? Psychonauts?" Eli giggled into his fist. "Damn," he muttered.

Mike looked nervous hearing Eli's thorough catalog of their botanicals and pharmaceuticals. Drake seemed bored. Ziggurat watched intently, but I couldn't read any emotion in him. The rest of us steeped in the tension that hung in the air between these four boys. May sighed in irritation and opened the oven, pulling out a tray of oatmeal raisin cookies that she started scraping onto a plate.

"So, why you here tonight, Eli?" asked Drake.

"Me? I'm just here to wish your sister a happy birthday. Happy Birthday, May!"

"Thanks," said May without looking back at him.

"You invited him?"

"No. Lucy did. She takes him where she goes. To keep him out of trouble."

"Is that okay?" Lucy asked. "I thought you said it was okay."

"Is it okay?" asked Eli. "Okay, is it okay? Okay, May?"

And a strange silence followed, punctuated only by the scrape of the spatula across the cookie sheet.

"Yeah," said Drake, finally. "It's cool. Ain't it, Ziggurat?"

"I don't got no problem with him," said Ziggurat, his first words. His voice was lower, deeper than I expected. "Fact, I wish we known you was comin'. O's a little low, you see, and you know we only get it from your brothers."

"Not my brothers, no, those Chalks," said Eli. "Yeah, we can hook you up Monday, maybe. That cool?"

"Better be," said Ziggurat.

Mike seemed to relax a little.

"What's that, anyway?" asked Eli. He was looking at another Tupperware, unlabeled, with a tiny label, sitting on the windowsill behind the table. A half-dozen paper blotters floated at the bottom, in a thin liquid. "Oneirine?"

Ziggurat and Drake tensed.

"No," said Drake. "Actually, we're playing around with the O-Sugar a bit. Cutting in some salvia."

"Is that that shit on your front porch?" asked Eli.

Drake laughed. "Yeah, man. Salvia divinorum. It makes for ... I don't know ... it's a little bitter and dark, you know. The trip is. Not as heavy as what you guys do with it."

Eli laughed. "Salvia divinorum! Ain't that like from the jungle or some shit?"

"Sim, amigo," said Mike. "Brazil cloud forest."

"Exotic! You ain't gonna improve on our process, though. Ain't gonna improve on Akawe. Shit, I'll kill your suspense. No secrets between friends. We cut ours with nightshade. Take some from my dad's backyards even."

"Nightshade?" asked Mike, interested.

"Not a lot," said Eli. "Too much of it kills you. See, the O-Sugar is made out of ecstasy and nightshade. The atropine and scopolamine in the nightshade give you this sort of doomy feeling. Sense of death and dread. The loss of your whole identity, your whole you. But the MDMA makes it all fun and good, like the destroying is all part of God's plan, and don't you know God is good and all that."

"It works," admitted Ziggurat. "Crazy, but it works."

"Yeah," said Eli. "Like a real good slasher flick. Who thought our horror could be so happy? The shit sells, man. Keeps the Chalks in business, and not too bad for Ash, neither."

Drake folded his hands behind his head.

"But hey," said Eli. "We appreciate your experimentation. Let us know if anything works for you. We're always wanting to make the trip better, you know. More of a ... deep and profound thing, right?"

Drake gave a small nod. Ziggurat smiled. So did Eli. Mike watched everyone. He took his hand off the table, and I realized that a handgun was sitting there, ready to be picked up or used. But only if needed. Only if. That meant, counting Eli's, there were at least two guns in this room, and for all I knew someone was thinking about using one.

"Okay," said May briskly, "my cookies are all ready, and this is *my* birthday party, and I don't want to stand here all night and listen to y'all brag it about your drugs and pills. Come on. Let's go on downstairs."

May led the way, and Lucy, Eli, Chris, George, Nick, Lisa, and I followed her through the door and down the stairs, leaving her brother and his friends behind.

"Nice shades," Drake said as I passed him.

As we made our way down the carpeted stairs into the Third Substage, Eli probed tentatively at the back of Lucy's pants, but she slapped his hand away. A corrugated metal wall stood at the bottom of the stairs, but this was nothing but a bit of masking to screen the room beyond. We walked around it, and the rest of the basement came into view.

The unfinished room had some decent furniture – a plush rocking chair and some faux-leather sectionals – but the light came from a naked bulb overhead and was mostly sucked up by the unpainted cinderblock walls. The foam ceiling panels had been painted pink, though. So was the hard concrete floor. I caught a glimpse of an adjacent laundry room through a small wooden door, its walls darkened by the graphite streaks of what looked like mold on the walls.

May hurriedly closed the door to the laundry room and crossed to a mid-century credenza, polished to a fine-gloss and smelling like chemical lemons, where a boom box player sat next to a TV. She put on a cassette – 2Pac – and then taped a piece of blue cellophane over the light bulb. Through my sunglasses, the room shaded blue on blue.

Chris, as disgusted by May's lighting effect as she was by everything else that May said and did, liked the music anyway and started to dance.

Eli went up to one of the narrow windows and looked out into the yard where the fog was swirling. Then, a moment later, he turned and looked at me again. I finally understood. Eli didn't know what to do about me. He wanted to threaten me because I had somehow gotten the sunglasses, but his instinct was to try to win my trust and manipulate me. Plus, he was probably wondering how I had taken them. *Someday I have to make Selby tell me how she stole them back.*

I realized then that I believed in God after all. At least for the moment. Just twenty-four hours earlier, I'd been standing in the holiest of holies, an Arcadian Wendy's, and watching the reflected sunset in a glorious froth of snow and flame which I, alone, adored. Now, my sins had landed me in the ninth circle of hell – the Third Substage of May and Drake's basement – while Eli Ostyn, an actual son of God, was maybe planning to kill or torture me because I'd stolen some special sunglasses from his dead mom. Maybe I deserved this punishment. I had taken them from a dead woman. I hadn't, I told myself, known that she was dead. I hadn't, I lied to myself, known that they were hers. At any rate, Selby knew what she was about. Her threat against the Ostyns had already unfurled with perfect proximity and symbolic oomph.

Now the party was finally starting to shape up the way May wanted. Nick helped himself to some of her dry cookies, and Lucy and George danced with Chris.

Why not? I thought. *I'm in Hell. I might as well dance.* I went out onto the hard floor and started dancing with the others. *And, really, why stop at dancing? I could go all the way. I could head out in a whole 'nother 'rection.* I was, I knew, on a margin. I could go either way. There were two. Ways. There were only two ways. The first way had been Michael's way, Quanla's way, Omara's way, my parents' way; the good grades and maybe college and all that, which I guessed I meant to recover through hard work and powerful Charisma. But the other way had its own temptations. I *could* abdicate aspirations. I *could* murder the yearning and take my place with Eli and Drake and the other older boys in this small pink house. I could convincingly assemble dysfunction from the fringe of the nominally functional life I'd enjoyed until the last few months and pretend I'd been born into their ranks. I could make a home for myself deep in their shadows. I could become a reluctant pimp or a freelance mastermind. I'd had an Akawe address for my whole life. Wasn't that also my birthright? I'd have to *look* at things differently, though. I'd have to turn my back to everything I'd absorbed as *normal, good, stable, sane.*

Chris has lost her frown when she'd found the beat, while Lisa's unbound chest bounced as she danced. Nick seemed spaced out, bobbing his head, barely aware of the others around him, while George held himself close, crisp nods, tightly tied. May danced careless and languid while Lucy studied her own movement, trying to refine it, to find the music with her limbs and rhythms. I was above them all. Eli was removed. He was alone, looking out the window. I was the king by default. *But am I?*

What if Eli took two steps and joined us again? After all, he could drive. He was a gangbanger *and* a pimp – he'd said so – and, also, he looked better than me and knew how to smile fast and talk as sharp as a silk ribbon snapping. Then again, I was wearing his mother's handmade teashades, way better than John Lennon's or Ozzy Osbourne's, and if that couldn't swell my balls, what at else possibly could?

Eli's mind was somewhere else at that moment. He was still staring out the windows at the dancing fog as if it embodied a higher reality of sex and stimulation. *Fine with me, Eli. You can fuck the atmosphere. I'm content with actual flesh.*

Hearing my thoughts, Lucy obliged and bumped her hips on mine, and I was grateful. I'd gone out with Omara for more than a year and had never even seen her naked. And I had actually had sex with Crystal, but she never once called herself my girlfriend. We'd been "summerfriends." But two years ago, when we were still kids, Lucy had gone out with me, and we had shared, and I had spoiled it all by being selfish and jealous.

That thought shocked me out of delusion.

I couldn't be like Drake or Eli. It was the difference between my family having a little money and their families having no money. The difference between seeing what happened on the street and being what happened on the street. My advantages were like tattoos; I couldn't simply shrug them off. If I tried to force my way into the world those older boys had inhabited since birth, I'd get killed or, worse, humiliated.

Meanwhile, Lucy had taken her own cosmologic tour of what had seemed exotic to her. Gary's Pentecostalism, Eli's ghettoism, her own parents' absenteeism, and here she was, 1996, more fierce and gaunt and disoriented than she had ever been before. But her hair was starting to grow out again, so there was that.

"You gonna ask May out again?" Lucy asked.

"We don't got nothing in common," I said.

I felt her ass pressing against my crotch through my pants, and it excited and confused me at the same time. Somehow, for as different as we were, and the different trajectories we'd sought out, I felt like we somehow understood each other in a way these others could not.

"May is kind," Lucy said. "You need kindness, John. Maybe you can learn to give some back to her."

"Aren't you kind?" I asked.

This question surprised her, and she didn't have an answer right away.

"I thought I was," she said, finally, "But not really. At least, I'm not kind like Eli is kind."

"Is he kind? Really? It seems like an act to me."

"No. It's an act for us. Because it doesn't cost you or me anything to be kind. It's just something we can do to look good. But when Eli's kind, it's expensive. It can come back on him. And still, he chooses to be kind. I mean, a lot of the time."

"Would you ever go out with me again?" I heard myself asking. "I mean, I'm not asking you out. I just mean ... in a different universe or something? If I was, like, better."

Lucy thought about this.

"I don't think so," she finally said. "You didn't mean to be bad, but you weren't good for me. You were bad for me."

"So. Who you gonna get with now?"

"Nobody. Nobody deserves me. You know?"

"I think you've changed."

"Have I? What about you? Have you *changed?*"

The song ended, and Lucy wandered off. Our quick talk had left me feeling disoriented. Maybe depressed. I tried to come back from it by throwing myself into the party. Now I was dancing with Chris, and she was grinding *deep*.

Now I was dancing with Lisa. Moving my feet. Now I was dancing with George and Nick.

And when I asked Chris about L.A., about why she left and how she wound up in Acheron of all places, she didn't really answer me. She just told me that her ex-boyfriend was a Crip, and that's why she wore blue from head to toe. Since everything was blue to me, I lifted my sunglasses for a moment and saw that, yeah, all her baggy clothes were blue.

"Ain't that make it easy to pick 'em off?" I asked.

She shrugged. "Bloods do it too."

"Sounds like bullshit to me."

"Don't care. You want my asshole, you best wear blue."

"What?"

"Everything's shit here. Jesus, I fucking hate it. It's the middle of fucking nowhere. There, I had people. How old are you, anyway?"

"Fifteen."

"Fifteen? Jesus shit! Now I'm all squaggy. I'll be back."

She left for the bathroom. George handed me his flask, sympathetically. I took a swig. I looked up at the ceiling, and the sprayed pink ceiling panels seemed to be oozing heavy beads of blood through their blackhead pores. I put my shades back on. George shook his head.

May changed tapes. Something new and innocent to shove the bloody tears back into the ceiling. The Macarena. The Electric Slide. The Train. I heard its thrill out the window. It was close now. *Lestrade must be right next to the tracks.* The same old train, carrying parts for cars, moving over to the factories. The few that remained.

"She don't drive a Aubrey!" barked Lisa. "She don't drive a Aubrey!"

"No," said Chris. "I ain't from Akawe, remember? I don't give a shit. But I do drive a Chevy."

"Oh," said Lisa. "Well, that's cool."

The Jump.

May danced quietly alone, eyes closed.

I danced and asked Nick a question.

"Have you heard the frequencies in the songs they sing?" he asked me. "There's a higher frequency, beyond the one you notice. The frequency you hear with your ears is talking about loving each other, breakup songs, frontin', bangin', drugs, and all that. The frequency you hear with your brain can tell you to do all sorts of things, and you'll never know it."

I danced and asked Lisa a question.

"I don't talk shit!" she snapped. "I don't talk unless I got something to say! Why you talk so much? Damn! You can't even drive and you expect me to talk to you!"

I danced and returned to George frequently for sips from his flask.

More time floated by on currents of sappy music. May went upstairs, braved the older boys, and came back down with a pitcher of orange juice. Mike followed her downstairs, asking her what she wanted for her birthday, and had she gotten what she wanted, and what she was going to do this weekend. Also, he wanted to see what her party was all about. Pretty soon, Mike was dancing with the girls in the middle of the room while I went over to the credenza to grab fistfuls of cookies and dolphin crackers.

I gave George a look.

He shook his head. Held up the flask with its cap off, turned it upside down, and a single lonely drop to the floor.

"Dammit," I said.

"This shit was full a few hours ago!"

"You musta been thirsty."

"I think you drank most of it." He laughed nervously. "You're welcome!"

Eli crossed over to the washer and dryer, which had been dragged out of the laundry room and shoved into a dusty corner. He lifted the lid on the washer, peeked inside, let it drop.

A few feet away, Mike wrapped his arms around Chris' and Lisa's waists, and they swiveled toward him.

Now Eli pulled his t-shirt up over his nose and wandered into the laundry room, studying the sump pump and the patches of mold spreading wild over the walls.

Nick wormed in vain, humping the dance floor.

George was looking for a wall or a column to lean against.

And then I saw May kneeling. Someone had scattered crumbs from one of her cookies, and she was collecting them in her palm, her brows furrowed in disgust. Finally, the task completed, she crossed to a trash can and brushed her hands carefully clean. I suddenly felt sorry for her. All she had wanted was a fun party with some food and dancing, and all of her guests had brought all of their mess and drama down into the basement with them.

"Want to dance?" I asked her.

"Sure," she said.

As we danced, Eli returned to his moody window and looked back out into the night. Lucy crossed over to him, and they spoke quietly and quickly to each other. Lucy's gestures grew and flew, but Eli seemed taciturn. His hands rested in his pockets. May closed her eyes again. She wasn't careful about where she stepped, and she kept bumping into me and stepping on my feet. George and Nick and Lisa were each dancing on their own. I couldn't see Mike or Chris, though. They had disappeared. I became aware of a burning plastic smell. May noticed it at the same time.

"Oh no!" she said.

The overhead light had melted through the blue cellophane, and now its remnants were blackened and smoking. May reached up and ripped it off.

"I hate this!" she said. "It's ruined now! It's all ruined! Everything is just ruined! Everything is just wrecked."

Lisa came over to us.

"It's okay, May," she said. "You can dance anyway. It's still pretty down here. Everything looks all pink now."

"Where's Chris?" May demanded, her frustration suddenly changing into anger.

Eli looked over with a grin.

"She's in your laundry room fucking your brother's friend," he said.

Nick croaked out a laugh.

"Not cool," said Lisa.

May stomped over to the laundry room door, which was now firmly shut again. She banged on it.

"Mike!" she yelled. "Chris! Come out now! This is my party!"

George danced passively in the middle of the room.

Eli looked out of the window again.

"Looks like the fog is clearing up now," he said. "When I drive you home, John, I'll be able to drive even faster. I can drive as fast as I want."

His teeth seemed like daggers, and I shivered. But Lucy put on a cynical smile of her own, reached into Eli's belt, and pulled out the black handgun. Eli seemed unsurprised, and watched her. May and I also watched her, though I don't think we understood, yet, what we were looking at. Lucy turned the machine over in her hands, examining it from every angle.

Suddenly, she held the gun up in both hands, finger on the trigger, and pointed it at Eli's chest.

George stopped dancing. May and Nick and Lisa froze in place. Nobody moved. Nobody understood. We were paralyzed and terrified, but maybe also just a little bit eager. *For what? What the fuck is going on?*

Eli backed toward the window, lifting his hands in surrender.

"Don't go popping off half-cocked, ho," he said.

"You haven't danced at all tonight," Lucy said. "Bet I could make you dance now."

Eli chuckled and nodded his head.

"I could make you strip your ass naked and go running out into the snow. I could make you do anything I wanted."

"No," Eli said. "Not anything."

Someone has to say something, I thought. *Nobody is saying anything. Nobody is doing anything. I have to say something.*

"Lucy," I said. "Put the gun down, okay?"

Lucy kept her eyes on Eli.

"Why?" she asked. "This is all just a game, right?"

She looked around at us and pointed the gun at her own belly.

"It's all just a game isn't it?" she said.

She smiled, and it was hideous, like she hated everyone and everything. Eli laughed. A dry laugh. George laughed, though his was the laughter of stifled panic. May and Lisa and Nick and I stayed where we were, quiet.

"Right here?" Lucy asked us, tapping the gun against her stomach. "It would be like a diet! No? Well, how about here?"

She pointed the gun at her heart.

"A lot of blood," she said, pensive about it. "But not messy enough."

She tilted the gun down. Pointed it at her crotch.

"How 'bout this?" she asked. "I mean, we're all bleeding out, right? Like, all the time."

Lucy looked at me. She glanced over at Eli. He shrugged. She looked at May. May's eyes were wide and wet. She gave her head a little shake. Lucy's smile widened. She was really enjoying this, I realized.

"Well, okay," Lucy said. "I mean, if you're not going to help me decide, I guess I'll just have to decide myself."

She lifted the barrel of the gun and slid it between her lips.

"You know that bitch ain't loaded, right?" said Eli. "I wouldn't load that fucker in Drake Dunham's house. I'm not an idiot."

"Oh yeah," said Lucy, her words distorted as she tried to talk around the metal muzzle. "I know it isn't loaded."

Her teeth clicked down around the barrel as her brow furrowed in concentration.

She looked at May.

"Lucy –" May began.

Then Lucy pulled the trigger.

The gun clicked.

"I told you it wasn't loaded," said Eli.

George threw up on his shoes.

"Oh, shit!" said Lisa.

I lunged forward and grabbed Lucy's hand.

"Ow!" she yelled. "Let go of me, you asshole! It was just a joke!"

Eli stepped in and pried the gun from her fingers, and slid the gun back into his belt. Lucy wrenched herself free and stormed up the stairs. May followed her, along with Nick and Eli.

George hunched over, hands on his knees, looking at his own puke and giggling raggedly.

I crossed to the closed door and shoved it open. The smell of mold and mildew poured out over me, making me stagger for a moment.

"Shut the door!" yelled Chris and Mike in the darkness.

I groped around on the floor until I found a damp towel and returned to the pink room, slamming the door behind me. Lisa and I wiped up George's vomit while he clutched his head and moaned.

"Why would she do that?" he asked us. "Why did that happen? Did she really know it wasn't loaded?"

He was asking the precise questions I wanted out of my brain at that moment. I was trying to focus on the vomit and forget that I had ever known a person named Lucy. I just wanted to put more time between *that* moment and the present before I looked at the thing directly.

"She knew it wasn't gonna go off, man," said Eli. I hadn't realized he was still in the room. He was perched on the uppermost stairs, looking down at us. "That's just a game we used to play at my house. To scare my little sister."

I looked at Eli through his mom's sunglasses. Haloes of blue surrounded him.

"Fuck you," I said.

I heard a snotting sound. George wiped his nose with his sleeve. He was starting to cry.

"You need some water," I said.

"Sure, I ..."

"Go on upstairs."

He went up the stairs, followed by Lisa. I was alone.

I glanced out the window Eli had been studying all evening. He had said that the air was clearing, but it looked to me like the fog was still thick, mingling with the crusted snow.

I heard the soft sound of voices coming from the laundry room.

I threw the towel in the trash and went up the stairs.

When I got out of the Third Substage, I heard voices shouting. Eli and Lucy. At first, I thought that they were shouting at each other, then I realized that I was hearing two different conversations. Lucy was standing in the bathroom, crying and shouting at May, who stood beside her and rubbed her shoulder. In some other room, I heard Eli shouting at someone else. Ziggurat or Drake, I assumed. I wished that someone would shout at Daryl to turn down the TV; the same deranged music was circling through the air. *He still hasn't beaten that fucking level?*

"And I can't keep up with him," came Lucy's voice. "He won't even return my calls."

"You got a living room!" roared Eli.

"He keeps slipping away. And I even dream about him sometimes, but he's always gone."

"You got a shitty little house!"

"She doesn't care, and he went away ..."

"We got hundreds of houses all over the city!"

"So, I just sit in my room and stare at my walls."

"I could put an assassin in any one of them and take you out whenever I want, wherever you go!"

"It doesn't stop. It just keeps going. Year after year. It never ends."

"Who you think happened to Kid Zero? Who you think did the Undertakers? Who put the Chalks on top? Who took out the DM? It wasn't the Masters or the fucking Akawe PD! No. You go downtown, the colleges, hospitals, the organ-eye-zations, see the suits run that shit, but you go out in the hood, the projects, the factories, they're ours. Little bitch you think you own these hoods? We got paper and blood to prove it's ours. All of it. And we know what you're doing. What you've been trying to do since the beginning!"

"And my walls are, like, white, but sometimes? Sometimes I feel like I'm not looking at them but looking into them. Like they're these, these white holes or something opening into like nothing."

As I stood alone in the kitchen and the voices raged on, I felt myself moving over the card table stacked with drugs and plants. I lifted my shades to take a closer look. Drake and his friends had been careful with their packaging. Every Tupperware and every packet was neatly sealed and cleanly labeled, though the names had been written in code. It looked like gibberish. Eli had known what he was looking at, but I wasn't able to read a thing.

Still, it was easy to find the O-Sugar. It was in the smallest container in the back, near the edge of the table, filled with a handful of light blue pills, tiny and round, carefully stained with a pink x and o, superimposed, in case anyone forgot that O-Sugar came from the Chalks.

"Who thought our horror could be so happy?"

I'd seen horror. It circled in my blood and would never leave me for my whole life. If O-Sugar meant that horror and happiness could coexist, I finally started to understand why it had sold so well in Akawe, and in other forgotten places, however bad the side-effects might be.

Quickly, so that I wouldn't have time to think about what I was doing, I grabbed three pills of O-Sugar and put them in my mouth. I swallowed once and swallowed again, and it was all going down into my stomach. I ran over to the sink and turned it on. I laughed. In May's shitty little house, the water was clear. I drank and drank until the taste of the pills was gone.

I hurried into the living room where Eli was still shouting at Drake and Ziggurat. They watched him, arms crossed, unimpressed, unworried. Nick and Lisa and George were here, watching the inferno of Eli's rage. Daryl was gone, which explained why he hadn't beaten the level of Megaman, though the music from Sigma's fortress still swirled around us.

"You know where our coats and shit are?" I asked.

Drake gave a nod. "Probably on May's bed," he said.

I hurried into May's empty bedroom and got my coat. I slid it on and turned around. Eli was standing in the doorway. He seemed suddenly timid. Deflated and apologetic now that the party no longer demanded a performance from him.

"I know what you did," he murmured. "They're killers, John. Ziggurat and Mike. And Drake, he ... he's not a killer, but ... it's not like he can stop them."

"What do you mean?"

Eli leaned in, looked deep into me with his eyes, black and huge through my shades.

"The O-Sugar you just took," he whispered. "Give me my mother's sunglasses. And I won't tell them."

What did I do? I thought. *Everything. Everything I've done tonight has been a mistake. A horrible mistake.* And the vast horror I felt in my chest expanded even further, expanded without bound, painted the floors and the walls and the whole world blue because I had consumed horror, and now I could never escape it.

"You really don't have a choice," Eli said reassuringly.

I took a deep breath.

I removed the sunglasses and folded them, and put them in his hand. Now his eyes were agate-colored again, and the blue world was ordinary.

Eli put the sunglasses in his shirt pocket.

"Thank you, John," he said. "I'll put some O-Sugar from my stash in the box to cover what you took. How many did you take?"

"Three," I muttered.

"Three?!" Eli laughed sadly. "Fuck man, you better get somewhere safe and sit down. Sit it out. You're going to see some shit tonight. You just traded a hundred dollars of O-Sugar for a pair of sunglasses that aren't even yours. That's one hell of a deal."

Eli stood aside for me to pass, and I went down the hall. He followed me but turned toward the kitchen.

"Eli!" Ziggurat was saying.

"Hold it, dog," Eli answered.

"Wait," someone else said from the bathroom, but I didn't want to stop, I didn't want to talk to anyone, so I hurried past and into the living room. I gave everyone a quick wave, shoved my feet into my shoes, and banged through the door and out into the front yard. I kept my eyes down so that I couldn't accidentally look at the freakish Jesus mural.

May caught up to me on the sidewalk.

In her hurry to catch me, she hadn't put on any shoes. She was standing in the snow in her socks. She wrapped her arms around her chest.

"Where are you going?" she demanded.

"I got to go," I said. "I got ... homework!"

"Okay. Okay. I'm ... I'm sorry. You ... you got a ride?"

"I want to take the bus!"

"Okay. Um. Thanks for coming to my birthday party, John. I hope that you had a fun time."

I wanted to think that this was just May being stupid. That she really did think I could have *possibly* had "fun" in there. But I knew that, this time, she understood the irony in her words. She knew that I was miserable. She knew that we all were.

"Is Lucy okay?" I finally asked.

"I should go back to her."

"I understand. Happy Birthday, May. Thanks for inviting me."

She leapt, toe to toe, back through the snow toward her porch.

When she got there, she turned around to look at me.

"You are a good person, John," she said.

"No, I'm not," I said, "but thanks anyway."

May opened the door and went inside.

I was alone with the Jesus mural.

What's the point. It sees me. I might as well see it.

I looked at it.

The mural was just as horrifying now as it had been before. It was a universe of pain and hunger. The wide-open mouth, throbbing with nothing but scattered radiation, a growing emptiness between galaxies, and a void that should have been filled with love.

There was nothing here, and nothing was coming.

Into the wilderness, my feet beat the sidewalk.

A grassy median ran down the middle of Armstrong Boulevard, planted with ragged junipers and withered phlox and *a phlox on both your houses!* Snow-covered sidewalks, hiding the compacted ice beneath. The wind whistled in my ears, and I drew my coat tighter. I didn't have a hat, or gloves, or scarf. I hadn't expected it to get this cold. I hadn't planned on being outside for long. I didn't know where I was going. I just knew that I had to get away from that house and the people inside it.

Armstrong ended against Lestrade, which extended to the right as a boulevard with a huge median, much larger than the street itself. I imagined that neighborhood kids played football here when it was warm out, but tonight there weren't any human footprints crossing the fields. Just the scattered tracks of dogs, rabbits, and deer. To my left, Lestrade ran as a two-lane road pressed between the cold glowing houses and the swampy margins of Carnival Lake. I didn't like the darker spaces off in that direction, so I turned right instead.

I crossed Hooker Ave.

I'm sure nobody ever tells any jokes about that. Eli said that this was the original Black neighborhood in Akawe. Is this Sycamore Grove? If so, why do they call it Lestrade?

I crossed Smith Avenue.

I passed a windowless church and some more houses. Maybe Eli was right. Maybe the fog *was* starting to clear. Above the mist, a wider canopy of stars began to emerge, but I couldn't keep my mind on the heavens. I couldn't keep thinking about the neighborhood, either.

I knew, eventually, I was going to think about Lucy. I was going to remember how I had ached after her and had even *been* with her in seventh grade, and then I would turn over, and over, the question: had this seed of furious despair been growing within her this whole time? After she had dumped me, I had felt like I had failed her by being a selfish asshole. Now I started to see that my failure had been much bigger and deeper than that.

Who are you? I had asked myself about Lucy two years back when she had swallowed the note in Mr. Kolin's class.

Who are you? I had repeated two months back when she showed up at Eastern High School with her hair cut short.

And the terrible thing was, I still didn't know. I got that she felt spiteful and miserable and wronged and misunderstood. But there was so much that I didn't understand, and it was mostly my fault. Because ever since I had met her, I had been trying to impose some interpretation or other upon her, and since she wasn't the kind of person to shout in my face when I fucked it up, she inevitably resembled what I was looking to see.

But Lucy had *wanted* to be seen. When she had told me about her sixth-grade suicide attempt, she had *wanted* me to understand, and I hadn't. And when she had put Eli's gun into her mouth, joke or no joke, she was telling us, along with all of the other things that she was telling us, that we *didn't* understand. That we hadn't really tried. That when she hurt, she hurt alone.

I clenched my teeth and pressed my hands against my mouth to stop the wail I felt welling up inside me.

But I couldn't stop this cold despair, so I punched a tree with my naked hand.

My knuckles split and blood filled the cracks. I felt a shudder of pain jump up my arm.

I shook it out.

I made the sign of the cross.

It was an impulse, but it felt right.

I crossed Ledbetter Avenue.

Three pills of O-Sugar I had taken.

One for the Father.

One for the Son.

One for the Holy Spirit.

Eli had told me that I was in for quite a night.

The cold and the bitter wind had stopped bothering me. My hand, after that brief flash of pain, had stopped hurting. *Is that the O-Sugar? Or George's Maker's Mark? Or is it adrenaline?* I didn't want to spend the rest of the night crying and hitting trees. Then again, maybe *that* was the drug talking. Or maybe it was just that seeing Lucy put a gun into her mouth – *why did you do it?* – made my own problems pathetic and forgettable.

I crossed Monk Street.

The further I went, the more decrepit and ancient the neighborhood seemed. I passed a small business strip floating up against the boulevard. An empty shoe store. A closed hair salon. Split juniper bushes. I hadn't seen a single car. I was, it seemed, the only living creature out on Lestrade that night.

I crossed Spring Avenue and thought about how I had lost the blue-bottle sunglasses. Now they had been taken from me for a second time. I thought about Eli, who had lured girls and women away from their homes, and how I hated him. I thought about EZ, who had long ago chased me through my own neighborhood with a knife in his hand, and how I hated him. And, I thought about God Ostyn, the myth that I had never met, and how I hated his family and his manipulations. My hate for that one father, his one son, and the nervous spirit that he had adopted and disfigured in its soul. They all hung in the air around me like a threat, and I hated them so much my mouth tasted like metal.

By now, there weren't many buildings left, just a few old frame houses with oversized radio antennae hanging out over the ghostly snow. Open fields swept away on the far side of the boulevard like a great midway. The fog had cleared enough for me to make out the muddy, ice-crusted shores of Carnival Lake behind some low-rise apartment buildings. Off to the left, past the lake, I saw silver orbs illuminating I-292 high above the water.

I wanted to get back home. To Agit Street. I wanted to go upstairs and crawl into my bed. But I wanted this without my parents' hurt and disappointment, so I wasn't going to do it. I wanted to go back to May's house and ask for a ride back to Adam's, but I didn't want to see Lucy after what she had done. I didn't want the winter, but I wanted it. The winter wanted me, and fuck it, it could have me.

Anyway, it's never possible for anyone to return anywhere after they've left.

Returning is impossible.

Time is travel.

Eventually, Lestrade Boulevard died. Maybe the city had reduced and killed it because it didn't want anyone to learn the place's history. Maybe Sycamore Grove was supposed to have been forgotten. And so, as I finally approached the edge of the neighborhood, Lestrade took a turn and became a simple two-lane road, not even marked, its name lost.

I followed.

Where are you going?

I want to go home.

You have no home.

More houses, old houses, cold houses, blue houses, more railroad tracks – *so this is where trains pass when they carry in the parts for the cars we used to build here* – and big black sheds sheltering big red spools of cable and corrugated metal. Some sign sparkling neon blue bled out into that slushy, dismal mess. *Why neon?* There weren't any businesses to advertise here. This was an in-between sort of place that didn't know what it was supposed to be. Liminal. A rime-frosted chain link fence. Interstitial. Tiny houses, abandoned and trashed, of course. *How did this happen?* The ice crystals were blue, too. A big security gate, padlocked shut. I came to an intersection. Poulsen and Lemnos. This was Poulsen. I turned onto Lemnos. Another marginal road. The city had cut off the power to the streetlamps overhead. *Why not? Nobody lives here.*

I went on with the blue neon glow washing over me and over the slushy puddles.

Lemnos led me onto a bridge. At first, I thought I was crossing Carnival Creek, but the sound beneath me wasn't that of water covering rocks. It was a hush-rush, occasional, once, twice, and again. Cars. No, this was an expressway overpass. I'd reached I-292. A few blocks back, I had seen it, elevated on a bank above the lake. Here it had sunk beneath the level of the streets. I walked up the middle of the road, then looked through the chain-link mesh to the north and saw the monstrously huge interchange between 63 and 292, some ways off; four levels of six-lane expressways and their connecting ramps running north, south, east, west, winter, summer, spring, autumn, another overpass, another. To the left of the interchange, it must have been a mile away, rose the Pyramid and the Olan Foundation Building. No Akawe Rise. *You're long gone,* I thought. Now I knew, sort of, where I was.

I crossed Lemnos to look out toward the east. Very close, maybe a hundred feet away, or maybe less, there was a trestle, heavy steel, rusted iron. I looked down at the cars again. They were all driven by Akawe people, which meant that they were mostly built by X Automotives, which meant that some of them – still – had been built – in part, at least – in Akawe. By Akawe people. But now they were leaving. The cars and the people. They were driving out east, toward other places, and some of them weren't coming back. As I watched them abandon us – these cars, these drivers – my feet felt heavy and rusted in place, like the tin woodman. Moving was hard. It was easier to stand and stay.

A train passed on the trestle across from me. I knew this train. I had known it my whole life, when I was four years old and when I talked with Selby about my sunglasses, and when I was thirteen and talked to Lucy about the girls she drew. It was a freight train carrying the parts for cars, and it moved slowly across the trestle. The trestle was red-green, but the train was blue. It rolled away from me to the north, but it came toward me too, going bluer and bluer. I looked down at the cars passing beneath me. Yes, they were leaving, but some of them, too, were blue, and the blue cars glowed, and approached me, floating, praying for me as they came through the thickening fog.

I heard footsteps.

Someone was standing on the corner of Paulsen and Lemnos, studying the signs. He was grown, but not an adult. He might have been about my age. He was wearing a bulky coat, but no hat, and he looked tired, very tired. He paused for a moment, studied the street signs above him, then turned on to Lemnos, this lonely, car-forsaken overpass.

He approached me.

He was blue, and he stared at me.

With a shock of terror, I realized that he was me.

John Bridge stood before me, his hands cracked with the white cold, his hair a mess, his eyes weary and wary and afraid.

"What are you looking at?" I asked. I didn't like the way he stared right through me, as if I wasn't even there.

He didn't answer.

Instead, he studied the blue neon light reflecting off the slush at his feet, then crossed the road and looked out at the interchange and the downtown skyline. Then he crossed to stand beside me, and I backed away as he approached. He looked down at the cars passing underneath. Then he looked up at the train that had passed, that was still passing, and that was blue. Then he looked back down at the cars.

"What are you looking at?" I repeated.

"What are you looking at?" he said and looked off to his left.

"What are you looking at?" I repeated.

"What are you looking at?" he said, and seemed to be listening to a faint reply, something that was real, but that was too soft for me to hear.

"What are you looking at?" he said.

Then he turned and looked at me with his dark eyes, his un-sunglassed eyes, blue light superimposed on his brown irises. "I don't know," he said.

"Yes, you do," I said. "You're looking down there. At those cars. They're going."

"Yeah."

"They just want to get out."

"Can you blame them?"

"No."

"That was pretty fucked up what happened back there at May's."

"I don't want to talk about it."

"I mean with Lucy."

"I said I don't want to talk about it!"

"What makes you so sure?"

"Because the expressway doesn't have a billion fucking potholes."

"You sure that's what you should be worried about?"

"What should you be worried about?"

"What should you be worried about?"

"What should you be worried about?"

"What should you be worried about?"

"What should you be worried about?"

"I'm not worried about it."

"Then why do you keep talking about it?"

"So that I don't talk about the shit I'm actually worried about!"

"You don't want to talk about it."

"I don't want to talk about it."

"You don't want to talk about it."

"Shut up."

"Eli Ostyn."

"No."

"Ezekiel Lang."

"No."

"God Ostyn."

"Jesus, shut the fuck up!"

"Yeah? What's that?"

"Potholes, I guess. Where they are. That's okay. I get it. I'm glad you're worried about those things. Someone needs to talk about the potholes."

"Are you scared?"

"I feel sad. Are you scared?"

"I'm terrified."

"That's good. You should be scared."

"Fuck off."

I ignored myself, and then I was gone. I was alone again.

Or was I? Which me had left and which had remained? Was the real me the one who had stuck around? Or were we both real?

This shit is stupid, I thought, and I put my hands in my hair again. *This isn't anything big,* I thought. *This isn't that different from acid. What a dumb drug.*

I looked out through the chain-linked diamonds. The cars were gone, but they were still there, and they were blue, and they were quivering beneath me, reluctant to leave. They wouldn't leave until I allowed them. The train was gone, but it was floating where it had been a moment ago, bright and blue, and it wanted to come toward me. I was gone, but I knew ...

That it all comes down to God. Yes. That. *He is responsible for all this.* I hesitated. *For everything?* I didn't know. But he was responsible for Eli pulling Cora onto the streets. Which meant that he was responsible for Selby infiltrating his fucked-up family. Which also meant that he was partly responsible for Eli's manipulations of Lucy. And he was even more responsible for what he had done with Selby. His son Quint molesting her. He, or someone he knew, murdering her dad. He, or someone he knew, sending EZ after Selby and me. And then there was the thing with Drake. *I knew Drake got O-Sugar from the Chalks, but Eli says he got it from EZ. And that means that he got O-Sugar from God. And Eli said that they made it too strong back then. Jesus, how much did they take?* I shuddered as I thought about Drake's plunge from the hospital roof. *How much evil is in three pills of O-Sugar now?* My fist was clenched. Blood was running between my fingers. I didn't look down to see whether it was red blood or blue. I didn't want to know.

"You fucked him over," I told the night. I spat the words out: "You fucked us all over."

The pointless kindness of Eli pecked in my brain. The breath of EZ fluttered in the wind. The gaze of God swept over all.

"I know what I have to do," I told the night. "I have to kill them. I have to kill all three of them. I have to kill God. I have to become the antichrist."

I heard a swishing sound from behind me. I swung my head around.

A car was coming along Lemnos Street, and I was standing in its way. When had I stepped into the road? I heard the parting of the slush as the car hit the overpass. It had angry blue lights. The headlights grew. They were becoming blue. They slowed and stopped, maybe six feet away from me. The driver honked. I stepped out of its way. The car was waiting, but lifting my feet felt like lifting lead, and time slowed.

I took one aching, hard step, and then another. The third step brought me to the sidewalk again. I turned to watch the car as it receded across the overpass, but it was already gone. Its red taillights were already vanishing around the corner. But then they seemed to shiver, and I concentrated on them. They were the tapering rectangles of some hulky 80s car, and as they moved away, they shaded from red to orange and then yellow. They suddenly seemed to grow. To be shading green. To be growing into me. Flowing into me. I blinked. When my eyes opened, the car was gone, along with its taillights. I looked around. I wasn't in the middle of the overpass anymore. I was on the far end, where the car had gone. *But when did I finish crossing the overpass?*

I walked on, slow step after slow step, through the snowbanks and the next intersection. Bott Street. To my left, the road had been fenced off, and just past the fence were monster-sized heaps of slag and rusted crates. Glowing cones of snow crowned each pile, but then I realized that these were not snow but piles of putti smiling beneficently down upon me. Their chins tilted in unison, gesturing the other way, to the right.

A block later, there still wasn't much to see. Just some shattered warehouses with open dumpsters, also crowned with the glittering cherubs. They were all watching me. They seemed to be laughing at me. I crossed Sphenic Steet, where one stop sign stood as stoic as a beefeater, and the next angled drunkenly toward the creamy earth. By now, it was practically raining putti. They were pouring out of every abandoned opening. They climbed onto each other's shoulders, and their eyes shone a cold white. I smelled plastic burning. I was short of breath. I imagined a mighty sheet of plastic pulled tightly across my face. I finally made it another block and left the hordes of angels, though I still heard their giggling and discord behind me.

Up ahead, I heard drumming. It pulled upon me, deft and sympathetic. My chest swelled with emotion. There were tears in my eyes now. The drumming boomed like thunder across the horizon. I followed the sound until I came to Valley Street. Unlike the other streets I had crossed tonight, Valley was thick with traffic, and there weren't any lights or crosswalks here. I had no idea how I was supposed to get across. Every step felt like it took me a year, but the cars hadn't slowed down at all. In fact, they seemed to be speeding up, glowing blue, accelerating.

Then I saw four children watching me from across the street. At least I guessed that they were looking at me. It was hard to say because they didn't have any features. No eyes, noses, or mouths. Just blank sheets of skin.

"You have to come over here!" they said to me. "You have to hurry! This is the way you have to go!"

"I can't," I said back. "I'm walking too slow."

"Don't walk. Just think about it. Just imagine that you're over here with us!"

I closed my eyes and opened them. I stared at the opposite corner of Valley and imagined myself standing there, and suddenly I was. Somehow, I had safely crossed the street.

Now the children surrounded me. They were younger than I was. Three, four, five years old. Facial features started to grow upon the children. Eyes, noses, ears, and mouths. I saw Michael, Adam, Quanla, and Selby.

"What are you doing here?" I asked.

"We're here to help you out," they said in unison.

"Where do I go?"

"Keep following the drums."

"It's hard to walk."

"Your arms and feet don't work well because of the drug," said little Michael.

"Imagine where you want to go," said little Quanla.

"It's easy to go where you want," said little Adam. "It's easier than walking."

I imagined myself back at Chuck's house. I imagined myself in Adam's living room.

"It isn't working," I said.

"Start with something easy," said little Selby, her voice bell bright. "Look at the sidewalk there."

I did. It was gray, at first, then shaded toward blue, then purple, and then space collapsed and I was standing there.

"See?" said Adam mockingly. "Told you."

I continued to phase forward haltingly, and my stomach lurched with each shift. I went two sidewalk squares at a time. I wondered if I was hallucinating this movement, this awkward shifting, so I looked behind me. There weren't any footprints behind me, so I clearly wasn't walking, but it wasn't like I had teleported or vanished, either. I saw furrows in the snow, as if I had been dragged forward. I looked forward again and kept moving.

I finally made it to the next intersection. The drumming was louder here.

"Follow the drums!" said little Selby from behind me.

She was blue, now, faintly iridescent, and a white fire filled her eyes, like flames reflected through glass. Quanla, Michael, and Adam had vanished.

"Why are you still here when everyone else has gone?"

"I'm not here!" she said, indignant.

Selby fluctuated, shifted colors, cerulean and indigo and sky blue. A depthless azure. She nodded me forward.

I swept myself farther along the street. I arrived under the green walls of the Treemonisha Club. The shouts and laughter were coming from within. A cymbal crashed. Someone screamed in laughter. Bass chords synchronized with the fabric of the walls. But the pummeling drums came from another source. They didn't come from the club. They sounded more like bongos now, and they blew in out of the darkness across the street.

"You know what to do," said little Selby.

I looked up at the sign to the club. As I concentrated, a thin veneer of mist settled upon it, then started to shine and shine brighter, bright blue, and the rust on the sign flaked away. The inky lettering blackened. A neat, blue-and-white awning flew together over the concrete porch. The chipped blue bricks repaired themselves. Darkly gleaming fresh blue paint coated the Treemonisha Club from crown to foot.

"You're right," I said. "I do know what to do."

"Who on God's earth are you talking to?" asked a woman. I hadn't seen her. She was middle-aged, Black, a little round around the middle, wearing a blue skirt that was probably actually blue, and she looked at me with both concern and skepticism.

"Nothing," I said. "Sorry. I was just looking at that sign."

The woman shook her head, tossed her cigarette, and went inside.

"Come on!" little Selby insisted. "You know what to do!"

I looked across the street, into the darkness.

I looked at the sidewalk across the street, and I was there.

I looked at the snowy field, and I was there.

I looked a bit farther, and now I was fully immersed, beyond the pale umbra of light that shone out from above the porch of the Treemonisha Club.

Urbantasm: The Darkest Road

I went farther, between the twin hills, beneath the cathedral of trees, toward the final ridge that banked against the expressway.

This was where the auditorium had been, where Lucy had taken my friends and me in seventh grade. Andy Banner would never sell it: it had finally been demolished. Nothing at all was left except for a large rectangle of furrowed dirt.

The drums were close now, but their sound was still muffled. I concentrated, and a new world started to assemble in this forsaken hollow.

The air blurred. Shining blue bricks congealed and converged. They built skyward, assembling richly stained window frames, concrete plinths, limestone entryways, and mosaic tiles. The entire auditorium and the attached school rebuilt itself in spectral blue until it was just as I had seen it in seventh grade. But the building's resurrection didn't stop there. The dead, dried leaves scuttled back through the empty windows, which de-shattered themselves into polished planes of glass. The crumbled masonry climbed together into a neat blue grid of brickwork. The dust and grime of the place cleansed itself as well, and I saw floors slick with mop water, the air quivering with heat, the sound of radiators kettling, the lights buzzing softly. And with a shock, I recognized the auditorium not as the abandoned building I had visited in seventh grade but as a place where I had seen a concert when I was much younger. I was witnessing the full memory I had started to recover in scraps at the Wendy's in the sunset. Yes, I had gone here with Michael and Selby, and yes, I had run away from my parents – yes! – and when I got away, I saw the whole city turn blue before my eyes!

The drumming stopped.

"But I didn't do O-Sugar when I was four," I said. "There wasn't any O-Sugar when I was four. It hadn't been invented yet!"

I waited for Little Selby to say something – to help me – but she didn't answer. I looked around. She was gone. I turned back.

I tried to reach out and open one of the doors to the auditorium, but my hand was heavy at my side. I imagined myself inside, and then I was, the broad windows rising up all around me, the dull blues and browns of the mosaic tiles reflecting my face back like fuzzy mirrors. I saw the door to the men's bathroom, and I imagined myself inside, and then I was.

I saw myself, four years old, standing at the urinal. Then, beside me, I saw the drummer, slight of build, kinky hair, all glowing blue except for the teashade sunglasses he wore on his face. They were plain blue. Nothing fancy about them. Just ordinary sunglasses with blue lenses.

"Why you wear 'em inside?" asked the young me.

He talked to the man with the blue sunglasses. He told the man that he had been running.

"Why?" asked the man.

"I was chased."

"By your papa?"

"Yeah. And by dead things."

"Really. And what did the dead things look like?"

"They were blue dead things, and they were from before, and they went backwards, and everything was blue."

Then the man with the sunglasses stared at young John for a long time.

Finally, he did his best to answer, "Those ghosts want to go away from you, but you run up and catch them. That's how you see them. How, I don't know. They are moving ghosts and leaving ghosts. Sometimes I catched them too, a long time ago. A long way away. They fly fast."

"They wanted to get me," I said. "To kill me like they killed my Aunt Ellie. That's why I had to fly away from them."

"No. They only go away from you. If you saw them it's because you catched them as they were going away."

"Did they saw me?"

"Of course, they can see you. How else would they run away from you if they didn't see you?"

And I stood still and watched the conversation, trying to commit every word to memory:

"John," the man said, "you asked why I wore my glasses inside. I wear my glasses inside, so I don't see them. I know they see me, and I know they're there, but now I don't see them, and they don't bother me. You see, they're all blue, so any blue glasses can hide them from you."

Suddenly, I understood what Eli had done. The perverse cruelty that he had buried beneath his infamous kindness. Yes, he had taken the blue-bottle sunglasses back because they had belonged to his adoptive mother, but he also knew that they would have protected me from the worst effects of the O-Sugar. They would have mitigated the *insanity* of what I was experiencing now. That was why he had smiled through his white teeth as he had put the shades in his shirt pocket.

The man with the sunglasses went on: "In the village where I am from – it's far away – everyone there saw moving ghosts. A long time ago, my sister met a Christian man, and they went away so they wouldn't see the ghosts anymore. Then my brother went to try and find them. My sister and the man of God. Then I followed them, too, but I can't find them either. I took the path through the garden. I went through city after city. The last city was this city. Akawe. Now that I'm here, I see the ghosts again. It is the first time I seen the ghosts since I left my village. So maybe, if you, if your family leave this city, then maybe you won't see the ghosts anymore."

"John. Wear the glasses so you don't get scared. But more important: Be a good man. Love your family. Keep yourself clean. Then the ghosts can't scare you or hurt you, even without blue glasses. Do you understand my meaning?"

Young John nodded.

The man took off his sunglasses.

He gave them to John, who put them on.

"Let's go now," the man said.

They left, but I remained. I stood where I was, remembering everything else that had happened that day. After the concert, Selby and I had traded the sunglasses, trying to hide the blue ghosts that we saw all around us. But not Michael. Michael hadn't seen any ghosts.

I felt the wind pricking against my arms. I looked around me. The bathroom had gone, the auditorium had gone, and I was standing in the empty field once again.

I knelt and vomited. Putrid pulp poured from my mouth and burned a patch in the snow. My mess spread into a pancake shape, and from that foam emerged a blistered face with wide eyes and an angry mouth. The fog began to stink, like burning sediment, an autumny smell. The smell soaked through me, and I discovered myself standing on another street, and the world was fading in around me, putting on its blues, too blue now, becoming violet, so violet that it bled black and emerged again as blue. I was standing just a few blocks from my house, and it was late summer.

I saw myself in seventh grade, limping down a driveway, ragged and panicked. I was wearing the bottle blue teashades. A man came down a driveway, and his face was peppered with gray stubble, but I thought he had the face of a corpse. I knew that all his blood and circulation was just a clever disguise.

"Where did you get those sunglasses?" he asked, and all of the bloodthirsty dogs in the universe howled with him.

I took the shades off and put them in my pocket.

The man turned his watch and reflected blue sunlight into my eye. I squinted and looked down, and the man laughed cold.

"It's EZ," I told myself, but I didn't listen.

The man pulled the knife from his boot.

"It's EZ!" I screamed at myself.

EZ started to walk toward the younger me, but I ran up to an old pickup and snapped off the antenna, holding it out in front of me like a sword.

The man stopped.

"Where did you get those sunglasses?" he asked.

"From your rotting mother, you dickweed," I said.

"Just leave me the fuck alone!"

"Do you want to fight?" he asked.

"Your brother raped my friend, so I want to fucking kill you."

"I ran away from the fight, dumbass," I screamed.

"And I followed you," he said.

I walked backwards toward the nearest house.

"Someone," I yelled, "is going to hear those dogs and come and see what's going on. And they're going to see some tall faggot threatening me and they're gonna call the cops."

"Most definitely. What's your name? Where did you get those sunglasses?"

"Leave me the fuck alone!"

"I'll find out. I'm always able to find out."

"Fuck off!"

And I turned and ran up the driveway.

EZ Lang didn't follow. He stood there, watching, for a long time. Then he put the knife back in his boot and lit a cigarette. He stretched and took a few drags, scanning the surrounding houses.

"I hope you get cancer and die," I told him.

EZ blinked in surprise. He took the cigarette from his lips, studied it for a moment, then dropped it and ground it underfoot. He sighed, turned, and strode off into the sunlight. When he was gone, I knelt to pick up the cigarette, but the ground was suddenly dark. I couldn't find anything down there.

I found myself standing on the corner of Hastings and Church on the night of my first junior high dance. John Bridge was standing there, and Michael Loss, and Adam Miller, all of us looking anxious, like boys in over their heads. I was going to be the courageous one. I was looking off into the distance, trying to decide how to get back home. Something had caught my attention and had frightened me. It was an empty space off to the north, and I didn't know what it was. But *I* knew what it was: I was looking toward Eden. Toward the Hell House. Reflexively, and in panic, I raised mental walls of web and weal against that part of my imagination, because I did not want to go there, I did not want to go *there*, I did not want to go to the Hell House when I was drowning in the blue froth of O-Sugar.

"No!" I yelled at myself. For a moment, I thought I looked back at me. *Am I blue too?* I wondered. I looked down at my hands.

They were shimmering, quaking, trembling with blueness.

They were insects.

Cockroaches and centipedes were becoming my arms and hands, sliding in and around my bones and muscles. I tried to shake the bugs off before they completely became me, but the more I shook, the heavier they were. I lifted my arm to my mouth and started crunching down upon the wriggling insects, crushing hundreds of little bodies beneath my own mandibles, feeling my chin streaked by their fumbling blue blood.

Two figures took me by the arms and led me down the street.

I still couldn't move my feet, so they were dragging me. They were shaded blue and orange, and they were glowing. They were both naked, and he had an enormous penis that pointed arrow-like up toward the clouds. She had an engorged vulva and a swollen belly. They were young and powerful.

"Who are you?" I asked.

"I am Inshushinak," the man said, "but you can call me Big."

"I am Išnikarap," the woman said, "but you can call me Place."

Then, they let me go, right there in the road, somewhere on the margins of town, the South Side or the West End where there weren't any sidewalks, and the gravel roads stank of drowned worms and loam. Big got to work. He double-palmed his massive dick and used it to dig a hole. He must have chosen the perfect spot – a patch of spongy earth covered with careworn grass – because he quickly hit the aquifer – a spring even – and the crystalline water welled and bubbled up for him. Then Place carefully spread her legs and opened herself up, and I saw a small band of humans tumble out, exhausted and bewildered, but happy to be alive. They were wearing rags. They immediately fell to their knees and started drinking from the fountain that Big had dug.

"Don't worry," said Place, and she rested her hand upon their backs.

"Where are we?" I asked Big.

He nodded toward a shaggy house with an attached cinder-block building. Lucy's house and the attached Tent and Tarp shop. I floated away from Big and Place. I floated around the house until I was standing on the small drive that ran past both buildings. Seventh grade John was there again. Lucy was coming up the walk. It was Thanksgiving Day.

"So, anything exciting ever happen in the Akawe Tent and Tarp Shop?" I asked.

Lucy stopped for a moment, her face fleetingly registering open surprise and terror, and gave a sudden shake before stepping toward my parents' car. And I saw on my own face the planting of a seed of horror about what might have happened in that building.

"It isn't that!" I shouted at myself. "It's worse than that. It's so much more worse than what you're thinking!"

And I fell onto my knees and cradled my bleeding fist, while Lucy's phantoms multiplied and spiraled about me in overlapping blue circles placing handgun barrels into their waiting mouths.

I wailed and tore at my face.

Two people were waiting at the bus stop across from Lucy's house.

They stared at me in shock.

Suddenly, I stood in the blue effigy of Mr. Kolin's classroom while myself and a bunch of other students listened to his raving.

"This is what you have to understand," said Mr. Kolin. "When X Auto closes one of their factories, when they take the jobs away and demolish the factories, they leave behind all the junk they put in the soil and the water over all those years."

And he said: "I know. I've been measuring this, myself. Carbolok, Octolok, paints and sealants, PropylOsirin, advanced polymers ... you aren't going to read about these in your textbook, but they exist right under your feet. You walk upon them every day, and they get on your shoes and in your laundry and they are trying to kill you."

"And what about you?" I asked.

"Trying to kill you, trying to kill you."

Mr. Kolin's voice reset, over and over, like a scratched record.

"Did the Ostyns kill you?" I asked him.

"I'm a science teacher," he said. "I am a science teacher. I've been down to Cartierul, where you've got twenty years of storm sewer runoff from the Old Benedict, all that dirt just soaking in PropylOsirin and Octolok."

"Mr. Kolin?" I asked. "Mr. Kolin!"

"In fact, I've been submitting this all to the EPA, which does not seem all that interested. But this isn't years ago. This is last year. Mercury causes birth defects, mental retardation, and, if it's bad enough, your skin peels off. Any of you have friends down in Cartierul? They ever go outside barefoot?"

"Mr. Kolin?" I bellowed. "Did they kill you because of this? Were you murdered?"

Mr. Kolin opened his mouth to speak, but all that came out was a bubble of blue blood that burst and flooded over his desk and dripped down onto the floor.

All the phantom kids screamed and pushed their desks backs and covered their faces.

I heard delicate laughter high over my head.

Cora's forgotten laughter.

Some dumb joke that Adam had told once upon a time.

The birds congregated, flapping fast as they went, covering suns, and erasing everything.

I looked to the birds. Looked through the birds. Fell through them. I knew, somehow, that this wasn't a hallucination. I was actually falling up. Compressing space at such a rate, simply by looking to the sky, that I felt myself projected into the air. It felt like a tornado, only I could slightly control this. Pick a point. Lower myself gently back onto the ground. If I wasn't careful, I'd smash myself onto the pavement instead. But I kept spinning up, up, getting distracted, spinning up. Then I realized, with certainty: *Drake and his friends didn't want to kill themselves, but they thought about it. For just one moment, they imagined themselves going over the edge of that hospital. And that was enough. It compressed the space between them and the edge. Projected them outward. Then, gravity worked. They went down. They died. Except for Drake.*

And since I'd caught myself thinking about the hospital, I was there.

St. Christopher's Hospital had been demolished, but it rose before me now, with crystalline white-blue bricks climbing six stories with a cross-shaped footprint. I floated myself up so I could see the roof.

Adam and Michael and Selby were there, and so was I. I was looking over my own back as we sat in a circle holding hands. We flickered blue, crackling through like bad reception, our voices garbled, though I could understand us anyway in the storm-cadenced summer breeze.

We all breathed deep. Started to hum. The rest came instinctively as if this was the most natural conversation in the world. For a long time, our humming was so quiet that our voices were indistinguishable, but as the moment stretched, as the sound built, I started to pick out layers. We merged and separated, in and out, like spiraling knots, and then the spiral continued on as our mouths opened. The humming became an 'ah.' The 'ah' became an 'oh.' The 'oh' became a scream, and the whole bright blue darkness rang with our terror. And then, just when my head was finally going to split open with all of the horrified noise, it stopped.

The silence hung on.

For a long moment, nobody moved.

Then, with a steady gaze, a gaze specific in its focus and intention, Selby lifted her eyes and looked over the edge of the building, where I waited.

"Selby," said the thirteen-year-old me. "What is it?" I reached out and touched her shoulder. Her eyes went wide, and she looked between the thirteen-year-old me sitting on the rooftop and my present self, floating in the air and watching us.

"But there's two of you!" Selby said, and she slid backward until she was up against the lip of the ledge.

I saw myself tense.

"What?" I asked angrily.

Selby moaned. I was staring at her. Now she was looking beyond the two John Bridges.

"It's coming!" she said with a kind of whispered urgency. "It's getting closer, and fuck, it's coming!"

I trembled at the tone in her voice. I looked over my shoulder and saw what Selby saw.

Thousands of urbantasms were converging upon us from every point above and below. I saw the phantoms of everyone who had ever been born or who had died or who had suffered at that hospital, animated by anger, charged with passion, their resentment coupling with the frissive currents. And then, in the midst of that cyclone of the dearly departed, I saw a searing white light flying out of the west, burning and billowing. *It* was coming. It was coming from the dark house on Eden Street.

"I don't want to go there!" I shouted. "I don't want to go there, I don't want to go there, I don't want to go there!"

And when I shouted, Selby screamed right back at me. "Get back! Get back! Get back! Don't touch me!"

I had to get out. I had to leave. I had to get out. I was out.

I was sitting with Selby and myself on her front porch late at night. Fog hung heavy against the limp grass under the viaduct, and crickets sang from every side, and the cherry sparked as John and Selby passed the pot pipe back and forth.

"Have you ever seen something that was destroyed?" Selby asked. "Like destroyed and gone? And you see it right in front of you? Like it still exists? Only it's blue or purple. And you can see right through it."

"Like a ghost?"

"No. Because a ghost is a spirit and a soul, you know? A ghost can think and talk and do things. These are just ... just, like. I don't know. Images. Like a photo. Or, I don't know, more like ... if you look at the sun for a second and then look away, you still see the circle glowing in front of you? Like that."

I understood that the urbantasms were like photographs or films. I knew that they weren't technically alive and couldn't think for themselves. But the borders that separated the living from the urbantasms now seemed to be a lot less fixed than Selby had said. Might we not be urbantasms ourselves, projections of a superior mind, riding our own fixed trajectory through the expanding universe until our essence was fatally dispersed? Might others see us as we saw the urbantasms? Angels, perhaps? Possessing devils? And if this was what we were, what about our intelligence? What about our agency? Did we have identities or souls? Or were we just brief congruities within the relics of an explosion that had happened billions of years ago?

"I don't think I've seen that," John said. "I mean, not that I remember."

"You're wrong," I said.

"Manole – Macewoudd – saw them," said Selby. "And I don't remember much about him, but I do remember that. I remember him telling us kids about it. He said he saw them all the time in Cartierul. More than anywhere else he had ever been. He called them urbantasms. Urbantasmele. Because he saw them in the city. In Cartierul, where the city has pretty much disappeared, and it's all muddy and swampy. He saw urbantasms here. He saw the whole living city all around him. It scared him."

Is Manole – Macewoudd – God? I wondered.

I looked up from the conversation, and I saw what Manole claimed to see. Shattered houses flew back together in clouds of dust and plaster and wood and brick. People came in and out of the swinging doors, banging windows open and shut, living their lives, as oblivious to the two teenagers on the porch as they were to me. The moment elided time. Everything was episode and vignette. I knew that everything I was seeing had once happened, and was still happening, and would go on happening forever. Everything about it all was blue.

"Even just seeing something does do something," said Selby. "I mean, if you see something – if you sense it – then you know that it's there. That it exists. And you can think of what it is in any choice you make after that. You know?"

"The past tries to run away from us," she said. "But he discovered you could run up behind it and catch it. And also, the urbantasms told him that Akawe was a true city. He said he couldn't see them in most cities, but he could see them here, and that made a difference."

"I mean," she said, "any city is just a place where there are a lot of people living whatever – their lives – all together. Right? So, a true city with urbantasms would be, like, everyone is all together, and all time is all together, and everyone is part of one big thing, all together, and that big thing is the city. Is Akawe."

"And you remember all this from when you were four?!" the younger me asked.

But I crouched in front of Selby. I reached out to brush a bit of her hair to the side, where it had fallen in front of her face.

She shrugged as if to chase off a mosquito as it alighted upon her neck.

I held my hand where it was, an inch away from her skin.

She blinked.

I pulled my hand back, and stood, and paced the porch as Selby and I continued the conversation.

"Kill that," Selby finally said, waving at the pipe. "It's later than you think."

A minute later, Selby and the younger me exchanged a chaste hug, and I turned and crossed the field and climbed the shadowed stairs that took me to the top of the viaduct. Selby and I stood alone together on her porch.

"I don't know who you are or why you're here," she said. "But if you aren't evil, I hope that you will say a prayer for us."

This was about when the last clasp of my control unhooked. I wasn't steering the ship anymore. No deliberate shift from one memory to another. No guidance by snowy putti or faceless children or glowing angels. Now I lurched violently from vision to vision, the urbantasms tearing through me as I went.

I knew that these encounters could *not* be arbitrary. Someone or something was trying to steer me. To *teach* me something. I tried to marshal my thoughts in the midst of pandemonium. Selby and I had hallucinated blue before. We had hallucinated as children, almost a decade before anyone had heard of O-Sugar. So what was O-Sugar? How was it made? What was happening to me?

Selby shut the door in Celesta's face. She turned back to face Michael and me.

"It's 1996. Happy New Year, my dear, sweet best friends. Now: stay away from the Ostyns. Stay with each other. Love each other. Trust each other. Everything is fucked up. Everything is crazy. Everyone is going to die. We're all going to die. But let's not die for a little while. Let's not. Please?"

"I don't want to go where this is taking me," I said.

"You are a good person, John," said May.

"No, I'm not. But thanks anyway."

"It's going to be all right."

"No, I'm ... wait, what?"

"I said, 'It's going to be all right.' Everything is made by God, right? So how can it not be all right? I mean, it has to be all right!"

"It's hard," I said.

May laughed.

"Well, of course, it's hard!" she said. "Nobody said it was going to be easy."

She leaned toward me and kissed me gently on my forehead.

"Why don't you look out for me, and I'll look out for you?" she said.

"I don't want to go there."

"I'll see you when you get back. It won't be like this forever."

I closed my eyes. I took a deep breath. I opened my eyes and looked around me. I was standing on the edge of the South Street Viaduct, looking down over Cartierul. To my right, the Pyramid. To my left, the road that would have taken me home. It was almost dawn, it was after dusk, it was this night, and it was the night before I had started junior high. This wasn't where I was meant to go, however. This was only a staging area. Before the blue-hued curtain came up on O-Sugar's last act of the night.

I took one more breath.

Now, I was ready.

My silent coach arrived. It was a faintly glowing '59 Valentine Formosa. Its headlights cast eerie green beams through their emerald-cut glass, while the grid of its platinum grille glittered like a set of symmetrical silver teeth. Its jagged rims spun like the march of time. It was a rigid-finned coupe, its paint glimmering with the golden richness of fertile mud, and a set of jade dice swung from its rear-view mirror.

When the coach had come to a halt before me, the headless chauffeur – no bleeding, it was simply as if his head had been erased – shifted into park, got out, and held the passenger door open for me. I climbed inside. The vehicle levitated into the air.

As I stretched across Akawe, I looked down at the city passing below. I saw skeletal trees and snowy fields, the ice-glazed river, and frost-specked houses. Then factory rubble. I forced myself to look up. To lean forward in the open air. I waited for the moment when it would finally appear: the final stop.

The Hell House appeared as a speck on the horizon. It grew and grew, utterly alone in its waste of slag. That flaked-up farmhouse, broken, shattered, sunken, spotted, hollow, catastrophic, lost, and absolute.

This time, a single bright white light shone from a second-story window.

I had arrived.

I stepped onto the splintered porch and walked in through the open door.

No candles or lamps lit this darkness, but a soft blue light suffused the air. I stood in a drafty, narrow hallway, spiced with the wet scent of sediment. Rectangular arches opened into rooms on my left and my right, and a set of stairs rose directly in front of me.

I climbed the creaking stairs to the second floor.

When I had reached the top, I stood in another hallway lined with shut doors. A blue-and-amber light streamed out through the crack at the bottom of the farthest door.

I walked to it.

I opened the door and went inside.

On the other side, I found an almost bare gray room, all wood, small, with the ceiling higher than the length or width of the walls. To my left, a window looked out toward the west. To my right stood a wrought iron torchiere with a Corinthian motif, a single light bulb beaming from its top, golden, surely, but blue when I looked at it.

Between the lamp and the window was a rush-cushioned wooden chair with splintered spindles.

In the chair sat a worried-looking old man, white and bald, his chin pepper-stubbled, his head glistening in the light of the lamp. He held a glass of brown liquid in his crotch and pointed a rusted shotgun in my direction.

When he saw me, the man wheezed a sigh of relief and lifted the gun toward the ceiling. He decided that it was safe to risk a quick sip of his drink, but it sloshed in his trembling hand. He returned the glass to his crotch and wiped his chin with his right arm.

"I was expecting the mulatto girl." His voice was gravelly with phlegm.

"Are you God Ostyn?" I asked.

"Just God," he said. "Who are you?"

I didn't answer.

"You aren't the wheelchair kid. Are you the boy who took Ruth's sunglasses? You aren't wearing 'em now. Eli take 'em back? Or was it Ash? You're still breathing, so probably not Ash. You must have had quite a night, but you knew to come here, so you know something."

He took another drink.

"How do you make O-Sugar?" I asked.

God laughed, and it was a wet wheeze that seemed to get stuck in his throat.

"When I was in the army," he said, "I served with a rabbi and a grammarian. One day, we all went into a bar. The rabbi told us about how the entire Torah was waiting to be interpreted, and that it had more secrets than anyone knew. *He* told us that there were as many miracles in the blank spaces as in the words. Then the grammarian said, 'that's why you should always put two spaces after the end of a sentence.'"

He chuckled at his joke.

"What is Octolok?" I asked. "What is PropylOsirin?"

"Keep telling me what you know," he said.

"Why are you hunting us?"

"Hunting *you?*" God said. "You think *I'm* hunting *you?* Can you really not understand that *you* have been hunting *me?* Why else you think I'm sitting up here in my own house – *my* Empyrean – waiting for *her* to turn up and slit my throat?"

"What," I sneered. "You're scared?"

"Anyone who isn't scared is insane."

God took another drink. A big drink.

If I just wait long enough, maybe he'll black out. Then I could finish him off with his own gun. I stood where I was.

"I mean," I said. "Maybe you deserve that. To have your throat slit or whatever. Did you kill her father?"

"Who?"

"George Demnescu."

He waved his hand dismissively. "He fell. Dumb drunk. Construction is dangerous. Drinking is dangerous." He raised his glass in a silent toast.

"Did your son molest her?"

"I didn't believe it when I heard it," he said. "Would you like a drink? It's bourbon. You look like you could use one. I've seen the urbantasms for years. Seeing them is like going to sleep with the living and waking up with the dead. After a while, they're all you see. After a while, you don't know the difference."

"No, thank you."

God nodded understandingly.

"I'm old now," he said. "You're young. *She's* young. You're all ... full of vigor. Just like my children. You can all fight and struggle, but I am tired. I don't have fight left in me anymore. Did you know that this house used to be at the very center of a neighborhood? It was the busiest, most crowded neighborhood in the city of Akawe. Now, I am the last one left. They were able to get all of the Blacks to leave, but they couldn't make me leave."

"What is it you want? To take over the Chalks? To make a lot of money? *What?*"

God laughed again.

"Jesus Christ," he said, "you don't understand at all. Take over the Chalks? Why would I want that? Jesus, you couldn't pay me enough. And money? Don't you think there are easier ways to make money than inventing a drug and selling it to people who don't have any money?"

"Well, what is it then?"

"You think you understand, but you haven't even reached the shore of knowledge." God grinned. "I make my sons memorize sacred scripture. It doesn't matter which of them you talk to, and they have several different mothers, but you can know that they're mine because of the things they say and the way they talk. It is who they are. It is who I have made them."

God took a drink.

"You are in my house. You do not have the right to ask me any question, and I do not have to answer anything. But, since you came in here speaking and not shooting, I will answer one question for you. One question will not hurt me, and I cannot imagine that the answer will help you or your friends. So, I will tell you: what I want is to leave. What I want is to go away. I have been here from the beginning. I have been here since times before anyone can remember, when this place was even emptier than it is right now, and I can tell you, someday it is going to be that empty again. This has been my prison, and I want out. And after all this time, you are not going to prevent me from leaving. Nobody has ever prevented me from doing anything I want to do. Not once I have finally decided to do it."

I listened as he spoke and tried to etch all of his words in my memory, in case I could make better sense of them after the drug subsided. In case he was mistaken, and there really was something in his proclamations that I could use.

Having spoken, however, God had evidently run out of patience with me. He leaned forward and carefully set his drink on the floor. Then, straightening up, he again put his hands around the shotgun and lowered it toward me.

"Now," he said. "Unless you have something else that you want to tell me, I think it is time for you to leave me in peace."

I held up my hands and slowly backed toward the door.

"At least I know where to find you now," I said.

"Don't bet on that," God answered.

I woke with the sun full in my face and the sky a wash of blue. I lay on my back in the snow, arms wide and spread-eagled, a snow angel. My pants were stiff with piss, my right fist was bloody, my joints were sore, my body was cold, and pain banged through my head. The sun looked fuzzy overhead, but at least I could see colors other than blue. I got to my feet and started walking.

I almost walked right off the edge of a cliff.

Shit! Shit! I was standing on top of a large building, black topped. Brick. With a hazy sprawl of parking below and a neighborhood of small houses beyond. I was on the roof of Radcliffe Junior High School.

I staggered back, then squinted, trying to see better, but my eyes were all wrong. Still, I could make out, barely, the snow undisturbed all around me. I had no memory of climbing up to the roof. I knelt, ignoring the cold and willing my head to clear. The dizziness eased a bit, though not the pain. My eyes were still fucked. I concentrated, trying to identify the fuzzed-out forms all around me.

I vaguely made out the triangular shape of an antenna descending to the parking lot.

I crossed over to it, stamping new tracks as I went and trying to think of what had happened after my conversation with God. I couldn't remember anything. I made it to the antenna and wrapped my palms around it. I looked down, and I had no sense of the distance to the ground below, so I sat down again and tried to clear my mind some more.

If I could get past all of the corrupted cells and the fear, I had learned a lot the night before. One: Lucy had pretended to attempt suicide. Or maybe she wasn't pretending, but I wanted to say that she was for the moment. If she was just pretending, then maybe there was still some hope. Two: Eli knew and didn't care. His famous "kindness" was bullshit. Three: God Ostyn didn't give two shits about running Akawe. He wanted to leave. *So why doesn't he just leave?* Four: God Ostyn owned the Hell House, which he had called "my Empyrean." *Is that its true name?* Five: When I had arrived, God had been expecting Selby. Though he knew, more or less, who I was. He also knew about Drake. Six: The Chalks get O-Sugar from the Ostyns. The Chalks get *all* of their O-Sugar from the Ostyns. Seven: Ziggurat and Drake were doing something with their stash of O-Sugar, and Eli took it as a threat. Eight: *I drink too much. I do too many drugs. I stop that shit today. For fucking real this time.* Nine, and this was the big one: As a four-year-old living in Cartierul, Selby and I had seen urbantasms, and they had looked just like the urbantasms I had seen on O-Sugar. Mr. Kolin had found traces of PropylOsirin and Octolok in his soil samples from Cartierul. So were the urbantasms a product of those drugs, whatever they were? And if so, did they have something in common with O-

Sugar? Like, did those three drugs all share the same chemistry or something?

With my eyes closed, I found that I was able to think quite clearly.

Even better, maybe, then I had been able to think in the comfortable warmth of my bedroom.

Selby's life was in danger.

Lucy's life was in danger.

Mine too, probably.

Who else was caught up in this drama? Drake obviously was. What about May? Were there others? Who knew?

And was I really going to kill God, and EZ, and Eli? The Ostyns were killers. Even if I wanted to, could I? Wouldn't they just kill me, instead? I still felt the anvil weight of my hatred of that family, but in the daylight it was leavened by an equally heavy fear.

I had to do something, but I couldn't know what until I had a better understanding of how it all fit together. Selby knew more, but I couldn't count on her to tell me. I'd have to figure it out on my own. So, there was an urgency to undertstanding. A bleeding urgency.

The pain in my head had finally subsided. Now, it was only as bad as an ordinary headache. I opened my eyes. The antenna was just as fuzzy as it had been when I'd first seen it. *I hate this shit, but I can't wait anymore.*

I stood and took a piss, marking the junior high school as my territory. *The South Side doesn't belong to God*, I thought. *The South Side belongs to Adam and Selby and Lucy and me!* I zipped up, grasped the antenna with both hands, and swung myself over the edge. *Fuck a fear of heights.* I started climbing.

A minute later, my feet touched the ground.

I crossed the empty space and crossed the street. I kept rubbing my eyes as I went, but I still couldn't read any street signs, so I had to rely on my memory. I walked two long blocks into the sun and two short blocks toward the morning. I finally got to Adam's house. I fumbled around with my key until I managed to unlock the door.

Grandma M was in the kitchen, doing the dishes.

"Adam's not here," she said.

I kicked off my shoes and went past her and upstairs to the bathroom.

The door was locked.

"I need the bathroom when you're done," I said.

When fuzzy-faced Ophelia got out, I went inside, hurriedly washed my face, and dunked my head in ice-cold water, washed my crotch and legs, toweled dry, then felt my way down to the basement where I stripped in Adam's

473

room. I put on a pair of his underwear, khakis, a t-shirt, a sweater, and socks. His clothes were too tight on me – the hems of his pants were high around my ankles – but it was the best I could do. I went up to the kitchen, and threw my old clothes away. I tried to read the clock above the stove, but I couldn't see it.

"What time is it?" I asked Grandma M.

"10:10," she said. "You okay, John?"

"I'm fine. Thanks. Where's Adam?"

"I think he's over at his Grandpa A's with his mom."

"Is she staying there now?"

"They've got her set up in some motel, but she's meeting them for breakfast every day. Not at their house. At the coney island."

"Well, I've got to go. Will you tell Adam I'll catch up with him at school?"

"I'll do that."

I put my boots and coat back on and went outside again.

I walked fast. By now, I knew that I didn't need the street signs. I knew every road by heart. I didn't want to risk meeting my parents, so I followed Debs west across Whitmore, then South, and past the prim houses of Ashburn Hills down to the river. I crossed a footbridge, made my way through the park, and continued on through South Village, chancing a dash across Aubrey Street, even though I couldn't tell whether any cars were coming or going. I finally made it to St. Brendan's Church. I passed through the lobby and into the nave. I crossed myself with holy water, and it felt warm against my numb fingertips. I genuflected and took a seat near the back.

That morning, more than usual, I felt like I really was in the presence of something holy. Something watchful but patient, that contrasted with everything I had heard and seen the night before. Something that understood but withheld judgment. As the priest droned on, I ran through my plans in my head.

When the Mass was over, I stood at the back, squinting to make out a pair of familiar faces in the crowd and praying that my parents weren't with them. It worked. Michael and Mabel were coming toward me, and it looked like they were alone. She was wearing a floral scarf, and I saw Michael hesitate a moment when he saw me.

"John," said Mabel. I couldn't see her mouth moving, but I recognized the voice coming from the direction of her smudged face. "Are your parents here?"

"No," I said. "I was wondering if maybe I could spend the night at your house tonight."

The next hour gave me no margin for error. If Aunt Mabel realized my eyes were fucked up or that I'd been taking drugs – *any* drugs – she would have called my parents, and that would be the end of it. I didn't even want to think of what my parents would do. Pull me out of school? Confine me to my room? Move us all to Kearsley, or wherever?

I was sweating with effort as I carefully followed Mabel and Michael to their car, just squinting a little to resolve the silver Benedict handle, to grip it casually, to push the button. I got in and fastened my belt by touch. I heard the door slam and realized that Michael was sitting beside me and Aunt Mabel was in front. The car moved.

"You look pale, John," said Mabel as we pulled out from the parking lot. "Are you sick?"

"Just tired," I said. "I didn't get much sleep last night."

"You'll get more tonight. Michael isn't doing anything but homework for the rest of the day."

We merged onto the expressway. We left Akawe. Left Acheron. Got into the subdivision in Parc Pierre. When I got out of the car, I felt the larger lawns, the larger houses, the newer houses, cool brick and beige siding, spreading out around me, circuited into the wired cul-de-sacs. I stretched my arms and felt relieved. Maybe God was powerful in Akawe, but he wasn't out here in the suburbs. I squinted my eyes again and followed Aunt Mabel and Michael inside.

"You know," I said, "I am really tired. I think I might just go and lie down."

"We can pull out the couch bed in the basement," said Mabel.

"You don't have to pull it out. Just give me a pillow and a blanket, and I'll be fine."

I went down and slept for I don't know how long. It wasn't a great sleep – knots in my neck – but it was better than the snowy roof of Radcliffe.

When I woke up, I saw that the small windows had gone dark and the room was dark, too.

"John," said Mabel.

"Yeah?"

"Your mother is on the phone for you. You can pick it up from the wall over there."

I stumbled over to the wall and lifted the receiver. I heard Mabel hang up upstairs.

"John?" came my mother's voice. It was tense, though I couldn't tell from the tone whether she was angry or not. I realized that I hadn't heard her voice in almost a week.

"Yes?" I said.

"I'm glad I got you. Chuck's mom called me. She said you were going to call her last night?"

"Yeah. I forgot."

"So, you aren't staying there anymore?"

"No. I'm staying here at Michael's tonight. Duh."

"And how are you going to get to school tomorrow?"

"What do you care?" I said. But as I spoke, I realized that it would be risky to piss her off. "I'll take the bus up East Street. That's easy enough. Or, I don't know, maybe Mabel will give me a ride."

"I see. And where are you planning on staying tomorrow night?"

"I don't know yet. I'll figure it out."

"That isn't responsible."

"Yeah, tell me I'm not responsible!"

"This is stupid, John. It's asinine. I'm coming to pick you up. You're coming back home."

"No, I'm not."

"Excuse me?"

"I'm doing fine on my own. I'm fixing my problems, okay? I'm ... doing my homework! I'm already doing a lot better this semester. But I don't want to go back there. Not yet!"

"You can't just bounce around from house to house, John!"

"If you force me back, I'll tell father about you."

"Excuse me?"

"You were right about me skipping school, and one of those days, you brought your new boyfriend or whoever back to the house. I heard you talking."

"What?"

"Yeah, he said something about buying a chandelier, and you were both worried about the neighbors seeing you or some shit."

Silence from her end.

"You remember any of this?" I asked. "Mother? Why were you so afraid that someone would see you?"

"You can't talk to me like this," she said, her voice soft and still. "You can't threaten me."

"I'm not threatening you!" *She's trying to claim the moral high ground? She's trying to talk down to me? Hypocrite!* "I just don't want you, or Father, of all people, around me while I try to figure my shit out. You have too much shit of your own. So, you two figure your shit out, both of you, and I'll do the same, and when I have, I'll give you a call! Don't call me back; I'll call you when I want to talk to you!" I slammed the phone down so hard that the receiver cracked the plastic cradle.

I waited for my mother to call back. For my Aunt Mabel to come back down and get me again. For the shouting to start.

But she didn't call back.

I spent the rest of the night acting.

For dinner, we had some chile recipe from New Mexico, which was a bit hard for me to eat with my jacked eyes, although it helped that Michael seemed to be having trouble with it too.

"That's good," he panted, wiping his face with his napkin and taking a sip from the tiny glass of wine Mabel had given him.

After dinner, Michael dove into his homework at the dining room table. My vision was getting better, but it still wasn't good enough to read. I had left my backpack at May's, so I just pulled a book off the shelf and pretended to read. I needed to talk to Michael alone.

When Mabel finally left the room for a minute, I leaned toward Michael: "Come down and meet me at 3 am, okay?"

Michael gave a quick nod.

When Mabel returned, I said goodnight to them both and went down into the basement. I unfolded the couch-bed and put on the TV. The Red Wings were playing the Penguins, but all I saw were shadowy shapes gliding across a white background. It was strange to think that just twenty-four hours before, I had been climbing into Eli's car. That all of those hours of peril and ache had only just passed. That one day had made me into a different person. Different, but safe for the moment. The familiar sounds and smells of Aunt Mabel's basement were a world without end away from May's basement with its mold and its pink floor and ceiling, to say nothing of the blue storm raging outside. *But won't I have to go back into that storm again?*

I fitted the sheets and got out a pillow and comforter. I lay down and fell asleep again at once. It felt like only a moment had passed when Michael was shaking me awake. I blinked in the television light. The game was long over, and now an infomercial was flickering across the screen.

"Turn on a light," I said. "Turn it off. The TV."

Michael turned on the fluorescent overhead light and clicked off the TV.

"Anything to eat down here?" I asked.

He went over to a small shelf, shuffled around, and brought back a fistful of wax pop bottles, each filled with a few drops of fruit juice.

"Is that it?" I asked.

"I could go upstairs and make you something. You want some nachos?"

"Don't bother."

I bit the top off the bottle and spit it into the trash can. I tried to make out its color.

"It's blue," Michael said. "Raspberry. They're the best ones."

I sucked down the juice. Then I went back to the trash can and threw it in.

"Any pop?" I asked. "Real pop?"

Michael went upstairs and came back down with a couple Cokes. I popped mine open and took a long pull. The carbonation burned my throat. Michael's fuzzy face didn't move. I knew he was studying me.

"So, how you doing?" I asked. "What are you up to?"

"I'm okay," he said. "I guess. Parc Pierre still sucks. I finally got together with Abbey, though. She's the bomb. I mean, she's cute and, you know. Nice. She's nice to me. She likes computers. She's a computer programmer. She takes them apart. Like, for fun. Why are you acting so weird today?"

I sighed.

"You think I'm acting weird?"

"Yeah."

"Like how?"

"Your eyes sort of wander around like you're trying to find something, but they never settle. And then upstairs, when you were reading? I don't think you were even reading. You know it was one of my mom's engineering books. It's all, like, Calculus and stuff."

"Did your mother notice?"

"I'm right, huh? No, I don't think she noticed. I kept it to myself."

"Thank you. It's important, Michael. Are you sure she's asleep right now?"

"Pretty sure."

"Okay, look, I'm going to tell you some heavy shit, and then I need to ask you some heavy shit."

"Okay."

"Can you keep it all a secret?"

"Yeah!"

I wasn't sure how to begin, so I decided to just get the worst of it out of the way.

"You remember that girl May that I was going out with last fall? Last night, I went to her birthday party, and when I left, I took a bunch of O-Sugar."

Michael sucked in his breath, and even with my blurry vision, I could see that his eyes were wide, so I hurried on.

"I'm better now. I mean, I think I'm getting better. The only thing is that I can't see real well; my eyes are all fuzzy. That's why I couldn't read, but I think they're getting back to normal. Last night, I could only see the color blue, and it was everywhere. Tonight, I can see other colors; I just can't make out details."

"Jesus, John," Michael said. "That's, like, one of the worst drugs you could do, you know?"

"You know about it?"

"I mean, it seems pretty bad to me. I was trying to find out more about it after New Year's Eve at Selby's. It's killed, like, twenty-five people in just the last year. People have gone blind from it. Some people have killed themselves or tried to kill themselves. It really screws them up. You remember that kid and all his friends who jumped off the roof of St. Chris' a couple years ago?"

"Yeah, I do, and that's actually part of it all. That kid is May's *brother.* Drake! But I don't think they jumped."

Michael sat down on the pull-out and drew his knees up to his chin. I caught him up on what had happened at May's house. How Selby had given me the sunglasses, and then the weird conversation that Eli had had with Drake, Mike, and Ziggurat. What Eli had revealed about the ingredients in O-Sugar. But when I got to Lucy's moment in the basement, I stopped short. I still didn't want to think about that. I didn't want to look at it. I just had to swerve around it because it was more monstrous than anything else that had happened that night.

"I was curious," I told Michael. "About the O-Sugar. After all that time, all that talking, I just needed to know what it does to a person."

"What does it do?" Michael asked.

I told him about my night shifting through the city. I told him about my conversation with God. When I was finished, he sat where he was for a long time, thinking.

"Deadly nightshade?" he finally said. "Eli really said there's deadly nightshade in it?"

"Yeah, and, like ecstasy."

"Well, that explains why it kills people. I mean, deadly nightshade will kill you. It can also make you blind. That's why your eyes are so messed up right now. Why would they put deadly nightshade in a drug they wanted to sell?"

"Oh, it all makes sense when you actually do the shit," I said. "It's like a sort of horror that mixes with happiness. The nightshade gives you the horror, and the ecstasy makes you happy, so they, like, balance out."

I felt the skeptical silence wafting off Michael.

"Whatever," I said. "That's not that weird. *Here's* the weird thing," I said. And I told him about the hallucinations Selby and I had had as children. I told him about Mr. Kolin's studies of soil contamination in Cartierul. The fact that Cartierul used to flood every month or two. The fact that the urbantasms appeared again when I had taken O-Sugar.

"I think I know what you're thinking," Michael said. "You think that because these drugs were in the ground when you and Selby got sick —"

"We didn't get sick."

"I mean when you saw the blue things, and then you saw them again just now – on the O-Sugar – so you think that one of these drugs —"

"Octolok and PropylOsirin."

"Right. You think that one of them is used in O-Sugar?"

"I mean, wouldn't that make sense? And if they are, and we can prove it then maybe we can ..." *What? Call the police? Murder the Ostyns?* I had a feeling that the actions I was going to take would terrify me, but I still couldn't know what to do until I knew what O-Sugar was and why I had felt its effects as a child.

Fortunately, Michael's thoughts were elsewhere.

"Weren't you saying that God was scared of Selby?" he said. "I mean, from what you said, it sounds like she's the one who won't leave them alone."

"I don't trust him. I think he's lying about a lot. But I *do* think she wants to kill him or something. I mean, she didn't tell me that. But she thinks that he killed her dad. I mean ... I think she's probably right."

Michael let out a big breath. "You know," he said. "You were hallucinating. It could just be that, I don't know, that you were hallucinating about these things because they were on your mind? That it wouldn't have anything to do with the drug?"

"No offense, Michael, but you don't know what you're talking about. I did some drugs with Adam, okay? I did acid, and I did this fruity hippie drug he gave me. They both gave me hallucinations. Look, I've never seen *anything* like all this crazy stuff that was happening with the O-Sugar. I mean, I was, like, I felt like I was teleporting. I'd feel like I was floating through the air, and I'd look back, and there wouldn't be any footprints, just marks like I'd been lifted up and dragged through the snow. I felt like I was just *appearing* different places, and then suddenly I was there. Traveling through space and time!"

"I hate that you're doing drugs, John. You were always better than that. Until now, I mean." He sighed. "Well, did your science teacher say anything about where he thought the two drugs came from? I mean, how they got into the soil."

"He blamed it all on XAuto."

"Right, I know ... but there's a factory near Selby's house, right? Near where you're talking about?"

"Yeah. The Old Benedict. It was a foundry, in one part, and then powertrain and Tool and Die a long time ago, and some other stuff."

"That's what I thought," said Michael. "I might be able to find out some of this."

"Really? How?"

"Well, my mom's an engineer for X Automotives, isn't she? She teaches at the Institute, right?"

I hadn't even thought of this.

"Those drugs you said ..." Michael continued. "Octolok. PropylOsirin. Those sound like trade names. If they are, that means that they've got a patent which could tell us a lot about them. And I can probably find out some about them at the XAI library. I mean, maybe it isn't anything ... maybe there isn't anything to find out. But I could look."

"Yes, Michael. Please look! I have to know. I don't know how to fix this without knowing the truth."

"The truth? Huh. Well, anyway, even if it is true, I don't know what you're going to do about anything. But I'll try to find out."

"That's okay."

"Are you staying here all week?"

"No," I said. "Just tonight. I have to stay with someone where I can take an easy bus to school."

"You'll have to call me, then, maybe in a couple days. Maybe even a week. But I'll tell you what I can figure out."

"Thanks Michael."

"I'll only do it on one condition."

"Yeah?"

"Never, ever, ever do that shit again."

I laughed bitterly.

"I promise. I'll never take O-Sugar again unless you want to try it with me."

By the time morning came, I finally started to feel like myself again. I still couldn't understand small print – my textbooks would be a challenge – but I could read the faces and expressions of the people around me, and that was enough to get me through the day.

Still, faint traces of blue light trailed objects whenever they moved. Colors shaded slightly downward whenever I stared directly at something. Worst of all, I kept thinking I saw people standing in my peripheral vision, staring at me. They, too, were blue. I knew that they were urbantasms. They had *been* in the past, but now they had hollow eyes. Once again, I found myself wishing that Eli hadn't taken the special blue sunglasses.

Aunt Mabel dropped Michael off at Parc Pierre High School – a huge new building that held more students than any high school in Akawe – and drove me back into the city. She let me off near the front door of Eastern.

"I hope you're back with your parents soon, John," she said as she pushed the button to unlock the door.

I didn't know what to say, so I just gave her a quick nod and shuffled off toward the school. I needed to shake these blue shadows. I needed to get through my classes. I just needed an ordinary day for a change. When I got to my locker, I grabbed the two textbooks I'd left there and started digging for some loose sheets of paper so that I could take notes.

"John!"

I jumped in surprise, and the blue shadows fled.

May was standing right behind me. She was holding mine in her hand. She was frowning, her brows knit together. "I brought you your backpack, okay? You left it at my house, okay? I thought you would want it. Because it has all your school stuff in it. It has all your clothes in it, too!"

"Thanks," I said.

I reached for the backpack, but May wouldn't let go. I couldn't tell if she had forgotten that she was holding it or if she had changed her mind and decided to keep it. I pulled. She finally let go. The backpack hit me in the chest.

"You know!" May said, like she'd been holding these words in check but hadn't thought of what else she wanted to say. *Are you about to lecture me, too?* I turned back toward my locker.

May reached out and tapped me on the shoulder until I turned back around.

"We were really worried about you!" she said. "You left, but you didn't tell me that you had taken a bunch of O-Sugar!"

"You found out?!"

"Eli told us –"

"That motherfucker."

"And Drake counted it and –"

"And now he wants to kill me."

"What?! No! Jesus, he is *not* a gangbanger. I mean, you do have to pay him back, like, a hundred bucks, but *no* he isn't going to kill you. But you were already gone! We went out – Ziggurat and me – we went out *looking* for you and we couldn't find you *anywhere*, and we were worried you'd fallen, or got runned over by a car, or got killed or something."

"Why did you go looking for me?"

"That's how my party ended, John. Happy Birthday to me! It was *such* a great birthday party, wasn't it? So, I'm glad I finally found you, and was able to get you your backpack back because you need it, okay? Dammit!"

"I'm sorry," I said.

"It doesn't matter, okay? And here are your sunglasses back, too! Eli had them! Lucy and Drake made him give them back!"

She put the bottle teashades into my hand. I stared at them. Just like that, they were mine again.

"Like Drake needs more reasons to piss off Eli," I said.

May sneered. The expression was so comical, I couldn't help laughing. She started walking away.

"Wait wait wait wait!" I said.

She turned back toward me, reluctantly.

"I'm sorry," I said. "I was messed up that night. That whole thing with Lucy. I can't even ... Jesus, I can't even talk about it now. I just. But yeah, you had to feel like you had to take care of everyone there. And it *was* your party. I'm sorry."

May seemed to calm as I spoke. Her shoulders were still tensed up around her neck, though.

"What is Drake doing with the O-Sugar, May?" I asked.

"I don't care, okay?" she said. "Not even a little. It almost killed him. Everyone thinks that he and Jamo and Sapphire and DeeDee and TK all jumped off that roof, but they didn't. It was the O-Sugar that did it."

"I believe you," I said.

May let her shoulders drop. She seemed exhausted. Too many waves, too much wind, too much work, constant.

"I just want some cherry lip balm, and a new sweater, and people to stop killing themselves, and each other. That's the only things I want. Nothing else."

I watched her as she left. Then I unzipped my backpack and started unloading my textbooks into my locker. I noticed that my *Lord of the Rings* books had gone missing. Maybe Eli had taken them, too. One last payment in exchange for everything else he felt I had taken from him.

I was tempted to put the sunglasses on at once and erase the urbantasms from my vision. It would have made the day easier. But I also had to think about who might be watching me. I had now had the sunglasses taken from me twice. I meant to keep them this time.

In the last few minutes before school started, I hurried down the lawn behind Eastern, crossed the pedestrian overpass into the Happy Hunting Grounds, and pushed into the thickets of oak trees flanking the rutted tracks. I found a dead tree that was recognizable from a distance, and I hid the sunglasses in a hole burrowed beneath a swollen bole. I covered them with a flat gray rock.

I still caught blue shadows watching me from behind the trees, but I'd just have to live with them. On the way back, I scanned the classroom windows for faces, but they were empty. I wondered again about what I could do to protect myself and my friends against the Ostyns, but all of my answers sounded implausible or ineffective. *Borrow one of Grandpa M's guns and shoot them? Call the police on them?* It didn't matter. I couldn't do anything until I heard back from Michael. I tried to push Lucy and the Ostyns from my thoughts to focus on schoolwork, but as the day wore on, I found myself thinking more and more about May.

I mean, my thoughts weren't coherent. There wasn't any sort of story in them. I'd start out saying her name in my head, and then I'd imagine her face, and then my thoughts would range out into the imagined haze of some sunny summer, and after a while, I'd return again, filled with wonder, but without memory. And I'd repeat this. And repeat. She moved me.

I didn't want to bullshit myself. This felt something like the electric thrill that had gone through me when I had looked at Lucy in seventh grade. It also felt like the deep sense of rightness and contentment that had filled me when I'd been with Omara in eighth grade. And the feeling contrasted, powerfully, with the *wrongness* of everything else going on around me. The horrid urbantasms.

But could I trust these feelings? In the past, I had trusted them too fully. I had stopped paying attention to everything else, and right now, I really *needed* to pay attention. Besides, I'd already gone out with May once. Selby was right when she'd described us as "the dumbest couple ever." I wondered if I just wanted to rest from everything, and May's warmth was the best shelter I had found.

That's why I asked her out before. This is different. She's changed. Or maybe I'm just noticing something that I never noticed before. May's life wasn't fair, but she didn't seem to care. Her outlook was the opposite of mine. My life had been fair to me, in all of the most important ways, but I still got pissed off about stupid shit. It wasn't good for May to care so little about herself, just like it wasn't fair for me to care about myself so much. And I wondered whether we might fit together in this. If we were friends, or if we were ever more than friends, would I take and take as she gave and gave, and so we'd both become worse people through each other? Or was it possible that she could teach me to be less selfish, and I could teach her to be a bit less selfless?

I just want to do something nice for her, I thought. *Fuck it.*

At the end of the day, I caught Adam at his locker.

"I need to borrow some money," I said.

"Jesus, John, everyone wants a piece of me right now. What do you want it for?"

"Important stuff. I can tell you later."

"Drugs?"

"No."

"I got a twenty. I guess I don't need it right now."

"Is that all?"

"John, you even gonna pay me back?"

"It's fine. I'll take the twenty. Thank you. Hey, by the way, I need to crash at your house tonight. Is that okay?"

"Fine."

And so, I went to my classes and took my buses, and I saw the fabric of the city embroidered before me as I went.

It happens like this on any winter day:

The sun rises over downtown. Its modest towers catch the radiation climbing over the frozen river, its searing silhouette along the pointed peak of the Pyramid, casting manmade things into outspread black shadows and charging the sky from gray to fire. In Bellwood, Ken Lessard slowly draws back his charmeuse curtains. Nova scours his teeth, the toothbrush churning the paste into a minty froth. Majenta binds her feet into tall black boots. Ties the black leather laces into a double-knotted bow. Nova slides the floss, bites it off, swirls mouthwash, and spits and rinses, and takes a pull of bottled water. Majenta stomps on out of her house. Omara walks down the salt-streaked sidewalk, knocking the snow aside with her faux-fur boots before climbing into her dad's minivan. A dozen desecrated driveways recede into the morning. At the bus depot, May puts in her student-discounted twenty for the month, and the machine feeds her a pass printed on thick, yellow paper. Smokers stand outside, adding their own soot to the atmosphere. At the airport, Ken's dad arrives for an early morning flight to Atlanta. He rides the elevator with Carla. She's in uniform, and when she gets off she stoops to pick up some scraps of paper that litter the polished tile floor. May climbs onto her bus and it groans out of the depot. Diesel fumes rise in the quickening cold. They put a sulfurous bite in the clear air the men with the crutches breathe as they stand in the blue and clutch their coffee. Traffic jams along 292 as Aunt Mabel makes her daily commute to XAI. Standing traffic never lasts long in this city that has lost half of itself, but still holds over a hundred thousand distinct souls. A hundred thousand stories. My father stops at the Constellation for a couple eggs over easy with hash browns and rye toast. He sits and sips and watches the jagged-edged shadows diminish, giving way to sunny brilliance. Teen boys rap in brick back alleys, clapping their hands to keep the beat and to keep warm, their bodies taut, their blood pumping, their voices cutting, their limbs strict and supple. My father laughs at his waitress's joke. Little kids hurry into the basement kindergarten classroom at St. Brendan's School. Red and blue and gray cars streak past the fast glass East Street windows, then the bridge's humble hump, steam lifting off of the river's face, the shards of ice turning eddies, the blood that burns through icy fingers held to lips under hot breath, the kindergarteners going outside now and shoving each other off piled mountains of snow. Now Ken's father scans the departure schedule for delays. High-frequency speculation on stock trading is all about aspirational plans for the newest model Passway, more chrome, worse mileage, but that's okay; it'll be a retro-throwback crazy-ass look with four-wheel drive as a bonus. The Bellwood elite love their bonus views of all that furnace heat hissing across Akawe from some big-windowed space way up high, high, high in the Olan Foundation Building. Or from the top of the escalators at the Basadena Valley Mall. Kitty-corner diagonals across Jordan and East streets when traffic lulls for one short moment. The Passway! What colors? Blue and gray and black and blue, but phase out the gold. Nobody buys a Passway and goes with the gold. Looks more beige anyway. A sparkly beigey. At the credit union, Quanla's mom counts out cash into a customer's hand. An X exec allots seven million to test market a greater proportion of fully-loaded Passways in the Southern and Pacific West markets. On the corner of Orion and Olympia, Juanita stamps her feet in the snow. Recess is over! Back inside! Trucks trundle all over everywhere, dumping salt as they go. Class is out at Southern Michigan, and the masses of students pour out of the buildings, all of them with their fists plunged deep in their pockets. The sun shifts upward. Public defenders climb into their cars, off to depositions. Semis unload crates of produce and budget brand Hamburger Helper into the supermarkets; one on the North Side, one on the South, two to the West. Down the escalators. Through the food courts. The planes are finally taking off into the astral cold. The clock flies. The cars race. The neighborhoods thrum off exit ramps. Off student-choked glassed-in pod-walkways linking the classroom buildings. Space-age corridors. Atomic reveries. Reflections like liquid metal. The sun is now as high as it's going to get. Perfectly framed in junkyard concertina haloes out on the far Northwest Side. Time races in this busy city. Clerks stamp through the pockmarked snow. Pigeons cluck and bob over a spilled sack of Cheetos. City Hall boils with black-coated moms and dads here to pay their bills late before the fines get any worse. Before the city shuts off their water. Before their electricity goes. Before their gas naturally evaporates into this sparkling atmosphere. Teachers throng the sidewalks on Campus Akawe, crowding into the convention center. Dogs lie around a blanket furnace grate. Pace around it, even. Drive around with the windows down, even though the windchill is subzero, because this is audacity! Spinning tides and skyscrapers hiding skies. Airplanes leave the earth. At the Constellation, my father talks through an informal interview with some pipefitters working out in Acheron. Azure out and about. Good food. Heavy. Eager policemen, happy because violent crime and the endless paperwork always sinks just a bit during a cold snap. Cars hum through the parks. At the school, lunchtime. Trays of crackers and chocolate milk. Billowing resin. Coffee cloudy with cream. Get some gas. Eat a coney. Get that key lime pie. Sway with the blue and green. Eat every citrus bite. Spin the carousel. Off to class. Don't be late. Praise the sky. Stop for a brownie just off East. Meeting adjourned. The bell rings. The light is green. The clock is ticking. The fish are swimming luminescent in their salty tank. Homework time, art time, make it the truth. Spin the sky. Swim in circles. Build a baby. Breathe through gills. Race along. Make a heartbeat. Build the spinning sky. The skies want a storm, and they won't be still. Old men play checkers in the yellowed gym of a community center. Pickups skid along the 63/92 interchange, where they hit a patch of black ice they didn't see because they go too fast. The sinking sun spears them. A baby waits for an airplane to take her back home to Birmingham. Bop the sun. Spin it. Take the bus on out to Meijer's. Left turn signal, play. The baby bobs to a beat she hears in her head. Dance the skied range. Drive out through the suburbs with a half-million Basadenans. Kick at hacky-sacks. Decelerate under overpasses because that ice will rise up and catch you again if you don't. The clouds stalk. Paint with chalk, a smiley face. No ice past the overpass, so you can crush seventy, eighty, ninety. Faster than the skies. Faster than a chalked-out sun. Faster than the clouds coalesce. Faster than Darius in his pitiful Daphne. Faster than the execs drive their golf balls in the Acheron inflatable winter dome. Car auctions. Armies of Salvation. Civic comeuppance along the curb. Clouded curbs. B-boys breaking in the gym because it's too cold for another recess today, and the Truman sixth-grade kids had to hang inside. A parked cloud. A long line drive. A tilt-a-whirl. A slip on the ice. A classic, cadet blue Aubrey convertible. An airport croissant. Dryers belching clouds out onto city streets. Evergreen needles, a welcome relief. They're real. They smell ripe. Pineapples arrayed in a pyramid shape. Brick gym backflips. The sky dome umbraed by hazy margins. Spam on sale. Fresh cuts cost more. The execs sip Gray Goose and Blue Nun in the winter garden on the highest floor. They see the haze recede. Omara gets home, and Selby, and Qunala too. They see the haze advance. A hundred-plus train cars ride across Valley Street near Starville, backing up autos a half-mile and more. Cloud gray. At the Treemonisha Club, some old-timers order the first beer of the night, waiting for the Pistons game to flick into life on the one mounted TV. The skies dim. May gets on the bus to go back home. Adam is out at a bowling alley. He rents his shoes at the counter. My mother is out for a jog. She puffs her way through the icy neighborhood, looking for houses with the lights on, activity, optimism, effort. Adam rolls a spare. The machines pick up the pins and reposition them. Chuck's mom shows up for the shift change at Proctor Hospital. My mother turns back toward Agit as the sun starts to go down. She likes running. She thinks it's bracing, refreshing. The sun goes lower. The sky goes indigo. Students are leaving the late classes now. The clouds have given up their storm for the day. Late-day programming. Soap operas and grainy game shows. Overpass shadows. The Big Wheel. Daily Double. Bankruptcy. Commute back home. Stripped and sunsetting fields of corn and soy, frostblasted. Taking the curves too fast again. Tomorrow will bring us closer to summer, so don't stop moving! Bouncing clouds. Twirling sirens. Hazy lengths. Video rental. Hurried and hallowed. Hollow hopes consume caffeine, bucket by bucket. Sunglasses on. Stop jogging. Retie your shoes. The wet laces trail out somewhere. Leave rivers of wet on the tidy tile floor. Cheer. Jump. The sky is orange and now purple. The clouds mass, and Ken Lessard slowly draws back his silk charmeuse curtains. Flash bright! Jump up! Skyline affire, Pyramid to Southern, Two Rivers to Olan, Hellburger's to the Arcade! Teamsters ready up for long hauls. Shop rats get up for the post-pm binge. Clouds lace their boots with fire. Planning committees dry puff breath like dusty laundromats that welcome long-day weary tenants. The Basadena Mall is burning from the friction of a thousand restless soles. Fold your new clothes once you go back home. Wash them before you wear them. Set them to the west before you ready for the east. ATM transactions. Liquor store gummy bears. The sky as violet as the deepest of seas. Angler fish headlights. EKG fangs, a cause for concern, but not panic, not panic. Moon halo twirl. This night. Oncoming. Streetlights accelerate. Spin and merge. Gold and white. Up and down. Lansing or Detroit. The spasm ramp.

Akawe was a big world, and nobody could imagine all of it, or tell even a tenth of its secret stories.

I got off the bus at the corner of Ash and Huron, deep on the East Side, and crossed the parking lot to the Ash Mall. A giant plexiglass clown hung from one of the parking lot lights, its bolts bronzed with rust in the late afternoon sun. I went in at the Dollar Depot, went out into the main corridor, past the hockey shop, past the coney island and the consignment store, and turned into a dusty novelty shop.

It was dim in here – no windows – and the air smelled stale. Every inch of the walls was covered in blacklight posters. A glass counter ran the length, with rings, necklaces, steel-studded wrist bands, bongs and pipes, and decals on display. A rustling voice sang about revolution across the speakers of an old stereo in the corner. I breathed it all in for a moment, feeling how unexpectedly wonderful everything had become over the course of the day. I had taken my eyes for granted, but now I could *see* again. The last of the O-Sugar had finally faded. It had faded in time for me to see May! I felt happy and laughed out loud. The clerk, a shaggy-faced man wearing a Confederate t-shirt, stared at me.

I found a box of lip balm on the counter. $1.25. I stopped briefly at a rack of tinted sunglasses priced $3 a pop. There weren't any sweaters in here, but I saw a whole wall of t-shirts emblazoned with pot leaves and the names of bands.

The sunglasses and the lip balm were easy. I could buy a t-shirt instead of a sweater, but I had no idea what kind of music May liked. I had a feeling she was fine with all of it, so that meant I was looking for shirts that just looked cool. I thought she'd laugh at the classic swollen Stones tongue popping out from between the bulging lips. The loopy Nirvana smiley with x'ed out eyes, or Dr. Dre glaring out from some golden disk. The problem was, they all cost $25, which meant I couldn't afford any of them even if I didn't buy anything else. I finally lucked out in the farthest corner of the store, where a large cardboard box had been stuffed bottom to top with Natalie Merchant t-shirts. They weren't really what I was looking for, with her sullen mug frowning out over fisted fingers, but ...

"How much are the Natalie Merchant shirts?" I asked.

"T-shirts are twenty-five," said the burnout.

"You ain't gonna sell two hundred or whatever Natalie Merchant t-shirts. How about fifteen?"

"How about twenty?"

"I only got twenty. And I need that lip balm and a pair of sunglasses, too."

"Fine. Fifteen."

I took the crumpled shirt up to the counter. I added a tin of cherry-flavored lip balm and some pink teashades. The man rang me up. It came to $20.41.

"I told you I only got twenty!"

"That's Uncle Scam in that cash register, rippin' you and me both off."

"Yeah, fine, but I still don't got any more money."

"Fine, fine, give me the twenty."

I left the mall, crossed the parking lot again, and followed Ash back into the city. It was cold out, but my motion warmed me. The sun was setting now, and the streetlights had already come on. Lights were winking on in the occupied buildings along the strip. Even when Akawe had been rich and offered up leather upholstery to warm suburban asses, Ash had always been a bit seedy. I had known it was the last place in town where I could stretch twenty dollars this far. I passed a few clubs – gay – metal – bus stops, strip malls, thrift stores, pawnshops, gas stations, and 7-11s. Gold and weapons. Jewelry and music. Then the red-light district – several brightly painted windowless buildings of metal and stucco with a steady stream of middle-aged men passing back and forth between their cars and the mirrored doors. And, of course, the usual burnt-out stacks of bricks and rubble where a business had stood a year or two back. The weed-choked vacant lots. I finally got to the corner of Lestrade Street.

From there, it was just another ten minutes to make it to Armstrong Boulevard. I found May's house easily and saw that her sidewalk had been shoveled. I ignored the mural and climbed the ramp to the porch. I held my breath for a minute. *What if Drake answers?* I wondered. I knocked on the door.

May answered.

"John?" she said, real surprise in her voice. "Hi!"

"I got you something," I said.

I reached into the bag and put the lip balm into her open hand. May stared at it. She kept staring at it.

"I wanted to get you a sweater. But I couldn't ... today. But I got you this."

I handed her the Natalie Merchant t-shirt. She put the lip balm in her pocket and unfolded the t-shirt over her chest, looking down at it.

"Who is she?" she asked.

"I don't really know? She's in some band. I thought you might like it."

"I do like it. I want to hear her now."

"And since I couldn't get you a sweater, I got you this, too."

I handed over the sunglasses.

"Happy birthday," I said.

By now, the sky was fading fast. May looked at me. She didn't say anything, but she was studying me, long and carefully, and as she watched me and I watched her back, I realized that the gift had done what I had hoped. I had made her happy. And her happiness made me happy. And I just wanted.

I just wanted so badly ... I can't even find words for it now, because it wasn't the same as wanting sex or wanting to kiss her or to hold her hand, or for her to tell me how important I was to her. I just wanted to *be* with her. I wanted her to *be* with me. I wanted to go back in time and take back every hurtful thing I had ever said or done, not just to May, but to anyone. Because I wanted May to love and to value me, and anything that might have diminished her opinion of me was something I hated.

"Thanks," she said.

"You're welcome," I said.

We stood there for a moment as the twilight got darker and the wind picked up around the little house.

"It's cold," she said. "Do you want to come inside?"

I felt a twist in my stomach. I knew that Drake was in there.

"I should get going. I'm staying with Adam tonight."

"Do you want a ride?"

I hadn't even thought of this, but the day had exhausted me. I had spent all of my energy again, and all of my money, and I didn't want to take two buses to spend more than an hour getting back to the South Side.

"Yeah," I said.

May smiled.

During Geometry the next day, I got called down to the office. I figured that it was my parents trying to corner me at school. For all I knew, they were waiting for me there. As I walked, I tried to rehearse some kind of answer. Some way to say "no" and shame them into retreat without naming any names or bringing the office staff into the mix. For a second, I thought about fleeting the school and running off to ... *where?* By then, I was already outside the main office and visible through the window in the door.

"John Bridge?" the secretary asked when I walked in. She was sitting at a low desk adjacent to the main counter. She held a mug of tea in one hand and a phone receiver in the other. I walked around the counter, and she handed me the phone.

"Hello?" I said.

"Is this John?" came a man's voice.

"Yeah. Who's this?"

"It's Charles."

"Who?"

"Charles Letts. From the youth theater."

"Oh, hey! I'm sorry. I don't know why I didn't recognize your voice."

"I've been trying to get a hold of you. I left a couple of messages on your answering machine."

"I'm not living there right now," I said. "I got kicked out." It wasn't *technically* a lie.

A pause from the other end. "Jesus," he finally said. "Are you okay?"

"Yeah, I'm fine. What's going on?"

"Well, um. I wanted to make sure that you're coming to audition for the play. To act."

"Oh my god, I forgot all about that! Did I miss the auditions?"

"If you did, it would be fairly cruel for me to interrupt your school day just to tell you. Auditions are tonight. Can you make it?"

"Um, yeah. I think so. What is the play about?"

"It's an original piece. We're calling it *Teen Age Riot*, and it's about what it's like to be a young person living in Akawe today. With the unemployment. The contaminated water. The schools closing. There's a lot people have to say about all of that. I just realized we were mostly hearing about it from adults. August and I had really hoped to get you involved."

"What time does it start?"

"Six o'clock."

"I'll be there."

The secretary took the receiver without looking up. She put it back in its cradle. She was looking over some papers.

I didn't think I should stay at Adam's again that night. I didn't want my parents calling me there or, worse, stopping by. Also, I didn't have the money to pay Adam back. He wasn't going to bug me about it, but I was starting to feel like I was ripping everyone off. I didn't want to go back until I could pay him back.

I figured I had also closed the door on Chuck's when I'd forgotten to call Tammy after May's party. Which was too bad; I liked the noise and warmth of Chuck's small house. It was a good place to do homework. Wherever I went, I wanted it to have that comforting feel. I didn't want to be alone. I wanted to be surrounded by friends.

"Excuse me," I said.

The secretary looked up at me.

"Could I make one more call? It's about getting a place to stay tonight."

She turned the whole phone toward me and went back to her tea.

I hesitated – held my breath – and punched in the number, and, after a few rings, Mark Adams picked up.

"Hi, Mr. Adams," I said. "It's John Bridge."

"John," he said, clearly surprised. "Nice to hear from you. It's been a while. How are you?"

"Very good, thanks. How are Darius and Quanla?"

"Um, they're doing fine. They're in school, of course. Wait, you're in school right now, aren't you?"

"Yeah."

"Is everything okay?"

"Pretty okay," I said. I held my breath for a moment. *No turning back.* "But I'm not staying at my house right now ... with my parents."

Mark was quiet for a moment.

"I see," he finally said.

Now that I was actually talking to him, I felt selfish and embarrassed. Why *did* everyone have to bend over backwards to give me a place to stay? Maybe I *should* just slip into a vacant and take on the cold. But I was too sensible to go off alone and too proud to go back home. The only option left was prostrating myself before my friends' parents.

"I was wondering if there's any chance I might be able to stay with you all for a few nights."

"I don't know, John. Don't your parents want you back at home with them?"

"I stayed at Adam's last night. They'd rather I stay with you guys than him."

"When you say 'stay' ..."

"I don't mean for long. Just a few nights. Not long at all. I'll be good for any food I eat."

"Oh, I'm not worried about that. I just can't imagine –"

"If you thought I could stay 'til the weekend, I'll be able to work out something else. I don't want to make things hard."

"No. Not at all, John. Yes, you can stay here for as long as you need. I'll have to run it by Kimmy, but I'm sure she won't mind. I will want to call your parents and let them know where you're staying."

"Thank you, Mr. Adams," I said.

The secretary watched me over the rim of her mug.

On my way to lunch, May surprised me at my locker. She was wearing the t-shirt I had bought her. She swept her finger across the lip balm and ran it along my lips.

"This is for you!" she said.

I tasted wax and synthetic cherry flavoring.

Then, May took my hand and dragged me – her almost running and me just trying to keep up – all the way to the cafeteria, where we found Lucy sitting at an empty round table near the corner. I heard her annoyed sigh as I took my seat. I didn't want to stare at her, but I didn't want to seem like I was avoiding staring. I smiled at her in an exaggerated way. I didn't want her to talk about what had happened at the party, but I'm sure she knew everything that I was thinking.

"How are you?" I finally asked, normally.

"It's as good as it gets," Lucy said.

She poked at a rubbery slice of pizza with her spork.

"Are you doing anything after school today, John?" May asked. "We could all do something together. I still haven't taken you to that McDonald's on Ash!"

"I want to," I said. "But I can't tonight. I've got auditions."

"For Mr. Agape's play?"

"They're doing another play?"

"They're doing *West Side Story*," said Lucy. "The school doesn't have any money for it, so Mr. Agape is paying for it all on his own."

"That's pretty crazy."

"Yeah, he's very noble. I'm sure all of your new friends are trying out."

"I'm pretty sure you are all of my friends," I said.

Lucy rolled her eyes.

"I mean," I said, "except for Adam. And Michael and Chuck. And ..."

I shut up, too late.

"Please don't be mean to each other," said May.

"I didn't say shit!" said Lucy.

"I didn't mean nothing," I said. "I'm auditioning for a play at Akawe Youth Theatre."

"Oh, that sounds like fun too," said May.

She got up to buy herself a pop.

As soon as May was out of earshot, Lucy leaned across the table and hissed at me: "Are you going to play her again, John?" she said.

"I ain't playing her!" I snapped. "I never played her once, okay?"

Lucy frowned and leaned back.

"I thought you *wanted* me to get back together with her!"

"Yeah," she said. "I said that, but I didn't think you were actually going to do it."

She didn't talk to me again for the rest of the meal.

As I moved through my day, Charles' sonorous voice beat a steady tempo in the back of my brain. I imagined the acrid dryness of the stage fog, and Fresnel lights strained teal and magenta through industrial gels. Scouring latex paint off my hands, beneath my nails, with sawdust in the air. I missed the weirdness and queerness and openness of the people at the theater. Their gathered confidence. Those typed-and-stapled rules confirming that students and teachers alike were *professionals*. As professionals, they were all *going somewhere*. This was where I had first thought that it might even be possible for me to go to Chicago.

Now, Charles wanted *me* in the production. He had called me *multiple* times, at home and at school. I was important to them. Both Charles Letts and May Dunham had decided that I was someone worth bothering with. Their efforts argued against the blue currents in the surrounding air.

After my magnet class, I caught the bus to Campus Akawe and sludged the last block to the theater. One of my socks crunched snow and turned wet. I knelt and inspected my boot. The seam had split at the heel. The other boot was also starting to split. How much more winter did I have left? Two months? It could keep snowing until the middle of April. How much longer did Lucy have, or God, or Adam's mom? It didn't matter right now. I could warm myself in the heat of the theater.

The lobby was unlocked, but nobody else had arrived yet. I cleaned out my boot in the bathroom and wrung my socks out over the sink. I brushed my hair with my hands in the mirror. I went back and sat on the floor with my back against one of the giant windows that looked out over the commons. The flagstone floor was cold, but air from the furnace blew warm around me. Auditions wouldn't start until six, so I started on my homework. I dissected proofs and chewed on a package of Saltines that May had given me after lunch. I got thirsty, but the drinking fountain had been shut off, so I took a chance slurping water from one of the bathroom sinks. I finished my math and started on biology. The assignments in Mrs. Clark's class were getting harder and harder, like she'd given herself a mission to flunk as many students as she could. Eventually, the sun sank behind the museum across the street. Other kids started showing up.

I tried to focus on my homework, but it was getting harder and harder as the din of conversation rose around me. I caught myself grinning. I knew a lot of these kids. They had been my friends for more than a year now, though I'd mostly ignored them since the start of ninth grade. Again, I felt like an asshole, but at least these kids would forgive me. Shit, they wouldn't even think that there wasn't anything to forgive. I wasn't surprised when I caught a fist prodding my shoulder. I looked up to see Nova as the last licks of sunlight blazed across his orange dreads.

"Hey, man!" I said.

"Hey," he said. "Didn't think you'd be here."

"Why not? I been here plenty."

"Not lately. Word is you was kicked out by your parents."

"You want to know the truth about it? Kinda yeah, kinda no. I mean, my mother kicked me out, but I don't think she really meant it. I think she thought I'd want to come back. But I didn't. I mean, I haven't."

"Street sleepin'?"

"Fuck no!" I laughed nervously. "In this cold?"

The cold was right there. Waiting. It was right on the other side of the huge surrounding windows.

"Freeloading at Adam's?"

Freeloading? I thought. *Yes. That's what I am. A freeloader. Or a sucker. Or ...* "Some of that. But I've only been there a few nights." I coughed and thought. *Why am I trusting Nova? I thought I didn't like Nova.* I realized that Nova alone had held out for me after I'd dropped all of my other new friends. "Mostly, I've been staying out by Hastings with some other people. I'm going out that way tonight."

"Damn, man. That bus ride'll kill you. I always figured you were the stable one, and Adam was gonna get himself fucked up. Now it looks like the opposite, right?"

"No, I still think he's probably more fucked up than I am."

"Are you kidding? He's taking care of his mom *and* his grandma! And did you know he has a boyfriend now?"

"*What?!* No, he didn't tell me!"

"Well, maybe he didn't have a chance to. You *did* only mooch off his grandpa for a few nights."

"How long they been, um, together?"

"A week, I think. This dude from the Catholic school. Name's Dylan."

499

"Holy shit!"

"I know. He's very shy about it."

Maybe he was, but I couldn't understand how Nova knew and I, Adam's best friend, didn't.

A minute later, August opened the double doors leading into the dark auditorium and invited us inside.

At some point, I'd figured out that Charles and August were more than just "roommates," although they never said anything to indicate otherwise. As we entered the auditorium, I wondered if Adam and Dylan would be able to be more open in whatever future they had together. And then I wondered about Nova. By then, I'd realized that he wasn't really as straight as an arrow, but the word "gay" didn't seem to stick to him either. None of us knew how to talk about these things. We just felt our way as best as we could.

Since the last play, the lima bean green block walls had been repainted in shades of light and dark gray. The space seemed more adult now. More serious. From what Charles had told me, this sounded like it was going to be a serious play.

I took a seat next to Nova. Chris and Shannon were sitting a couple rows ahead of us and waved. Majenta was here too, though she didn't wave. There were close to a hundred kids here, but I knew Jeremy from Western, Lavonte and Diamond from Southern, Peter from Northern, and Crispin from the Junior College. Clare from Sellers, Laura from Elmwood, Brisbane from Owen, Johnny from Parc Pierre, and Katy from Sterlingville. I knew another dozen or so kids by face, even if I couldn't remember their names.

Charles got up in front of us. He hadn't changed much in the last year. He still had the same tidy mustache and a thin crown of blond hair. Maybe that hair was grayer than it had been before, but I still figured he was a bit younger than my parents.

"A few years ago," he said. "I had an idea that we should do an 'everything' play about life here in Akawe. I mean, you have all seen a lot here, haven't you? I certainly have. Now obviously we aren't going to be able to actually do a play about 'everything,' and it isn't going to be *about* everybody, because this is a youth theater. Obviously, it couldn't just be a 'normal' play, because how is a play like that going to talk about all the – well, the difficulties happening in this city right now."

People were listening. It wasn't like class at Eastern where we shouted down the listless subs. We could see Charles in the beaming house lights, and we all cared about what he had to say. He went on:

"This year, we sent surveys out to all of the ninth graders in the Akawe Public Schools, and asked them about the challenges they've been through. About their families. About the lead in the water, and the fires, and the serial killer, and the school closings, and the demolitions. I'm sure you know it better than I do, but these are a lot of things for young people to have to live through. Those surveys are the basis of this script and of this production. Everything you will read comes straight from the surveys we sent out. We got almost a thousand of them. If you get cast in the play, these are the words you'll be reading."

I wasn't an actor. I felt more comfortable with tech. But I went up on stage and faced the auditorium. The stage lights were bright on my face. They were hot. Directors always warn actors about the focused heat of those powerful lamps. A nimbus of gold came between myself and everyone watching. It was easy to forget that I was addressing a small group of auditionees, and to imagine that I was talking to an audience of several hundred people. They would be older, most of them. Suburbanites. White people. They would mostly be people who had left Akawe when things had started going south. Who had left us all behind. I started reading the words I'd been given:

"I almost shot my sister –" My voice broke.

Holy shit, I could have been reading for Adam. *That happened.*

I read ahead. *I am reading for Adam. This must be from the survey he filled out.*

Everyone was waiting. I fixed my eyes on the red exit sign. I didn't want to cry. I wanted to say these words and go home. I wanted to give this audience a truth without giving them more of myself. A look at the *people* they had left behind. A look at the situations and decisions that we face every day. I wanted them to *get* us. But I didn't want them to *claim* us. We weren't *theirs*. We belonged to *ourselves*.

I started again:

"I almost shot my sister. She was standing outside my house and banging on my back door, and I thought she was someone else who was going to come in and hurt me. I didn't know who she was, but I pointed a gun at her anyway. I am so glad I didn't pull that trigger. I'm stupid all the time, but I was never as stupid as I was that morning."

Riding the #9 out to Quanla's felt a bit like going back into the past. I had been to her house dozens of times during elementary school when I held Quanla in my mind like a sacred star too perfect to understand. Now, many of the neighborhoods that separated us had been torn down. I rode through the Old River District. Poplar Street, where the old lumber barons had built their Victorian mansions. Some of these had been rehabbed, rebuilt, refinished. More of them had been boarded up or demoed. Westward, the ranch houses of South Branch flowed into the Hastings Corridor, and we passed the Palisades just a few blocks from Chuck's house. Quanla lived further out near the city limits, where the fast-food chains and liquor stores were still going strong. If each block had been pitted with a few vacant lots, the rest had neatly mowed lawns in front of prim brick and vinyl-sided houses, smiling out. Waiting for spring.

The Adams' green cinderblock house had certainly not been built with the same sense of status as the others on the block, but today it was in better shape than any of them. Mark came to the door as soon as I knocked. The man never seemed to age. He had a heavy mustache, straight out of the 70s, and his smile was warm and genuine.

"Glad you're here, John," he said. "It's almost ten."

"I'm sorry," I said. "You know the buses. I got here as fast as I could."

"Come on in."

"You talked to my parents?"

"Yeah, yeah, they know you're here. Wish it wasn't like this, but come on."

Nothing to do but go in. I crossed the threshold and kicked off my shoes. We found Kimmy sitting in the living room with Darius and Qunala, their faces illuminated by the tv. As I entered, Quanla looked at me out of the corner of her eye, and I saw her curiosity.

"We're watching *Shawshank Redemption*," she said. I perched myself on a chair and took a handful of popcorn. I didn't want to look at anyone. I ate and got another handful. I hadn't had anything to eat since lunch except that pack of Saltines. We watched Tim Robbins burst out of the mud, covered in rain and shit.

"Guess we're near the end," I said.

The movie finished.

"We're off to bed," said Kimmy. "Don't stay up too late."

"John," said Mark. "There are some sheets and blankets in the closet there. Make yourself comfortable. If you want, I can give you a ride to school in the morning. You're right. Those buses take a long time."

"Thank you," I said.

Kimmy and Mark went upstairs to their room, leaving me sitting with Quanla and Darius. He was reading some piece of crumpled paper he'd fished out of his backpack. Quanla watched the endless sequence of names as they scrolled up with the movie credits. *Are they trying to think of something to say?* I wondered. *Well, I'm not going to say anything first.* But then my stomach growled angrily. I covered my belly with my arms, but Quanla and Darius busted up laughing, and I started laughing too.

"Sorry," I said. "I'm starving."

"We've got Hot Pockets," Quanla said. "Mom keeps 'em as snacks for herself, but I don't think she'll mind or even notice if you just take one or two."

"Ham and cheese okay?" asked Darius.

"Sure," I said.

Darius led me into the kitchen. While I microwaved the Hot Pocket, he grabbed me a bag of Cheetos and a couple of cheese sticks. I felt relieved. I had worried, in the silence, that they were pissed off at me. Darius rocked on his heels while we waited for the microwave to ding. I found myself remembering his quiet, diligent work in Ms. Ropoli's classroom, and then I remembered him dancing with her at the rave.

"So," I asked, "you bangin' my old social studies teacher?"

"Shhhht!" he hissed sharply. "Shit, man! They don't know about her!" He gave his head a sharp jerk toward the stairs. He looked at me seriously. "You didn't know Q knew, either. You know what happens to snitches!"

I laughed. "You never did shit to snitches, Darius!"

"There's a first time for everything," he muttered. "Besides, I remember how you flipped on her. You should go talk to her, John. She likes you. Respects you a lot as a student. And I get you were pissed off about shit, but she wasn't able to deal with it well because you've just got six teachers, and she's got, like, two hundred students."

"She tell you this?" I asked.

"No. Just what I figured out. You're both dumb to be pissed off at each other, if you ask me."

When we got back, the credit scroll had finally finished. Quanla turned off the television.

"You know," she said. "I know all about Ms. Ropoli."

"Yeah, but you don't know her," said Darius.

"No, *you* don't know her. You just think you do. As long as you don't know her, like, Biblically."

"Get your mind out of the gutter!"

"So you aren't, like, going out with her?" I asked.

"What is this, the Spanish Inquisition?"

Quanla laughed. "You know nobody expected us."

Darius laughed despite himself.

"Angela really likes me," he said. "She wants to help me get into college. She says she can help me with that ... and it's good, you know, because my parents never went to college."

"So ..."

"My Independent Study. It's about the Water Disaster. She's saying if we finish it in time, I can send it in with my college applications. She thinks it has a good chance."

"She know you call her by her first name?" asked Quanla.

"Angela Ropoli," he said. He shrugged. "That's her name."

For as much as I had obsessed over Quanla over the years, I'd never given a lot of thought to Darius. He was her older brother. Like Selby's older brothers, Darius got to do things that the rest of us didn't. And like Selby's brothers, he usually ignored us or complained about how we annoyed him. I now realized that he was a world apart from them. George Demnescu moved with confidence and swagger. Demetrius sat in attitude and rebellion. But Darius' attitude was a front. He didn't believe it. I still thought of him as the kid with the driver's license who gave my friends and me rides all over town. I had a feeling that the jocks and bangers at Southern didn't think too much of him.

"Are you thinking," I said, "like, you graduate and tell her how you feel, and since you're not a student, she might want to ..."

Darius glared at me. Quanla was watching me too.

"I mean," I said. "She is divorced."

"Yeah, her ex-husband's an asshole."

"What else do you know about her, John?" said Quanla.

"She isn't from Akawe. She doesn't understand. But I think she tries to. I mean, I think she tries too hard."

"Can we please talk about something else?" asked Darius. His discomfort had grown as the conversation went on. I didn't want to press him anymore, but I felt as reluctant to talk about my secrets as Darius was to talk about his, so I turned my questions upon Quanla.

"What have you been up to?" I hurriedly asked her. "I haven't talked to you in, like, forever."

Quanla smiled, and I knew that she had noticed my evasion.

"Like three months."

"How's your singing?"

"It's funny you'd ask that. When I got to Southern, I wanted to join the AV Club. I've been watching a lot of movies, you see, and wondering about how they do the special effects. Wondering about how they write the scripts, cast the actors. You hear about a film and how, they'll say, back in the 50s or something, 'they shot it on a tiny budget of like $50,000.' And that always sounded like a lot of money to me. So, I wanted to understand that too. Well, I got to Southern and found out that the AV Club closed down years ago. They just never took it out of the student handbook."

"Same thing happened with me and the Chess Club at Eastern!"

"Right. Well, anyway, there's my English teacher, Mr. Bedford. And he likes movies too. We read *Romeo and Juliet* in class, but I think he was more excited about showing us the Zeffirelli version than he was in talking about Shakespeare! Anyway, I asked him about the AV Club, and he said that if I wanted to restart it, he'd be the faculty contact. I put up signs and made an announcement on the PA and talked to people, and we got five or six kids to join. And it's been really wonderful, John. We meet once a week, and we put together these screenings that we have after school once a month, and none of it costs anything – I mean, we don't have any money – because everything is free or donated. And I'm hoping that this spring we can have this screenwriter and TV casting director from Detroit come and talk to us. But it *is* taking a lot of time. And with that, and homework, something had to go ... and it was singing!"

"And your mom let you?"

"She was pissed!" said Darius.

"Yeah," said Quanla. "She said I had to keep singing, and that was that. But I told her no. That I was going to run away if I couldn't be in AV Club. She wasn't happy about that, either. But she finally agreed to it, and we had a good talk about it a month ago. She said I've got my whole life to worry about how to earn my bread. If I want to learn about something I love, it's good for me to do it now."

"That's hard advice," I said.

"It's good advice. Not everyone can make money doing what they want. But anyway, that's that. You're acting like you don't want to talk about, but you know that what I want to know. Things at Eastern. With you and Selby, and Michael, and Adam, and Lucy."

I couldn't dodge any longer, but I took a long breath to think. I didn't want to tell them everything. I decided to start with what was easy: I told them about how Michael had gotten a girlfriend but was still having a hard time adjusting to Parc Pierre. I told them about Adam's reunion with his mom. I even pretended to know all about his new boyfriend, Dylan.

It was harder with Lucy. I didn't want to share the worst thing – the essential thing – because it felt like a violation of her privacy. And because it meant, again, looking at *what had happened* and saying it out loud.

"She just broke up with her boyfriend," I finally said. "She's having a shitty year."

I didn't have much to say about Selby, either. I didn't want to give away her secrets, and I hadn't really hung out with her at all except for at her New Year's Eve party.

"She's doing fine, I guess. You know her; she's always going through some shit."

"And what about you, John?" asked Quanla.

And what about me? This girl I like that I dumped two months ago? This play I auditioned for that hasn't been cast yet? O-Sugar? The Ostyns? Urbantasms? My parents? Blue shadows following me through the day since I took the drug?

I looked anxiously into the corners of the room, but the shadows there were ordinary shadows.

"I'm just trying to make it through the winter," I said. "My father started drinking again when he lost his job. And my mother's cheating on him. Last month I just kind of went crazy from it all. I skipped school a lot, and I did a lot of … drugs. My grades got really bad. But more shit kept happening. My mother told me to leave. And I left. And now they want me to come back. And I keep saying, 'not yet.' I don't want to go back until I've figured my own shit out. Until they've figured their shit out."

Quanla's face fell when I mentioned the drugs, and the feeling was even worse than when I'd told Michael. But I didn't let myself look away from her because doing the drugs had been my decision, and I needed to own it. When I finished, Quanla took a deep breath, and she looked more tired than she had before.

"Isn't it crazy how fast everything just falls apart?" she said. "Your parents always seemed really happy to me."

"Yeah, I thought they were too. I knew they were stressed out and busy and broke, but … I mean, not that long ago …"

I thought about Christmas vacation. Sleeping on the floor when the power went out. Painting my room.

"Whatever," I said. "I'm not going through anything too bad. Other people have it a lot worse."

I thought about the warmth and companionship I had found with Adam, and Chuck, and Michael, and now here. I thought about all of the cold and empty houses, waiting. I shuddered.

But Quanla said: "What you're going through is still a big deal, John. Don't minimize it. You're strong, John. You're strong for still trying. For going to school. For trying out for plays."

"Whatever."

"It's true."

"She's right," said Darius.

I looked at them, smiling in their confidence and reassurance. I measured their real innocence against the feigned innocence of Eli Ostyn. *No way,* I thought. *I'm not going to tell them about urbantasms and suicide and contemplated murder. They want to be happy tonight, and they deserve to be.*

"Actually," I said. "There is something else going on. But it's weird. There's this girl."

"Oooh," said Quanla, her voice teasing, "and your parents don't even know!"

"I think she's retarded," I said.

They laughed.

"No, listen, I ... I'm serious. I mean, I don't know if she actually is 'mentally retarded,' because I don't know how they measure that. But she is really, like ... she was held back, and I don't think it was because she was skipping class or anything. I don't think she was smart enough to ... I mean. She isn't a burnout. She doesn't do drugs, I don't think. She just ... her brain just ... I don't even know what I'm saying."

"And *you* like her?" asked Quanla.

"I don't know why. I feel better when I'm with her. It's like she cares about people too much. But you don't meet many people like that."

"I always thought Michael was kind of like that."

"No. I mean, I get what you mean about Michael. And Elizabeth, too. Jesus, I miss Elizabeth! Why didn't we keep in touch with her?" I shuddered at the memory of Elizabeth at the rave. "But Michael and Elizabeth, they care for everybody, and that includes themselves. May cares about everybody else, and it's like she forgets herself. I feel weird about that. I don't know what to do about it. I don't think I've met anybody else like that before. And the thing is, I think she likes me too. She makes me feel like I'm seen. I hope I make her feel like she's seen. You know? But then I also look at the things she talks about.

Baking cookies and lip balm and McDonald's, and she lives in this weird little house with this messed up mural, and –"

"If you connect with her," said Darius "If you *can* talk with her ... I don't know, John, does it really matter the exact things you're talking about? Or whether she's been held back or whatever?"

I thought he had a point. But maybe he didn't, and I didn't care, because I was just bending things that way, because I really just wanted to go out with May.

By morning, my vision had finally recovered, and the blue tracers and apparitions had faded away. I was fully in the ordinary world again, and I felt a powerful temptation to try to be normal. Was I *really* going to move against God Ostyn? What about Selby's plots? Yeah, they had spilled into my life, but I could probably ignore them if I was determined. What about Lucy's agony? But that was a huge thing, bigger than me. What could I do about that, even? I didn't *have* to think about these things.

If I wanted – and I *wanted* – I could think instead about May Dunham and *Teen Age Riot*. I knew that Michael was reading up on the chemicals and that the sunglasses were safely hidden in the hole of the tree, and that was enough for now.

By now, I'd managed to sell most of my teachers on my seriousness about schoolwork this semester. At least the teachers who were left. Mr. Russell vanished at the end of the semester, and Mrs. Dimitri had soon followed. Now we had subs who didn't know the lesson plans or anybody's names.

Days passed. I saw Selby in the hallway, but as she had asked, I avoided talking to her or looking at her. I put off calling Michael. I told myself that he could use the extra time to continue his research. I did call the theater and discovered that I had been cast in Ensemble A, whatever that was supposed to mean. Our first rehearsal wasn't going to be until the following Monday. That meant that my Friday was free. I had something that I wanted to say.

"Hey May," I said at lunch after Lucy had left.

"Yes?" she asked.

"What are you doing after school tomorrow?"

"I have to drop my dad's car off to get the transmission fixed, and then I have to walk to my mom's house."

"Is that going to take a long time?"

"Oh, yeah. It's a long ways."

"Oh. Because I was wondering if you'd like to go out with me on Friday."

"Do you mean on a date?"

"Yeah. I do. Do you want to go on a date with me?"

"Okay. Do you want to go on a date to drop off my car?"

She looked off through a far-away window, and the light glowed upon her face. I could guess what she was thinking: dropping off her car wasn't a romantic evening ... but could it *be* romantic if she did it as a date? I realized that I knew the answer.

"I'll go anywhere with you," I said.

"It could be fun," she admitted. "We could get something to eat and walk to my mom's. We could get cold, but we won't because we'll bundle up!"

"Yes. I can't wait."

The night passed.

I had dreams about swollen faceless women giving birth to water-filled plastic bags. Grocery bags tied at the top with tight knots. After the bags came out, the nurses and doctors punctured them with serrated knives and the salty, grainy water spilled out onto the tiled floor. I woke up with a taste of copper in my mouth.

I got dressed.

I brushed my teeth.

I imagined the smell of balled-up diapers and the rainbow-colored stickers on the charts at Proctor hospital, where Chuck's mom worked. I imagined Adam's Grandpa A shooting a feral dog that had charged him outside his house. I imagined Quanla's dad showing up to work at Starr City, putting on his gloves and safety goggles, and blowing the metal shavings from his worktable. I saw pastel clouds overhead. I touched raw circuitry. It all felt strange and dear to me. These places and things. Even the tragedies. Because I had witnessed them and they had witnessed me, and we had partaken of each other. We had all been together, and now we were becoming something else. The whole world felt cold and dear and strange.

The day finally ended, and the bells rang, and everyone slammed their lockers shut, and it was time to meet May and leave the beautiful, haunted school together.

May shrugged on her coat but left her backpack behind.

"No homework?" I asked.

"I don't do it on weekends," she said. "It's too hard, and there's no point. I don't like it, okay? Are you going to hold my hand?"

"Sure."

Our palms kissed. The doors parted. It was warmer than I'd expected outside, though a wind cut against us from the west. I was looking for the beat-up Aubrey, but instead, May took us to a glittering brown Benedict. Its trunk was black, and the passenger front door was red. Other than that, it was your standard-issue mid-80s Armada. The kind of huge, awful car that your grandparents drove to the Republican fundraiser. We got in.

"Is this your car?" I asked.

"It's actually my dad's," May said. "He wanted me to get it fixed before he got home."

She turned the key, and the car roared into life. We did a gentle donut and turned out onto Valley Street. The car wasn't going very fast, but it sounded like it was about to spit its engine out through the hood, so May put on her hazards and coasted along at an easy ten.

"It hasn't been normal since my dad and his friend Curt tried putting hydros on it."

I shook my head. I couldn't believe this shit.

We drove south, and the view to our left was filled by the sprawling mass of Starrville, its brown, corrugated walls and stocky smokestacks as tall as anything downtown, with hundreds of freight cars parked out front. On our other side, cars flashed north and south on I-63. We finally cleared the factories, and Valley curled away rightward, over the creek and under the expressway, and became Starr Highway. We passed the Unitarian Church, a plain-looking building with a half-timber veneer and giant vertical windows that looked out over a wooded lot. A hundred cars packed the parking lot. A placard read:

THE SEEDS OF HOPE
WORDS WITH GAYLORD NELSON

"It doesn't look like it now," said May. "But this car used to be way pimped. But the stereo got stolen." There was a black hole in the middle of the console. "But it would just blast out the song about the chariot coming down."

"You mean like church music?" I asked.

"No, the other one."

"The funky one?" I was trying to remember my mother's record collection.

"No!" she said, exasperated. "The *other* one! The one where he's cutting off peoples' heads and leaving them all over."

"I don't remember that one."

"My dad would take us all out to Sellers, and we'd get ice cream. I'd get the strawberry ice cream with a cherry on top. Cherries are my favorite fruit, John, okay? Don't forget that. It's important, in case you want to buy me something sometime."

We crossed Aurelius, then turned right onto Whitmore. This was *my* neighborhood. What would happen if we ran into my parents? How would I introduce May? What would they say? What would *she* say? How could I protect her from their cynicism?

"Hey May," I said. "Where are you getting your car fixed?"

"Just up here a bit."

"Is it anywhere near my house?"

"I don't remember. It's all up here!"

As it turned out, the body shop was less than two blocks from Agit Street. I could almost see my house from the parking lot. I *could* see Bennett's house. *Where is it?* It was gone. *Has it been demoed?* A pile of snow-crusted, hard-graveled dirt was all that remained of the unfortunate house. *Holy shit. I've only been gone for, like, two weeks.*

We dropped the car off, and May gave the cashier an index card with her dad's pager number written neatly in blue ink on the top line. We started our walk back south along Whitmore. As we passed Agit, I anxiously looked down toward my own house. Yup, the car was there, but I didn't see anyone in the windows, so I guessed we were safe. Then we passed Radcliffe, and I remembered how I'd woken up on the roof on the morning after May's birthday party. I finally relaxed when Whitmore bent southward and aimed itself toward the suburbs.

We passed the Kaleidoscope Coney Island. It had gone out of business two years ago. Although the inside hadn't been much to look at, I had memories of the building's glittering marquis, with metal lettering mounted upon a frame of illuminated multicolored plastic. After the restaurant had closed, someone had cut the marquis down and hauled it off. They had replaced it with a pale banner promising a new Middle Eastern restaurant "OPEN SOON," but another year had pressed against the vacant restaurant, and eventually the new sign had also crumpled up and vanished into the wind.

"So, I've met Drake," I said. "But I haven't met your parents. What's your mom like?"

"She's a doctor," May said. "She's very busy. I don't see her a lot. She's kind of a bitch."

We passed the Bread Loaf bakery. I still remembered when my father had taken me in to buy donuts on windy spring afternoons after Mass. The bakery had held out for many years, but it had finally failed, its windows dark, its doors destroyed.

"I like holding your hand," I said. "But my hands are getting really cold, and I can't feel my fingers anymore."

"Yeah, mine too."

We put our hands in our pockets.

"You could kiss me instead," May said.

I leaned in and kissed her. Her lips were waxy from the cherry balm, and I smelt the faint scent of cherries before the damp wind stole it way. This was our first kiss, and it felt like summer.

We started walking again. The sun was already starting to slide down the sky, lending its golden luster to May's face, her sharp profile rippling across the burnt-out contours of every smashed building we passed.

"Are we going out?" I asked her.

"No," she said. "You haven't even asked me out, and I haven't said 'yes!'"

We walked, and while it was clear what I was supposed to do next, I wanted to hold the question in the future for another moment. To enjoy the anticipation of something happy and good.

"Will you go out with me?" I finally asked.

"No," she said. "You asked me out before, and I said 'yes,' and you weren't very nice to me. So, I don't think you get to ask me out a second time."

We walked on for another block without speaking, and I was turning her words over in my head. Was she right? Or was she teasing me? *She could be both right and teasing me*, I thought. In either case, I trusted her, but my heart was pounding hard.

We passed the broken ruins of a supermarket.

We passed the eroded foundation of a former notary public.

We passed a used bookstore, still fully stocked, with dusty paperbacks climbing its windowsills, but the place had been padlocked for months.

Whitmore Road was clearly following the trajectories of Trevithick and Intervale and Orion into ruin. *Who would ever claim this?* I wondered. *Who would ever want this?*

Connor Coyne

"Are you in love with me, John?" May asked.

I didn't think I was allowed to answer with anything other than a yes or a no. I also knew that I was supposed to answer honestly. So, I stopped walking. I let her words fill me. I let them fill my whole body so that I could become the words of the answer that I gave her. We stood on Whitmore Road. And yet, for all Whitmore's racked torment, the horizon started to swell the sun, and its ambering glow transformed the snow into crystalline sand. The wind stilled for a moment. The sky was cloudless and clear, the blue of sunlight scattered, not the blue of urbantasms. And May was with me here. And nobody else seemed to see this as we saw it. And we were alone together in it all.

"Yes," I said. "I do love you."

"I love you too," she said.

We passed an empty ice cream stand, its windows pocked with massive holes.

We passed an empty tattoo parlor whose front door had been wrenched from its hinges.

We passed an empty dog grooming salon, its bricks graffitied with sloppy tags.

"Will you go out with me, John?" May asked.

And then my heart exploded through my chest and painted the entire street, the shuttered businesses, the houses and lights, the salty soil, the massed clay, the bedrock, and saturated the sky.

"Yes," I said.

May smiled, put her hand in my coat pocket, gripped my hand, and squeezed.

We didn't speak for a long time after that. There just wasn't anything else that we needed to say. The silence bound us instead of holding us apart. After a few blocks, May started humming some song I vaguely recognized but couldn't place. She picked up a stick and trailed it through the snow as we went, etching hieroglyphics whose secret meaning could be easily decoded, but only until the warmth returned. And I tried to study everything I saw.

It was as if everything had transformed, intimately and irrevocably. Black birds perched upon the splintered tips of telephone poles. Desolate storefronts leaned into their own shadows. Smoking sedans packed the salt-streaked parking lot of the fishmongers' shop, one of the few businesses still open on Whitmore.

"Do you like fish?" asked May.

"Fried fish," I said.

"You ever eat there?"

"Not yet."

And so we came at last to Starr Highway again, and I witnessed the crumpled napkins on the sidewalk at the Taco Bell, and the African braid shop with its glass frosted from steam inside, and all the tracks of the passing cars that pressed the ice cream snow into slush. The sun continued to sail west before us as we walked the hills that led past the fiery spires of the Temple Medical Center.

"My aunt died there," I said. "She had cancer. She was too young."

"I'm sorry your aunt died," said May. "I don't like hospitals."

And then we reached the river, and we stood in the middle of the bridge and watched the water flow beneath us as the ice cracked into fragments, taking their first tentative turns on the long journey that ended at the sea.

We finally reached a tiny drive-through coney island with a cemetery stretching out behind it. It was called the Coney Planet, and while I didn't see any cars in the parking lot, a line cook was doing his dance behind the fogged glass.

"Here we are!" said May.

I squinted in through the windows.

"It's a drive-thru," I said. "There isn't anywhere to sit."

"Yes, there is."

She pointed to a couple of circular red tables bolted to the concrete patio in front of the drive-thru. They each sported their own red-and-white-striped umbrella, even though it was the middle of February.

"Are you kidding?!" I said.

"You've got gloves, don't you?"

"No, I've just got my pockets!"

"You can have mine."

"No, that's okay."

We sat down.

"Are you going to order for me?" May asked.

"Yeah. Um ... I don't have any money."

"That's okay. I've got some."

She gave me a twenty.

"I'll pay you back," I said.

"Why would you do that?"

"What do you want?"

"A cherry Coke and a gyro, please."

She pronounced it "jie ro," but plenty of people do.

I went up to the window, and the bored line cook took my order. I came back with two trays: one with May's food and one with my coney, coffee, and fries. We ate. The coney was all right. The coffee tasted like water, but at least it warmed my hands. I laughed a little.

"This is a strange date!" I said.

May rocked in place and nodded.

"I love the gyro sauce," she said.

"I think it's pronounced 'you row.'"

She shrugged.

"I still love the sauce."

May took another bite and laughed before swallowing. She started to cough on it. For a moment, I thought she was going to choke, but the look of alarm on my face must have amused her more because she laughed and coughed even harder. Soon her nose was running, and there were tears in her eyes. She wiped them away, still grinning.

"Do you know?" she said when she had finally recovered. "One time, I went to the drug store and bought a pair of reading glasses because I thought they would make people think that I was smarter?"

"What?"

"Yes, I did! You know how in movies and on TV the smart person always wears glasses? They always do! Well, people were always saying how dumb I was, so I got this pair of glasses, and I started wearing them so people wouldn't know or say any more about me."

I didn't know what to say.

"I thought it was working," she said. "The glasses. But then Drake told me it wasn't. He said that they were only making things worse. He told me that I had to listen to the way people say things. Not what they say, because they could just be lying if they're saying, like, they like your hair, or they like your outfit, or you're so nice. But how they say it lets you know what they really think of you. Like who they are looking at when they say it. Or if they make their words sound really long and stuff. I really thought about that a lot, what he told me. I didn't forget it. Anyway, I know smart girls. Some of them even have STDs. They're supposed to be smart, but they don't even know how not to get them! But some of them are nice. But most boys are mean to you."

I wanted to tell May that I had never called her stupid, but I had, many times. Just that week, I had told Quanla and Darius that I thought she was borderline retarded.

May continued: "Drake and my dad tell me I'm stupid, but they don't mean it to be mean. My mom also tells me I'm stupid, and she does mean it to be mean. God. Thank God I don't live with her very often! I know so many people think I'm stupid, so I always start out thinking that people think that, but some people I don't think do. You probably do. Though I believe you that you love me. I know that Selby thinks I'm stupid. I don't think Lucy does. There are just ways I can tell. She looks at me when she is talking to me. And she doesn't say her words strange like Drake told me people do. I don't think Eli thinks I'm stupid, either. And I do *not* like Eli. He is not a good person. But he is good in that way, I guess."

"What do you think?" I asked. "Do you think you're stupid?"

"I don't know!" Her voice was loud, and her eyes wide. Her arms flew out in exasperation. "Which I guess means yes, because a smart person would know if she was stupid, but a stupid person would never know, right? And if I'm so stupid – like a retard – like how am I even supposed to even know if I *am* one? Right?! I just don't know why people are mean, though. Like they are mean to Drake because he's in a wheelchair, but then they were always mean to him, and I know I see people being mean to my dad, too!"

"But May, at your birthday party, you understood what was going on with Lucy, and I didn't. I don't even think Eli did! You did, and you were the one who was able to calm her down. I mean, I didn't even want to talk to her. I didn't even want to look at her after what she did, and it had to seem just as awful to you as it did to me, but while I took a bunch of drugs and ran off, you stayed with her and tried to make her feel better! Doesn't that make you smarter than me? And better than me? I mean, like a better person? I mean, doesn't that make you smarter and better than anyone else at your party?"

"It isn't the same thing, okay?!" she said. "Anyway, I'm going to eat my food now because I'm hungry."

We ate in silence for a few minutes.

"Did anyone tell you that I got tricked into sex?" she said.

"No."

"Yeah, because I'm stupid!"

"I don't think –" I started. *Ugh. Does it matter what I think?* "Lots of people we know have gotten tricked. You don't have to be stupid to get tricked. For some asshole to –"

"Yeah, well, some boyfriends really hate that, and dumped me, and called me a slut after they heard about that, so ... you ... if you think –"

She suddenly hit the table. I was quiet, but she thought my silence was ambivalence.

"It wasn't my fault!" she said. "Even if I was stupidm it wasn't my fault, and even if I wasn't stupid, it still wasn't my fault, okay?!"

"I know. I know. Of course, it wasn't your fault."

"And you don't care?"

"I kind of want to kill the fucker that tricked you, but it doesn't change how I see you. Anyway, I had sex too. When I was thirteen. I wasn't tricked. But it didn't feel very good, either. I mean, I worried about a lot."

"Uh huh. Well, I just want to tell you all this stuff now, so if you're going to dump me, you can do it now, and I won't have to worry that you'll hear about it and want to dump me later."

"No. I don't."

"It wasn't serious when you asked me out before because before, I could tell you didn't mean it. The way you asked me. But this time, you're serious, and I'm serious, so just don't lie or be mean, okay?"

"Can I hug you?" I asked.

"Yes! Please hug me!"

I leaned over the table and hugged her. She hugged me back, hard. My coat knocked my coney and fries onto the ground, but we held each other for a long time. Finally, we sat down again. She began carefully wrapping her gyro in the wrapper again.

"Are you going to pick that up?" she asked, pointing to the trash on the ground.

"Um, yeah, sure," I said.

I gathered my garbage and carried it over to the trash can.

"People should try to be clean," she said. "Will you please go and get me a bag for my leftovers like a gentleman does?"

I got her a bag from the checkout.

"Thank you," she said.

By the time we started walking again, the sun had set, and the world had gone purple and gray. We followed Starr Highway west across Elmwood Road and into the quiet side streets of South Branch. That's where things started to go sideways for me.

For a moment, I didn't understand what was happening. I felt a lurch in space, the sidewalk shaking under my feet, and my vision exploded in violent phosphenes. Then I caught the blue ghosts gliding by on every side, watching me as they passed, and I knew what corner I'd turned.

"Shit," I said.

May's hand tightened around mine.

"What is it?" she asked.

"I, I ... fuck," I muttered. "They're here. They're all around me."

Space collapsed beneath me, and I felt like I was being folded into another, distant part of the universe. I saw rotting wood collapsing into rotting wood collapsing into an improvised blue coffin that clapped itself together around me.

May's hand got tighter.

"You're having a flashback," she said. "It's the O-Sugar."

"It can do that?" I said. "I didn't think I'd have to deal with this shit!"

"You don't get to decide. It decides, not you. This happened to Drake. Hold my hand. It isn't real."

"It's real! I can taste wood in my mouth!"

"It isn't real, John. It isn't there."

I heard syncopated drums strumming angrily across the contracting space. I smelled humus and rain. I saw my Grandfather Richter's blue corpse floating before me on a cloud of blue fireflies.

"Shut up," he croaked. "It isn't real." He was lying in his bed.

His bed had a mattress of twisting maggots. His blanket, a canvas of woven worms. It was all blue and purple.

"Do you have your sunglasses with you?"

"No! I hid them! So Eli couldn't get them!"

"Then close your eyes. Close your eyes, and I will guide you."

I closed them. My grandfather vanished, but I could still feel space lurching and twining around me. May held my hand tightly.

"Anyway," she was saying, "you took three. Usually, people just take one. It's bad, and I hate it. It almost killed Drake, and now it wants to kill you. Stay standing. Breathe. Now count to eight."

"What?!"

"Count to eight with me. One, two –"

"Why we gonna count to eight?"

"Because it'll help you feel better."

"How is counting to eight gonna help me feel better?!"

"Because eight came after the rest."

I didn't have any idea what she was talking about.

Still, we counted together: "One. Two. Three. Four. Five. Six. Seven. Eight."

And again: "One. Two. Three. Four. Five. Six. Seven. Eight."

And again: "One. Two. Three. Four. Five. Six. Seven. Eight."

And again.

May was right. As we counted, my breathing settled, and the quaking earth beneath me did as well. Slowly, I felt time calm around us, moving at its usual ebb, without tide or swell.

"Do you think you can walk?" May asked.

"I think so," I said. "Yes. I can. I can walk."

"You know that this is going to keep happening to you, right?"

"What? This?"

"It happened to Drake for months. It still happens to him sometimes."

"How often does it happen?"

"I don't know. A lot. You'll have to get some more sunglasses, okay? You'll have to keep counting to yourself when it happens."

"Are we far from your mom's house?"

"Not far now."

When it was built, probably right after the Second World War, May's mom's house in South Branch could have been a clone of her dad's house in Lestrade. But things had changed over the years. While the Lestrade house fell apart (except for the Jesus-negative mural on its front wall), the South Branch house had been frosted pristine, a rosy shade of beige, with neat yews and a red maple planted against the curb. Stairs climbed from the driveway to a small concrete porch under a filigreed wrought-iron awning.

May led me up to the front door and knocked.

"I have a key, but she likes me to knock," she explained.

By now, I was standing on my own, and my eyes were open. I keep muttering the numbers to myself, though.

A woman opened the door and glared at us. She had May's eyes and complexion, but she was smaller, barely five feet tall, and she looked at us as though we were cockroaches scurrying across her floor. I tried to smile and look her in the eyes.

"What are you doing here?" she asked May.

"I'm staying the night today," said May. "Remember? I had to drop off dad's car. He's getting back tonight."

"And you couldn't walk back there?"

May laughed. "That's a really long walk, mom!"

Her mom stepped back inside, leaving the door open behind her. May went inside, and I followed. We were standing in a warm living room – it was sweltering, really – with a white shag carpet and the TV playing *Jeopardy* loudly in the background. The air smelled thickly of cloves.

"God dammit, close the door, May!" said her mom.

May ran around me to close it.

"Who is this?"

"This," said May, "is my boyfriend."

"He's your boyfriend?"

"Hi," I said.

"Yeah," said May.

"Since when?"

May took my hand.

"I asked him out today, and he said yes."

"Day one," said the mom. "Let me guess. You met her yesterday."

"No," I said. "I met her, like, six months ago."

"Uh huh. You have a name, 'boyfriend?'"

"His name is John Bridge!" said May.

"Kitty Smith," said her mom.

I held out my hand, and she gave it the most tepid shake ever. She moved over to a coffee table and picked up a mug of what looked like cold tea. Kitty took a drink. The bag had been steeping for so long that the water had turned black.

"Can I get you some tea, John?" she asked.

"Um, sure. Thanks."

She went off into the kitchen. May looked at me, sighed, and sat down on the couch.

"Something wrong with your eyes, John?" came Kitty's voice from the kitchen.

"No!" said May. "He's just tired. And allergic."

"Uh huh."

I heard a microwave beep. Kitty came back in with a steaming mug of tea and pressed it into my hands. I took a sip. It was hot and watery. The steeping had just begun.

"Maybe I should have a look, then," she said.

"No, don't do that, Mom," said May.

"You a stoner, John?" asked Kitty.

"No," I said.

Kitty sniffed.

"She just wants to look at your eyes," muttered May, "because she's an Ayur ... a doctor."

"I'm an Ayurvedic Physician," said Kitty. "The only one in Basadena County. Real medicine. Better than the stuff they peddle at ... those ..." She waved her hand.

"She means the hospitals," May added pointlessly.

"There are hundreds of them around here. Those doctors. Those nurses. There's only one of me."

I nodded. It seemed the polite thing to do.

"You aren't spending the night here, John," said Kitty. "So, don't even ask."

"Mom!" said May.

"Don't worry," I said. "I wasn't going to ask."

"Oh, I wasn't worried," said Kitty. "What did you tell her?"

"What?"

"Is he friends with Drake?"

"No!" said May. "He doesn't even know Drake."

Kitty took a step back and looked at me for a long moment.

"Open your eyes wide, John."

May seemed beside herself in embarrassment, but I obeyed. I looked over Kitty's shoulder, where a small crack split the beige paint in the otherwise seamless wall.

Kitty gave a little grunt.

"I'm not a stoner, Ms. Dunham. I'm just tired, and the bright light hurts, you know?"

"It's Ms. Smith," said Kitty. She picked up and lit a clove cigarette. "You're lucky I was home, May. I've been working at the Mission all day. I had the locks changed like I told you. If you'd have gotten here a half-hour sooner, you'd be locked out."

"I know I told you I was coming tonight," murmured May.

"You need a ride home, John?" asked Kitty.

"No," I said. "I'm not going too far from here. It's an easy walk for me. It was nice to meet you ... Ms. Smith."

Kitty gave me an insipid smile.

May walked me out to the porch. Kitty stayed inside.

"Are you sure that you're okay to get back where you're going?" May asked.

"Yeah. I'm staying with my friends Quanla and Darius ... they're, like, a mile from here, I think. It isn't far."

"I wish I could walk with you."

"I'll be fine. But do I get a kiss?"

May kissed me.

"Goodnight," she said.

"No," I said. "It's a bad night. Because now I'm leaving you. I want to have the last few hours back. I want to have them over again. It won't be good until I get to be with you again."

"What about the bad parts? Your flashback? Or when I spazzed out at the restaurant?"

"Everything is better if I just get to be with you."

"You're sweet."

"You don't even know what you've given me, May."

"Well ... maybe sometime you can tell me."

523

I couldn't spend forever basking in the sunshine of May's morning. The O-Sugar flashback had reminded me of everything else in the atmosphere. When the weekend ended, I'd be back at Eastern with Lucy and Selby and the shadows of Eli haunting the halls. Moreover, Kimmy and Mark Adams had somehow figured out that my eviction from my parents' was more of a self-imposed exile than I had suggested. After they got home from church on Sunday, they told me that they wanted me to meet with my parents again. In person. I didn't want to. I felt like I was running out of time and options.

I caught myself eyeing the phone, wondering if I should call Chuck or just walk over and throw myself on Tammy's mercy. *"Sorry I didn't call like I said, Ms. Coppo, but I was tripping balls."* Or maybe it was time to take a gamble and head back to Adam's. *"Tell me about Dylan, you fucker."* For a moment, I thought again about Chris and Shannon Allard. We'd gotten along fine. But I hadn't talked to them much since I'd broken up with Omara. My "new" friends had now become my "old" friends, or maybe they were just the ignored middle children. I felt weird about asking the Allards for help.

The next day, after school, I took the bus to AYT for our first rehearsal. I took a seat in the house and looked at my other friends filling out the other rows around me. There were a few dozen of us. This was a big cast. Anticipation buzzed through the air like electricity. *"What are we going to do – what are we going to be – here?"* The air was busy with sense and anticipation.

"So, you got in too, huh?" said Nova, sitting down next to me.

"Hey," I said, shifting gears at once. "You think I could crash at your place for a few nights?"

"No foreplay, huh?"

"None whatsoever."

"Yeah. I was wondering when you were going to ask, actually."

Charles got up on the stage, holding a clipboard.

"Welcome," he said, "to the first rehearsal of *Teen Age Riot.*"

The script was unlike anything I had ever read, even at AYT, and this was the same year they had adapted *Candide* for little kids. Really, we were reading more of an advanced outline than a script. The premise was that the young people of our city were subjected to inhuman conditions, and that this sucked, and that we all had a collective responsibility to address the problems in our midst. Simple enough, right?

The script, then, consisted of a sequence of short monologues separated by sprawling arrays of stage directions. Some of these had been arranged on the page in parallel columns to distinguish actions taking place by different ensembles in different areas simultaneously.

"Different areas," in this case, didn't mean downstage left and upstage center. No, when the audience arrived in the rain-soaked parking lot (the production was scheduled to open in April), we'd escort them inside, not through the lobby, but the door to the scene shop. There, our guests would be metaphorically stripped of their identity, made to wear gray sackcloth, separated from their friends and family, and sent into the audience with their seats randomly determined.

During the actual show, each scene consisted of three parts: a poem recited over a shifting kaleidoscope of music, a short sequence of spoken monologues, and then a choreographed sequence. The cast was divided into speakers and dancers. I was one of the speakers.

Each scene was predicated upon dangers visited upon Akawe, represented by the four classical elements. The danger of earth was contamination and rust, the metal in bullets, the cracking shells of factories and houses. The danger of water was flooding, lead contamination and *legionella*, E. Coli and trihalomethanes; all the nasty things that had gone into our water supply. The danger of fire was arson, of course. The danger of air was a mystery. Pollution, maybe? Charles hadn't figured that one out yet. It was a problem with the script, and it clearly frustrated him to be this far along with such a big problem looming.

In the first scene, we presented the four elements as "obstacles" threatening the city's teenagers. In the second scene, the obstacles had evolved into "hazards." In the third scene, hazards became "threats." In the fourth scene, threats coalesced into "calamity." The fifth scene hadn't been written yet, but it assumed that calamity had been survived. Survival had given birth to hope. The sick vine had been destroyed, leaf, stem, and root, but the seed of a healthier plant remained. It was up to the adults in the city to protect their children. It was up to the children to plant and nourish the future.

If all this sounds insanely arcane, well, it was, but the music, choreography, and especially the words we read, culled from the surveys of ninth graders, smashed through the abstraction:

"I can't sleep at night. Train wheels grinding all night long."

"My sister's scared of monsters, but I'm scared of who's going to hurt my sister."

"I don't like it when the house is cold, but I like it less when the house is dark."

"The bat house is across the street. Bats come out all the windows at night. Once when my friend got shot at, he ran into the bat house to get away, and all the bats flew out of their windows that moment. There were too many bats to count. My friend got away. That time."

But Charles believed that an audience could only *understand* if these words were spoken by young actors who *knew* what they meant. We were, he told us, the *best* actors to pull off this script, because we wouldn't simply be reading, but witnessing. That was why he had called me at school when I hadn't returned his calls to my home. They didn't need me to act in *The Cherry Orchard.* They didn't need me for *Candide.* They needed me for this.

"Right now," said Charles, before he sent us off on our break, "this script is not a fixed thing. It can and will change. And I want *you* to be instrumental in the way it changes. We will all be working on choreography, on line readings, on blocking and notes, and tech. It's a bit like a music box sitting on a shelf. Until you wind it up and let it go, you don't know what sort of music it's going to play."

I started to feel, again, the long-forgotten thirst that had driven me to audition for every play I could in eighth grade. That had made me ask my parents about the theater programs at every college I could think of. Not just a desire to escape from the ruin around me, but to become something larger than what I was alone. But *this* time, the escape and the becoming and the ruination were all tied up in each other. We were going to speak. We were going to testify. And our testimonials might become a part of others' becoming.

During the break, I went up into the lobby and looked out through the big window at the naked tree branches tossing in a sudden wind. *In here*, I was reading words off a page, and it made me want to get *out there.* Out there, I'd fight the Ostyns, and fight for my friends, and cling to May, and that made me want to come back *in here.* In here, I could tell the world about everything we fought every day.

"John," said August. He was standing in the doorway to the scene shop. "Will you follow me for a moment?"

He led me past the set pieces, each of them being quickly cut out of large sheets of thick plywood, and down the stairs to the costume shop set up among the pipes and valves in the basement.

"Will you try these on, please?" he said, handing me a pair of thick, black boots.

"What scene are these for?" I asked. "I thought we were doing the show barefoot."

"We are. We have a few extra pairs of boots, though, and I noticed that yours are kind of falling apart."

Nova lived in Maplewood, a subdivision on the outermost edge of the East Side designed to keep the rest of Akawe at arm's length. Only one street connected the neighborhood to Huron Road to the west, while another crossed Arcadia Creek by a one-lane bridge. Even though this neighborhood had been built for white folks, Black people had started to move here in the 70s. Then the whites had left all at once. But Starville remained just across Woodward Road, with its thousands of cars and jobs. The factory's paint shop had been assembled right upon the boundary line, and cloudy waves of atomized plastics crashed like broken surf over the humble houses and all of their backyard evergreens. The schools weren't so bad out here, but the cancer rates were through the roof.

I'd met Nova's mom a few times, and I knew that she wasn't going to have any problem with my staying for however long. She worked at Sellers High School and made art pieces that got displayed downtown. They were strange square skins of leather stretched between rustic wood frames festooned with feathers and dragged with lines of soot. She kept some of them mounted on their eggplant purple walls.

"I can give you a week here," is what she told me when I explained my situation. "Ronald's uncle will be staying here next week, and I'll need the couch for that. You can't miss school, though."

"I haven't missed a class since I got kicked out," I said, which was true.

"Still," muttered Nova. "We'll go clubbing on Huron soon as I find you a fake id."

My new home.

My fifth home that month.

I was running out of homes, but I planned to keep running for as long as I needed.

John
I had a lot of fun with you on gong
lets go agin ok
ware do you want to go???
I like the mall becase there is everething there
but we coud go someware ellse if you want too
How was your weekend?
My dad got back from Briton and got his car its all fixed
He and my brother got in a fieht becase Drake wantid a ride to
Micheals and my dad said he coud not take him.
So drake hid his paint brushs haha!!
I love you so mush.
I am so sad that you are not here now.
I wish we could be togeter all the time.
Love,
May

The world had become disturbed once more. Adam had vanished again, and I called Carla and his Grandpa M and his Grandpa A, and nobody was able to tell me where he was. I tried to make eye contact with Selby when I passed her, but she was always looking somewhere else. I saw plenty of Nova at rehearsal and the house, but he was always on the phone or flirting with Jamie, the student stage manager. He did get me a fake id, though.

Sometimes, Lucy joined Mary and me at the lunch table, but she barely talked to us. She talked a lot about what she hated.

"I hate Mr. Esper," she said. "I hate the snow." "I hate music." "I hate my brother."

"It isn't all so bad," said May. "I have a brother too. Do you want my slice of pizza?"

"Don't walk on eggshells around me," Lucy said. "I don't need to eat with you, you know."

With a hard deadline to find another place to stay, I made a list of all the people I hadn't asked yet, and they were each impossible for different reasons. There was only one person left I could think of to ask: Bill Chapman, and he lived in the Os. I only had three options now: to go back to my parents, to go into God's neighborhood, and to go out into the cold.

I ground my teeth and called Bill.

"John!" he said. "Hey! I never thought you were going to call me finally."

"Yeah, I'm sorry it took me so long, and honestly, I'm going to look worse now because I'm calling to ask for some help. Do you think I could maybe crash at your house this weekend? Just for a day ... I mean, a night or two? I got kicked out of my parents. I just need, I don't know ... a couch or something."

"Wow! You're lucky, John. My cousin's been staying with me a lot of the time lately, and *he* always sleeps on the couch, but he's gone somewhere else right now. So yeah, you can stay here!"

"I don't need to stay there tonight. I'll be there Friday."

"Hey, that's great! I'm super excited! I'll ask my mom for some money. Maybe we can get Little Caesar's. With Crazy Bread!"

I felt sick when I hung up my phone. I wondered whether Bill had had any run-ins with the Ostyns.

I didn't have any flashbacks that week, but I was worried about them all the time. I always caught a glimpse of a blue jacket or a hoodie moving down the hall ahead of me and wondered: *Is that normal? Are things changing?*

One day, Eli showed up at Eastern again. I saw him giving Drake a high five – they must have made up or pretended to – and then he met Lucy at her locker, and they laughed together. Rich, resonant laughter that came from deep in their bellies. He caught my eye and winked at me.

I knew I'd been stalling. I needed to call Michael and find out what he had learned, but I kept not calling him. If he told me, I might have to do something, and now I just wanted to wrap myself in *Teen Age Riot* and May. I wrote her long notes and slipped them through the slats of her locker.

May,
I didn't realize your dad was gone for so long. What does he do in Brighton?
Do you help Drake out a lot getting places?
We should definitly go to the mall. But you'll have to give me a ride because I don't have a car or gas money even. I'm sorry. I would ask my parents for some but you know. When I get some money I'm going to pay you and everybody back. This winter it's like I've lost so much but people have done good things for me and I have to pay them all back. I already owe you more than I can say. I don't think I can ever pay you back for what you have done for me. But I want to try.
I love you.
I'm just here at Nova's house. I think it is snowing. It is 10:30 PM. I like his house. I wish I could stay here longer. I'm seeing so much now. I have to tell you about the things I am figuring out because there are a lot of them. I have to tell you what I know about Selby and your

brother and Eli's family and O-Sugar. I worry a lot about Eli and his family. I don't think they are good for people we know. I have to tell you about what I remembered from when I was real young. Four years old. I saw blue ghosts and now I am seeing them again. Do you believe me? It will mean so much to me if you believe me.

I'm glad things are so clear between us. I am not happy but you are the way to being happy. If I woke up tomorrow and you were gone, I would face a wasteland. It is so strange because my parents have been together since I was born but now this year I think they don't like or love each other any more, and they don't seem to like me, either. That's why I had to leave home.

I don't know if I could love anyone else in the way I do you because you are the first person who looks at me and seems to see me really and when I look at you I see you too. I don't think I saw people when I looked at them before, but you have made it so I can see everyone for who they are. Not just you. Do you feel the same way? I want to make you happy. I want you to care for yourself. You can't just care for other people. You can't let them be mean to you or take you for grantid. I don't want to take you for grantid.

When I think of you I think of what you say to me and how you have been treated but how you love your family and take care of people. I can smell the hair spray in your hair. I taste your cherry lip balm. I feel your eyelashes on my cheek when we kissed. They are the best I have ever known, anywhere, and I will never know anything better than that. I am sure of it.

Sometimes I think a storm is coming. But what does that even mean haha it doesn't mean anything! But I believe it anyway. I don't know what it'll do. Something big is going to happen with God and Selby and everyone else and I want to be with you when it happens so we can get through it together. Do you feel this? Tell me. I love you.

John

P.S. Could you pick me up after school at Northern?

That's what I wrote her on Thursday night after a long and frustrating rehearsal; hours of standing in space, crossing the space, saying some lines, saying them again. After I dropped the note in her locker, I felt embarrassed that I had shared so much of my feelings and paranoid that I had put so much about Selby and the Ostyns in writing.

I checked my locker for a reply after every class, and every class that passed without a reply, I felt more and more upset that May hadn't written me back.

Right before I got on the bus to Northern, I finally found a note.

Johnny-O,

Where you been? I keep calling and calling and you never call me back! Anywho, I'm at Eastern today w my girlfriend (social not carnal) and I wanted to leave you this Very Important Note.

I am having my 16th Birthday Party on SAT. MAR. 2ND from 6 or 7 or 8 PM until the BREAK OF DAWN. This is THE LAST PARTY! ANYWHERE! EVER!

(It's going to be like every party in every movie / TV when the parents are away and the teenager hoodlum rascal thugz get into all sorts of mischief and get caught or don't because their parents are out of town and don't even know only my mom IS out of town and SHE KNOWS!!!)

So bring whoever you want!

Because we won't have a keg!

We'll have KEGS!

Kisses,

Deeez Nuuutz (Crystal)

Ten minutes after the final bell had rung at Northern, I saw May's Aubrey roll into the teacher's parking lot. She waved at me. As I crossed toward her, I had to swerve around potholes that could have swallowed a car. Some were filled with water, but muddy ice covered most of them.

"Hi," said May after I'd climbed in. "I'm so happy to see you!"

"I'm glad to see you too!" I said. "Did you get my note?"

"Yeah!" she said. "I liked it."

"You liked it? Is that all —"

She pulled me into a kiss. The mingling of cherry balm and vanilla glossed the edge of my anxiety.

"I said too much in that note," I said. "I told you too much. I said too much."

"I liked your note, John. I said a lot in my note, too."

"But all that stuff about Eli, and —"

"I know about Eli," she said. "I know he is dangerous."

"How dangerous is he? I mean, isn't his father worse? Or his brother?"

"Eli uses people, John. But everybody uses him, too. So, he has to think that using people is normal. That's dangerous."

"Are you afraid of him?"

"Not for myself. But this is all sad stuff. Don't you want to go somewhere else?"

"Yes. Anywhere."

"Good. I want to take you some place special!"

I still felt the presence of the Ostyns hovering nearby, but the Coolio song about cruisin' came on the radio as we left Northern and the Os. Then blackbirds sang and their wings healed. May and I went downtown. We parked on the street outside the windowless AT&T tower. No need for windows. No offices or rooms on the inside. Just switches and circuitry. In its prime, Akawe had paid to dress up even this concrete mausoleum with fake black vertical windows, tapered panes of onyx sheen, confident diamonds, a matrix of mossed copper and gray slate. From the very top, a tower of white sutured cubes rose around a black spiral staircase to arrive at a massive platform, a landing pad for dark helicopters or UFOs.

"That's my favorite building in the whole city," May said during a break in the kissing.

"*That?* Why?"

"I like to think that angels go there. Plus, did you ever see a building like this one before?!"

I hadn't.

A police car pulled up behind us and chirped their sirens.

"Aw, shoot," said May. "I hate when they bother me."

"Is it No Parking here?"

"Probably? But don't they have other things to worry about?"

We left the city and went to the mall.

The parking lot was half-full of shoppers filling the crunch between school's out and lights out. It must have gotten warmer today because gray spikes of grass broke through the snow here and there. The sun had already started slipping behind the bitter brick of the Hudson's battlements.

We went inside. I remember what we did, but not why the time passed so quickly. Chinese food, sports socks, scarlet-on-black at Hot Topic, black coffee from the Beanery. Tweens doing somersaults in the kiddy play space standing in the white-lit tropical atrium in the shadow of Sears. These moments – extraordinary because I was spending them with *her*, and because she tattooed her presence on all this suburban whatever – were passing fast. Before I realized it, the sun was going down, the mall was closing for the night, and May and I were walking out into the dusk.

"Ouch!" she said a few minutes later, when the seat belt buckle poked her shoulder from behind.

"Sorry," I said.

"It's not your fault," she said.

I sat up.

"It's getting cold in here," I said. "We should turn on the heat."

"I don't want to waste the gas," she said.

"So what if we waste the gas?"

"We might run out of gas."

"So?"

"If we did, I would make you go walk and get us more gas. You would have to do it all on your own!"

"I wouldn't care."

"You should care! It's cold out. It's windy. Too windy!"

"It's not like it's gonna blow me away."

"It might. It blows wherever it wants."

"I don't care where it blows."

"You might look around, and suddenly you're somewhere totally different, and you don't even know where, and you can't even do anything about it!"

She laughed. This was a joke, I guess. But I saw that she knew I was worried, and it made me angry at myself that I had worried her.

The sun finally vanished for good.

The sky turned Easter pink and purple.

The whole American Midwest was rolling into the dark.

May and I shifted our positions, but the seats were uncomfortable no matter how we arranged ourselves. As the light faded, it got harder and harder for me to see her face. Instead, I imagined Bill's lonely house looming out of the twilight. I had never been to this house before. What would it look like? What would it feel like? Why was I going into God's neighborhood again? Why couldn't May and I just live together at the mall, stealing our meals from the food court, and wearing all of the expensive clothes? Why did we need families and addresses? Why couldn't everything just take care of everything?

"I don't want today to be over," I said. "I don't want to be alone without you."

"You're shaking, John," May said. "What's wrong?"

"Everything that's not you," I said. "Everything that I wrote you in that note. God, what's going to happen with our friends? What's going to happen with my parents? What's going to happen with us? Where am I going to live? I just don't want to be alone!"

"Then don't!" she said. Even though it was dark in the car, something about the way the distant light silhouetted her suggested a smile. "Come back to my house and stay with me!"

I took a deep breath.

"Couldn't you do it?" she asked. "Come back me with me to my dad's? He won't mind. Drake won't mind. They've brought people over. For months sometimes! You can move in with us, and you can live with us long as you like, and we can love each other and be with each other all the time every day. We'll be together at school *and* at home. It would be wonderful!"

I *could* do this. I had everything I needed in my backpack. My backpack was in the trunk. But ...

That was the house where Lucy took the gun and Eli took the sunglasses and I took the O-Sugar. And that's the house with the fucked-up Jesus painting on the wall. Jesus Christ. I was worried about a storm coming.

535

Returning to that house would be like going into *the storm.*

"You don't want to go there because of what happened there before," May said. "At my birthday party."

"It isn't your fault," I said.

"But you don't understand," she said. "It isn't a bad house. It's a good house. My brother and my dad are good people. They take good care of me, and they'll take care of you too. That house is where Drake and my dad got better after bad things happened to them. And after Lucy ... scared us all in the basement, it was upstairs that I made her feel better! Trust me. Come home with me, John. I love you. We need to be together. I mean, we should get to live together. Don't you think so?"

At least I knew May's house. At least I knew what was inside it. At least I knew that one of its people loved me.

"Okay," I said.

My unease returned as soon as May had clambered back into the driver's seat and turned the ignition.

The radio chirped on in the middle of a rap with a woman singing far above her range. May drove us over to a pay phone near the Hudson's, and I borrowed a quarter to call Bill. I got his answering machine.

"Hey, Bill," I said. "Um. I'm really sorry, but it looks like I'm going to be able to stay at my girlfriend's this weekend. I guess that means more Crazy Bread for you? I'm really sorry about not letting you know sooner. It just, um, came up. We have to hang out soon, I promise. I'll see you at school."

My hand was shaking as I hung up the phone. I climbed back into the car, and we cut out through the rapidly emptying parking lot. Cars jammed Aurelius all the way from the Hooters to Chuck E. Cheese, and a hundred brake lights glittered like predatory eyes in the dark, but May was a capable driver, and she knew the city well. She glided across three lanes onto the I-92 entrance ramp, changed lanes again to merge onto 63 North, passed into Akawe, passed Eastern, passed downtown, and took the exit onto Ash Highway. Just a few minutes after we had left the mall, we were turning onto Armstrong Blvd., and the metallic taste of panic flooded my mouth.

When May turned into her driveway, the headlights unerringly found the painted Jesus looking right back at us. Its chubby, boneless arms begged me for a vinyl hug. Its empty blue eyes promised me a whole silent universe of entropy and rending. "Accelerate into me," I imagined Jesus saying.

"Here we are," said May, as if I needed to know.

I pressed the button on the seatbelt, and it clicked. The nylon cord made a zipping sound as it slackened. The passenger door crunched shut. I was moving with deliberate steadiness, but why did I feel so cautious? Was it because May was about to invite me to meet her dad and ask him to let me live with her? Was it because Drake was inside, and he knew what I had done there? Or was it something else? I tried not to look at the Jesus. Jesus was looking at me the whole time.

May cheerfully hooked her arm in mine and led me to the door. We went inside.

May's dad and Drake were sitting in the small living room, watching the big tv. The sound had been turned way down, but they were watching the news. A bomb had gone off in London. Drake sat in his wheelchair near the hall, while May's dad lay on the sofa.

"Hey, May," said the dad. "Who's your friend?"

"This is my *boy*friend," said May. "His name is John. John, this is my dad, Key."

Key Dunham was somehow exactly what I had expected May and Drake's dad to look like. He wasn't tall, but he was so slender that he gave the impression of height as he sprawled across the couch. Even as he reclined, I felt a tension in his sinewy frame that also suggested Drake's hidden strength. Key had a small mustache and stubble on his chin. His hair was as scrambled as May's was coiffed. He was wearing a KC Chiefs baseball cap, and dirt crusted the bill. There was something sharp about his eyes, like he never really relaxed. Like he feigned relaxation.

"Nice to meet you," I said and stepped forward to shake his hand.

He gave mine a limp shake.

"Likewise," he said.

"Dad, is it okay if John stays with us for a while?" May asked. "His parents kicked him out, and we're in love."

I stood up a little straighter. I wasn't sure I trusted Key and Drake with this information yet.

"You're in love, huh?" said Key, piercing me with that canny glance of his. "What's your address, John? What's your dad's name?"

"It's okay, dad," said Drake, without looking up from the tv. "John ain't with the Chalks. Or anyone else, for that matter."

"You know this boy too?" asked Key. "You didn't say nothing."

"I'm still on the O. My thoughts aren't clear. Anyway, she's been staying with Mom this week. She ain't my business every day."

"You're on O-Sugar *now?*" I asked.

For the first time, Drake looked at me. His eyes weren't focused, but now I knew why.

"Yeah," he said.

"Why?" I asked. This drug had almost killed him the first time he'd tried it – and it *had* killed his best friends – so why would he go back for more?

"Don't ask me questions," Drake said. "I got questions for you."

"Yeah," said Key. "I got a few questions myself."

They were both staring at me. May seemed a little embarrassed. She was looking at the floor.

"May," said Key. "Go get that pizza in the oven. Drake, you help her out."

"I already had a day," said Drake.

"Do it!"

They went on into the kitchen. I could hear Drake sniping at her: "You didn't shovel the walk. I can't get to the garage when you don't shovel the walk."

After they were gone, Key made a simple gesture to a chair near the front door.

"Have a seat," he said.

I sat down.

"Take off your coat," he said.

I took off my coat and laid it across my lap.

"My daughter said that you're in love. Are you?"

May had already told him, but it wasn't like she had lied or anything. It wasn't like she was wrong. "I, um ... yeah. I mean, yes."

"Yes, what?"

"Yes, I am in love."

"With?"

"With May. I'm in love with May."

"You met her mom?"

"Yeah."

"What did you think of her?"

"I ... um ... it was nice to meet May's mom?" I had no idea how to answer this question. Kitty had been unkind to May and rude to me, but I wasn't about to say that to May's dad.

"And she was happy to meet you?"

"I don't think I'd say that."

"She ain't happy to meet nobody. Last question for now: What do you think of my painting?"

"Your painting?"

"Yeah. The mural I did on the side of the house. It's of –"

"Jesus?"

"Yeah."

I stopped to think. I knew that this was some sort of a test, but I had no idea what he wanted from me. In the end, I figured he'd know if I was lying. I decided to just tell him the truth.

"I'm sorry to be rude, Mr. Dunham ... but I think it's pretty messed up. I mean, it's very colorful. But it freaked me out the first time I saw it, and it freaked me out again today. I ... I don't know. Why did you paint it?"

Key studied me for a moment, then folded his arms behind his head in a gesture of extravagant ease.

"You answered those questions alright, John. You aren't embarrassed of May. Plenty of people are. Plenty of her boyfriends, even. You think Kitty's a bitch, because everyone does, but you want to be careful with me and not hurt May's feelings, so you play it soft without lying. And when I ask you a hard question, point-bank, you give me a straight answer. Good job."

I was a bit annoyed that I was once again taking the New Boyfriend Essay Test. It didn't seem to me like Kitty and Key were perfect parents, either. But there was no point making another enemy tonight.

"Thanks," I said.

"What I do for a living," Key said, "is painting. I'm a painter. I paint houses. Insides. Outsides. Sheds. Decks. Walls and molding. I'm pretty good, too. I painted that Jesus mural three years ago when I was coming down off some bad shit. It's the ugliest motherfucker I ever seen. I don't paint over it. I leave it there, always, so I see it every day, and know what I was. That painting has kept me sober so far. He sees everything, you know!"

"You were going through withdrawal ... and you decided to paint? You painted ... that?"

Key smiled. He clearly liked talking about this, and I suspected that he talked about it often. "I don't believe in the divinity of Christ," he said. "I believe that Jesus was a poet and a philosopher. But back then, I'd been Reaganed and Bushed and Clintoned. I'd been brushed back into that corner. There are mushrooms growing in our basement, you know? It fulfills its purpose, even if it looks like an exploded piece of Play-Doh. Yeah, you can stay here, long as May wants you to. But this is clear: you're good to her, you do what I ask, you do what Drake asks, got it?"

"Yes, sir," I said.

I'd never called anyone "sir" before, but I could sense that it was what Key was looking for. He even flashed me a little smile.

"Good," he said. "I never made up some shit like this house is whole or happy. But this house is healthy. This is a house for healing."

We all went into the kitchen and sat down around the card table, which had been pushed into the middle of the room. May opened the oven and pulled out a boxed pizza with onions, black olives, and Italian sausage. We each got two slices with a pile of microwaved tater tots and cans of RC. May muttered a little prayer that nobody else echoed, and we all started eating quietly.

As we ate, I started to understand Key and Drake a bit better, and I started to understand Kitty a little, too. They had all seen people take advantage of May. They probably assumed that I wanted something more from her than a relationship. That complicated things for me, too, because while I *did* love May, I also *did* want something else. I wanted to know what Drake knew about O-Sugar, and the Chalks, and above all, God. I wanted Drake to tell me everything so that I could understand Selby's plan of attack and figure out how to save her – how to save all of us – from the Ostyns. But I wasn't sure how to bring it up.

"John," said Drake. "You dosed O times three, right? Then Eli took away your sunglasses. How was that? What did you see that night?"

"Oh, Jesus, Drake!" said May. "He doesn't want to talk about that!"

"It's okay," I said. "I don't mind. It was my dumb thing to do. And Drake, I'll pay you back for those as soon as I can."

"Yeah, good. They weren't for free. That shit's expensive. So, what did you see?"

"I saw blue things."

"What blue things?"

"Imaginary things. Like from my past. And impossible things. I knew they were hallucinations. And I saw things around me kind of turn blue and move around."

"Yeah? How did they move at you?"

"What do you mean?"

"Did they move away?"

"No. They moved toward me."

He nodded.

I went on, "It was like I moved without walking."

"It was *like* you moved without walking." He flashed me a grin. "Three of those pills is a lot. It only takes one for tripping balls. I've taken two a couple times, but –"

"You do it a lot?"

"Almost every day."

Drake was smiling. He had an attitude about it. Like he was proud.

"I'm surprised you do it every day. I'm surprised anyone does it. It felt pretty shitty to me."

"Yeah, that's the nightshade. Jesus' shit, I couldn't believe when Eli told us that. That makes it all nightmares, you know? But they say that it's part of the whole experience."

Key wasn't paying much attention. The conversation seemed to bore him. May, on the other hand, stared at the table and seemed to be completely embarrassed by all three of us. But Drake kept looking right at me. It was time for me to put a few cards on the table if I wanted to get anything back.

"You know," I said, "it wasn't the first time I've seen that, either."

"You did O-Sugar before?" Drake asked.

"No," I said. "That was the first time. But when I was a little kid, I lived down in Cartierul. You know, the Romanian neighborhood? My friend Selby lived there too. Anyway ... I saw the blue ghost phantom things then, too. Just the same as they were a couple weeks ago. She saw them too."

"When was this?"

"It was like ten years ago or something."

Drake chewed his food quietly. I couldn't read a thing from his face.

I went on: "The night I took the O, I also met a guy in an abandoned house. He was weird. Told me his name was God."

That worked. Now Drake was staring at me, unblinking.

"You *met* him?" he asked.

"He had a gun and a drink, and he told me he was expecting someone else."

"It was me," Drake said. "He was expecting me."

No, I thought. *You are wrong.*

"Why would he be expecting you?" I asked.

"Well, that's a fucking mystery, ain't it?" asked Drake.

I had to give him a little bit more. Just a little bit more. I had to give him enough to open up to me.

"I think he wants to hurt some of my friends. He told me so. I need to figure out what he's about so that I can protect them."

Drake laughed, hollow. "You can't protect them," he said. "You can't protect anyone. You don't have to fake with me, John. I know what you know.

I know you know that two years ago, I took the first O-Sugar that anyone made, and my friends and I went off the top of that hospital."

"How do you know it was the first O-Sugar?"

"My supplier told me it was a test. He said he tried it out and wanted me to try it out before they started selling it. They were making it stronger back then. Anyway, you saw our collection. You know we're trying to decode that shit. But I never get to the bottom of it. I think I'm getting close, and then ..." He clapped his hands together, then swept them apart, flicking his fingers like he was trying to get water off of them.

May wasn't staring at the table anymore. She was watching both of us.

"*They* said," said Drake, channeling the ethereal, invisible *they*, "that the drug made us crazy and suicidal. *They* said it *made* us jump."

"But you didn't jump," I said.

"You want me to tell you?"

"You don't have to tell me. I know. Also, I went there. I went up on that roof with my own friends, the summer after you fell. We got into that hospital and went up to the roof and saw what you saw."

"You saw ghosts?"

"We weren't on O-Sugar, but we felt them. We knew they were there."

"There was ... something ... about up there ..."

"Maybe it was real ghosts!" burst May.

"There's no such thing, sis," said Drake.

I wasn't so sure.

Neither was Key. "I bet it was real ghosts," he said. "There are ghosts, you know. Thing is, they ain't what you picture them as. Spirits floating around ... the minds ... the trapped souls of dead things? Like you say, Drake, 'no such thing.' But there is such a thing if you can feel something so strongly that its teeth poke in all around you ... that they're, like, gnawing against your skin."

"But we didn't jump."

"You thought about it," I said. "All that loneliness up there. Nothing but the height, and the night, and the ghosts, and you and your friends all alone up there in the dark. I don't think anyone could go up there and not think about jumping. I think that place would make you kind of want to jump even if you knew you weren't going to."

"But we didn't jump!"

"You didn't have to," I said. "The drug did it for you. Because when I was on O-Sugar, I didn't have to walk places. I didn't have to make a decision.

As soon as I thought about it, I was there. You thought about being over the edge, and ..."

Drake stabbed at his tater tots and took a bite. He took another stab and dipped it in ketchup.

"You know things," he told me. "You want to know more. Is that why you're here?"

"No," I said. "I'm here because I love your sister, and I don't want to go back to my parents."

May looked at me with such a depth of compassion, such understanding, that it almost overwhelmed me. Drake didn't notice.

"God Ostyn ain't a ghost," he said. "He's a man. And a monster. Don't fuck around with him. Or Eli. Or EZ. Or Ash. Or any of the others. They'll kill you. Any one of them. Or all of them, all together. You know God keeps them all living in garbage, don't you? But he fixes all of his kids up with perfect teeth. EZ told me that living things need strong teeth to stay alive. God buys his kids their teeth so they can feed on flesh."

After dinner, we went back into the living room and watched *Groundhog Day*, then played Mega Man X for an hour or so. Eventually, Key went off to his room. A few minutes later, Drake disappeared into the bathroom and didn't come back out.

"I want to play you my music before we go to bed!" said May. "I am so excited that you're staying here with me, John. I'm so excited that we're living together now!"

She took my hands and drew me off to her room – that tiny, pink, immaculate room with the white-framed bed – and locked the door behind us. She put on a cassette tape with music she'd recorded off the radio: Boyz II Men and R. Kelly.

"Who were you with," May asked. "Up on the hospital roof?"

"Selby," I said. "And Michael, and Adam."

I was shaking. I wasn't sure what caused it, but I couldn't stop.

"Why did you go up there? It's the worst place in the whole world, okay?"

"I can think of some worse places," I said. *The Hell House, I mean, Empyrean.* "I don't know. It was a bad week. I was wondering about stuff. It was a long time ago. Did you ever go up there?"

"No. No way. I don't go around places like that. I don't like the abandoned buildings."

Did *I* like them? I did seem to spend a lot of time in abandoned places. Why didn't they bother me like they bothered her? On the other hand, it was hard to completely avoid that emptiness in Akawe.

"I think your dad was right ... about the ghosts."

An angry God pushing out with two arms, flinging the universe wide. A malignant God, gripping the universe in two fists and pulling it to shreds. Ripping the fabric. Scattering all the stuffing. Dark energy. Phantom energy.

"I had a good day with you today," May said. "I can't believe it's dark out, and we're here in my room here together. We're going to *be* together! All that other stuff ... my brother, and O-Sugar, and ghosts and that hospital? It's really bad, okay? Let's not even think about it, okay? Let's think about good things."

"Yeah," I said.

I stood near the door, trembling.

May turned on a desk lamp, closed her curtains, and turned off the overhead light. She untucked her shirt, then pulled it up and over her head. *So is this happening now?* I wondered. *Are* we *happening now?* My heart was fluttering, but I didn't want to fuck things up like I had with Lucy. I didn't want that emptiness that had followed sex with Crystal. May didn't seem to notice my doubt, though, so I lifted my polo shirt over my head and dropped it on the bed. I crossed my arms across my chest. I was self-conscious about my pallor. I was a little self-conscious about my weight.

May folded both of our shirts neatly, then put them in the wicker hamper for dirty clothes. She did the same with her pants. She seemed so confident. Carefree, even. I was shaking more and more now. I felt like I was going to shake into pieces. I took my own pants off, and folded them, and set them in the hamper with the shirts. May unhooked and removed her bra, and lay it neatly over the edge of the hamper. I could have looked at her then. But I looked at her desk instead. Looking at her would have felt like taking an irreversible step, and I wasn't sure ...

Out of the corner of my eye, I saw May slipping her fingers beneath the elastic band of her panties. I interrupted her quickly, to stop her:

"Are we going to sleep without any clothes on?"

"Isn't that, like, the whole point?" she asked.

Maybe the frankness of her question surprised me. But it gave me a chance to tell her how I felt:

"I don't want to have sex," I said. "I mean, not right now."

"Okay," she said. "We don't have to. Do you mind sharing the bed with me, though? If not, I could get you some blankets for the couch."

"No," I mumbled. "I think I would like to share the bed with you."

"That's good. It's very comfy. A lot comfier than the couch. Anyway, I want to be close to you."

"I want to be close to you, too."

"You don't have to look away from me, you know. We're just people!"

I looked at her.

"I think you're beautiful."

"Thank you. And you are very handsome!"

In the middle of the night, I woke into another flashback.

I kept my eyes shut, but I knew what was happening in the darkness. I felt the space contracting between subatomic particles. If I opened my eyes, I would see collapsing space and converging ghosts. But keeping my eyes closed also caused problems. A frenzy of images spiraled through me, dancing behind my eyelids, and so Joan Crawford jigsawed with Ingrid Bergman, and they were both annoyed, both furious, shaking their pointer fingers at me, asking me why I didn't just open my eyes and fall into the Truth that I had created by drinking that drug down a couple weeks back.

A monster eagle, striped red and white, gripped me in its arms, flapped its wings, and set off. I hung upon a precipice at a great height and saw below where peaks and mountains jutted up through the mist. There was the overpass where I had stolen Eli's mom's sunglasses – *was that her body in the shadows?* – and there were the streets where EZ had chased me. There was St. Christopher's hospital, resurrected from its azure demolition, and here was May's house on Armstrong. I also saw my parents' house on the hill of Agit Street while Cartierul swirled down in the wet. The Empyrean stood the tallest of all, notwithstanding its actual nonscape. It straddled a monstrous eyrie spiking far above the illuminated fog. And yet, the fog swirled about the base of the Empyrean. I realized that the fog was made out of ghosts. It was made out of urbantasms.

"Is it another flashback?" May murmured.

"Yes," I said, and I was surprised at how breathless my voice sounded.

"Are your eyes shut?" she asked.

"Yes," I said.

"Good. Keep them shut."

And with her left arm across my chest – against my pounding heart – she reached up and brushed my hair back with her right hand. Kissed the back of my head and placed it beneath her chin. Pulled the warm blankets tighter against us both. My heart was in her palm. Her understanding kept it beating. The bright fog receded. With May's arms around me, I held the flame of the flashback in the palm of my hand. All I had to do was clench my fists, and its fragile light would go out.

But while I knew that May hated the drug, I did not. For me, the drug had become a tool. A terrifying tool. I *had* to understand what had happened to me eleven years before. I *had* to discover what Selby and Drake and the Ostyns were doing, because I already sensed that their efforts would all converge in some catastrophe. I had to go deeper into the hallucination, so I didn't snuff it out. I opened my eyes. In the shadows of May's nighttime room, perfectly clean, everything pristine and ordered, blue things moved upon me.

But I saw important things, too.

Like, like, like, Nebuchadrezzar killed, but it all became sand, right?

And so I saw a cluster of men and women come together in a windowless room, plain walls, beige walls, and pour themselves cups of lukewarm coffee, shake in a bit of non-dairy-creamer, and entropize the stuff with candy-colored straws as they traded plans that transcended legality.

"They haven't protected us," they said.

"They said they were going to protect us," they said.

"What about those out on the West End? What about the Os? What about the projects?"

"Remember back when Reuther brought racial justice to the table? That was radical but not radical enough! Remember when Meany tried to throw out the corruptionists? I never seen an egg as clean as that fine man's eggy head!"

"He was a ton of things, but not an egg head!"

"He was a ton of things ..."

"We can't see."

"We've got to feel our way without seeing."

"If we don't got eyes, we got to feel with our hands."

I reached out and tried to feel with my hands.

"We got to try and salvage what ain't been lost."

"We can't let them take any more. We got to salvage what ain't lost."

"Salvage is our name."

"Salvage."

So, they called themselves Salvage, and they were dangerous and good. On official union rolls, Salvage would have been flagged as an erratic upstart caucus or, worse, as wildcats, but they couldn't flag it precisely because it still *was* informal. So, any sudden movements to salvage the tattered remnants of what had once been the tens-of-thousands-strong X Automotive Workers Union occurred with blue-light, blue-fire pow-wows in the late dusk of Hunters Park in the Os, or the predawn of Holborn Park on the West End. They would bide their time and circulate their petitions on coffee filters through which they later steeped strong stuff to further indoctrinate the unsuspecting rank-and-file. They wanted to launch a strike that would hit harder and dig deeper than that dustup over the Little Passway dies in '94.

But how am I hearing this? I wondered. *Or am I imagining it?* No, I was just building connections based on what I had already caught. I had witnessed things. I had overheard them. Tonight the drug was driving my recall.

May tightened her arm around my chest.

"Garota de Ipanema."

In certain zones of Rio de Janeiro, where X Automotives had colonized the Fifth Brazilian Republic as a market for Aubreys, there were a few favelas, liminal spaces not crammed high up on the mountainsides like their elder siblings, but pressed close against the walled shores of the auto factories. Children there sometimes saw the crashing waves of Ipanema rushing upon them, blooming bromeliads and foaming glory trees, all blue, even though they lived far from these things. Sometimes, the blue ghosts of beachgoers strode out of the sky and stared at them. A blue-flamed sacred heart beat deep within the soapstone breast of Christ the Redeemer.

Why were there urbantasms in Rio but not in São Paulo? What did X Automotives have to do with it? I hadn't even known that you could buy Aubreys in South America.

"Salvage Brazil," I said. "Salvage Akawe. Salvage. They call themselves Salvage!"

"Shhhhh," said May.

I saw a blue garbage truck.

"Macewoudd!" I said.

Then I saw something else.

It was the last thing revealed before the vision released me, and I collapsed back into May's embrace and the actual world.

I saw Selby climbing rickety stairs. I saw her creeping down a dusty hall. I saw her pass silently through a splintered door. She clutched a small oil lamp in her hand, and she was deep inside the Empyrean.

"You can't get her!" I shouted. "You can't get me! You can't get her! You can't get us! We'll kill you! We'll kill you!"

"Shhhhhh," whispered May. "One two three four five six seven eight," she said. "One two three four five six seven eight."

When I woke, I saw the sun beaming coldly through a part in May's curtain. I dressed and went to the bathroom. Brushed my teeth and combed my hair. When I got back to the bedroom, May was sitting up in bed, smiling lazily.

"I got to make a couple phone calls," I said. "You got some quarters I can borrow?"

"You can use our phone, you know," she said.

"They're private."

She shrugged, went over to her dresser, and fished some coins from a shallow tray.

"You're coming back, right?" she asked.

"Yeah. I'm staying here now, remember? I'll be back in like a half-hour."

I walked through the living room where Drake and Key were watching TV. They ignored me while I put on my shoes and coat and went out into the morning. Another heavy snow had fallen overnight, and neither the street nor sidewalks had been cleared. The sky had been swept of clouds, however. Blue shot through like flawless sapphire, but the sun was hard and the shadows were still long.

I pushed my way through the drifts and eventually made it to Lestrade, which had been plowed. I walked in the street until I got to a beauty salon already humming with early-morning activity. I found a payphone out in the parking lot.

I made my first phone call. I called Michael. Aunt Mabel picked up the phone.

"John?" she said. "Where are you?"

"Nowhere! I'm fine!"

"Your mother said you were staying with this kid named Noah? Is that where you are?"

"His name is 'Nova.' But anyway, I'm staying with my girlfriend now. I haven't missed a day of school, by the way!"

"Call your parents, John!"

I finally persuaded her to put Michael on.

"I've been trying to get a hold of you," he said, annoyed. "It hasn't been easy, because I haven't wanted your parents asking a ton of questions about you, but I wasn't sure if you were ever going to call me, either!"

"I'm sorry, Michael. It's been a strange few weeks. May and I are going out again. But we'll have to talk about that later. What did you find out about Octolok and Propyl-Osirin?"

"That's awesome. Congratulations on your girlfriend! Anyway, the other stuff. It hasn't been easy, you know. Here, let me move the phone."

A full minute of rustling and clatter, then Michael picked up again.

"I'm in the basement now. Look, you should be careful what you say because it's real hard for me to talk about it with my mom around without her wondering what we're up to."

"Sorry."

"So, I found out about Propyl-Osirin. It was this toxic compound that X was using in their headlights, but it ended up wrecking them instead. Then because X disposed of them improperly, they got into the ground and poisoned a bunch of people on the East Side, and there was a big lawsuit about it. You see, mercury is a part of synthesizing Propyl-Osirin."

"So, when Mr. Kolin said he found Propyl-Osirin in Cartierul ..."

"Yeah, that would be kind of a big deal."

"Okay. That's something. Do you think you could use it in O-Sugar?"

Michael was quiet for a moment.

"I don't see how you could," he finally said. "I mean, maybe you could, but I don't see *why*. I don't think it would add anything to the drug. It would just make making it more complicated. And it could poison people ..." Michael was quiet a moment longer. "But actually ... no, you definitely couldn't. Because people got mercury poisoning from trace amounts of Osirin in the soil. And you'd get a lot more than trace amounts if you were using it in O-Sugar. And nobody who has been on O-Sugar has gotten mercury poisoning. And that's something we would have heard about in the news a long time ago. You know?"

"Okay. Well, it's good to know that it isn't that. And, I guess it's also good to know that the dirt in Cartierul can make people sick."

"Yeah. Someone should tell Selby."

"I'll tell her. What about Octolok?"

Michael sighed.

"I'm still working on Octolok. It was used in manufacturing some Aubreys and Benedicts in the late 70s and the early 80s. They used it as an adhesive. It was really strong, and they didn't need a lot of it, but there was an organic ingredient that, I guess, they could only get from this one specific place, and it was really expensive to get, so they discontinued it after a few years. Also, it wore out, I guess. It was one of those ideas that seems really great, but that just doesn't pan out. I'll figure it out ... most of this stuff is on microfilm in the library at XAI, but it's still taking longer than I thought. Can you call me back in a few days?"

"Sure, sure, no problem. Hey, tell Abbey I say 'hi.'"

Michael laughed nervously.

I hung up and called Selby. I was getting cold, so I put the phone in the crook between my head and shoulders and kept my hands in my pockets. When Aria handed the phone over to Selby, I already felt a wave of relief.

"Hey," I said. "It's me."

"John," said Selby. "You staying with that orange-haired friend of yours?"

"Not anymore," I said. "Did you see God Ostyn last night?"

"What? Last night? No, I've never met him. I mean, not yet."

"Did you go to his house? The one on Eden Street?"

"No. I was here."

"Good. It wasn't real."

"What wasn't real?"

"O-Sugar flashback."

"Jesus, John. What's happened to you?"

"I'll tell you what I've figured out if you tell me what your plans are."

"I'm keeping my plans away from you so that I can keep you safe."

"I'm not worried about myself."

"Then worry about Lucy, and May, and everyone else you spend time with."

"If you don't tell me, then I can't help you. Anyway, I think I'm getting close to figuring out how O-Sugar is made. Michael and I are figuring it out, and if we get some help from Drake ..."

"Yes! Do that, John! Have Michael and Drake help you with it. It is very important! It is almost the most important thing. But be really, really careful, because if any of the Lang-Ostyns find out that you're trying to figure it out, they'll kill you."

"Yeah, that's what everyone keeps telling me, over and over and over. But they already know that Drake is trying to figure it out. Or, at least Eli does."

"If Eli knows, then they all know. But Drake is smart and hooked up with Ziggurat, and they aren't going to do shit to that kid. Not out in the open. So, I'm not worried about Drake. I'm worried about you."

"Are you and Drake, like, working on the same thing?"

"No. He's got his score to settle. I've got mine. But what he's doing

552

could help me out, you know?"

"Oh, by the way ... see if maybe you and your family can get checked for mercury poisoning. There's some really nasty shit in the soil around your house, and I just found out about it."

"You just found out about that? I've known about that for years."

For so long, the interminable winter had been my enemy. These months had felt like the longest of my life. I thought back to the first snowfall on the night when my parents had thrown the party for the Renfest kids, and I had been dating Omara, and learned that Selby was helping Cora escape to her aunt. I had become a different person since the snow had started falling.

But something had changed since May's party, as I traveled between beds and couches at six different houses. Winter now felt precious to me. After all, May and I had discovered each other in the heart of winter. Whenever this winter finally started to melt, it would also mean that our moment of encounter was fading. I didn't care that it had already been winter forever. I wanted winter to go on. I never wanted the flowers to blossom again.

When I got back to May's house, Drake and Key were still watching TV. I didn't feel embarrassed as I took my shoes off and went down the hall to May's bedroom. She was up and dressed now, sitting at her desk. Her room smelled like synthetic cherries and aerosol hair spray.

"You aren't Catholic, are you?" I asked.

"No," May said. "Are you?"

"Yeah."

And for some reason, I thought back to my last confession, which had happened more than a year before. It had been right at the end of the summer of '94, when Omara and I had just started dating.

"Bless me, Father," I had said, "For I have sinned. My last confession was like a year ago or something. I've done some bad things, and the thing I feel the most bad about was that I took some food from my parents' fridge ..." It had been a carton of eggs. But I didn't tell him what I had done with those eggs. How some kid from AYT had driven us around town, and we'd pelted everyone we passed. People just walking along the sidewalks. A haggard man riding a rusty bike, with all of his everything in the pack on his back. And I had felt guilty as I'd received absolution. In my mind, the more venal sin of fudging of my confession cloaked the graver sin – my cruelty – and it all felt rotten and vain within me, and so I had decided not to bother with confession anymore. They were just too confusing, and worse, they didn't *feel* good.

But May would have been disappointed, not by the lie, but by the cruelty.

"Let's listen to this!" she said brightly.

A piano played. *Ping ping ping pa ding.*

It was Mariah Carey.

That afternoon, May and I finally went to her favorite McDonald's on Ash Highway. It had recently been remodeled with a Hollywood motif, with pink-and-yellow wallpaper where Jimmy Dean looked over my shoulder as I ate a McChicken sandwich and leaned across the booth to kiss May.

The next morning, May was up before me.

"You got to get up!" she said. "I've got a surprise for you. You've got to dress up nice. Let me grab you one of Drake's sweaters!"

Drake had a muscular chest but he was also taller than I was. The sweater was tight across my stomach, but I still had to cinch up the sleeves.

We made our way through the neighborhood to the Church of St. Benedict the Black. It was a Catholic Church that I had never heard of; a small church with a green copper roof and abstracted squares of shaded glass filtering soft colors into the sanctuary. The place was packed for its single Mass, but I saw less than a dozen white people in there, not including the priest. The service ran for an hour-and-a-half, but May sang fervently and a little off-key.

"I thought you said you weren't Catholic," I whispered.

"I'm not," she hissed back. "But I thought you'd like to come here. I've been passing it for years, but I've never been inside!"

When we went up the aisle to take communion, I decided not to tell May to cross her arms in front of her chest to receive a blessing instead of the bread. If anyone's soul was prepared to receive Christ's body, I figured it was May.

That afternoon, Drake called me into the kitchen alone.

"You don't got no money, do you?" he asked.

"No," I said. "Not now."

"Well, you can't just stay here, eating our food, all that, and not do nothing, right?"

"What do you want me to do?"

"I'm going to write up some notes. I'll tell you some locker numbers. You memorize them. Drop the papers off at the lockers. You'll do this early. A half-hour before school starts. You'll do it quickly, and then you'll go the library and read or some shit."

"That's it?"

"You do that for me on Monday, you're straight. You can stay here, eat our food, whatever. I don't care, neither does my dad."

"What is it? Drugs?"

"No, man, it's just pieces of paper with numbers on them. Like I told you. But don't talk about them, and don't talk to me at school."

That evening, Key made us cheeseburgers, singing Jimmy Buffet as he went, while May went outside to shovel the walk.

"I can do that for you," I said.

"It's my job!" she said, annoyed, though I couldn't tell whether she was irritated that she had to do it or that I had offered to help her out.

Key laughed. This man was made out of bad jokes, whiskey breath, off-kilter religiosity, and a sawblade laugh. I didn't trust him at all, but it was impossible not to like him a little.

That night, we all watched a taped episode of Jerry Springer, then went to bed.

When I crawled into the bed with May, we made the cool covers warm, holding each other in silence. For some reason, I started crying, and then May started crying too, and we both cried until we stopped and fell asleep.

For the next week, my dreams had the clarity of waking action, while my days were vague and indistinct, except for a memory of mingled anxiety and love. I went to play practice. May worked on her homework and watched tv. She baked cookies, and I did the dishes. We started to teach the secrets of how we'd been shaped.

But then, when that was over, I remembered my conversation with Selby, and how she had told me to help Drake reverse-engineer O-Sugar. I was too science stupid to do it myself. I needed to get Drake and Michael together in the same room, which was too weird to think about. There was only one way to do it. I had to call my father.

He picked up the phone, said "hi" in a dusky voice, and asked me how school was going.

"What about you?" I asked. "Any luck on the job search?"

"Couple interviews. No offers yet, though."

It was already the most normal conversation we'd had in over a month.

"We want you to come home, John," he said.

"I'm not ready yet," I told him. "But soon." I wasn't sure if I was telling the truth or not, but I needed to not piss him off. I needed him to help me get Michael to May's house. I knew my father, and I knew my Aunt Mabel. She relied on his judgment when it came to "marginal neighborhoods" in Akawe, and he would be looking for a chance to be on my team. We talked about X Auto, the Red Wings, and the weather. By the time I hung up, I was pretty sure my father would help me.

Then I called Michael.

"Come over to May's tomorrow," I said. "I know you can't spend the night. We're going roller-skating."

"You said it isn't that great a neighborhood," Michael said. "My mom won't want to drop me off there."

"It isn't that bad. But you're right; you don't want Mabel bringing you. She wouldn't like Key's ... painting. Get my father to bring you. He hasn't seen me in a month. He'll bring you just so he can talk to me. He'll also want you to tell him all about what I'm up to. Tell him whatever you want, just not about the bad stuff. Tell him about May. And how hard I'm working in school. But, yeah, if you call my parents and ask my father to take you, he won't say no. Then ask your mom."

"Well, fine, I can do that. You're lucky I don't have anything planned with Abbey. But why do you want me to come, for real?"

"I want you to tell May's brother about everything you found out about Octolok and Propyl-Osirin."

"You think we can trust him?"

"Selby thinks we can."

"You think we can trust Selby?"

That was the question, wasn't it?

I went to class and handed in my homework.

I went to rehearsal and memorized my lines.

Outside, the weather warmed just enough for a swollen mass of cold, wet air to push into Michigan from the northwest. Some of the forecasters were even predicting blizzard winds and record snowfall. They called it "Snowmageddon."

The snow did not increase during the day. Perhaps there were moments when the clouds spat out some flecks of ice, but otherwise, it was easy to miss the sky getting darker, even as the sun rose across the sky. As afternoon turned toward evening, the snow and the wind increased, and soon the world outside looked as hostile as Hoth.

After school, I spent a lot of time looking out of May's bedroom window. I didn't know what my father would say to me, but I wasn't about to leave May's house. Not now. I decided that if he tried to make me leave, I was going to run through the backyard, leap the chain-link fence, and vanish into the twilit neighborhood. I'd take my chances with the blizzard, instead.

I kept checking the driveway, and it was always empty.

Finally, I went into the kitchen and was helping May wash the dishes when I realized that Michael was standing in the doorway, his coat dripping snow, his face red and puffed up.

"Your dad's out front," he said. "He wants to talk to you."

"Take off your boots!" yelled May.

I tossed down the towel, passed Michael as he stammered his apologies, and slipped on my own boots at the front door. Out front, the lights of the Benedict were so bright that it was hard to see the car itself. Just two twin suns illuminating the currents of snow howling down the purple night. I went around to my left, so my father had to lean over and roll down the passenger side window.

"Hi," I said, because it was the easiest thing to say.

My father was clean-shaven, which was strange ... I was used to seeing him stubbly or with a beard.

"I haven't seen you in a month," he said, his voice tremoring.

"I'm doing okay."

"John, don't think I'm going to make a big deal about it or anything, but I have to ask you ..." and he gestured at the mural on the side of the house, "what is *that?*"

"That's Jesus."

"It is?"

"See the crown of thorns? It's easy to tell when it isn't a blizzard. May's dad painted that."

"Oh. Okay. Yeah, I guess I can see that. Is May's dad ... is he okay?"

"He's pretty weird, but he's okay."

"Some people would say *we're* weird," he said with a nervous chuckle.

"They would," I said. "We are."

My father cleared his throat.

"Will you get in the damn car and talk with me for a minute?"

The snow was blasting against my neck and running down my collar, but he could see me hesitating.

"Come on, John, it's not like I'm going to drive away with you and leave Michael here."

Fair point. I clambered into the car.

"Look," he said as I slammed the door shut. "You know that we could make you come home anytime, right? I mean, we have legal custody of you. There are laws –"

"But you can't just –"

"Jesus, don't interrupt me. Just listen for a moment, okay? This is important. We haven't done this. We could have dragged you home at any time, but we haven't done it. Early on, the first few days you were gone, we mainly left you alone because we didn't want you to run away. We thought, well, at least you're with friends ... at least you're getting taken care of. We were worried if we tried to make you come back, you might do something ... reckless."

"You keep saying 'we.' Does Mother feel the same way?"

His eyes flashed with momentary anger. "Yes," he said. "She does. She loves you very much."

I gave a little nod, but just so that he would keep going.

"After a few days, we realized that this wasn't the only problem. I don't know, maybe you just have us figured out, and you know how to make us do what you want, but you mostly – not always, but *mostly* – stayed with someone we knew and trusted and let us know where you were. Your mother has been calling the school every day, and we know that you haven't been skipping. We also know that you're doing a lot better in your classes."

"You've been spying on me."

"Of course, we have!" my father said. "Are you kidding me?! Someday, you'll have a kid, and you'll do the same damn thing. We *love* you, and we *need* to know if you're doing okay."

"I'm doing fine."

"You're really lucky. You know that? If Adam left his grandparents, you think he would have the number of options that you have? What about Selby? How many of your classmates do you know who could just ... freeload ... off their friends' parents for a whole month? Huh?"

"You aren't telling me anything I don't already know. Anyway, I think I know what they're going through better than you do."

"Maybe you do. Anyway, all I'm saying is, we're trying to work things out now, your mother and I, and we need to work them out with you too. If that takes a while, okay, fine, we don't like it, but it is what it is, as long as you're in school and doing your homework and staying safe and staying off the streets. But you can't cut us out. You have to stay in touch with us. And you have to know that, whether it takes a week or two weeks or a month, you're going to have to come home sometime."

"Do I? Do you think you can make me?"

"Your life will be a lot easier if you do," he said. "And as the first step toward an armistice, I want to invite you and your girlfriend, May, over for dinner tomorrow. I strongly suggest you attend."

"What if I don't?"

"Well, I guess that's up to you. We're all rebuilding, John. Do you want to be a builder? Or a bulldozer?"

It made a kind of stupid picture in my head, but when I took a moment to think about it, I was surprised how true, how moving, the image suddenly seemed. Houses repainted, re-shingled. Houses reduced to dust. *Jesus, am I going to get emotional over everything now?*

"Last week, I went down to Wojewódka's for pączkis," my father said. "I thought I would just stuff my face and eat them all, but then I thought it would be better to save some for you. Even though Ash Wednesday is over, I thought you, and Michael, and May might like some. Will you come over and join us for dinner? You don't have to stay ... but will you come?"

I thought.

I sighed.

"Fine," I said.

Another pair of twin suns appeared behind us. It was a tiny, beat-up Starr with a few boxes of Domino's stacked in the back.

"That's our dinner," I told my father.

"Eat up," he said. "Have fun."

He gave a valiant attempt at a smile. I gave a little nod. I went back down the driveway, gave the driver Key's money, and took the pizza inside. The Starr backed out and drove away, followed by my father's Benedict, both of them struggling through the slurry treads.

Inside, I heard Michael talking, fast and excitedly.

"But Octolok might be the thing!" he was saying. "It's an adhesive. And you already know that there's an adhesive, right? That something's bonding the alkaloids to the MDMA, but nobody knows what!"

"Yeah, yeah," Drake was saying across the table. "But the problem is, I mean, the problem always was ... the bond breaks down. Like we break it apart, and what do we have? We have nightshade. And we have molly. The other thing? The thing the makes you, like, teleport, in your brain? Turn everything blue? That just vanishes along with the bonding agent. I don't know what it is or where it goes."

May sat between them, cheek leaning on her fist, looking like the most bored person on the planet.

"Jesus, Michael," I said, dropping the pizza on the table and taking a slice. Everyone else leaned in for some food. "I said to wait until we were all here."

"John," said Drake. "Your cousin is a fuckin' genius."

He seemed a lot warmer toward Michael than he did toward me.

"He ain't that big a genius," I said. "I was the one told him about them in the first place."

"Yeah," said Drake, "but he had to look up that shit, those patents and stuff, to find all this out."

"I'm surprised you trusted him so easy. You've known him about five minutes!"

"He's not the one I needed to know," Drake said. "You are. And I've been watching you all year."

"Why?"

"Back when you started seeing May the first time, I asked about you. Found out you knew Selby Demnescu. Sometimes she seems tight with Eli.

Sometimes not. I had to know about you. I had to be sure."

"So now you trust me?" I pressed Drake.

"I don't trust you," he said. "But I know you. And Eli never would have done to any friend what he did to you, taking those sunglasses. And because I know you, I can trust your cousin."

"That doesn't make any damn sense!"

"You want me to *trust* you, maybe you want to tell me what Selby Demnescu is doing with the Ostyns? And you want me to be down with you bangin' my sister –"

"I ain't bangin' her," I said.

"We aren't having sex!" said May.

"I don't trust you," Drake went on. "But I know you want me to be okay with you. You get your Einstein cousin to figure out this shit I been working on for years, and he turns it up in a few weeks. And he ain't lyin'. I knew O-Sugar had some weird adhesive holding everything together. I just didn't know what. Here's what I don't get: Michael, what made you look up these two chemicals ... these two things used by XAuto?"

"He didn't know that. *I* know that." I stabbed at my chest with my index finger. "I told you. Selby and I started seeing the blue ghosts when we were little kids. I realized that was the same thing I saw on O-Sugar. And an old teacher of mine told me that the dirt down there had all kinds of Propyl-Osirin and Octolok in it. *I* remembered."

"I don't care if the stuff makes you trip ... the blue ghosts," said Drake. "I have to figure out the secret you-know-what. The thing that makes like the teleportation thing. The thing where you think you're someplace else and then suddenly you're really there."

"Yeah," I said. "That was fucked up."

"It's got something to do with deadly nightshade," said Michael. "I'm sure it does."

"That's just part of the deal," said Drake. "The nightshade is there for you to *enjoy* the drug."

Michael shook his head. "Nightshade kills people. Nightshade makes them paranoid and freaked out."

"It's a weird drug."

Michael shook his head. "No," he said. "I don't think so. I don't think that the nightshade is there for you to enjoy it. There's got to be another reason for it. An important reason. Something that has to do with the whole thing."

"You don't really know, Michael," I said. "You've never done O-Sugar."

"When are we going to go skating?" May asked.

"How about right now?" said Drake.

The snow was flying twice as fast as we made our way out to May's car. Drake's wheelchair cut new ruts in the snow that had fallen in the few minutes since May had shoveled, and she held the door for him as he hoisted himself into the passenger seat. I helped May pack the wheelchair into the trunk, and then Michael and I got into the back. May climbed into the driver's seat and backed the car down the driveway. We curved into the cloudfall and onto Lestrade. Nothing had been plowed, and so we crept along like slow-riding pimps. May's knuckles were white as she squeezed the wheel, and the wipers swept fast from side to side. Their dismal squeak.

Eventually, we made it to Valley Street and from there on to East Street. It *had* been plowed. After May had gained the inner lane toward Parc Pierre, we picked up a bit more speed. We made our way through the East Side, and every time we stopped at a foggy red light, May glanced back and shot us a smile.

"You shoulda told me we were just going back to Parc Pierre," said Michael, when the brick buildings had spaced out, and Acheron had faded into the distance behind us.

"I didn't know where we were going," I said. "Drake told me about this."

Eventually, we turned into a large lot dominated by two hanger-like buildings. One was a large, low, squat: Quasar Bowling. One was narrower, higher: Simón Rollivar's, the roller skating rink.

"Drop me off at Quasar," said Drake. "Then y'all can go skating while I meet with Ziggurat."

May stopped the car in front of the bowling alley.

"Is twenty enough?" Drake asked.

"We might want to get something to eat or play some of the games," said May.

"Thirty?"

"And if we want to come over here and do some bowling ..."

"Forty?!"

"I'll have some change for you ... if you do give me forty."

Drake pressed a couple twenty-dollar bills into her hands.

Michael and I got out and took the wheelchair from the trunk. Drake pushed his door open and swung himself into the chair, then lifted his legs, first the right and then the left, into the guides and footrests. He slammed the door and wheeled himself up toward the bowling alley. Michael and I got back in the car, and May found a parking spot halfway between the two buildings. We all walked toward the skating rink.

"I love roller skating," she said. "Sometimes they have cotton candy there, too."

When we got inside, the DJ was in the middle of an 8os set – Berlin, the Telefones, Loaded Dice, Cheap Trick – even though most of the kids there were our age or younger. May paid for our skates, and we put them on and clumsily made our way onto the current that pulled us counter-clockwise under the high dim ceilings.

As we roll-staggered along, May and I took hands, and Michael tried to keep up.

"If we ever go to Japan," said May, "they'll try to sell us sushi, but we need to get something else instead because raw fish is gross."

"Why would we go to Japan?" I asked.

"Don't you want to go to Japan?"

"Yeah, sure, I'll go anywhere. I just don't know why you're talking about it now."

"The music makes me think of Japan."

"*This* music?" I heard Michael mutter behind me.

"What else do they eat in Japan?" May asked him.

"I don't know," he said. "Wasabi?"

He shrugged and almost fell over in the process.

May was more sure on her feet than either Michael or me. "Because," she was saying. "All of the best cartoons are the Japanimation cartoons. That's what Mike says. Mike, my brother's friend," she explained to Michael. "But my dad says that it was the Japan cars that made all the factories close around here. Is that for real?"

"Yes? Kinda? Not exactly?" I murmured.

"Like people wanted to buy those Japan cars and not the American cars?"

"I mean, that part's true."

We made another couple circuits.

We kept passing a girl: pale, tall, a bit heavy, with tangled blonde hair and thick glasses. On the third pass, she gave us a small wave.

"Michael, is that your girlfriend?" I asked over my shoulder.

"What?" he asked.

566

"Is that Abbey?"

"Um, yeah," he said. "I waved to her."

"That's your girlfriend we just passed?" said May.

"Um ..."

"You've got to introduce us!"

Michael seemed reluctant to say or do anything, but it didn't matter because May spun around and caught up with Abbey on the next pass. They talked quickly, Abbey nodding and waving, and May beckoned for us all to leave the rink.

When we were back on the carpet, I took a seat. My feet felt heavy with the skates, and my ankles ached.

"Um," said Michael. "May and John, this is Abbey. John is my cousin. He's going out with May. I know Abbey from high school."

"You're lucky you got Michael," I said, nodding his way. "He's a real pimp. He tears shit up in the Os whenever he's back in town."

Abbey laughed nervously. She looked confused.

"Well," she said. "I've got to go. I'm here with my sister; I'd better not let her get ahead of me too much."

She went back on the rink.

"What, you guys fighting?" I asked Michael.

"Not exactly ..." he said.

"Let's start skating again!" said May.

She pulled me to my feet.

"I'm gonna sit here and rest a few minutes." I heard Michael's voice diminishing behind me as May pulled me along.

An ocean of blue swirls had been painted along the cinder-block walls, with brightly abstracted trees rising above in a rainbow of colors. Several American flags hung at regular intervals. It all blurred as we sped along.

"So, all the Japan cars," May was saying, "here's what I think. If all the people with all the money would just share it, then it wouldn't matter. If they wanted, they could just keep the factory shut down until people wanted cars from it again – I mean, American cars – and they could just turn everything on again. All the machines. And then the workers could come back. I know, I know, it isn't free. Because maybe people want Japan cars now, but maybe, someday, they would decide that they wanted cars that our parents would make, or, I don't know, maybe they could get rid of the factories or put in a garden, or a mall, or a movie theater!"

Just ahead of us, a balding middle-aged white man fumbled along on his skates. He glanced at May as she spoke and tried to stifle his laughter.

"You got a problem with something?" I said.

He held up his hands to demonstrate harmlessness. He looked genuinely embarrassed. "No, no," he said.

"I don't care how old you are," I said. "Don't laugh at her."

He looked awkwardly between the two of us and the floor as he rolled along. On the next pass, he left the rink.

"Hey," said May. "Don't do that, okay?"

"He was laughing at you, you know," I snapped.

"I don't care. I don't want you to get in a fight about me. It's stupid. Especially if it's someone's dad."

"I'm sorry. It just ... it pisses me off when people are mean to you. I keep telling you; you can't let people walk all over you!"

"I'd like to visit Japan," May murmured.

We made another couple circuits around the rink.

"You remember Mike?" she asked. "My brother's friend?"

"Um, yeah?"

"I don't normally think about him very much," May said, "but I am now because it was one year ago today that his brother Cedric died."

That wasn't what I was expecting her to say.

"I'm sorry," I said. "What happened to him?"

May was quiet for a minute. I noticed the way our bodies swayed with the pace of our skates. I could keep myself moving, but I wasn't graceful, and I heard the clatter every time my skates hit the floor.

"Cedric got shot," May said. "He was parked outside a club waiting for his friend. Not Drake, another friend. He was going to come out of the club and meet him and go home. Anyway, Cedric was sitting in his car. Nobody heard it, though. The friend came out and saw that he was shot. Someone shot him from behind. They don't know why. I mean, they couldn't find out why because they never found out who did it! He did have some money taken, though. But they shot him through the back window of his car. It was really sad. Drake went to the funeral, but they had the ... the coffin was closed, you know?"

We made another circuit.

I watched the whir of the Parc Pierre kids as they circled the rink, clunking on and off, radiating away to play video games, or to buy pop and nachos, or to go to the bathroom. They were younger than us, mostly, and their arms and legs were bare and unscarred. Their voices were higher than ours. They laughed a lot.

I saw the middle-aged dad who had laughed at May. He was off the rink now, and he'd found his daughter: a skinny blonde-haired girl who looked like she was probably twelve or thirteen. He was buying her a bag of popcorn. Suddenly I felt so sad and tired. I didn't want to think about anything. Not the chemical composition of O-Sugar, or Michael's weird girlfriend ignoring him, and certainly not Cedric's closed-casket funeral. I wanted to sleep.

"Let's go get Michael," said May. "I want to go bowling. Do you?"

"Sure," I said. "Fine."

We collected Michael, changed out of our skates, and crossed the parking lot to Quasar. The snow was coming down even thicker than before. May's Aubrey had already been covered again. Now it was identical to all of the other cars in the parking lot.

There were still a dozen bowling alleys in Basadena County, mostly peopled by aging shoprats, but Quasar was where all the suburban kids went. The newish carpet was patterned with nebulae phasing in and out among red, purple, yellow stars, and bright pink Saturns encircled by lime green rings. Polished lockers and rows of bowling balls lined the walls, along with claw games, video games, and slot machines packing the dark back wall, and behind that, the darkened cave of a bar scarcely illuminated by low hanging faux-Tiffany lamps. I saw Drake and Ziggurat warily circling a pool table. Silent in concentration.

"Ziggurat wants to open a supermarket," said May.

"What?" I asked.

"He says if Drake figures out the O-Sugar, and they make a bunch of money, the feds could bust him for tax stuff and get our parents in trouble too. So he says what he's gonna do is give the money to his neighbors, so it's just a little bit for each one, and then they'll all pool the money, and it won't look suspicious, and they'll open a supermarket up on Arlington or something for all the people who live out there and don't have a car."

"What do you think about it?" I asked.

"I don't know. I mean, I guess it makes sense. It would be nice for all those people to have a supermarket. But I wish Drake wasn't in it, you know? I wish he'd just leave it all alone, okay?"

"Does it bother you?" Michael asked, "that we're helping your brother? John and me?"

May shrugged. "It doesn't matter if I do," she said. "You're doing it anyway."

"You must trust us a lot," Michael said. "To trust us with your brother like that. I mean, you love him a lot?"

"Most of my life, Drake's been there for me when nobody else has. Not even my mom. Not even my dad."

"I feel awful!" Michael exclaimed and put his face in his hands. "I lied to you!"

"What?" I asked.

"I lied to you! I lied when I told you Abbey was my girlfriend. I mean ... she is ... my friend. But I never asked her out. We aren't going out. We're just friends."

I hadn't guessed. But it didn't surprise me either. What was Michael thinking about when he wasn't looking up obscure chemicals for me? He felt all alone in his new school, so he had lied about a friend to make his life there feel more meaningful. I felt bad for him. I felt bad for Abbey. I wanted him back at Eastern, where he belonged.

"Everyone has someone," Michael said. "I don't have someone. I had someone ... Juanita! But that was two years ago. I mean, I think that was my one shot. I don't know how I got it. I'm too fat, too weird, and so I had a chance, and I blew it. I totally did."

May sat down at Michael's side. She put her hand on Michael's back.

"What was it that happened before?" she asked. "How did you start going out with Juanita?"

"Oh, she had a boyfriend, and he wasn't being very nice to her, so I stood up for her, and after that, we just, I don't know, started going out. We went out for two months and one week. It was the only time I've ever gotten anyone to go out with me."

"So, she went out because you were wonderful to her?"

Michael stared at May.

"I mean," May said. "You were wonderful to a girl, and it worked, and she went out with you. Couldn't you just be wonderful again?"

"I wasn't *that* wonderful..."

"Or maybe a girl will be wonderful to you, and you'll say, I like you! See, Michael? Anything can happen! It can even happen at a roller-skating rink. Or a bowling alley. That's why I'm glad we came out. Even with all the snow. Things can happen at a party. Nothing's going to happen when you're just sitting in front of your TV."

"I guess ..."

We went up and rented our shoes. We picked out our bowling balls. We bowled and did pretty badly. Michael ended up getting a few pins here and there and a single spare. I got two spares and a strike. May beat us all with two spares and two strikes and no gutters. She got more points than the two of us put together. I could've done better, but I was thinking about what she had said, what I had seen, all week long, all night long.

"Hey!" yelled Drake from the bar. "John's cousin!"

Michael turned in his direction.

"Come here," said Drake. "I want you to meet someone important!"

Ziggurat was smiling. Michael set down his bowling ball and went into the bar. I saw Drake handing over his pool cue.

"So, May. You said that someone tricked you into sex," I said. "Was it Mike?"

May sighed.

"I don't want to talk about the time I got tricked," she said. "I don't need to talk about that. But you're right that I slept with Mike. You guessed that."

"It was just a hunch I had ... after you told me about Cedric."

"It wasn't supposed to be like a secret."

"And it isn't like I need to know. I slept with this girl Crystal, and you've never asked me about that!"

"Well, you're with me now."

I nodded. I stared at the lane. I felt jealousy in the back of my mouth, and for a moment, I wanted to throw the ball down the lane, but the game was over. The pins were racked up in the dark.

"Does it bother you?" May asked.

I can't help it; it does! I thought.

"Only a little," I said.

"You know," May said. "You're always telling me not to let people treat me bad. I don't think it's very fair of you to be mad at me about something that happened before I even knew you, and anyway, you did the same thing with somebody else."

"Just let me think for a moment," I said. "Not even for long, just for, like, a minute."

I turned the bowling ball in my hand. Felt its weight. I took it to the rack and set it down. I returned.

"I wasn't ever mad at you about it," I said. "But that doesn't even matter, because you're right. You're completely right. I'm sorry. It shouldn't bother me, and I'm not going to let it bother me."

"That sounds like a good deal. I don't want us to have a fight about stuff like that ever, okay?"

Somewhere, the wind cut a branch from its tree, and the thing split a bunch of power lines, and all of the lights in the bowling alley went out, and now we were in darkness again.

We joined the caravan of vehicles leaving the drifted parking lot. When we finally made it back to East Street, the snow had blown across the road, obliterating all signs of lane and curb. May pushed farther east into Parc Pierre in the hopes of catching 292 back toward Akawe, but when we got to the entrance ramp, it was blocked by a jackknifed semi, with several cars thrown like toys in its wake.

We pushed on through the howling dark until we made it to Intervale Road and turned toward the city. The farther we went, the more black shapes we saw in the margins: rebellious cars that had fled the road. While we'd been inside, the air had gotten colder, the snow drier, and the wind harder until its speed was able to strip shingles. Nobody spoke – we all felt tense – but May aimed straight between the tender rays of sulfur lamps marking our humble runways.

"You probably should have just dropped me off at home," said Michael.

"Well, it's a little late now!" I said.

When we pulled into the driveway, all the lights were off, and the painted Jesus wailed silently at us.

"Do you want me to shovel the ramp for you, Drake?" May asked.

"Don't mess with it tonight," Drake said. "Just get as close to the back door as you can."

When we'd all finally made it inside, May rummaged around in the drawers until she found some flashlights. She went into the basement for linens, but Michael, dazed from the long drive back to this cold, dark house, dragged the couch pillows into May's bedroom and fell asleep at once on the floor.

"Oh," said May, holding an armful of blankets and sheets. "I was going to have him sleep on the couch."

"We could wake him up," I said hopefully.

"No, that's okay. We can just sleep in our clothes tonight."

I finally found my anger for Michael.

When morning arrived, the snow was deep, but the sky was clear again. Without the furnace, the house had started to cool, but it wasn't *that* cold yet. We wrapped ourselves in coats and sweaters and tried to wait out the power outage.

Key, heroically, walked clear from Armstrong to Ash and came back with a big bag of McMuffins (seven), hash browns (nine), and coffees (three). "I just told 'em to give me what they had all ready," he said. "Eat up."

We ate.

We heard a knock at the door.

I answered it and saw Justin Ray on the other side with snow shovel.

"Hey John," he said. "I thought you was stayin' with Nova."

"No," I said, "That was a week ago. More than a week ago."

"So, you're going out with May again?"

"Yeah, and I'm not on the rebound! I don't want to be with *anyone* else."

"Cool, man, cool. Don't flip your shit. I'm just sayin' what I heard. Hey. It's better than May and Leigh up in that trailer park, right?"

"Sure," I said, though I didn't know what he was talking about. "What are you here for anyway?"

"I live, like, a block from here. Sometimes, Key pays me to shovel his walk."

"Key!" I yelled.

Key came over.

"Here's five," he said, wrapping some money in Justin's hand. "Don't tell May I had you do it." Justin nodded and started shoveling.

"You know, I could do it," I said.

"She'd never forgive you," he said. "But she needs a break, you know?"

Throughout the day, things incrementally returned to normal. This power outage had been less severe than the last. We all cheered – even Drake – when we heard the microwave beep followed by the low hum of the furnace in the basement. I rubbed my hands together until they were warm. I was glad to be out of the cold, but it freed my mind to worry about tonight. What would my parents think of May? Would they try to pressure me into coming home again? But even more elementally, I was worried about going into the house on Agit Street, because I felt that I had been a completely different person the last time I had lived there.

Michael spent hours lying on his stomach in the living room, drawing out schematics of letters surrounded by dots, dashes, and equal signs. N, O, O, OH. H3C. N. O. O. OH. Squiggle lines and hexagons.

"What's that?" I asked.

"Trying to figure out O-Sugar," he said.

"Maybe he's got the right idea!" said May. "If you can help me with my homework, I can help you with yours?"

"I thought you didn't do homework on the weekend," I said.

"Maybe if you help me out, I can!"

We spent the rest of the afternoon conjugating Spanish verbs and listing out the nutritional benefits of the four food groups. It did distract me from my anxiety, but eventually the sky started to darken again. My armpits got sweaty with nervousness. May laughed, unworried. My father pulled into the driveway, and I introduced him to May in the front yard, and everything was going as well as it could. Michael came out, we all climbed into the car, and my father drove us across Akawe to Agit Street.

"That's our house," said my father.

"Oh, I know," said May. "I drove John over here to pick up his things when he moved out."

My father hesitated, trying to understand why she'd say something like that.

"Well, here we are," I said, climbing out of my seat almost before the car had stopped.

I found my mother standing near the door, a smile plastered on her face, her hands out, clutching, almost grasping, needing something to do, waiting to take our coats. I sloughed off mine and handed it to her. May was right behind me.

"Oh, thank you, Mrs. Bridge! I'm May!" she said.

"Call me Theresa," said my mother.

"Like Mother Theresa?"

"Hardly," I said.

My mother didn't say anything but took May's and Michael's coats and hung them all on the coat rack. My father came inside.

"It smells wonderful in here," he said.

"It's smelled like that all day," my mother said. "You're just noticing it now because you've been out."

"What are we eating?" I asked. I felt awkward. Like I was at a stranger's house.

"Chicken and dumplings," said my mother.

We made it, somehow, through the stale air of the living room – *Was it always so dry in here? So dusty?* – and into the dining room, where the shamrock green walls glowed in the steady light of two taper candles. After my mother had brought in the food and drinks, we all sat down, with my parents each at a head of the table, Michael with a side to himself, and May and me side-by-side.

Then, everyone but May made the sign of the cross, and we all clasped our hands.

My father started, "Bless us, oh Lord, and these thy gifts which we are about to receive, through the bounty of Christ, our Lord. Amen." Then, symbolically, he added, "Would anyone like to add anything?"

"Yes!" said May. "I would. I just want to pray for everyone I love and care about. My boyfriend, John. His cousin, Michael. And their families. And my brother, so that he doesn't get killed, and my dad so he doesn't go back to jail, and John to get along with his parents, and Michael to finish the problem he's working on. And everyone who was out in the cold."

May spoke solemnly, eyes closed, while my parents stared at her in surprise. When she finished her prayer, she opened her eyes.

"Doesn't anyone else want to add anything?" May asked.

"Yeah," said my father. "I'll add a few things. I pray for all the poor, and all the hungry, and all the lonely, and all the forgotten. May they find wealth, and nourishment, and companionship, and memory. All the good things that help to keep us all alive. And I pray for everyone with X, everyone with XAWU, everyone in Salvage, everyone in Akawe, to make it through this hard and dangerous time safely. And I pray for John and Michael and May to know that they are always welcome here and that they never need to be alone or scared. Amen."

"Amen!" said May.

"Amen," said my mother, Michael, and me.

Something was filling me up inside, and all I could think of was that it was like my mother's chicken and dumpling dinner: something nourishing and reassuring. But I had to pack these feelings in to make it through the night. I would look at them later. I also had to ask my father about Salvage sometime.

"Thank you," my father said, "for your prayer there, May. You know, I always ask if anyone wants to add anything, but nobody ever does. I like it this way. I like for us to take a moment and name off the things that matter."

"We never pray at my house," said May.

"Do you have a church?" asked my father. I gave him a glance. "I'm sorry, it's okay if you don't. I mean, it's just something everyone used to ask about."

"No," said May. "Not really, but when my dad was getting himself clean a while ago, he painted Jesus on the side of our house. But my brother doesn't believe in Jesus. He believes in Superman. I believe in Jesus, I think, but I don't really have a church. But last week, I took John to church at St. Benedict in my neighborhood."

"Really," said my mother. "St. Benedict the Black, right? I didn't even think that church was still open."

I wanted to change the subject. The last thing I wanted to talk about was God.

"What's with all the water bottles?" I asked. "You guys buy out the Meijer's?"

Cases of bottled water had been stacked in the corner of the dining room. There were more cases in the kitchen, as well as a clunky chrome Culligan filter fitted to the sink.

"We got them from the National Guard," my father said.

We took a few minutes to eat. While we were eating, we didn't have to worry about what we were saying.

"So, Michael," said my mother. "What is the problem you're working on?"

"The what?" asked Michael.

"May said you were working on something?"

"Oh, that." Michael blushed deeply. "It's just a chemistry problem. My chemistry class is pretty hard, so ..." He took a big bite to keep himself from talking more.

The chicken and dumplings were perfect. Salty and just slightly sweet, moist and thick, a smooth buttery roux, the light bite, light texture, spongy flesh, warm and rich and full in my stomach.

"Dinner's really good, Mother," I said.

"Thank you. I haven't made them in a while, so ..."

I tried to sneak a glance at the cuckoo clock, but my eyes landed on my mother's face instead. She wasn't really into makeup, but she had put some on tonight, and I knew that it was to cover up her tiredness and worry. To cover up the shadows under her eyes. She noticed me looking and answered with a question about *Teen Age Riot* rehearsals.

She kept asking me questions, about school, about Adam and Chuck and Quanla and Nova, then about May and Key and Drake. I knew that she wasn't really worried about any of my friends, though. Not tonight. She was worried about me. It was me making her tired and worried more than anything else, and for the first time, I felt guilty for refusing to come home.

And then I felt like I was seeing her for the first time in my life, not as my mother at all, but as a wise but exhausted woman in her 40s, who was poised, who noticed all sorts of things, but who worried too much, and who mostly kept her worries to herself. Who felt like her worries were devouring her. I wanted to say something to reassure her, but the words I imagined seemed idiotic or insufficient, so I just kept thanking her for the meal.

"It really is really good," I said.

My father, on the other hand, had a simpler worry; he was worried about silence. Whenever he wasn't chewing or shoveling food into his mouth, he was talking. I was happy when he started talking about Salvage, a radical XAWU caucus that had been simmering in the background for years but which had finally come to a boil with the plant shutdowns of the last year.

"The only question is whether XAuto is going to leave a couple thousand jobs here in the end or whether they're just going to end it all for good!"

In response, Salvage intended to strike everywhere at all times, to forge new ties with the urban poor, the Blacks, the rednecks, the broken down, the East Side, South Side, North Side, and West End, and make common cause against the corporate sentience that had obliterated their past and future. My father respected and admired Salvage. He also feared them a little.

"You can't eat idealism," my father said. "Still," he went on. "They've held on to their dignity. You can't eat idealism, but food won't feed your sense of worth, either."

Michael didn't talk much more than I did.

May talked a lot, though. She told my parents about her home in Lestrade, how much she liked Eastern but disliked the teachers and kids and classes and homework and mornings and hallways. She told them about Drake, how much he loved her and protected her, and how she had to shovel the sidewalk too much. She told them that she loved to bake. She wanted to be a baker when she finally graduated. Or maybe a veterinarian. Or maybe the hostess at the Bob Evans on Outer Road, except only if they could give her a chair to sit in when she got tired.

And my parents thought that they were subtle with the glances they exchanged. May didn't seem to notice. Neither did Michael. But I noticed. *Is this real?* they were wondering. *Is he still planning to go to college at all? In Chicago? How is that going to work with this new girlfriend, who isn't planning on going anywhere?*

They didn't ask May how old she was, but she was obviously at least a year or two older than me, although she was in ninth grade, and didn't seem to understand the difference in the training you need to become a veterinarian versus a hostess of Bob Evans who, by the way, does *not* get to sit down on the job. Even though they didn't say these things, I knew they were thinking them, and I found myself starting to swell with anger against them.

"May is great," I said. "She already takes so much care of her brother and her dad. They're great too, but May does all the cooking in that house, and most of the cleaning, too."

"Thanks, John," May said. "It's a lot easier since you are there. Since you are helping me with my homework. I usually do my homework, but I don't worry about getting the right answers. I wouldn't have time for it with all the other stuff. But since John moved in with us, I'm able to get it all done. Your son is a very good person, Mrs. Bridge."

My mother smiled.

My father pushed his seat back from the table, excused himself to the kitchen, and returned with a grease-stained white cardboard box.

"We have three pączkis left," he said. "They might be a little stale, but I resisted eating them, just for you three. There's a lemon, a custard cream, and a raspberry."

"I want lemon!" said Michael.

"Give May the raspberry," I said. "They're the best ones."

"Awww!" said May, and she leaned over and kissed me on the lips.

After we had eaten our pączkis – a bit of leftover sugar dusting our lips and cheeks – my father turned out all of the lights so that only the burning candles illuminated our five faces. My mother wasn't smiling. She was watchful. Michael looked confused. May, eager. My father went into the kitchen and came back with a pearl-colored white coffee cup.

"John," he said, "I'm guessing that you missed out on Ash Wednesday this year."

I nodded, confirming his suspicions.

"Well, I was giving out ashes this year, so I did a bad thing. I stole some of them –"

"You stole them?" I said. "The ashes? From the church?! Holy shit, Father!"

"He put them in his pocket," said my mother, trying to hide her smirk.

Michael was scandalized.

"Holy shit!" I repeated.

"I wasn't trying to steal! I did it for you! Do you want some ashes or not? It's up to you."

"Yeah, I do. I guess ... I probably need them right now."

Without another word, my father came over to my chair and knelt before me. He dipped his thumb in the coffee mug.

"Um ... remember that you are dust, and to dust, you will return."

He sketched a soot cross on my forehead.

"You look beautiful with that, John," said May.

"Would you like some ashes, May?" my father asked.

"Yes, I would," she said. "I truly would."

He said the words, and she closed her eyes.

"Amen," she said, sparkling in her voice.

My father looked at Michael.

"No thanks," he said. "I already got ashes."

And Michael looked suspiciously at my father's coffee mug.

Before we left, I went into the study and dug through boxes until I turned up *The Chronicles of Narnia*. I slipped them into my backpack on our way out to the car.

That night, May and I tossed and rolled together, close in the darkness. When the sun came up, the snow sparkled like crushed gemstones. May and I took showers, microwaved some Eggos for breakfast, slabbed them with butter and sugar, and went back into her room. It was a long, lazy day, and we talked about our friends. What was happening with them? I called Chuck and Quanla and Nova to find out what they had been doing since I had left their houses. Chuck wanted me to come back; he said his mother had been easier on him about chores while I was around. He told me that Tammy would forgive me for bailing on them. Quanla asked me about a used computer store opening on Whitmore Road. At Nova's, nobody was at home.

I tried reaching Adam again, but neither Carla, Grandpa M, or Grandma A knew where he was. Was he staying with Dylan? Had he vanished Up North again? Somewhere else in the city?

Selby had gotten suspended that week after getting into a fight at lunch. Evidently, an 11th grader had said something about her little sisters, and Selby had slammed the girl's head into one of the cafeteria doors. Before the fight had been broken up, there had been blood and hair on the floor.

After weeks of chewing my tongue, I finally asked May: "Do you think Lucy is okay?"

"I don't know," she said. "She won't tell me."

"Do you think ... at your party. Do you think she knew that the gun wasn't loaded?"

"I don't know."

"Maybe it was just a joke. I mean, if so, it was a pretty fucked up joke, but –"

"She isn't combing her hair anymore. I don't think she's even washing her clothes anymore."

We sat in silent for several minutes, and the rooms beyond were quiet, too. I felt like May's whole house was mourning Lucy now.

"Can't we help her?" I asked.

"I don't know how," said May.

I thought, for a moment, about the room just beneath us where Lucy had ... and I wanted to think about anything else.

"I brought us some books," I said. "I thought you might like them. Do you want me to read to you?"

"Yes, please."

So I read *The Lion, The Witch, and the Wardrobe*, and May listened. For a while, she drifted in and out of sleep, but she woke in time for the beavers to save the children from pursuit, and laughed when Santa Claus made his appearance. We ate dinner in her room and finished the book before midnight.

"There's another!" I said. "Should I start it?"

"No. Let's save it for tomorrow."

That night, May and I rolled and struggled to keep the covers on us. The air that kissed our skin was cool and raised bumps and tiny hairs. Key was right: this *was* a house for healing. I looked up at the shaded windows, their own dark blue, and it triggered another O-Sugar flashback, but this one was softer, gentler than the others. I stood at the planetary pole, barely tilted against the orbit, and so the sun skimmed the horizon, perpetual dawn, perpetual dusk, and day and night didn't exist there. To travel toward the equator was to create a night and day, so I contracted distances. Made it all-at-once. I combined the revelations of Drake with the revelations of Miss Pavilik. God had ordained the universe to self-destruct, but O-Sugar had given us the power to defy God. He could stretch space all he wanted, but when we imbibed, we defied him, and folded the expanding space back into place. If time really *was* travel, then, maybe, with practice, we could bring the past into the present. Not a perfect past that we would relive with nostalgia and sentimentality, but a broken past that we would finally have the wisdom to repair.

I softly started to count to eight.

May woke and started counting with me.

The next morning, we found that another storm had come through, quietly and without wind. It had dropped another six inches of snow, and school was canceled. May didn't bother to shovel the walk that day because the fridge was full, and nobody was going anywhere. We lay around and ate and watched TV and read *Prince Caspian*. The children switched into the ruins of Cair Paravel and followed their leonine guide toward shelter at Aslan's How.

That night, after we had twisted and touched again, under the covers, her and me, I activated the O-Sugar again. I realized that I was learning to control it. Maybe some chemical – maybe this Octolok Michael was researching – had gotten lodged in my brain, and I'd finally unearthed its location. Maybe I could turn the thing on whenever I wanted. All of the visions I'd had for years – all those stories I'd picked up from Selby and Adam and Quanla and Chuck – felt fierce and real. God and his family. Big and Place. The girl with the gold-green swimsuit who had become the woman with the gold-green dress. The Nain Bleu. They were all real, and they moved about the world with different names. I closed my eyes, counted to eight under my breath, and visions went away.

"If we have school off tomorrow," I murmured into May's back, "do you want to go sledding?"

"Sure."

"I always went sledding over by XAI. The golf course."

"Oh, no. Are you kidding? The hill at Eastern is way bigger."

School was canceled the next day. It had gotten so cold that the buses wouldn't start. May put on a lot of lotion and perfume after taking her morning shower. She sculpted her hair. We got in her car and rolled out carefully, slowly to Eastern, and went sledding down the big slope, which really was twice as big as any of the hills in South Village. We fell off our sled and rolled over and over in the snow, kissing before we got back up. When we were done, we stopped by my parents'. My mother was at work, but my father was happy to see us, and he made us hot chocolate and threw a plate of frozen cookies in the microwave. He asked May more questions: about her favorite classes, her favorite music, her favorite TV shows. He waved to both of us as we left.

Back at May's house, I read her *The Voyage of the Dawn Treader*.

I read quickly. Skipped sentences. Skipped whole paragraphs, I was so anxious to get to the end of it all. To the ocean of sweet water. With the lily pads. With the sand bar and the great beyond.

That night, I wanted to imagine myself onto a blue-black beach, where the sand would be so fine that it would twinkle and reflect the glittering fragments of the stars overhead, and maybe the sand would be the actual stars, scattered across dark galaxies, but May kept me present in her room.

"I think it would be a very good idea if we had sex now, okay?" she panted in my ear.

"I do too," I whispered back. "I do ... um ... but I don't have anything ... for it. You know?"

"I don't either," she said. "I don't care. I don't have AIDS, John!"

"That's not what I'm worried about."

"Oh. Does it mean ... because your parents are Catholic. Should we get married? I mean, I love you. Can we get married? I'm seventeen! I'll be eighteen in just a year!"

"No! I mean, I'm only fifteen. No way we can get married now. My parents would flip their shit. But, I mean, I don't care about that."

"But then, what are you worried about?!"

She was breathing heavy, sad, frustrated. I don't even know how I was breathing. The stars were crowding out my eyes. I hated that I was spending all of my everything trying to think clearly then, because I didn't want to be

583

thinking at all. I wanted to absorb this moment totally. I wanted this moment in May's bedroom to become every moment and every time.

"I'm worried about ..." I said. "May, what if you got pregnant?"

"Oh ..." she said, and fell on her back, looking up at the ceiling.

It took a moment before I realized that she wasn't going to say anything else.

"What's wrong?" I finally asked.

"Well," she said. "You know what is better than anything? Even better than cherries and cookies, and even better than sex? Babies are better. And people have been having babies forever. That's how you know that God wants to have people on the earth. That's like the real getting married, okay? And if we had a baby together, you and me, that would make us just like we were married, and nothing about this has to be real anymore, and it can be something better, I mean we can! You know? And if we had a baby together, you and me, we could take care of it, and take care of us, and make it happy, and the baby would love us, just so, so much!"

Now, I really did feel dizzy. She meant it. Every word that she said. The sounds were stirring in her throat.

"May," I whispered. "I can't have a baby. I'm ... Jesus, May, I'm sorry, and I do love you so much, but Jesus, I'm only fifteen! I'm not ready for that! Are you ready for that?"

"Other people are! Younger than me!"

She started crying.

I held her.

We didn't speak again that night.

But when we fell asleep, we dreamed together. We spoke in our sleep and walked in the night, all night long. The horizon had turned purple with solar radiation, but the stars were bright overhead, and the moon waxing gibbous, cheering us on, her silent mouth wide with joy and sadness. Michael walked with us, and he thanked us for letting him join us on our sacred travels. We would have invited Selby, but she had already departed. I remembered sprinklers, and shopping carts, and an old man dancing with a mop. May and I whispered. We kissed. We held our breath. We held heartbeats. At the end of the night, I said goodbye, and I clambered up the neat, new shingles to my bedroom.

The next day, school was canceled again.

I read May *The Silver Chair* very quickly. We finished by lunchtime. After we ate, I read her *A Horse and His Boy*. I skipped whole chapters and managed to finish in just two hours.

"This is the lame one," I said, waving *The Magician's Nephew* in the air, but I read the first two chapters, until the world destroyed by the Terminators shattered. Then we just flipped through the rest of the book, looking at the illustrations.

"The last one is the best," I said, rooting around in my backpack for the final book, but *The Last Battle* was nowhere to be found.

"I'm sure I got everything off the shelf!"

"It's okay," said May.

"I probably lent it to Bill Chapman, and he left it on his floor, and it got cat piss all over it! They always had animals running all over their house ..."

"It's okay, John. I was kind of starting to get confused by the whole thing, anyway."

Then, in the evening, sitting in the living room and watching *Wheel of Fortune* with Key and Drake, we heard a knock on the door.

Michael was standing outside, shivering and red-cheeked, with an expression of frigid defiance.

"How did you get here?" I asked him.

"I took the bus," he stammered. "It's really fucking cold outside."

Michael came inside. He stamped his boots then diligently removed them. He reached into his coat pocket and took out a black rectangular thing, slightly curved, with what looked like thick black ropes hanging from it.

"I did it," he said. "I figured it out. I know how to make O-Sugar."

Michael strode into the kitchen, followed by Drake and May and me. My cousin found the silverware drawer and grabbed a butter knife. He sat down at the table and wedged the blade into the slim side of the black rectangular shape. I squinted at it.

"Is that ... what is that?" I asked.

"A brake pedal," said Michael. "From a 1979 Aubrey Pacific. I had to spend half of yesterday freezing my ass off at a junkyard to get this. I only talked the guy out of it because he knew he wasn't going to sell the car anyway. It was all rusted out and missing two doors. He had some mean dogs, too –"

"Michael!" I asked. "What's going on?"

May was watching. Drake held his chin in his palm, balancing curiosity and guarded skepticism.

"What's going on?" Michael laughed. He turned and shook the brake pad in my face. "You're my only friends! I'm not going anywhere in my life! I can't even get any girl to even look at me! But you know what? The feds couldn't do it, and the Satanic Masters couldn't do it, and even you couldn't do it, Drake. I did this. I did it! I figured out O-Sugar!"

Michael turned his attention back to the brake pad, which was proving more stubborn than he had expected, however hard he scraped.

"Octolok," he said, "comes from a tree in the Gulf of Papua, in these swamps near the ocean. They call it the blunat tree, and it's sorta related to the nipa palm. It's crazy. It's a palm tree that grows with its trunk beneath the ground, so all you see are its branches, which are all twisted, and they even don't always have leaves. If you ever saw it, you probably wouldn't think it was alive, except for the fruit, maybe. I tried to get a picture of it, but I couldn't find one. But the wood isn't anything special. The fruit is useful."

"What do you mean?" I asked. "Can you eat it?"

"I don't know. I don't think so? The fruit is this sort of ball of ... I guess it must look like a little apple? I mean, I had to guess. I got all this from a lot of patent filings. And it isn't like they describe things, exactly, so you can picture them in your mind. They, mostly, are just telling you what they use and how they use it."

"Okay."

"Inside the fruit, there is this really sticky sort of paste. It's really good at binding things together. The military tried to use it for repairs and stuff, but when they would mix it with other things in the lab – to preserve it or transport it – the chemical would break down. I mean, it never really worked right when they altered it like that."

Michael had finally managed to pry the pad shims apart, and he began rhythmically scraping the knife along one of the two narrow sheets.

"After World War II, a lot of those guys who worked for the army went to work for the auto industry, and some of them went to work for X. Some of the big guys at X Auto remembered this plant and its crazy adhesive properties, and so they made a patent for a resin from the tree. They found a way to preserve it by encasing it in molecular plastic. It only took a film of a few molecules of this mixture to hold car parts together. It was, like, the strongest glue ever while it lasted. Problem was, it didn't last forever ... it eventually decayed. The parts started to peel apart. And the plant was really hard to find. They couldn't ever manage to grow them anywhere else, which doesn't make a lot of sense, since it was easy enough for them to replicate the soil conditions and all that. But anyway, it was super expensive to just get this stuff, so they only used it for, like, four or five years. But the organic-synthetic compound I described? The resin they used as an adhesive? They called it Octolok. And this is it."

Michael held up the knife, and we saw that it was coated with a thin black paste from the brake pad.

"Drake," Michael said. "You got some molly?"

Drake hedged. He was excited, I could tell. He was breathing fast. But he'd been trying for too long and had been disappointed too many times. He didn't want tonight to let him down. Not when *Wheel* was broadcasting from Hawai'i with two sisters competing and one of them pregnant with twins!

"Come on," said Michael. "We gonna crack this code or what?"

"Yeah, yeah, fine!" said Drake. "Go get it, May. From the laundry room."

May frowned in disgust but went down into the basement.

"And you got some nightshade?"

"Yeah, I got that, but it doesn't matter because I don't know the secret ingredient."

"Shut up, Drake. We've got the secret ingredient!" said Michael.

Drake rummaged through some drawers and handed Michael a small vial.

"That's tincture of nightshade," said Drake. "I got that from a pharmacy, not cheap. Careful with it."

May came back upstairs with a small bag of crystals.

"May," said Michael. "Crush that up into powder. Drake, I'll need a scale and your oven, and some tweezers."

"I got that," said Drake. "But we usually just use the hot plate."

Michael thought, "Yeah, that's fine," he said. "Bring it over."

He plugged in the hot plate. I could feel the heat radiating off it as the coils started to glow.

"You got a piece of metal or something?" asked Michael. "I don't want to wreck your hot plate."

"Just use this!" snapped Drake, dropping a quarter onto the hot plate. I had never seen him so impatient.

Michael wiped the paste from the knife onto a scrap of napkin. He put it on the scale.

"Five milligrams," he muttered. "Too much." He pinched off a bit of the paste with his tweezers, then weighed the rest again. "Three milligrams." Another pinch. "Two milligrams. Perfect. I mean, I'm kind of guessing, but I think that sounds right."

Drake nodded, his excitement growing.

Michael scraped the paste onto the quarter.

"Scopolamine," he muttered.

Drake handed him the vial.

"Scopolamine?" I asked.

"In the deadly nightshade tincture. They go together."

He put a dropper into the vial, took out a little bit of the liquid, and dropped it onto the Octolok.

"May, you done with that?" asked Michael.

"I think so ..." she said.

"Just measure out a bit ... like ... I'm not sure ..."

".75 milligrams," suggested Drake.

They weighed out grains of molly and brushed them onto the quarter.

"Now we wait."

"When do we add the secret ingredient?" asked Drake. "What *is* the secret ingredient?"

"There isn't one," said Michael. "Actually, no, wait, that isn't exactly true. There is a secret ingredient ... but it's not what you'd think. See, this is how I figured it all out, and it took me weeks and weeks, but it makes sense. You know the feds have been trying to crack this, and as far as we know they haven't been able to. I mean, we haven't heard anything in the news about that. There hasn't been a bust to take out the Chalks. But they can hire any chemist they want to do this stuff. Also, you know that the FBI's got to have gotten invoices from all of the industrial companies, to see if anybody was buying way too much of something. And you know they got into the Chalks, no problem, so it wasn't anything that the Chalks could figure out. No, the chemical had to be something *really* weird, being used in a weird way, for it to have stayed a mystery for this long. So, I knew I had to start with something that nobody would figure out easily, you know?"

Michael paused to see if we followed. I wasn't sure that we did, but he kept going.

"John told me about Octolok and Propyl-Osirin in Cartierul. I already told you what I figured out about the Propyl-Osirin, but Octolok was a lot trickier. You see, the feds and XAuto, they never thought of it as anything other than an adhesive. That was all they ever used it for. All they ever knew about it. But there was this book mentioned in the patent that talked more about the blunat tree. It said it was published in Akawe. And that confused me because, you know, nobody here publishes books! Turns out this guy, Tito Maus, had written it as his memoir because he was exploring Papua with Michael Rockefeller. But he never got it published. He just made up a few copies and showed them to people he knew. That included the people filing the patent for X Auto. But another copy wound up at the library. So, I was able to read that there. And Tito talked about how he met with some tribes up there – some of them were cannibals! – and he ate the blunat fruit with them and had these crazy hallucinations just like you were saying, John. Like the people on O-Sugar have been having."

Michael squinted down at the flakes and gel on the quarter. It was starting to liquefy. Starting to slide together.

"So, Drake, I started wondering what you actually *knew* about O-Sugar. I mean, you didn't know that Octolok was in it, but you did know about nightshade and MDMA. Eli told you, right? He said that nightshade gave the drug a horror, but that it was, like, a good kind of horror. Only that didn't make any sense to me. Deadly nightshade can kill you, real easy. It messes you up. Messes up your eyes... like yours were, John. And it's a kind of drug called a deliriant that makes you feel like shit, terrified, horrified ... I almost took a bunch of nutmeg to feel it myself, but I chickened out because I heard it was so bad."

"Nutmeg ain't that bad," muttered Drake.

"That's where I had to think about the job the Chalks do. Because John told me, the Chalks can't *make* O-Sugar, but they sell a lot of it! If you're some dumb teenager, you might take some random drug just to try to get high, but if you're a street gang trying to make money, a drug that'll straight up *kill* people is a liability. So, whoever is making the drug wouldn't use nightshade if they didn't *have* to. It makes O-Sugar more dangerous and less salable. So that meant that the nightshade had to be important for some *other* reason. And it is. The blunat tree has the resin they use for Octolok in it and scopolamine. When they process the resin to make Octolok, they strip away the scopolamine.

Octolok is just an adhesive. It doesn't do anything else. But when you bond it to scopolamine again, and then a person eats it, like, then it's a lot like what happens if you eat the fruit. And then it kind of, I don't know, breaks the laws of physics!"

"What?" asked Drake and me.

"Yeah!" Michael cried. "I know, I know, and that's what's really messed up. You know how they say time travel isn't possible? Or, like, in science fiction books, if you go, like, near the speed of light, time slows down for whoever is going fast, and it's slow everywhere else? Well, that's kind of what is happening right inside the fruit of the blunat tree. The way the Octolok resin and the scopolamine interact pulls space together. It isn't *really* an adhesive like, say, glue at all. No, it's like some sort of phantom Frankenstein chemical that shrinks the space around its atoms and molecules, because of the way it's all wrapped up in itself. But it shrinks them so much that time actually is slower in the middle of the blunat fruit than it is on the outside. That's why the tree stays fertile for so long. The fruit, I mean. After the tree has gone dormant or even died, it could still have fertile fruit for years and years. So the blunat tree evolved this, somehow, I don't even know how, as a way of conserving energy. You break the fruit apart, and you can take out some sticky stuff that X tried to use for their brakes before they realized it wasn't cost-effective. But you add scopolamine back into it, just like we're doing right now, and then you eat it, and, somehow, you can consciously direct both those things: the squeezing time part and the squeezing space part. I mean, I guess, like physics, they're both pretty much the same thing. But anyway, according to Tito's book, it basically blue shifts everything. The more you take, or the more you concentrate on it, the more it slides toward blue on the color spectrum. And the more you take, the stronger it is. Because you're pulling time and space *toward* you."

Drake didn't say anything.

"But what about the hallucinations?!" I exclaimed. "I saw my grandpa decomposing! I saw little kids without faces!"

"That's the deadly nightshade. I mean, just because O-Sugar lets you stretch space-time doesn't mean that the chemicals won't have an effect on you. Remember, Tito hallucinated when he ate the blunat fruit. When you take O-Sugar, you're still on scopolamine, and you're still on ecstasy."

"I get it!" said Drake. "Yeah! That's why there's molly in it. The MDMA is something they had to add to make people enjoy taking the drug. It was there to offset the nightshade!"

"That's right," said Michael. "You take Octolok and mix it with scopolamine – with nightshade tincture – and you get a drug that does something that no other drug on the planet will let you do: stretch space and time. But it still has the shitty side effects of making you hallucinate and get sick and horrified and paranoid. So, you add MDMA to make it fun to take.

There isn't any secret ingredient. There's only those three. The secret ingredient is what those three chemicals do when you put them all together."

Drake wasn't able to sit still anymore. He started rolling around the room, first toward Michael near the hot plate, and then the sink where he looked out the window toward the sky.

"Then that's what happened," he said. "To Jamo and DeeDee and TK and Sapphire and me. That was what happened! We were up on top of the hospital, fucked up, scared shitless, and we looked out over the edge, and suddenly we were there! You're ... you're saying that the drug actually moved us over the edge?"

Michael answered clinically.

"Yeah," he said. "You all *thought* about going over the edge. Your thoughts compressed space. The space beneath you stayed as it was. If someone else was there, it might have looked for a moment like you all blurred and stretched out in different directions. But you weren't moving. Space was folding. When you were over the edge, there wasn't anything holding you up, so you fell."

"I," said Drake. "Fuck, I ... I don't know. I been working on this for two years. I could have kept working on it for the rest of my life and never figured it out."

"I got lucky," said Michael. "John told me about Octolok, and my mom has a job where I can look stuff like this up."

"The Satan's Masters have been at it for years! The FBI! The Chalks!"

"I mean, I could be wrong about all of this. I haven't tried it myself, and I'm not going to." He gestured to the quarter. "But this batch is all done."

Drake tapped the quarter to make sure it had cooled, then picked it up between his thumb and index finger. He looked at each of us in turn, gave May a furtive grin, then licked the paste.

"I think that's about as much as you get in one of the pills you were talking about," said Michael. "I hope I'm right."

"You want me to get you some sunglasses?" I asked. "For the urbantasms? The blue ghosts?"

"Nah," said Drake. "I've done O-Sugar a few hundred times. I don't need sunglasses. I'm going to my room. I'll know if it's legit."

Drake rolled on down the hall and disappeared into his bedroom. He shut the door behind him.

An hour passed without any sound coming from Drake's bedroom.

May, Michael, and I sat at the kitchen table, glancing at the clock, nervously telling jokes and stupid stories, looking at the floor or out the window into the dark backyard, glancing at the shut bedroom door down the hall. Waiting.

Eventually, Drake rolled out with an unreadable expression on his face.

"It works," he said. "This is it. This is O-Sugar."

And then his face broke into a thousand fragments of smile and laughter, and I saw bright, crooked teeth, centuries of mirth, and joyful hate. Drake went over to the counter and pulled a Glock out from under the sink.

"This is it," he said. "I'ma break them down like acid!"

Michael and I flinched and half ducked behind the table, while May watched her brother impassively. With strong arms, Drake hoisted himself up onto the counter, pushed the window open, and aimed the barrel up toward the sky.

"DeeDee!" he shouted and fired. "Jamo!" he shouted. "TK! Sapphire!"

Pop! Pop! Pop! Drake returned to his wheelchair, breathing heavily. He set the gun on the counter and turned toward us.

"Michael!" he said, and my cousin flinched a little. "You are a friend, Michael!"

He took Michael's head between his hands, looked him closely in his eyes, then kissed his forehead. He sat back again.

Michael stared at him.

"May!" Drake said. "Is the sidewalk clear?"

"Yeah! It is."

"Let's go. It's Open Mic at Treemonisha tonight. I want to celebrate, you know? We'll free all those ghosts. Yours and mine. TK and Cedric. Sapphire and Leigh."

May laughed nervously.

"I'm buying!" crowed Drake.

Michael and I had a moment alone on the sidewalk while May helped Drake into the car.

"So," I said, "you think Selby and I hallucinated as kids because there was Octolok in the soil? In Cartierul?"

"It's the only thing I can think of."

"Because of the Old Benedict over there."

"They made Aubreys. The time was right. The factories are right between the river and Sellers Creek. Cartierul is at the lowest elevation in the city. There's got to be all sorts of stuff in that soil."

"But you said that Octolok on its own wasn't anything but, like, an adhesive."

"Yeah," he said. "It's just an adhesive on its own. It has to bond with a tropane alkaloid like scopolamine to do anything to a person."

"Then how did Selby and I hallucinate? How did we see the blue things? Where did the ... the nightshade whatever come from?"

Michael flung his arms up. "I don't know, John! Maybe nightshade grows down there? Or maybe it's, just, the hand of God or something giving us a clue he knew we'd need down the line, but ..." He looked for more words but couldn't find them.

"John! Michael!" called May. "Come on!"

We went out to the car.

By now, I had been to the blast-faced, green-bricked Treemonisha Club several times. I had seen it as a four-year-old in the summertime when I ran from my parents and the blue ghosts. I had seen it in seventh grade when Lucy had taken my friends and me into the abandoned auditorium across the street. I had seen it after I'd started high school when I danced with my friends in a haze of smoke and funk. And I had seen it a few weeks before when I was coming into my own on three pills of O-Sugar with music chiming through the dark.

I had never been inside.

I could hear the music as we parked at the end of a long line of 80s Benedicts, Aubreys, Starrs, and Buicks. I heard bass. I heard drumming. Strings jangling. Drake cut new ruts through the drifted snow, pulled the door open, and waved us inside ahead of him.

I didn't see any bouncers at the Treemonisha Club, and nobody seemed very interested in enforcing the "members only" rule. The dim, narrow room was packed with a crowd of maybe thirty or forty people. I saw low, water-stained ceilings. Budweiser posters, half of them sporting bikini-clad women posing around stock cars. Christmas lights ran along the tops of the wall. Groups of old men, mostly Black, all grizzled, sat at the bar nursing little plastic cups, while Black and white men and women, 20s, 30s, 40s, filled the small Formica-topped tables drinking beers and rum Cokes and listened to the band.

The band!

Now I recognized the music. This was a straight-up funk band, and maybe I should have figured it out sooner by the fact that the bassist was the real diva onstage. He closed his eyes in opulent indulgence as he spidered his fingers across the strings like some sophisticate might have caressed a harp at her Campus Akawe recital. The permanently purple-tinted Fresnels, six or eight feet from his face, painted him royal, his crimsoned instrument clutched knuckle white under the sweaty heat of his back-and-forth swaying. Behind him, the drummer was encompassed by circles – not only the planetary shapes of his drums, but a large cymbal that had been sliced like a lemon twist and hung over the AstroTurf-covered stage. The shade-wearing keyboardist – were they blue shades? – was he on O-Sugar even? – played on down and up and down again, marching like dancing ants upon the floors of the world. A tall, strong Black woman with straight hair pulled back with a scrunchy made of pearls sang bleak blues, but driven, driven, driven before the one, the one, the one.

It was her version of Hooker's "My Dream."

"What do you want, honey?" asked the waitress after we'd taken a seat at a table halfway back. She was beautiful, she wore glasses, and she reminded me slightly of my mother. For that reason, I was pretty sure she wasn't going to serve me alcohol.

"Just a pop," I said.

Everyone nodded for the same, except for Drake, who asked for a Jack n' Coke.

"Everything falls apart," he said, "but this place don't fall apart."

He took a sip of his drink. "I wouldn't be nowhere without the three of you," he said. "My sister who saved my life. Her boyfriend who told me what he saw as a kid. Her boyfriend's cuz who told me what goes in the drug. It's you three and Mike and Zig. You take me into the future."

May gave another nervous laugh. "Don't let Ziggurat know you called him that. He won't like it."

The music rang out, low and light, contradictory tones reconciled through sympathetic frequencies. The light dimmed. I pulled on my straw. The carbonation burned in my throat.

"John," muttered May in my ear.

Her voice sounded unusually husky. For a moment, I thought that tonight might be the night we would finally have sex.

I went in to kiss her, but she nodded her head away.

"Isn't that your father up at the bar?" she asked.

I looked over.

Yup, that's him. He was sitting closer to the stage, up on a stool, facing the bar, his chin in his hands, swaying his head from side to side in tune with the music.

"Don't you think you should go talk to him?"

"No," I said. "What if he's drunk?"

"Go talk to him!" she said.

"Hello, father," I said, taking a seat next to him at the bar.

He looked over at me in surprise, then at my drink, then at his own, then back at me.

"Hi," he said. "So. This is what you're up to when you aren't staying with your mother and I? Going out to bars on a school night?"

"Yeah. Good music here," I said. I didn't want him to lose track of the fact that he was the one being tested here. Not me. "Trade drinks with me?" I asked.

"Okay," he said.

He slid his drink over to me. I slid mine toward him. We both raised the glasses to our lips and took a long sip.

"I'm proud of you, John," he said. "They probably would've served you here if you just asked."

"I wish I could say I was proud of you. This is gross. What, you got Diet Coke?"

My father shrugged ruefully.

"I'm trying to lose some weight," he said.

"You can have it," I said.

I pushed his drink back toward him.

He slid mine toward me.

"How often do you come here?" I asked.

"I used to come here all the time ... before you were born. When your mother and I were dating. Then I just came a couple times a year. Since things got weird with your mother and you left, I try to make it every Wednesday."

"Wednesday?"

"Yeah. Open Mic Night. Usually, the house band just does some funk, but every so often, someone else goes up. In fact ..."

As if on cue, the band wrapped up their set and called a girl named Cass up to the stage. Cass was slight and slender and graceful, and probably still a teenager, but just barely. She was Black with ringlets of hair spiraling down her shoulders. Cass was going to college in Oklahoma. Cass was a student at the Ann Lacy School of Dance. Cass had grown up just a few blocks away on King Avenue. Cass was just back for a few days for her aunt's funeral, but she couldn't come back to Akawe without stopping in to see her friends at the Treemonisha Club.

Now I don't know shit about tap, but when Cass started moving her feet, and the band matched her with a Cuban beat, and the drummer pulled out a trumpet from beneath his kit and hit it hard, the clapping then staccato cascade from heel and toe as she stepped about, turned in place, arms whirling like turbines before clasping or clapping before her, behind, the thin film of her gray skirt moving with the music too – this was a dance costume, and Cass had shown up ready to step on stage – I felt like I must have been sitting in some polished theater of a much larger, more prosperous city. I wondered how many of the scars on that battered stage had come from secret geniuses buried beneath the many layers of Akawe. Cass finally stopped dancing, and everyone clapped and beat their tables. I heard May's voice raise in a whoop of praise.

"Wow," I said.

"Yeah," said my father. "Pretty amazing. That sort of thing happens here all the time."

Cass took a seat, the band leader invited us to buy a drink or leave some money in the tip jar. He invited us up for his brother's potluck birthday at the club that Saturday, then slid smoothly into the next song.

"You know the story of this place?" my father asked.

"I know it's a jazz club."

"It was more than that! We used to be on the circuit between Detroit and Chicago. So we got all the big acts between their biggest shows. They'd stop in time to time, play at the XAWU Auditorium. Or Campus Akawe. Places like that. But of the time, those were all-white audiences. They only sold tickets to whites. Keep in mind that most of these musicians were Black, too."

My father stopped to take a sip.

"Anyway," he went on, "since Blacks weren't welcome at the big concert halls, they'd go out to clubs in their own neighborhoods. Here in Sycamore Grove, you had Four Cross and Blue Diamonds over on Brighton Road. And the Treemonisha was the oldest and the most famous. After Basie or Satch or the Prince of Darkness played for a few thousand downtown, they'd come up here and play, and you'd be so close you could reach out and shake their hands. People'd stay here all night long. They wouldn't go home until the sun was coming up!"

We didn't say anything for several minutes.

I glanced over my shoulder to look at May. I was hoping she was looking at me. She wasn't; she was watching the band murder the beat. She was electric in wonder at that music. She was so lovely that the aching I had carried within me for weeks crossed through my chest and spilled across my whole body and out into the room. I was watching her so intently that my father startled me when he spoke.

"It is ... remarkable, John," he said, "to see you like this. To see you openly care about someone like this. Like I see you with May."

I looked at him.

"I don't know May well," he said. "But I'm seeing you – with my own eyes – thinking more about someone else than about yourself. And I'm so glad I'm seeing that because there were days I didn't think I ever would."

"Well," I said, slowly, sliding my glass around with my palm. "It isn't like it did you or mother any good. Thinking about others. You still ended up ... you know." I didn't look at him.

It took him a long time to answer.

"No," he said slowly, drawing it out. "That isn't true. God, I hope you don't think that. Your mother is the most wonderful thing that has ever happened to me in my whole life. And I don't think that anything better will ever happen to me between now and when I die. You come pretty close. Meeting your mother and having you. Those are the two best things in my life."

"You think so ..." I said, worrying that I was being too obvious.

"John," my father said abruptly. "I know everything you think I don't know."

I looked at him. He was usually so emotional, but not now. He had almost a sort of deathbed serenity about him. I wondered if this was the expression his oldest sister must have worn when he had come to her with his troubles. I saw my father's face, and I thought of my Aunt Ellie.

"I know," my father said. "Things you saw and heard at our house recently have hurt you. It looks and sounds bad to you, but it isn't, maybe, quite as bad as it seems. You can't understand, John, but you have to believe ... it's very difficult to be married to an alcoholic. You can't ever trust completely. And a drunk who can't get drunk on alcohol will find himself getting drunk on other things. You probably think I always had a short temper, too? And that's when things are going well. When you are also living in a house that you hate, when you are working hard, and the person you are married to isn't earning money anymore, when he just wants to drink all the time, when you think your kid is out of control, when nobody in that house seems to like or trust one another anymore, when the power goes out, when you can't drink or take a shower in the water ... these things are all stresses. Little stresses add up to something big. Something huge. Denial and disappointment. See, you're still young. You understand violence and hate. You see someone get mistreated, and you know what that means. But you still don't know yet about that kind of slow disappointment that just builds up over years and years of hoping for something better and not getting it. But I know. You'll be stronger than me as an adult, I know. Who knows ... maybe you'll be stronger than your mother, too? She has been through a lot."

"What about the chandeliers?" I said.

If he *really* knew everything that I did, he would know about the strange man who had lured my mother out to buy chandeliers, and he would know what that meant.

"What about them?"

I guess he doesn't know ...

"I told her we couldn't afford them," my father said.

"She *asked* you about it?"

"Why wouldn't she ask me?" He thought about my question for a moment. "John? What exactly do you think you know?"

I hesitated. But he had *said* that he knew everything that I did, and he evidently knew about the chandeliers.

"I was skipping school one day," I said. "I came home and hid in my room. And I heard *her* come home. And there was a man with her. And they were talking, like. You know. Like they were *close*. He kept talking about buying her all sorts of things. He said you needed to buy chandeliers. He was worried about you or the neighbors seeing them."

I waited to see the effect my words would have.

My father looked into his mug for a long time. Then he laughed bitterly. Then he took a large gulp of his Diet Coke. Then he laughed again, this time with mirth and irony.

"John, you're young," he said. "There's a lot you don't understand, and you definitely owe your mother an apology. She was at our house with a realtor."

Now it was my turn to be confused. *Does he even get what I'm telling him?*

"A realtor?"

"Yeah. Yeah. No, she didn't tell me. She wanted to keep it from me. She wanted to get everything all worked up and then surprise me with it when I'd feel like I'd have to say 'yes.' What you heard was them talking about how to sell our house."

"She wasn't —"

"She was just trying to sell our house, John. So we could move somewhere else. Safer. Cleaner. With better schools."

I stopped and recalibrated everything in my mind. I replaced my mother's deceptions with her frustration and desperation: a desire to get away from this house and city so strong that she had started making plans on her own. In a way, this made me angry, too. Now, I felt I didn't *want* to leave Akawe. There was too much of myself wrapped up in this city. But I couldn't resent her for it. Moving away from this broken place was something she would have honestly wanted, as a wife, and a mother, and a woman with hopes of her own.

Still, I had to wonder how I had made the mistake in the first place. I had found faithlessness because I had been looking for it. Because my father had been deceiving me, and I had been deceiving both of my parents, so naturally, I expected to find the worst kind of deception in my mother. And then I felt shame, because she had known what I had suspected. After all, I had accused her over the phone. *How am I going to apologize?* I wondered. *Am I even going to apologize?*

"And *are* we going to move?" I asked instead.

My father sighed.

"Not right now, but I don't want to lie to you either. We decided the time isn't right. But things have gotten bad. At some point, they might just get too bad for us to stay. Your school isn't doing too good. Our house is the last on the block. The water. These fires. And I still don't have a job, and your mother's job doesn't pay that well. So I won't lie to you, John. Someday soon, yeah, we might be looking to move."

"I don't want to move."

"I understand why you feel that way."

I closed my eyes and absorbed all of this. I still wanted to go home to Lestrade Street. To return to the little house with its freakish mural and May's tiny bedroom where we had made a shelter for each other. But I also missed my home on Agit and wondered how empty my bedroom must have felt without me. About the paths my parents took through that house without me there to keep them company.

"I'm sorry, John," my father said. "For all the hurt we've put you through."

"I'm sorry, too," I said. "I lied to you. And I wasn't trying in school. I just ... I gave up for a while. But when I left, I found my friends, and I got into that play, and I found *her.*"

"Don't be too hard on yourself. We're all just cracked glasses trying to carry water. I love you, you know."

"I love you too. And Mother."

"Then ... will you please move back in with us?"

For a moment, his serenity split, and his face looked anxious.

"I ..." I didn't want him to crack. I had to tell the truth. "I think I will, soon. But I'm not ready to leave May yet. I'm working hard in school. Getting good grades. Going to rehearsals. Handing in all my homework. Everything. But I'm not ready to leave her yet. You don't even know all the things she's done for me. You don't even know how deep it goes ... the trouble people are in. People I care about. You don't know how they haven't been loved and the things they have done – the stupid things – because *they* are miserable."

Urbantasm: The Darkest Road

My father nodded, blinking back tears.

"It's okay," he said. "I'm not being sarcastic, you know. It's okay. If you know you can come home – if you know why you should come home – I believe that you will. I believe that you will come home soon."

I didn't answer. I looked back to May again.

This time, she was looking at me with a concerned expression and a timid smile. It was like she was worried that she was going to break something by smiling too broadly, and the way her eyes dwelt on me, moving across my cheeks, my nose, my brow, my neck ... it seemed like she was trying to memorize me one atom at a time.

"Well," said my father. "I'll let you get back to your friends. I should get back home to your mother."

He finished his drink and left a ten on the bar.

"Call me in the next few days," he said. "Okay?"

"Okay," I said. "I will."

He went out into the wind.

The sound of static crackled through the PA.

"Mr. Esper, is John Bridge in your class?" said the tinny voice.

"Yes," answered the teacher.

"He has a phone call in the office."

When I got there, the secretary – Miranda – handed me the phone.

"It's your mom," she said.

"Hello," I said into the receiver.

"John, you asshole, I've been trying to get ahold of you for almost two weeks!"

"Oh, hi, Mom."

"Yeah, it's me," said Crystal. "Didn't you get the note I left you?"

"Yeah. Sorry. I forgot it."

"You forgot my birthday party? You fucking asshole! Well, it's going on tomorrow, so you better come."

"What time?"

"I don't care. Anytime, after, like, six. Or seven? It's the last party ever. There are going to be kegs. Plural. Like, multiple kegs. So many of them. So, bring people. Anyone you want. I want there to be as many people at my house as we can fit in my house, and then I want there to be some more! You got it? It isn't February anymore. It's March now. Winter is dead. Vive la Spring!"

I looked out of the narrow window at the grainy banks of snow, several feet thick.

"I'll see if I can make it."

"Whatever, I can't believe you never wrote me back or called. You're a jerk. Go to hell! See you tomorrow!"

"You go to hell!" I said and hung up.

The secretary was staring at me.

"Sorry about that," I said.

The truth was, I wasn't even sure that I wanted to go to Crystal's party. Before everything else that had happened that winter, a "last party" with multiple kegs would have been the sort of thing I anticipated for weeks. Now I was leery. It didn't sound any better to me than a night at home reading with May. I hadn't mentioned the party to anyone else yet, because I wanted to keep my options open.

Besides, many things were in motion that week. Adam turned up at school again and gave me a casual wave in the hall.

"Sometime you disappear like that, I'm not even gonna notice anymore," I said.

"Sorry, man."

"You want to tell me about Dylan?"

"Sorry, man. Shit's been crazy again. My mom is out. Dylan is in. That's where I've been. He doesn't go to school here. I've been with him over at Jordan."

"Are you gonna switch schools or something?"

"No way. I can't afford Jordan. Plus, some kid thought he saw a demon there last year, so they had some dude perform an exorcism. A real fucking *exorcism!*"

Adam tried to turn his neck a hundred-and-eighty degrees.

"Ow!" he said.

Even though I was still frustrated that he kept vanishing without a trace, I was glad to have him back. By way of apology, he agreed to drop a note into Selby's locker for me.

It read:

S,
I finished my Chemistry homework in Parc Pierre. In English, we're talking about dragons. In History, we're talking about Mesopotamian temples. They've got all the answers. They're going to write them all over the chalkboard. If you want to compare notes, we should study together sometime.
The Boat

Drake had told me to stop distributing his notes around the school. He went out with Mike and Ziggurat at night and didn't come back until four or five in the morning. From May's bedroom, I could hear the front door sliding open, scraping scraps of ice into the yard.

I was starting to hope that maybe my part in all of this was drawing to a close, and even without murdering anyone. If the Chalks lost their monopoly on O-Sugar, it would weaken both them and the Ostyns. Drake had also learned that the feds had been waiting to crack down on the Chalks until they had found the source and composition of their homegrown drug. I was hoping that between the hammer of the law and reaping by other gangs, the Chalks would follow the Undertakers and the Demonik Mafia into oblivion. I could put my full energies into school, the play, and May.

This was already a lot. By now, the *Riot* cast was practicing five days a week, including Saturdays, with three-and-a-half-hour rehearsals. Warm-ups. Choreography. Monologues. Choreography. Monologues. Notes. It was more intense than school because I cared about it more.

The show was scheduled to open on April 19th. The complexity of the tech elements – because the audience was to be physically dispersed from the parking lot through different parts of the theater, while the actors also moved between the stage and the house – meant that we were literally reading our lines on bits of half-assembled scaffolding. Meanwhile, Charles and August kept slipping in new bits of script, making cuts, securing rights to new pieces of music, and rearranging the order of the scenes.

"When are we going to choreograph the Air sequence?" asked Maggie, the choreographer, after one exhausting rehearsal.

"I don't know," said Charles, rapping his fingers against his scalp. "When I figure out what the Air sequence is all about?"

And so, we worked the other scenes intensively, navigating around an empty conceptual space, a void, that we knew was going to be filled, at some point, with something revolving around "Air."

When I was at school, I couldn't stop thinking about the play, but while I was at rehearsal, I couldn't stop thinking about May. There were two girls at *Riot* who knew May. They knew that I was dating her, and they didn't like her. They went to Southern. Their names were Tonya and Daph.

On Saturday afternoon, the day of Crystal's party, I went to rehearsal. I found myself standing with the rest of the actors on the scaffolding built over the back row of seats. I stood next to Tonya, and as Charles was giving some notes to another actor down the line, she leaned over and whispered, "When you going to dump May? She's no good, you know."

"She's not stupid!" I hissed back. "Most people don't even know about it!"

"Stupid? Who said anything about stupid? I don't like her 'cause of what she did to my friend's mom."

"What are you even talking about?"

"My friend got taken from his mom because of what your girlfriend said. Because she's a snitch!"

"Quiet offstage!" snapped August. He glared at us for a long moment before returning to the lighting cues.

"Ask her about Leigh Hollister," hissed Tonya. "She'll tell you. If she even remembers her name!"

When I got back to May's house, Key was off on a job, and Drake was out with Ziggurat. I found May sitting on her bed, cradling a book in her lap.

"You spent a lot of time reading to me last week. I found this book I used to read each night before I went to sleep. It's a wonderful book. It's short, but it's perfect for going to sleep."

The book was *Goodnight Moon.*

"Do you want me to read it to you?" May asked.

"Sure," I said.

I took a seat on her bed beside her, and she read. I heard about the big green room. I heard about all the sounds and the delicate small objects that separated the bunny from darkness and rest. May's voice murmured like snowmelt, and the air was still, and the light was soft. She said goodnight to nobody.

The last page had been torn from the book.

"Haha," she said. "I must have ripped that one out when I was little. But I think we can guess how it ends. How was your day?"

"It was fine," I said. "Did you ever know someone named Leigh Hollister?"

"Oh," said May. "Her."

She set the book gently on her desk, picked up a can of pop, and took a drink.

"Leigh's a girl," she said. "I mean, she's a woman. She used to be our neighbor. A few years ago, my mom lived here, in this house, and my dad and Drake and me lived in the trailer park over by the strip clubs. Leigh was our neighbor, and she watched Drake and me sometimes when my dad was gone."

"When I was at rehearsal, this girl from Southern – Tonya – said that you did something wrong to Leigh."

May's eyes got wider.

"No," she said. "I didn't do anything wrong to Leigh. At least, I didn't mean to." She took another drink of her pop, although it looked to me like the can was empty. "But I think I know what you're worried about. I don't like it, okay? I don't like talking about it, okay?"

May wouldn't look at my face. She was looking at a nothing on the carpet.

"But ... look," she said. "Okay, I'll tell you about it. Haha! I mean, I can't not tell you about it, right? You're my boyfriend! Oh. So, I don't know what happened, but a year ago? I think a year ago? It wasn't long after Drake came home after his ... fall. Anyway, Leigh's parents came over here because they wanted to talk to me about her. They asked me a bunch of questions about back when I lived near her, and she was my babysitter, and they decided that they were going to take Leigh's kids for themselves. I mean, they took them from Leigh! But when they were all fighting about it, they must have said about me because after that, people kept calling our house and trash-talking me for snitching on Leigh and getting her kids taken away from her. Only I didn't mean to snitch on anybody. I didn't mean for Leigh's kids to get taken away. So, I bet one of Leigh's kids misses her and was talking to your friend in the play and told them I'm a horrible bitch who got them taken from their mom!"

"Okay, they did say something like that," I said. "But I don't understand. Why did Leigh's parents want to talk to you? What does that even have to do with her kids? What, did you help her sell drugs or something?"

"No, no, I was too young for that. It was because when she was babysitting me, I was yelling and crying a whole lot, so she poured a bunch of gas in a bucket and told me to sit and smell it."

"What?!"

"That was what they wanted to know about. They were trying to decide that she wasn't a good mom or a good babysitter, and I guess they were talking to all these people who knew Leigh, and someone they asked told them about me, so I don't know how they found out, okay, and I don't know why it was such a big deal, but they wanted to know about it, okay?"

"She ... wait. You mean gasoline? She poured gasoline in a bucket and told you to huff it?"

"No, she didn't say huff. Just that it would feel good, and it would help calm me down."

"And you did it?"

"A mom told me to do it! She was my babysitter, okay? She said it was okay, so why wouldn't it be okay? It wasn't like she was giving me O-Sugar or something! I mean, Jeez, everyone else around me is doing heroin and O-Sugar, and Drake and my dad all acted like this was just as bad –"

"It is just as bad!" I shouted. I closed my eyes. Splayed my hands. Tried to control my breathing.

"What do you mean?" May asked slowly. "I knew it had to be bad, but it isn't against the law or anything. I mean, they let you buy it at a gas station."

"I think it's just as bad for you as that other shit," I said. "I think it might even be worse."

She was staring at me.

"But it isn't a drug," she said. "I don't understand. I didn't drink it or anything. I thought they just wanted me to show that she was ignoring me instead of watching me or something. I mean, it wasn't like when Drake gets on O-Sugar, and he sees ghosts and stuff. It isn't like those flashbacks you get. This just made me feel warm and tingly, okay? Like, you know, when you close your eyes, and you see stars? And, I don't know, it made me feel loved, okay? Kind of like there was this big fuzzy love all around."

"Did your dad know what was happening?"

"He thought I smelled like gas but just told me to go and take a shower, and I did."

"What about Drake?"

"I mean, Drake knew, but he didn't really notice the first time."

"The first time –"

"Um ..."

"How many times did this happen?!"

"I don't know. A few ... a ... it was summertime, okay? We were having lemonade!"

"When did it stop?"

"Well, I mean, so Drake told dad, and dad stopped sending us over there, and that's when it stopped, okay?"

Now May was looking at me and I was the one who didn't want to see her face. Now *I* was studying nothing on the carpet.

"John?" she said.

I didn't know what to say.

"I'm sorry, okay?" May said. "I should have known I did something real wrong, okay? Because why would all those people have been so mad at me if I didn't do something so wrong? But I don't know anything about it. I ... what ... um, what does it do? The gas?"

"It's bad for your brain," I stammered. I wanted to answer her without hurting her, but there was no way to do that without lying. "It's like ... I think it makes it so you can't remember things. Or, it makes you so you're like ..."

"Oh," she said. "Okay."

And we stood in silence for several moments.

"So ..." she said. "You think that Leigh is the reason that I'm ... like this. Why I don't do good in school. And I can't write and remember stuff. Why people think I'm a retard."

"I don't know. Maybe?"

"So, this is the secret."

"What secret?"

I looked up. May was standing by her window now, looking out, her arms at her side, her fists clenched.

"I was so worried that you would get upset or mad about the sex stuff, or about Drake being a drug dealer, but it isn't even that! It's this stupid thing. You're all upset about this stupid thing my babysitter made me do when I was a kid!"

"I didn't say it was your fault," I said. "I don't think it's your fault. I think it's Leigh's fault. It *is* Leigh's fault!"

May turned to face me now.

"Don't say that, okay?" she said. "Leigh was very stressed out! She didn't have a car! And she had her own kids! It was crazy! And I really was noisy and didn't do what she said! She had to find a way to calm me down, okay? Nobody could, okay?! But I get what you are thinking, what you must be thinking, okay, because if this, this, this gas made me stupid like you said, then maybe I wouldn't think that would be the thing that would make you upset, but if I hadn't done that, then maybe I would have known to tell you about it, so we wouldn't have this stupid, this stupid, stupid right now, but I was stupid, so I didn't tell you, and anyway, it doesn't matter, okay? Because I was already stupid! Before she did that! I was already stupid, okay?"

"How do you know?" I asked. "It just makes me so mad that someone would hurt you like that! That anyone would tell a little kid to do that!"

"I'm sorry, I'm sorry, I'm –"

"I said it's not your fault! Fuck Leigh! I hope she dies! I hate her more than anyone! I hate her more than any of the Ostyns! And I hate Drake, and I hate your dad for not stopping her!"

"You, you –" May said. "You can't say that, okay?! They're my only – they're! You shut up, okay?!"

"Why the fuck didn't they call the police on her? That's child abuse!"

"Oh, you're really stupid to say that, you are! That's a stupid thing to say! And you can't talk about Drake like that! He was the only one! The only one! Anyway, it doesn't matter about Leigh, because I said, I told you, I said, I was already stupid!"

May was shouting now. She stood planted by the window, her fists balled at her side, her eyes wide and glaring.

"I don't want anyone to treat you like that!" I shouted back.

"Go away, you idiot!" May screamed. "Go away, okay?! I was already stupid! I hate you! I hate you all! Leave me alone, you idiot! I was already dumb! Go away! I hate you all! Leave me alone! Go away, you idiot! I was already dumb, and I hate you all! Go away! I was already stupid, and I just hate you!"

I left May shouting in her room. I had made it back to the living room and had put my coat and boots on when I realized that I didn't know where I was supposed to go. My head was raging, and I knew that anywhere I went, all I was going to want to do was pace and hit things. I might even cry. *Jesus, I don't want to cry in front of anybody,* I thought. *Not after this.*

So where would it be? Bill's? Adam's? My parents'? Another long, pointless walk in the dark?

I could go burn down Leigh's house, I thought. *Dump a bunch of gasoline on it and just light a match. That would be ironic.*

It was such a stupid thought that I laughed at it. A bitter, hateful laugh. But I had already kicked off my boots and crossed into the kitchen.

I picked up the phone book.

"I don't suppose you have a listing here, Leigh?"

I flipped through the book.

HOLLISTER, LEIGH   3613 LESTRADE ST.

"Son of a bitch," I muttered.

I ripped out the page and stuffed it in my pocket. I put the phone book back, palmed a book of matches, and returned to the living room. May had stopped shouting, but I heard muffled sobs coming from behind her shut bedroom door. Again, my chest filled with incandescent fury, and I tasted metal in my mouth. I put my boots on again. I stepped outside. I carefully shut the front door.

I tried to ask myself the same pragmatic questions: *Where am I going? Adam's? My parents'? Bill's?* But instead of walking out toward Armstrong, I found myself passing the Jesus mural and heading into the garage. There, I found a red gas can sitting on a dusty shelf near the lawnmower. I stared at it for a minute, imagining how I might spend the rest of the day. *I can't just go walking down the street with a gas can. Everyone would remember that afterward.*

A couple planks of wood rested on a sawhorse, and on them rested a large glass peanut jar filled with scavenged nails and screws. I dumped the hardware into a flowerpot and then carefully filled the peanut jar with gasoline. It was big enough that I was probably able to pour out a quart but small enough that I could hide it in the folds of my coat. *I won't be able to waste any,* I thought. *But if the wood is dry, and I'm careful how I start it, this should be enough.*

I screwed the lid back on the peanut jar. I set the gas can back on the shelf. The stink of gasoline was on my fingers and everywhere around me. I smelled them and imagined May – little kid May – sitting in a dimly lit corner, her head bent over a bucket of the stuff, with that ancient stench curling through the air. Curling through her brain. I wanted to hit something, but instead, I slid the jar under the side of my shirt, then wrapped myself up in my coat.

Am I really going to do this? I wondered. *If I stop and think about it, I probably won't do it. So if I'm going to do it, I'll have to do it now, quickly, and without thinking.*

I started walking fast, down the driveway, toward Lestrade Street.

I was walking fast because I was afraid of my thoughts, and I tried not to think about anything except closing the distance between myself and 3613 Lestrade. I must have passed May's favorite McDonald's on Ash, and the coney island that served all of the johns after their late-night fixes, and the housing projects that had taken in all of Eden's exiles, once upon a time, but I don't remember any of that. I remember the snow underfoot, hard now because it had lain where it was for months, compacted, pocked, and pitiless. I walked quickly, but I had to walk carefully because there wasn't any sidewalk here, and the cars surged past me.

And then I was there. It had been a short journey. And maybe, though I had resolved not to think, my brain had been doing some secret work in its unseen alcove. When I set out, I hadn't known whether I really was going to try to burn down Leigh's house, and I still didn't know when I arrived. But I had realized that this decision was in the palm of my hand and that Leigh was as powerless to contest me as a young May had been powerless under Leigh's care. This would be *my* decision. Maybe, like God Ostyn, and the God of the Bible for that matter, I would be an angry God and punish my enemies with fire and destruction, or maybe I would say, "let him who is without sin cast the first stone." Would I be as devious and unrelenting as Eli, or would I forgive, as May forgave, even when forgiveness was unearned and unasked for? I didn't know. But *I* would decide. It was up to *me*. As I walked, I felt my power, and that power felt *good.*

There was nothing between 3611 and 3615 Lestrade Street. Those two houses, little cookie-cutter things, like Key's house and Kitty's, were dilapidated beyond their years, with broken windows and sagging siding, though there were lights within and cars in the driveway. But between them, there was no structure – not even grass – not even snow – just a little rectangle where a tiny house had been ripped apart by huge machines that crushed the dirt until it could not support any life.

I yelled raggedly and threw the peanut jar at this sad patch of soil.

The glass smashed, and the gasoline pointlessly splashed against the hard ground.

I couldn't burn down a house.

I couldn't burn down anything.

Spring really was on its way; even with all of the snow on the ground, the sun was still hours from setting by the time I made it to Adam's house. When I got inside, I found Adam in the living room alone with the curtains drawn, the blue tv light flickering upon his face. They were trying to sell him some sort of fancy colander.

"I kinda thought you'd be out with Dylan," I said.

"He dumped my ass."

"Sounds like a real fucking asshole."

Adam tried to stifle his laugh.

"I wish you had told me about him," I said. "I mean when you started seeing him."

"I'm sorry."

"I mean, I should have kept up with you more."

"You seem to have a lot on your plate."

"So do you. What happened with your mom?"

"She's in Lansing now. I don't know what's up. She's staying with a friend there, I guess. She didn't tell us she was going. She just called us after she got there."

"Are you doing okay?"

"No. You?"

"Not even a little. You want to go to a party?"

At that, I saw a little light stirring in Adam's eyes.

"Maybe? Probably? Whose party?"

"Crystal Galitz. You remember, my *summerfriend*. She says it's going to be huge. She says I should bring as many people as I can."

"You bringing May?"

"Not this time. I think she maybe wants to take a break from me tonight."

"Huh. That why *you're* not okay?"

"Let's just start calling people."

We called Selby first. She bragged about her suspension from school, told me that the world was ruined, and said that yes, she would come to the party.

"Who's driving?" she asked.

"I want to ask Quanla along. Will you call her? She wants to hear from you. Invite Darius. See if he can drive."

Then we called Chuck and Nova. Chuck had a dance performance that night, but Nova said "yes." We called Selby back. She had good news: Quanla and Darius were coming, and Darius would drive. She also had a surprise.

"I decided it was time to make up with Lucy."

"You called her?"

"She's coming too."

"She's going near a car with you?!"

"Maybe we'll both throw you in the trunk."

A half-hour later, Darius' Daphne was fuming in the driveway.

"Let's ride," he said.

I wasn't sure what I expected from "the last party ever," but if I could just dance and yell and discharge some of my cold fury, I might even make it through the weekend without doing anything even more reckless.

When we got to Crystal's, we found a police cruiser on the parkway, its blue lights turning. Seven or eight kids, upperclassmen, stood around it, shouting and cheering, while two boys circled each other warily, sneakers sunk in the snow, hands balled into fists, their breath smoking with the challenge. Another kid stood between them, his hands braced between the combatants, his face pivoting between them.

"I ain't parking at this!" said Darius.

We went around the corner, where a long line of cars crowded the street. Darius finally found a spot a block later, and we walked back to Crystal's house. When we got there, the fighting boys and their mediator had left, and the police lights had stopped twirling. The kids still stood there, in their pajamas and coats, their slippers and scarves, holding Solo cups which they filled from a keg sunk in a snowdrift.

"Want some beer?" asked a matchstick-legged white boy.

Darius took a cup. I waved one away.

We went up onto the porch where a Black girl with long braids handed out leis.

"Welcome to Crystal's party," she said. We all got leied and went inside.

We went into the living room, which was packed thick with twenty, maybe thirty kids, no place to sit, practically no place to stand, everyone leaping in concert, causing the floor beneath them to croak in warning. A shaggy band, wedged into a corner, their backs against the windows, their amps up against the kids' knees, lit by a blue and a red light, ground out rough rhythms.

"Holy shit," said Nova. "Your friend got Twisted Amphibians to play?"

The guitarist kicked the fuzzbox and sounds scuzzed Robin's carpet worse than the muddiest of sneakers. But as we pushed our way farther into the room, I realized that the floor had been completely covered in beach towels. Large drawings of volcanoes, oceans, and palm trees had been painted on multi-colored poster boards and hung along the walls. A lot of the partygoers were wearing costumes: a bequilled St. Sebastian, a collegiate communist with his red-and-yellow megaphone, the bride of Frankenstein with a bouquet of dead flowers, a sword swallower, the sergeant major of the color guard, a clinical receptionist, and a licensed practicing nurse, Marcel Marceau, Ellroy Blues, Asbestos Lady, Marvin the Martian, Red McKenzie, and the sun, the sun, the sun. They were all moshing, leaping, crashing, grinding, floating in the sonic air shot through by the frequencies of the Twisted Amphibians. I passed a bulldog wearing a crimson and gold sweatshirt. He growled at me, then commenced licking himself.

"Holy shit!" I said.

"Sorry about that," said a boy holding the dog by the leash. "Brutus, down!"

"What's with the dog?!"

"SMU just beat Ferris State, and we borrowed their mascot!"

We sidled across the floor into the dining room, carefully, although the Lizards drove their instruments further, into a cloud of feedback, making Adam and Quanla flinch into the table, causing a model of the Great Wall of China built out of empty Vernor's cans to come down in a metallic clangor.

We found Crystal in the kitchen. A girl grabbed a boy by his collar with her left hand while her right dumped a bowl full of brownies down his shirt. They ran out, followed by a new horde of kids. With the space cleared, I saw a hairy 40-something white man with a thick black mustache trying to pry the glass top off a coffee table. Somehow, some poor kid had gotten trapped beneath it. She sat and calmly read a comic book while waiting to be freed.

"So, what do you think of my party?" Crystal asked. She was wearing Guinness pajamas and a set of Sunkist sunglasses.

"This is insane!" I said. "You know you got a cop car out on your front yard?"

"Oh, yeah. Don't worry about that. That's just Gus. He's here in case anyone calls the cops."

She gestured to the man with the mustache, who strained as he pulled at the tabletop. I noticed that he was indeed wearing a blue police uniform and had a black gun strapped to his side.

"So, you're Crystal?" asked Nova hoarsely.

"Yeah. Nice to meet."

"I'm Nova. Happy birthday!" he said. "And congratulations! Holy shit, I can't believe you got the Amphibs!"

"They're just the warm-up act. Get yourself something to consume. Nothing harder than grass or booze; I don't want anyone going to the hospital."

I looked over my shoulder at my quieter friends. Selby was grinning behind me. Lucy frowned. Quanla was starting to move to the beat. We'd lost Adam and Darius. "What have you got?"

"Beer," said Crystal. "Gin-n-Juice, Spanish Fly."

"Anything without alcohol?"

"I think there's some milk in the fridge if you want."

I left Selby and Nova to talk to Crystal, and I took a plastic cup from the counter. I poured myself some milk from the fridge and stirred in some strawberry syrup.

I turned around just in time to see Gus finally pry the table off the nerd trapped underneath.

"Thank you so much," said the nerd, but Gus popped his arm back and drove a slice of starlight yellow birthday cake straight into the nerd's face. The nerd retaliated with a slice of pineapple upside-down cake. I put my hands up and retreated, backing my way into the dining room again.

Now that the beer cans were out of the way, some girls were dancing on the table. Quanla was with them. Lucy stood in the corner, looking sullenly at nothing in particular.

"Cheer up!" I told her.

"You cheer up!" she said.

I climbed up onto the table to dance with Quanla. The Amphibians finished their set and started packing up. Crystal turned on her stereo and started blasting Dre.

A thin white woman wearing a purple blouse and a purple scarf festooned with a Russian doll sequence of nesting yellow cubes made her way slowly through the room, saying, "Wayne State University, looking for Crystal Galitz. Is Crystal Galitz here?"

A group of boys and girls made a ring around the table, taking out their drivers' licenses and bingo cards to stage a friendly game of suck-and-blow.

In the living room, someone turned on the television, and someone else retaliated by smashing its bulbous screen with a well-timed fastball.

"John! Quanla!" came a small voice.

It was Adam.

We looked down at him from the table.

"You don't know this, but there was this asshole named Brick who always made Dylan's life hell back when they were in junior high at Maturin."

"So?" I asked.

"This kid was a real taint to him, John. He tried to set the shed in their backyard on fire."

I didn't want to say anything about that.

"Anyway," Adam went on, "he lives right over there. Just on the other side of the expressway. And there's this girl Darcie goes to school with Crystal. She hates Brick, too. I guess his whole family is on vacation now. They're going to go trash her house. I really want to go."

"You should go!" I said.

"You should come!"

"I don't want to go and just trash someone's house," said Quanla.

"What if that house belongs to a really terrible person?"

She shook her head.

Crystal's voice rang out from the living room. "I want to welcome our next musical act, all the way from Southern California! Thank you for coming to help me celebrate my birthday, guys! Let's welcome Gordon Strozier!"

Wild cheering.

"Yeah!" shouted Quanla.

The drum machine kicked in with handclaps, block drops, syncopated, echoing.

"Damn!" I said. "I kinda want to stay for that."

"John," said Adam. "Come with me. Someone just needs to rage against something for a few minutes, you think?"

"I do?"

Adam jerked his head emphatically at Lucy, who was watching the moving room with a glazed expression.

"I don't think she'll come with me on her own," Adam said. "But if you were to come, John ..."

"She doesn't even like me," I said. "I mean, as a person."

"She likes you as much as anyone. You're one of the only people she talks to anymore."

I sighed. I climbed down from the table.

"Okay," I said. "Just let me use the bathroom, then I can go."

I took the hall to the bathroom, where, a year-and-a-half ago, I had changed, soaked, into Crystal's mother's nightgown, but I didn't get a chance to pee. The room was packed with kids who had dressed themselves in Crystal's black towels.

"Friends! Lankhmaris! Countrymen! Lend me your fears!"

It was the same nerd who had just been trapped under Crystal's kitchen table.

I washed my hands in the sink, squeezed through the crowd, and found

Urbantasm: The Darkest Road

Selby, Lucy, and Adam at the front door.

"You're coming too?" I asked Selby.

"Hell yeah," she said.

We turned out through the door, passed the empty police car and the discarded keg, the boot-trampled snow. We passed the Southern High School varsity basketball players borrowing a shotgun from a Jordan kid, ready to fire shot at a ruined concertina. An old wino with a snotty beard was plucking at the back of their letter jackets, asking if he could just have a turn, just one shot, because this was his old hood and all.

Darcie and her sister, Macy, were waiting for us in their VW Bug, an old hippie hatch, badly rusted and smoke-choked. The windows came down. I saw two pale and dark-haired white girls, and they could have been twins. Darcie was coughing.

"Trouble with your Audiovox?" asked Adam.

"Athlete's foot," said Darcie. "Old socks. Mickey's on the rocks. Hotbox."

We crowded in and vrooomed away right before the wino took his shot, and the sludgebath began.

The car swung east along FDR, found the expressway overpass and made it to the other side, turned west, and dropped us off in front of another tiny house with a skinny maple tree in front.

"I'll go park," said Darcie. "I'll be right back."

We stood there a moment, hands in our pockets, worried and wary. This was usually a busy street, but it was empty right now. The windows of the neighboring houses were dark. There was nobody there to see us, but nowhere to hide, either. Darcie appeared on the corner. She came toward us, taking off a backpack and opening it to reveal a dozen rolls of toilet paper inside.

"Let's go, homies," she said.

We launched the toilet paper over the branches, high and low, over the shining porch light, the boxwood under the front windows, the fence on either side. We threw them so they would unspool fast. Darcie, Macy, Adam, Selby, and I ran as fast as we could while Lucy stood and watched. Then, when I was standing near her, Lucy reached out and tugged at my arm.

"What's up?" I asked.

"Follow me," she said.

I followed her up the driveway. She hoisted herself up over the shadowbox fence into the backyard, and I followed. It was a small backyard, with most of the lawn taken up by an aboveground pool.

"Things okay with you and May?" she asked.

"What do you mean?"

"She's not here tonight."

"I don't think this is her kind of party."

"So, nothing going on with you two right now?"

"We had a fight. It sucks."

"Were you an asshole?"

"You know, I don't think I was this time. But I know why she's mad at me."

"Maybe you should –"

A floodlight came on. Lucy and I froze where we were. We breathed for long moments in the still.

"It's just a motion detector," Lucy said. "Get it."

I climbed up onto the back porch and unspun the floodlight until the bulb popped out. I gave it to Lucy. She stepped back and launched it through a basement window. The glass shattered. A dog barked in the distance but quieted after a moment.

"Holy shit!" I hissed.

We listened. No sounds of cars. No sounds of traffic or voices. Just the lowing wind. The sound of an amber sky. Lucy went up to the broken window and started kicking out shards of broken glass with her foot.

"What are you doing?" I asked.

"See if you can find a hose," she said. "Hook it up."

And with that, she dropped onto her belly and lowered herself through the broken window.

The spigot was easy to find near the back of the house. The hose wasn't as easy. I looked around outside, then tried the garage, but it was locked. A few hours after I'd been thinking about burning Leigh's house to the ground, I was reluctant to join Lucy in window smashing. But a light had come on in the basement, outlining silhouettes on the side of the garage. I made out the serpentlike trail of a hose near a back fence. I dragged it over to the spigot and screwed it on.

A minute later, Lucy threw an old towel over the jagged edge of the window and hauled herself up and out.

"That's B and E," I said. "You're a rebel."

"Give a rebel yell," she said. "You find a hose?"

"Yeah. What were you doing?"

"Turning on their water."

"Why?"

"You'll see. Go turn it on."

She unlatched the gate and dragged the hose out. I turned the spigot, and I could hear the water gurgling through. I followed Lucy into the front yard.

"Hey," said Macy. "Where you been?"

Selby eyed us nervously. So did Adam. Their bodies told me that they thought Lucy was about to turn the hose on them. For all I knew, she was.

Instead, she took aim at the tree, pressed her thumb down over the nozzle, and water jetted out, hitting the long strands of toilet paper, plastering them back along their branches, coating it all in a stream that would harden into ice in a few minutes.

"Damn girl," said Darcy. "You're cold. Stone cold."

As if in answer, Lucy turned the hose on Darcy. She laughed as the spray covered her, then Lucy turned it on Selby. Macy and I rushed Lucy, wrestled the hose from her hands, pulled it away as she fell on her back in the driveway, sprayed her with the icy water, and we all laughed and kicked and grunted and blew our noses out into the cold air. Finally, Adam pinched back the hose.

"You're fucking insane, Lucy!" he said. "Fucking crazy!"

Lucy grinned, a stream of blood running down the middle of her chin.

"I put some towels on the back porch," she said. "Let's get back there before anyone sees us."

We went into the backyard and dried ourselves while Adam, who hadn't gotten wet, poked around the garden. He found a set of five or six lawn gnomes and a ceramic Elvis.

"Fuck Brick," he said and threw Elvis into the pool.

We heard it shatter.

We hurried out then.

We walked quickly down the block until we'd gotten back to Darcie's car, and we packed in and set off into the night.

"Do I go right back to the party?" Darcie asked.

"No!" said Lucy. "You should go, go, go!"

"Where should I go?"

"Everywhere!"

So we went.

The white lights and bright windows of the party stores shot forth illumination like constellations by which we could navigate. While Darcie didn't drive as fast as Eli, she drove fast enough, and the green and red lights blurred and fuzzed as we whirred beneath their buzz. It was enough for me to see the fire in my friends' faces and to know that the same fire burned within me. We weren't just made to fear and regret. We were made for motion.

I rolled my window down. I wanted to feel everything more sharply. In less than a month, this bitter cold – this bitter breath – would be gone, finally gone, after so long, after forever, maybe in a week or two, or maybe even in a few days. The spring was coming.

We went over expressways. We went under expressways. If we went far enough in this direction, we'd arrive in Detroit. If we went farther in that direction, we'd get to Chicago.

"John," said Lucy. "I think you've grown up a lot this year."

"I think Lucy's full of shit tonight," rasped Selby.

"What about me?" asked Adam. "Have I grown up a lot?"

"No," said Lucy. "You're still short."

"What time is it?" I asked.

"It's after midnight," said Macy.

"I think I'm ready to go back to the party now," said Lucy. "I'm not done with that party."

As we walked up the sidewalk, we saw a Bajaj – the *Hamara* kind – burst through Crystal's front door, stagger down the porch, and exit through the front yard. The teeming masses roared in approval, and just like that, the Last Party had attained its apotheosis.

By one o'clock, more people were leaving than were arriving.

Someone ordered a pizza, and I ate some.

Someone emptied out of the tortilla chips, melted the necessary cheese, chopped up the necessary jalapeños, and set it out.

For a while, I fell asleep on a couchlet in the basement.

By three o'clock, more people were leaving, and nobody new was showing up.

By that point, we were deep into the *Ghostbusters, Highlander,* and the *Reality Bites* phase of things. We'd fallen into the canned music phase of things. Gordon Strozier was long gone, and Melvin Riley had never bothered to show up.

And then, at four in the morning, with sunrise so much closer than sunset, someone resorted to the White Album, and I knew I was a long, long, long way away. What could I do? *I haven't had anything to drink tonight except strawberry milk and bottled water,* I thought. *So why do I feel like I'm drunk?*

At five o'clock there were less than thirty people left at Crystal's house.

At six o'clock there were less than twenty. Darius and Quanla had finally departed.

At seven o'clock in the morning, it was Selby, Lucy, Adam, Nova, Crystal, myself, and maybe six or seven other people.

Everyone was as tired as time, but I wanted to stay awake until spring arrived.

Winter had run its course, and now I wanted to bury Leigh in my heart.

I wanted to lie with May in *my* bedroom.

I wanted to grow up with May and marry May and bring new life into the world with May.

Instead, I sat cross-legged in Crystal's dim living room and played Truth or Dare with friends and strangers.

Crystal and a boy named Trent had to kiss. A girl named Renee had to call another girl and tell her what a ho she was. Selby and Lucy had to swap clothes, meaning that Selby's sleeves hung out over the end of Lucy's hands, while Selby was unable to pull Lucy's shirt down over her stomach.

Nova had to strip down except for a long t-shirt and go running around the outside of the house barefoot.

"How you feel, Supernova?" Crystal asked him when he got back inside.

"Blue," said Nova. "Balls."

After Adam dared Renee to moon a car going by on FDR Drive, she had it out for him. When she called on him (it took a while; no callbacks), she made Crystal fetch a cucumber from the fridge and told Adam to give it a blowjob. Adam did this with relish, making Renee far more uncomfortable than himself.

"John!" said Adam.

"Truth," I answered.

"No," he said. "You ain't picked nothing but truth since we started."

"Yeah, and I'm the only one who hasn't made an ass of himself."

"C'mon, pick dare, or go to sleep."

"No. Truth."

"John, he has a point," said Crystal. "The point of the game is that we all have dirt on each other. It isn't right for you to have it easier than anyone else."

I wasn't buying it.

"No," I said. "You're talking about a game called 'Dare.' This game gives me a choice. I choose Truth."

"Okay," said Adam, almost dismissively. "I give up. What's the worst thing you ever did?"

The question confused me in its simplicity. I had done many bad things. The worst hurt I had given had come from moments of indifference or carelessness. People you care about mostly know you don't hate them. But when they find out that you don't care, that you haven't heard or acknowledged them: that wounds. And so I thought about all the times I let Adam mock Michael as gay, or when I had been thoughtless with Omara, or, worst, when I had downplayed Lucy's torment in the Tent and Tarp Shop. But it was the moments of cruelty and malice that had wounded my conscience, and that made it harder for me to be a good person in the world. And that was an easy memory to call up: I remembered when I had shut May in my locker. That moment of cruelty had been defused, but only because May had forgiven me. If that had been done to most people— if it had been done to me – such a moment would have festered and swollen and consumed me with a desire to injure in return. That May had forgiven me that cruelty impressed me. That she had forgiven Leigh both amazed and appalled me.

But that train of thought led me to my answer.

I knew what I had to say.

"The worst thing I've ever done," I said. "It was yesterday. And that's hard because there's shit I did years ago that I still feel bad about. I've stolen from people." I thought of Ruth. "I've ignored people." I thought of Lucy. "But yesterday, my girlfriend told me about someone who had hurt her. And instead of staying with her or trying to help her feel better, I decided that I had to get revenge on this person. Not for my girlfriend. For myself. I felt like I wanted to be powerful. I wanted to be in control of something for a change. I wanted to hurt someone who deserved to be hurt. So ... I got a bottle of gasoline. I mean, I poured it into a glass jar because I didn't want to be seen carrying it. And I hid it in my coat, and I walked to this woman's house. And thank God, the woman's house wasn't there. I mean, it had already been demoed for whatever reason. So, there was nothing there to burn down. It really pissed me off. And you know ... if I had burned it down, and I had hurt or killed someone inside, my girlfriend would have blamed herself. And it could have come back, on her or her family. It could have come back on me, and then how would my parents have felt? My teachers? Jesus. I'm so lucky that house was gone when I got there. So yeah. Maybe it's just because it only happened yesterday, but ... I think that's the worst thing I've done. But I'll tell you. I've seen a lot of evil now. And I still want to destroy something."

Nobody said anything.

I couldn't tell whether they were perplexed or angry or unimpressed.

"Lucy," I said.

"Yeah?" she said.

"Truth or Dare?"

"Truth."

"What's the worst thing you've ever done?"

I wasn't testing her, exactly. I wondered if she would mention her suicide attempt in the Tent and Tarp shop or the night of May's birthday party. I thought that those were probably the worst things she had ever done, but I wasn't sure that she would have agreed with me.

"That's easy for me to answer," said Lucy. "Although you'll probably think it's lame. There was this day three years ago when my mom had to work a double shift, but we were late on the water bill. So my mom gave me extra bus fare and an envelope with the water payment, and all I had to do was deliver it to City Hall so we wouldn't get our water shut off. Of course, I forgot! So, what did I do when I remembered the next day? I hid the envelope under my bed. I just pretended that I had delivered it. I mean, I even told her that I had. Like, what did I think was going to happen?! I think I meant to go the next day or something, but I forgot then, too. So, like, a week goes by, and then all of a sudden, they shut off our water. And then my mom was super mad. We paid again right away, but after they shut off the water, it can take them a long time to turn it back on. It took them two weeks or something. We didn't have any water in our house that whole time. We had to buy a bunch of water just to flush the toilet."

"Really?" said Selby, with a disgusted tone of voice.

"I think that's your mom's fault for not paying in the first place," said Trent.

"Yeah, I've done way worse than that," said Crystal, with a dismissive toss of her head.

I studied Lucy, trying to understand.

She shrugged. "I told you it would sound lame. You weren't in that house with me, so you don't get to say how bad it was."

Lucy sighed.

"Selby!" she said.

"Yeah?"

"Truth or Dare?"

"Why not? Truth!"

"Haha! You know it! Well, Selby, what's the worst thing you've ever done?"

"It isn't thinking about burning down someone's house but not actually doing it," said Selby. "And it's definitely not forgetting to pay someone else's water bill. No, I've been doing it for years, and I'm doing it right now. I just really want to kill someone who deserves it."

"Yeah?" said Lucy, challenging. "You want to kill someone who deserves it? Well, so do I! But if they deserve it, then it isn't a bad thing, is it? Not as bad as what John did. Not even as bad as what I did!"

And she moved her foot back and forth along the carpet while Selby glared at her.

Now, the silence was thicker than it had been before. The fun had left the game, the night was over, everybody was exhausted, and the sun was getting ready to rise. Nobody wanted Selby or Lucy to explain what they meant by their answers. Maybe that's why nobody jumped in to say, "No call backs," when Selby returned to Lucy with the words, "Truth or Dare."

Lucy thought it over for a moment, then grinned.

"Dare!" she said.

Selby jumped to her feet.

"I'm glad you said dare," she said. "John has been such an asshole tonight, saying 'Truth,' 'Truth,' 'Truth,' every fucking time. Help me throw him out in the snow."

I tried to get to my feet, but Lucy leapt onto my back. She was lighter than me, and maybe I could have wrenched myself free, but Selby was taller and stronger than I was. She grabbed me by the ankles, and was pulling them out from under me when Nova and Trent joined the pile. Nova ran up behind me – I couldn't see him, but I heard the sound of his breath – and he grabbed the elastic band of my underwear and tore them upward so hard that they ripped. Lucy had wrapped her legs around my waist and grabbed for my arms as I tried to stand. Adam was tickling my stomach. Selby finally got a hold of my feet, and Crystal grabbed my hands.

They staggered the half-dozen or so steps to the entryway, and Renee held the door open while my friends flung me out into the yard. Snow covered my hands, bloody and scraped, and fell down my back and ass crack. I was barefoot, and my feet stung with the cold. I squinted. It was bright out. The sky was blue intense. Almost as sharp as if it was an O-Sugar flashback. *Is it a flashback?* No, this was a real, present-tense blue, in a bitter, end-of-winter sky. The sun had just erupted over the trees and fields, and it shot blades of blue-gold light into my face. Everyone was crowding onto the narrow, stone porch, laughing at me.

I didn't wait.

I ran up the walk and wrapped my arms around Selby's waist. With a heave of adrenaline, I flung her into the same snowbank where I had just landed. Then I shot forward, grabbed Lucy, and lifted, her feet kicking pointlessly in the air, and threw her into the snow as well.

"Quick! Quick!" yelled Crystal, and I heard the door slam shut behind me.

"No! No!" wailed Lucy, standing up on her pale white toes. "Open up!"

Selby went up onto the porch and started banging on the door. "Open up, assholes!" she yelled.

I calmly picked up a clump of powdery snow and shaped it into a snowball. I threw it, and it hit Selby right in the middle of her back.

She turned to face me.

Lucy turned to face me.

I turned from them and ran, and they pursued me.

It was the most blue I had ever seen. The most blue and the most bright. The most illuminated. I ran, and they ran, and we ran after and from each other. It wasn't the devil chasing us that morning. It wasn't God Ostyn who had driven us out into the cold. It was the real God. The true God. A full eye. Witnessing us and judging us for what we had done.

"I just really want to kill someone who deserves it."

"Well, so do I!"

"And I still want to destroy something."

We ran.

Down! Down! Across FDR and I started to climb the chain-link fence separating me from the interstate and passage out of Akawe, earth-cradled and blue-illuminated, but Selby and Lucy were on me, full of rage, their mouths contorting, and they grabbed the back of my shirt and threw me onto my back, into the snow again. Selby started throwing stones and snow at me, and Lucy stabbed at me with a narrow branch she had picked up. Spiky brambles. Scraps of concrete and bits of glass and anything else they could pick up with their hands.

"No!" I yelled, and stumbled to my feet, and realized that I was bleeding, dripping blood into the snow. I got up, slipped, slid down, got up again, cold numb, their two faces, lacerated pain, and they drove me to my feet, and I ran, and they ran, and again we ran against and with each other.

We ran for real, into the city, barefoot along the icy pavement, and I heard their urgent breath. Lucy caught the edge of the curb with her foot and went sprawling into a drift. When she came up, her dark hair spidered across her face, and her eyes were wounded, unquenched. Meanwhile, Selby's empty and hungry face floated toward me. It was all blue snow, blue face, blue looks, empty eyes. Then Selby started laughing as she ran.

Why is she laughing? I wondered. And then I realized that I was laughing too.

We ran at each other. We threw snowballs like little kids. We all wanted to murder each other, but we didn't have knives or guns. All we had was snow. I wanted to cry. I wanted to speak. I wanted to breathe. I wanted to stop breathing. I didn't. Instead, I ran.

Where were we running?

Not to any house that would care for us.

Not to any car that would take us home.

Toward a nothing, a final darkness, an escape.

Lucy yelled at us as she ran, but we didn't hear her right.

"Don't you know?" Selby heard her say.

"You don't know," I heard her say.

God, it was so bright out. God, I thought your occultation was a fearful thing, but that was before I beheld the blinding terror of your illumination. Of having to bear witness to every awful thing. So hard and so bright. So bright and so cold. The throb. The blood. The shaking scared.

Urbantasm: The Darkest Road

Scarred. Running to God. God, I swear. God, I pray. God, hear us. Christ, hear us. Christ, graciously hear us. God, the Father of Heaven, have mercy on us. God, the Son, Redeemer of the World, have mercy on us. God, the Holy Spirit, have mercy on us. Holy Trinity, one God, have mercy on us. And pray for us. God, we ran. God, we ran faster than anything else you have ever created. Even light. Even time. We outran everything. Nothing could catch us. Not anymore.

URBANTASM

Book Four:
The
Spring Storm

Connor Coyne

URBANTASM

Book 4: The Spring Storm

by Connor Coyne

Urbantasm: The Spring Storm is the fourth and final book in the magical teen noir serial novel inspired by the author's experiences growing up in and around Flint, Michigan.

The stage has been set. The chessboard awaits. Against a background of love and friendship, of hard-won grades and groundbreaking plays, John and his friends are ready to claim their lives, their futures, and their city. They have identified their adversary: a mysterious man who calls himself "God" and manipulates the Chalks street gang through the influence of his children. John has also unlocked the secret of O-Sugar, a mysterious drug with the ability to distort space. But God wields a powerful influence throughout the city of Akawe, and nobody seems to understand his true motives or intentions.

As the ice and frost of a long and unrelenting winter finally crack under cold, torrential rains, frozen things begin to stir again. The brutal murder of one of John's friends and the abrupt disappearance of another signals that the moment of action has arrived. Who will survive this dying city, and how will the experience change the survivors? Akawe has been unstable for decades. A bit of lift and heat and moisture is all it needs to build a spring storm.

I wish to thank God, whose compassion is bottomless, my wife Jessica, my parents Shannie and Gregory, my late Grandma Coyne, and my brothers, sisters, family and dear friends, and mentors who have supported me over many long years.

I also wish to thank the team that made this project possible. Although just one name appears upon the cover, books are a collaborative affair, and this one wouldn't exist without the help of Paul Lathrop, Hosanna Patience, and Sam Perkins-Harbin. I need to give a special mention to editor Kelsey Ronan, who joined the team *in media res*, and without whose warm, generous, and incisive critique this book would now feel incomplete.

For me, *The Darkest Road* is the core of the story, in the sense that this is where we finally learn who these people are, deeply and essentially. In that spirit, I need to thank the those who have shared knowledge and experiences that have made the telling possible. I want to thank Shawn Amidon and Rebecca Holm for their deep-dives with me into our 1990s memories of the Michigan Renaissance Festival. Similarly, both Steve Mintline and Margo Halligan were extremely helpful in excavating the recent history of Flint Southwestern Academy. Melodee Mabbitt, Gary Fisher, John Brent Wilson, and Nic Custer were all fonts of wisdom on Flint's Eastside, and I went back to that well often. The same credit goes for Bob Campbell and Lottie Reed's reminiscences and insights into the Floral Park / Kent Park / Elm Park / Sugar Hill neighborhoods on Flint's South Side. In September 1999, Martin Jennings and the staff at Flint Central High School (especially the librarians) allowed me to work at the school on a brief internship, and this gave me the chance to witness firsthand the glorious Theatre Magnet program at work. In writing about Romania and Romanians, I am indebted to Dr. Adrian Poruciuc who taught me as part of a cultural immersion program at Universitatea Alexandru Ioan Cuza in 2000, and Andrea Cure here in the states. In writing about the Porajmos – the Romani genocide – I am thankful to Dr. Michelle Kelso, as well as to Donald Kendrick, author of *In the Shadow of the Swastika*, and to many others. When it comes to the Flint Water Crisis, I lived through that event along with many friends and neighbors. Yet much of the scholarship, commentary, and activism surrounding the crisis were illuminating even to those of us experiencing it. With that in mind, I want to thank Nayyirah Shariff, Desiree Duell, Anna Clark, Ben Pauli, and so many others for their ongoing efforts to promote Flint voices and justice for Flint. On a lighter note, I want to thank Lindsay Crawford and Lisa Worf for taking me to honest-to-God raves in Flint and Detroit (though not in warehouses, alas), and Bill Holland for sharing his own treasure trove of knowledge and referring me to the writing of Dan Sicko. My father and Dave DeVoe were always eager to share stories about their time working for General Motors, and just when I think I've heard it all, they surprise me with something new! Adam Moore helped me to understand the mechanics and pragmatics of municipal public policy, especially in a revenue-starved city like Flint. Finally, I want to boost three writers, entrepreneurs, and fellow travelers whose local work was timely and relevant to the development of this novel: Egypt Otis of Comma Bookstore, Tyler Bailey of Whaley Reclaimed, and LaTashia Carter-Perry of 4 Kids Like Mine. Your support and encouragement, and your own energetic work are what make Flint such a wonderful place to be a writer.

Once again, I wish to recommit my thanks to everyone mentioned in previous acknowledgments, including members of the Gothic Funk Nation, the Moomers crew, Scavhunt gangs, University Theater friends, faculty from the New School and the University of Chicago, and all the quality people from Flint Youth Theatre, the Flint Public Library, St. John Vianney Catholic Church, the Unitarian Universalist Church of Flint, the Flint Community Schools, Powers High School, and the teachers I was blessed to learn under at Flushing Junior High and High School.

And since this book is filled with places so resonant in life and memory – places where kids from many different backgrounds met and mingled and forgot their cares for a few hours – I want to raise a cheer for their real-life counterparts, so dear and so priceless: Paradise Express at the Dort Mall, Galaxy Lanes, Rollhaven, the used bookstore on Corunna Road, the corridors of Genesee Valley, and Christ the King Catholic Church.

Long live Flint!

ABOUT THE AUTHOR

Photo by Eric Dutro

Connor Coyne is a writer living and working in Flint, Michigan.

His first novel, *Hungry Rats*, has been hailed by Heartland prize-winner Jeffery Renard Allen as "an emotional and aesthetic tour de force."

His second novel, *Shattering Glass*, has been praised by Gordon Young, author of *Teardown: Memoir of a Vanishing City* as "a hypnotic tale that is at once universal and otherworldly."

His essay "Bathtime" is included in the Picador anthology *Voices from the Rust Belt*, edited by Anne Trubek.

Connor represented Flint's 7th Ward as its artist-in-residence for the National Endowment for the Arts' Our Town grant, through which artists engaged ward residents to produce creative work in service of the 2013 City of Flint Master Plan.

Connor's work has been published in *Vox.com*, *Belt Magazine*, *Santa Clara Review*, and elsewhere. He lives with his wife, two daughters, and an adopted rabbit in Flint's College Cultural Neighborhood (aka the East Village), less than a mile from the house where he grew up.

Learn more about Connor's writing at ConnorCoyne.com

Made in the USA
Monee, IL
23 September 2021